BILLIONAIRE WOLVES OF MIAMI — THE COMPLETE COLLECTION

A WOLF SHIFTER PARANORMAL ROMANCE COLLECTION

BILLIONAIRE WOLVES SERIES

CHARMAINE LOUISE SHELTON

CONTENTS

*About Billionaire Wolves of Miami — The
Complete Collection: A Wolf Shifter Paranormal
Romance Collection*   vii

JAGGER THE TEMPTATION
A Wolf Shifter Fated Mates Paranormal Romance

About Jagger The Temptation: A Wolf Shifter
Fated Mates Paranormal Romance   3
Chapter 1   5
Chapter 2   15
Chapter 3   24
Chapter 4   33
Chapter 5   41
Chapter 6   49
Chapter 7   59
Chapter 8   65
Chapter 9   74
Chapter 10   83
Chapter 11   90
Chapter 12   100
Chapter 13   111
Chapter 14   120
Chapter 15   130
Chapter 16   141
Chapter 17   151
Chapter 18   160
Chapter 19   174
Chapter 20   182
Epilogue   186

RUST THE REJECTED
A Wolf Shifter Rejected Mate Paranormal Romance

About Rust The Rejected: A Wolf Shifter Rejted Mate Paranormal Romance	191
Chapter 1	193
Chapter 2	203
Chapter 3	213
Chapter 4	222
Chapter 5	229
Chapter 6	239
Chapter 7	249
Chapter 8	257
Chapter 9	266
Chapter 10	276
Chapter 11	287
Chapter 12	298
Chapter 13	308
Chapter 14	315
Chapter 15	329
Chapter 16	338
Chapter 17	348
Chapter 18	357
Chapter 19	366
Epilogue	371

TAG THE REDEMPTION
A Wolf Shifter Fated Mates Paranormal Romance

About Tag The Redemption: A Wolf Shifter Fated Mates Paranormal Romance	377
Chapter 1	379
Chapter 2	390
Chapter 3	400
Chapter 4	410
Chapter 5	419
Chapter 6	427

Chapter 7 436
Chapter 8 443
Chapter 9 453
Chapter 10 463
Chapter 11 472
Chapter 12 480
Chapter 13 489
Chapter 14 499
Chapter 15 510
Chapter 16 519
Chapter 17 530
Chapter 18 547
Chapter 19 554
Epilogue 560

VIGGO THE OBSESSION
A Wolf Shifter Fated Mates Paranormal Romance

About Viggo The Obsession: A Wolf Shifter Fated Mates Paranormal Romance 569
Chapter 1 571
Chapter 2 580
Chapter 3 590
Chapter 4 599
Chapter 5 608
Chapter 6 616
Chapter 7 626
Chapter 8 635
Chapter 9 644
Chapter 10 655
Chapter 11 667
Chapter 12 677
Chapter 13 686
Chapter 14 698
Chapter 15 708
Chapter 16 718
Chapter 17 731

Chapter 18 737
Chapter 19 746
Epilogue 752

Next in Series Signy's Mates: A Wolf Shifter
Fated Mates Reverse Harem Romance 757

Also By Charmaine Louise Shelton 759
About Charmaine Louise Shelton 763

ABOUT BILLIONAIRE WOLVES OF MIAMI — THE COMPLETE COLLECTION: A WOLF SHIFTER PARANORMAL ROMANCE COLLECTION

Enter the spicy and luxurious world of the Billionaire Wolves of Miami for plenty of steam, drama, and tension.

Contains the complete Miami series:

Jagger The Temptation: A Wolf Shifter Fated Mates Paranormal Romance
They say the heart knows, but what if it's impossible...

Rust The Rejected: A Wolf Shifter Rejected Mate Paranormal Romance
Can I heal the tortured heart of my fated mate, even though she rejected me?

Tag The Redemption: A Wolf Shifter Fated Mates Paranormal Romance
What havoc can my shy, curvaceous human assistant wreak on my structured life? Drive my wolf feral.

Viggo The Obsession: A Wolf Shifter Fated Mates Paranormal Romance

I'm the playboy prince who vowed it would never happen. Then it did. And she became my obsession.

Scroll up and one click **Billionaire Wolves of Miami** today.

Their steamy love stories are HEA standalones in the sizzling Billionaire Wolves Series of interconnecting stories featuring wolf shifter fated mates and rejected mate romance. Get a glimpse of each couple's dynamism in other books.

Visit CharmaineLouiseBooks.com

CHARMAINE LOUISE SHELTON

JAGGER

THE TEMPTATION

ABOUT JAGGER THE TEMPTATION: A WOLF SHIFTER FATED MATES PARANORMAL ROMANCE

They say the heart knows, but what if it's impossible...

I'm the leader of my pack—the Billionaire Wolves of Miami. A wolf shifter who has it all—money, power, and she-wolves who vie for me to claim them. Sounds good? Not exactly. I long for my fated mate.

When my wolf senses detect her unique scent on another male, I lose it. Then memories forcefully blocked for ten years flood my mind. Memories of a young witch. And not just any witch—the future High Witch.

She's the one my wolf howls for, my fated mate. Now, I have to find her and prove it to her. Again. A second chance for us.

Too bad wolves and witches are not allowed to mate...

You've heard what they say about cats and dogs? Yeah,

well, crank that up by a thousand percent for wolf shifters and witches.

No one is happy about this revelation. But that's too bad for them. My heart knows what it wants and that's her. Again.

Their steamy love story is a standalone in the sizzling Billionaire Wolves Series of interconnecting stories featuring wolf shifter fated mates romance. Get a glimpse of their dynamism in other books.

Anthem: "Never Tear Us Apart" INXS
https://www.youtube.com/watch?v=AIBv2GEnXlc

Visit CharmaineLouiseBooks.com

CHAPTER 1

"THE QUARTERLY NUMBERS show an increase in profits. More than projected because of the opening of the beachfront resort in Charleston earlier than planned. The general manager reports the property sold out for the first four months…"

I nod as my Vice President of Hotels and Resorts for Larson Enterprises, Inc. continues his update. My mind focuses partially on his presentation.

For the last few weeks, I can't seem to focus. I don't know whether lack of sleep causes the lapse or something else. Dreams of another dominate my nights. They remain just out of reach, on the fringes. But it's their silent pleas for help that keep me tossing. A vibration from them of fear and sadness draws me closer. My instinct kicks in, and I want to save them, protect them.

Each dream brings me closer to them. But they remain

just out of reach. I wake tangled in silk sheets. An arm extended as my hand reaches for them. Last night I called a name. However, as the last vestiges of the dream slipped away, the name dissolved with it.

I growl low in my chest in frustration.

My COO shifts his gaze to me. His wolf senses picked up my displeasure with ease.

I shake my head at Tag Dahl.

He cocks his head at me.

As my best friend, he's known me since we were pups. Born within a few weeks of each other—him to our pack's enforcer and me to our Alpha—Tag knows me as well as I know myself. I haven't mentioned my dreams to him, not that he'd think me nuts. No. I just don't know what they mean and if they warrant a conversation for analysis.

And Tag would delve into their meaning.

As my beta, he's my right-hand man. Anything that involves me and can impact our pack, he wants to solve the puzzle.

But this one will remain under wraps until I figure it out. So, I shake my head again and turn my attention back to the presentation. Even as I will my mind to pay full attention. I remove my personal hat. Then I firmly affix the one for my roles as CEO and Chairman of the Board of the luxury hotels, fine dining, clubs, and lounges company my family founded in Miami.

An hour later, a persistent Tag strides along with me to my suite of offices in The Larson Tower on Biscayne Bay. We pass through the executive floor as staff—wolf shifter and human—acknowledge us. The unaware humans often stare in awe at our formidable sizes. We're both six feet, seven inches of pure muscle and move with predatory grace. We nod in return but continue without pause.

I know Tag wants to find out what's up with me. I'll

allow his henpecking since we're so close. Otherwise, I do not tolerate others in my business. No. One.

"Alpha, you have a few voicemails, sir."

"Thanks, Ginny," I respond to my administrative assistant as I open the double doors of my office. "Kindly hold my calls."

"What's up, Jagger?"

I bite back an irritated growl—lack of sleep will have you pissed, even at your best friend who only wants to help.

"You want a drink?" I ask as I unbutton the jacket of my bespoke three-piece Brioni suit and stride to the bar cart. It's after five-thirty, and I can use a stiff one before I head out to Club Sol & Mani for some much-needed sexual relief.

"Sure, thanks."

I take my time pouring two fingers of scotch into the Baccarat crystal tumblers. Absolutely no rush to have Tag pick at my psyche. My ears pick up his almost silent huff, and I chuckle to myself.

"Don't delay this conversation, Jag. You've been off for a few weeks now, and I've given you space," he says, then nods his thanks for the liquor. "What's up with you?"

Again, I allow him to question me, even though I'm his Alpha and my word is final.

I lower myself onto the dove gray tufted leather sofa in the seating area. Tag takes a chair opposite and places an ankle over a knee. I sip my drink as I consider my words. He knows better than to interrupt at this point.

"Dreams."

He cocks his head at the simple one-worded respsonse. I shrug and take another sip.

"For the past few weeks, dreams invade my sleep. Every. Single. Night. Someone's in trouble. But I can't catch their name or where they are to help them," I sigh and stare out the window.

The panoramic view across Biscayne Bay with jet skiers and megayachts on its dazzling surface out to the azure Atlantic Ocean helps to quiet the inner turmoil my wolf and I sense. He turns his massive silvery white head to stare at me with accusatory ice blue eyes. It's as though he knows something I don't and pissed I'm not aware. I run my fingers through my white blond hair as I think on it, then shake my head. No clue.

"What do you recall?" Tag asks as he leans forward and places his elbows on his knees, the scotch tumbler balanced between his sizable hands.

I shrug.

"A brightness in the background prevents a clear view. I know it's outdoors since I hear the hum of insects and feel the warm sun on my skin. Naked skin. So, I must have shifted and returned to my human form."

Another sip of scotch, and I stand to pace my office.

Instinct tells me these are no ordinary dreams. But each morning I account for the whereabouts of my pack, and no one turns up missing. Not knowing who calls for my help drives me and my wolf mad.

I growl and toss back the rest of my scotch. A few long strides and I refill the tumbler.

"No one in our pack seems in trouble. I'll stop by the she-wolves' residences on my way home just to make sure. A few of our unmated males flew to New Orleans for the weekend. I'll shoot a text to them and make sure they didn't get into anything on Bourbon Street."

With a nod of agreement, I hold the decanter up. Tag declines a refill—ever the responsible one. Fine. It's not like wolf shifters can get drunk. Well, not too much. Our systems process substances differently from humans. All the better for us, especially when I'm in this pissy mood.

"Well, you know they say fated mates can have dreams

about the other. The more frequent and intense they become, the closer the pair gets to their first encounter," Tag says. His emerald green eyes scan my face for a reaction. He knows I've waited all these years for my fated mate—and will continue to do so.

Despite my father's damn near daily persistence, I issue the claiming bite and complete the mating bond with a single she-wolf. The last eleven years of nearly nonstop mating runs, with the she-wolves in my pack and those from nearby cities—hell, even overseas. Or galas at our hotels and mixers at our clubs, an accidental encounter, all to persuade me to select a she-wolf as my mate. None of them tempt me in the slightest.

All the she-wolves desire to bond with me. Then the supposed prince—and they were eager to lose their slippers and thongs for me to pick up——now the Alpha of the Miami Wolves Pack. Correction, *Billionaire Wolves of Miami* as the other packs refer to us. With good reason, since we're the most powerful pack in the South.

Several millennia ago, Scandinavian Viking wolf shifters sailed from the Old World and landed along the East Coast of what's now the United States. The six packs headed by best friends who sought new lands moved throughout the continent to form territories with ours settling here. We maintain close ties with our brethren through friendship, mating, and business. Plus, our Ruling Council gatherings keep us informed of happenings throughout the packs.

And even going that far and wide, I have yet to meet my fated mate. However, I will wait for her.

Hell, my wolf demands it as he gets agitated when he senses a she-wolf's burgeoning interest. Sure, he'll sit back while I fuck since it fills a need and doesn't equate to being mated. Wolf shifters—male and female—have strong sexual appetites. We don't have the same hang-ups as humans over casual sex, no sex before marriage, and whatever other bull-shit they come up with. It's a part of our lives, just like eating or breathing. A need we won't suppress. Particularly with the built-up tension raging through my body. However, his pacing and snarls have increased recently, too.

So maybe Tag is on to something.

My *fated* mate.

A she-wolf whose scent I was born with teasing my nostrils. When she appears, I will recognize her by her distinct scent. No other will bear her uniqueness. Someday we will meet. I will give her my claiming bite, and we will have our mate bonding ceremony for all the clans to witness. I will make her mine forever.

The thought she may be in trouble makes my blood boil and my wolf snap his teeth, ears flat to his head. Our protective instinct on high alert.

So, I won't give up on finding my fated mate—or on us. No matter how many times my father bugs me about the need to bond with another. I'm no longer the teen who had to obey.

I am Alpha now.

~

"WE'RE HERE, ALPHA."

I glance up from my mobile screen and out the tinted window.

So focused on business emails, I didn't notice my driver pull my Black Badge Rolls-Royce Cullinan into the driveway for Club Sol & Mani Miami. The flagship of six exclusive, luxury, members only BDSM clubs Larson Enterprises owns sits on Ocean Drive directly across from the Atlantic Ocean in a South Beach historic, beachfront gated mansion.

"Great, thank you, Cole," I respond. "I'll take it from here and will text when I'm ready to go home."

"Yes, Alpha. I'll get the door for you."

I wave him off and reach for the handle, only for the club's valet to open the door. A nod to Cole and a thanks in the form of a hundred to the young wolf shifter, and I stride to the scrolled wrought-iron and glass doors of the Spanish-style mansion. Laughter from members as they frolic in the mosaic-tiled pool within the sun-filled courtyard floats in the balmy evening air.

"Good evening, Alpha," the doorman says with a respectful bow of his head. I shake his hand and palm off another hundred. He thanks me as I move on.

"Hello, Alpha!" The two she-wolf greeters chorus cheerfully as I walk through the opulent lobby to the elevators. Another two C-notes and I'm on the elevator headed to my personal suite.

Tonight, I'll play in privacy rather than amongst other members in Exhibition where demonstrations and performance rooms provide entertainment—or inspiration. Nor will the Dungeon do, despite my affinity for the spacious section devoted to public forms of BDSM play. Those not in the lifestyle may think it's a medieval dungeon for torture with the St. Andrew's Crosses, spanking benches, chains suspended from the ceiling, and more. To me, the pieces and assorted whips, floggers, canes, and implements are only to be expected.

The soft thrum of sensual music greets me as I step out of the elevator and into the hallway. The rhythm vibrates through my core as intended to amp arousal for what lies behind the closed doors of the eight private suites. Members can reserve them in advance should they prefer the same privacy I wish for tonight.

Each suite decorated by theme has various BDSM

pieces, implements, and toys. A nice variety of options to choose from. However, my suite remains for my personal use only.

I press my palm against the plate by the door of the corner suite, and the locks disengage.

"Good evening, Alpha."

My head jerks up. What the fuck?! I allow no one in my space without my consent. My ice blue eyes adjust to the candlelit room. On my custom-built mahogany wood, king-size bed cornered by four thick carved posters and a brass lattice canopy with rings strategically attached sits a she-wolf from my pack. And not just any she-wolf. The sable-haired hellion.

"Melissa, what the fuck are you doing in my suite?!" I snarl as I stalk towards her.

She jerks back as though slapped but recovers quickly. Fully naked, she rises from the bed with the prowess of a wolf in hunt mode and slinks towards me. Amber eyes glow in the candlelight. She tosses her waist-length sable brown hair over her shoulders. Her sleek figure with high perky tits tipped by puckered rosy nipples, flat belly, narrow waist, slim hips, and long, toned legs would make any male salivate.

Not me.

Even though I planned to fuck her tonight—after I *invited* her to my suite—my stomach churns at the thought as my wolf growls low in his broad chest. He's not happy, nor am I.

Melissa is one of my regular sexual partners. We scratch the itch for each other from time to time. However, it's not like we're exclusive. Many a she-wolf join me for carnal pleasures. As Melissa has with other males. And I've made it clear I am not interested in bonding with her.

But after this stunt, this may very well be the last time I

hookup with her. If she thinks she can enter my domain uninvited, she's confused. And I will speak with the club manager about her gaining unapproved access.

I have no intention of giving Melissa any ideas.

Not happening.

For one, Melissa thinks she's the alpha since the other male wolf shifters in our pack bow down to her beauty and succumb to her whims. I won't have it.

Not to mention she's a bully. Another trait I will not tolerate. I treat everyone in our pack with respect. They may not be my equal, but I don't make them feel less than.

And the most important reason… She's not my fated mate. The only wolf shifter who will enter my domain as she pleases.

My wolf agrees with a flick of his feathery tail.

"Melissa, I have told you we fuck. Nothing more"—I raise my hand to stop her response—"You have no right to enter my personal suite without my permission. None. Get dressed. I will inform the club manager not to allow you entry ever again. This is it. Do you understand?"

She blinks, then her mouth opens.

I fold my arms over my chest and stand with feet spread far apart in a dominant manner as I pin her with an arctic gaze.

Naturally, Melissa glares back and mimics my stance as her eyes blaze golden fire.

"Jag—"

"Alpha! Alpha, Melissa. And do not forget it. We may have fucked. But you will respect me as your Alpha. Get. Dressed. And. Go. Now."

She lifts her chin in defiance, then reconsiders when I slap my sizable palm on my muscular thigh. Her eyes widen at the warning. Then she scurries to the chair and gathers her clothes to her flushed chest.

"Yes, Alpha!" She exclaims.

With a stern eye, I watch as she dresses quickly.

Melissa stops at the door and glances at me over her shoulder. Her oval-shaped face pinched with worry. She knows she took it too far this time.

"Sorry, Alpha," she whispers, then opens the door and leaves.

I sigh and sink onto the bed.

Well, there goes the idea of releasing tension. More just built up.

With his tongue hanging out from the side of his mouth, my wolf yips. Ice blue eyes gleam with mirth. It's as though he laughs at my misfortune.

I growl at him and slump back on the navy blue silk pillows. My thoughts drift to my conversation with Tag. Perhaps fate doesn't want me with another since my mate will appear soon. My eyes close on a sigh.

Where are you?

CHAPTER 2

 *age*

"HELLO, darling. You came to my mind. How are you?"

Aaaw, so touching.

My heart should flutter as I swoon to the floor, so overcome by my loving fiancé's sweet concern. But it does not. At. All.

Fortunately, we're not on FaceTime, as Rupert Ravenheart prefers to communicate with me since he's miles away up in New York City and I'm in Miami. Otherwise, he'd notice the tortured expression on my face. And yes, the long-distance romance does very little to make my heart grow fonder for him.

Many females would consider me crazy to not fall at Rupert's feet, so taken by his masculine beauty and magnetic personality.

I can admit he's model handsome. A flawless, clean-shaven sculpted face, shoulder-length, straight jet black hair with equally dark obsidian eyes that draw you into their depths. Six feet, six inches of sun-kissed skin cover his lean-muscled frame.

But…

Rupert does nothing for me. No desperate yearning when I gaze at him. Not a sizzle of erotic electricity when our fingers touch. No sense of loss when we're apart—miles or separated by rooms. What I've always expected of my mate. A passion that lingers on the fringes of my thoughts that arouses me when I let it wash over me in pleasurable waves. But with Rupert. N.O.T.H.I.N.G.

And I know why.

My mother Prudence Waters.

He's a part of *her* plan for *my* life. A plan created the moment she felt the spark in her womb when my parents conceived me. Just as her mother did with her at her conception. As the first-born females, our futures never vary from generation to generation in all our millennia.

We're immortal witches—the rarest of the rare—who stop aging at twenty-nine. Our line descends from witches who left Nubia—the land south of present-day Egypt and north of Sudan, and its civilization predates both—millennia ago. Their migration led them to this continent. Covens dispersed to various areas of what's now the United States, Canada, and Mexico. Some went even further to Central America into Latin America. My ancestors established our coven in the area of present-day Miami.

In our matriarchal society, it's the eldest daughter who replaces her mother as leader of their coven. And in my case, the additional roles of High Witch—since we're the most powerful coven of all, even beyond the continent—and the head of the Witch Council. It's expected of me to carry the mantle—rather, in our case, to wear the Waters Talisman—and stick with the plan.

Marry Rupert Ravenheart. In a week...

Aargh!

At my birth, my and his mothers betrothed us to bond the covens of the South and the Northeast—the second most powerful. Rupert is the eldest son of their coven's leader and five years older than me at thirty-three. For the last ten years, we've been officially engaged with a ring and a date. A date for my twenty-second birthday, then my twenty-fifth, and now my twenty-eighth.

Yes, each time I found an excuse to delay the intended nuptials. I wanted to graduate from Spelman College, then for them to coincide with a quarter of a century. Now, my mother put an end to me dragging my feet with the pronouncement of the wedding date with invitations sent to those worthy of attendance and a gown selected. Again, no input from me. At. All. I certainly wouldn't have chosen a pouf of a princess ballgown.

Not that I care since I dread the coming day, anyway. At the very thought of it, my head feels like a sledge-hammer hit it and my stomach roils. I have to take a nap just to clear my mind. And it's only gotten worse as the day nears.

Aargh... Aargh!

I close my eyes and inhale deeply to clear my musings before I answer Rupert. My eyes open on the exhalation, and I paste a smile on my face. They say if you smile when you talk it perks up your voice. We'll see.

"Oh, how sweet of you, Rupert. I'm well, thank you."

"Wonderful, darling! It's always lovely to hear your voice. So, I'm glad I called..."

He rambles on, none the wiser of my false cheer.

"—saying, Sage? Darling, are you there?"

His questions draw me back to his conversation.

Quickly, I recover.

"Y—Yes, of course, Rupert! I have a vendor call in a few minutes. Do you mind if I ring off?"

Silence follows my question, and I squirm in my seat.

Does he notice I'm lying? I mean, he is a witch and has magick. I just don't know what—never bothered to ask, really.

"Not at all, darling," Rupert replies at last, then snaps his fingers. "Ah, yes, I just remembered! Enjoy your bachelorette party tonight. Do nothing naughty, darling."

I cringe as my eyes squeeze shut. Tightly.

Aargh!

The party slipped my mind, of course.

"I won't!" I squeak.

Another beat of silence, then Rupert asks, "Sage, are you sure you're okay?"

"Absolutely! But, listen, I have to go. Talk soon, Byeee!" I press the end button on my mobile and drop it on my drafting table. The heels of my palms cover my eyelids as I practice my deep breathing exercises.

"Sage, are you okay?"

I jump at the voice behind me and spin around on my stool. If it weren't a feminine tone, I would have thought Rupert used teleportation to get here in moments. Instead, I find my younger sisters—Willow and Lillie—in the doorway of my office above my Sage's Gems & Jewels luxury custom-made jewelry boutique in The Waters Tower Mall.

I wave my hands and shake my head.

"Yes, yes, I'm fine. A bit of a headache, that's all," I respond as I hop off the stool and hug the identical twins. "What brings you here?"

Willow and Lillie turn their heads towards the other, do some twin-mind communication, then swivel at me. Their narrowed emerald green eyes—so like mine, a maternal trait —scan my face.

I try my best to remain stoic. But I sense heat rising beneath my toffee-colored cheeks. With my extraordinary powers, I could fashion a glamour to disguise my flush. But magick doesn't work on family members and mates. The Twins would see right through the temporary guise. Then they'd really question me. And I don't need it right now.

"Hello? You didn't answer my question. Not that I mind you coming to see me. But what's up?" I ask to end their analysis.

They nod as grins spread across their beautiful faces, again so like mine.

Many people think we're triplets, even though they're four years younger. Add our mother to the group, and we're quadruplets. We're so similar, it's like peering into the mirror at our individual reflections. Our heights hint at who's who with The Twins five feet, four inches, me an inch taller, and our mother two more than me.

While my sisters and I vary the styles of our waist-length ebony curls, Prudence wears hers wound in a bun at the nape of her neck. Some would think it's severe, but the hairstyle serves to highlight her sculpted cheekbones and flawless toffee-colored skin. My mother is stunning and doesn't look a day older than twenty-nine despite being centuries old. No glamour needed.

"Party time, Ms. Bride-to-Be!" Lillie exclaims as she claps her hands.

Willow throws her hands in the air and wiggles her curvy hips. "Yes! We are going to have a blast tonight, Sage!"

"I can't believe you haven't pushed the wedding date back again. Mother was not playing with you this time!" Lillie giggles as her eyes shine and her dainty nose crinkles.

"Third time's the charm—no pun!" Willow adds, doubling over with laughter.

If only they knew the level of torment that besieges me. But I'm resigned to my fate.

Unconsciously, my hand touches the Waters Talisman.

The necklace imbued with magickal powers to protect and to heal passes down from one High Witch to the next. It also serves to signify her roles and importance within our community. Over the millennia, some wearers re-set it. However, the original gems never change. Currently, the large turquoise stone with agate around it is set in white gold. The creator chose the gems based on their properties. Turquoise known as a sacred stone of power, luck, and protection. Agate to transform negative energy into positive and to enhance perception and analytical abilities. All qualities beneficial for a High Witch who must remain strong, clearheaded, and decide for all.

I wear the Waters Talisman with pride and dedication. In this instance, I seek its soothing and calming qualities.

My mobile chimes for the delivery of a text message, and I'm thankful for the interruption. As The Twins chatter on, I pick my mobile up from the drafting table. A genuine smile brightens my mood as my cousin and best friend's name appears on the screen—Anala Azar.

Hi! Just landed on my way to your penthouse duplex. Make sure the wards will allow my entry. Love ya! A.A.

Although Anala is a powerful elemental witch who controls fire and a badass vampire hunter, she prefers to fly on her private jet instead of teleportation. Don't ask…

"Who has you grinning? *Rupert?*"

And just like that, my stomach twists.

Aargh!

～

"THIS MUSIC IS PUMPING! I'm hitting the dance floor to shake my thing again," a tipsy Anala announces after she applies gloss to her pouty lips.

She, along with Willow, Lillie, and a few friends from our coven sip mojitos and cosmopolitans gathered around our VIP booth at the opening night for the exclusive Club Hati. My girls vowed to make my bachelorette party a fun night. I go along with the tasty drinks and pulse-pounding music.

My gaze roams around the opulent club full of the glitterati. Celebrities, socialites, fashionistas, and billionaire tycoons wear their sexiest, most revealing outfits. Bottles of top-shelf liquor and magnums of champagne sit atop the tables in booths like ours.

Partiers pack the dance floor with their booty shaking as they grind and gyrate to the DJ's booming tunes. Those not fortunate to have a booth stand two deep at the three bars or perch on stools at high-top tables surrounding the dance floor.

"Hold on," I shout over the music to Anala. "I'm coming with you!"

We weave through the crowd as the heady scent of various perfumes and colognes mixed with sweat assails our nostrils the closer we get to the dancers. I love it! The sensuous, undulating sea of bodies calls me to revel with them.

Anala and I make quite the sight as we dance in the middle of the crowd. Anala in a glittering fiery red sequin tank dress that skims the tops of the toned thighs of her five-eight-inch frame. Her ample bust nearly spilling over the top as she raises her arms overhead. She tosses her mane of ebony curly hair over her shoulder. Brown eyes dance with delight. She draws appreciative stares from the drop-dead gorgeous guys closing in on us as she seductively shimmies to the beat.

I match her moves with some of my own as I drop it low. The silver spangles of my fitted, strapless mini dress catch the LEDs like a spotlight. My shoulders shake as I rock back up to stand tall in my strappy sandals. Lost in the beat, I jump when brawny hands grip my hips to pull me against a massive chest. Trapped in the man's hands, I can only peer over my shoulder to see his face.

Golden amber eyes stare down at me from more than a foot above. Long silky caramel hair frames an angular face with a five o'clock shadow kissing the firm jaw. He smirks, and his eyes flash.

Well, damn.

"*Si, hermosa,* damn is correct," he rumbles in my ear. "You are a siren in your itty-bitty dress."

His warm breath sends goosebumps to the surface of my feverish skin slick with sweat from dancing for hours. The sensation of his thick dick grinding into my ass as his grip tightens on my hips nearly causes me to swoon. Whether it's the cocktails or the heat, I have the sudden desire for the man in whose embrace I shiver to have his way with me. Then I shake my head and pull away from him as my stomach clenches.

Will any man do? I wonder as he bows his head and makes his way through the crowd.

"Hey, are you all right?" Anala asks as she leans towards my ear. "He was hot as hell, Sage! You're not married yet, honey. You could've danced with him. Live a little!"

Her chocolate brown eyes sparkle with naughty intentions as she tracks his movements across the dance floor.

I follow her gaze and see him talking to three other big, beautiful boys. Their eyes shift to Anala and me. Grins that can only be called feral spread on their faces. They nod at us.

Anala wiggles her fingers.

I shiver.

"Anala, I'm not feeling too well. It's time for me to call it a night," I tell her as she half listens to me, too enthralled by the hotties. I take her arm and tug. "Come on. Let's go back to our table. Then I'm leaving."

I drag her from the dance floor and back to the VIP section. She giggles and follows along, swaying her hips in time to the music.

"Hey! We saw that guy grinding on you, Sage. Way to go, sis!" Willow says as Anala slips onto the white leather banquette.

Lillie frowns and asks, "Yeah! Why didn't you dance with him? He was smoking hot!"

I glance back towards where the guys stand. They still watch us and wave before I swing my head back around.

My girls laugh at me and call me a boring prude. They remind me—as Anala did—my wedding isn't for another seven days and I should enjoy my freedom.

Sadly, I couldn't agree more. Yet, even the hunks—as gorgeous and tempting as they may be—don't do it for me. No more than Rupert.

Aargh!

Willow and Lillie drag me back to the dance floor just as I sit on the banquette. Their shenanigans and laughter prevent me from asking my driver to take me home pronto. Those thoughts fade away as more attractive—albeit drooling—guys pivot towards us. With a shrug, I let go and dance. The wedding is days away, and I will have fun now!

CHAPTER 3

 agger

"Wow, I can't believe you actually came to the opening party, Jag. I figured you'd grump out as usual. Welcome back to the fun side of life, bro! Hey, maybe you'll even get laid!"

I growl at Viggo—my younger brother by two years at twenty-six—who winks an ice blue eye at me as I stalk past him to the floor-to-ceiling windows perched above Club Hati's dance floor. It teems with gyrating bodies. Scantily clad females, metrosexual males, macho types—wolf shifter and human—all vying for attention. And to get laid.

With a snort, I turn back to the interior of the club's office. Tag holds up a bottle of scotch, and I nod. I could use a stiff drink. My fingers run through my white blond hair and tug at my scalp.

Fuck!

The dreams have been incessant. Back-to-back every night this week. I can almost make out her face. Her, since the bright light lessened enough to show a petite, curvy female—although her face remains hidden in shadow. The urgency in her pleas for help drive my wolf and me mad!

"Here, looks like you need a drink."

I scowl at Tag as he hands a Lalique crystal snifter to me and chuckles. With a tilt of my chin in thanks, I stalk back to survey the club.

Viggo did a great job, as always. As the President of Clubs and Lounges for Larson Enterprises, Inc., this sits in his wheelhouse. My fun-loving and smart brother regularly increases profits for his division. So, he can get away with his dumb ass quips. To an extent.

I sip on my scotch as I watch the happenings below. The others—including Rust, my other best friend—sit around and shoot the shit. They're used to going out regularly. Except for Tag, who, like me, keeps a low profile most of the time.

I notice Enrique—one of our pack's deltas who runs messages between our allies and our enemies—cozying up to a stunningly beautiful female. Unfortunately for him, she thwarts his advances. I chuckle and take another sip of my scotch. Even though he's off duty, I have to follow up with him on a recent task.

Moments later, he enters the office in response to my text message.

"*Buenas noches*, Alpha," Enriques says. "You wanted to—"

A menacing growl thunders through the office as my wolf fights to spring free and launch himself at Enrique. My hands grab the sides of my head as the scent of my fated mate fills my nostrils. The scent of the Everglades after a spring rain woody and earthy with a hint of sea salt carried on the breeze from the Atlantic Ocean.

And the scent of *my* fated mate covers *Enrique*.

"What the fuck?!?!?!" I roar as I lunge at my shocked

delta. Multiple hands grip my arms and waist. I fight them and advance, only to get pulled back. "Get the fuck off me!" I focus on Enrique and shout, "Where is she? Where the *fuck* is she?"

"Who, Alpha? Who do you mean?" He asks as Viggo swears while he, Tag, and Rust pin me to the floor.

I glare up at Enrique accusingly.

"Sage… Sage Waters! If you fucked my fated mate, I will rip your fucking throat out and eat your beating heart! Right out of your chest"

I LEFT *my brother Viggo and my best friends—Tag, Dylan, and Rust—behind at the pack's camp in the Everglades so I could have time to myself. My wolf continues along a path in the Everglades at a jog. Then stops mid stride with a paw still up in the air. He turns his head left and right, then tips it back to scent our surroundings.*

I notice his pause in movement. But it's his whine followed by an excited yip before he tears ahead that rouses me. I push past the fog of self-pity and sniff. My heart races faster than my wolf.

My nostrils fill with the scent of the Everglades after a spring rain woody and earthy with a hint of sea salt carried on the breeze from the Atlantic Ocean. Sage! My fated mate is here! With another yip, I engage fully with my wolf.

We reach the same clearing as the first time we laid eyes on our fated mate. Sage faces us, having heard our arrival since we didn't bother to hide our approach through the trees. The corners of her mouth lift slightly as she watches us dash towards her. We stop, and I shift amidst crackling and a flash.

"Sage," I breathe, suddenly afraid she's a figment of my imagination. My eyes scan her face as my hands clasp her upper arms. She's solid, not a wispy illusion. Thank fuck!

"Why did you leave without a word?!" I ask, not bothering to hide my anger. "You could have at least said something. I've been going out of my damn mind. Do you know what happens to a male wolf shifter whose mate leaves him??? We go insane with grief!"

I rant on as Sage stands there held tightly in my grip. I won't let her go so easily.

"Are you all right? Did I hurt you?" I continue in the silence.

Her mouth opens, then closes as she blinks back tears.

Oh, great. Now I made her cry. Damn!

I pull her against me and rumble deep in my chest as one hand strokes from the top of her curly head to her round ass. An ass my palm itches to spank. Hard. How dare she run away from me—us?! It won't happen again. Or I will punish my fated mate. Soundly.

Sage winds her arms around my waist as she presses her forehead against my chiseled eight-pack abs. She's so tiny compared to my brawny frame. The perfect package.

"I didn't mean to upset you, mate—"

Her entire body tenses at the word mate. She loosens her hold on me and tries to step out of my arms.

Not happening. No.

I bend my knees to align our eyes. Her emerald greens filled with tears stare back at me woefully. Her lower lip quivers.

"Sage, you are my fated mate. Period. There is no denying us. Witch, wolf shifter, it does not matter," I tell her as I squeeze her hip bones. "How did you feel these past two weeks?"

Her eyes close as pain etches across her gorgeous face.

I squeeze her hip bones again, and she jumps.

"Open your eyes and look at me. Do not hide," I command.

Her eyes pop open as my mouth forms a perfect O in surprise at my tone of voice. Yes, I'm going all Alpha male on you, bad little fated mate, I muse.

"Tell me."

She takes a deep breath, then lets it out on a heavy sigh. But her eyes remain on mine.

"Not good. Not good at all. I ached for you," she starts, then lowers her voice. "I had more dreams."

I cock an eyebrow, and she tells me about them. I ponder their meaning for a moment. Then shake my head to clear it. Nothing matters except for my beautiful, fated mate being back in my arms. Where she belongs.

My fated mate awakens the most fierce side of my protective and possessive instincts. She's unfurled a carnal desire beyond anything I've ever felt before, deep in my soul. Mine! Only mine!

I pull her close and kiss the top of her head. Her unique scent fills my nostrils, and I sigh. Peace at last. Whatever we have to face, we will do it together.

My fated mate, my wolf, and me.

For now, I'm content to hold Sage Waters in my arms forever.

"Jagger Larson! Get away from that witch!"

"Sage Waters! Step back from that wolf shifter!"

My head snaps up as my wolf snarls and bares his teeth, ears flattened to his massive skull, ice blue eyes flash. A ferocious growl tears from my chest as I yank my fated mate behind me. My instinct to protect Sage heightened by the unexpected arrival of my father and, I guess, her mother. Their angry demands make my wolf claw to the surface, ready to fight for our fated mate.

"Mother!"

"I mean it, Sage. Step away from that beast, now!"

"Jag—"

"No!" I growl as I face down my father. Both pairs of ice blue eyes spark. "Sage is my fated mate! We will never part! Ever! I don't give a damn what either of you say!"

My father nods at Sage's mother.

She raises her hands as her lips move...

"Mother, no! Don't—"

Sage's words cut off as she crumbles to the ground, still as a stone statue.

My roar shakes the tops of the pine trees. I lunge for her mother. As I spring into the air, I loose my wolf, canines bared for the kill.

Her mother's emerald green eyes widen for a second, then narrow as her incantation focuses on me.

My wolf whines in mind-blowing pain, and we drop at her feet. The last thing I see is the face of my fated mate staring sightlessly towards me. An anguished cry forms in my mouth but never comes out.

As my memories flood into my brain—triggered by the scent of my fated mate—a formidable strength courses through me. I throw Viggo, Tag, and Rust off me and leap to my feet. I ignore their shouts as I race from the office. Like a mad male, I search the club for my fated mate, only stopping to scent the air. I catch a trace of it near the hall leading to the restrooms.

Mate!

I push past the patrons, paying no heed to their complaints. As I reach the door for the ladies' room, it opens. Chest heaving and wild-eyed, I stare into the gorgeous face of my fated mate, Sage Waters. With a feral growl of mate, I grab her arm and pull her towards the back exit.

SAGE

"Now, I am going home. You guys can't kidnap me, you know—"

My sentence ends abruptly as the most beautiful male

I've ever seen grabs my arm and pulls me down the corridor. So stunned, I can't react. My feet follow him as I hear Anala curse behind me. But he's too fast for her to catch up to us.

He slams a door. We burst into the night.

My senses return.

"Hey! Let me go!" I scream as I tug against his firm grip.

He's humongous. All muscle. Well over a foot taller than me, at least six, seven, I guess as I stare up the length of his broad back to his white blond head. He faces away from me. But somehow, I have an inkling I know him from somewhere.

He ignores my cries and tosses me over his shoulder with ease.

Startled, I take a moment to understand what just happened. Then I flail my legs and punch his back with my fists. Three cracks on my ass stun me still. What the hell?!?!?!

"Hey! Put me down, or you'll be sorry!" I scream. We're not supposed to use our powers in public. But being kidnapped proves an emergency situation. My fingers tingle as I invoke a spell to stop him cold. But damned if it doesn't work. I try again to no effect.

My mouth drops in shock at the failure of my powers. Dumbfounded, I barely react when he places me on the passenger seat of a sports car and secures me with the seatbelt. The soft thump of the door closing breaks my fog.

I yank on the seatbelt as he slides in from the driver's side. Frantic to get free of the hulking male, my fingers react clumsily, and I fumble with the metal.

"Sage..."

I turn just as his nostrils flare as he inhales deeply. Then his mouth crashes on mine. Surprised, my lips part on a gasp. His tongue invades my mouth. It sweeps around as though tasting me, then tangles with my tongue.

My body sags as my brain short circuits. He literally kisses me senseless.

And I love it!

I lean into him, straining against the seatbelt.

He rips it free. Webbed cloth and metal tear like cotton in his sizable hands. He pulls me onto his lap. My knees straddle his hips, and the hem of my mini dress rises up my thighs.

I mewl as the thick bar of his dick presses against my lower lips even while his mouth plunders mine. As though my body has a mind of its own, I grind against him. My nipples pucker, and my core gushes to prepare for the beast hidden within his trousers. All thoughts of getting away from him melt under his wicked tongue and now his hands as they slide along my flanks and cup my heavy breasts.

His thumbs brush the distended tips. I arch my back and mewl into his mouth. He growls and nips my lips.

I cry out in carnal bliss. One hand leaves his silky hair to snake between us. I must have him. Now! He growls again and shifts in the seat to give me better access. My fingertips brush the tip of his ginormous dick, and it grows even larger as it pulsates against my hand.

"Sage!!!"

I jump at the sound of Anala's voice.

The giant male growls savagely at the interruption. The vibration in his powerful chest runs through me. I mewl and cling to him, ignoring my cousin.

She bangs on the window.

I glance through the tinted glass, not sure I want her to rescue me.

The engine purrs to life, and the car leaps forward.

I bring my gaze back to—my captor?

He peers around me as he speeds the car down the alley and away from the club. His ice blue eyes flick up at me for a second.

I get dizzy under his possessive stare. My thighs tremble around his hips.

His hand pats my ass, and I gasp.

"We're going home now, Sage."

How the hell does he know my name? Better yet, what the hell does he mean by *going home*? Who's *home*?!?!?! I don't even know who the hell he is!

What's worse?

I don't even mind.

CHAPTER 4

Jagger

I IGNORE the incessant vibrations from my mobile in the pocket of my trousers. Viggo, Tag, and Rust better back the fuck up and stay out of my business. I have to secure my fated mate at our home.

My eyes flick to Sage as she sits beside me in silence. Her gaze remains directed outside the window as I navigate my Bugatti Chiron along Ocean Drive, headed towards my bayfront mansion on Moon Island—my pack's private island in Biscayne Bay, South Beach.

I guess I should be thankful she hasn't demanded I pull over and let her out. Not that I would. I found my fated mate again, and I will never let her go. Denied Once. Never again.

Light from an overhead streetlamp glints on a diamond engagement ring.

A growl of possession rumbles in my chest. My fingers

tighten around the leather steering wheel until my knuckles whiten. I burn to rip the damn ring off and toss it out the window as we speed along MacArthur Causeway. Then howl in triumph as the ring sinks beneath the inky black waters of the bay to disappear forever.

Just like the fucker who put it on her finger will once I get my hands—or paws—on him.

Sage jolts in her seat and swings her startled gaze to me. Her eyes search my face for the cause of the growl.

"Sorry, baby," I say as my hand slides from the steering wheel to the top of her thigh. At the touch of her warm, bare skin, my cock twitches confined within my trousers. I bite back a pained groan.

Sage nods and returns to the window. She doesn't shift under the weight of my palm. She lets it remain on her leg. I give it a pat and a squeeze.

Another win.

We continue the intimate connection until I turn off the causeway and pull up to the wrought-iron gates for the entrance to Moon Island. Two members of our security team sit in the guardhouse. Their eyes glow in the supercar's headlights. They recognize my car and wave.

Any other time, I'd lower my window and return the gesture. But I don't want them to see my fated mate just yet. Despite me being Alpha, many in my pack will complain— or worse—their Luna is a witch and the High Witch, nonetheless. Too damn bad.

The gates' sensor detects its counterpart installed in my car, and they swing inward. I drive through and along the main road to my mansion.

Residences ranging from ranch style to two- and three-story line the road. Some front Biscayne Bay, while others have interior views. On the other end, in the interior of Moon Island, a mini town offers options for those who prefer not to leave our protected land. A school for younger members of the pack, restaurant, deli, pizza shop, beauty salon, and barber shop are available.

I glance over at my fated mate to gauge her reaction to her new home. Still quiet, she stares with no outward response. I'll take it as another win.

When we roll onto the driveway covered in stone pavers for my Spanish-style ten-thousand square foot mansion, my fated mate leans forward in her seat. The landscaping lighting scheme puts a golden glow on her toffee-colored face. Her emerald green eyes dance over the mansion's front lit by strategically placed decorative sconces and pot lights. Then shift to the water fountain in the center of the circular driveway. Her eyes widen at the large marble wolf on his haunches with his head tilted back for a howl. From his mouth, water jets to the sky. Lights enhance the beauty of the feature. Her curious eyes skitter to me, then back to the fountain.

I hop out of the car before she can say a word.

Sage takes my hand as I extend it to help her from the low supercar.

My nostrils flare at the scent of her arousal as her legs swing to place her feet on the stone pavers. She's so small, even in her fuck-me heels she only reaches my chest. My eyes close briefly on an inhalation. My cock weeps.

I keep her hand in mine as we walk to the front doors. They open when I place my other palm on the plaque. She enters ahead of me with her head held high, as though accustomed to coming home. The swish of her long, ebony curls draws my eyes to her round ass in that tiny excuse of a dress.

Who else besides Enrique held her close enough to feel her lush body? A possessive growl rumbles.

My fated mate tosses a glance at me over her shoulder as

her heels click on the marble floor on her way to the opposite wall of accordion glass doors.

"Would you care for a drink, Sage?" I ask to distract her.

She shakes her head, never turning from the captivating sight of Biscayne Bay at night as lights from the surrounding islands and South Beach glow all around. Her curvy body silhouetted against the glass. I admire her view much more than the one outside for a moment, then turn to the bar. I need a drink.

My fingers run through my hair to adjust its wildness before I pour two fingers of scotch in a Baccarat crystal glass.

As I come up behind my fated mate—close enough to sniff—she turns her head towards me slightly.

"You're a wolf shifter."

She states it rather than asking for my answer.

"Yes."

Sage turns fully and takes the tumbler from my hand and tosses back the entire drink. I blink in surprise as she swipes her mouth with the back of her dainty hand.

"You said, 'mate.'"

"Yes."

"As in *me* being *your* mate?"

"Yes."

She nods her head at my empty tumbler. "Another."

I return her nod and stride towards the bar. My wolf senses detect she watches me intently. But she doesn't utter another word. As I stalk to my fated mate, her eyes glide over me from head to toe while her face remains expressionless. Back in front of her, she takes the drink and sips once before she turns to the view.

"You know my name. What is yours?"

"Jagger Larson."

"And this is Moon Island. Am I correct to assume you're the Alpha of the Miami Wolves Pack?"

"Yes."

She nods once and takes another sip, then cradles the tumbler to her breasts.

"How do you know my name and I'm clueless of yours?"

"Your mother wiped our memories with my father's permission."

At that, Sage pivots to face me. Her emerald green eyes wide with shock—and dare I say anger? They scan my face. I maintain an open expression so she can sense no guile in my words. She cloaks her emotions and takes another sip, then nods.

"When?"

"Ten years ago."

"Did you claim me before she... Before she did what she did to us?" She asks with a wave of her hand. I shudder at its similarity to her mother's actions so long ago.

"No."

She nods.

"But... I made you mine another way."

I place my hands—that have itched to touch her again since we entered our home—on her grip-worthy hips. My lips trace the side of her face as they seek the delicate shell of her ear.

"I made you mine when I took your virginity, *mate*."

She gasps and trembles in my arms.

"You are mine, Sage Waters. Then and now. I will claim you and make you mine forever."

Her emerald green eyes stare up at my ice blue ones.

"Well, we have two insurmountable problems. You're a wolf shifter, and I'm a witch," she says, then raises her left hand between us. "And I get married in seven days."

~

SAGE

JAGGER'S EYES WIDEN, then narrow to glowing sapphire slits as they flick from my face to the engagement ring on the left hand I hold up.

During the ride, my head cleared. Well, as much as it could, considering his intoxicating masculine scent—a potent combination of pheromones, sweat, and yes, a primal wolf—allowed. I realized he must be a wolf shifter.

He emanates the sensual power and confidence of a lethal apex predator—a wolf shifter or a vampire. The feral growls—that send shivers along my spine and moisten my core—tipped the scales to the wolf shifter. The water fountain in front of his mansion confirmed my suspicions.

Despite our apparent sexual attraction to one another, a wolf shifter and a witch can never be mates. Not now, not ever. Especially since he's the Alpha of his pack and I'm the leader of my coven, High Witch, and head of the Witch Council. Talk about triple whammy...

All beings in the overall paranormal world know of one another. We'll even work together to achieve a common goal we can accomplish better together. It's not as if we live in our separate bubbles and don't interact. Hell, my bachelorette party was at a club with wolf shifters, and I danced with a few of them.

However, witches frown upon shifters of any kind. Some even refer to the wolf shifters as mangy dogs. The snobbish belief they're less than our kind since we predate them. Hence, the rivalry goes back millennia. It's ingrained in most of the elder witches.

Me, not so much. I don't despise shifters. Obviously,

since I just wrapped my heated body around their sexy as sin Alpha. But I know I could never become involved with one. My future mate is Rupert Ravenheart. I sigh and shake my head.

"There's no getting around who we are. What that means for any chance of us being mates, Jagger. No matter what this attraction may be, you and I can never be—"

"NO!"

His roar rips through the air. The veins in his thick neck bulge as his anger punches the air. He clenches his fists and storms away from me to pace the floor of the living room.

I watch, unafraid. Deep in my heart, I know Jagger Larson would never hurt me. He's dealt with this longer than I have. Wait a minute!

"Obviously, you recovered your memories. So, if you knew we were mates, what took so long for you to find me? I mean, we're both in Miami. You know my name and who I am. It makes little sense," I say as the thought occurs to me.

Jagger turns to face me. He stalks over and towers over me. His sizable, calloused hand cups my face as he leans in and nuzzles my neck. He murmurs against my skin.

I shiver from his warm breath and soft lips. A mewl followed by his name escapes my slack mouth.

He rumbles deep in his chest—not so much a growl. Rather, a sound that soothes as the vibrations roll through me.

"Your scent, baby. I lost it along with my memories until tonight. I do not know what happened. All I know is I scented you on one of my male wolves and nearly killed him for touching what is mine. The memories returned immediately at the recognition of my fated mate's unique scent. *Your* unique scent, mate."

I gasp, shocked Jagger thinks we're *fated* mates and not

just a regular pair. To be the one linked to him through time forever?! This is a lot more dangerous. And impossible.

I back away from him, shaking my head.

He advances, ice blue eyes flash with a predatory gleam as they lock on my wide emerald green orbs. The rumble in his chest increases.

My butt hits the wall of glass behind me.

His forearms lift to bracket either side of my head. He leans down, soft lips hover over mine…

With the sound of his soothing rumble in my ears and the whisper of his lips on mine, I land on my bed. A strangled cry bursts from my lips. In the seconds it took for me to use my magick to teleport from Moon Island to my bedroom, the ache for the wolf shifter pulses between my thighs.

My magick works. It just doesn't work on him.

I roll to my side and cover my flushed face with my hands as a desperate moan slips past my trembling lips. Can we be mates after all? *Fated* mates???

Impossible for a witch and a wolf shifter!

No, we can never be.

And what the hell did my mother do to erase *my* memories *and* my scent? What caused the scent to return now but not the memories? Why did Jagger regain both, and I didn't?!

CHAPTER 5

"Bro! What the fuck happened to you last night?!"

"You didn't answer your mobile *and* turned on the perimeter alarms around your mansion?"

"What the fuck, Jag?!!"

I ignore my brother and best friends now, just as I did last night—and this morning. My mind still reels from reconnecting with Sage and from her disappearance. Again! She pulled that same shit the last time when I was about to issue the claiming bite on her. Having a powerful witch as a fated mate may prove my undoing.

My hands ache to hold her against me again. To feel her heat against my skin. Hear her soft moans of carnal pleasure.

Fuck!

I jump up from my desk chair and slam my fists into the pockets of my suit trousers. I spin to face the view of

Biscayne Bay outside my office window. My sudden movement and back to the others silence them. Bunch of nags.

My eyes close as I visualize my gorgeous fated mate. How I burn to have her beneath me as I thrust my cock into her sopping wet pussy and my canines sink into her flesh. Her sweet taste lingers on my tongue from the kisses we shared. I want to plunge it into her spasming pussy and feast on her abundant juices.

Fuck!

My fists clench. I want to bang my forehead on the window in frustration.

I started to confront my father. Then decided it's best to wait until I have Sage back at my side. I want to make certain she's aware I will never let her go. I had to prove us to her before, and I'll do it again. Even if I have to give up all I own to make her mine.

"Alpha, a Sage Waters is down in the lobby asking to see you, sir."

A smile spreads across my face as I pivot and press the intercom to answer Ginny.

"Allow her up, thank you."

I stand and glare at the Three Stooges.

"Out!"

They squawk but leave. I follow them out as I slip my suit jacket on and stride to the elevator. Ask and you shall receive.

The guys grumble as they disperse. Viggo and Tag to their offices while Rust—our pack's doctor and an emergency room doctor at the hospital—strides along with me.

"Listen, Jag, I'm not trying to get in your business"—he pauses when I cock an eyebrow and growl menacingly—"Whoa, bro! Let me finish."

"Fine," I respond with a nod. I value their opinions even if I choose to disregard them.

"Sage Waters is the High Witch. That's pretty taboo. Is she a tryst or more?" Rust asks as his hazel eyes scan my face. When I respond more, he runs his fingers through his shoulder-length dark ginger hair. A curse falls from his mouth. "Damn, Jagger. I'll support you whatever you decide. But that's a huge ask of the pack, bro. You sure you want to go there?"

"Absofuckinglutely!" I nod again as we stop in front of the elevators.

"Okay, bro, I'm with you and I know Viggo and Tag will feel the same way."

I slap him on the shoulder and smile.

The elevator dings its arrival, and the doors open.

My fated mate steps out. Her eyes find mine immediately. I notice a flicker of what I hope is desire before she glances at Rust and back at me.

"Jagger, I hope I didn't disturb your day," Sage says smoothly. I love the way my name rolls off her tongue. "Thank you for seeing me."

"Sage, you will never disturb me," I assure her. I place my hand on her waist and lean in to brush my lips across hers, unable to deny myself the pleasure of the intimate caress. She allows it but pulls away to glance back at Rust.

"Sage Waters, this is Dr. Rust Ingolf, our packs' doctor. Rust, this is Sage Waters, your Luna and my fated mate," I make the formal introductions with an emphasis on Luna.

Sage's eyes widen briefly before she regains control of her features. Rust blinks but extends his hand.

"Luna, I am honored to meet you, and to welcome you to the Miami Wolves Pack," he says with a respectful bow. "If you would be so kind as to excuse me, I must return to the ER."

Now Sage blinks but shakes his hand as she replies, "Of course, a pleasure to meet you, Dr. Ingolf."

Rust bows deeper, nods at me, and steps onto the elevator. As the doors close, the fucker winks at me with a smirk.

I bite back a snarl and place my hand on Sage's lower back to guide her to my office. My fated mate walks beside me with her head held high, regal, as though she recognizes she's the other half of the pack's Alpha.

The human staff don't pay any attention as my fated mate and I walk across the executive floor. However, the wolf shifters track our movements as they sense her level of comfort amongst them. I eye a few of them, and they have the common sense to lower their eyes.

Ginny jumps to her feet with wide eyes when she notices our approach. Apparently, the grapevine reached her already.

"Mr. Larson, sir, should I hold your calls?" She asks as her eyes flick between Sage and me.

I nod, "Yes, Ginny, thank you. In fact, why don't you take your lunch early?"

She blinks, then nods. "Yes, Mr. Larson, as you wish, Alp—I mean, sir!"

Ginny scoots from behind her desk, grabs her handbag, and rushes away without a backwards glance.

Sage laughs under her breath.

"Please don't tell me I scared the poor she-wolf away, Jagger."

I push open my office doors as I shake my head.

"No, baby, she's overwhelmed to see her Luna so unexpectedly," I respond as I usher her through the double doors. "I'm glad you came. I was just thinking about you and how you disappeared on me. Again."

Sage turns and stares at me. I brace myself for her denial of being fated mates.

"I can't deny we're fated mates, Jagger."

My mind reels at her admission. But I keep a straight face and wait for her to continue.

"I used my magick to try and stop you from carting me away from the club. Twice. Each time my magick failed me. Keep in mind I am an advanced witch with unimaginable powers. Yet, they did not work on you," Sage says with an elegantly arched eyebrow. "Only a family member can rebuff a witch's magick... or their mate."

My heart soars through the roof! I want to pump the air with both fists as my wolf bounds about the office. But again, I hold back a response.

She continues.

"I have an appointment to speak with my mother in thirty minutes. I plan to question her about her involvement ten years ago. Since her actions involved you, I came to offer you the opportunity to accompany me."

Now, that's a surprising turn of events. Her choice of the word "confront" lets me know she doesn't plan to sit back and allow her mother to get away with what she did to us. To make us lose ten years together. For what? Because she's a witch and I'm a wolf shifter? Fuck that!

"Let's go," I respond, determined to move forward at all costs. I gesture towards the door beside a shelf where my private elevator waits and place my hand on Sage's lower back as she passes me. She glances over her shoulder at me and arches her eyebrow. But I apply more pressure to guide her forward. She doesn't step away from me.

The wins keep piling up in my favor.

As we wait for the elevator, I shoot a text message to my security detail to tell them to meet us in the garage. Once on the elevator, I admire my fated mate from behind my aviator sunglasses.

She stuns in a white suit with a pencil skirt that hugs her ass oh so right. I want to run my fingertips along her inner thighs up to cup it through the back slit. Beneath the one-button jacket a white silk demi-cup bra plays peekaboo. Damn. Her tits grew. My palms itch to mold to the D-cups as I suckle her tantalizing brown nipples. Hard.

Like my cock, as it punches the zipper of my trousers. I adjust its burgeoning length down my thigh. Soon I will bury my cock balls deep into my fated mate's sweet pussy and bathe her womb with my seed. Our one time so long ago will not be our last. The thought of her fucking fiancé going where I was first makes my blood boil.

Sage glances wide-eyed at me over her shoulder.

I stare back as though a vicious growl didn't slip between my clenched teeth.

She shakes her head at my denial and faces forward without a word.

The elevator doors ping open to the garage level. I place my palm on her lower back and guide her towards my Lamborghini Aventador J. Sage stops.

"What's wrong, baby?" I ask as I glance around us despite no sense of a threat—and it better not be on my territory. Karl, the head of my personal security and our pack enforcers, stands beside one of the two SUVs with the rest of my team inside. He glances around, ready to take out any threat. Seeing none, he nods at me. I turn to Sage.

She steps out of my reach and faces me.

"My car isn't on this level. I need to go to it, Jagger."

I shake my head and remove my sunglasses so she can see the seriousness in my eyes.

"Sage, when we are together, I drive. In fact, I will select four of my security members for your detail. They will rotate in pairs so you will have coverage at all times when you and I are apart. As the Alpha's fated mate and Luna to our pack, a good deal of my enemies may target you. I will protect you by any means."

Her mouth opens and closes before she responds.

"That won't be necessary"—she puts her hand up to stop me from speaking—"Jagger, understand clearly. We cannot act on being mates—"

"*Fated* mates, Sage," I cut in with a growl.

She sighs and shakes her head.

"That may be. But it's impossible, Jagger! *Please*! Let's just speak with my mother—" She stops and shakes her head again as she steps past me. "This was a mistake. I'll go alone—"

"The hell it is!"

I grab her arm and spin her on her sky-high strappy sandals. She wobbles, and I grip her hip with the other hand. I bend my knees so we're at eye level. She must have missed how serious my expression was a moment ago. She'll see it *clearly* now.

"Sage, it is not 'impossible!' You. Are. My. Fated. Mate. We will speak with your mother and my father to clear their bullshit up. Then I *will* issue the claiming bite, and we *will* have our mate bonding ceremony. Is that *clear*?"

She narrows her eyes, but I remember another chastisement.

"You used your teleportation magick to get away from me twice. Do. Not. Do. It. Again. We will communicate and not run away. Or I will put you over my knees and spank your bare ass."

She gasps at the punishment, then narrows her glittering emerald green eyes. I match her with flashing ice blue ones, giving her a glimpse of my displeased wolf. We glare at one another for what seems hours. Each refuses to back down. But I am Alpha, and she will obey me.

"You will do no such thing. Or *I* will find a way to cast a spell to make your dick shrivel up and fall off."

My fated mate issues her own threat.

I throw my head back and bark a laugh. Oh, she's not the sweet little Sage Waters of ten years ago. She's still a little thing compared to me, but feisty. My cock hardens to the point of pain, eager to make her mine again. With a smirk, I press my lips to her ear.

"That's not what you said ten years ago, *mate.*"

A gasp bursts from her lips as her pupils dilate and a scarlet flush spreads across her toffee-colored cheeks.

I snicker and take her elbow, leading her to my supercar.

"Come, you've tarried long enough. Let us not keep my mother-by-bond waiting."

"I am telling you, Jagger, when we speak to them, that's it—"

"Come along… *mate.*"

Sage's grumbled curses as she follows make me laugh harder.

But the thought of what awaits us makes my wolf snarl.

age

"WHAT'S THE ADDRESS?"

"If I were in my car like I should be, you would follow me and not need the address!"

Jagger throws his head back and barks out a laugh. Again. His stunt irritates the hell out of me. Some wolf shifter Me Tarzan, You Jane nonsense! Like I need *him* to protect *me*? I scoff and give him the Brickell address for The Waters Tower, then fold my arms under my breasts, staring straight ahead.

I feel the warm breath before his words wash over me.

"You're so feisty now, *mate*. I hope you're that worked up when I have you beneath me in our bed. Not that I minded your soft mewls as I drove my cock deep inside your virgin pussy ten years ago," Jagger murmurs in my ear, ending in a throaty groan.

My entire body quivers as my core drips arousal onto

the gusset of my silk G-string. My eyes flutter closed as I press my thighs together to ease the ache my fingers failed to satisfy last night. Or this morning. Damn this wolf shifter!

He laughs huskily as the supercar's engine purrs to life. He weaves the shiny red-hot number through traffic with ease. At stop lights, people gawk at the Lamborghini sans roof, windshield, and windows. Just two seats in this beauty. Jagger takes no notice of them. His eyes fixate on me. I ignore him.

We pull up to The Waters Tower's residential side. His security details stop behind us. The burly wolf shifters gather around the supercar. One opens Jagger's door.

The valet's jaw drops as he rushes to open my door. He barely greets me as I take his proffered arm. He hops back when Jagger rounds the front of the supercar with a growly, "I've got her. My men have the car."

If this is how he'll behave with me as his—

I cut that thought short. I cannot allow myself to think in that way. We cannot move forward with being mates. Period. A shake of my head clears it.

Jagger places his palm on my lower back as he glances around us. He needn't worry about any threat here. My wards protect The Waters Tower from humans and paranormals. He and his men will only gain entry since they're with me. Otherwise, the wards would repel them.

"Good afternoon, Ms. Waters."

I return the doorman's greeting as he eyes Jagger and the others surreptitiously.

The doorman, valet, and the rest of The Tower's residential staff are witches. The thoughts running through his mind question the wolf shifters' presence and Jagger's hand on me. It was bad enough hearing the wolf shifters' thoughts at Larson Enterprises when they saw me with their Alpha. This will only be the beginning, I think with a sigh. Then correct myself once again. Not the beginning or anything, Sage!

Jagger follows my lead to the private elevators for my family's residences on the seventy-fifth through eightieth floors—the penthouse levels. I nod at the coven members as we pass and ignore their thoughts.

Jagger must sense the tension rising in my body. He moves closer to me as his sizable hand strokes my back as we walk further into the lobby. Just for a moment, I allow myself to lean into his strength. He rumbles deep in his powerful chest. With each wave of vibrations, the tension lessens. I sigh, relieved once the elevator doors close.

"Although we're not mated—yet—I sense your unease, Sage. Our bond is stronger as fated mate than as a regular pair. You must recognize our connection. Do not deny us. We are stronger as one, and we will need to work together to overcome the challenges your coven and my pack will raise," Jagger says. The passion in his ice blue eyes burn into my very soul. He pays no heed to the two members of his security team. They don't flinch at his reference to me as his fated mate, just stand at the ready.

"Jagger, let's take it one step at a time. Please," I respond, even though my heart constricts. "There's so much to consider, so many involved beyond your pack and my coven. I'm engaged to the son of the second most powerful coven's leader. Due to marry in six days, remember?"

His eyes flash sapphire, and I see his wolf make his presence known—rather, his displeasure.

"You. Are. Mine!"

Before I can correct him, the elevator doors open to my parents' duplex penthouse on the top two floors, one above my duplex with my sisters' residences on the floors below. I shake my head and walk into the entry foyer.

Jagger's menacing growl makes my hand hover in front of the doorbell. I glance over my shoulder to see his handsome face twisted in anger. His men bear the same expression.

"Jagger, not—"

"My father is here."

My head swivels forward just as the double doors open. My mother and an unfamiliar male stand inside staring at us. He's a replica of Jagger from the imposing height to the white blond hair and ice blue eyes. Eyes that glare at his son.

"Jagger!"

"Father!"

They speak at once.

I glance between them, then face my mother. She stares at me, expressionless. My lips purse as I bite back what I dare say would be a growl. I blink in surprise, then refocus and step forward.

"Mother, obviously, you know the reason for our meeting. So, let's not waste time. What do you think gives you the right to wipe our memories, and how did your magick work against me despite me being a member of your family?"

Her eyes narrow a fraction at my demanding tone and pointed questions.

I don't give a damn! She had no right to interfere and to such an extreme as to use magick against her own daughter. Unforgivable.

"Sage, watch your tone with your mother."

I look beyond her to find my father and another unexpected person. A woman who must be Jagger's mother sits with Wyatt Waters in the living room. My blood boils. They really came prepared. No matter. They're wrong, and we're right.

"Wyatt, no need. Sage is just overwrought. What with her wedding in a few days, it's understand—"

"There will be no wedding!!!" Jagger's thunderous declaration cuts my mother's words off, and the room falls silent. "Sage is *my* fated mate! Your magick kept us apart for ten years. No longer!"

"And do not think to try it again, Mother. I am High Witch now, and you will face punishment. Besides, I placed protection spells on Jagger and me. Ones I learned from the ancient grimoires. You will not break them," I add, as my fingers flex at my sides. I don't want to fight with my mother or anyone else. But I will protect Jagger and myself.

Prudence's eyes flick to my hands, a slight curve to the corners of her mouth.

"You do understand a witch and a wolf shifter will never bond as mates. Especially, as you remind me, you are the High Witch. The coven will not stand for it. Nor will Rupert's. You will not reject the son of the second most powerful coven's leader for a"—her emerald green eyes blaze as they flick towards Jagger and her lip curls in disgust —"*beast.*"

Chaos erupts as Jagger and his men snarl. His mother jumps to her feet—teeth bared—and his father growls.

I place my hand on Jagger's heaving chest. He glances down at me. His wolf contorts his face. Even without magick, my simple touch calms him as he takes a deep breath and relaxes. Then I face my mother.

"Enough with the insults, Mother. So beneath you, don't you think? Perhaps I need to remind you again. I am High Witch. Tread lightly. And that goes for you, too."

My gaze turns to Jagger's parents.

"You will no longer interfere, either. What Jagger and I decide is our choice. You took it away from us ten years ago. Never again."

Their beings shimmer, then fade.

~

Jagger

"WHAT THE HELL?!"

It's like my body dissolved, floated through a tunnel, then merged back together. My head swivels on my neck as I take in my surroundings. The view of Biscayne Bay. Tile floors. Oversized caramel-colored tufted leather sofa. My living room.

Next to the bar, Sage stands completely at ease as she pours healthy portions of scotch into two Old Fashion tumblers. She turns and struts towards me.

"You'll get used to it… I mean… the sensation will wear off," she says as she hands a glass to me. "I wanted to get us out of there and someplace… ah… safe."

Her cheeks flush, and she lowers her eyes.

I take the glass and grasp her chin between my thumb and index finger to raise her gaze back to mine. The calloused pad of my thumb brushes over her plump lower lip, tracing a pattern.

"Baby, I'm glad you consider our home 'safe,'" I croon as the rumble in my chest soothes her. "Here or in my arms. Where you belong."

She sighs and closes her eyes.

My palm moves up to cradle her soft cheek. She presses into my hand and places hers on my chest. My skin tingles beneath her touch. Instantly, I'm as calm as she.

We stand for a moment, savoring our connection.

"You were a badass back there, baby," I murmur. My lips skim the top of Sage's silky head and down to her other cheek. I angle her face to bring her lips to mine. I inhale her unique scent as our lips hover a hair's breadth apart. "You're right. The choice is ours and ours alone. And I choose you, Sage Waters. I can do nothing else. You are my fated mate, whether or not you like it. You know it."

Her soft breath teases my lips.

But I wait for her move as in my mind I command her to give in to me—to us—at last. The breath I held expels on a sigh as she turns her head aside and sidesteps me. I close my eyes and inhale deeply to pull my wolf back from claiming what he knows is his, despite her reluctance. I can control my beast. The question is how long do I want to.

I turn and watch her walk to the accordion glass doors as she did last night. This time, the sun glitters on the aqua blue waters of Biscayne Bay and forms a brightness around her body. She sips from the tumbler as she stares sightlessly through the glass. I wait.

"By the way, I sent your men to the SUVs," she says, then pauses for another sip. "Jagger, even though we're connected, you and I cannot move forward. A wolf shifter and a witch? An Alpha and the High Witch? No. Impossible."

My wolf growls and claws to break free. Sage—startled by the anger of my wolf—spins to face me. Her emerald green eyes widen as she watches me disrobe. I yank at the full Windsor knot of my silk tie and shrug out of my Tom Ford suit jacket. My fingers already shifting scrabble with the platinum cufflinks.

"Wh—What are you doing?" Sage asks, a tremor in her voice.

"Run… Going for a run."

My response emerges guttural as my shifts continues. I tear the custom shirt in two from my body. Sage's pupils dilate at the sight of my muscular pecs, chiseled eight-pack abs, and white blond trail disappearing into the waistband of my trousers. Yeah, what you're missing, baby. I snarl and toe off my A. Testoni Oxfords and Pantherella socks. Claws snatch open my fly, shedding the trousers and black silk boxer briefs. My thick cock slaps my abs, the bulbous tip at my belly button. Oh, so hard and ready to claim my fated mate. I throw my head back with a roar.

I allow my body to relax and accept my wolf to take over. My other half lives on the fringes of my being. Always ready to spring forth at my command, then retreat at my will. An ability born of our kind so long ago and marks us different from full humans.

The sensations of my bones reshaping and muscles lengthening to shift me from my human form to that of my great silvery white wolf block out all else. Crackling and a flash find me on all four massive paws within moments.

I swivel my enormous head to pin my ice blue eyes on my fated mate.

She stands transfixed. It's been ten years since she's seen me in wolf form. Her eyes scan me from snout to the tip of my feathery tail. Every inch of my body feels the intensity of her stare. Tingles ripple through me.

I ache to go to her. To rub my body on her. Scent her.

No!

My head shakes, and I pivot, bounding across the living room floor for the side door. My giant paw slams the button, and the hand-carved wooden door depicting a wolf opens. I race across my lawn, staying beneath the cover of palm tree fronds. My destination is the center of Moon Island.

Another perk of our private island provides a safe place for members of my pack to run in wolf form unencumbered. We run as a full pack in the Everglades a few times a month. The vast expanse and relative safety the subtropical wilderness offers makes an ideal setting for our numbers.

However, now, the island's oasis calls to me. I need to outrun the frustration my fated mate causes and the desire to claim her and to deal with the consequences—her ire, the witch hunt, my pack's disapproval—later.

I run past fragrant gardenia and jasmine bushes. Their floral scents fill my nose. But don't hide the unique scent of my fated mate. I might as well be in the Everglades after a spring rain whenever she's near. I snort and dash between some palm trees.

Glimpses of other pack members in wolf form appear amongst the foliage. Not wanting to be disturbed, I increase my speed and head towards the other end of Moon Island. I run for what seems hours. A normal wolf would have tired by then, muscles strained to capacity. As a wolf shifter, my body heals quickly unless silver is involved. Then it can be fatal.

Unfortunately, the pain in my heart doesn't abate as I throw myself through the side door and shift. I grab a pair of black joggers from the antique armoire filled with post-shift clothes. Not that I mind being in the buff. Another distinction between shifters of any kind and humans nudity is natural.

I run my fingers through my wild hair as I stride down the hall towards the kitchen for a bottle of water. The woody earthy scent with a hint of sea salt carried on the breeze from the Atlantic Ocean fills my nostrils. Not just the lingering whiff of my fated mate's prior presence. No, the actual tantalizing fragrance emanating from her warm, lush body—

Fuck!

My cock hardens to the point of pain as pre-cum seeps from the swollen tip. I palm my junk with a groan. The thought of rubbing one out flits across my mind. But her scent draws me to the living room. I adjust my aching cock and follow her scent trail like a lovesick puppy instead of a fucking savage wolf.

I'm so screwed and not in the right way.

CHAPTER 7

age

A WARM TINGLING ripples over my skin. My nipples scrape against the white silk of my demi-cup bra as my chest rises on a deep inhalation. I close my eyes to steel myself for the male who drives me crazy with need.

The unsatisfied ache in my body blasts into me. I shudder from the impact as my core heats and moistens with my arousal. Oh, how I want to give in to Jagger Larson. My fated mate.

I close my eyes as I sense his presence closer. Near enough, the sexual tension crackles between us fed by pulses of erotic energy. Pulses that vibrate in my core. His all-male scent intensified by the sweat from his run envelops me.

"Sage, I expected you to have left."

He steps closer to loom over me as I lie on the caramel-colored tufted leather sofa. His ice blue eyes a deep sapphire drag over my body beneath a white cashmere oversized throw. He cocks an eyebrow at my suit jacket draped on the back of the sofa, then locks on my hidden breasts. A rumble rises from his chest.

My eyelids drop. But I catch myself and snap them open as I rise to a seated position. The throw slips from my shoulders. I catch it against my breasts.

Jagger lowers onto the large wooden coffee table. His thick, muscular thighs bracket my legs as he leans forward and wraps his fingers around my wrists. With a shake of his head, he pulls my hands away from my body.

"Never cover yourself from me, Sage. You are an exceptionally beautiful female, and I want to admire you always."

A shiver takes me as his rough voice licks at my skin. My mouth falls slack at his commanding compliment. Already peaked nipples bead tighter, and my breasts grow heavy under his hungry gaze.

"Jagger…"

His name comes out as a plea instead of the firm tone I intended to have with him when he returned. We need to talk. Seriously. Not dance this sensual tango.

I clear my dry throat and try again, more forcefully this time.

"Jagger."

The confident tone inspires me to continue despite his heated gaze on my lips as he licks his own full mouth. A flash of a long canine shoots a thrill through me.

Aargh!

"Jagger, we must talk."

I almost waiver when his sizable hands stroke the tops of my thighs as his legs press into them from either side. My eyes beg to stray to his sculpted chest and washboard abs. The white blond happy trail beckons to me to gaze lower. Lower to the magnificent bulge tenting his soft joggers. A damn flagpole stands tall. A pole I ache to climb and ride.

Sage Waters! I yell at myself to remain focused on the issues at hand. And there are many. Too many we may not be able to overcome.

Aargh… Aargh!!

His molten sapphires nearly crumble my resolve. But I persevere.

"This mating thing—"

His low growl makes me swallow and start anew.

"Us being mates—"

Another growl corrects me.

"Us being *fated* mates—"

He rumbles and smirks appreciatively.

"Goes beyond the two of us," I press on, ignoring the scowl on his handsome face. "Hear me out, please."

He nods begrudgingly, and I continue.

"We have responsibilities—you to your pack and me to my coven and all witches. Not just to lead, but for succession."

Jagger cocks an eyebrow, and I wonder how much of the male is present and not the wolf.

"You are the Alpha of the Miami Wolves Pack. You must mate and produce an heir. A male wolf shifter to carry on your family's legacy."

He gives me a slight nod. His hands still caress my thighs while his thighs press into them. I blink to ignore his erotic distraction.

"And as the High Witch, I must produce a witch daughter who will take my place and lead our coven and head the Witch Council."

He raises his eyebrows as if to say, right. I sigh because I must make him see how wrong for each other we are as mates—fated or otherwise.

The next part brings tears to my eyes. I glance away and take a deep breath. Jagger lets his hand move from my thigh to cup my chin and turn my gaze back to him. His eyes scan my face while my eyes flit everywhere but at him. He rumbles in his chest, and I sigh—this time in ease. I gather the courage to go on.

"You do not realize something very important about me, Jagger. I still don't have my memories. So, I don't know if we had this discussion before."

I pause and stare him straight in the eyes.

"I am an Immortal Witch. My twenty-ninth birthday is in five days. At that age, we stop aging. Forever. You saw my mother. She's hundreds of years old and gets mistaken for my sister every day."

My throat clogs with the tears causing me to pause. I close my eyes. A tear slips from the corner of one.

Jagger catches it with his thumb and leans over to brush his lips against my eyelids. I tremble beneath his soft touch.

"I know wolf shifters—all shifters—live much longer than humans. But I cannot imagine watching you getting old and—" My throat refuses to release the word, and I bow my head as the tears flow freely. They drop to my lap as I shudder.

Jagger moves from the coffee table and sits beside me, pulling me onto his lap. He buries his face in my hair as his arms band around me. I bury my face in his muscular chest and cry.

I cry for the thought of watching him age. For the messed-up fact we cannot be together. For my desire to be with him and hell, fuck it all! But I can't. We can't. A wellspring of tears flow from my eyes as I finally let it go.

Jagger holds me for an indeterminate amount of time. His rumbles help to soothe the ache in my heart. But not the passion burning in my core.

I want him. And I want him now.

~

JAGGER

I HOLD my fated mate as my mind absorbs all she's told me. The only thing that stands out is her desire to be my fated mate. The obstacles she keeps insisting upon do not matter. At. All.

Sure, we'll face opposition. But I give zero fucks. If my pack fights me on their Luna being a witch—the High Witch—then fuck them, too. I meant it when I said I will give it all up for my fated mate. The Fates would not pair us if we did not belong together. We may not see the reason now. But there must be one the Fates see we need to be together for.

The same goes for the witches. I couldn't care less. It's Sage's call with them, and I will support her in whatever she decides.

Our pups. Well, we'll cross that bridge when it happens. Hell, we may not have males or may not have females. We won't know until we try. And I damn sure am bursting to get on with that part of our mating. I want to see Sage's belly swell with my seed. Grow round with my pup inside her womb. My cock thumps in agreement.

But she's in her head too much with this whole situation. Not saying I'm irresponsible. Not at all. I know my responsibilities and take them seriously. But I will *not* allow them to supersede my relationship with my fated mate.

In an ideal world, the witches and my pack would accept Sage and me as fated mates. We would move forward and live as one in peace. But if it calls for more, my wolf and I will do what we must to protect our fated mate and our relationship.

I have to get her away. Give us time to be together with no outside influences. To reconnect. I hope being alone will help her regain her memories. Something may trigger them, like her scent on Enrique did for me.

A smile spreads across my face as I realize just the solution.

"Sage, I understand what you say, and I do not disagree. Except that I will sacrifice all for you—for us," I say as I sit back and cup her wobbly chin in my palm. "We need to spend time together, away from everyone and everything else. Reconnect. You and me. Come on my boat with me. Let me show you how good it will be between us. Five days. Just you and me, Sage."

She studies my face. I keep an open expression, so she sees no guile. In my mind, I chant for her to agree. After a moment, she nods.

"Okay, Jagger. I will go."

My heart leaps in my chest. I can't help the silly grin on my face as I pull her tight to my chest and bury my face in her silky curls. Her scent washes over me, and my wolf howls with passion.

I will persuade my fated mate nothing matters but us. Or turn the world upside down.

agger

"Oh, my goodness, Jagger! You said your boat, not a megayacht! It's incredible."

My fated mate's squeal of delight makes me grin.

After I told Tag to step in as my second to handle the pack and work while I take the next few days with Sage, I drove us in a golf cart to Moon Island's private marina. Karl and my security team followed. We walked along the dock to the tender where a crew member waited to ferry us to *Moonbeam*. It dwarfs the other boats members of the pack dock in slips. The 465-foot silver megayacht gleams in the afternoon sunlight. Five decks tiered from the back with a long front to accommodate a helipad.

Twenty cabins sleep up to thirty-six guests. For entertainment, it features a beach club with a garage for water sports toys, fitness center, spa and sauna, swimming pool and hot tub, media room, bowling alley, and a game room.

Multiple living spaces include salons, wet bars, dining rooms, library, and an office with a conference room I can conduct business. I designed the megayacht with my pack in mind, wanting to provide the members with a luxurious water respite.

Now, *Moonbeam* will serve as our getaway.

The rest of the crew greets us on the lower deck as the tender nears the megayacht's stern. Lined up in their dress whites, the captain steps forward as the others stand at attention. He's a former naval officer who still loves the sea. Along with the others, he's a member of our pack.

"Alpha, it's been a while. So good to see you, sir," Captain says as the tender slips beside the much larger boat. While the bosun helps secure the tender, Captain reaches out to lift Sage to the deck. "Welcome aboard, ma'am!" He smiles.

"Thank you," she responds with a giggle as she smooths her suit jacket and pencil skirt.

"Good to see you too, Captain," I say as I step onto the boat and take my fated mate's hand. My wolf growled at his hands on her, even if polite. "This is Sage Waters. Sage, this is Captain."

He tips his hat and turns to introduce her to the rest of the crew. The Chief Stew holds a tray of mojitos. We take glasses with thanks. The chef tells us she prepared a late lunch of grilled Maine lobster and king prawns with cilantro lime butter and grilled vegetables and salted caramel pie for dessert.

I turn to Sage and ask, "Do you want a tour first or to eat lunch?"

She's already grinning, emerald green eyes sparkling with delight. "Absolutely lunch! I will never turn down a delicious meal. Thank you, Chef. We can tour after to burn off such a decadent dessert!"

With a smirk, I lean over and press my lips to the delicate shell of her ear. "I have a much better plan to 'burn off' calories, *mate*. Besides, I do not want you to lose one centimeter of your hot, curvy body."

She shivers. I place my hand on her lower belly and press her ass against my erection. The very same one I've sported since I found her still in our living room. I nip her lobe and step away. She gasps and sways. My hand grasps her waist and steadies her as a wicked chuckle makes her tremble.

With their wolf sense of hearing, the crew avert their eyes. The Captain hides his smile with the turn of his head as he instructs them to get ready to leave Biscayne Bay. I requested he charter our voyage to the Florida Keys. My fated mate and I will have plenty of time to ourselves and to enjoy the sights of the coast, then explore the Keys.

Before we return, I will claim her fully.

She bends over and removes her fuck-me heels, then holds them by the straps.

I band an arm around her waist as I lead her up to the deck for outdoor dining. She wraps her arm around my waist and snuggles against me. A grin spreads across my face as she tucks into my side perfectly.

Another score.

How they do it, I don't know. But the Chief Stew and Stewardess beat us to the deck. They greet us with a mixture of fresh citrus fruits and melon for a refreshing appetizer salad. We exchange our empty mojito glasses for crisp and dry rosé wine. It pairs well with the starter and main dish.

Over lunch, our conversation flows comfortably. We don't discuss her concerns. Rather, I tell her about our destination and the fun to have on the megayacht—besides hours of making love, of course. It's as though ten years haven't passed. We're at ease with one another. As expected of fated mates.

My hope is Sage senses our connection is undeniable and worth fighting for.

After lunch, I take her on the tour. The megayacht impresses her as I knew it would. Once again, she's comfortable in the space. Walking about with ease. Until an hour later, when we arrive at the primary cabin.

"Oh, so where will you sleep?" She asks as her eyes flick from the king-size bed to me and back.

I chuckle and yank the collar of my t-shirt over my head. I toss the unwanted garment to a chair and stalk towards my fated mate. My blood heats with each step. Like the apex predator I am, her startled gasp and the sweet scents of fear and arousal mix to heighten my desire to take her without reservation however I choose. Now.

In a few strides, I stand before my fated mate and stare down into her wide emerald green eyes. Her swallow audible to my wolf senses. But her gaze doesn't waver. My hands reach out. Fingers make quick work of the single button on her suit jacket. I push it from her shoulders. It slides to the carpet.

Her brown beaded nipples stand out in bas-relief against the white silk of her demi-cup bra. I drop my head to suck one into my mouth through the fabric. She moans. Her fingers dip into my hair as mine slip around her hips to unzip her pencil skirt. It too slides to puddle at her bare feet.

While my mouth moves to the other plump nipple, I grab her hips. My fingers dig into the soft flesh as I anchor her in place. Thumbs trace the edges of her G-string along her mons. I tease her lower lips with a few flicks beneath the white silk. She mewls and grinds her slick pussy against my thumbs.

I growl and rip the scrap of silk from covering her pussy. The pinch of the fabric on her sensitive skin makes her cry out. I drop to my knees, throw her thigh over my shoulder, and plant my face at the treasure box between her thighs. My nose burrows between her wet folds, and I inhale. Deeply.

My mouth waters from her tantalizing scent.

Mine!

I lash my tongue in a zig-zag pattern across her slippery seam, then angle her pelvis to reach along the perineum to her puckered hole. She hops on one foot as the tip of my tongue rims, then probes the forbidden spot. The gasp of my name rolls off her lips, straight to my engorged cock. Its head plus several inches pushes past the waistband of my joggers like a heat-seeking missile aimed for her cunt.

"Jagger! What are you do—"

Her question ends abruptly when my tongue spears into her dripping pussy as my thumb and index finger pinch her swollen clit. Her back bows as she wails. Juices gush into my eagerly waiting mouth as her first—of many I have planned —orgasm rocks through her. As her pussy walls ripple along my tongue, she falls forward, torso draped over my head.

The near suffocation is worth it to taste the sweet nectar of her climax. I gulp it down, already craving more. I add a finger to aid in my feast. It mines for more golden honey as the tip strokes the sensitive spot on her front wall. And as expected, her inner thighs squeeze my ears like a vise as another orgasm hits. I can barely hear her cries over the sounds of my munching.

I continue my delectable feast until my fated mate wobbles on her standing leg, despite me bracing her with my arm looped behind and around her thigh. Her hoarse voice begs for no more after many orgasms.

In one swift move, I rise to my feet with her a quivering mess over my shoulder. Two fingers dabble just inside her slick folds, enough to keep her on the edge as I stride towards the bed. The bed in which *both* of us will sleep. Later, that is.

I toss her onto the middle and salivate as her D-cup tits spill from the tops of her little silk bra. The plump nipples stare back at me, and I growl as I tear out of my joggers. Her hooded eyes linger on my cock as it bobs against my washboard abs. I fist the base and stroke upwards a few times. Her tongue moistens her lips.

"Oh, I'll fill that hole, too, mate."

Her gaze jumps to mine as her eyelids flutter. I smirk.

The mattress dips as I knee my way towards her. My smirk widens when her knees splay out to welcome my advance. I drop kisses from her ankle up her calf, behind the knee, all the way up to her slack mouth. I cover it with mine.

My tongue sweeps inside to tangle with hers. I swallow each of her moans possessively. She reaches for me. But I twine our fingers and lift our hands to either side of her head as I remain planked over her. When my fingers brush the engagement ring on her finger, I rip my mouth from hers with a growl.

"Mine!" I snarl as I sit back on my haunches with her left hand in mine and tug the offensive piece from her finger. I toss it to the floor, then pin her with my hardened gaze. "You will marry no one but me, Sage Waters. Me!"

She opens her mouth to speak, but I shake my head.

"Enough! You know the Fates plan for us to be together. I will not succumb to madness brought about by separation from my mate—from *you*! And damn sure not because you married another."

"Jagger, I agree."

⌒

HIS EYES POP at my admission.

"I cannot marry Rupert," I continue, then place my finger on Jagger's lips when he starts to speak. "But I am not ready to complete the bonding with you yet. Let's do as you said earlier and spend the next five days together, alone. You also said you would show me how good it will be between us."

I wrap my arms around his neck and pull him down to me. He's stiff in my arms, but I persevere.

"I'm here. With *you*. Now show me," I purr with my lips against his ear as I arch my back and secure his narrow hips between my welcoming thighs. My wet core throbs as it rubs against his thick cock, coating it with my arousal.

He groans and relaxes in my erotic embrace. Then he raises his head to stare into my eyes.

"One question."

When I nod, he continues in a gruff voice, "Have there been many others?"

Oh, my possessive fated mate…

"Only you, Jagger Larson. And I can't even remember what happened. Make up for it," I say, then nip his lower lip as I undulate my hips. "Now."

His ice blue eyes flash deep sapphire. A glimpse of his wolf appears in their depths. Its hungry eyes devour me. Jagger blinks, and it's gone.

Is it crazy I want to see more of his feral other half? To feel the raw power it exudes as it takes me?

Jagger doesn't give me a moment to ponder the sanity of my questions. His hands grip my hips and lift them.

Balanced on my shoulders and the back of my head, I clutch at his forearms. My eyes dart from his face to his dick, that's even bigger than it was a moment ago. Long, thick, and veiny with a shiny bead of pre-cum on its deep purple tip poised at the entrance to my core.

"I can't be gentle with you now, mate. My wolf and I demand all from you, and we plan to take it."

Before I can express agreement, his hips drive forward, and he impales me on his ginormous cock. A strangled scream rips from my throat. He's so big. Too big. My fingernails dig into his forearms as my back bows. I'm torn between pushing him away and pulling him deeper.

Once again, he decides for me.

Jagger's firm ass flexes beneath the heels of my feet as he thrusts to the root of his cock.

My head twists from side to side as his bulbous tip brushes my cervix. And I thought he was inside of me fully before! A guttural groan escapes my mouth.

He leans over my body and captures my mouth with his for a demanding kiss. His tongue takes possession as it licks around, then prods my tongue. I have no choice but to tangle with him. I moan and give in. He growls in triumph.

My lower half registers his dick as it pulsates inside my core. The inner walls stretch to accommodate his massive girth and length. They match his carnal rhythm.

"This pussy is mine, mate. Only mine. Mine forever. You will never forget *this* memory of my cock claiming you."

His gruff voice filled with possessive-driven lust makes me mewl in response as my pussy clenches down hard on his cock.

"Fuck, yeah..." He groans in my ear. "So tight. So wet. You like how my giant cock claims every inch of your little pussy. *My* pussy."

"Oh, Fates..." I moan as my core spasms. The unexpected orgasm sends shock waves through my body, from my core and along my limbs to my fingers and toes. They dig deeper into his forearms and curl as my body revels in the throes of carnal passion.

"So responsive, mate. But we've only begun."

That's the only warning Jagger gives me before he withdraws to his tip, then snaps his hips forward to fill me to the root again. His heavy sac slaps my ass. I yelp and hold on tighter as the brutal force shifts my body up the mattress. Pillows cushion the sides of my head.

Jagger becomes a machine as his hips piston repeatedly. One of his arms bands around my waist as the palm of the other slams on the headboard. His solid torso flattens my breasts as he locks me to him for a mind-blowing ride.

"You are mine, Sage Waters. All mine," he growls against my ear. His warm breath sends a shudder through me. "Tell me you are mine!"

I gulp air into my mouth to refill my lungs.

"Answer me!" He bellows as his thrusts turn barbaric.

My pussy clamps down and gushes, so aroused every time he gets forceful with me. I did not know I would respond to such a rough manner. And I love it!

"Uh. Uh. Uh. Uh."

I can't verbalize too far gone for words. My body only feels his raw intensity—the demands he makes of it to accept his claim. I'm on the edge of the abyss and want oh so badly for him to mark me, make me his in every way.

Tears leak from the corners of my eyes. They land on his cheek, and he lifts his head to stare at me. He nods, realizing without me having to speak just what I feel—and need.

"Give in to us, Sage," Jagger says, emphasizing each word with a thrust and drag of his giant dick inside of my soaked and ravaged core. His eyes flash, and the wolf appears again. "MINE!!!"

He lowers his mouth to my neck.

CHAPTER 9

agger

SAGE'S TEARS trigger my wolf. I can no longer hold back. Nor deny what is ours to take. Our growls unite to form one all-encompassing word.

"MINE!!!"

I lower my head and nuzzle her neck. She mewls and turns her head to the side giving me better access to the juncture of her neck and shoulder. My cock swells at her submission and increases its pace to pound her into the mattress.

The serum to lodge my scent in her skin permanently and to enact the transformation of her into a wolf shifter drips on my extended canines. My gift to my fated mate, and Sage Waters will be my mate forever. We can never part once I issue the claiming bite. Or I truly would go crazy and lose control of my wolf. Or worse.

My thick fingers circle her slim throat like a collar to

lock her in place. It will be painful, and I don't want her to jerk away, potentially causing damage from my canines. Add in Sage isn't a wolf shifter capable of healing immediately, and a misplaced claiming bite can prove dangerous.

I angle my thrusts to hit her G-spot, ensuring optimal pleasure. It triggers an orgasm for my fated mate. As she screams my name in carnal passion, my canines sink into her delicate flesh. Her moan morphs into a pained cry. Instinctively, she tries to pull away from me. But I tighten my grip on her throat and rumble in my chest to soothe her.

My mouth gapes, and I bite down again with an added shake of my head. The bite must be deep enough and fill her with an ample amount of serum. She writhes beneath me as pleasure from my pounding cock overtakes the pain of my claiming bite.

Her moans trigger my release.

A tingling at the base of my spine shoots to my balls and down my shaft, where my knot forms at its base. My mouth disengages from my fated mate's neck as my head lifts towards the ceiling. A victorious howl rings out as my knot locks her to me and the first ropes of my seed jettison inside of her womb.

My grip moves to cup her ass. Our groins melded together will not allow one drop of my seed to slip from her pussy, for I will put my pup inside of my fated mate this day. The rhythm of my strokes slow but doesn't stop as her greedy pussy milks every bit of my seed.

The stretch of her pussy by my knot causes her pain. She babbles incoherently as she clings to me.

I stare down at her, and my heart swells. Sage is the most beautiful being I've ever seen. She glows as though lit from within. A sheen of sweat coats her toffee-colored skin flush with her arousal. Long, silky strands of ebony curls stick to her neck or fan out around her head. A contented sigh slips past her Cupid's bow lips. I made her blissed out, I muse with a smirk.

My eyes land on the claiming bite. Saliva fills my mouth, and I lean down to lap at the wound. Properties in my saliva will help speed up the healing process. Now, we'll have to wait for the transformation to complete.

My knot remains embedded at her pussy entrance. I have no wish to break our intimate connection, even if I could. But her much smaller frame can't continue to bear my weight. I wrap an arm around her and roll onto my back. She snuggles her cheek against my chest with another sigh. My hand strokes from her back to her ass and up again as more rumbles vibrate from my chest to soothe my fated mate.

Sage Waters, my fated mate forever.

With that thought in mind, I drift off to a peaceful slumber.

I awake on my side wrapped around Sage with my erect cock nestled between the crack of her round ass. I groan as I lean into her, wanting to envelop her with my body. Fuck! She feels so damn good. So right in my arms. Where she belongs.

I brush curls from her neck to stare at my mark. The indentations from my canines prove easily discernible. No one can mistake her for being unmated. I nuzzle against her soft skin and inhale deeply. My face splits into a grin at our combined scents. My wolf's feathery tail thumps in approval as he sits on his haunches guarding our mate.

"Jagger?"

"Yes, baby?"

I growl when she tries to slip from my grip. She giggles as she swats at one hand on her tit and the other cupping her pussy. She stills and moans when a thick finger slips between her slick folds, already wet for me. Her ass grinds back against my erection.

I seize the opportunity and flip her beneath me on her hands and knees—ass high, head low. A snap of my hips, and she mewls as my cock bottoms out inside her tight little pussy.

"You do not leave our bed without my permission, mate," I chide, cock plunging in and out with absolute precision. My torso lowers over her back to bring my lips close to her ear. "Or I will punish you soundly."

Her pussy clamps down and strangles my cock. We groan in unison.

I rear back up, dick still deep, and smack her ass. Left, right, right, left. Never in the same spot. Yet close enough to elicit a baby howl from my fated mate. I grin. Yeah, baby howl away.

My hand snakes around her hip and collects her juices. I rub her clit with her natural lube, and she cums with a scream. She bucks against my hand as her fingernails shred the sheets.

"Oh, Fates, Jagger!" She cries as her pussy squeezes the life out of me. "You're so big. Fuck!"

What a stroke to my ego.

I go all out with a punishing rhythm between my cock in her dripping pussy and my palm on her reddened ass cheeks. She writhes beneath me, screaming through one orgasm after the other. I mount her like the feral beast I am, then spill my seed deep within her womb, pussy locked to me by my knot.

I lower us to our sides as we catch our breath and heart-beats return to normal.

"Jagger, I wanted to go to the bathroom," Sage says accusingly.

I nuzzle her neck as I rumble. She sighs and relaxes against me.

"You wild boy… Don't think your little sounds will hold my bladder."

I chuckle, and she joins in. Moments later, soft snores let me know she's asleep again. With my fated mate wrapped in my arms, I close my eyes, sated.

~

SAGE

SUNLIGHT DAPPLES THE STILL, smooth surface of the pond. No wind whispers through the saw grass along its rim. A great egret spreads its snowy white wings as it silently takes to the sky. It glances down at me as if to say, you should leave too, if you know what's best. Instead, I watch it fly into the distance.

I return to my walk. The Everglades give me peace and tranquility. A place I retreat to when my mother's demands of perfection drive me crazy. I shake my head to dispel the bad vibes in my special place, then slip a loose ebony curl behind my ear with a sigh.

But as I continue along the path between the pine trees, the hairs on the back of my neck rise. I don't change my pace. Instead, I focus on my surroundings, now eerily silent, as though a predator lurks. My ears pick up the silent tread of a four-legged creature. One that appears to be stalking me.

My direction detours from the close proximity of the pine trees back to the open expanse surrounding the pond. The water remains without a ripple. Even the insects quiet as I approach. Whatever follows scares all.

But not me.

I pivot quickly to face the four-legged creature I sense will follow me into the open, unafraid of me or of anything else. I expect a Florida panther creeping behind me. They're known for their stealth and preference to bite the back of a person's neck to break the spine. Face-to-face, I'll have a better chance at defending myself against the lethal predator.

My eyes widen at the sight of a ginormous wolf as it pads into the clearing. Its silvery white coat gleams in the early morning sun. Ice blue eyes should freeze me. Instead, they send a frisson of carnal heat through my body. A tremor follows in its wake. My mouth falls slack on a gasp.

Instinctively, I know it's a male wolf. But unlike any regular wolf. Although beautiful unto themselves, this wolf is majestic. The most incredible thing I've ever seen—and I've seen all kinds of stuff.

He lopes towards me with nostrils flared as he scents the air. His formidable size brings his massive head nearly to my shoulder, where I stand at five feet, five inches. Only needing to tip his head up slightly, his eyes remain locked on mine.

In their icy depths, I see a hunger—and not to devour my flesh. A yearning that tugs at my heart and zings my core. A low rumbling from the depths of his broad chest washes over me. Instantly, my body releases the tension built from his unexpected appearance. My eyes flutter closed as I sway.

Warm wetness and silky fur on the side of my neck stills my movement as my eyes pop open. I gasp. My heartbeat slams against my ribcage, frightened by the nearness of his exposed canines to my delicate neck.

I take a step back.

He rumbles and matches my movement.

My heel catches on a rock, and I fall on my ass. I swear I see a flicker of laughter in his eyes as he steps between my legs. On their own, my bent knees butterfly to the ground to allow him closer access. He stands above me and once again nuzzles my neck, inhaling deeply.

This time, I mewl when his textured tongue swipes my sensitive skin. My nipples pucker against the thin cotton of my white t-shirt. I cry out as my core moistens and clenches with need. Then yelp when his nose nudges the front of my black leggings, flush against the apex of my thighs.

A low growl emanates from his mouth as he drags his ice blue eyes up my quivering belly, lingers on my heaving chest, and stops at my flushed face. He licks his muzzle from one side to the other as though he tastes me on his tongue. Another low growl sends a shiver down my spine. His pheromones waft around us, matching my arousal.

A crackling sound and a flash appear.

I blink.

A gorgeous male stares at me. A naked, muscular, gorgeous male stares at me. As my eyes travel the length of his body, I notice his giant dick thumps his eight-pack abs. A pearl of pre-cum glistens from the slit of its bulbous tip.

I close my eyes. Too much to take in for a virgin like me.

"Mine!"

His rough growl snaps me back.

My eyes open and meet his.

His gaze dip to my chest, then back at my face. A hint of a smirk plays at the corners of his lush mouth. His fingers grip the collar of my t-shirt. With the flick of his wrists, he rips it from neck to hem. The soft bra rends in two to expose my breasts to his lust-filled gaze.

My lips part on a whimper.

His mouth crashes onto mine. That same wicked tongue sweeps inside, demanding my tongue tangle with his. I comply. The low rumbling increases and vibrates on my heated skin.

I cry out, but his mouth swallows my plea.

Whether a plea for him to stop or to claim me as his, I'm not sure. What I know without a doubt is this wolf shifter intends to have his way with me, his captured prey. I shudder as his mouth leaves mine to trail licks and nips across my jaw and down to the column of my neck.

The press of his canines against my throat draws another yelp from me. He rumbles to soothe me once again. I relax as he continues his carnal path over my collarbone and down to my heavy breasts. The achy nipples beg for his sinful mouth to engulf them.

He does.

His tongue curls around one distended tip to suck it into his wet, warm mouth. He flicks his tongue over the tightened bud as his mouth widens to take in more of my ample breast. Savage snarls and grunts issue from his mouth as he feasts on my breast, moving from one to the other and back again.

I writhe beneath him as my fingernails dig into his broad back. My core fills with my slick arousal, drenched and ready for him to claim me completely. To take that gigantic dick and mark my virgin body as his and his alone.

My wetness must call to him since he leaves my sore nipples to skim his lips over my flat belly and down to my mons. The forceful rip of fabric precedes his hot mouth on my most vulnerable flesh. My back bows and my hips rise on a scream as he licks from my slick slit to my engorged clit.

Sizable, calloused hands press my hips down to the soft ground. Fingers slip around to grip each butt cheek as his wide shoulders press my trembling thighs apart. Settled in place, he devours me.

Lusty grunts mingle with the squelching of my abundant juices to fill the surrounding air. Even I can scent my arousal as my head tosses side to side and desperate moans pour from my mouth. I want more. I want that dick!

But locked in place by his powerful hands, I can only lie there and take what he gives to me.

A tingle builds in my lower belly and spreads through me. My breath hitches in my throat. My core tightens as my toes curl, still inside of my hiking boots. Sight and sound disappear as the wave of a massive orgasm crests.

I scream until hoarse as wave after wave knocks into me. My body convulses and my eyes roll to the back of my head. My fingers claw at his long, white blond hair. Whether they mean to pull him away or bring him closer remains unclear. My mind too blown by the deep-seated throes of my first non-self-induced orgasm.

Between gulps of my gushing core, he raises those magnetic ice blue eyes to my hooded emerald green gaze. He rumbles, and the vibrations from his chest skitter across my heated skin, leaving goosebumps in their wake.

"Mine!"

With his eyes still locked on me, he takes a last lick of my swollen lower lips and crawls up my body. The corded muscles of his arms and shoulders flex beneath his skin.

I inhale deeply, knowing what comes next. He'll claim my virgin flesh as his own.

Planked over me, he nuzzles my neck, sending ripples of erotic energy along my spine. His lips brush my earlobe as he murmurs, "Mine."

He reaches between us to grip his turgid length and align it with my core. His eyes find mine—

"Jagger! I remember! I remember everything!"

CHAPTER 10

agger

"Yeah, baby! You got it, Sage! Fly, baby, fly!!"

I yell through the megaphone as I stand on *Moonbeam's* aft deck.

My fated mate zips past me with her feet strapped in special boots that use a propulsion mechanism from the jet ski guiding her flyboarding experience. It's her second time doing the extreme sport and the first session of our trip. She's become good at it in a short time because of her increased strength—one difference her body has experienced in the last few days since her transformation began. She swears she's not using her magick to control the water. I'm not so sure since it seems to carry her along. I shake my head and chuckle.

A grin and thumbs-up serve as my fated mate's response.

I grin even more than she does as I watch her plump ass

in a red string bikini bottom when she passes the boat. A life jacket covers her lush D-cup tits. I'd have to chew out the eyes of the crew should a tit pop out of her string bikini top from the jostling of the powerful propulsion. Only mine!

My wolf nods his massive head in agreement. When she first stepped off the boat, he whined, concerned for her safety. I assured him our mate was fine. Now he watches her —and the crew—intently. Ready to spring forward to rescue her.

How quickly she healed from my claiming bite surprised us. We were even more shocked by how it triggered the return of her memories. All of them. We spent hours talking as we sat in bed, and I fed her meals. She admitted she wanted more then but was afraid of what her mother would do. Well, now we know the lengths our parents took to keep Sage and me apart for ten years. Fuck!

She sensed my anger and soothed me with kisses all over my face until I fell back against the pillows with laughter and allowed her to ravage me. The one time I let her take the lead in our lovemaking. As an Alpha male, to give up control is beyond my comprehension. But I spoil my fated mate. I've been too long without her to not let her have her fun. Plus, the pleasure is mutually conducive. My wolf nods, with his tongue lolling from his mouth in agreement enthusiastically.

My only concern is she hasn't shifted yet. She tells me her magick may block the ability. We won't know until more time passes. I know wolf shifters whose human mates' transformation didn't give them the ability to shift. But my wolf aches to run with hers. We'll just have to wait and see.

Tomorrow is Sage's birthday. We return to Miami the next morning. My stomach churns. I shake off the negative thoughts as I remind myself I am Alpha of my pack, and they will obey or pay the price. Sage is their Luna, and they better respect her.

We have talked little on the subject of what happens when we return. My plan is for her to move into our mansion on Moon Island. Immediately. We can have our mate bonding ceremony to complete our mating. If she wants a wedding too, we can do it then or at a later date. But we will have the ceremony now. Whomever isn't for our mating can go fly a fucking kite—my parents and hers included.

I bring my attention back to Sage. She laughs as she flies higher and higher, carried by the propulsion. She signals the crew member on the jet ski, and he brings her down to the water's surface. I dive in and channel my inner Michael Phelps to reach her in a few powerful strokes.

"That was incredible! I can't wait to do it again!" Sage enthuses, floating on her back as I take the boots from her feet and hand them to the crew member. "I could go all day, but I'm hungry."

I chuckle and cup her face. My mouth descends on hers for a toe-curling kiss as we tread water. I can't get enough of my fated mate—of us. It's been perfect. I couldn't ask for anything more.

Her arms wrap around my neck as she returns my kiss with a fiery passion of her own. My cock hardens in my board shorts. She feels it and lifts her legs to draw me close to her body. Her hand reaches between us, and she frees my cock, then aligns it with her pussy.

"But I'm more hungry for you, Jagger Larson," she purrs against my lips.

I growl and thrust forward, breaching her folds in one swift motion. Her tight pussy encases my cock from root to tip. My eyelids close to absorb the carnal sensation. Her pussy walls flutter as they expand to take in every one of my thick inches. I groan in pleasure.

My fated mate proves to be insatiable. Always wet and ready for me to take her, no matter how rough or gentle. And I'm more than willing to oblige her needs.

As I do now. I band my arms around her and pump up into her pussy. The water churns from my powerful thrusts. Her soft cries like a red flag to a bull. I must take her. All else fades—the crew, the boat, the world.

"Oh, Fates, Jagger!" She screams as she cums undone so beautifully for me. Her pussy clenches on my cock, and she wails.

I'm right with her and throw my head back for an earth-shaking roar. My seed floods her pussy like a geyser. She shakes uncontrollably as her orgasm rocks throughout her body. Since we're in the water, I suppress my knot. With a groan, I slip out of her pussy. I kiss her mouth like a possessed male before I urge her back to *Moonbeam*.

She all but glides on the surface ahead of me. Yeah, she used her magick. I follow along at a slower pace.

Once we're back on board, I dip down and put my shoulder into her midsection to put her over my shoulder. Sage giggles and slaps my ass. I return the love tap with a few smacks to her ass. She yelps and wiggles it. Another thing I learned, Sage loves punishment. I won't go so far as a pain slut, but she's a natural submissive. I can't wait to get her to Club Sol & Mani. Explore more of her sub side as her Dom and to introduce her to the BDSM lifestyle. I grin as I carry my fated-mate-cum-sub up the stairs to the outdoor dining deck for lunch.

"I can walk, you know," she says when I put her on her feet by a chair. "No need to carry me about like a sack of potatoes, Jagger."

I nuzzle her neck and murmur, "You're too gorgeous to be a plain old sack of potatoes, Sage, mate of mine."

She giggles and swats at me with a linen napkin as she sits. I round the table and sit across from her. The Chief Stew appears with ceviche for our appetizer. The Stewardess fills our wineglasses with a chilled rosé. We thank them.

"You're welcome, Alpha, Luna," they chime in unison.

Sage blushes at the acknowledgment the crew adopted since they spied my claiming bite on her neck. Bikinis and strapless maxi dresses do nothing to hide my claim of my fated mate. I smirk as I lift a spoonful of ceviche to her lips.

At first, she complained about me feeding her. After a few spankings, she learned her lesson and takes her meals from my hand without issue. I sense she enjoys it. Again, a natural sub. And I love it. In fact, I love her more than life itself.

I haven't spoken the words yet. But I will tomorrow.

~

SAGE

"HAPPY BIRTHDAY, MATE."

I lift my arms overhead and stretch my muscles, sore from countless hours of lovemaking over these past few days. I turn my head and open my eyes to find Jagger on an elbow staring down at me. The expression of love so raw on his handsome face, my heart constricts. Neither of us has said those three words. Although our bodies shouted them for us again and again. I smile and cup his face.

"Thank you, Jagger," I respond.

It's still hard for me to say mate, and I know he notices

but hasn't mentioned it. We are fated mates, with no doubt. However, I worry still. Before I can delve into negative thoughts, Jagger moves over me.

His forearms bracket my head with his palms cradling its crown. Ice blue eyes scan my face before he lowers his full mouth to mine. The kiss is slow and touches every inch inside my mouth until his tongue teases mine to join with him. I do.

Breathless and toes curled later, he pulls back to gaze at me. I raise an eyebrow questioningly.

"I love you, Sage Waters,"

My heart skips a beat.

"I love you so much it hurts. I've never felt this way before. Other than ten years ago. I'm so thankful to the Fates they brought us together again, baby."

He reaches under his pillow and pulls out a little black velvet box. His gaze flicks back to me before he pushes the sapphire cabochon closure. Nestled in a black suede pillow, a gigantic pear-shaped diamond ring winks at me. The sunlight through the cabin's windows shines on the platinum-set stone for a dazzling display of rainbows.

I gasp.

"You are my fated mate, Sage Waters. No one else will ever do for me. You bound my heart the moment I spied you in the Everglades ten years ago. You took my heart then. Now. I've given you my claiming bite and here is my ring—a family heirloom. We will complete our bonding with the mate bonding ceremony and a wedding, if you wish."

His sincerity proves my undoing.

I fling my arms around his neck and bury my face against his skin. I inhale his masculine scent as I pray we can get through the challenges we'll face once we return to Miami.

He must sense my stress and rocks his cock into my core. I sigh and spread my legs to give him full access. I need him to take me. To remind me I am his and his alone and no one can separate us as they did ten years ago.

Our lovemaking is full of passion as we lose ourselves in the other. As we cum as one, I cry out his name.

"Jagger! I love you."

CHAPTER 11

 *age*

Why are you being so tight-lipped? Where are you?

You have your last fitting for your wedding gown? Where are you?

HELLOOOOOOOOOO...

Sage, what's up? I'm coming to Miami sooner. I can't believe you're not telling me, your bestie, what's going on.

Sage! Rupert is going crazy trying to contact you! You haven't even told your fiancé where you are? Come on already...

I SCROLL through many text messages from my sisters and Anala while Jagger and I ride in the tender back to the marina.

Before we left, I sent a text message to Willow—who, as the second oldest—stands in for me in my absence. I didn't give her a reason I was taking five days off. Only that I would be unreachable unless it was an emergency. I've never taken time from my duties. So, I don't feel bad about dropping out of reach. Besides, my connection to our coven would alert me to any danger. However, I increased the wards as a precaution.

The sense of peace from the few days of happiness Jagger and I shared blows away like dandelion pappus on the breeze. In its place, the original reasons we can't be together resurface. The tension creeps up my spine like a frigid chill. I shiver despite the ninety-degree weather and sunshine streaming around us.

I allowed myself to indulge in what our life together could be like if not for Jagger being a wolf shifter and me a witch. His pack and my coven won't stand for our mating. I can empathize with Juliet on a deeper level, not just feeling sorry for her and her forbidden lover.

"What's wrong?"

Jagger's question as he wraps a powerful arm around my shoulders pulls me from my musings. He leans over to peer at the mobile screen. A low, feral growl makes me shiver.

"I don't give a fuck how 'Rupert is going crazy.' I forbid you to see him. Enrique can return the ring," Jagger says with finality as he sits back, arms folded over his massive chest, and stares ahead.

My mouth opens, then closes, unsure of what to say. I can't simply have someone else return the ring. This calls for a conversation. One held in person. It's already bad enough. Plus, I bear Jagger's claiming bite and ring a day before my wedding to Rupert. I don't want to cause further ripples in my coven's relationship with his coven, especially since it's the second most powerful.

How the hell do I tell Jagger?

He'll never go along with me meeting Rupert alone. And I cannot allow Jagger to be present. What a mess that would become!

So, I remain quiet as I go back to my text messages. I don't respond to them yet. What's mentioned will give me a heads up to what I'll face when I return to The Waters Tower. The first instance that caused Jagger's ire.

He wants me to move in with him now. I told him I need to settle things with the wedding. Of course, he went all possessive and snarly. But I didn't back down. I must do it my way.

The tender pulls up to the dock, and a crew member hops onto it to secure the line before we disembark. Jagger gets out and extends his hand to me. I glance up at him, nervous at what I may find. His unreadable expression makes me hesitate until he cocks an eyebrow. I nod, more to convince myself I'm doing the right thing than to acknowledge his questioning gaze. My hand slips into his, and he pulls me to stand before him, held tight to his body.

I lift my gaze to meet his eyes, hidden by sunglasses. I chew on the corner of my lower lip knowing he's about to freak out. Again, I press on. I stand on tiptoe and brush my lips against his chin, the closest spot I can reach.

"I'm not running away. I told you I have to go."

As Jagger shimmers, he squeezes me closer and growls for me not to go. Then he fades away. His anguished howl pierces the absolute depths of my soul.

I land on the bed in my penthouse duplex. Immediately, I sense his loss. My arms wrap around my body at the sudden chill. I close my eyes to focus on my inner strength and inhale deeply. With an exhalation, I sit up and stride to my en suite bathroom for a shower.

Dressed in a wrap dress with a silk scarf tied around my neck artfully and sky-high strappy sandals, I leave my bedroom for part one of my task. I shoot a text message to Willow, Lillie, and Anala asking them to meet me in my coven offices.

Not a second passes before their responses come through and my mobile rings. I ignore the text messages and send the call to voicemail. Instead, I use my teleportation magick to enter my offices, determined to get this part finished ASAP.

Situated on the floor below Lillie's penthouse, my coven offices share the vast space with Willow's office, several conference rooms, and our coven's grand hall. Anala has the ability to teleport, but not within our coven's wards. So, I have time before my girls arrive.

With that in mind, I send a text message to my fated mate.

I'm at The Waters Tower. Please don't be mad. I have to do this my way. I love you. xo S

I blink and the three dots show he's texting a response.

You should have let me come with you. I am not pleased with your decision, Sage. I do not want you anywhere near that witch.

I hear my girls before my door opens. Quickly, I respond.

Please, Jagger.

I close the app while the three dots appear and stand, a hand pressed against my aching heart.

"Sage! What the hell?!"

"You are *so* wrong for not answering not one of us, Sage!"

"Sage, what's going on?"

I remove my hand from my chest and gesture towards

the sitting area. My sisters settle on the chairs, and I sit beside Anala on the sofa. Their eyes focus on me. I nod.

"I cannot marry Rupert—"

"What?!"

"Seriously?!"

"What's going on?"

I raise my hand to stop their onslaught of questions. Once they quiet down, I speak.

"Jagger Larson Alpha of the Miami Wolves Pack is my fated mate."

An uproar ensues. I sit back and wait for them to clear their systems. They notice my silent reaction to their shouts of denial and shut up. I continue.

"I cannot marry Rupert."

I wait out more screeches of disbelief.

"Is that why you wear the scarf, Sage?"

Naturally, Anala—who's the wisest of the three—asks as she flicks her gaze between my neck and my eyes. My sisters gasp. Lillie jumps up and tugs at the scarf. It unwinds from my neck to reveal the marks left by Jagger's canines. She covers her mouth with a trembling hand.

"Sage… no…" she cries as her eyes widen. She glances at her twin for support.

Willow jumps from her chair to get a closer look. She shakes her head and sighs.

"Sage, you know it can't work out between a wolf shifter and a witch. Especially you, Sage. What the hell were you thinking?!"

She returns to her chair and plops down with her eyes closed, as though the sight of Jagger's claiming bite proves too much for her. Lillie follows suit with a sigh.

Anala watches all but says nothing.

I clap my hands and lean forward to pin each of them with an intense stare.

"Okay, now that we're past the news… I need to know if Jagger and I will have your support or not. I will not pressure you in any way. However, know this… I would support you no matter what, especially for a fated mate. We cannot know the reason the Fates pair couples. We can only go by what they decree or suffer from the loss of the fated mate. And I will tell you, being here with you and not with Jagger pains me more than I thought possible."

They exchange anxious glances. The Twins connect on a deeper level. One can see their internal dialogue play out. I wait patiently for their answers, knowing I will continue with or without their support. It would be better to have them on my side when I inform Rupert, then the coven.

"How sure are you of being fated mates?" Anala breaks the silence.

"Absolutely. Ten years ago, Jagger and I first met and realized our connection. Mother and his father found us, and Mother cast spells to erase our memories despite us telling them we're fated mates," I say, then pause to gauge their reactions.

Willow sits forward with her eyebrows raised.

Lillie's mouth drops open.

Anala nods her head, neither surprised nor concerned. Again, she speaks first.

"How could Aunt Prudence use her magick against you?" Anala's eyebrows raise surprised my mother can use her magick against a family member.

I sigh before I respond, "She didn't tell me. But I'll figure it out."

"So, if you lost your memories, how is it you know now—"

"Wait a minute! Is that who kidnapped you from the club?!" Anala leaps to her feet as her question cuts Lillie off.

"That wolf shifter who carried you away and drove off with you?!"

Her eyes burn molten chocolate with her inner fire as she stares at me. Her fingers twitch as though she holds her two curved blades. Undoubtedly because of her reliving Jagger carrying me over his shoulder out of the club and ignoring her at his car's window.

"Yes, he is the one. That night, he caught the scent of his fated mate, and it combated the spell. His memories returned, and he sought me out. My memories returned after he issued his claiming bite."

"Well, damn," Anala says as she falls back to the sofa. "You have my support, Sage. But he better not mess up."

I smile at my bestie, then turn to my sisters.

"Fine," The Twins say in unison.

Lillie sits up with wide eyes and asks, "Oh, Sage! Does Mother know?"

Anala and Willow turn to me.

I nod and relay the encounter in my parents' penthouse duplex. My girls sit enraptured, then confirm they're still with me despite my parents' reaction. Pleased, I hug each of them before I move to part two of my task. Rupert.

"Sage, darling, I was so worried about you! Where have you been?"

I turn my head as Rupert leans over to kiss my lips. His mouth glances off my cheek. A frown mars his handsome face as he settles in the chair opposite mine.

"Are you all right, Sage?"

I nod and clear my throat.

"I'm fine. No need to worry, Rupert. Shall we order?" I respond as I lift a menu to ignore his deepening scowl. "I recommend their chicken paillard with arugula and tomatoes. It's tasty. The server can go over the specials, if you prefer."

He's silent as he studies my face. His obsidian eyes narrow at the scarf around my neck. A second later, he cocks his head as his nostrils flare. A slow breath leaves him.

"Sage, am I mistaken, or do I smell a male wolf shifter on you?"

Rupert's question doesn't surprise me.

Wolf shifters are not the only beings with heightened senses. Which is the reason I attempted to mask Jagger's scent embedded in me. My girls didn't take note of it. But a male—as intended—will detect another male's scent on a female. However, I had hoped to get further along in lunch and our conversation before Rupert noticed.

Aargh!

"Rupert, we need to talk," I respond, then stop when the server appears at the table. I wait for her to complete the list of specials while Rupert stares at me, transfixed. When she leaves, I return his gaze. "Shall we continue our conversation here or upstairs?"

I wanted to meet with him surrounded by others. But it's best to avoid a public scene.

Without a word, Rupert rises, places his napkin on the table, and comes around to help me from my chair. A smidgen of hope unfurls in my belly. Perhaps this will go better than I expected. He places a palm on my lower back to guide me from the restaurant.

We move in silence through The Waters Tower Mall to the separate entry for the residences. I try to slip from Rupert's hold—as subtle as it is—unsuccessfully. Each time, he moves closer and applies more pressure. The tension in the private elevator is palpable.

I glance from beneath the thick fringe of my eyelashes at him in the reflection of the doors. He remains impassive.

We step out into the entry foyer of my penthouse duplex. I place my hand on the plaque, and the lock disengages. Rupert reaches around to hold the doors for me. I duck under his arm, careful not to touch him in an intimate way.

"Would you care for a drink?" I ask as I move towards the living room. My heels click on the marble tile. The only sound in the space rings loud in my ears.

"Sage, you're not wearing my ring. What is going on?"

I turn to face Rupert. He remains by the doors. Enough with this dance. I take a deep breath and reach inside of my Bottega Veneta woven clutch. I hold out his ring as I answer him with sincerity.

"Rupert, I became aware of my fated mate again after ten years, during which they concealed our memories from us. Had I known, I would have called off the pairing between you and me years ago. I'm sure this news comes as a surprise to you as it did for me. But I sincerely hope you understand and harbor no ill will towards me, my fated mate, and my coven. If the roles were reversed, I would not stand in the way of you and the destiny the Fates put forth."

He stares at the ring, then lifts his blank obsidian eyes to my face.

I find it unsettling he shows no reaction. As I open my mouth to speak, he steps forward and plucks the ring from my palm as he responds.

"Sage, you are correct. I would never have expected this news," Rupert starts, then he draws up even taller than his six feet, six inches. "I cannot deny your belief in the Fates. Therefore, we must call off the pairing and make our covens aware. Most of the guests arrived yesterday. A message should suffice. I expect you will handle the situation while I return to New York. I doubt anyone will linger to interfere in your newfound happiness. And I suppose you are happy, Sage?"

I nod, then verbalize a positive response.

He inclines his head.

"Well, then I bid you farewell, Sage Waters."

Rupert pivots and strides out the doors.

I hurry after him. The elevator doors close as our eyes connect. Once again, he shrouds his emotions. A shudder runs through me. But I shake it off.

My hope is it ends here.

CHAPTER 12

"I GET IT, bro. But you can't start a war with her witch fiancé—"

My ferocious growl cuts Tag off. My beta raises his hands, palms out, head bowed in submission. He chances my wrath by continuing.

"No disrespect, Alpha. But we have to be strategic and not let our emotions come into play. I can't say I know what it's like to have my fated mate away from me *and* with another male. However, I get your need to protect what is yours. I suggest we go to The Waters Tower and see if we can get word to her through the doorman. I doubt we can pass through the protective wards to enter the building."

I study Tag with narrowed eyes. What he says makes sense. But the pain caused by separation from my fated mate wrenching through me muddles my thought process.

My wolf and I can only focus on getting to our fated mate and ripping out that witch fucker's throat.

"Alpha?"

Tag's question brings me back from blood-thirsty visions of a shredded *Rupert*.

My beta speaks the truth. I nod and growl for the two of us and my security team to leave Moon Island. On the way, I call Sage's mobile only for it to go straight to voicemail. With a snarl, my fingers fly across my mobile screen as I type a text message.

I am on my way. You cannot stop me.

The sound of splintering glass fills the inside of my SUV as the grip on my mobile threatens to crush it. I loosen it at Tag's cocked eyebrow, then slam myself back against the supple leather seat. My eyes close as I try to temper the beast inside of me.

"We're here, Alpha."

My eyes pop open, and I reach for the door handle. It opens from the outside by Karl, the head of my security team. His eyes scan the area as I jump from the SUV to the sidewalk in front of The Waters Tower. My head goes back as I inhale deeply, hoping to catch a whiff of my fated mate. Nothing. I growl low in my chest and prowl towards the doorman.

It's the same one as the other day. A flicker of recognition crosses his face, then he raises his guard as he eyes me and the wolf shifters behind me. The doorman stands taller and squares his shoulders, ready to defend his High Witch.

Fuck him.

"I know you remember me with Sage Waters. I need to get a message to her. Now."

The doorman doesn't even flinch at my command. He shakes his head and tells me no.

Tag's hand shoots out and grabs my arm as I lift it to

throttle the fucker in front of me. Then his eyes show a bit of fear as he sees my wolf leap to the surface and alter my appearance. The fucker trembles visibly and backs away towards the doors.

"Hey! What's going on here?!"

I whirl around, eyes flashing sapphire barely containing to my wolf. He paces and snarls with canines bared as his tail flicks back and forth. He's eager to get past the doorman and to our fated mate.

"Move out of my way!"

I step from behind my security team to find the source of the angry voice. My eyes widen at the sight of a female witch with chocolate brown eyes ablaze as though an internal fire fuels them. Her mane of ebony curls swirls around her head by the power that emanates from her body. She's a powerful one. And she's the one from the club—Sage's friend. She can help us.

The witch's fiery glower lands on me. Her eyes narrow as her lip curls.

"You! You owe me an apology," she says, arching an eyebrow as her arms fold beneath her breasts.

My men growl. She pins each of them with a death glare, then cocks her head at me. Lips pursed, she waits for my response.

My wolf gnashes his teeth. But in a flash of clarity, I realize this witch is the only hope I have of getting to my fated mate. It will pay to make the witch a friend and not a foe. I tell my men to back down as I approach her.

She throws her head back and laughs throatily. Then she glares at each of them and me.

"You think I need your help, wolf shifter? I am a skilled *vampire* hunter. They nor *you* frighten me in any way," she scoffs. "Now, apologize or move."

I bite back a retort. She smirks at my inner struggle. The

heat in her eyes softens to a glow full of mirth. Okay, she's a badass. But she's not fucking with me out of spite. She's testing me. Fine.

"I apologize for my behavior towards you at the club"—her smirk widens, but I hold up my hand—"However, I will never apologize for taking my fated mate."

The witch scans my face for any artifice. Finding none, she nods.

"Apology accepted, Larson. I already pledged my support of your pairing to my cousin and best friend"—now she holds up her hand to stop me from speaking—"However, should you hurt Sage in any way, I will end you. Period."

Tag tenses beside me. But I wave him and the others off.

She has every right to say what she said. I respect her honesty and loyalty. Not to mention she supports Sage and me. A valuable advocate for us to have on our side. I incline my head to the witch, and she smiles.

Then her eyes widen as she stares over my shoulder.

I spin around. Through the glass exterior of The Tower, a tall male with jet black hair walks beside a woman with his hand on her lower back. The couple heads towards an elevator.

Fuck. Me.

My vision tunnels on them as they step through the elevator doors. The sound of rending fabric fills the air. My wolf breaks free in an instant. We charge forward only to bounce back and land on our rump. My massive head shakes, and we rush ahead.

"Larson, you cannot get past the barrier I erected. You must calm down and shift back."

My wolf and I round on the witch.

She stands within a circle of fire, two flaming curved swords in each of her hands.

"I will help you. So, do not make me use my powers against you and your men. Do you understand?"

My wolf growls, hackles raised, and flicks his feathery tail. I glance around and notice people walk past us as though we do not exist. They don't bump into the barrier nor notice the circle of fire within it. Tag and my men dart their gazes between the witch and me. I throw my head back and let loose an anguished howl, then force my wolf to retreat. He snarls but obeys while he paces on the fringes, ready to come forth anew.

"Great, now how the hell do we enter the building with you buck naked, Larson?" The witch giggles as she covers her eyes with a dainty hand free of the sword. "And I have no interest in seeing my bestie's mate's family jewels. Eww!"

Tag chuckles as he instructs one man to get the extra clothes we keep in the SUV for times like this one. The witch waves her hand.

"Never mind, I'll take care of it. You need to look sharp and make a good impression as we enter The Tower," she says as a well-tailored, three-piece suit and the appropriate accessories cover me. "Oh, and I'm Anala Azar of the Northeast Coven, by the way."

"Thank you, Anala, nice to meet you officially," I say with a smirk, then introduce her to Tag and my men.

She nods, and the barrier disappears. "Shall we?"

We follow her inside. As much as my wolf wants to snap at the doorman, I maintain a stoic expression as we pass him, holding the door. He mumbles a greeting to Anala. She nods but doesn't slow her pace.

And she is correct. The witches who come and go in the lobby eyeball our group as we walk to the elevator. Some stare openly while others ogle surreptitiously at us. Their whispered exclamations clear with my wolf senses. The others give her and us a wide berth. I follow Anala's lead and ignore them.

"Now, listen to me carefully and swear you will not lose control again. And that goes for all of you. Or I will invoke a spell you will regret," Anala says while we wait for the elevator. When we affirm our agreement, she continues. "I will take you to Sage's sister Willow's penthouse, one floor below Sage's residence. Then I will reach out to Sage and let her know we are here. It will be up to her to come get you."

My mind envisions all the things that fucker *Rupert* can do to my fated mate while we wait. A growl rises from my chest. As though reading my mind, Anala speaks again.

"Listen, I understand, Larson. But I know Sage. She will not allow Rupert to do anything untoward. She made it crystal clear to me and to her sisters *you* are her fated mate. All three of us support her and you. Do this my way. Trust me," she says fervently.

"Fine," I bite out.

She offers me a smile and steps onto the elevator. I must say, the male who captures this spitfire will be one lucky bastard. Beauty, strength, loyalty, compassion, all admirable traits in a mate. I wonder if the Fates could favor a male from my pack. Anala's laughter confirms she can read my mind. I grin back at her as the elevator doors close.

Soon we step off to an entry foyer. The double doors fly open, and two witches run out.

"What's going on?!"

"Does Sage know?"

I do a double take and realize they're identical twins who resemble Sage. They must be her sisters. I offer them a smile as Anala bustles them back inside and beckons for us to follow.

She recaps the events as I pace the living room. My

patience hangs on by a wolf's hair. The twins turn to me as one.

"You better be good to our sister..."

"Or we will use every ounce of our power to make you suffer unimaginable torture for all eternity."

Damn. Even my wolf shudders at their vow.

"I love Sage and will do nothing to hurt my fated mate. That I swear," I respond wholeheartedly.

"We will hold you to your word, Jagger Larson, Alpha of the Miami Wolves Pack," the twins state in unison.

"So will I."

My wolf leaps to his feet, tongue lolling from his mouth as he wags his tail and whines. I whirl around to find my fated mate behind me. Two long strides and she's in my arms, my face buried in her neck. I inhale deeply to check for the other male's scent on her. Only a trace from being in his presence, no lasting impact. Thank the Fates!

"I see you met my sisters Willow and Lillie and my cousin Anala again," Sage says with a laugh. "And believe me, they mean what they say. So, don't mess up, Jagger Larson."

"I won't," I answer gruffly, then pull back to stare down at her. "What happened with him?"

She shrugs and leads me to the sofa. She waits for everyone to sit, then recaps their conversation. When I growl at certain parts, she squeezes my hand and smiles at me reassuringly.

At the end, I don't trust the fucker. I glance at Tag. He nods, understanding I want eyes on *Rupert*. Our pack has close ties to the New York one. So, we'll have their support once I speak to their Alpha. I add the conversation as a mental note and tune back into my fated mate.

"—a message to the wedding guests and speak with the coven. I need to get those tasks completed right away. I don't want word to spread before I get a handle on the situation. Anala, I'll need you to gauge the New York coven's reaction. Will you return home now?"

Anala agrees and gives Sage and the twins hugs before she smirks at me and leaves the penthouse.

I can't help but to admire her fearlessness.

"Sage, I wrote a letter for you to provide the guests after you told us the wedding was called off permanently. Here, let me get it for you," the twin named Lillie says as she leaves the living room.

While she's gone, Sage instructs Willow to call the coven for a meeting in two hours. I grumble to myself, not wanting to wait any longer to get her home. But also glad she's taking care of things with a quickness. I hope it goes smoothly.

Lillie returns, and Sage makes a few changes to the letter. By Sage's magick, she disperses it to each person. They decide to make one for coven members unable to attend the last-minute meeting.

A little over an hour later, Sage and I enter her penthouse duplex. While we go up to her bedroom suite, Tag and my men go to the living room. As soon as the door shuts behind us, I spin her around and pin her to it.

My fingers untie the belt of her dress. The silk slips open to reveal her lush curves. D-cups fill a black lace bra. Her flat belly leads to hips with the strings from her black lace G-string around them. I yank the cups down and lower my mouth to feast on her plump brown nipples.

She mewls as I lap at one. It tightens beneath my tongue. I flick the distended tip, then nip it. The bite of pain makes her back arc from the door as her fingers dive into my hair.

I pull back with a pop from her tit. With a flick of my wrist, the dress falls to the floor. I use the belt to bind her wrists. I open the door and toss the end over the top, then close it. Sage hangs suspended, arms overhead, toes wiggle to reach the floor. I step back to admire my work.

Her chest heaves as she pants and stares back at me with hooded eyes. Fingers flex into fists, grasping at the air. My ring on her finger sparkles with each movement. She squirms while a crimson hue licks along her breasts as I continue to watch her body react to the restraint.

"My beautiful, fated mate. Mine!"

I grip her hips and crush her mouth with mine. My tongue pushes past her lips and sweeps through her mouth. I groan at her sweet taste. Her tongue probes mine, and I allow them to tangle. My knee wedges between her thighs to press against her hot pussy.

She grinds down on a moan as I swallow down greedily. Her arousal fills the air as her juices coat my trouser leg. I flex my quads, and she groans at the added friction. Her humping becomes erratic as her orgasm barrels towards her.

I step back.

Her eyes fly open. Dazedly, she searches my face.

I shake my head.

"You disobeyed my command, *mate*," I tsk. "You will only cum when I tell you. *If* I tell you. And I'm inclined not to give you the release you crave."

"Jagger... *Please*," she cries, body shaking poised on the edge.

I ignore her plea and unhook her bra. Her delicious tits spill free from the cups as the front closure opens. I pinch both nipples, then rub them between my thumbs and index fingers as she pants through a slack mouth. My mouth returns to lave, suckle, and nip each one of her pebbled nipples until she's on the verge of another orgasm.

She throws her head back against the door and blows out a frustrated breath when I step back again.

"Jagger! Be fair! I had to do it my way," she cries, emerald green eyes plead for her release.

I move close to her again. My lips ghosts over hers, then trail lower—over her collarbone, between her tits, down her belly—to land on her laced-covered mons. A warm breath blown over her swollen slick pussy lips makes her shudder so hard, her shoulder blades bang against the door. A wicked chuckle puffs more air on her sensitive folds. She groans, eyes closed, head back.

A growl follows the ripping of the skimpy lingerie. It grows savage as I bury my face in her soaked pussy. My tongue pushes past the slick folds to lap every inch. Her thighs quiver on my shoulders as my fingers dig into her ass, locking her in place.

So intense, she still manages to buck as I devour her. My snarls join her cries. Her knees squeeze the sides of my head as her inner walls flutter. I increase my ministrations, tilting her pelvis to drive deeper into her core. A nip to her engorged clit, and she begs me to let her cum.

I jump to my feet, keeping her legs on my shoulders. Her body bent in half, I impale her on my thick cock. She screams as she cums all along my turgid length.

"You. Are. Mine. Sage. Waters. Mine!" I punctuate each word with a feral thrust. I continue to pound into her pussy as she climaxes again and again. "Do not disobey me ever again, Sage!"

I roar her name as my heavy balls draw up. One final thrust rocks me to the balls of my feet, thick thighs and firm ass flex. My cock spews copious amounts of seed inside of her womb. Once again, I pray for my seed to take root for my pup to fill my fated mate's belly.

Before my knees buckle from the ferocity of my release, I open the door. The silk belt slips from above the door. I close it and sag to the floor, twisting to put my ass down and Sage in my lap. She curls against my heaving chest with a sated sigh. I kiss the top of her head and let my eyes drift shut.

We can remain in blissed-out peace a moment longer and regain our strength before the meeting with her coven. The Fates know we'll need all our energy to face the next steps, including my pack.

CHAPTER 13

agger

"What is the meaning of this nonsense?"

"Are the rumors true?"

"Is that even allowed?"

"Wow! A wolf shifter as our High Witch's fated mate?"

"I saw him and a bunch of other mongrels strut inside of our coven led by Anala of all witches!"

"And they're lurking around here like they own the place!"

"How did the Northeast Coven react to the news? What did Rupert say?!"

. . .

My wolf senses allow me to hear every spoken word members of Sage's coven utter despite me being in the room behind the High Witch's dais.

My wolf growls at each insult. An occasional remark by a member who sounds supportive brings me hope. Typically, the older witches complain while the younger ones appear more open. But with them being Immortal Witches, it's hard to distinguish who's of what age. Only their comments help to differentiate one group from the other.

I glance at Sage.

Showered and freshly dressed in an aqua blue suit with a pencil skirt and flesh-tone heels, she exudes power and beauty. She explained as an elemental witch of water, the colors of the ocean—the largest body of water—emphasize her connection to the element. My chest fills with pride to see her claiming bite uncovered. An unspoken acknowledgment to all our status as fated mates.

When we arrived ahead of the coven, she asked for space. Now, she sits on a chair with her eyes closed. A serene expression set on her lovely face as her mouth moves soundlessly.

My wolf and I stand not too far from her, keeping one eye on our fated mate and the other on the door leading to the coven's grand hall. Tag stands beside me while two of my men stand at the door leading to the hall and the one leading to Sage's private entry and the elevator for her family's residences. Several other enforcers cover areas throughout the floor and outside her penthouse duplex. Others remain on standby in vans outside of The Waters Tower. My wolf and I will protect my fated mate at all costs.

Even though Sage told me she heightened the level of

protective wards around us, her sisters, and Anala—even though she's in New York. Sage's powers know no bounds.

However, the Alpha in me demands I have a hand in her safety. I also spoke with Garrett Moen—Alpha of the New York Wolves Pack—to not only monitor *Rupert*, but to watch Anala's back. Whatever may hurt my fated mate falls under my purview.

My gaze shifts to Willow and to Lillie across the room. That includes her younger sisters. I assigned enforcers as their security detail. Although they denied needing protection because of their powers, I insisted. Sage told them to just give in like she did with her new detail. They agreed for now. I chuckled to myself and thought forever, little ones.

Lillie senses my eyes on her and lifts her gaze to mine. She arches an elegant eyebrow. I shake my head and turn back to my fated mate.

She stirs, then her emerald green eyes open. They find my ice blue gaze on her, and a beatific smile spreads across her face, lighting her from within with a warm glow.

"It is time," Sage says as she rises. She pauses next to me and angles her face for a kiss. I slant my mouth over hers and impart a kiss full of love, protection, and desire. When I step back, I catch Sage by the waist to steady her on wobbly legs. She grins at me. "Wow, thank you."

I smirk and brush my lips over hers as I rumble in my chest. Her eyes close on a sigh as her fingers tighten on my suit jacket—a new one she whipped up after our shower. And I can't wait for this meeting to end so I can have back in my arms. Alone in our home.

"Okay, lovebirds. Let's go, already."

Willow's comment with an exaggerated sigh, cuts into the bubble I share with my fated mate. I bite back a possessive growl.

Sage nods and smooths the front of my jacket, then pats

my pecs with the corners of her lips curled up in a mischievous grin. Then she straightens her shoulders and walks with her head held high to the door leading to the coven's grand hall. Voices erupt as she enters.

My men and I are to wait until she calls me forward. The uproar of the crowd makes it difficult for me to heed my fated mate's request. A vicious growl rips from my chest. I pace behind the now closed door like a caged wild wolf separated from his fated mate—exactly what I am. Even it's only by a door. Tag and my men stand alert for any sounds of distress.

Sage's voice rings clear.

~

SAGE

"I WILL HAVE ORDER. *NOW.*"

My emerald green eyes blaze as I pin several rambunctious members of the coven with a look of unbridled power. It surges over me and into the grand hall. Most of the vociferous ones have the respect to avert their eyes and bow their heads. I make note of them and of those who meet my gaze unfazed. However, all stop speaking at once and take their seats.

I wait until the entire room settles before I sit on the center chair reserved for the High Witch on the dais. Willow lowers to her seat on my right. The coven secretary sits at a table at my left to the side of the dais. Lillie sits in the first row opposite us, back straight, head held high like her sisters.

My eyes scan the crowd. Our parents did not join the meeting—at least not yet. I send a prayer to the Fates for

Prudence and Wyatt to not cause any conflict. With a deep breath, I call the meeting to order.

"Good afternoon. It is 5:00, and I call the meeting of the Coven of the South to order."

The secretary calls each member's name from the coven roster and marks those present and those absent on her laptop. When she completes her task, she announces the number present. I'm not surprised to find all but a handful in attendance. I'm sure those gathered notice the obvious absence of my parents.

I shake it off and get to business.

"As you may now be aware, I called this meeting to inform you of my decision to cancel the pairing between Rupert Ravenheart of the Northeast Coven and me—"

Angry voices rise. I silence the room with a flick of my fingers, then continue.

"Last warning. Should anyone speak out of turn, I will eject you from this meeting," I state as my eyes rove over those in the grand hall. No one dares to open their mouth. "Whatever you may have heard, I will now tell you directly the events that led to this final decision."

I proceed to recount what happened ten years ago, ending with the return of my memories. A few murmured words of shock ripple through the members. They glance at one another in disbelief at my mother's actions. I assure them of the veracity of my words.

If it were not for Jagger being a wolf shifter, I am certain the coven would have agreed with me unanimously. However, after I open the floor to comments, those known to despise shifters—particularly wolves—rush to the two microphones.

I take a deep breath and brace myself before I recognize to speak a male witch around my mother's age.

"Sage, I must say how incredibly disappointed in you I

am. We expected more from you as part of a long line of esteemed High Witches. And you've taken a wolf shifter as your mate," he says, lip curled in disgust. He glances around the room for a show of support. Several members nod and murmur their agreement. He turns back to me. "And where is this *mate* of yours? Hiding behind your skirt?"

A ferocious growl rips through the air as the door to the Hight Witch's chamber bursts open, nearly tearing from its hinges. The grand hall erupts in shouts and screams as Jagger—followed by Tag and the security team—enter the space.

I jump to my feet and stare at Jagger, silently begging him to control himself and his wolf. Now is not the time to lose it. His flashing eyes land on me, and he stalks forward. He stops with his body angled between the rest of the grand hall and me. His chest heaves with the exertion to hold his wolf at bay.

"And *this* is what you expect us to accept, Sage?"

The witch's snicker causes Jagger to flex his fingers. I place a hand on his back. His muscles taut with beneath my palm. Through our connection, I sense his anger. It burns and threatens to upend the grand hall—the world, if need be —to protect me.

I step from behind him and face the witch.

"You know not the depth of a fated mate, Cyrus. So, no, I do not expect you to accept the bond Jagger and I share necessarily. But you will respect it and him. Do not belittle your status in the coven for petty displays."

Cyrus bristles as I recognize the next speaker. He opens his mouth to protest. But I silence him with a stare. He moves aside and returns to his seat. Those around him lean in to whisper. I make note of them too.

The speakers continue with those against and those in support of Jagger and me. Others voice their concerns about offending the Northeast coven. After more than an hour, I call for the last speakers. No one steps to the microphones.

"The meeting stands adjourned. The time is 6:30," I say, keeping my voice firm and clear, then rise from the chair.

Jagger and his men who stood the entire time behind me follow me towards the smaller room. Tag steps forward to enter it ahead of me. He scans the space, then nods it's clear for us to enter. Willow and Lillie join us.

"Fuck—"

I raise my finger to my lips and shake my head at Jagger, then gesture for us to continue to the private elevator. Once the doors close, I take a deep breath. Jagger rages, all but yanking on his white blond hair. I don't interrupt him.

We step off to my entry foyer. The enforcers at the double doors stand aside to give us access. Jagger tells them to remain alert while Tag speaks to the ones stationed around The Tower.

"I find it unnerving Mother and Father didn't show. What do you make of it, Sage?" Lillie asks as we sit in the living room.

A ragged sigh slips past my lips as I slump back against the silk sofa. Jagger stops his pacing and sits beside me. His arm goes around my shoulders, and he pulls me into his side. I close my eyes as he nuzzles my hair. His rumbling soothes me.

Reluctantly, I sit up. We'll have time later to cuddle... I hope. A shudder runs through me at the thought of not being with Jagger. But judging by the reaction of the coven, I can't say for certain how things will end up. I pat Jagger's muscular thigh when he sits up and stares at me questioningly.

"They must stand firm in their beliefs still. I have not heard from either of them. So, your guess is as good as mine. I would hope they won't incite any conflict," I respond. "However, I was pleased to see so many members offer their support. This comes as a shock. I'll give the coven time to absorb the news, then meet again."

I glance over at Willow, where she stands by the wall of windows overlooking Biscayne Bay and the Atlantic Ocean beyond. Her shoulders hunch around her ears as tension emanates from her. I stand and go to my younger sister.

Jagger cocks an eyebrow. But I shake my head and walk to Willow.

"Hey, Willow. What are your thoughts?" I ask quietly as I slide the door open to the wraparound terrace.

She hesitates, then follows me outside. We stop at the glass divider and lean on the railing. I wait for her to answer.

Willow shrugs.

"I have to admit some of their points are valid, Sage. Especially the lineage of the next High Witch, your daughter," she starts, then casts a sidelong glance at me. I keep my face expressionless, not wanting to discourage her from speaking unhindered. She takes a deep breath and continues. "I love you and want what's best for you. But the coven can't remain strong if it's divided. Then there's the Witch Council to consider."

Willow stops and takes a deep breath as her eyes continue to stare out to the ocean.

I hold my tongue.

"But you're right. The news comes as a shock. Once members have time to think on it—given you provided the full story—they may change their minds. It's a matter of waiting, I suppose," she says, then pushes off the railing. "It's been a long day. I want to soak in a tub with lavender essential oil and a glass of Cabernet Sauvignon. Do you mind if I call it a night?"

I mimic her move and stand as I shake my head.

"Of course not," I respond and put my arms around her for a hug. "Thank you, Willow, for your honesty. Never think you cannot come to me, no matter what you think my reaction may be. Above all, you are my sister, my blood. Do you understand?"

I pull back to search her face. She lowers her eyes. But raises them to meet my gaze and nods.

"Aaw! Sister's group hug!"

Lillie's arms fling around us.

"Boy! What a day, huh? Time for a bath and wine. Heck, maybe even the entire bottle!" She says with a light laugh as she loops her arms through ours and leads us back inside.

I walk them to the elevator, not reacting to Jagger's raised eyebrow as we pass him. Once in the entry foyer, I give my sisters another hug and bid them goodnight. When the elevator doors close, Willow meets my gaze with forlorn eyes. A shiver runs through me, and I wrap my arms around my waist.

Muscular arms cover mine as a firm chest presses into my back. I sigh and lean into my fated mate. His strength washes over me as his rumbles soothe the sorrow in my soul. I close my eyes and pray to the Fates Willow will not turn against me too.

"Let's go home, beautiful mate of mine."

Jagger's huskily spoken words save me from the moment of despair.

I nod my head in agreement as my heart constricts. At this moment, with my parents and now potentially my sister in opposition to me and my fated mate, this does not feel like home anymore.

CHAPTER 14

"WHAT IS THIS? The Wolf, the Witch, and the Wardrobe? You have more clothes than me! Where will I put mine?"

My fated mate's questions followed by giggles float from within my dressing room.

It's nice to hear a light air from Sage. Since last night, she's been sad and doubting herself. But I keep telling her she's a badass and those in her coven who oppose us can fuck off.

After the meeting, she used her teleportation magick to bring us, Tag, and my enforcers within The Tower to my mansion on Moon Island. The others drove back in the vans. She didn't want a skirmish as we left through the lobby. I agreed because they would not hold me responsible for my wolf tearing through some witches if they threatened my fated mate or my pack.

Once my enforcers pledged to stand by my side, they left

Viggo, Tag, and me to discuss the next steps, including a pack meeting. They were no more thrilled than I was with the outcome of the witches' meeting. Tag voiced his concerns of the pack accepting Sage, standing with me should the witches retaliate, and whether someone may challenge me as Alpha.

His last concern made my wolf bristle—ears flattened to his skull, canines bared. A savage growl issued in warning. My lip curled as I snapped out a reminder, I will finish anyone who dares to challenge me. No one will keep me from my fated mate. No. One.

But I will give up all to keep Sage by my side.

I wonder if she will do the same.

"Seriously, Jagger. You're not a wolf shifter, you're a clothes horse!"

Sage's snorts as she doubles over in a fit of giggles washes away the negative thought. She leans against the doorframe and wipes tears from the corners of her eyes. My silk robe swallows her petite body. Then she pauses as the disquiet in my mind passes along our mating bond.

Each day, it gets stronger. Our feelings transmitted along the tether that binds us as a mated pair.

She rubs her chest as her eyes scan my face.

I won't let my unwarranted doubt worry my fated mate. So, I stalk towards her until her butt hits a wall and her mouth opens in a perfect O, then cage her between my forearms.

"A horse, huh? Is my cock not large enough for you, *mate*?" I ask, our noses inches apart.

Lust explodes within her emerald green eyes as a breath escapes her open mouth. She blinks and shakes her head.

"Oh, no, you won't flip my words, Jagger Larson. I said nothing about your dick. Only the amount of clothes you have and no room for mine," she replies.

I chuckle and brush my lips over hers. She melts against me. But I stand and take her hand.

"You missed something, *mate*."

Sage gasps when I open a door on the other side of the bedroom. Her eyes dart around the space as she takes in the all-white Carrara marble bathroom. A walk-in Roman shower big enough to hold four, an extra-large silver wolf-claw-foot tub, a single vanity with an adjacent makeup table, and a separate water closet for the bidet and toilet.

I usher her inside and towards another door.

Her eyes shine as she scans the dressing room. A hand-carved white island with a white suede top and drawers sits in the center. Three walls accommodate racks and drawers for clothing. Shelves for handbags and shoes flank the door. In one corner, a trifold mirror surrounds a raised platform.

Sage steps forward and skims her fingers over the designer day dresses, skirt suits, blouses, and evening gowns. She opens drawers and smirks at the Agent Provocateur lingerie and playsuits laid out on silk liners. When she turns to face me, her mouth drops open at the dazzling array of Hermès Birkin bags—red Togo leather, matte black alligator, the impossible to get Himalayan with diamond details. She steps forward, entranced.

Now, I smirk.

"Satisfied, *mate*?"

"Jagger! Why didn't you show me last night? When did you do all of this? And you bought the correct sizes!" She exclaims as she throws her arms around my neck, wiggling her curvy little body all over me as she dances on her toes. "Thank you! Thank you!"

"I believe we had other things on our minds…"

I cup her ass, lifting her to grind my burgeoning erection —hung, but not horse size—against her pussy mound. My mouth catches hers as she plants a kiss on my cheek. A nip followed by a lick has her wiggling for other reasons.

"You like?" I say gruffly in her ear as I thrust my hips upwards, holding her down against my cock. I respond to her mewl with a wicked chuckle. "Let's see how much."

I stride towards the center island and sit my fated mate on top with her ass cheeks on the edge. When I press my palm between her tits, she leans back on her elbows. Hooded eyes stare up at me. They follow as I lower my face between her welcoming thighs. We maintain eye contact as I swipe the sides of my silk robe away from my reward.

The calloused pads of my thumbs drag along the edges of her bare mons. The delicate flesh quivers in their wake. So responsive, her pussy lips begin to glisten with her juices. My nose twitches, full of her instant arousal. I groan, hungry for the succulent taste of her.

My thumbs pull her lower lips apart to expose her slick core. I stare at it transfixed, as it winks and weeps for me.

"Jagger... I need you..."

"Hush, baby, I know what you need and when you need it."

Sage whines as her head falls back, eyes squeezed shut. My hand snakes out, fingers curl around her throat. Her eyes pop open.

"Eyes on me," I command as I tighten my grip. Her breath catches as I continue. "I want to watch you break for me."

Her pupils dilate.

Moisture coats my other thumb. I glance down to find her pussy gushed at my words. I lean down and purr as I lap at her sweet juices. My eyes never leave hers as my tongue swirls to capture every single drop.

"Unnhhh... Jagger. Oh, right there. Oh!" My fated mate's cries of carnal passion urge me to probe deeper with slow, long licks. A few well-placed nips add a bite of pain to her pleasure. She writhes and moans louder. Her eyes remain locked with mine.

However, my eyes want to roll to the back of my head in pure ecstasy. Her taste and arousal so divine, I can barely contain myself—or my wolf. The tip and several thick inches of my cock poke from the waistband of my joggers. I feel pre-cum collecting on its mushroom tip. My cock wants in on the action.

Who am I to deny it?

But I'll wait. I want my fated mate soft and dripping for me before I mount her from behind. With a groan, I add my fingers to the mix. One, then two drill into her pussy while my tongue wraps around her distended clit.

"Jagger! I… I can—can't hold back," my fated mate cries anxiously as her wide eyes plead with me.

I blow a puff of air over her slick folds before I respond, "Cum for me, my beautiful mate. Cum for me now!"

She screams as my teeth nip her clit and my fingers spear her pussy. The knuckles graze her G-spot. Her eyes flutter closed as her body convulses and her pussy clamps on my digits. She writhes as I lap at the flood of juices. I press my palm above her mons to make her still so she can focus on the pleasure rippling through her body. Her screams turn into a baby howl.

I spring to my feet as I yank the tie on my joggers. My aching cock bounces out. I grip its base and plunge my length into her quivering pussy. She's so tight as her pussy clenches, it takes effort to fit all of me inside of her. I feed it to her inch by agonizing inch. My wolf snarls. He wants all in. Now.

My fingers strum her clit to keep her orgasm on high until I'm fully seated. Her pussy continues to flutter around my length as I thrust with wild abandon. I want to pound the worry and fear from her body. Hell, from mine too. All that matters is we are one. Whole. Never apart again.

Her cries and moans please my wolf. We make it our mission to bring absolute pleasure to our fated mate. My hips circle as I change the angle to drive deeper. I pull out and flip her around with a few smacks to her round ass before I plow back into her. My torso presses hers into the center island. Her hips held aloft by my tight grip grind into the edge with each brutal thrust.

"MINE! Dammit! MINE!" I roar.

My fated mate shudders at my frenetic outburst, even as her pussy clamps on my cock. We groan in unison. I keep pumping, intent on finding my release. My knees shake as the first zap of erotic energy hits my lower spine. It zings to my balls and out to the tip of my pulsating cock. It thickens more than possible. With a savage roar, ropes of my seed shoot into her womb.

"You. Are. Mine, Sage. Waters. MINE!"

I bury my face in the side of her sweat dampened neck. My cock pushed to the maximum inside of her pussy. She babbles an incoherent response as her fingers twine with mine on either side of her head. Our pants mingle. Heartbeats race.

We remain locked as one until I step back and watch as my cock slides from her well-used pussy. She groans louder than me with longing for more. I tap her pussy lips and smirk as my seed dribbles from her core down the curve of her ass. I scoop up some on a finger and press it to her slack mouth. Her little pink tongue darts out to lap the digit clean. I groan as my cock twitches, ready to go again.

Alas, we cannot. Duty calls.

I slip the robe from my fated mate and scoop her into my arms. As I carry her to the Roman shower, she nuzzles against my chest with a contented sigh. I wish we could stay at home in bed. But we have the pack meeting to attend in an hour.

Her plump brown nipples tighten as I bathe them with a soapy sponge. I'm torn between suckling them and getting her washed and dressed. Instead, I take a deep breath, then groan when her arousal fills my nose. I shake my head and re-focus on my task.

"Jagger, I can do it," Sage says as she reaches for the sponge. "How much time do we have? We can't be late."

Even in her post-coital haze, my fated mate's concern is for us. I lean over and brush my lips against hers as I assure her we have plenty of time. She gives in with a sigh and leans against the marble wall.

Quickly, I wash her, then myself. She protests when I carry her from the shower. But I ignore her and dry her soft skin with a heated towel. Sage makes her way to her dressing room. I swat her ass just to fuck with her. She covers it with one hand as she scowls at me over her shoulder. Hips sway to a natural rhythm as she walks away.

I leave her bathroom for my dressing room. When I reemerge, Sage stands by the window dressed in a three-quarter sleeve, navy blue dress that accentuates her curves and falls below her knees. The boat neck reveals my claiming bite. Strappy sandals lengthen her toned legs and give her ass an added boost. Her ebony curls flow down her back. She turns as I enter the bedroom.

"Don't you look dapper, my Alpha," my fated mates says as her appreciative eyes scan me from head to toe in my custom Brioni suit.

My heart soars at her possessive use of my title. I grin and respond huskily, "As do you, my Luna."

I extend my arm, and she loops hers through it. In the entry, Viggo, Tag, Rust, Karl, and my security detail wait for us. I pause to introduce Sage to my younger brother before we leave the mansion.

Calls to my youngest sibling, Signy, went to her voicemail. I haven't had time to question my sister. My hope is we'll speak after the pack meeting. Unless, of course, she's sided with our parents. I shake my head to clear the negative thought and stride towards the front doors.

Instead of golf carts, Suburbans wait to take us to the clubhouse. I agreed with Tag it's best to have the protection of an entire SUV and not the openness of the golf cart. I lift Sage onto the back seat, then circle around to the other side. She takes my hand as I sit beside her. Tag drives and Viggo rides in the passenger seat.

It's quiet as we ride to the center of Moon Island. The clubhouse appears as the lane opens up. The two-story structure accommodates our meeting space, recreation rooms, and a grill that serves burgers, fries, shakes, and other backyard-style food.

A few golf carts and cars sit in the parking area. Most members walked from their homes.

Viggo nudges me as I reach to open Sage's door. He inclines his head towards the side of the clubhouse. I follow his gaze.

Melissa struts towards us. Her amber eyes locked on me.

I mutter a curse under my breath. I've ignored her calls and text messages ever since her unexpected appearance in my suite at Club Sol & Mani. It didn't occur to me she would find a pack meeting as the time to approach me. Fuck.

Distracted, my hand hovers over the door handle. A moment later, the door bumps into me as it opens from the inside, just as Melissa reaches me.

"Jagger, why haven't you answered my calls and texts?"

She demands, lips formed in a pout. "Do you want me to grovel or what?"

Sage's body brushes against my back as she slides from the SUV.

I don't even have to turn around to see her face to gauge her reaction. Her surprise comes through our tether, loud and clear. I send back reassurance in hopes to diffuse the situation.

"Who the hell is *she?*" Melissa snarls. Her amber eyes flash with streaks of gold as she glares at Sage. "Oh, so is *she* the reason you stopped fucking me, Jagger?"

My fated mate stiffens beside me.

"Now is not the time, Melissa. Go into the clubhouse," I command.

When she hesitates with her wolf hovering at the surface, glaring at Sage, I issue a warning growl. The sable-haired hellion jumps. She walks backwards, keeping her narrowed eyes on Sage.

Other pack members take notice and pause before entering the clubhouse to watch the exchange with interest. Tag steps forward and gestures for them to go inside. Their curious gazes flick between Melissa's retreating figure and me. A few cock their heads at the sight of Sage, noses lifted as they scent the air.

I put my arm around her waist and pull her against my side.

"Don't worry. What the she-wolf said is not true. I will explain later," I murmur in her ear. I keep my voice low to avoid others hearing us with the enhanced reach of wolf sifter ears. When Sage nods, I relax.

We enter the clubhouse and head for the meeting space. It accommodates our entire pack, set up with tiered seating and two aisles that lead to the raised platform. Already filled, Sage, Viggo, Tag, Rust, Karl, and I stride down one aisle while my enforcers line the walls. I bring Sage onto the dais with me. She sits in the chair reserved for the Luna. I had it placed there from storage earlier. She crosses her legs and smooths her dress over her thighs before she lifts her head with her back straight and stares out at our pack.

Murmurs arise. Members shift in their seats to get a better view of the female who sits beside me as my mate. I raise my hand to call for silence.

"That's Sage Waters! She's the High Witch!" Melissa's angry snarl reverberates around the space just before she shifts into her wolf and leaps towards the dais.

Then all hell breaks loose.

CHAPTER 15

age

"Viggo, Karl, get my fated mate out of here. Now!"

Karl grabs my arm. The huge wolf shifter lifts me to my feet with ease.

However, my eyes never leave the she-wolf named Melissa. Her sable-haired wolf races towards me with ears flat and snapping jaws. Around her, others shift into their wolves or rush to their feet. Shouts blend with the sound of ripping clothing and claws scrapping the stone floor.

In my periphery, Jagger tears through his suit like tissue paper as his great silvery white wolf charges forth with a blood-curdling howl and canines bared. On his other side, Tag's massive brown wolf paws the floor with his ears flattened to his head. Rust's huge red wolf snarls and snaps his jaws. Standing between me and the mad she-wolf, Viggo morphs into a giant red wolf. His ice blue eyes flash silvery, and his lips curl in a snarl as he takes a defensive stance.

My lips move on instinct.

Melissa yowls when her wolf slams into the invisible barrier I erected around the dais. She bounces back as her limbs flail to gain purchase on the stone. When she rights herself, her amber eyes shoot venomous daggers at me. Blood pours from her muzzle. She paces along the barrier snarling as she attempts to find a weakness.

There is never a weakness in my magick. She should know since she outed me as High Witch. I watch her dispassionately.

The space falls quiet as others stop and stare at me. Karl's grip on my arm lessens until I extricate it from him gently. I move to Jagger's side. His wolf stares up at me. Through our tether, he sends his love and admiration. I return it tenfold.

My fated mate would risk himself and his pack to save me. With no uncertainty, I now realize I will do the same for him. If the coven decides against our mating, then I will walk away with my head held high and Jagger by my side.

I smile at him, then turn to sit in my chair.

～

*J*AGGER

I watch my fated mate settle back on her Luna's chair—a position she just cemented with one simple move. She meets my gaze and bows her head in a sign of respect for my role as Alpha. I grin as best as I can in wolf form—more sharp teeth than curved lips.

Then I swing my head around to face my pack. My parents don't appear amongst those gathered, nor Signy. Despite my disappointment, I don't let it impede my control over my pack. I eye each member until they lower their heads in submission. All but a few—including the sable-haired hellion who started the ruckus—return my stare as wolves and in human form. I throw my head back and howl. It bounces off the walls around the room. I continue until members join in.

Our song continues a moment longer, then I command my wolf to recede. He does so reluctantly, not wanting to leave our fated mate. I assure him she will be more than fine. When I stand on two feet, I notice some members followed my lead and shifted. I eye those who remain in wolf form.

"Shift. Now!" I bellow, drawing on the force of my Alpha command.

Some do so immediately. Still others hesitate. Their eyes filled with hostility focus on my fated mate. I issue a warning growl, and they sift. But once again, Melissa defies me.

I glance at Sage over my shoulder. She nods and releases her barrier spell. I stalk towards Melissa. Tag and Rust stride beside me while Viggo and Karl stand by my fated mate. When I reach Melissa, I grab her wolf by the scruff.

"Shift. Right. Now!" I command with a rough shake for each word.

She hisses and snaps her jaws.

"Last warning, Melissa," I say in a deep voice that brooks no disobedience.

Still held by the neck, she releases her wolf, then glowers at me.

"She's a *witch*! Look at how she hurt me with her *magick!*" Melissa whines as she rubs her nose. Blood trickles from it. But already her enhanced healing ability repairs the damage from her face-plant into Sage's invisible barrier. Melissa's face reddens more from embarrassment than from harm.

"Serves you right!"

A she-wolf who Melissa enjoys bullying shouts from her seat.

"Yeah! You finally met your match this time, Melissa!"

Another she-wolf yells from the back row.

The space fills with more voices—those for and those against. I release Melissa and raise my hand for silence. At once, everyone stills. Meanwhile, her anger and jealousy roll off her in waves.

"Those who shifted go to your lockers and dress, then return so we can begin the meeting properly. Five minutes," I pronounce. Without a glance at Melissa, I pivot on my heel and stalk towards my fated mate. Viggo and Karl give me nods as they move from Sage's side to enter the room behind the dais for clothes. Tag and Rust wait for me.

"I apologize we're not as well behaved as your witches," I say as I crouch in front of her, ashamed by my pack's outburst. She shakes her head. My hands slide up her legs, needing to feel her. "Baby, are you all right?" I ask

She smiles, and responds, "Yes, my Alpha. Thank you for protecting me."

I rumble in my chest. She bites the corner of her lip, then widens her eyes at my erection standing tall between us. I shrug with a smirk, accustomed to being naked and aroused after a shift.

"Oh, no! No one sees my mate's stuff!" Sage declares. A microsecond later, I'm fully clothed in a fresh version of my suit. "Hunh. Much better."

I chuckle and stand, brushing my lips over hers.

"Thank you, my love," I murmur against her lips. My heart skips a beat at the word love.

Sage smirks and says, "You can thank me properly later. But first, duty calls."

I turn and survey the space. Everyone who shifted

returned clothed and sit waiting for the meeting to begin, including Melissa. A hush descends as I scan the room. I take my seat.

"Now, the meeting begins. Any further disruptions will lead to that member being banned from the meeting and dealt with as I deem necessary," I say, as my eyes land on Melissa. She flares her nostrils but remains quiet. "I called this meeting to inform you of my fated mate."

Murmurs arise again. More subdued this time. But I will allow no interruptions.

"Need I remind you to remain silent until called upon?" I ask in a low, deadly voice. I wait until I hear not a sound. "Many of you know my strong desire to mate with only the female the Fates chose for me. Ten years ago, I was in the Everglades…"

By the time I complete the recap of our story, the entire room sits in stunned silence. I allow them time to digest this information. Most of them flick their gazes to study Sage. She sits like a queen on her throne. Poised and regal with an open expression to offer trust and serenity to our pack.

"Alpha, may I speak?"

I look towards the center of the meeting space. An elder wolf shifter stands, awaiting my approval to speak. I've known him since I was a little pup, and he's always been kind to me. He's of an indeterminate age, having been around since my grandfather was Alpha. Bo earns the respect of the pack for his wise council and unbiased opinions. I'm eager to hear his reaction to my news.

"Yes, Bo, come forward and say your piece," I respond.

He walks to stand before the dais. His eyes move from me to Sage. He inclines his gray head at her.

"Luna, I know your people, your grandmother, in fact. She was a wise witch who understood the importance of respect amongst paranormal beings. You remind me of her, even in the short time I've seen you. You have grace and control. Knowing how powerful your grandmother was, you could have easily destroyed our pack with a flick of your fingers. You did not. Instead, you controlled the situation, then stepped back for our Alpha to perform his duties."

Bo turns to face the rest of the pack as he continues.

"And perform his duties, Alpha Jagger Larson shall, as he has all these years. It is not as uncommon as you may think for a wolf shifter and a witch to mate, particularly with fated mates. I support our Alpha and our Luna. May the Fates bless them with many strong pups."

Bo faces Sage and me again and bows his head before he returns to his seat.

Rumblings begin, and I issue a warning growl. The room falls silent again.

More pack members come forward to speak. All remain respectful. The most vehement concern is for the Alpha's bloodline. What happens if our offspring can't shift? How can a witch lead a pack of wolf shifters? What if they don't want to stay with the pack and choose the coven? Fortunately, not one challenges me as Alpha. Then Melissa asks to speak. Not having a choice, I allow her request.

She makes a show of approaching the dais. Her lithe figure outlined in a gossamer slip of a dress. At one time, the sight of Melissa would have awakened my cock. Now, it lies flaccid against my thigh. The only pussy it wants is my fated mate's delicious core.

Melissa tosses her waist-long sable mane when she stops before me. She licks her lips seductively.

"My Alpha--"

Through the tether, I feel Sage's irritation at Melissa's innuendo. I send back reassurance and love to settle my fated mate.

"—please accept my most humble apology for my behavior," Melissa starts and pauses for my recognition. I give a grunt. A brilliant smile spreads across her face as though I proposed marriage to her. Then she continues. "The appearance of another female surprised me, given the fact you and I were intimate for years—"

My growl cuts her off. She blinks, glancing around, feigning innocence.

"I… I mean you and I mated many, many, many times—"

"Melissa, do not attempt to make more of the fucking than what it was. I made myself very clear to you it was to satisfy a need, no more than food or water does for the body. You agreed and 'mated many, many, many times' with many, many, many other males in this pack and in others. Correct?"

I raise my gaze to those gathered.

More than a few males voice their agreement. I glance back at Melissa. Her face contorts as her wolf battles to come forth. I cock a warning eyebrow at her as Tag growls. Her nostrils flare.

"Whatever, *Alpha*! However, I issue a challenge to the witch," Melissa spits out, teeth bared.

Gasps ring around the space. Even I'm shocked. I feel Viggo, Tag, Rust, and Karl glance at me.

"*My* Alpha, may I speak?"

My head swivels on my neck so quickly, the room spins. I stare at Sage as I push across the tether, begging her to let me handle Melissa. My fated mate ignores my pleas as she sits forward and meets my shocked gaze with her determined one. I nod, unable to verbalize a response. Sage hasn't even shifted yet. Unless she's allowed to use her magick, how can she beat the pugnacious she-wolf? The challenging pair makes the rules, not the Alpha.

Fuck!

Sage shifts her gaze to Melissa.

"I do not know you or the situation you had with my fated mate. However, I can understand your desire to keep him. Jagger Larson is a wolf shifter any female would be proud to call her mate—in the bed and out of it. To that I can attest to many, many, many, *many* times."

Snickers from the room make Melissa's face flame crimson as Sage turns the sable-haired hellion's words on her.

"I accept your challenge"—my fated mate holds up a finger when Melissa speaks—"on one condition. You will abide by whatever decision the pack Alpha decides afterwards. Agreed?"

Melissa's eyes narrow as she considers Sage's words.

"Agreed. However, you cannot use your witch's magick!" Melissa declares as she folds her arms under her breasts and smirks in triumph.

I sit forward. But Sage speaks.

"Agreed, as long as you do not shift. We meet female to female, barehanded."

The smirk slides from Melissa's face, then she shrugs.

"Fine, *witch*! I don't need my wolf to beat you."

Sage nods her head and rises from her seat. I jump to my feet. But she lays a hand on my forearm and smiles up at me. Love floods across our tether. My wolf snarls as he paces. I pull on every source of my control to stop myself from snatching my fated mate and racing from the clubhouse straight to our mansion. Hell! Straight to *Moonbeam,* so we can sail away.

The pack moves outdoors to the patch of grass reserved for situations such as this one. However, females rarely step onto the grass in a challenge. I scowl as I take Sage's hand and follow.

Melissa stands in the middle of the patch buck naked.

Sage ignores her display. In an instant, her navy blue

dress changes to a catsuit and her curls form a tight bun on top of her head. Barefoot, she steps on the grass.

I join them in the middle and have them agree once more to the challenge and terms. Neither one hesitates. I tell them the challenge lasts until one of them yields to the other. Females may not fight to the death. They're too valuable to the future of a pack. The Alpha decides if the loser remains or sends them to another pack. When my last plea down our tether goes ignored, I step off the patch.

With a feral growl, Melissa charges arms outstretched, and long fingernails directed at Sage. A second before contact, she steps aside. Melissa barrels forward and bumps into a she-wolf, who pushes her back onto the patch as she shouts for the bully to take her beating.

Wild-eyed, Melissa glances around for Sage. Another attempted charge fails. The grace with which Sage leaps aside or pivots draws praise from the pack. However, she remains focused on Melissa. The next time she rushes at Sage, instead of stepping aside, she spins and drops to the ground with a scissor kick. The move knocks Melissa's legs from beneath her. Sage pounces onto Melissa's back and pins her arms to her sides. She flails, but Sage holds firm.

"Enough! Yield, Melissa. Now!" my fated mate commands as she holds strong to the sable-haired hellion.

Melissa screeches as her body bucks to toss Sage from her back. Realizing the gig is up, Melissa mutters yield.

Sage leaps backwards to land in a crouch, then stands a distance from Melissa and next to me. My fated mate smiles up at me and winks. I wrap my arms around her, lift her from the ground, and bury my face against her neck.

The pack breaks out in raucous shouts, stomping feet, and wolf whistles. The voices of every single one of the she-wolves and some males Melissa subjected to her bouts of bullying rise higher than the rest. Someone begins the chant of 'Luna' and others pick it up.

Melissa stands and faces us with her head bowed awaiting my judgement.

I look at my fated mate. She puts her hand on my chest and murmurs the decision is for me to make. I turn to Melissa.

"Melissa, what do you have to say for yourself?"

Surprisingly, she doesn't puff up or yell.

"I apologize, Luna, Alpha. I promise to behave and hope you will not force me from the pack," she mumbles.

I consider her words, then respond.

"Apology accepted, Melissa. As Alpha, I never want to lose a member of my pack. However, if necessary, I will transfer the offending member to another pack if they will take them."

Melissa shudders, a small cry escapes from her mouth.

"This is not your first offense. But I will grant you the opportunity to prove you will be a peaceful member of the Miami Wolves Pack over the next few months"—her head snaps up with wide eyes—"Should you stray to your old ways, you will no longer be welcome amongst us. Do you understand?"

Her mouth opens and closes as her gaze darts between my fated mate and me. Sage maintains an impassive face. Melissa looks at me and nods.

"Yes, Alpha, I understand. Thank you, Alpha," she responds gratefully.

I nod, then lift my gaze to my pack.

"Does anyone else take issue with Sage Waters as my fated mate or me as your Alpha?" My eyes rove over the crowd.

Many speak up to support our pairing. Others don't hold my gaze. I make note of them. Then announce the meeting is over. I swoop my fated mate into my arms and stride towards the Suburbans. Viggo, Tag, Rust, Karl, and the enforcers follow us.

Once inside the SUV with Sage on my lap, I ask her how she learned her defensive moves.

"I train with a witch who's a world champion MMA fighter," she replies with a shrug. "I have to defend myself with more than my magick."

I chuckle, then hope it won't be necessary for her to defend herself at all as my thoughts return to those who oppose our pairing—witches and wolves.

CHAPTER 16

"You disobey me, mate. I do not agree with your return to The Waters Tower. And damn sure not without me!"

Sage jumps when my bellow rises to the ceiling as we stand in the living room of our Moon Island mansion. But she recovers and folds her arms beneath her lush tits as her eyes narrow on me.

We're deadlocked in our first argument. She insists she must return to normal activities to avoid giving the witches any reason to complain about her, or worse. I don't trust those fuckers and want to keep her close and safe here on Moon Island. With me!

"You see! You see! That's why I told you we couldn't work! We have responsibilities—you to your pack and me to my coven and all witches. How can I do my role when you want to confine me to your side?! Yet you can go about your duties uninterrupted."

Sage throws her hands in the air as her temper matches mine in intensity.

I stumble back at the force of her words as much as their meaning. How could she go back to her past doubts at this point? We're bonded dammit! She bears my claiming bite. The only part left is our mate bonding ceremony and wedding, if she wishes.

No! I refuse to let her backtrack on us.

I stalk towards her. She stands her ground with hands on her hips and emerald green eyes blazing. They waver as the sound of my deep-chested rumbling reaches her ears and the unconditional love I send through our tether caresses her heart. By the time I reach her, she melts into my embrace.

One arm bands around her waist, holding her close to my chest while the other hand strokes her back. My lips brush across the top of her silky curls as I murmur words of love to my fated mate. She trembles and tightens her grip on my back.

"I'm scared, Jagger. I just don't know what they'll do—"

My protective growl cuts her off. But she shakes her head and continues.

"No, I don't mean as in harm me. Rather, they demand I step down as the leader of the coven, High Witch, and head of the Witch Council. I don't know what I would do! Aside from my jewelry making, my entire life centered on training for the roles. I never imagined a different one. Well, not until you."

Sage lifts her face to stare up into my eyes.

"You changed everything, Jagger Larson. The course of a life pre-planned for me by my mother from the moment she conceived me. I love you. And if it means I lose my coven to keep you, then I will. But I have to try and make both work. So, I must go to The Tower with my head held high and your claiming bite and ring on my finger. I hope you understand, Jagger."

She ends with tears spilling down her flushed cheeks.

With a ragged cry, I crush my mouth to hers. My tongue pushes past her quivering lips to possess her. I want to drive away her fears and replace them with our love and our combined strength. Together, we can surpass any challenge. I pour every ounce of my passion into the earnest kiss.

"Fuck, baby. I love you so much it hurts! Never fear. We stand together as one. Okay?"

Cupping her beautiful face in my sizable hands, I speak the words as I kiss the tears away from her cheeks. She sobs but nods. Watery eyes stare up at mine, shining bright with uninhibited emotion.

"I have to go, Jagger," Sage whispers.

"I know you do, baby. But first"—I scoop her into my arms and head for the stairs—"I'm going to show you just how much I love you, my fated mate."

The corners of her lips curl up slowly. I bend my head and kiss her again, then bound up the stairs three at a time. And my scent will cover her to warn every single one of those male fuckers to back the hell up.

"What have you heard from Signy?"

At my question, Viggo averts his ice blue eyes—so like mine and our father's. Then reaches up and pulls his red, shoulder-length hair into a ponytail. Pack tattoos on the buzzed sides of his head stand out in contrast to the pale skin. He uses the move to bide himself some time.

Great. So, it can't be good. Hopefully, Signy meets us for a run in the Everglades, as I requested. While Sage goes to The Tower—with Njal, the head of her security detail, and three others after I instituted my Alpha command—I want to connect with my siblings. Get them away from the rest of our pack, particularly from our parents.

Viggo re-affirmed his allegiance to me.

Signy? No word.

As I turn from my Sikorsky S-92 Executive Helicopter to get back in the golf cart and ride to my mansion, I see Signy driving towards us. Her waist-length ebony hair pulled into a ponytail flies behind her like a banner as the wind whips past the open top of her white-on-red Porsche 911 Carrera Turbo Cabriolet. She parks next to my golf cart and hops from her supercar. Shield sunglasses block her ice blue eyes, so I can't gauge her mood.

Instead, I watch her body language as she struts towards Viggo and me. At five feet, nine inches, her long, toned legs eat up the distance between us. She moves with predatory grace and power, unwavering. When she stands before me, she bows her head in a show of respect.

"Alpha, I apologize for being late. A mechanic had to change the tire—"

"Yeah, because you drive too damn fast!" Viggo cuts in with a frown on his handsome face.

Signy takes her sunglasses off and gives him a scathing look. Then she turns back to me.

"Anyway… Here I am. As commanded," she says.

I bite back a retort. She came. So, that's a good sign.

"Let's go," I say instead and gesture towards the helicopter.

The pilot steps aboard while the flight attendant stays beside the aircraft. She climbs in after us and closes the door.

"Would you care for a beverage or a snack, Alpha?" The she-wolf asks. When I decline, she asks my siblings. Viggo winks at her and nods. Signy rolls her eyes at our brother's flirtatious behavior and declines. The flight attendant disappears through the door leading to the galley and cockpit.

I settle back in the plush leather chair and pull out my mobile to check for a text message from my fated mate. Finding none, I send one to check in. I grin as she responds she's fine since Njal—the Giant—shadows her everywhere she goes.

A cough interrupts my response.

I glance up to find Signy staring at me with pursed lips. I cock an eyebrow in question.

She huffs and folds her arms across her chest.

"Did you summon us here so you can chitchat on your mobile or for some other reason?" She asks.

Again, I let her snide remark go for the sake of peace. Besides, I don't want my flight crew to overhear a personal conversation with my siblings. I shake my head at Signy and mouth, not now.

She sits back with a scowl and takes her mobile from her white leather Chanel backpack. Viggo and I exchange glances. He shrugs and pulls out his mobile. Fingers fly across the screen as he grins at whatever he reads. For the rest of the twenty-minute ride, our little sister ignores us.

Unlike Viggo, Signy doesn't work at Larson Enterprises. She lives the pampered life of the daughter of a former Alpha and sister to the current one. It's our fault since she's the only girl and the baby of our family at twenty-four, four years younger than me. The rest of us coddle her.

When our father wanted to strengthen an alliance with a pack out west, he told her she would mate their Alpha. For obvious reasons, she lacked attraction to the much older male whose mate had died and left him without an heir. Readily, Viggo and I stood up for her. We insisted she have more time to find her fated mate, just as our father did with our mother. He agreed, if reluctantly.

Now, I expect Signy to offer the same support for me. I glance over at her as she rises to disembark from the helicopter. She still wears the scowl from earlier. I sigh.

Ordinarily, she's fun-loving with a good sense of humor. Smart and independent. A joy to be around. However, she still lives with our parents in their waterfront mansion on Moon Island. Named for our mother Sigrid—a Viking name for victory. Signy means new victory.

Well, I hope to triumph over her apparent disapproval of my mating with Sage.

Viggo follows Signy with a parting wink to the flight attendant. She blushes and busies herself with reordering the cabin. He chuckles. I chuff him in the back of the head and growl. He smirks. Fucker.

Signy stands with her hands on her hips.

"Are we doing this or what?" She calls out over the sound of the rotors as they power off.

"Good luck, bro," Viggo murmurs under his breath.

Yeah, tell me about it…

I glance around the area cleared for a helipad near our pack's camp in the Everglades. It's the place we come for pack runs and trainings. For generations, the virtually untouched area of the subtropical wilderness allows us the freedom to be in our wolf form without prying eyes. Over the years, the original pack grounds grew from temporary cloth shelters to simple wooden cabins and now to luxurious residences scattered around the Alpha's house and clubhouse. Glamping—or glamorous camping, as Signy—calls it.

A few families and enforcers choose to remain here, not wanting the hustle and bustle of Miami for their principal home. On days like this one when the humidity is low, the sun sits in a cloudless sky, and fresh air abounds, I don't blame them. My thoughts move to bringing my fated mate here for a few days to ourselves once everything settles, especially since we first met near to here.

"Greetings, Alpha!"

I turn to find the wolf shifter I put in charge of our property striding towards me. I shake his extended hand and clap him on the back.

"Good to see you, Ulf!" I respond.

"After your run, we'll have a good meal ready for you. My mate's excited to cook for our Alpha and his siblings. She's prepared some of her specialties just for you," he says with a broad smile.

"Thanks to you both. We appreciate a delicious home-cooked meal any day!"

I turn to my siblings and tell them to go to their cabins and leave their things before we shift, then meet outside of my cabin. They nod.

Once inside of my residence, I send a text message to my fated mate. She responds all is well. Relieved, I strip out of my t-shirt and jeans before I shift. My giant silvery white wolf pads to the door and slaps the button. The hand-carved wooden door depicting a wolf opens. I bound out to meet my siblings. My wolf yips in excitement to be free.

I run up to Signy's wolf—a black beauty with a white patch on her back—and pug her flank where it's ticklish with my muzzle. Her stiff posture relaxes as I continue to poke her beast. After a while, she gives in and yips before hopping into the air, tongue lolling and eyes bright.

A wave of relief rolls over me at the sight of my little sister being her normal self with me. Then I stumble side-ways. A glance over my shoulder reveals a red wolf with its lips pulled back in a toothy grin. Viggo!

I rush him and we tumble to the ground, rolling around like we did as pups—and still do occasionally. Signy's wolf bounces around us, getting in a nip to our flanks or rumps, dodging our swatting paws with ease. Then she yips and bounds towards the tree line.

Viggo and I give chase.

Hours after traipsing through the wetlands, hunting, and lying in the sun, we return to the cabins. We separate to shower and meet back at my cabin. Changed back into my t-shirt and jeans, I call Sage. She answers on the first ring.

"Hi! How's it going?"

I grin as her love flows through our tether, even at the distance of nearly thirty miles. My wolf thumps his tail in happiness.

"Good. I haven't spoken to Signy yet. But she loosened up once we shifted. Her wolf was easygoing. Hopefully she will be too."

We talk a bit longer until I hear my front door open and the voices of my siblings as they talk smack to each other. I ring off from my fated mate with promises to devour her tonight. I end the call to the sounds of her giggles, then bound down the stairs.

"Whatever, Viggo! You don't understand," Signy says as she punches him in the chest.

He doesn't flinch and shakes his head at her.

I glance between the two.

They clam up until I cock an eyebrow—Alpha command wafting off me.

They eye each other. Viggo arcs his hand through the air, signaling Signy to proceed. She growls at him and snaps her head in my direction.

"How could you, Jagger?! I mean, a witch? Really?! What a total mess! She's—" She yells as her ice blue eyes flash.

I cross my arms over my chest. I gave her leeway before. But no one will disrespect my fated mate. No. One.

"Signy, I suggest you consider your choice of words very

carefully when you speak of my fated mate," I tell her, drawing on every ounce of my steely Alpha command.

My younger sister's eyes widen as her mouth flops open like a fish pulled from the water. She scans my face. Seeing no room for argument, she lowers her head and mutters to herself.

Naturally, my wolf senses pick up her words of 'arrogant,' 'selfish,' and 'not fair'. I wait for her to get herself together. She strides to the living room and throws herself onto a leather sofa. Eyes stare up at me.

"Jagger, Mom and Dad told me all about your *fated mate* and how you lost it over her years ago. They had to consider our pack over your… your… sexual desires," she says with a lip curled in disgust. "And now, you flaunt her in front of our pack and let her hurt Melissa?! How could you, Jagger?!"

Viggo steps forward, ready to defend me. I raise my hand to stop him. He slumps into a chair, disappointed eyes fixed on our younger sister.

I stride over to the sofa and sit beside her. Obviously, our parents filled her head with bullshit. Had she come to the meeting she would have heard my side of the situation, not one meant to cast my mating with Sage in a horrible light.

"Signy, do you truly believe me capable of whatever you were told I did?" I ask quietly as my eyes stare into hers.

She squirms under the intensity of my gaze and glances away. After a moment, she shifts her gaze back to mine. She studies my face.

I keep an open expression to allow her to see no deceit, only her brother, the one who cared for her all her life. Who wants nothing but the best for her.

"Well, that's what they told me," she responds at last.

I shake my head.

"Do you trust me, Signy?"

She hesitates, then nods.

"Well, then, let me tell you what really happened…"

Like the pack members in the meeting, Signy voices outrage at the lies our parents told her. She apologizes for not speaking to me before—believing their lies—and vows to support Sage and me. My little sister throws her arms around my shoulders when I forgive her.

I hold her close and thank her for standing by my side.

Viggo comes over and grabs us for a group hug. Signy's eyes shine through her tears as she expresses how grateful she is to have us as her big brothers.

A knock on the front door separates us. Ulf enters to let us know lunch is ready. We thank him, and he leaves.

I turn to my siblings and grab them close again. Our foreheads touch as I thank them for their love and support.

We stand as one. I can only hope Sage's siblings will continue to do the same for her.

age

"HONEY! It's been a shitstorm up here. I came back as Tabitha returned from Miami. A category five hurricane, I tell you! She was beyond pissed! Even Rupert cowered at her rage"—Anala blows a breath before she continues—"The coven met to decide what to do. Of course, they gave me and others connected to you the side-eye. I know they had a second meeting to really discuss things. For now, they only said Rupert decided to take a sojourn through Europe for an indeterminate amount of time. To lick his wounds, no doubt..."

I listen as Anala fills me in on the reaction of the Northeast Coven to the news of me calling off the pairing with Rupert and mating with Jagger instead. It's worse than I thought. If it angered the second most powerful coven, the Witch Council will definitely get involved. I hope they'll listen to me and consider the part of Jagger and I being *fated* mates, and not some randy teens wanting to sate their desires despite the impact on others.

That's exactly why I'm so glad I followed my intuition and came back to The Waters Tower. I didn't use my teleportation magick. With my head held high and back straight, I entered through the lobby. From the valet to the doorman and the coven members milling about, they watched my every move. I acknowledged them with my regular greetings, not allowing them to see they fazed me at all.

Only within my penthouse duplex did I let the walls crumble. My body shook as I thought back on the hostile faces and recalled their snide remarks about me being a mangy wolf lover and forsaking my lineage and coven. It hurt me to my core. My own coven could turn on me so easily after knowing me all my life. And especially as their leader.

I didn't let on my dismay to Jagger whenever he sent a text message or called. It's best he focuses on his pack and reconnecting with his sister Signy, whom I haven't met yet since she's not thrilled about the pairing any more than my coven.

And I haven't heard from nor seen my parents and Willow. Who knows what they're up to? Their silence unnerves me. But my disappointment with Willow pains me even more.

I thought my own sister would stand beside me, show strength and support in the face of the covens and the Witch Council. But no. She's ghosted me. I never would have thought she'd ditch me.

My eyes close to block the pain. I take a deep cleansing breath to clear my head and tune back in to my bestie. At least Anala stays in my corner. She's my eyes and ears for the happenings up north, even if they hold secret meetings without her present. She's well respected in her coven. Hell, even feared by many. Anyone who can successfully kill vampires proves a force to be reckoned with.

"—shifters from the New York Wolves Pack slinking around me. When I caught them in a trap, they confessed Jagger asked their Alpha to watch my back. Give your mate my thanks. Even though I don't need their help, I appreciate his concern."

My heart swells with love for my mate, knowing he reached out to another powerful Alpha to look after my cousin. Jagger is so good to me. Suddenly, I get a burst of love through our tether from him. I was careful to suppress my sadness and let my happiness come through our bond. Thankfully, he only picked up on the positive and not the negative. I send my love to him and sit back with a smile on my face.

"Thanks so much, Anala. You don't know what it means to me you're sticking by Jagger and me. I don't want to cause any trouble between you and your coven. So, only do what you deem necessary. Don't push it on my account," I tell her.

She huffs. I can picture her eyes rolling as her full lips purse.

"Sage, never mind all that nonsense. What's right is right and what's wrong is wrong. Period. A fated mate bond is nothing to ignore or try to deny. I hope one day to meet my fated mate. And I tell you now, I won't let him go for anything. Nothing at all!"

"I'll remind you should you ever forget, Anala Azar," I say with a grin.

Voices outside my office at Sage's Gems & Jewels catch my attention. I tell Anala to hold on as I go see what's happening. Lillie stands toe to toe with Njal. The giant of a wolf shifter—his Viking name literally means giant and suits him perfectly—stares down at my younger sister impassively. She glares at him, then sees me at the open door.

"Sage! Tell this behemoth to let me into your office right this minute!" Lillie exclaims as she stomps her Manolo Blahnik covered foot and points her finger up at Njal.

I stifle a giggle at her tiny frame compared to his, well, giant one. Then beckon for her to come in. I wink at Njal over her head. His face contorts into what may be his version of a smile but resembles a grimace. I close the door and shake my head as I raise my mobile to my ear.

"Hey, Anala, Lillie just came in. I'll call you later. Thanks again," I say.

"Anytime, honey. Tell Lil I said hi!" Anala responds before she ends the call.

I relay the message as I follow Lillie to the sofa. She nods. A worried expression mars her pretty face.

"Talk to me, Lillie, and don't hold back. I want to hear all you have to say," I tell her as I clasp her hand and squeeze. I sit back and wait.

Between her slender fingers, she twists the hem of her Roland Mouret dress. Distress clearly outlined on her face as she opens, then closes her mouth. She shakes her head, and her mane of ebony hair falls across her profile like a silky curtain. She sighs, then shifts on the sofa to face me.

"Sage, I love you so much and hate what Mother did to you and Jagger. She was wrong to go about it the way she did."

My heart sinks. Lillie—my little sister—would have preferred a different method to block me from my fated mate? Oh dear, this is not good at all. I bite my tongue to prevent myself from speaking.

She continues, unaware of the pain she just inflicted on my heart.

"I mean, Mother should have given you a chance to defend yourselves, at least listen to you before going to such extremes. Erasing your memories? For ten years? Wow! Just wow."

Lillie reaches for my hand, and I let her take it. She doesn't notice how limp it dangles in hers. She squeezes.

"Jagger seems like a really great... uh... wolf shifter. I'm sure he cares for you. But do you think it's worth it? To have our coven, the Northeast Coven, and undoubtedly his pack in an uproar for just the two of you? It's kind of selfish. You know what I mean, Sage?"

I yank my hand from hers and sit up.

"No, Lillie, I do not know what you mean! What I know is you've changed your mind and want to clear your guilt by making me think I'm the one who's wrong. I. Am. Not. What I am is surprised at you and at Willow. How many times did I have your backs when Mother tried to run your lives? How many times did I bite the bullet and take the brunt of her demands to keep my *little sisters* free from her? Need I remind you? And Willow? Wherever the hell she may be! Anala—our *cousin*—has my back and my *sisters* do not."

To hell with this bullshit!

I snatch my mobile from the coffee table as I jump to my feet, then storm to my desk. Ignoring Lillie's sobs, I put my laptop in my handbag and head for the double doors. I open and close them without a backwards glance at my sister seated on the sofa still.

Njal takes one look at my face and having heard our conversation with his enhanced wolf hearing nods and gestures for the other enforcers. He leads the way to the elevator. As we walk through my boutique, I send a text message to the manager letting her know I've gone home and will be unavailable until tomorrow.

I keep my head high and back straight as I walk surrounded by my wolf shifter security detail past humans, witches, and any other paranormal beings who bustle about The Waters Tower Mall. But the moment the door closes on the Suburban, I shrink into the soft leather with my face in my hands and cry.

~

JAGGER

PAIN PIERCES my heart so deeply I choke and press my palm to my chest.

Sage!

I jump from my chair at the table where my siblings, other pack members, and I sit after eating lunch. My hands fumble in my jeans pocket for my mobile. I press her number conveniently saved in favorites since my hands shake with the powerful urge to shift and free my wolf, who howls.

A few rings come across the line before she answers just as I was about to call Njal. I sigh in relief, then snarl when I hear her tear-choked voice warble.

"J—J—Jagger..." she cries pitifully before a sob breaks over the line.

I turn to the table. Viggo has his mobile to his ear as he stands beside Signy. Her worried eyes scan my face. Viggo motions for me to follow.

"The flight crew heads to the helicopter now," he says, eyes flashing silver, then he turns to Ulf. "Thanks for lunch."

Signy rubs my arm as her long legs trot to keep pace with my long strides.

"Whatever it is, Jagger, we have your back. Don't worry, big brother," she says vehemently.

I nod as I turn my attention back to my fated mate.

"Where are you? Are you hurt? What happened?" I bark.

She takes a breath and tells me she's in the SUV with Njal and is safe. As she recounts her conversation with Lillie, my blood boils and my wolf claws at my skin to break free. I tamp him down as we board the helicopter. No one needs my wild wolf pacing within the confines of the helicopter, no matter how spacious it is.

No sooner does the flight attendant close the door than the pilot lifts off. We zip back to Miami in less than twenty minutes. All the while, I soothe my fated mate. The helicopter hovers over our side lawn just as her Suburban pulls into our driveway. With a nod to my siblings, I jump out and roll as I hit the grass, then leap to my feet, running for the side door.

"Sage!" I bellow as the door slams into the plaster. Pieces fall to the tile as I rush to find her. I sigh in relief when she hurtles towards me and flings herself into my outstretched arms. "Oh, baby, baby. It's okay. I'm here now."

I croon to her as she trembles. Her sisters really did her wrong. And I thought Signy was a lost cause.

Over Sage's head, I notice Njal. He watches with a steely glint in his gray eyes. His wolf also flexes beneath the surface of his skin.

It pleases me he cares so much for my fated mate and his Luna. I nod and send him my thanks through the bond I have as Alpha with my pack. His massive chest rises on an inhalation as he wrestles control of his wolf. He returns my nod and spins on his heel to leave the mansion.

"Come on, baby, let me take you upstairs. I'll draw us a nice bath so we can soak. Okay, baby?" I murmur against the top of Sage's head. She nods, and I scoop her up. I call out for the smart home system to run the bath water with essential oils.

By the time I carry her into my bathroom, the tub is full of warm water ready for us. I set Sage on the navy blue terrycloth bench in the center of the bathroom. I cup her face and kiss her lips softly before I put cool water on a washcloth and dab her tear-stained face. She closes her eyes and leans into my gentle touch.

We undress each other as I rumble deep in my chest to soothe my fated mate. Her eyes aren't so much sad anymore as they are resigned. I hate she feels that way, but I don't pressure her to talk now. It's time for our bodies to speak the only words necessary. Those declarations of the special love only a fated pair can know.

And to hell with anyone who doesn't understand.

Once we're naked, I carry her to the bath and step in. Keeping her close to my chest, I lean my back against the side of the copper bathtub, then arrange her in front of me with her back to my front. My long, muscular legs stretch out along the sides of her slim ones. I keep my arms wrapped around her, just beneath her full breasts. My lips trail open-mouthed kisses along the side of her neck.

Sage leans into me and rests her arms on top of mine. She tilts her head to give me better access to the column of her throat. She moans as I press my lips to my claiming bite. The wound healed nicely, allowing the mark to show clearly.

As I cup her breasts now heavy in my hands, she mewls and drags her fingernails over my scalp. I shudder from the erotic pain. My already turgid cock thumps against her spine. I pinch and tug at her nipples, gauging her desire.

She moves swiftly to straddle my thighs. Water sloshes to the marble floor. She reaches between us and fists my cock. Her thumb rubs over the mushroom head as she rises to her knees to align the tip with her pussy.

We groan in unison as it breaches her folds and she sinks back onto my thighs. Her hips circle to help with the tight fit as her inner walls clamp and drag my cock deep inside. I grab her hips and pull her down as I thrust up. She throws her head back and cries out my name. My mouth closes around a pebbled brown nipple presented to me as her breasts rise. Her hips undulate as I suckle.

Her fingernails dig into my shoulders as she finds her rhythm. Up and down, she bounces on my cock as she rides out her frustration. I hold her hips to keep her balanced and meet each of her violent slams with a brutal thrust of my own. My hooded eyes eat up the sight of my gorgeous fated mate. I'm more than happy to endure her vexation.

With a guttural moan, she climaxes and falls forward, face buried in my neck. Warm pants lick across my sweaty skin. Her tight, little pussy spasms along my cock, choking my release from my heavy balls.

I yank her down and grind up until I bottom out. A feral roar rips from my throat as I unleash a torrent of my seed in her womb. White light dazzles behind my eyelids, squeezed shut as the orgasm rages on. The aftereffects ripple through me, refusing to end. I take them with low groans slipping from my slack mouth.

After we return to Earth, I bathe my fated mate, then myself. I dry us off before wrapping us in heated terrycloth robes and carrying her to our bed. I pull the cashmere blanket from the foot to cover us. She cuddles against me with her cheek and palm on my chest. I rub her back and rumble to her.

"The coven and the Witch Council want me to step down and Willow to take over and pair with Rupert."

Well, I'll be damned.

CHAPTER 18

age

"It's all right, Jagger. I just need to walk and clear my head. And if you feel anything over our bond, don't worry and let me be. Lots of emotions will well up, I'm sure. But I'll be fine and won't leave Moon Island. Promise."

My super-protective fated mate narrows his ice blue eyes as he scans my face. He wants to keep me in our bayfront mansion until the meeting later today. I tell him not to worry. The witches can't harm me or get to me here.

I placed protective wards around Moon Island, the Everglades camp, and Larson Enterprises. Now that I'm a part of the pack—their Luna—it's my responsibility to keep them safe with my magick. Despite Jagger's knowledge of my precautions, concern mars his handsome face.

I lift my hand and cup his cheek as I send calm through our tether.

He closes his eyes and leans into my palm with a sigh.

Emotions play across his face as he considers my words. Eyebrows dip, nostrils flare, lips move in silent internal debate. Finally, resignation. His eyes open to pin me with an intense stare.

"Fine. But Njal will follow you"—he raises his hand at my protest—"he'll keep his distance. Or you can stay here. Any one of the many rooms can provide the space you need."

Quickly, I shake my head and agree to Njal's shadow. Then press a kiss to Jagger's full lips. His tongue darts out to deepen the connection, but I pull back with a wry smile. My fated mate won't lock lips to prevent me from leaving. No, ma'am!

He growls low in his chest as I dart away. I wiggle my fingers over my shoulder as I hurry towards the side door. No more than a few steps outside and I sense Njal behind me. I glance back. Yup, the Giant follows. I offer him a smile, and he inclines his head.

As I follow the stone-paved path beneath palm trees, I close my eyes and let the floral fragrances of the gardenia and jasmine bushes fill my nose. The scents mingle with the saltwater air wafting in from the Atlantic Ocean. The splash from the wake of jet skis as they fly by and the horn of a cruise ship drift in from Biscayne Bay a few yards away.

Being on Moon Island feels like a whole other world separate from the bustle of Miami around it. A serene oasis filled with lush foliage provides the perfect respite. And that's what I need to prepare myself for the meeting.

I still can't believe the phone call I received from my mother as I rode from The Waters Tower to Moon Island. She told me as the prior High Witch it was her duty to inform me of the coven and Witch Council's recommendation and of my opportunity to speak before them. Recommendation? Bullshit!

The brief interlude broken, my eyes snap open as I fist my hands and storm forward.

How dare they *recommend* ousting me and replacing me with my own sister? How could she accept? Whose bright idea was it to begin with? Prudence? Tabitha? Rupert? Hell, Willow???

I tromp along the path, barely aware of my surroundings. Wild thoughts run through my mind on a loop.

Should I refuse and fight back? What if I ignore their *recommendation* and carry on as usual? Should I seek supporters within the witches and stage a revolt? Would the wolf shifters back me?

I throw my head back and scream until I have to stop for a breath.

Aargh!

Birds startle and take flight from the palm trees. Lizards dive from the path into the underbrush. A few members in wolf form howl.

My skin feels tight. Fingers twitch. I glance around and find I'm a few yards from the bay. The sparking azure blue water calls to me. With a wave of my hand, the tank top and yoga pants morph into a teal blue bikini as I race forward.

The minute my feet touch the water, a sense of relaxation washes through me. I scramble over the slippery rocks to reach where it's deeper. Raising my arms overhead, hands together, I dive in. The sound of Njal's gruff voice calling my name fades as the water covers my ears.

My element cleanses me with each vigorous stroke as I swim parallel to Moon Island. The source of my magick binds with me. It covers my skin and fills every cell. My heartbeat thrums boldly in my chest. I swim faster as I circle the island. Time and distance become meaningless as I lose myself in the revitalizing water.

When I rise from Biscayne Bay, my mind is free from

turmoil and my body vibrates with renewed power. Peace fills me. I am ready.

Njal stands at the edge of the grass. He watches me as I stride towards him. Not one to talk, he nods when he's satisfied I'm okay. I return his nod and continue to the path.

I let the water seep into my skin as I head back to the mansion. When I step onto the stone pavers, an older wolf shifter greets me with a respectful nod. When he lifts his face, I recognize him as Bo from the pack meeting. I smile and extend my hand.

"Hello, Bo. I'm glad to see you. I want to thank you for your kind words at the pack meeting. Do you have a moment to speak with me? I'd like to ask you about how you knew my grandmother."

"Yes, Luna. In fact, I came to speak to you. I understand you have a meeting with the coven and the Witch Council?" He takes my hand and pauses for confirmation.

I'm shocked he knows. Only witches were told about it. I doubt any of them would have leaked negative information about the coven, especially to a wolf shifter. I don't ask who told him and confirm the meeting.

He nods and gestures for us to walk.

"If you do not mind, Luna, I would like to attend the meeting as your guest. And obviously as your and the Alpha's supporter," Bo says.

Again, he catches me by surprise. But Jagger and I could use all the support we can get and show a united front to the witches.

"Absolutely, Bo. Jagger and I would appreciate you standing with us. You're a respected elder of the Miami Wolves Pack. Your opinion holds value. The meeting is at one. We can pick you up on our way to The Waters Tower."

Bo shakes his head.

"Unnecessary, Luna. I will meet you at your residence.

Until then," he says, then bows his head and walks the other way.

I watch him go. He nods at Njal, then continues down the path.

Well, that was a welcome surprise, I muse to myself. We can add Bo to our list, along with Anala, who told me she'll be there ready to rumble. The corners of my mouth begin to lift, then spread into a broad smile.

The better it gets, the better it gets.

My step is light as I continue on to the mansion. A few feet from the side door and it opens wide. Jagger stalks out, a scowl on his face.

"Sage! Where are your clothes?! You walked around the island in a skimpy ass bikini?!"

I throw my head back and laugh.

Correction, my super-*possessive* fated mate…

"You okay, baby?"

Jagger squeezes my hand resting on his thick thigh as we ride in his Black Badge Rolls-Royce Cullinan bound for The Waters Tower. His ice blue eyes filled with concern study my face.

I cup his cheek and smile.

"Yes, my love. I will fight for my positions and not allow them to take what is rightfully mine. I've worked too hard and been too good of a leader for them to think they can toss me aside over their narrow-minded beliefs."

My fated mate grins and presses his forehead to mine.

"And I'm right by your side, mate of mine," he murmurs.

"We're here, Alpha."

Karl's voice draws Jagger and me from our bubble. He

nods and presses his lips to mine. Then sits back and straightens the knot of his silk tie.

The doors open, and we step out of the SUV. I close my eyes and take a deep breath. Instantly, the sounds of waves breaking on the shore fill my head. My element seeks to calm me and maintain my strength.

Jagger takes my hand and cocks an eyebrow. I nod reassuringly, and his shoulders relax, if only slightly. He turns and—with an air of determination—leads me to the front doors of The Tower.

Not only Bo joined us for support. Viggo and Signy—who I met briefly as we climbed into the SUV—came to support their brother. Tag and Rust stand with their best friend. While Karl, Njal and some other enforcers provide security.

The doorman's mouth gapes like a fish floundering for air. We stride by him as he holds the door open. I feel his eyes drilling into the back of my skull as I go through the lobby, headed for the elevators. I draw up to my full height, not allowing the weight of his glare to drag me down.

At the elevators, our group splits to enter two cars. We reach the floor for the coven's grand hall simultaneously. Witches who linger in the lobby turn to stare. They point and whisper, eyes wide at the arrival of several wolf shifters.

Two of the members who function as security step in front of me. Eyes full of menace.

Jagger steps between us as Viggo, Tag, Rust, and Karl flank him. Njal and the enforcers stand beside Signy and me.

"Move away from my mate," Jagger growls. His wolf roams beneath the surface.

"You have no right to be here," Morris, one witch, says. "Leave now."

"Morris, unless you wish me to cast you from your rank, back away. Now," I say as I step between Jagger and Tag.

Morris sneers and responds, "You have no autho—"

I silence him with a flick of my wrist. His hands fly to his closed mouth. Eyes wide, he pokes the sealed seam of his lips in an attempt to part them. I narrow my eyes at him and scan the faces of those gathered.

"I have every bit of *authority* as I am the leader of this coven and the High Witch. Do not disrespect me, my fated mate, or my pack," I say fervently.

Silence ensues.

I take Jagger's hand and step forward. He tightens his grip and walks beside me. The rest of our pack follows. Inside the grand hall, more stares and murmurs greet us. I ignore them as I continue to the dais.

A row of chairs stands before it, separate from those for the coven. Members of the Witch Council turn in the chairs to watch our approach. My mother, father, Lillie, Tabitha, and members of the Northeast Coven sit amongst them. Willow sits in her seat beside my chair on the dais.

For a moment, my heart constricts. Jagger squeezes my hand and sends love through our bond. I square my shoulders. The sounds of waves increase. You've got this, Sage! I cheer myself.

"Sage! Jagger!"

I pause and turn towards my bestie's voice.

Anala blazes a trail through the crowd behind us. Her chocolate brown eyes shine with her internal fire. My pack makes room for her to reach me. She pulls me into a hug, then smiles up at Jagger.

"I saved seats for everyone right behind them," she says with a glare at the others. Some of the council members have the grace to lower their eyes. "You take your *rightful seat*, Sage. I put a chair behind yours for Jagger, your *fated mate*. The rest of you come with me."

My heart swells with love for Anala. She winks at me and leads my pack to their seats.

"Come on, baby," Jagger murmurs low so only I can hear.

I nod and press on.

Those seated in the additional row know better than to question me and say nothing as Jagger and I pass them. We settle in our seats. I nod at Willow. She hesitates, then returns my polite gesture. I look out at those seated in the grand hall.

Quickly, the last of them take their seats. I turn to the secretary, and she nods.

"Good afternoon. It is 1:00, and I call the meeting of the Coven of the South to order."

After the secretary calls each member's name and marks those present, I'm not surprised to find all members in attendance. Each visitor stands and gives their name. My pack follows once the witches speak. The secretary adds them to the list on her laptop. When she finishes, she announces the number present.

Here we go…

"As you may know, Prudence Waters, the prior High Witch informed me of the coven and of the Witch Council's recommendation. They wish for me to step down as leader of the Coven of the South, High Witch, and head of the Witch Council. They wish for Willow Waters of the Coven of the South to replace me and to pair with Rupert Raven-heart of the Northeast Coven."

Who's notably absent, I muse to myself.

Silence encompasses the vast space.

"First, I ask the speaker for them to stand and explain their reasoning. Then I will respond," I say, and shift my gaze to those seated in the additional row.

Their heads turn to my mother, of course.

Prudence rises from her chair. Her emerald green eyes focused on mine. It's incredible how much we resemble each other. Thankfully, I did not inherit her stony heart. She nods at me, then pivots to face those gathered.

"Thank you to all who came out for this unexpected situation," she says and pauses as she turns her gaze to individuals. "Sage Waters has turned her back on her coven, her fiancé, and all witches for the most selfish reason. Her lust-filled desire drove her to mate with a *wolf shifter*."

Amidst the cries of the coven, Jagger's anger bears down on our bond as he struggles to maintain control of himself and of his wolf. Ferocity pours from his body. I glance at our pack as they stir, feeling his ire through their connection. Jagger takes a ragged breath as he wins the battle.

I sigh in relief. We need to remain cool and calm. I send my plea through our tether. He nods.

"We do not agree with Sage's decision, as it is not conducive for the wellbeing of the Coven of the South or for the role of the High Witch and head of the Witch Council. In addition, her selfish decision negatively impacts the relationship between the Coven of the South and the Northeast Coven. We stand by our recommendation and put it forth to the Coven of the South to vote, then to the Witch Council."

She turns to me with a gleam in her eyes and continues.

"We have witnesses who wish to be heard."

I meet her gaze with a cool one of my own.

"They may speak now."

She nods her head at a witch who stands beside the side door. She opens it, and Jagger growls low.

I watch, shocked, as his parents step into the grand hall. Signy gasps in the silence. But I keep my eyes on Marcus and Sigrid.

They shift glares between Jagger and me. Then a snarl rips from Marcus' curled lip when he sees Viggo and Signy standing.

"You dare to defy your father?" He bellows at his daughter.

Signy lifts her chin and responds, "I stand by my brother and my Alpha, Jagger, and his *fated* mate, Sage."

"As do I," Viggo growls.

The rest of the pack jump to their feet and voice their support.

Reluctantly, I raise my hand and call for order. They settle down immediately. I turn to Marcus and Sigrid.

"You may speak."

He steps closer. But Jagger rises and growls, "That's as far as you will go." They lock eyes. Jagger's power as current Alpha thwarts his father. He curls his lip. But stays where he stands. He turns to the crowd.

"I am Marcus Larson, the immediate past Alpha of the Miami Wolves Pack. We do not condone the mating of—"

"You do not speak for the pack. We held the meeting you did not attend, and they recognize Sage as their Luna. Do not challenge me, or you will fail," Jagger declares, standing tall beside me.

The males glower at one another. Once again, Marcus bows before Jagger's strength. He steps back.

Prudence jumps to her feet.

"How dare you run our coven's meeting, *wolf shifter?*" She shouts, emerald eyes flashing. She spins on her heels and faces the grand hall. "This is exactly what we fear. The *wolf shifter* will control Sage and thus the coven, council, and all witches! We must end this threat now!"

The space erupts with shouts.

I stand and silence them all.

"No one shall speak unless recognized as per the rules of

decorum of this coven," I say. When they nod in compliance, I release the spell and turn to my mother.

"Are you finished with your explanation for your recommendation, Prudence?"

"Yes, I am!"

I ignore her snippy tone.

"We have heard you. Now, you may sit," I tell her and wait to take my seat until she sits on hers. With a huff, she lowers herself. I return to my chair.

"My response is such witches abide by the rules set forth by our ancestors, rules adapted as time requires. Such as changing the rule only witches of the same gender may mate to allow any gender to be as one. Regarding witches mating with wolf shifters or any non-witch being, nowhere in the histories of this coven or in any of the ancient witch texts does such rule exist."

I turn my gaze to those in the additional row.

"Your recommendation is not valid, as I have broken no rule by mating with Jagger Larson."

They huddle and murmur amongst themselves.

"Excuse me, Luna and High Witch, may I speak as a witness?"

I glance over at Bo. This elder continues to surprise me.

"Yes, Bo, respected elder of the Miami Wolves Pack, we may hear you," I respond.

He steps before the dais and faces the grand hall.

"Yes, I am a respected elder of the Miami Wolves Pack. And I am also a descendant of a female witch of the Coven of the South and a former beta of the pack—"

Witches and wolf shifters speak at once.

I'm so shocked, I forget to correct the outburst. Jagger nudges me, and I snap to.

"Silence! Now!"

The noise dies down, and I gesture for Bo to continue.

"Thank you, Luna and High Witch. I know this may surprise most of you. However, a few of you know more than you care to admit, obviously. Besides myself, there are more like me everywhere than you realize. Is that not so, Eliphas, Holly, Blaise?"

Bo pauses to point out several witches, even one on the Witch Council. Their mouths open but they think better of it and remain silent. He shakes his head, disappointed at their reluctance to admit their lineage.

"The stigma associated with the love between a wolf shifter and a witch forces those pairs and their offspring to hide, even in plain sight. Those spurned also carry a grudge and try to prevent others the love they themselves could not have. Isn't that correct, Cyrus?"

The most vocal witch now sits hunched in his chair, silent, while his eyes shoot daggers at Bo.

"Luna and High Witch, I knew your grandmother, a powerful woman who thought for herself"—he throws a glance at my mother and shakes his head sadly—"she would never have condoned the actions of those opposed to your mating with our Alpha. In fact, she told me of the foretold prophecy of a wolf shifter and a witch fated mates whose pairing will change the course of both pack and coven and whose offspring will rule both."

Now, even I gasp aloud along with others. Jagger takes my hand. We look at each other, unable to speak.

Bo clears his throat, and the space falls silent. Everyone leans forward to listen. Again, he turns to my mother.

"I am surprised you did not know since they passed the knowledge down in secret from one High Witch to the next," he says and waits for her response.

She lowers her eyes and whispers, "I know."

I jump to my feet and rush across the dais. Caught off guard, Jagger catches up to me and takes my arm.

"Why? Why would you erase our memories and cloak my scent if you knew, mother?! How could you?!" I shout.

She winces.

"I didn't want the prophecy to come to pass. It's just not right!"

My father rises and towers over my mother.

"Prudence Waters, you had no *right*! You are wrong! You abused your power and nearly ruined our daughter. I will no longer stand for you to hurt her for *your selfish* reasons!" He says as his voice rises in anger.

"Nor will I!" Lillie says as she throws a withering look at our mother and rushes to my side. She takes my hand and presses it to her forehead. "I am so sorry, Sage, Jagger, please, *please* forgive me!"

"We forgive you, Lillie," Jagger and I say in unison.

"Me, too."

The small voice comes from behind us. We turn to find Willow with tears streaming down her cheeks as she hurries towards us. She throws her arms around my neck and sobs as she begs for my forgiveness.

I hug her tightly and cry along with her. Lillie throws her arms around both of us.

"Sister's group hug!" She says through her tears.

"Well, this is all fine and dandy for you all. However, my coven expects recompense."

I blink to clear the tears from my eyes before I face the leader of the Northeast Coven.

"Tabitha, the plan you and my mother designed for my life failed. There is no coming between fated mates. Any witch will be happy to have Rupert as a mate. But do not expect me to force anyone to pair with him as recompense. I expect our covens to continue amicably, as we have for centuries. Do you have an issue with that expectation?"

She flicks her gaze at Willow.

My sister moves behind me and Jagger's bulky frame. I reach back and touch her hip to let her know I have her back. I wait for Tabitha to speak.

She sucks in a breath and exhales slowly.

"No, Sage, I do not have an issue. Our covens will continue in harmony with yours. You have my word," Tabitha says as she inclines her head.

I return the gesture of respect.

"Wonderful," I respond, then turn to the grand hall. "Does anyone else wish to step forward as a witness or to object?"

Not a beat passes before someone claps. Others pick up the applause until it thunders around the grand hall.

"Well done, *mate*," Jagger murmurs in my ear.

I shiver and bite the corner of my lip.

Further correction, my super-*sexy-as-sin* fated mate.

CHAPTER 19

age

"I NEVER WANTED any part of your roles or to pair with Rupert. Eewww!"

Willow scrunches her dainty nose as her eyebrows dip.

"Oh, yuck! No sloppy seconds for this female!" Lillie adds with a grimace on her lovely face.

I laugh at the Twins not just because of the faces they make. But because we're back together again, as sisters should be always. Stand by one another as one. Sure, we'll have disagreements—hopefully none as big as the last fiasco. However, we'll not lose sight of what we are to one another.

It's been a week since the coven meeting. Jagger and I stayed at my penthouse duplex the first few days to make sure the coven remained stable and no one incited any animosity. Several members came to speak with me in private to express their concerns, whether for or against Jagger and me.

However, all were respectful and left with a better understanding of us as fated mates and less negativity towards wolf shifters. I'd rather they speak with me than plot behind my back. Fortunately, no one brought up my removal from my positions.

Bo's disclosure did a lot to change many minds—witch and wolf shifter. He stayed in one of the guest apartments and met with coven members, particularly the elders who knew my grandmother. His revelation of the prophecy surprised them—but none more than Jagger and me.

Jagger had him repeat every detail of the prophecy. The idea of a wolf shifter and a witch fated mates whose pairing will change the course of both pack and coven and whose offspring will rule both intrigued him.

I could sense from our tether his excitement for me to become pregnant. I'm surprised with all the lovemaking we've done—with and without his knot locking our pelvises —I'm not with child. It makes me a bit nervous. But I know the Fates have plans for us that supersede ours. My mother and Tabitha can vouch for that!

Prudence…

I haven't seen my mother since she left the grand hall. Her face covered in shame as those around her whispered about her actions. She attempted to keep a straight face. But her body language spoke volumes. Aa tightness around her eyes, shoulders slumped slightly, back not ramrod straight. Subtle differences to her normal formidable carriage I could detect.

Conversely, my father pulled Jagger and me aside right then and apologized profusely. He even expressed regret for allowing my mother to run my life for years. He allowed it because she reminded him she was in control constantly. So, he focused on Waters Corporation. He pledged himself to me and vowed to stand up to my mother should she seek to overthrow my positions. We thanked him, and he left to find my mother.

Sigrid approached us after my father stepped away. The former Luna and Jaggers' mother asked to make amends with us since the prophecy changed her mind. Her hazel eyes were full of remorse as she stared at her son's hard expression.

I let Jagger take the lead on this one. It's up to him should he forgive his parents. But Sigrid—like my father—seems to have followed what her mate told her. So, I'm inclined to accept her apology. Jagger is still undecided.

His father… Well, not so much.

Marcus refused to join us when Sigrid beckoned to him. He glared at me, then at Jagger, when he issued a warning growl. With a snarl, his father spun on his heels and left the grand hall. Sigrid offered excuses for him and hurried after her mate. We haven't heard from them. Viggo told us they flew to their residence in Key West. Jagger shrugged, disinterested in his parents or their whereabouts.

"And who the hell would want Rupert, anyway? He's always creeped me out. I'm telling you, something sinister always lingers in those obsidian eyes of his."

Anala's comment pulls me from my musings.

My cousin and bestie never wavered from my side—ride or die. And I love her for it. After the meeting, she popped back up to New York. She even used her teleportation to get there fast and not the commercial planes she prefers. She only returned yesterday and told me the Northeast Coven was not pleased with no replacement by one of my sisters for Rupert. But the legacy intrigued them.

Enough so that some of their members came forward to admit their descendancy from witches and shifters, even some of the big cat shifters. As it turns out, word spread amongst all the covens and more admitted their connections. I believe Bo reached out to them and urged them to step forward.

When he joined Jagger and me for dinner the other night, Bo explained more of his background. He's not fully immortal but can live much longer than wolf shifters. Silver does not kill him because of the witch's blood in his body. He said more like him will feel comfortable coming forward now with the most powerful Alpha wolf shifter and High Witch as a fated pair. Bo asserted we will have their support. We told him they will have ours. He said he's just pleased the prophecy has come to fruition.

I smile in the mirror as I agree with him wholeheartedly.

My white maxi dress floats around me as I twirl on bare feet to get a glimpse of all angles. The gossamer light fabric shows just a hint of my body's curves. The strapless neckline shows off my fated mate's claiming bite. White jasmine flowers twine through my loose curls. Their symbolism of love, beauty, and sensuality sum up this moment perfectly.

The mate bonding ceremony between my fated mate and me.

Jagger and I will proclaim our love and commitment to one another in front of our families, closest friends, and members of our pack and coven. We decided to have a more intimate affair for this special occasion. Our formal wedding will happen in a few months, with invitations sent to the six wolf shifter packs, covens across the globe, and to the Witch Council. Already RSVPs have returned, with everyone responding yes. We'll hold it at a Larson Enterprises property in Miami.

But our mate bonding ceremony? Only one place can serve for us—the Everglades.

We're bringing it back to where it all began ten years ago. When a young witch and a young wolf shifter first experienced the love and passion of their fated mate. Where Jagger made me his. Now we complete our bond as one.

"Sage? Are you ready yet?"

Signy enters the sitting area of the primary bedroom suite in Jagger's cabin. My future sister-in-bond smiles at me as her ice blue eyes take in my dress.

"You look amazing, sis! I—I can't believe it," she says as tears shine in her eyes. "Jagger waited so long to find you, then lost you, and now you're together. Oh, Fates! I hope I can find my fated mate soon."

Willow, Lillie, and Anala throw their arms around her as they too express the desire for their fated mates. I beam as I watch my closest family take to one another so easily. Then say a prayer to the Fates my girls will find the unequivocal love I share with Jagger.

Another knock at the door, and I call for them to enter.

Prudence Waters. My mother.

Aargh!

She must see the dismay in my face because she rushes forward with her hands up, palms facing out. She's stopped by my girls as they place themselves between her and me.

"Sage, please, I—I don't mean any harm. I want to apologize and wish you well. Jagger—"

"I said she can come to you, and I will be right behind her—"

"NOOO!"

"Jagger! You can't see Sage before the ceremony!"

"Don't come in, Jagger!"

"Go back, brother!"

He chuckles and the double doors open despite Signy and Anala putting their weight against them. But instead of Jagger, Njal enters the room. The Giant steps between my mother and me. He folds his bulging arms across his massive chest and stares down at her. He stands at least a foot taller than her five foot, seven inches.

She blinks, then gazes around him with pleading eyes on me.

"Have your say, Mother."

She nods and licks her full lips.

"Sage, I was wrong and should never have done what I did to you or to Jagger. My fear and bias towards wolf shifters blinded me. I understand now how very wrong I was. I can only hope with time you will forgive me and allow me to be the mother I should have been to you all along."

Tears slip from her eyes. And in them I find no guile, nor do I sense ill will from her. I use my magick to double check. Nothing bad. I nod.

"I accept your apology, Mother—"

"So do I," Jagger says from behind the doors. "But if you don't mind, I want to complete the mate bonding ceremony. Now."

Everyone laughs at his demand. Even Njal's lips twitch. He guides my mother from the suite. She glances over her shoulder at me as he hustles her out. A watery smile lights her emerald green eyes. I smile back. With a wave, she's gone.

"Now, *mate!*" Jagger says with his Alpha command.

I jolt as it hits me.

"Yes, my love. We'll be right out."

"Ready, Sage?"

I glance up at the sound of my father's voice. He smiles at me as he enters the sitting room.

"How beautiful you look, sweetheart," he says as his eyes shine with unshed tears. "You're my first daughter to have her mate bonding ceremony. You make me so proud to be your father."

I take the tissue Willow hands to me and dab at my eyes. So much happiness flows through me at this moment.

"Come, Sage. Unless you want that mate of yours to storm in here and carry you to the ceremony bower," my father says with a raised eyebrow.

I giggle and loop my arm through his.

"As much as I love for my fated mate to carry me, I'd rather walk to meet him at our ceremony bower."

My girls go ahead of us and out the door of the cabin.

Although Jagger and I wanted to have our ceremony in the Everglades, we decided to keep our special place by the pond private. So, as my father guides me out the door, my eyes land on my fated mate a few yards away at the center of the camp.

Across the distance, his ice blue eyes pierce my very soul. So full of love and longing, I blush. The tether pulsates with his emotions. I return them tenfold. He smirks.

My father and I don't make it far down the aisle before Jagger stalks forward and lifts me in his arms with a possessive growl. He rumbles in his chest as I wrap my arms around his neck and bury my face against his skin.

The guests clap and stomp their feet. Wolf whistles fill the air. Suddenly, white jasmine petals fall all around us. Their fragrance mingles with that of the wetlands.

I glance up to find my mother smiling as her fingers wiggle in the air, causing more flowers to shift in the breeze. I mouth thank you, and she bows her head. A symbol of peace I'm grateful for since I never wanted to battle with my mother.

"Time to complete our bond, *mate*."

Jagger's husky baritone sends shivers down my spine. I shudder in his arms and tighten my grip around his neck.

"Yes, mate!" I respond enthusiastically.

He chuckles and strides towards the ceremony bower

made from items found in the Everglades. Branches, twigs, driftwood, and colorful wildflowers mix for a beautiful bower. He lowers me to my feet, and we face one another, hands clasped together.

"Sage Waters, I claim you as my fated mate to protect, love, and cherish for all time. To bear my pups and to lead our pack with me as the Luna. I love you, Sage Larson Waters, my fated mate!"

I swallow back tears of joy, then clear my throat to respond.

"Jagger Larson, I claim you as my fated mate to protect, love, and cherish for all time. To bear your pups and to lead our pack with you, our Alpha. I love you, Jagger Waters Larson, my fated mate!"

The clearing explodes with shouts and howls of jubilation.

Jagger lifts me in the air and swings me around. I throw my head back and give my best howl. He joins me for a song of love. Then he carries me back up the aisle and straight to our cabin. More wolf whistles and howls punch through the air.

"Jagger! Where are you going?"

"Taking you into seclusion for a week, *mate*," he growls, with eyes flashing as his wolf rises to the surface.

"But our guests… lunch…"

"MINE! NOW!"

He pushes the door open with his foot and races up the stairs three at a time. I hold on as I giggle.

But when my fated mate strips me of my ceremony gown, I'm no longer laughing. Only lustful moans, mewls, and screams of his name fall from my mouth. His knot swells behind the wall of my core to lock us together. The first jettison of his seed shoots deep into my core. Instantly, a spark glimmers in my womb, and I gasp.

 agger

"Hi, baby. What are you doing out here? You know you can't run off like that, *mate.*"

Sage smiles at me as I scoop her from the porch swing onto my lap. She nuzzles against my chest and purrs with contentment.

"You call sitting a few feet from the front door of our cabin running off? Jagger, you are too much." Her words come out muffled as her mouth trails kisses along my neck.

The warm breath makes me shudder. I rumble deep in my chest as my hands roam over her lush curves. Covered by a maxi dress. I growl in frustration.

"And you're in clothes. Seclusion Rule number two you've broken. *Bad* mate!" I chide as I spank her ass cheek.

She yelps and wiggles on my lap, waking my cock for another round. And I'm all for it. One hundred percent!

Since we made love after our mate bonding ceremony,

something about Sage has fueled a hunger in me I've never experienced before. I don't know if it's because she's all mine finally, we have the bullshit with our pack and coven behind us, or just being in love. Fuck if I know. But I'm not complaining in any way, shape, or form.

But today marks the last day of our seclusion. The pack will arrive soon for a night run to celebrate our bonding. It's a tradition I cannot deny them. I grumble just at the thought of having more than our enforcers, Ulf, and his mate—who cooks for us—around. Fortunately for the males, they've kept their distance knowing the protective instincts of an Alpha go off the charts when he takes his mate to seclusion.

And mine are even worse given the fact we had to fight so hard to stay together. Ten fucking years apart, then dealing with those still wanting to keep us separated. I was on the verge of an all-out war or walk away from all of it. Thank the Fates it's all settled on both sides.

"Does that mean you're going to punish me, my Alpha?"

My fated mate's question captures my attention. She wiggles her round ass on my lap. My cock gives her what she seeks as it thickens and lengthens along her hip. She purrs and presses kisses against my stumbled jaw. Her mouth leaves a scorching trail as it makes its way to cover mine.

I slant my mouth over hers for a dominating kiss. She moans as my tongue slides into her wet heat and sweeps around to taste every bit of her. On a mewl, she lifts her tongue to tangle with mine. I groan and shift to place her back on the swing and kneel between her spread thighs.

She stares up at me, panting for breath. I stare back as I hold the base of my cock and push the swing back. On the return, I impale her on my dick. Then repeat the move. As the swing arcs back and forth, my fated mate cries out in wild abandon. Her fingers grip the edge of the swing as her chest heaves. On a return, I lower my mouth to bite her plump brown nipple through the gauzy fabric of her maxi dress. She wails.

We continue our adult version of a day at the playground until I drag out multiple orgasms from her quivering pussy. She slumps back against the swing in a state of sheer euphoria. Her eyes hooded. Lips parted. Thighs twitching. I blew my mate's mind.

With a roar, I plunge into her soaking pussy once more and cum so hard *my* mind blanks. I slump over her and bury my face against the crook of her neck. My tongue darts out to lap at the sweat coating my claiming bite. The night of our mate bonding ceremony, I reenforced it with a fresh claim. Lest anyone not notice my first mark.

The distant sound of laughter filters through my carnal haze. I growl. The pack arrived. Damn!

"Now, baby, you'll stay here with Njal, the rest of your security detail, and some elders who chose not to shift for the pack run. The pack understands you haven't shifted yet. They still love their Luna, as do I."

A secret smile plays on my fated mate's gorgeous face. Her eyes shine as she stares up at me in the clearing outside of our cabin. The rest of the pack—some in human form, others as wolves—wait for my signal to bound off for our celebratory run. I squeeze her hip bones where my hands rest as I raise my eyebrow in question.

"What are you not telling me, Sage Larson Waters?" I ask using my Alpha command as leverage.

She gnaws on her bottom lip, eyes wide.

I squeeze again as she hesitates, and she yelps and hops onto her toes.

"O—okay… Okay! I can shift now."

My mouth drops open. What the hell? When did that happen? Better yet, how did I not notice?

She giggles, and I realize I spoke aloud, especially since the pack turns to stare at us. I ignore them and wait for Sage to answer me.

She places my hand on her lower belly. The shine in her emerald green eyes increases with unshed tears. I frown, concerned the dinner we ate earlier upset her stomach. But it was only grilled fish and vegetables. A light fare prior to the pack run. She passed on the Chardonnay—

"Jagger, the night of our mate bonding ceremony, I felt the spark indicating we conceived."

I stare at her blankly. What?

She shakes her head and speaks again.

"Jagger Waters Larson, I am pregnant with your pups!"

My eyes snap to her belly, where she cups my hand against it. I glance back up at my fated mate, and she nods.

"Twins, a male and a female. *Your pups*," she whispers as the tears leak from her eyes.

I fall to my knees in front of my fated mate, the mother of my unborn pups. *My life!*

My forehead presses to her still flat belly. Now tears gather in *my* eyes as I murmur thanks to the Fates. Sage runs her fingers through my hair as my entire body shakes with emotion. I barely register the pack as they raise a song of joyful howls to the star-studded sky above.

I place two kisses on my fated mate's belly, one for each pup. Soon it will grow round with my heirs. At that moment, I know the foretold prophecy will come to pass, and I will allow no one to stand in the way of my pups' futures. No. One.

EPILOGUE

he Everglades

THE RAVEN GLIDES on the air currents. Its glossy ebony wings spread wide as it circles above the tops of the pine trees. Its obsidian eyes flick across the wetlands below. The raven sees every movement as the female and male stand amongst the others. Just as it had for the past seven days and six nights. It never strayed far from the pair.

Yet, they never noted it flying above or sitting on a branch, even on the windowsill of their cabin.

The raven makes certain to blend in as best it can despite being larger than the average raven and the closet population is in Georgia, miles away from the Everglades.

But the female and male pay no heed as they fornicate like feral beasts all day and all night long.

The raven's body shudders at the memories, feathers flutter.

It takes a last turn over those below, then settles on a tree branch high above them. Although close enough to hear their every word.

"Jagger Waters Larson, I am pregnant with your pups!" The female declares.

The male's eyes snap to her flat belly, where she cups his hand against it lovingly. Dumbfounded, the male glances back up at the female, who nods.

"Twins, a male and a female. *Your pups.*"

Even though it's a whisper, the raven hears it as though the female spoke to its face.

A croaking sound rips past its ebony beak. The raven almost falls from its hidden perch.

A few of those gathered turn in its direction. Their sharp eyesight detects the raven amongst the boughs of the pine tree. Heads cock curious as to the reason the raven would utter such a devastated cry.

Before they can approach, the raven leaps from its perch, ebony wings spread out, and it flaps hard to reach the star-filled sky above. Satisfied it's far enough from those below, the raven circles the female and the male once more.

With a parting strangled croak, it banks towards the north.

CHARMAINE LOUISE SHELTON

RUST
THE REJECTED

ABOUT RUST THE REJECTED: A WOLF SHIFTER REJTED MATE PARANORMAL ROMANCE

Can I heal the tortured heart of my fated mate, even though she rejected me?

By day, I save patients in the ER. At night, I'm the doctor for my pack—the Billionaire Wolves of Miami. I work hard and play even harder. A wolf shifter whose busy life should fulfill my wants. Yet, I long for my fated mate. When a carefully concealed secret reveals her, Dr. Natalie Moore rejects me. A needle hurts. But this pain… Ouch.

As an OB-GYN, pregnant women may surround me all day, and I care for them. But that doesn't mean I want any parts of being pregnant or having pups! So, I suppress my wolf. No male will ever claim and mate me. Until an unfortunate accident brings Dr. Rust Ingolf sniffing around me. He may be sinfully sexy and tempt me. But. No.

And then, there's my old pack I ran away from. The leader wants me and will stop at nothing to make me his mate. How can I risk another?

Their steamy love story is a standalone in the sizzling **Billionaire Wolves Series** of interconnecting stories featuring wolf shifter fated mates romance. Get a glimpse of their dynamism in other books.

Anthem: "Never Gonna Give You Up" Rick Astley
https://www.youtube.com/watch?v=dQw4w9WgXcQ

Visit CharmaineLouiseBooks.com

CHAPTER 1

ust

"Oh, my, Dr. Ingolf. What a big stethoscope you have, Sir. So long and hard. Ooo and look! It even has a shiny tip. Shall I blow on it to warm it for you, Sir?"

The submissive purses her full, glossy lips as she stares up at me from the velvet pillow between my feet. A rich chocolate brown rims her dilated pupils.

But it's the sight of her creamy pillowy tits overflowing the cups of her pink lace corset that makes my cock leak pre-cum. The perfect size to fit in my large hands and soft. Nothing against silicone enhancements. But the feel of naturally lush tits with pinchable plump nipples wins hands down—or hands full.

My mouth salivates as much as my cock drips.

The Alpha Dom in me knows I should correct the sub's forward behavior. I did not command her to fist my dick— only to kneel. Any other time, I would toss her over my thighs and spank her round ass. The globes on either side of the skimpy lace thong would match its color for a delightful rosy shade. My palm itches for the punishment.

Instead, I sigh and pinch the bridge of my nose—not a nipple.

I've had back-to-back nights as a critical care surgeon at Miami's busiest hospital emergency room. The urban location has more than its share of acute, life-threatening injuries that require immediate surgery. Trained to perform well under pressure, I never hesitate to pick up the scalpel to save a patient.

My duties require the utmost focus. I cannot allow distractions. A patient's life—many times their heart—is in my hands, literally.

So, when I have a rare night off from the ER and no one in our pack needs Dr. Ingolf, I don't waste it. I take advantage of the opportunity to revel in my dominate proclivities.

A trip to Club Sol & Mani Miami provides a safe space for those in the BDSM lifestyle. The luxury, members-only club on Ocean Drive owned by the Miami Wolves Pack promises a night of pleasure.

I let my gaze return to the sub. She winks at me. Uh. No.

"Oh, naughty pet, how you misbehave," I tsk as I tuck my cock back into my bespoke trousers and zip up. Her mouth droops in dismay. "I must let the resident Dom know you like to top from the bottom."

Her glossy lips pout as elegantly shaped eyebrows pinch together and mar her pretty face. The little she-wolf even dares to growl at my reprimand.

Well, damn. That will never do.

She yelps as I scoop her from the pillow and over my muscular thighs. Long blonde hair falls over her face like a silky curtain. Her hands scrabble for the floor while her shapely legs flail.

I trap them with one of mine and press a hand between her shoulder blades to still her movements. A deep growl of my own halts her wiggling. Then a swat to her left ass cheek makes her jolt.

"Enough with this, naughty pet. You will take your punishment like a well-trained Club Sol & Mani sub. Twenty spanks, and you will count each one. Miss one, and we start anew. Do you understand?"

She shivers as I add Alpha power to my words. The musky scent of her arousal flares. I inhale deeply. My cock throbs, and my wolf howls. Yeah, it's been a while.

"Yes, Sir. I apologize and will behave appropriately."

I smirk as my palm rubs the soft skin of her upturned ass. A moan slips past her lips, and her pelvis tilts to push her ass into my hand.

THWACK.

"You disobey during a punishment?"

Her ass lowers as she shakes her head. Blonde strands sway with the light catching the golden streaks.

"Words, naughty pet. I will have your words."

"N—No, Sir."

"Count, or we start from one."

"One, Sir." She replies immediately.

Halfway through, the intoxicating scent of her arousal permeates the air in my private suite. A damp patch of it spreads through the wool of my trousers. I rim her slick pussy lips with the calloused tip of my middle finger.

She gasps, and her greedy core clenches. Then she wails when I issue three successive spanks to her swollen folds. But she doesn't miss the count.

I thrust two tapered fingers inside of her pussy. It pulsates around the digits, sucking them in deep. So tight and wet. I stifle a groan. Too damn long.

"Twenty, Sir."

The sub ends on a choked pant.

I lift her to straddle my lap.

Tears stream down her reddened cheeks. Like her ass, they bear a crimson shade. I pull the Ferragamo silk pocket square from my suit jacket and dab her face. Chocolate brown eyes now softened lower to stare at my chest submissively.

"You did well, pet. Now, you will think twice before topping a Dom. Won't you?" I ask with a cocked eyebrow.

"Thank you, Sir. Yes, I will," she whispers.

"Good. Now, we fuck," I say as my hands cup her heated ass, and I rise. Quick strides take me to the sex swing. Even quicker, I strap her in.

Excitement shines in her eyes, even as she keeps them lowered. Her teeth nibble at the corner of her lip. Dainty fingers wrap around the black suede straps. Her thighs—slick with her juices—quiver in anticipation.

She doesn't have long to wait.

I unzip my trousers, and my aching cock springs free. It slaps back against my shirt. The engorged mushroom tip reaches my belly button.belly button.

Teeth marks dimple her lip as she moans at the sight of my well-endowed dick.

I fist its wide base and stroke up the veiny shaft once, squeezing below the head. Pearly beads of pre-cum drip to tile floor. Her lust-filled eyes follow their descent. I slip a condom over my cock. Her eyes snap to my face when I grab her hips and pull.

The sex swing arcs forward. We watch as her pussy swallows the length and girth of my cock. The tip parts her glistening folds, then disappears inch by delicious inch into her soaked core. When my heavy balls meet her heated ass cheeks, we groan in unison.

My eyes close. The sensation of tight, wet warmth

clamping on my dick makes my balls tingle. Finally. Fuuuck. I relish the moment before I withdraw to my tip.

The sub mewls in protest at the loss.

"Oh, little pet, I will satisfy you many times over. But you will not cum until I give you permission. Do you understand?"

"Yes, Sir, thank you, Sir!"

I chuckle wickedly and pull the sex swing forward to plunge back in. With each arc of the swing, her pussy flutters around my cock. Too much and I draw back, edging her until she begs my permission to cum.

The forceful thrusts pop her tits from the corset. I lean over and suckle the plump nipples. She moans as her inner walls clench around my cock. A few more thrusts, and my control hangs on by a thread.

"Now, pet! Keep cumming until I give you permission to stop," I growl.

She keens as her first orgasm causes her body to buck in the sex swing.

I grunt and growl as I fuck her through one wave after the other of her toe-curling orgasms until she's limp in the swing. Then I chase my release with a roar to the ceiling. My knees turn to jelly, and my still erect cock slips from her pussy.

She whimpers.

I slip the condom off and toss it in the discreet trash can. She watches with hooded eyes as I tuck my junk away, then uncuff her from the sex swing and carry her to the bed. With a sated sigh, she rolls to her side, curled up like a well-fed pup. I chuckle to myself as I head to the en suite bathroom for a warm, moistened cloth and clean her gently. I apply a soothing salve to her warm crimson ass cheeks, and she moans softly. Tucked beneath the silk sheets, I leave the contented she-wolf with a note beside her pillow to stay the night and enjoy breakfast.

I skip the shower and go downstairs to my McLaren P1 LM. The ride to my beachfront penthouse on Ocean Drive —where most pack bachelors live—brings me back to reality.

I let my mind wander as I drive along Collins Avenue, South Beach. And as my thoughts have in recent months, they go to what I long for to complete my life. No matter how successful I am in the ER or how many—or how few— nights at Club Sol & Mani, one thing still eludes me.

My fated mate…

~

"Hey, Big Red, you finally made it. Got held up in a storage closet by a hot nurse checking your vitals?"

"The Love Doctor is available for private appointments —one or multiple patients per session. Leave your name and number after the beep."

I growl in response to the jabs and guffaws of my best friends—Dylan Vang and Jagger Larson—as I enter the Wolf Den on Moon Island.

The hangout spot for the males on our pack's private island set in Biscayne Bay—the body of water behind the barrier island of Miami Beach across from South Beach. The Wolf Den offers every luxury amenity and boys' toys imaginable to entertain the males. A gym, steam room, sauna, bowling alley, game room, cinema, wet bars, and more allow us to relax in our true nature. No concern humans hear us growl when we lose. Or growl at Jagger and Dylan…

"Fuck off, losers. A human kid fell off a bike and fractured her arm right before my shift ended. A higher priority than shooting pool with you two," I say as I select a cue stick from the wall rack. "Her olecranon took the brunt of the impact while the lateral epicondyle of her humerus suffered distal fracture—"

"Okay, Doc, we don't need to hear your nerdy description of a broken arm. Get a drink and rack the balls already," Dylan says, rolling his amber eyes to the ceiling. "We're trying to have some fun here, you know."

Jagger chuckles and claps me on the back as he strides to the wet bar.

"Rack the balls. What'll you have to drink?"

I nod my thanks and ask for two fingers of aquavit—a nod to our Scandinavian Viking roots. Wolf shifters have a high tolerance for alcohol. It's not getting drunk for us. Rather, we enjoy the taste.

"D., you want a refill?" Jagger asks, then takes Dylan's old fashioned glass when he nods.

While I gather the billiard balls on the sand-colored felt of the modern desert pine pool table, Dylan sets the music playlist. I glance around the game room at the other males. Some play poker, laughing about a joke across the room. Four play pool at another table. A few gather around the wet bar watching a Miami Heat versus LA Lakers basketball game.

"Viggo and Tag can't make it tonight. Viggo had an emergency at one of his clubs, and Tag was too mysterious about his reason to bow out," Jagger says about our other best friends as he hands us tumblers.

He's our pack's Alpha in a long line of leaders of the *Billionaire Wolves of Miami*—as the other packs refer to us. With good reason, since we're the most powerful pack in the South. Several millennia ago, Scandinavian Viking wolf shifters sailed from the Old World and landed along the East Coast of what's now the United States. The six packs moved throughout the continent to form territories, with ours settling here.

Jagger continued the Larsons as our pack Alphas, despite Dylan's misguided challenge. Fortunately, the two reconciled recently. We've been best friends since we were pups. Now in our late twenties—except for Viggo, who's twenty-six—we can enjoy our friendship for decades to come. Including tonight, and it's the distraction I need.

The three of us play a few rounds of pool as we rib each other and talk about work. Aside from being the Alpha, Jagger serves as the CEO of Larson Enterprises, Inc. It's the source of our pack's wealth with its luxury hotels, fine dining, clubs, and lounges throughout our territory across the south. Dylan made his billions with an early investment and spends his time competing in an underground fight club in New York City.

Viggo and Tag work with Larson Enterprises as President of Clubs and Lounges and COO and are Jagger's younger brother and beta, respectively. Dylan and I chose to work outside of the company.

My need to be a doctor driven by wanting to care for our pack and the horrible memory of a male driven to madness because he never mated. A flash of the vision of him running wild as his wolf attacking other members in the Everglades—where our pack has a camp compound— makes me shudder. I hit the billiards ball at the wrong angle. It skips past the corner pocket and bounces off the top rail. Lost in thought, I barely hear Jagger.

"Damn, Rust! What are you aiming at? *My* balls?"

Dylan throws his head back and roars in laughter. Others turn to our table and grin at his infectious guffaw.

"Not the Larson family's jewels. The gods forbid!"

Jagger's ice blue eyes narrow at Dylan, who wipes tears from his eyes.

"You're a regular comedian, D. These jewels already sired fraternal twin pups with my gorgeous fated mate, Sage. And she would *not* appreciate any damage to my extraordinary package," Jagger says with a smirk.

I laugh. But inside, an ache stabs my heart.

After all these years, Jagger and Dylan found their fated mates—even with Dylan not believing in the concept. The lucky bastard claimed a beautiful Russian she-wolf. Jagger's Sage is the stunning and powerful High Witch of the Coven of the South turned she-wolf and our pack's Luna. Now, she wields never-before-seen magick because of his DNA mixing with hers. I delivered their twins despite Jagger's growling because a male was near his fated mate, especially being up close and personal with her most private areas. It's part of my responsibility to our pack regardless of the males' possessiveness of their mates, fated or otherwise.

I believe wholeheartedly in fated mates. Yet, I haven't found mine. Each year I get older, and the fear of the madness affliction striking me grows stronger. Meanwhile, two of my best friends enjoy the bliss of a fated mate bond. Damn.

"Yeah, well, my jewels filled my beauty with a pup," Dylan responds, then turns to me. "And you better not fuck up when it's time for her birth. I damn sure wish we had a female doctor. I don't want your eyes and your hands anywhere near my Sasha."

I shrug and say, "The she-wolves I care for do not differ from any other patient. I have no further interest than to help them with their medical requirements."

Dylan huffs and sips his aquavit, eyeing me over the rim of his glass. Then he pulls his mobile from his jeans pocket. A grin spreads across his face, and his amber eyes gleam as they scan the screen. His fingers fly across it as he types.

"Well, fellas, it's been a pleasure. But I gotta go. My fated mate requests mint chocolate chip ice cream, and I vowed to give her all her heart's desires. And then some!"

He claps Jagger and me on the back and strides towards the door.

Jagger's mobile rings. Undoubtedly, it's from his fated mate, based on the giant grin as he answers the call. With a not so genuine sorry to end our evening early, he gives me a salute and heads out the door.

I shake my head and glance around, trying to decide if I'll join the other males for poker or to just hang out. Instead, I finish my drink and go to my Bugatti La Voiture Noire. Another boys' toy, and the most expensive supercar in the world. Since I don't have a fated mate to lavish with "all her heart's desires," I might as well spend my money on the finer things for myself.

Once again, the ride back to my bachelor's penthouse leaves me yearning for the one who will complete me.

My fated mate...

CHAPTER 2

atalie

"Dr. Moore, your next patient arrived. Shall I bring her to examination room two now?"

So engrossed in the patient's medical chart on my desk, I startle at my nurse Thandie Ross' question. I glance up to find her standing in the doorway of my office.

"Oh! I didn't mean to scare you, Dr. Moore!" She says as her sepia cheeks redden apologetically.

I wave off her concern and shake my head.

"Not a problem, Thandie. I was caught up in her case. It's intriguing. Right in line with my specialty of critical care. Kindly take her to the exam room," I say, then arch an eyebrow. "And remember to call me Natalie unless we're with patients. I'm not into formalities."

She smiles and leaves.

I close my eyes and sit back in the chair. My mind drifts to my former pack out west and the drive for me to care for females who require the close attention and knowledge required for dangerous pregnancies.

"Amanda, you don't look too good. Your face is pale, and your breathing is labored. Are you sure you want to continue our walk? I think we should head back," I say as we reach the tree line surrounding our pack's land. "We already walked a mile, and I don't think we should go any further."

My older sister takes another step forward, then winces as she gasps and clutches her round belly.

I grab her arm to prevent her from falling. My gaze scans the area for a comfortable spot she can rest. A fallen Douglas fir catches my eye.

"This way. You can rest over there, then we're heading back. And do not argue, Amanda. I'll get the midwife to check on you."

Amanda nods as she grinds her teeth. Slowly, we make our way to the evergreen, where I help her sit gingerly. She closes her eyes and inhales, then exhales. The grimace disappears as she settles.

"Listen to me, Nat, no matter what happens, you take care of yourself. Don't let anyone force you to mate. We're not meant to be breeders. Dad would never allow this to happen if he were still alive and Alpha."

Tears sting my eyes, and I glance away. It won't due to upset Amanda—not now with her in distress. But she's right. Had our parents not died with so many other members of our pack from the unexpected affliction two years ago, Sam would never be Alpha or mated to Amanda. He defeated the other males, then took Amanda as his mate since she's the eldest daughter of the prior Alpha. I thanked the gods I'm four years younger at sixteen.

We sit in silence—lost in thoughts—until Amanda moans. She glances down at her lap, then up at me. The grimace returns as her onyx eyes—so like mine—widen.

"M—My water broke... Nat," she pants.

I turn towards the closest building. It's too far for Amanda to walk. She'll never make it.

"I'm going to shift and run to the midwife. We'll return with Sam and his pickup truck to bring you home. Don't follow me, Amanda, please!"

She nods as she sucks in a ragged breath.

I kiss her forehead—covered in a sheen of sweat—and step back to remove my clothes. I allow my body to relax and accept my wolf to take over. My other half lives on the fringes of my being. Always ready to spring forth at my call, then retreat at my will. An ability born of our kind so long ago and marks us different from full humans.

The sensations of my bones reshaping and muscles lengthening to shift me from my human form to that of my wolf block out all else. Crackling and a flash find me on all four paws within moments. My wolf appears with midnight fur and a white streak like my widow's peak.

I cast a quick glance at Amanda. Certain she's not moving, I dart away. My paws pound the grassy terrain as the salty air from the Puget Sound wafts past my nose. It's a rare sunny morning with no sign of rain. Nothing to impede my race to the midwife and Sam. Thank the gods!

I run straight to the older she-wolf's home. My howl as I approach brings her to the front porch. One glimpse at me, and she rushes inside. She returns with her bag and a dress.

"Here, Natalie, shift and change. Where's Amanda?" She says as she hands the dress to me. "Hurry, she hasn't looked good to me in days!"

My wolf retreats, and I pull the dress over my head as I tell her about Amanda. We hurry to get Sam from the Alpha's office. He's with his beta and a few other males. They leer at me as we enter. I ignore them and focus on Sam.

"Amanda's in labor! We need you to bring her back home with your pickup—"

"Why the hell did she go anywhere when I told her to stay her ass at home?! She never listens, no matter how many lessons I give that stubborn she-wolf."

My mouth gapes. Does he mean he hurts my sister? Why didn't she tell me?

"Shut your mouth and take me to her."

I blink at his harsh words but set the thoughts aside. My sister and the pup come first. We'll have time to figure out what to do about Sam after the birth.

We drive to spot and find Amanda on the ground with her back against the evergreen and her sweatpants beside the tree. Her knees bent with her feet wide apart on the grass. Her face contorts as she screams in agony.

"No time to take her back. I'll deliver the pup here. Natalie, you've watched me enough times to know what to do," the midwife says as she hurries to Amanda's side with me close behind her.

My sister doesn't register our presence until the midwife kneels in front of her and calls her name. Amanda opens her eyes and stares unseeingly. Another contraction hits, and she wails how much it hurts. Blood gushes to the grass.

The midwife checks her, then glances at me. Regret fills her brown eyes as she shakes her head.

Tears blur my vision. I grab Amanda's hand and whisper how much I love her, along with words of encouragement.

Sam growls.

"You better not die on me, Amanda! Deliver my pup and quit with your whining. You hear me? Of course, it hurts. Who the hell said it would be easy?"

Tears—not just from the pain in her womb, but from the heartless words of her mate and our Alpha—stream down my sister's flushed cheeks. Her entire pregnancy was rife with pain. Not one moment was idyllic for her. She did her best to ignore it. But I could tell by the sadness in her eyes she was not enjoying her *pregnancy. And the oaf of a male wolf shifter she mated with was of zero use to her.*

Like the other males in our pack, he only cares about his offspring. Their sole focus on increasing our numbers since so many of the pack died from the unexplainable affliction. Now, instead of cherishing the she-wolves, the males view us as breeders. And the gods forbid if a she-wolf fails to produce pups or ages out of fertility! She's tossed aside by her mate, and he chooses another. She becomes the head mate while the original moves to the side-lines and hopes he will provide for her, too.

The day my sister and her male pup died in childbirth marked the end for me. Instead of mourning his loss, our Alpha turned from their lifeless bodies to pin me with his intense stare.

"You will become my mate since your sister failed me."

That night after I buried my sister and her pup beside the graves of our parents, I left the only home I'd ever known.

I gathered some clothes and my savings—including the sizable inheritance from my parents. Without a backward glance, I left my pack's land. After years of witnessing the pain and the loss she-wolves experienced—even before the years prior to the affliction—I knew the gods wanted me to help females as an OB-GYN. It became my mission through the years at the University of New Mexico undergrad and medical school to excel in my studies. During my residency, I applied to positions far away from my former pack. Miami accepted me.

My eyes open with a fierce determination to help my patient and her unborn baby. As I have for the last twelve years, I use the tragic memory of my sister and her pup to urge me to do my utmost to care for other females. From finishing my studies early and succeeding in my residency until now, I do it all to honor my sister and the struggles of the she-wolves of my former pack.

I take a deep breath and exhale to clear my mind. Focused and determined, I leave my office for the examination room. Ready for the day's challenges.

"Natalie, Thandie and I are going for happy hour with a few others in the department. Do you want to join us? You'll get to meet more people and have fun doing it!"

Paloma Sabela Garcia—the OB-GYN department secretary—smiles at me as Thandie nods in agreement.

I consider their offer, then decline.

"Thanks ladies. But I'll have to take a raincheck. Too many boxes sit in my living room waiting for me to unpack them," I say, then grin. "You have no idea how many times I rotated three wrap dresses this week!"

They glance at each other, then burst out laughing. With a shrug, I join them.

It'll be nice to have girlfriends again. During school, I was too busy to bond with others. Without the pressure to do well and to finish early, I have time to spend with others. Just not tonight.

I watch them still giggling as they leave my suite of rooms.

After I complete notes in the charts for the day's patients, I head to my car. Fortunately, work study, scholarships, and grants covered most my education. So, I splurged on the pre-owned Volkswagen Beetle convertible. Now, I can enjoy the sunny Miami weather every chance I get. So, unlike the rainy Pacific Northwest. And I'll do anything to distance myself from that place.

As soon as the ignition starts, I press the button to lower the roof. Then pull my mane of midnight hair with its snow-white widow's peak into a ponytail and slip on a pair of oversized glamour girl sunglasses. The playlist of Miamiinspired dance music has me tapping my fingers on the steering wheel as I navigate through the streets.

I stop by the spot famous for its Cuban sandwich Paloma Sabela recommended. My mouth waters at the delicious aroma of ham, roasted pork, salami, and fresh-baked bread. At the checkout, the cashier suggests the Materva Cuban soda. I thank him and head to my car, more than ready to chow down.

It's a quick ride to my furnished, one-bedroom rental apartment. I chose a spot near the hospital for quick access in case I need to deliver a baby, or the mom may need help with little warning. The less time lost, the better in the cases of my critical care patients.

As I open the front door, my heart sinks. Box after giant box stretches from the middle of the living room to the two windows on the opposite wall. A few sit open with medical books, lingerie, or shoes spilling out. The side of one wardrobe box labeled dresses gapes open—items on hangers visible. I unpacked the ones marked for the bathroom for my toiletries and cosmetics last week.

And of course, I opened the most precious box that contains my special serum. A quick check revealed the glass vials and syringes remained intact. I couldn't fly with them. Too much of a risk should the TSA choose to confiscate the box or to question the serum's purpose.

I shudder at the thought of humans learning about wolf shifters' existence. Worse yet, they gain the knowledge I can't even share with my own kind. My formula and its purpose would cause an uproar in the entire shifter community. Its impact goes beyond wolves.

With a shake of my head, I put the thoughts aside and head to the eat-in-kitchen. A tiny mosaic-topped café table with two chairs sits in a corner by the window with a view of the park across the street. I set the bags of food and sodas on the countertop, then wind my way past the boxes for the bedroom.

It's not large. But the room fits a queen-size bed with nightstands on the wall opposite the door and a small, three-drawer dresser beneath the window. I can see the same view of the park as the living room and kitchen while I sit in bed.

I strip and let my hair down on my way to the bathroom on the other side of the bed. A quick shower helps wash away the day before I eat dinner. My stomach rumbles just thinking about the tantalizing Cuban sandwich. Yum!

Bundled up in a comfy robe and my hair up in a drying turban, I settle at the café table. My mouth waters at the delicious aroma of the meats blended with Swiss cheese, pickles, and spicy mustard. The sandwich is so large, I'll save the other half for lunch tomorrow.

My leg swings as I eat. Laughter bubbles up at the memory of my mother teasing me about being so greedy I'd swing one leg and hum in delight as I ate. The flash of her smiling face brings me a moment of joy before the sadness tries to creep in. Once again, I shake my head to dispel the negativity.

It's a fresh start, Nat. Don't dwell on the past, I chastise myself.

As I wash the dishes, the alarm on my mobile chimes with the ringtone for Creedence Clearwater Revival's "Bad Moon Rising." Hurriedly, I dry my hands as I grumble trouble will definitely be on the way if I don't inject my serum as scheduled.

From the time I left my former pack, I knew I needed to avoid all shifters. I had no desire to encounter them. Distance from the paranormal world prompted me to research a method to suppress my wolf. Various combinations of regular human medicines and trials finally resulted in a serum that hid my wolf, even from me. No scent detectable. Not a chance of a shift. The only downside is the loss of my enhanced healing and senses, including my ability to detect a shifter. But I'm free of my wolf with no way for others to find me. Safe to be me and to live my life as I choose—not forced to mate and breed. Just as Amanda told me.

Unless I didn't inject the serum on time each month. Then I would revert to a wolf shifter over a period of time. To test the amount of time I had before the reversion to my wolf, I skipped a scheduled dose. Each day, an element of my wolf appeared. By the seventh day, she returned fully. Without hesitation, I injected the serum. In two days, it banished that side of me again.

I do not know the side effects of the combined medications other than as they stand alone. However, the risk outweighs any negative result. It's been three years, and I have no regrets.

As an OB-GYN, pregnant women may surround me all day, and I care for them. But that doesn't mean I want any parts of being pregnant or having pups!

So, I turn off the alarm, slip my mobile in the robe pocket, and stride purposefully towards my bedroom. As I pass through the living room, I pick up the stepladder. Even at five feet, nine inches, I'll need the extra height to reach the rear corner of the top shelf in the closet where I put the box.

Atop the ladder, I collect the box in one hand while the other keeps my balance. As my foot lowers to the next step, the robe's belt snags on the corner of the ladder. I pull the belt loose, but the ladder teeters precariously. My heart clenches as in what seems like slow motion the ladder topples sideways, my fingers reach and miss the closet door, and I free fall to the tile floor. Eyes widen in horror as my precious box flies from my hand, arcs through the air, and crashes to the floor. The shattering of bone and glass followed by a wail echo in my ears.

Pain radiates along my arm. But it doesn't compare to the agony in my heart. The shattered remnants of the vials represent the last of my serum supply. An entire six months destroyed in seconds. Tears fill my eyes.

And now, I regret the loss of my wolf. My arm hurts like hell. I can't drive in this condition. Drawing on my strength and determination, I slip my mobile from the robe pocket and dial 911.

ust

"Dr. Ingolf, I hate to do this to you since your shift ends in a few minutes. But the EMTs brought in a doctor from the hospital who fell off a stepladder at home. X-rays reveal multiple upper arm fractures. She's in area five."

I curtail the flash of annoyance and replace it with a smile as I accept the patient folder from the ER nurse. It's not his fault, nor can I blame the patient. They have nothing to do with me on duty for almost twelve hours and mere minutes away from being off shift.

"Duty calls," I respond, saluting him with the folder, then stride towards the curtained area. Scanning the images, I wince at the type of fractures the patient sustained. Damn.

"Hello, I—"

My mouth drops at the luscious swell of an exposed breast. The more-than-a-handful—even for my sizable ones —mound peeks from behind a drab gray hospital gown. The opening reveals a heart-shaped birthmark on the inner curve of her breast. My eyes slide to the imprint of a plump nipple outlined against the thin cotton. My mouth salivates. Unconsciously, I lick my lips.

"Oooooo…"

The pitiful moan—not the kind I prefer to hear from a female—snaps me out of the unprofessional lust fog.

Dammit, Rust! What the fuck?!

I shake my head. Obviously, I need another night at Club Sol & Mani if I'm getting horny over a hurt patient…

"Hello, I'm Dr. Ingolf, Dr. Moore," I say, to continue my disrupted introduction. "Let's get a look at your arm. Shall we?"

Her eyelids flutter open and the most soulful eyes I've ever seen peer at me. Air rushes from my lungs at the intensity of her onyx orbs—even while full of anguish.

Unconsciously, I rub my chest.

"P—Please… The pain."

The nurse steps around me and raises a questioning eyebrow at me. I return my gaze to Dr. Moore.

"On a scale of one to five, how much pain—"

"Eight!"

"How well do you tolerate morphine, Dr. Moore?"

Her eyes close as she considers my question. Then she mutters under her breath and pins me with a fiery glare. Lightning flashes in the onyx depths.

"I've never had it. But give it to me. I'm a doctor, for goodness sake! I'll prescribe it to myself if I have to! Ooooo…"

Her eyes squeeze shut as she sags against the upraised bed.

The nurse stifles a laugh at her snippy command and glances at me for approval.

My inner Alpha Dom bristles at her bratty behavior. But

I ignore it since she's in pain—and not the erotic kind. I give the nurse a nod to administer the medicine via IV drip, and he leaves the curtained area. I hold back the fact a doctor cannot self-prescribe a controlled substance to themselves in the state of Florida. No need to upset her further.

Instead, I stride to the X-ray reader on the wall and place the images on the glass surface, then flick on the light.

"Well, *Dr.* Moore, the nurse will administer the morphine. Meanwhile, I'll explain the fracture to you and the next steps."

Her eyes open, then narrow at the images. A gasp escapes her mouth as she scans the breaks in her arm bones. For a moment, her in-charge demeanor drops, replaced by a small, sad female.

My heart goes out to her. The urge to comfort coming from out of nowhere.

"You had a nasty fall. I'm sure it must shock you even as a doctor. But it'll be all right, Natalie. I'll help you," I say as I offer her a comforting smile.

Her head jerks up to bring her gaze to where I tower over her at six feet, six inches. Gone is the vulnerability. Onyx daggers hurtle towards me as she sits up straight. Only a flicker of pain appears before she shutters her eyes.

"I do not need your *help*, Doctor Ingolf. Your medical attention to my arm will suffice. So, get on with it," she snaps. The curtain draws back, and the nurse steps through. His eyes dart between the two of us. She shifts her gaze to him, and her eyes drop to the morphine bag in his hand. Relief floods her face. "Thank you, nurse. There's one step in my treatment."

Well, fuck me.

My inner Alpha Dom gives me a dour face, and my wolf flicks his tail. Fine, two can play this game…

"Dr. Moore, I will reset the bones and place your arm in

a soft cast to allow room for swelling. You will return tomorrow for a fiberglass cast worn during the healing period—typically twelve weeks. More than likely, you will require physical therapy to regain proper use of the limb. The option to see an orthopedist to further your care lies with you. Do you understand?"

She blinks at my dominance. I catch a glimpse of submissive behavior as her eyes lower in deference with a nod.

"Words, Dr. Moore. I will have your verbal response."

This time, her mouth gapes as her eyes jump to my face. She studies me a moment. Emotions war in their dark depths—surprise, reluctance, confusion, finally irritation. Her chin lifts in the air. She scoffs.

"*Yes*, Dr. Ingolf."

My cock twitches of its own accord. I do my best to ignore the instant desire to punish her for continued bratty behavior.

An erotic vision of her torso braced against the bed, hospital gown flipped over her back, bare ass exposed, and her feet spread wide emerges in my mind. My palm itches to spank her soundly. It lands on the fleshy portion of a round globe with a resounding THWACK. A warm crimson shade blooms around my hand as I hold the heat in. She tosses her mane of ink black hair with a swath of white and cries out in wild abandon as her arousal flares. A succession of spanks lifts her to dance on tiptoe. She pants as aromatic slick slides down her inner thighs from her dripping pink pussy to puddle on the floor—

"Dr. Ingolf?"

Damn! Not again, Rust.

I shake my head to dispel the highly inappropriate vision, then turn to the nurse. I shift on my feet to adjust my burgeoning erection down my inner thigh. Thank fuck the white coat hides my cock. I use the patient file as an additional shield in front of my crotch. Then school my face despite the heat on my cheeks and clear my throat.

"Pardon. What did you say?"

In my periphery, Dr. Moore tilts her head as she inspects me. Onyx eyes narrow. Full lips purse.

The nurse eyes me, too. But he doesn't comment on my lack of attention. Instead, he tips his chin towards the IV pole.

"I administered the morphine drip. Her pain level on a scale of one to ten dropped to a four. She's ready for you to reset the bones. I can get the supplies you need."

"Excellent, thank you," I respond and turn to the patient —*not your fantasy lover, Rust.* "Dr. Moore, we will proceed..."

*N*ATALIE

D*R*. I*NGOLF RILES ME.*

"I'm sure it must shock you even as a doctor... I'll help you."

"Do you understand?"

"Words, Dr. Moore. I will have your verbal response."

Who the hell does he think he is?! So condescending! I'm not some damsel in distress who needs a knight to ride up on his steed to save her from a horrible plight. Well, sort of. But that's beside the point!

I'm a doctor. His equal. He owes me respect. The same he would afford a male doctor in my place. Not make me feel small and dependent upon the heroic Dr. Ingolf!

Males. They always put themselves above females. Think they know better for us than we do for ourselves. Speak to us in any manner they choose. Expect us to bow down to them. Controlling so and so Dr. Ingolf!

And no, his dazzling golden-flecked hazel eyes do not make my heart flutter in the least. Nor do my fingers flex to remove the hair tie and tangle in his thick, shoulder-length hair the color of dark ginger. His innate air of command does absolutely nothing for my nether bits.

All I experience is annoyance added to my pain.

"Ooooo!"

His hands pause as he realigns the bones in my arm. Even with the morphine drip direct in my vein, the movement of the fractured bones proves excruciating. No matter the tenderness with which Dr. Ingolf handles my arm, it still aches. Badly.

My enhanced wolf healing ability spoiled me. In all my youth of racing up steep mountainsides, leaping over felled trees in the forest, and charging across open fields, not one scrape or sprain set me back. Within hours, I healed completely. Even the scars faded to nothing. And I was off for another romp with my friends. Blissfully unaware of the amount of suffering my body could experience without my enhanced nature.

"Are you still with me, Dr. Moore?"

My eyes peek open at the sound of Dr. Ingolf's smooth baritone voice. *Those* eyes scan my face to gauge my discomfort. I whimper. Lost for a moment in their depths, I stare, no longer mindful of my disdain for the male. Until he opens his mouth again...

"The morphine only dulls the pain so much. Of course, it hurts. It's not easy."

Gah!

I growl low in my throat as my eyes narrow on him. I want to gnash my teeth. On his arm! Damn the male for sounding just like Sam! Unbelievable. Obnoxious. Rude. Oaf!

The descriptions roll nonstop in my mind as I grind my molars to prevent another whimper from my mouth. I will not give the good doctor any satisfaction of witnessing my torture, only for him to say something patronizing. Bedside manner, my ass.

I won't even close my eyes. Instead, my gaze flits about the curtained area as I tune into my surroundings. A baby cries to my right. Its father's murmurs of loving words reach my ears. Across from me, a human male in his late thirties holds his head between his hands. The nurse beside him asks questions about his motorcycle accident. A doctor walks past, trailed by interns. A female answers her question with confidence. While a scowl forms on a male's face. I roll my eyes in disgust. Gah!

"I realigned the bones. Next step in your treatment, the placement of the posterior long arm splint."

Without glancing at Dr. Ingolf, I nod and continue my observations of the busy ER. Out of the corner of my eye, I notice a slight smirk on his handsome face. Masculine with angular bone structure yet with soft, full, kissable lips. WHAT?!?!?!

It has to be the morphine kicking in for real now. The drug robbing me of all sensibility and restraint. I bite back a curse. The gods help me!

Fortunately, a commotion at the entrance to the ER distracts me. Three nurses rush past my curtained area while an EMT shouts for help. A female's cries mingle with the calls for a doctor STAT.

Dr. Ingolf's hands pause as they adjust the last strap on the splint. He cocks his head as though listening to something. His nostrils flare. A glow appears in his hazel eyes. He turns to the nurse.

"The incoming patient requires my expertise—"

"Let me guess, your gut instinct tells you?" Dr. Ingolf nods in response, and the nurse continues. "A lot of patients owe their lives to your gut instinct, doctor."

"True. And Dr. Moore is stable. You can put the sling in place and discharge her pain meds and a list of the orthopedic doctors," he says hurriedly. He glances at me, nods, and rushes towards the new patient.

At last, he's gone.

But why the hell do I feel at a loss?

Get a grip, Nat. What is this? Emergency Room Stockholm Syndrome, or what?

I barely listen as the nurse speaks to me. Carefully, he places the sling over my head to rest at my neck and loops it around the soft cast. A few adjustments, and I'm all set.

When he asks if I have someone who can take me home, I shake my head and yawn. The morphine and the late hour make me sleepy. He tells me to wait a bit, and I settle against the bed. My eyes shut.

"—still here? Did something happen after I left her with you?"

"No, Dr. Ingolf. She doesn't have anyone to take her home. I didn't want her to go alone, considering she only came in with a robe on. Plus, she's a hospital doctor. I felt responsible for her safety. I'm leaving now and can offer her a ride home."

"No, I'll do it. I left so abruptly, I owe it to her to check in."

My fuzzy mind absorbs the conversation on the other side of the drawn curtain. But I can't believe Dr. Ingolf just offered to drive me home. I should protest. However, I don't want to get in a rideshare with only my robe and the hospital socks. It has to be after midnight by now.

As my hand slides across the sheet in search of my mobile, the curtain parts. Dr. Ingolf strides in.

"Hello again, Dr. Moore. The nurse tells me you adjusted well to the splint. How do you feel after some rest?"

"H—Hello," I say with a dry mouth, then swallow to try again. "Hello, Dr. Ingolf. Fine, thank you. And I'll accept your offer of a ride home. I'm not inclined to take a rideshare at the moment. If you give me a second, I'll be ready to go. Oh, and thank you."

The little smirk appears on *those* lips again.

I ignore it and wiggle my way to the edge of the bed. Immediately, he reaches out to grasp my good arm. But I wave him off. Let's not go overboard with accepting his help.

He inclines his head and steps away. The curtain falls back in place.

Once again, a twinge of loss gnaws at me. I berate myself as I slip the hospital gown off and replace it with the robe. One arm through the sleeve and the other side draped over my shoulder. I tighten the belt. A glance down at my feet, and I shrug. I'll just have to make do with the socks and watch out for sharp objects.

A rumbling chuckle meets my ears as I step from the curtained area.

With a hip leaned against the nurse's station, Dr. Ingolf laughs with a young brunette. She bats her long eyelashes at him as her hand reaches to slap his forearm coyly. Their heads dip. His mouth goes to her ear. She covers her mouth with a dainty hand and giggles. She. Giggles. Typical male doctor, female nurse flirtation. Gah!

Just what I needed to witness to eliminate any ridiculous stirrings of attraction towards *Dr.* Ingolf. With a smirk of my own, I step forward.

"Ready," I say loudly.

CHAPTER 4

atalie

"THANK YOU AND ENJOY YOUR DAY."

I smile at the hospital dispensary pharmacist and pivot, only to bounce off a solid wall. A white coat over a pair of green scrubs blocks me. Hands steady me. Who the hell?

My head snaps back and up, up, up to find Dr. Ingolf staring at me questioningly. His hazel gaze flits from me to the pharmacist and lands on the bag in my hand before returning to my face.

I tighten my grip on my medicines as my lip curls defensively. Then I think about it and relax my features, offering him a cordial smile. No need to set off alarms with him regarding the contents of my bag.

Two days passed since my fall and the first I've been able to leave my apartment for the hospital. The ride home with Dr. Ingolf proved challenging.

He insisted upon carrying me from the ER to his SUV. *I don't want you stepping on glass and cutting your foot, Dr. Moore.*

And you don't want additional hours in the ER unnecessarily, do you? So much bigger than me and dominant, I had no choice but to let him have his way.

At the SUV, he placed me on the passenger seat and put the safety belt across my chest. I bit my lower lip when his knuckles grazed the curve of my breast. Instantly, the nipple beaded at his unintentional touch. He maintained a straight face. But I swore his eyes glowed. When he shut the passenger door, I moved as close to it as possible without plastering myself to the rich wood inlay. Being naked beneath my robe disinclined me from getting too close to him.

However, his masculine scent engulfed me—citrusy, musky, and spicy. Tempting. I let the window down and used the excuse of needing fresh air after all the time in the ER. He nodded with a slight smirk. I stared out the window and did my best to ignore the sexual attraction.

He stuck to generic questions about where I was from, how long I'd been at the hospital, did I like Miami so far. I skipped over details to my past and stuck with my college and med school period through the present. Very easy and detached conversation. Just what I preferred.

Once we arrived at my apartment building, he climbed out of the SUV and jogged around its front to open my door. With a firm grip around my waist and under my thighs, he hoisted me from the seat. For a second, our eyes connected. I was lost. Again. Fortunately, the spell broke when he asked me to push the door shut. The soft thud reminded me to squash any intention beyond doctor-patient care. All the better!

Despite my protest I could make it to my apartment from the lobby, he ignored me and strode to the elevators. With a scowl, I pressed the call button and the floor button once inside. Not wanting to add to the intimate connection of me being held bridal style in the confines of the elevator, my gaze glued to the floor indicator.

His warm breath tickled the top of my head. I ignored it. But the strong pulse of his heart against my breast caused tingles to zing throughout my body. The temptation to snuggle against him almost won. Fortunately, the doors slid open, and he strode into the hallway.

At my front door, I typed the code onto the electronic lock panel and pushed the handle. He stepped inside and glanced around. A frown marred his handsome face at the sight of the boxes. I gave up protesting at being carried and simply pointed to the bedroom door. He settled me on the bed and left for the kitchen. A bottle of water on the nightstand and instructions to take the pain medication every eight hours as needed and to keep my arm dry and elevated were his last words.

When I heard the door shut, I used the app on my mobile to activate the lock. With a sigh, I snuggled against the fluffy pillow—not Dr. Ingolf's solid muscular body.

Unlike now.

"Dr. Moore, good to see you getting about. I notice you wear the fiberglass cast. How's your arm?"

My cordial smile widens—more in relief he didn't call me out for the odd mixture of medicines he must have overhead me requesting based on his questioning reaction.

"Better, thank you, Dr. Ingolf. I just left the orthopedist. If we were in high school, I'd ask you to sign my cast," I respond with a grin. "Instead, I'll thank you again. You impressed her with your realignment of the fractured bones. As you said, twelve weeks should mend my arm."

His hazel eyes dance as he returns my grin. The overhead lights catch the shimmering golden flecks.

"Good to hear I know what I'm doing after all! Even better, you're well. I couldn't help but observe the boxes in your living room. Let me know if you want help to unpack, especially with your arm—"

He reaches into the pocket of his white coat and withdraws a pager. His eyebrows knit as he scans the screen. A hand rakes through his loose hair.

"Listen, I gotta go. You know where to reach me, *Dr. Moore*," he says as he rushes off.

I watch him jog down the corridor. His dark ginger hair and the white coat fly. Long muscular legs carry him away with ease. He's at least a foot taller than anyone else. So, it's easy to follow his path through the patients and the hospital staff. A few nurses stop to ogle him. My returned enhanced hearing picks up their comments.

"Dr. Ingolf is by far the hottest doctor in the hospital!"

"I wish I were his emergency..."

"What I wouldn't give for Dr. Ingolf to give me some tender loving care. Talk about a steamy bedside manner!"

A couple of them giggle behind their hands like starstruck fangirls.

Gah!

I shake my head, then pivot and stride in the opposite direction. I'm not due back in the office until the day after tomorrow. Which is perfect since I still need a few more medicines to complete my serum formula. The pharmacist expects the order to arrive that day or the next one. I just have to lie low in my apartment. The last thing I need is to come across a wolf shifter. Unconsciously, my feet hurry towards the exit as I clutch my precious cargo to my chest.

I make it home with no incident after I pick up Thai food for lunch. A glance around at the loads of boxes and I just might take him up on his offer to help. I make my way to the bedroom and store my medicine supply on a lower shelf in the closet—less risk of another mishap. Then change into my robe and settle on the sofa to binge on food and Netflix.

But my mind drifts to Dr. Ingolf. I searched for him on the hospital website. What else can I do all day with a bum arm? My curiosity revealed more about the good doctor. Rust suits him with his dark ginger hair. A rich shade that sets off his golden-flecked hazel eyes as he stares at the camera in his bio photo. Those clean-shaven, chiseled cheekbones and square jaw give him a strong masculine appearance. The full lips curve in a slight smirk to provide a glimpse into his confidence. Combined with his degrees from Vanderbilt University, published works, and multiple accolades, those in need of his expertise as a critical care surgeon can rest assured, they're in excellent hands.

Large hands with tapered fingers. Skillful hands. Hands I can imagine on more than just my arm.

The television screen fades as I focus on a revised version of Rust driving me home from the hospital.

His eyes flick between me and the road ahead as he weaves through traffic. I squirm in the seat to ease the carnal ache in my core. The lustful glint in his amber eyes shines in the light from intermittent streetlamps through the windshield. The corner of his full lips quirks up at my breathy moan.

A hand lowers to my thigh. Naughty fingers slip beneath my robe. The tips seek my swollen clit nestled within my folds, already slick with arousal. On a needy moan, my legs spread, giving them better access.

The thumb pad circles the sensitive nubbin, applying more pressure with each pass. My hips rotate in sync with its erotic rhythm. Moans and musk fill the interior of the SUV. Long fingers breech my folds. My pussy walls clench around them, drawing them deeper into my greedy channel. I drop my head against the headrest and arch my back as the orgasm dances closer.

A sharp pinch to my clit, and my thighs slam together, trapping his skillful hand as I buck against it. It's so intense, I damn near levitate. Stars flash behind my closed eyelids while my mouth opens in a silent scream.

As the ripples dwindle, I sag limp against the seat, thigh muscles slack, heart pounding. My breath comes out in warm pants. A cloud of condensation ebbs and recedes on the window. Eyes flutter closed.

"Such a good girl," Rust croons as he pats my pussy, then licks my juices from his fingers.

The television reappears as the fantasy fades. I blink, disoriented. Reality returns.

I growl and take a forceful bite of food.

Do *not* go there, Nat!

To open myself up to dating leads to love, then either or both parties wanting a committed relationship. One that leads to marriage, then to the male making demands of the female. He controls what she does with her life and her body. Forces the female to put her desires aside for his wants, including children, whether or not she wants them. Her health matters little as long as she produces.

Sam and Amanda—along with other mates in my former pack—are prime examples of that destructive relationship. The anguish he forced my sister to deal with breaks my heart. Her death and her pup's stillbirth finish any relationship I could ever want, even before it starts.

Sure, our father wasn't as extreme as Sam and his cohorts. But Dad persuaded Mom to mate with him despite them not being a fated pair. He was older and—as I learned later—didn't want to endure the madness unmated males experience after a certain time without a mate. He also wanted an heir to replace him as Alpha. They tried many times for male pups, resulting in my Mom's decline in health. A situation exacerbated by the unexpected affliction years later. So, once again, his needs supplanted my Mom's life.

I swipe tears from my eyes and reaffirm I want no parts of a male in my life, being pregnant, or having pups.

Not happening! Not now, not ever. And most especially not with *Rust Dr. McDreamy Ingolf*!

CHAPTER 5

Natalie

"I HAVE *a date with a guy my sister's husband knows. They work together at the firm. She swears the guy's cute and nice. Not at all like the one she hooked me up with the last time..."*

"This had to be the longest day ever! I cannot wait to get out of this waist trainer. Hourglass figure be damned!"

"Yes, sweetheart, Mommy will be home soon... No, you can't eat cookies before dinner..."

"Let's grab a drink after work..."

My palms press against my ears to lessen the banter from everyone around me. All. The. Way. In. My. Office. With. The. Door. Shut.

Gah!

Another day ushers in the return or improvement of a wolf sense. Some good, some not so great. Less pain in my arm and more shoulder mobility allows me to cover my ears. The healing process speeds up—though not quite as fast as during my full shifter days.

Two days ago, my wolf hearing restored. Also, not fully. I picked up the comments about Dr. Ingolf in the corridor easily—the level low. But now, the conservations around my office bombard my brain. A constant buzz I can't avoid. Not to mention the everyday sounds of doors closing, the clicks of high heels on the tile floor, papers rustling. They're all amplified, especially since it's been years since I had powerful hearing. It'll take a period of adjustment to reacclimate. In the meantime, I'll pick up ear plugs…

A less invasive buzzing in my white coat pocket draws my attention from completing notes in the day's patient files. I'm surprised Paloma Sabela didn't ring my office landline instead of paging me. But the message isn't from the department secretary. I grab my mobile and dial the number quickly.

"Hello, this is Dr. Moore. What's going on?"

"Dr. Moore, are you still at the hospital?" The ER nurse asks, then continues when I confirm. "Thank goodness! We need you in the ER STAT. A pregnant woman arrived with a knife wound to her abdomen…"

I fling the door open and race down the corridor as I listen to the details. Thandie steps from an exam room, and I yell I'm needed in the ER. She nods and rushes to the OB-GYN reception area to alert the staff. I end the call before stepping onto the elevator. My eyes close as I gather myself to prepare for a delicate case. Those around me disappear as I turn inwards and focus on my breathing.

The computer-generated voice announces the ground floor as the doors ding open. I rush out as I exclaim ER emergency and bypass the other passengers. My feet fly. I reach the ER and rush towards the operating room. The nurse waves me over and helps me scrub for surgery in the OR anteroom. I remove the sling from the damn cast to maneuver my arm as best I can. I ignore the slight twinge of pain. Patient first.

"Dr. Moore here. Give me an update," I announce as I stride through the door held open by the nurse.

Beeps from the machinery indicate a weak but steady heartbeat and an erratic one. My eyes go to the female patient. Tatters of her bloodied clothing lie on the floor. The metallic odor of fresh blood invades my nose. Her eyes remain closed in a pale face. An intubation tube protrudes from her mouth to assist with her breathing. The size of her belly puts her in the third trimester. I pray to the gods the knife missed the baby, and it's developed enough to withstand an emergency C-section. The mother, we'll see.

"Dr. Moore."

My eyes jerk to my left at the sound of Dr. Ingolf's baritone voice. Only his hazel eyes and his brawny frame offer distinguishing characteristics as the surgical cap, mask, and visor obscure his face.

"I stabilized the woman as best as I can, given the location and the severity of the knife wound. So, you'll have to work quickly to save the baby..."

As the lead surgeon, he goes on to update me while I check the baby's vitals. Thirty minutes later, I deliver the baby and close the C-section incisions. The knife nicked the little girl's shoulder and narrowly missed her head. The pediatric surgeon takes over the baby's care while Dr. Ingolf tends to the mother. I standby in case he needs help.

His skill level amazes me as he works swiftly to repair the damage inflicted by the knife. At times, his hands blur with movement. His intense focus serves the patient well. Not even a leaking abdominal aorta frazzles him. Less than half an hour later, the nurse rolls the mother from the operating room. She'll live to love her baby. Dr. Ingolf turns to me and smiles.

And damn if my heart doesn't flutter. A radiance about him after a successful surgery highlights the gold in his eyes. They glow internally. Enthralling me.

"You impress me, Dr. Moore," he says as he strides towards me. An air of confidence and masculine swagger exude from his being. Again, nurses peek at him behind their visors. But his eyes remain glued to me.

He leans over and his hand reaches out. My heart skips a beat as I gasp. He stifles a chuckle and inclines his head to the right of me.

"After you, Dr. Moore."

I glance over my shoulder to find his hand on the OR door. Color floods my cheeks as I lower my head and mutter a curse. For a moment, I thought he was reaching out to touch me. Get it together, Nat!

This time, he laughs out loud.

My head snaps up to find his hazel eyes twinkling.

"I think you got it together, Dr. Moore. I'm sure the mother will appreciate you saving her unborn child."

My cheeks burn as my gaze drops to his feet—enormous feet. How the hell did I speak aloud?! And why am I acting like those nurses?! But worse because I. Don't. Want. Him.

I nod and pivot, ducking beneath his muscular arm to hasten into the anteroom. He follows me to the biohazard bin and hamper. I avert my eyes as he removes the bloodied apron and the surgical gown. Briefly I imagine he strips to nothing but smooth skin and chiseled muscles, then beckons me. With a shake of my head, I toss my soiled garments in the appropriate place. Last warning, Natalie.

Determined not to make a further fool of myself, I remain silent as we move to the sink. Elbow to elbow, we wash our hands. Dr. Ingolf says nothing. But I sense he watches me out of the corner of his eye. Hurriedly, I dry my hands and turn to leave.

Others around us exchange words as they move about the anteroom. Their relief is palpable. I smile at them, also thankful we saved the mother and her baby. The anesthesiologist catches my eye. He saunters over.

"Dr. Moore, you did a phenomenal job with the baby. Smart and decisive. Are you done with your shift? A few of us are going for drinks. I'd love for you to come."

I detect the rapid beat of his heart. He's too eager for me to join him, which only means he wants more than I'm willing to give. No point in encouraging him. I open my mouth to respond when a muscular arm brushes against me.

"Actually, Dr. Moore and I have plans."

I glance up to find Dr. Ingolf towering over both of us. With a nod, he places a hand on my lower back and guides me towards the double doors. I offer a smile to the anesthesiologist. He stares mouth agape.

Out of earshot, Dr. Ingolf says, "I sensed you didn't want to go with him but didn't know how to decline without seeming distant. You can thank me for the save by having dinner with me."

I tilt my head back, surprised at his demand. The corner of his mouth curves in a smirk as his eyes glint with mischief. I can't help but to laugh at his gutsy move.

"Oh, you're good, Dr. Ingolf. Maybe too good. But I didn't want to join him, and I am hungry. So, I'll accept your demand to thank you over dinner."

He chuckles, then raises his hand. A black strip of cloth dangles from his fingertips.

~

DYLAN

. . .

She frowns at the cloth and shrugs a shoulder.

"Your cast sling."

Her onyx eyes widen as her mouth opens on a gasp. Color suffuses her cheeks.

The scent of her distress confuses me as much as her ability to move her arm with such ease mere days after her fall. I didn't want to distract her during the surgeries by asking about it. Rather, I explained it as her running on adrenaline, more concerned about the patients than her own wellbeing. However, I find it odd she left the strap on the counter.

"You've been using your arm despite the fractures."

Her face shutters as she reaches up to take the sling. As she places it around her neck and slips her arm through it, she responds in a clipped manner.

"Yes, obviously, Dr. Ingolf. I find it more important to focus on my patient's life than to worry about a bit of pain I experience. I do not appreciate you questioning me. Good night, Dr. Ingolf."

She spins on her heel and marches off.

My eyes narrow as I scent the air. She's holding back on the full truth. And I want to know why.

"Dr. Moore, my apologies for coming across as nosy. That was not my intent. Your rapid recovery surprises me. As a medical professional, I'm sure you must understand," I say when I catch up to her. Her pace slows, and I take advantage. "But you can't tell me good night until after dinner. That's ill form for a debt owed."

She swings her head around and scoffs. Her waist-long ponytail slaps me in the mouth better than her dainty hand ever could. A smile tugs at the corners of her lush mouth. Then a giggle bursts from between her lips. She raises a hand and covers her mouth.

"How apropos, Dr. Ingolf. Hopefully, that'll teach you to open your mouth unnecessarily."

I chuckle wickedly and lean down to whisper in her ear.

"Were we in another place, *Dr. Moore*, I would show you exactly what I do with a long ponytail."

She jerks back as she sucks in a ragged breath. Her pupils dilate to pure black. Cheeks redden a deep rose I'd love to see on her ass from my palm. A vision of my cock buried within the complete O of her mouth leads to a barely audible rumble in my chest.

Her eyes widen to inky pools.

For a moment, I wonder if she heard the sound, or if it's her response to my filthy words. Fuck unprofessional. This female drives me feral.

Again, I take advantage of her delay and place a hand on her lower back. She doesn't pull away as I guide her through the busy ER. I check out of my shift and head towards the exit. I don't trust she'll follow me once in her car. So, I stride towards my Range Rover P530 First Edition (LWB). The luxury SUV serves as my preferred ride for hospital duty. Fully loaded, but not one of my flashy supercars. I press the key fob, and the headlights illuminate the area as the engine purrs to life.

"Hold on. I have my car. I'll follow you," Dr. Moore says as her heels dig in. "It's just over there."

I tsk, and her elegantly arched eyebrows draw together.

"You may think I'm a nosy SOB. But I assure you, I am a gentleman. We will drive to the restaurant in my Rover. After, I'll bring you to your car and follow you home to ensure you arrive safely," I say in a tone that brooks no room for debate.

She lowers her eyes as her teeth tug on her lower lip. My cock twitches at another show of her reluctant submissiveness. Better still at the delicious vision of those teeth grazing my thick shaft to my plum tip before her tongue laps pre-cum from my slit. Oh, the things I would do with the feisty female. Her gaze lifts to mine.

"Fine."

I nod and move forward. Inwardly, my Alpha Dom smirks, and my wolf's tongue lolls out hungrily.

"After a complicated surgery, I'm famished, and one spot always satisfies my needs," I say as my eyes flick from the road to Dr. Moore. Her onyx orbs shine in the darkened interior of the SUV as she stares back at me. Their glow surprises me. As I open my mouth to comment, she speaks.

"And what spot would that be, Dr. Ingolf?"

I blink and return my gaze to the road ahead as the traffic light changes from red to green. The niggle in the back of my mind dissipates with the flow of cars.

"Ah, yes, Prime 112. A traditional steakhouse with a modern touch and contemporary menu known as one of the best in the world," I say, then glance at her. "Do you eat meat?"

She stifles a giggle and nods.

"I do and could use a tasty cut. My appetite for beef increased recently," she responds with an enigmatic smile. Her fingertips reach for the console touchscreen, and she tilts her head. "Do you mind if we play some music? It soothes me post-surgery."

I agree, thinking I could help her with that even better. She scrolls through the satellite stations until she selects one, then sits back, eyes closed, effectively ending the conversation.

When we arrive at the restaurant, the valet helps her from the SUV as I round the front. She thanks him with a warm smile. For a second, I wish she offered the beatific expression to me. As though sensing my thoughts, she shifts her gaze to mine, and her smile widens. Fuck if my heart doesn't stutter. I ignore it and place my hand on the small of her back, guiding her to the restaurant's doors.

"Dr. Ingolf! What a lovely surprise."

The host steps from behind the podium and extends his hand in greeting. We shake, and I introduce him to Dr. Moore. He double kisses her cheeks, then leaves us to get my usual table ready. It's a prime spot within the kitchen, affording the opportunity to watch the chef and her team prepare tantalizing dishes.

I guide Dr. Moore to the bar to wait for the host's return. She glances around, and I see the space through her eyes.

Typical of a top-tier steakhouse, it features customary dark wood and exposed-brick walls. But it stands apart for its sleek and superb design with white leather and low lighting resulting in a sexy decor. Up-tempo music in the background makes for a lively vibe. An eclectic mix of ritzy patrons mingle at the bar and dine at the tables. With business casual attire expected some of the clientele raise eyebrows at our scrubs. But I could give a fuck.

I pull out a Lucite and white leather high chair for Dr. Moore. She smiles graciously as she perches on the seat. I sit beside her and signal the bartender. She comes over, and we order drinks. I raise my tumbler of aquavit.

"Here's to saving lives and to new relationships."

She frowns as her lips part, then shakes her head and raises her mojito.

"Cheers, Dr. Ingolf."

I cock an eyebrow and place a hand on her forearm to stop her sip.

"Don't you think we're on a first-name basis now?"

Once again, her onyx eyes glint in the dimness as that mysterious smile tips her lush lips. She slips her arm from beneath my hand and brings the glass to her mouth. The tip of her little pink tongue moistens the rim before she sips.

My cock throbs, intrigued by the erotic move.

"Yes, *Rust*."

Fuck. Me. Or. What.

CHAPTER 6

ust

THE FULL MOON above casts shadows from the towering pine trees onto the ground as I pad through the dense undergrowth. A barred owl hoots perched on a bough. I glance up. It spreads its wings and leaps into the air. The predator soars before it swoops down. A rustling in a bush and a shriek followed by silence indicate it found its evening meal. The metallic scent of fresh blood fills my nostrils. They flare as I inhale, savoring the aroma.

My turn.

Deep in the Everglades, I hunt.

I trot ahead, careful not to disturb the twigs and rocks beneath my paws. My eyes scan the surrounding thicket. Ears swivel to capture even the most subtle sound. My head swings to the right at a low snarl. The moonlight glints in a Florida panther's eyes. Hidden in the scrub, it watches me. I issue a challenging growl as I stand my ground.

Nearly twice the size of a regular wolf, I have no fear of the night's new predator. Thick red fur covers my massive body. Vicious fangs dripping with saliva appear as my lip curls. I snap my teeth as hackles raise. Paws stamp the ground. Another ferocious growl, and the panther turns tail with a disgruntled hiss. It slinks away further into the underbrush. I watch its retreat still alert should it circle back. Satisfied it's gone for good, I prowl on in search of my evening meal.

Animals detect the presence of an apex predator and scurry from my path. I bide my time and lope along. I allow my wolf to decide our route, using his enhanced sense of smell as a guide. My nose twitches as it catches hints of a hare nestled in its form, a few white-tailed deer gathered beneath a pine tree, and rodents in their tunnels. I don't have an appetite for them tonight. We move on.

The pine flatlands give way to a marsh. The roots of coastal mangroves provide cover for West Indian manatees and leatherback turtles. I push through the sawgrass, searching the still water for any signs of alligators. I have no desire to tangle with one, especially alone without my pack.

None seen—although they can lurk beneath the surface —I approach the water cautiously. Eyes dart about as I lower my snout for a refreshing drink. A few laps and ripples appear on the moonlit surface. I jump back just as the might jaws gape open where my head bent low to the water. A growl rumbles from my chest as the alligator slithers back beneath the surface. Yellow eyes stare until the water engulfs its giant head. With a last glance, I trot back to the tree line far from the water's edge.

My ears prick up at snuffling beyond a fallen evergreen tree. I lift my head to scent the air. A feral boar! Just the challenge I seek for my meal.

Well aware of their dangerous tusks, I give it a wide

berth before I move closer. Remaining downwind to avoid it detecting my scent, I pad towards its rear. Also, out for its evening meal, the large boar lowers its head to use its tusks to forage for underground roots. Distracted, it doesn't notice me stalk, then pounce on its back. My canines sink into its neck as my claws dig into its flanks. Blood fills my mouth.

It squeals and bucks. I cling to it and shake my head, embedding my sharp teeth deep into its thick neck. Coarse hair pokes inside my mouth. But I refuse to let go. Snarls match its squeals. It drops to the side in an attempt to dislodge me. I use my back feet to clamber up. My unyielding grip ensures the feral boar rises with me.

My teeth meet its spine. I give my head a final jerk. The vertebrae snap. The boar collapses to the ground with a grunt. I loosen my hold and sit on my haunches panting from the effort to down the beast. My head goes back, and I issue a triumphant howl.

Sated, I find a stream to clean my fur and to rinse my mouth. As I shake remnants of water from my fur, my wolf whimpers. I glance around and find nothing of concern. A breeze blows across my fur like a lover's caress. My body shudders with instant carnal desire.

The touch of wind carries a scent I was born smelling the moment I took my first breath as a newborn pup. Earth, ferns, and fir trees mix with a hint of vanilla carried on the cool ocean breeze. The unique scent of my fated mate.

At last!

My heart races as I prowl in a slow circle to target her unique scent's direction. The low whine of my wolf increases to a joyful bark when the scent grows stronger further into the pine flat lands. I set off at a brisk trot.

Small animals scurry from my path. But they have

nothing to fear. I'm on the hunt for my fated mate. She will receive my bite, not them.

Her unique scent beckons me with a wispy curl leading from her to my nose. The closer I approach, the stronger the pull.

My cock thickens and lengthens to the point of pain. Seed drips from the bulbous tip. The serum to lodge my scent beneath her skin to mark her as mine permanently coats my canines. My body prepares to claim my fated mate.

Up ahead, my keen eyesight spots a flash of white amongst a cluster of dense pine trees. The moonlight reflects off the fur. As I draw closer, her entire body comes into view. A gorgeous, sleek she-wolf with midnight fur on her body and a white streak on her head. Unaware of my presence, she continues to dig, then to drag fallen boughs to cover the spot.

My wolf howls just as I detect more than earth, fern, and fir trees mixed with a hint of vanilla. A musky aroma fills my nostrils. My fated mate is in heat!

I bound into the small clearing beneath the pine trees where she prepares her nest. Her head jerks in my direction. A whine greets me as she backs away, frightened by my sudden appearance. I rumble deep in my chest to soothe her.

Instead, her body tenses. Dark eyes dart around the space, seeking an escape. Before she can move a muscle, I block her with my much larger body. She bares her teeth with a snarl. I return a dominating growl and stand taller. She bows her head and drops to her back. Vulnerable belly and throat bared to me.

I nuzzle her with my snout. Gone is the growl replaced by the soothing rumble. She acquiesces with a soft whine. I nudge her flank for her to rise. She rolls to her paws and watches me with her head lowered. I prowl around her in a circle. The rumble in my chest remains constant. She stands still. I breathe in her unique scent, mixed with the musk of her heat. Once again, I nuzzle her body—neck, flank, base of tail.

My mind reels. After all these years of aching for my fated mate and fear of succumbing to madness if I didn't find her, she stands before me, ready for me to claim and breed her. Thank the gods. My wolf howls in agreement.

With a possessive growl, I rise onto my hind legs and wrap my front ones around her waist and back legs. My thighs bracket hers.

She lifts her tail.

So, ready to breach my fated mate, I plunge my cock deep inside of her. She whimpers and paws the ground with her front feet. My feral growls fill the balmy night air as I pump my hips forcibly. Her slick eases my brutal strokes. As my heavy balls draw up, I open my mouth wide. The serum drips from my canines onto her midnight fur. The drops shine in the moonlight like a bull's-eye for my mark.

With a savage growl, I lower my mouth at the juncture where her neck meets her shoulder. I clamp down, piercing her flesh. She howls and wriggles. My front legs tighten around her waist as I grind my jaw to deepen my claiming bite.

The base of my cock expands to form my knot. Her pussy contracts as she whimpers from the painful stretch. We lock together. Molten heat explodes from my cock to fill her womb with my seed. I throw my head back and howl to the moon above. She joins me for a carnal song.

During the fifteen minutes my knot ties us together, I rumble in my chest to soothe her as she quakes beneath me. Once my knot deflates, we separate. I lick where my claiming bite left blood on her fur, then her snout. She returns my affection with licks to my head and flank before she limps to the nest. I follow close behind.

She curls up on the boughs, and I lie beside her. As my eyes drift closed, a chirping interrupts my slumber. I glance around for the bird with its incessant sound. An irritated growl pours from my mouth.

My hand flings out for my nightstand to stop the morning alarm from my mobile. Then my eyes snap open. I jump up to a sitting position and swivel my head.

Gone are the pine trees and the moonlit clearing beneath them. Instead of a nest made of boughs, tangled sweat-dampened sheets cover my legs. Fresh creamy jizz coats my cock, eight-pack abs, and pecs. Worse yet, my beautiful fated mate isn't curled up beside me, sleepy from my claiming. Aside from me, the king-size bed sits empty. And cold.

What the fuck?!

My damp palms press against my eyelids to clear my head. But the mobile continues to chirp. With an angry growl, I grab the mobile and jab the off button. I toss it onto the bed and throw myself against the pillows. My fists punch the mattress. I roar in frustration.

Only a wet dream. What a fucking tease!

～

*N*ATALIE

"Oooh, *GODS!!!*"

My back bows from the bed as my fingernails claw the sheets and my heels dig into the mattress. An orgasm so intense I lose my vision and my breath as it barrels through me. My body convulses as I fall back to the soaked sheets.

My pussy pulsates with delicious aftershocks. A warm puddle of my arousal lies under my ass.

I open my eyes, panting. My blurry gaze skitters around, expecting to see the giant red wolf amongst unfamiliar pine trees. Instead, my bedroom comes into focus. I cover my sweaty face with shaky hands. A moan slips past my lips as I taste his fur on my tongue, smell his wild musk.

It felt so real. His groin pounding against my rump, driving his ginormous cock deep into my tight pussy. The stretch and burn of his knot. The searing pain of his claiming—

My head snaps up as I touch the spot on my neck where he bit me. Relief washes over me. Nothing there. Even though an ache in the area makes me wince. I shake my head. It wasn't real. Only a dream. Well, nightmare.

"Natalie! You have to get the rest of the medicines. It's your wolf warning you."

I chide myself aloud as I roll from the bed and limp towards the bathroom.

Fuck if I don't feel his cock still inside of me. My pussy clenches at the thought. I growl and yank the glass shower door open. The warm water soothes the aches in my body. But does nothing for the turmoil in my mind.

Tomorrow marks seven days since I dropped the serum to suppress my wolf. And obviously, she's ready to merge with me completely.

But not if I can help it.

On the ride to the hospital, I begin to unwind as the sun warms my skin and the balmy breeze flows over me. At a red traffic light, I tilt my head back and close my eyes to revel in the Miami weather. My enhanced hearing alerts me to the movement of cars way ahead of mine. I take a moment to inhale deeply, then open my eyes on a slow exhalation. My increased sense of smell hasn't returned yet.

But I can detect the salt carried in from the Atlantic Ocean. Such a contrast to the coolness of the Pacific Northwest. And I love it!

Before I head to the OB-GYN department, I pick up coffee and a toasted corn muffin with butter from the hospital's cafeteria. It buzzes with activity. Visitors and staff mill about the glass-enclosed counters to select food and beverages or line up at the checkout. Beside a wall of floor-to-ceiling windows, people sit at tables. Beyond the windows, the view of the interior garden with its colorful flowers and palm trees brings a touch a pleasantness to a place often filled with sadness. I cast a last glance at nature's beauty and stroll towards the registers.

On my way to the elevators, I spot Dr. Ingolf—I mean *Rust*—striding towards the cafeteria. He's so damn handsome. His long, dark ginger hair is loose and glints in the overhead lights. Hazel eyes twinkle as he laughs. Full, kissable lips curve upwards. Broad shoulders fill out his white coat. Even beneath the basic scrubs, the flexing of his muscular thighs appears. Thick thighs save lives. And strong enough to—

Cut it, Nat! That erotic dream has you ramped up. Still.

I shake my head to displace lustful thoughts of the good doctor. With a clear head, I glance back in his direction. He's nearly at the cafeteria doors.

Just as I'm about to raise my hand to catch his attention, I notice a female doctor at his elbow. He leans over and whispers in her ear. A flush blooms on her copper skin as her brown eyes twinkle. She tilts her face up and smiles at him. He smirks as he pushes the door open and steps back to allow her to walk in ahead of him. His eyes follow her. Then he enters the cafeteria, and the door closes.

GAH!

Jealousy surges through me faster than a brushfire of dry

timber. My eyes narrow as my lips purse. A feral growl slips past them. My free hand forms a fist. I want to tear off this stupid cast and fling it at the happy couple. Wild-eyed and snarling, my wolf claws beneath my skin, eager to shred the female to pieces. The level of violence shocks me.

Air! I need fresh air!

I pivot on my heel and rush towards the hospital exit. I battle to restrain my wolf. Never has she behaved wildly uncontrollable. She remains on the fringes of my being and only comes forth when I summon her, then retreats as I bid.

My breath comes in shallow pants. The bustle in the lobby rings in my ears. I cover them and lower my head as my pace increases. I burst through the doors and jog around the corner. My eyes close and chin drops to my heaving chest. I bend my knees and slide down the wall. A tear slips past my eyelashes. Then sobs rack my body.

Gods, how I wish I could have a relationship with a male. Despite my bravado, I secretly yearn for a partner. Someone who cares for me and treats me with respect. Who loves me above all others. Wolves are not meant to be loners. We belong in a pack.

But it's just so fucked up how life treated me. My former pack's mentality damaged me. Ruined me for any possibility of a relationship. My wounded heart aches.

A light tap on my shoulder jolts me.

I lift my tear-filled eyes to find a human male asking if I'm okay. I nod and wave him off.

But I'm not. And it's the fault of my wolf!

Why did she have such a visceral reaction to Rust with that doctor? I had to hold my wolf back or she would have forced a shift. Not at all something I can allow, ever. And definitely not in front of humans. We're taught to control our wolves from the moment we're conscious of their presence within us. What the hell would trigger her?!

Mystified, I dab my face with a napkin from the food bag, then rise. I close my eyes and breathe deeply. Before I go to my office, I'll stop by the dispensary. The gods willing, the delayed medicines arrived. The risk proves too great without my serum.

CHAPTER 7

I smirk at the doctor as we enter the hospital's cafeteria. I have an hour before the start of my shift and decided to grab breakfast. She overhead me telling the ER nurses where to find me and asked to come with. Not one to deny a woman her desires, I welcomed her.

"I think I'll get a breakfast burrito. What about you?"

Undecided, I sniff the air for a scent that piques my tastebuds. Then stand gobsmacked.

Is it possible? Or a vestige from my carnal wet dream?

I spin in a slow circle with my head tilted back, nostrils flared.

Real or fake?

But damned if my wolf senses detect a faint trace of earth, ferns, and fir trees mix with a hint of vanilla carried on the cool ocean breeze. The unique scent of my fated mate on a she-wolf. Here. In the hospital's cafeteria???

Serum coats my canines as they extend to sharp fangs. The beat of my heart quickens and pulses in my ears. I stifle a groan as my cock grows down my inner thigh. Seed beads at the swollen tip. Fists form at my sides to restrain myself from throwing my head back and issuing a call to my fated mate.

Where is she?!

I scan the room. My eyes linger on each female. But none respond to the low rumble in my chest detectable by a she-wolf. She must have come and gone! I dash for the doors, ignoring the doctor's calls of my name. Carnal hunger for my fated mate supplants any need for mere food. My sole intent to find my fated mate. Now.

My wolf takes the lead to track her. The unique scent leads us to the elevators. As I growl in frustration, staring at the eight cars moving between twenty floors and the multitude of people, my wolf yips. I cock my head, then move towards the front doors of the hospital. Again, the scent picks up. Unfortunately, once outside, it dissipates in the wind. I stride back inside and pause, allowing my wolf to search for even the slightest whiff. Only the same trail back to the elevators.

I spend the next ten minutes popping my head into each elevator when it arrives on the ground floor. The humans stare at me, surprised by my unusual behavior. I ignore them.

A quick sniff finds nothing until the last car. The subtle combination of earth, ferns, and fir trees mixed with vanilla lingers in the air. I hurry inside and stand at the front. On each floor, I poke my head out for a quick whiff. Bingo!

Thirteen isn't an unlucky number!

I throw myself off the elevator and rush to the corridor.

It branches in two directions. A few feet down, one proves she didn't pass this way. I retrace my steps and jog to the other wing. The scent increases. And my urge to claim my fated mate rises with it.

My vision tunnels. The rumble in my chest returns. Every female I pass gets an inconspicuous sniff. None in the hallway bears my fated mate's unique scent. I double back and enter the offices. The process repeats. I close the door of a supply closet, then turn to the last door at the end of the corridor.

As I near it, a familiar voice reaches my enhanced ears.

"Are you sure the medicines will arrive this afternoon? I mean, their delivery keeps getting delayed. Is there a way for you to confirm now?"

Natalie? In the dispensary asking about medicines again? An odd assortment of medicines typically not used by OB-GYNs?

The niggling I had the first time I saw her in the dispensary speaking to the pharmacist returns. What the hell would she need them for? Not a patient. And she's not ill. It's highly inappropriate for doctors to use the hospital's dispensary for personal use. What is she up to? That reminds me of the quick recovery of her fractured arm and the glint in her eyes. None of it makes sense. Unless—

I'm so distracted by my thoughts, I don't notice her backing out the door until she bumps into me and yelps. Automatically, my hands reach out to steady her. The moment we connect, a bolt of electricity zings from my fingertips, up my arms, and straight to my pounding heart. A sharp intake of air carries the scent of my fated mate deep into my lungs. My cock twitches and leaks with seed. I growl.

She jerks her head around. Her wide onyx eyes meet my glowing hazel orbs. She gasps and tries to pull away. I tighten my grip and rumble in my chest. Her eyes flutter closed as she sags against me, mouth slack.

I ache to cover it with mine. Instead, I scoop her up and carry her to the empty supply closet. Her eyes pop open, and she protests. I silence her with a low growl. She shivers and glances away. Color suffuses her cheeks. Again, I fight the urge to kiss her and open the door, then flick on the overhead light. I continue to hold her close to my chest even after the door closes behind us.

"Natalie."

Her name comes out rough as my voice thickens with desire. She shivers and squirms. I bury my face in her hair. Then it hits me. Waist-long midnight hair with a snow-white widow's peak, just like the she-wolf in my wet dream. Except it wasn't a dream.

Fated mates often visit the other in dreams before they meet. The frequency and intensity increase the closer to them meeting in real life. A sort of bonding before the actual mate bonding ceremony occurs. In the dreams' vividness, the pair appear to be together in reality, not a dream—wet or otherwise. Sometimes they recognize one another. Often, they're not revealed, somehow shrouded or in wolf form, as with Natalie and me.

Dr. Natalie Moore. My fated mate. Fuck. Who knew? And how did I not detect her all this time?

"Put me down. Now!"

Her shriek rouses me from my musings.

"No!" I growl in response. "Tell me how you're an undetectable she-wolf. Now!"

"I have no idea what you're talking about! Let me go!"

"I will never let you go, Natalie. You are my fated mate. We belong together. You feel it as much as I do. I scent your arousal and hear the fast beat of your heart. The sooner you tell me what you've done, the sooner we can complete our mate bonding ceremony."

She freezes at my words.

I cock my head to the side to glimpse her face. But her hair covers it like a silky curtain. The bitter odor of fear rises in my nostrils. It overrides her arousal. What the fuck?!

"Natalie?"

Suddenly, she bucks her head. It crashes into my nose. Bone shatters as blood gushes. I stumble backwards and lose my hold on her. She slips to her feet and rounds on me. Onyx eyes flash.

"I reject you as my fated mate! I want no parts of you! Keep away from me!" She screams, then bolts for the door.

My hand flings out to grab her, but she wrenches to the side and evades my grasp. The door jerks open. She glares at me over her shoulder.

"I REJECT YOU, RUST INGOLF!"

She darts out the door. It slams shut. The sound of her feet pounding on the floor fades with the distance she puts between us. The thread that binds us snaps.

I throw my head back and howl in anguish, uncaring about the humans outside the door blood dripping down my front. My enhanced healing will repair my nose. But what about my broken heart?

Natalie

I panic.

Pure adrenaline drives me to the max. I run like the hounds of Hell chase me. Too scared Rust will follow me, I skip waiting for an elevator and head for the staircase. I hurtle down three steps at a time until I land on the ground floor. A peek through the door's window confirms Rust isn't lurking around, waiting to drag me away and claim me as his fated mate.

Fated mate!

Just my rotten luck the moment my suppression serum wears off, I stumble across a wolf shifter who's my fated mate *and* a doctor in the same hospital as me. GAH!

I yank the door open and rush out of the hospital, heading for the safety of my car.

But it's Dr. McDreamy…

I ignore my inner voice and my wolf, who howls in anguish. Most of all, I ignore the agony in my heart. To reject a fated mate bond is akin to ripping your heart out with your bare hands. The bond severs. But the pain can last forever. Or drive the male into madness. My forehead drops to the steering wheel.

The ring of my mobile startles me. I scramble inside my crossbody bag to retrieve the device. For a second I think it's Rust. But he doesn't have my number. Thank the gods! I check the screen. The number for the OB-GYN department flashes.

I glance at the time. Dammit! I'm late for the staff meeting.

"H—Hello?"

"Natalie, the meeting started. Are you on your way?" Paloma Sabela asks.

My mind reels. If I go back inside the hospital, there's a chance Rust will track me to my office. As much as I don't want to face him, I have no choice but to go. And then what? How can I work in the same place as him and risk him claiming me despite my rejection?

I shudder as flashes of Sam and Amanda, then him

turning to me, run through my mind. No way can I allow myself to be forced into a mating. I have no other choice.

With a heavy heart, I tell Paloma Sabela I need to speak with the head of the department after the meeting. She's surprised but agrees to let him know. After we end the call, I gather my strength and return to the hospital. I slip into the conference room and take a seat in the rear.

"Dr. Moore, you wish to speak with me?"

"Yes, Dr. Wright. Unfortunately, I have an emergency that requires me to leave Miami. I—I—"

My voice cracks. I swallow past the lump in my throat as tears fill my eyes. I hang my head, defeated.

"Dr. Moore, I'm sorry to hear that and to see you so upset. I hope everything works out," he says, then pauses.

I lift my gaze as I dab my eyes. He offers me a fatherly smile.

"Might I suggest you take a leave of absence for a month? You had a terrible fall yet continued to treat patients, even saved a mother and her unborn baby. You're new to the team. However, we value your contributions in the short time you've been with the department. I'll make an exception for your leave should you wish to take time off instead of resigning. We would rather lose you for a few weeks than forever. Why don't you go home and give me your answer in the morning? I'll have another doctor cover for you today."

I sag in relief. Time off would give me time to make my serum and restart my injections. Perhaps with my wolf suppressed, the fated mate bond will disappear. Rust and I didn't know about it all this time. So, the chances of it disappearing again are pretty high.

But is it worth it? Do you really want to give up your heart of heart wish for a partner in life? A pack?

Once again, I ignore my inner voice.

I take a deep, cleansing breath.

"Thank you, Dr. Wright. You're more than generous with your offer. I thank you and accept."

"Excellent. Human Resources will reach out to you later today. Take care of yourself. If you're ready to return earlier than expected, call me."

He rises from the chair, and I follow. At the double doors, we part with a handshake. I express my gratitude again, and he smiles, wishing me the best.

Before I leave, I tell Paloma Sabela and Thandie. They wish me luck as we embrace. I smile to myself, happy to have new girlfriends. In my office, I take a few things I'll need during my leave, then head for the dispensary. I tell the pharmacist I'll send a messenger to pick up the medicines, and he agrees.

Tasks complete, I head for the parking lot. I glance around, half expecting Rust to leap from around a corner and drag me caveman style to his den. My wolf whines as she stares at me with dejected eyes. Sorry, I whisper.

As I pass the emergency room entrance, I spot dark ginger hair shining in the sunlight. My heart clenches. Unconsciously, I slow the car down.

Sensing my stare, Rust turns his head from the patient on the gurney. Our eyes meet.

Electricity sparks through me. I gasp and turn back to the road ahead. My eyes dart to the rearview mirror, drawn like a magnet to steel.

Rust stands in the middle of the road, eyes locked on mine.

CHAPTER 8

ust

"DAMN, bro! What the hell's gotten into you?"

"You look like shit!"

"I'd say look what the cat dragged in, except we're wolves…"

"Did somebody steal your favorite toy, or what?!"

Jagger, Viggo, Tag, and Dylan double over and high five one another. Their guffaws fill the air as they sit on the terrace of Jagger and Sage's bayfront mansion on Moon Island.

I can't summon the energy to respond to my best friends' inane comments, especially when they're spot on. It's been three days since Natalie rejected me as her fated mate. When our eyes connected and she continued to drive away from me, my heart broke anew. It's been pure torture. A needle hurts. But this pain… Ouch.

An ER nurse had to call me back to care for the

incoming patient. Fortunately, it was a mild case of food poisoning, or I would have been beyond pissed with myself. For the rest of the day, I forced myself to focus. By the end of my shift, mental exhaustion set in. Not to mention the searing pain slicing my heart. The night proved no better. I tossed and turned with dreams of tracking Natalie only for her to dodge out of my reach.

The next two days, the pain from her rejection grew worse. Unable to concentrate, I took off two weeks starting today. The Director of Emergency Medicine was more than happy to approve my last-minute vacation request since I rarely take time off and bust my ass each shift. Plus, she took one glimpse of me and realized I needed a break.

Not wanting to stumble about my penthouse, I sent a text message to my boys to hang out. Hopefully, the distraction will ease the sorrow of finding then losing my fated mate after all these years. And stave off the madness I sense in my wolf. I rub my chest and drop onto a chaise lounge next to Viggo.

His ice blue eyes regard me. Those who don't know think we're brothers since he has long, red hair like mine. He wears his in a ponytail with the sides of his head buzzed. Pack tattoos adorn his scalp. A tribute to our Viking ancestors. Each of us—aside from Jagger—have paw prints on our pecs as symbolism for our bond as best friends for life.

He stretches his long legs in front of him and folds his bulging biceps across his chest.

"Speak up. What's going on?"

"I look like shit. I feel like shit. Not from the loss of a toy… But from my fated mate. She rejected me."

A hush descends. Hell, even the birds and insects stop chirping. A glance at each of my friends' faces reveals their stunned silent—eyes bug and mouths hang open. If I wasn't so torn up, I'd laugh at the sight of four Alpha males looking like cartoon characters.

"Your *fated mate*?" Tag asks, the first to recover from shock. Then his emerald green eyes narrow. "Where did you meet her?"

"Better yet, how the hell did you let her reject you? Damn!" Dylan chimes in.

Jagger sits forward, resting his elbows on his knees. He cocks his head to the side and studies me like his brother just did with the same ice blue eyes.

"Where is she?"

I shrug, then growl in frustration.

"Okay, start from the beginning," Jagger says.

I recall every detail from our first encounter in the emergency room to dinner after we teamed up to save the mother and her unborn baby to Natalie driving away. I even went to her apartment. She didn't answer, and I couldn't detect her scent. Since I couldn't sleep last night, I stood in the park across the street from her apartment and waited for hours, hoping to get a glimpse of her. Nothing. By the time I finish, their faces register pity and disbelief. Yeah, tell me about it.

Again, I rub the ache in my chest as I stare out over Biscayne Bay towards South Beach. The salty breeze from the Atlantic Ocean reminds me of Natalie's unique scent. I want to throw my head back and howl. My wolf whines.

Jagger opens his mouth to speak, then stands as a grin spreads across his face.

Dylan leaps to his feet.

"Hi, fellas! Sasha and I made too much popcorn for our movie night. We figured you might want some."

Sage followed by a heavily pregnant Sasha carries two giant bowls of buttered popcorn and a roll of paper towels.

They sit them on the side tables. Sage wiggles from Jagger's arms and faces me.

"Oh, Rust! Your fated mate!" She exclaims as she walks towards me. She sits on the foot of Viggo's chaise lounge and holds her hands out to me. When I hesitate and glance at Jagger, who growls, she rolls her eyes. "He won't bite your head off if you hold my hands, Rust! You're in pain. Let me help you."

"Don't tempt me," he retorts.

She giggles, and her green eyes dazzle like emeralds. Shaking her head, she gestures with her hands palms up.

I place my palms on hers.

She yelps and yanks away. Jagger leaps at me, but she holds up her hands and laughs.

"Gotcha!"

Her laughter turns into a squeal when Jagger swoops her up and places her on his lap as he sits across from me. She settles, then turns to me.

"Okay, now, seriously. I can help you. But first you must promise not to force Natalie to mate with you, or I'll shrivel up your manhood without hesitation."

I don't even bother to ask how Sage knows about my fated mate or her name. As the High Witch and super powerful, there's nothing I would put past her wolf-enhanced magickal abilities. If she can help me with Natalie, I'm all in.

"I promise, Sage."

She studies my face, then nods.

"You have to be very careful with your fated mate. She's wounded"—Sage holds her hand up when I jump to my feet —"Not physically. In her heart. She's had a rough time in life. I won't divulge any more since it's her story to share with you. Again, not to be forced from her. Go to her now. She rented a little cottage in Big Pine Key for the month…"

Amazed by Sage's knowledge, I whip out my mobile and type in the address. Jagger offers the pack's Sikorsky S-92 Executive Helicopter to transport me to the key quickly. I call the pilot, and he confirms he'll meet me at the helipad in fifteen minutes.

Before I race from the deck, Sage invokes a spell to fix my sorry ass. Gone are the limp hair, three-day beard, and bags under my eyes. A glance at my reflection in the infinity pool proves she brought back my handsomeness—if I must say so myself. I thank her and rush off.

An hour later, I stand in front of a white picket gate separating the road from a path leading to the cottage set amongst palm trees and flowering shrubs. It's tranquil with beautiful scenery. At once, a sense of peace envelopes me. I close my eyes and inhale deeply. A trace of her unique scent carries over the floral bouquet. Thank the gods.

I lift the latch and step onto the path. After I secure the gate, I jog towards the front door. Her scent grows stronger with each step. My heartbeat increases, and my cock punches the zipper of my jeans. As I reach the door, a distressed cry from the rear of the cottage reaches my ears. Immediately, I'm on high alert. My protective instinct kicks in. I race around the corner, ready to defend my fated mate. My wolf's growl joins mine.

"Natalie!"

I shout her name when I see her sitting on the step of the back porch alone.

One hand squeezes her bare thigh while the other hand holds a syringe poised above her leg. Tears stream down her flushed cheeks. At my urgent cry, her head snaps up. Onyx eyes widen as her mouth opens on a gasp.

I dart forward faster than humanly possible and snatch the syringe from her hand. She jumps to her feet, reaching for the needle. I lift my arm to the sky.

"What the fuck are you doing?! What drug is this?"

She flinches at my harsh tone.

I don't give a fuck! I will not allow her to harm herself. It's hard to cope when separated from a fated mate. But it's not enough to turn to drugs. If that were the case, then Jagger would have thrown my ass in rehab instead of me coming here. I scowl as I tower over her.

"Rust, it's not what you think. Please, just give it back."

"Not until you tell me what's in the syringe."

She swipes her hand over her face and walks up the porch steps. At the back door, she glances over her shoulder.

"Come inside. I don't want to talk out here."

I sniff the air. No deceit, only a profound sadness surrounds her. My mind recalls Sage's words about Natalie's wounded heart. Time to learn more about my fated mate.

~

*N*ATALIE

RUST FOLLOWS me into the house. I shut the door behind him and gesture towards the living room. I run my suddenly sweaty palms on the front of my strapless romper. When I glance up, Rust has a glint in his hazel eyes. His wolf is near the surface. I shiver and hurry to the kitchen for some bottles of water. When I return, he still has a wolfish expression on his handsome face. My wolf preens happy to be near our fated mate.

And fated mate, he is.

I couldn't bear to remain in Miami, knowing Rust was so close to my apartment. Its proximity to the hospital proved inconvenient when trying to avoid him. I didn't want to leave the state. A search on the Internet brought up the Florida Keys with Big Pine Key being the most mellow. Perfect for me to be alone and think about what I want to do with my life. More importantly if I wanted Rust in it. I booked the cottage for the rest of my leave.

When the medicines arrived from the hospital dispensary, I made my suppression serum and packed two vials and syringes. My wolf was back fully. All my senses returned. Plus, the inherent desire to belong to a pack and to have a mate.

I wrestled with the pros and cons for the last three days. Never alone again. Potential for love. No fear of Sam finding me and forcing me back to Washington since Rust's pack's Alpha wouldn't allow it to happen. But then I'd have to give up my career. Bow down to a male. Be bred for pups. Gah!

The days of debate are bad. But the nights filled with erotic dreams starring Dr. McDreamy keep me in a heightened state of arousal. My full breasts are heavy tipped with sensitive nipples. Constant pulses of my pussy walls clenching on air—or on my fingers. Dreams so real I wake sweaty and dripping. Double Gah!

Many times, I wonder if Rust aches for me as I do for him. Or if he found solace in the arms of that doctor or any of the nurses who fawn all over him. Worse yet, between their welcoming thighs. Talk about triple gah!

Then when I build the courage to put an end to the debate and my misery, Rust appears out of thin air! So, intent on my task, I didn't detect his presence. I nearly had a coronary.

Now, I stare at him and wonder. Was I about to make a terrible mistake suppressing my wolf again? He came for me. That counts as something. But how did he find me? I'll ask after I tell him about the serum and what forced me to suppress my wolf. And more importantly, drive me away from him—my fated mate.

"Here's a water," I say as I sit on the love seat. I shake my head at how apropos the name.

"Thank you," Rust says as he sits beside me.

His nearness engulfs me in his citrusy, musky, and spicy scent. He's pure masculinity as his long, muscular legs spread. His thigh presses against mine, and I have to bite back a wanton moan. It's bad enough my nipples pucker beneath the terrycloth of my romper. Their outline apparent since I don't wear a bra.

He cocks his head and sniffs. A feral growl rumbles in his chest as he pins me with a stare full of lust and possessiveness.

My pussy spasms.

"Natalie…"

I nearly cum from the silken baritone growl of my name dripping from his lush mouth. My eyelids droop as I breathe past my parted lips. Heat warms my cheeks and seeps into my pussy. I scent my own arousal. It turns me on more.

A large hand wraps around the back of my neck and pulls me forward. My wide eyes jump to Rust's flashing hazel ones. His mouth a hair's breadth away from mine. He sucks in my pants, then crashes his mouth on mine.

The world tilts.

White stars shoot behind my closed eyelids.

Sound ceases except for his growls and my moans.

All thoughts fly from my head.

My fingers bunch around the front of his t-shirt as I cling to him to keep from spinning into orbit.

His tongue thrusts inside of my mouth. It swirls around to taste every corner, then laps my tongue. Teeth nip my swollen lips. He tilts my head by his grip on my neck to better the angle for him to devour me whole.

The all-encompassing kiss goes on for what seems to be eternity. My lungs burn for air. I turn my head as best I can to catch my breath. Rust growls and trails open-mouthed kisses from the corner of my slack mouth, across my jaw, and down the column of my throat. When his canines graze the juncture of my neck and shoulder, I yelp.

Reality sets in, and I realize I'm somehow straddling his thighs perched above his hard, massive cock. It rocks up against my slippery pussy lips. Only thin scraps of cotton and his jeans separate us from mating.

My palms slam against his firm chest. It's like hitting a brick wall. He's oblivious to my sudden distress... Hot moisture drips onto my skin. His mouth opens wide.

"MINE!"

Oh, gods, no!

"Rust! Stop!"

CHAPTER 9

ust

"Rust! Stop!"

Natalie's scream freezes me. Her tiny fists pound my chest as she jerks away from me. She tumbles from my lap to land on her ass. Without missing a beat, she crab walks backwards until she bumps into the opposite wall. Her eyes full of fright watch me warily.

Still caught in a lust-filled possessive haze, I rise and stride towards her with my hand outstretched.

"NO! GRRRR…"

Her onyx eyes flash. The grinding sounds of bones reshaping and muscles lengthening fill the room. Her oval face morphs into a snout full of sharp teeth evident behind her curled lip as she snarls. As she moves to her hands and feet, her eyes never leave mine. Amidst a crackling, a flash, and ripping cloth, her wolf appears with midnight fur and a white streak like her widow's peak. The she-wolf of my dreams.

Except this time, her hackles rise, tail flicks back and forth, and she growls menacingly. No affectionate playfulness and damn sure no carnal desire apparent. She's prepared to attack.

Although she's larger than a regular wolf, she's no match for me, even in my human form. Especially when the need to mark, claim, and mate her ramp up my wolf and me.

But I set aside our bonding since something spooked her. I recall Sage's words and Natalie's initial plan to talk. With an inward groan, I rein in my wolf and lower my hand.

"Natalie, you are my fated mate—"

She growls and leaps with her fangs exposed and her claws extended. Her movement is clumsy, as though she and her wolf don't sync. Regardless, she's still capable of damage.

Instinct takes over. I dodge to the side. She flies past me and lands on the love seat, then whips around with a growl prepared to pounce. Oh. Hell. No.

"SHIFT!" I roar, instilling my Alpha command over my fated mate.

Already in the air, she crumples to the floor. Her wolf recedes immediately. She curls into a protective fetal position, covering her naked body as she trembles. Muffled sobs reach my ears.

My heart clenches. I drop to my knees and pull her onto my lap. My arms band about her body, pressing her close to my rumbling chest. She protests weakly. But eases against me as the soothing sound calms her. I murmur words of love against the delicate shell of her ear.

"Natalie, my heart, I did not mean to frighten you. Tell me what I did that spooked you," I say after her sobs slow to hiccups.

She squirms on my lap. Now it's my cock screaming for release.

I throw my head back and groan, "Babe, keep still, or I'll blow inside my jeans."

Her movements stop abruptly. The bitter scent of fear mixes with her unique scent.

Fuck!

Why does she get upset about sex? Did a male force himself on her? If someone did, I'll rip his fucking head off. In fact, both big and small! The thought makes me growl.

"Rust, just let me go."

I hold her chin between my thumb and forefinger as I turn her head to align our eyes.

"What did I tell you before?"

Her eyes dart away. But I wiggle her chin, and she glances back at me.

"I will never let you go, Natalie. You are my fated mate. We belong together. You feel it as much as I do. Remember?"

She nods. I cock an eyebrow.

The tip of her little pink tongue flicks out and sucks her lower lip inside her mouth. Her teeth dimple in the flesh.

My cock jumps in my jeans.

"Yes, *Rust.*"

Yeah, Fuck. Me.

"But I need to put on some clothes before we talk."

"You might as well get used to being naked, especially on my lap, Little Girl. When we are alone, I want you bare to me. I want to feast upon you with my eyes, mouth, fingers, and cock at all times. You are too beautiful to cover in unnecessary clothes that hamper my access. Do you understand?"

She bristles. Her wolf flashes in her eyes, ready to spring forth yet again. She slaps at my arms around her waist.

"You see! That's what's wrong with you male wolves! It's always about you and your needs. The gods forbid if a she-wolf has a thought of her own or her desires differ! I didn't let Sam force me to mate, and I won't let you either! No matter how much I ache for you!"

Her eyes widen in surprise at her last words. But mine narrow at the former.

"Who the *fuck* is Sam?!"

She startles at my possessive roar. Then regains her feistiness. She folds her arms across her full tits. The heart-shaped birthmark on the inner curve of her left breast catches my eye. I doubt she realizes she's made them more pronounce since she glares at me and doesn't hide.

"Do *not* yell at me!"

Okay, this is going nowhere. Reel it in, Rust. I suck in a breath as I close my eyes, then exhale as they reopen, focused on my angry fated mate. Crimson heats her cheeks. I do my best to ignore the tantalizing rise and fall of her heaving chest. Instead, I grip her waist and squeeze. She yelps and blinks. Now that I have her attention…

"Natalie, I know we have a lot to learn about one another. So, you wouldn't know I am an Alpha dominant. My kink is sexual control of my submissive partner to bring her ecstasy unlike ever experienced. I have no desire to control you outside of sex. Nor force you into anything you do not want. Even accepting my claiming bite to bond with me forever. I'll likely go mad. But rather my biggest fear than to hurt you. I do not know *Sam*. But I can assure you we are nothing alike. Do you understand?"

She studies my face for a moment and sniffs the air to detect any guile. Finding none, she relaxes.

"Yes, Rust, I understand. And you're right. From what I've seen and heard, you are an honorable male wolf who cares more for others than for himself. You're the complete opposite of Sam. That's why we need to talk. I want to explain things to you."

She pauses with an arched eyebrow and tugs on my t-shirt.

"As much as being your naked plaything appeals to me, I would rather have this conversation clothed."

I grin at her admission. She purses her lips.

As I grab the back of my t-shirt, I press my mouth to hers, then nip the plump bottom lip. She moans as I pull it before I yank my t-shirt over my head.

Through hooded eyes, she ogles my chiseled pecs and eight-pack abs. Her gaze follows the red feathery trail until it dips below the waistband of my low-slung jeans. Mesmerized, she drags a fingernail along the hair. Her eyes widen when my cock twitches in my jeans. And fuck if her sweet arousal punches the air between us.

I inhale deeply and lick my lips with a low growl. She blushes prettily and lifts her arms to pull my t-shirt on. My mouth salivates as her juicy tits jounce. The beaded rosy tips beg for me to suckle them. Hard. They disappear beneath the soft cotton, but their outline winks at me.

"Eyes up here, mister," she says as she lifts my chin up with her index finger.

I dip my head in deference, then raise it with a scowl when she slips from my lap to sit on the floor beside me. I catch her thighs and pull her back. She shakes her head. Silky midnight strands sway around her face and down her back. She runs a hand through the white streak and blows a breath.

"That anaconda you're packing is too much of a distraction. I need some space to think straight."

I chuckle and acquiesce. But I keep her legs over my lap. She rolls her eyes and stays put. Then she takes a deep breath.

"My name is Natalie Glenns, youngest daughter of deceased Alpha Conchar Glenns and deceased Luna Eilín Glenns, younger sister to deceased Amanda Dunne, née Glenns, and aunt to deceased pup Aidan Dunne of the Olympia Wolves Pack in Washington State."

My fated mate's eyes fill with tears and her voice stutters as she speaks of her family. She swipes the tears with her fingers and continues. I bring her fingers to my mouth and kiss each one, licking the tears into my mouth. She swallows and smiles softly as her fingertips stroke my lips.

"My parents died from an unexpected affliction two years before my sister and her stillborn pup died in childbirth. Many of our members died with my parents, as did many she-wolves who were forced to breed to increase our losses. Unfortunately, Sam Dunne fought for and won the role of Alpha after my father passed away. He forced my sister to marry him, as she was the eldest daughter of the former Alpha, and Sam wanted to benefit from the prestige of my family's legacy. The moment she took her last breath with Aidan in her arms, Sam turned to me and told me I would replace my sister as his mate. After I buried my sister and nephew beside my parents, I left my former pack that night."

Her lower lip wobbles as more tears flow. I lift her onto my lap, away from my now flaccid cock. She rests her head against my rumbling chest. The vibrations lull her. With fingers twined in mine, she continues to tell me about her desire to help pregnant women and their unborn babies. The long hours of studying at college and medical school to finish early and with honors, then performing well during her residency. Her goal to make her applications appealing to the best OB-GYN departments in the nation. And how she chose Miami since it's furthest from her former pack.

I tell her how I admire her drive and determination. She

smiles softly but puts a finger to my lips and shakes her head.

"I had no desire to be amongst wolf shifters and no interest in a mate or pups. To avoid detection, I created a serum to suppress my wolf"—I balk, and she shakes her head rapidly—"Let me finish, Rust. The medicines from the hospital dispensary are meant to replace my supply I dropped the night I fell from the stepladder and landed in the ER. With you."

She pauses to stare at me intensely. Sharp onyx eyes pierce my soul as she searches for any sign of judgment. I keep my expression open. She nods and goes on to explain the process and the return of her wolf.

My mind reels with her incredible discovery. Never have I heard of any shifter being able to suppress its animal half. Nothing in the Viking ancient texts I studied to learn their healing knowledge relayed anything of the sort.

Now, I understand how she went undetected by my wolf and by me. Plus, she couldn't scent me as a wolf shifter. Amazing but dangerous.

"Natalie, I doubt it, but I have to ask. Have you shared your serum with anyone?"

"Absolutely not. If it were to get in the wrong hands..." She lets her words trail off as we both know the impact the serum could have on shifters and humans. And with her being the only one with the knowledge, she's vulnerable.

I growl and hug her closer to me. She nuzzles against my neck, placing her palm over my heart. Her touch soothes me, and I bury my face in her silky hair.

"Now, do you understand my trust issues and negative reaction to you proclaiming us fated mates?" She asks softly.

I press a kiss to the crown of her head.

"Who can blame you? I get it."

"And I can never let Sam find me. I don't know what he'd

do. But the thought of leaving the other she-wolves under his and his cronies' thumbs sickens me. I just wish I knew how to save them."

I sit back to stare directly into her eyes. Mine glow with my wolf who snarls and paces.

"Natalie Glenns Moore soon to be Ingolf, you are my fated mate. I will protect you and our pups with my life. Any threat to you I will destroy. Fear no one. Do you understand?"

Without hesitation, she responds, "Yes, Rust."

"Good, girl. And you needn't worry about the she-wolves. We will call my pack's Alpha—about that fucker Sam's wrongdoings. I'm sure the Alpha of the Los Angeles Wolves Pack will not appreciate one of the packs within his territory harming she-wolves. We treasure our females. Those with mates—fated or not—and unmated deserve the pack's respect, love, and care."

"Rust, are you sure? Do you think they'll really help?" My fated mate asks eyes full of hope.

I nod and reposition her on my lap to reach into my pocket for my mobile. I pull up the FaceTime app.

"We'll call him right now. I don't want you to worry another minute."

She squeezes my arm as a brilliant smile spreads across her face.

"Thank you!"

Our gazes shift to the mobile screen. It connects with Jagger's on video.

"Rust. What's happening?"

"Alpha—"

"Oh, so, this call must be pretty damn serious for you to call me Alpha instead of Jagger—"

"Rust! You didn't upset her, did you? I warned you. Don't think I can't get to you from here!" Sage says as she leans over Jagger's shoulder to glare at me through the screen.

Fuck if my cock and balls don't shrivel just at the thought of Sage making good on her threat. I shake my head vigorously.

"No, Luna. I didn't upset Natalie. In fact, she's right here on my lap," I respond, adjusting the mobile's angle to include her face.

"Thank the Fates!" Sage declares.

Jagger pulls her onto his lap, and she leans against him with her emerald green eyes focused on Natalie to confirm she's fine.

"But we do have a major problem, one that involves the Los Angeles Wolves Pack."

Jagger sits up and narrows his eyes as they flash cobalt with his wolf near the surface. As Natalie recounts her story, his anger rises. At the end, he growls and assures Natalie the Los Angeles Alpha will rectify the situation immediately. She expresses her gratitude. He nods.

"Natalie, as Rust's fated mate, my Luna and I welcome you to the Miami Wolves Pack. Not only will your fated mate protect you, so will every male in our pack. I will finish anyone who dares to threaten you or to enter my territory to challenge Rust for you. More than likely, Magnus will punish the so-called alpha of your former pack, along with his followers severely. But do not worry about retribution."

"You will meet Sasha, another new member of our pack and the fated mate of Dylan—one of Jagger and Rust's best friends. It's her story to tell. But I guarantee it will resonate with you, Natalie," Sage adds.

Jagger nods, then asks, "Should we expect you back in a week after your seclusion? We can plan for a pack run in the Everglades to welcome Natalie officially."

"Yes! And your mate bonding ceremony!" Sage says as she bounces on Jagger's lap, clapping her hands. "I loved Jagger's and mine! So romantic!"

My fated mate stiffens on my lap and turns her head from the mobile screen. Tension fills the air. She tries to rise, but I tighten my arm around her waist. I cock my head and stare at her profile. She won't meet my gaze.

Jagger and Sage sit in silence.

"Natalie?" I ask.

She mumbles a response, and I pray to the gods my enhanced wolf hearing mistook her words.

"Natalie?"

She faces me and repeats words that sear my soul.

"I did not agree to mate you, Rust."

atalie

IF A FACE COULD COLLAPSE, Rust's would crumble to dust like a skyscraper hit by a dozen wrecking balls. His skin pales as his eyebrows dip over dimmed hazel eyes. The corners of his mouth droop. A gust of air puffs from between his parted lips. They move to form words, then close. He squeezes his eyes shut and shakes his head. When he opens them and stares at me, they're full of anguish.

My heart clenches.

"Uh, we'll let you go, Rust."

"And remember what I said about your manhood."

His Alpha and Luna's voices sound from afar as I stare back into Rust's eyes. He winces at Sage's words. I find them odd, but don't dare to ask their meaning while he's shocked by my response.

I'm a bit taken aback too. My reaction to his unexpected appearance and to our heated kisses proves I'm attracted to Rust. Hell, if I'm perfectly honest, my body burns for him.

My wolf rolled over and bared her vulnerable underbelly and throat to him. Well, after she came out to protect me when he tried to issue his claiming bite.

And that's it. I don't know if I want to be claimed. My views on being mated have changed since Rust. But I'm not sure I want to make that commitment. At least not right away.

He even admitted we don't know one another.

How can I just bow down and take his bite without a second thought? My former pack consisted of selected mates through alliances or choice before Sam forced she-wolves to mate. I've never witnessed a *fated* mate pair.

They're like a fairy tale where the two spy the other across a moonlit meadow and sparks fly between them. A sparkly tether appears at each one's heart and draws the pair together. Their hearts beat as one pulsing across the special bond. They embrace. The she-wolf tilts her head to the side, exposing her neck. The male wraps his arms around her, tips her backwards, and lowers his mouth to her neck. He bites, and she moans. They complete their bond by coupling as fireworks explode to twinkle with the stars above, and they live happily ever after. The End.

As I stare back at Rust, I wonder if we could actually be fated mates. Sure, he insists it's true, and I feel some sort of way about him. But forever is a long time. What if I give in now because he makes all these promises and later, he changes his mind? I'll end up stuck with him. Forever. Gah!

I glance away and attempt to rise from his lap. His arms tighten around me. When I face him, gone is anguish. Instead, gold flecks in his hazel eyes flash with his wolf. I blink at their fierceness and gasp at the pulse in my pussy.

"Already you forget I will never let you go, Natalie. Despite your hesitation, we belong together, fated mate. However, I won't beg you nor force you to accept my claiming bite. But you will tell me why you reject me. Again."

I lower my eyes as I nibble on my lower lip. How do I tell him what I want without contradicting myself? My lip pops from between my teeth as I yelp.

"Stop thinking so hard and answer with your heart, fated mate," Rust says as he squeezes my hip bones. He tightens his grip as I wiggle away. "Enough. Now, answer me."

As when he commanded I shift back from my wolf, words tumble from my mouth. I tell him my concerns about commitment, never witnessing fated mates, moving too fast, his promises being broken, all of it in one continuous stream. I let go and share it all. By the end, my mind clears. A sense of relief washes over me. I know what I want.

"Rust, I need time to get to know you and you me. It's not easy for me to forget wounds from my past and jump into a relationship forever. Your Alpha mentioned a week. Did you take time off from the hospital?"

"Yes, two weeks, actually, and I will extend it to four since you have the cottage for that amount of time. Let's stay here with no outside interference, no patients, no pack. Just you and me. I guarantee *you* will beg *me* to claim you before the end."

Somehow, I don't doubt it. But I don't admit it to him. Instead, I ask for what I've wanted from the moment I awoke drenched in sweat with a throbbing, soaked pussy.

"Fuck me, Rust."

RUST

"Fuck me, Rust."

My eyes bug out as my jaw hits to the floor. My fated mate giggles and places the tip of her index finger beneath my chin to close my mouth. She leans over and seals it with her lips. Her tongue licks around its edges, then along its seam.

On a groan, I cup her ass and pull her onto my lap. Her thighs straddle my hips. I grip the back of her neck to position her head at an angle for me to dominate the kiss. She needs to know from the start I'm in control. My Alpha Dom and my wolf growl in agreement.

I swallow each of her breathy moans as my tongue probes the wet warmth of her mouth. It thrusts inside and laps at her tongue. I groan when her hips undulate with the erotic rhythm I set. Her hot pussy lips rub against my burgeoning cock.

I guess she wears a thong since her juices soak my jeans. My fingers slip beneath my t-shirt to caress her waist and find the strips of cotton. I follow their trail to the patch of fabric covering her mons. A groan slips into her mouth when I feel her smooth and bare mons.

"Fuuuck, baby."

My teeth nip her lower lip as my thumb seeks her clit hidden by its hood. Slow circles make it swell. She gasps against my demanding mouth. Her pussy grinds down. I slide my middle finger past her slippery folds. She's so tight, my knuckle barely gets past. I jiggle it around to caress the sensitive spot on her front wall.

"Oh, *gods!*"

"Not the gods, baby. You're fated mate," I murmur against her panting mouth as I increase the strokes on her G-spot and engorged clit. Her cunt clenches and sucks my finger deeper as she screams.

My fangs descend, and the claiming serum drips along their length. I have to jerk my mouth away from hers to keep it from her neck. My vow to not force her and Sage's words prevent me from sinking my canines into my fated mate's flesh.

I cup her ass and flip us over, then settle between her trembling thighs. With a growl, I lower my mouth to drink from her gushing pussy. She bucks when the flat of my tongue strokes from clit to puckered hole. I growl and lay the flat of my palm against her lower belly and grip her ass with the other hand. Locked in place, she can only moan as I plunder her pussy with my tongue and teeth. My fingers spread her pussy lips wide. I flick my tongue up and down over her clit as I watch her.

After two more orgasms, her fingers tug at my hair.

"R—R—Rust… p—please…" She cries.

I lift my gaze up the length of her body. Our eyes connect.

"Tell me what you need, fated mate."

Bowing from the floor, her eyes close as she shudders. Another orgasm rips through her cunt, gripping my fingers like a vise. I wrap my tongue around her clit and suck. Hard. She wails. I swear she rips strands of my hair from the scalp. Ignoring the erotic pain, I swallow her juices in gulps. My eyes drag to her face. Her eyes remain closed. I spank her pussy lips, and her eyes pop open. The unfocused onyx orbs stare in my direction.

"Tell me!" I command. "Tell me what you need, my fated mate."

"YOU! I want you!"

My nostrils flare. I wipe my mouth of her juices on her inner thigh, then prowl up her body. My feral gaze never waivers as I keep hers pinned. One fist presses into the floor beside her head while the other hand tugs at the zipper of my jeans. My turgid cock springs free. I fist the base and drag my length along her sopping seam.

Her eyes roll to the back of her head. I growl, and she brings her lust-filled gaze back to mine.

"FUUUCK! Oh, Rust, Rust… Please fuck me!"

It's all the invitation I need. My tip lines up with her pussy. I bring my gaze to hers, wanting to see her reaction the first time I make her mine. Eyes wide and lip caught between her teeth, she watches me. My hands grip her hips and tilt her pelvis. I snap my hips forward and impale her on my cock in one swift thrust, buried balls deep in her tight little pussy.

She screams. Fingernails dig into the corded muscles of my forearms. Whether she pushes or pulls, I do not know. My instinct to take my fated mate and make her mine rides me hard. I growl her name with each pistoning stroke.

In return, her pussy walls clamp around my dick. It's a battle to withdraw as it sucks me in deeper. I groan with the effort. She syncs to my rhythm and rocks her hips to meet each of my savage thrusts. Her cries of passion match my possessive grunts and growls. It's a carnal symphony enhanced by the mingled musky scent of our fucking.

Before I give in to my own pleasure, I want another orgasm from my fated mate. One where she screams my name. I lick my fingers and reach between us. Thumb and forefinger roll, then pinch her clit as I nip the beaded tips of her tits through my t-shirt.

Her cry of my name while her cunt spasms around my cock makes my heavy balls fill with seed. The controlled thrusts give way to frantic hammering as I chase my release. A tingle at the base of my spine increases to a lightning bolt. It zips along my nerve endings as it travels to my balls and along my cock. With a ferocious roar, I drive into her soaked pussy one last time. Plunged to my root, I growl as my cock grows impossibly bigger and the base of it expands.

She hisses as my knot wedges behind her pelvis to lock

her to me. Her claws drag along my flanks as she howls from the stretch and burn. She thrashes beneath me, then keens when her pussy constricts for another orgasm.

It triggers my release. A long and low groan pours from my mouth as copious amounts of hot seed shoot from my cock to coat my fated mate's welcoming womb. Feral dominance and desire urge me to spill every last drop of my seed inside of her. I want her belly round with my pup.

"MINE! You. Are. Mine. Natalie. Only. Mine."

I punctuate each word with a determined thrust. Once again, I have to stop myself from issuing my claiming bite on my fated mate. It's a struggle as I force my fangs to retract while reining in my determined wolf. I close my eyes and howl.

She joins in as she clings to me.

Fully spent, I collapse on top of her. She holds me close and presses her lips to mine. Tears shine in her onyx eyes. I brush my lips against the lids and sigh. Our pants mix as I stare at my beautiful fated mate.

With enough air in my lungs, I wrap my arms around her and roll onto my back. Her smaller frame rests atop my much larger body. Her cheek over to my heart, I rumble to soothe her as I caress her back. She sighs and reaches up to twine her fingers in my hair. My knot will keep us connected for some time, so I allow my eyes to drift shut, content my fated mate rests in my arms. And this is no dream.

∼

NATALIE

· · ·

"BABY, why didn't you tell me? I thought you were tight. But I didn't realize—"

I place a finger over Rust's lips and shake my head.

"Please, don't. It was my choice. I didn't want you to treat me any differently than you did. I wanted all of you. Not a watered-down version because I was a virgin. Besides, no matter how gentle you may have been, that anaconda would still have split me in two!"

He chuckles and nips my finger.

"Split you in two, did I? How about we soak in the tub? The warm water will soothe your sore little pussy. And as much as it strokes my ego to know I'm the only male you'll ever know, I can rinse your virginal blood from my cock."

Naturally, my eyes go to his cock. It's so large I can't believe it even fits inside of me. And it's still erect! Suddenly shy, my cheeks heat. I can only nod as I avert my eyes from his crotch.

"Look at me, Natalie," he says in his commanding tone. When my eyes meet his, he directs his gaze to his cock. I flush deeper and nibble my lower lip. "Not my face, my cock. That's better. You have no reason to be shy with me or to avoid looking at my body. And damn sure not with me looking at yours. You said you want us to know each other. Well..."

He's got me there. I smile and stand. With a smirk, he tucks the anaconda away. I extend my hand to him. He takes it and rises. I squeal when he scoops me up, bridal style.

"Which way to the bathroom, fated mate? It's time I take care of you."

I tell him, and he strides out of the living room.

As we soak, I lean my back against his front. Rust makes good on his word. I all but melt as he washes and conditions my hair. His strong fingers knead my scalp, and I moan. It gets even better when he adds lavender-scented bath gel to a sponge and washes every inch of my body. But once again, I balk when he reaches between my thighs to clean my nether bits. He cocks an eyebrow.

"Last warning, Little Girl. Do not shy away from me—eyes or touch. Next time, I will take you across my knees and spank you soundly. Do you understand?"

My mouth gapes as my eyes skitter across his face. A serious glint in his hazel orbs lets me know he's not joking. No one spanked me as a child and certainly not as an adult. But instead of being outraged, my nipples pebble as heat pools in my lower belly. My pussy clenches. I bite back a moan as my thighs press together. The water sloshes over the sides of the clawfoot bathtub.

"Ah, ah, ah, Naughty Girl. Only I give you pleasure. You do not seek your own unless I give you permission. Now answer my question."

His reprimand adds fuel to the furnace raging in my pussy. He must sense my desire and maneuvers me to my knees with my fingers wrapped around the rim of the bathtub. He positions himself behind me and pulls my hips back. The head of his cock brushes along my wet slit. It nudges at my entrance, then sinks in slowly.

I moan wantonly as every vein, every ridge, and every inch of his long, thick cock strokes my inner walls. They suck him in greedily. At this angle, he goes deeper than before. I cry out. He fists my freshly cleaned hair and pulls my head back. My body bows and my pelvis tilts. He pushes in deeper as his mouth swallows my mewl.

Fully seated, groin to ass, his heavy balls slap my clit. I whimper in his mouth. He nips my lips. Long, even strokes of his cock have me white knuckling the edge of the bathtub. Again and again, he breaches my pussy with his slow drags.

I shudder as the first tingles of my orgasm surface. Wanting it to break, I push back against Rust.

He growls and withdraws. I cry out from the sudden loss and glance over my shoulder, only for his sizable palm to press between my shoulder blades. It holds me in place firmly. My mouth opens to protest.

THWACK. THWACK. THWACK. THWACK.

Instead of words, a startled yelp pops out of my mouth as his other palm spanks each of my ass cheeks in succession. Left. Right, Right. Left. It doesn't land on the same spot. But the sting blooms across my entire ass.

He wedges his thigh between my mine to widen my knees. The palm on my back presses down.

I should have known it wouldn't be good.

I nearly jump out of my skin when three of his fingers smack my swollen pussy lips. The squelching from my juices and the water minimizes the thwacking sound. But it does nothing for the erotic bite of pain. I bleat and try to move away. He holds me firm and leans over my back. Lips pressed to my ear, he speaks.

"For a smart little girl, you don't listen very well, Little Girl. Now, let's try this again."

He slides the palm on my back around the front of my throat. His other arm bands around my waist. In one punishing thrust, his cock fills my tight little pussy.

My mouth opens in a silent wail.

He withdraws, then slams back in. Over and over.

"Uh. Uh. Uh. Uh."

The only sound I can form as he sets a brutal pace. I love it.

My pussy flutters all along his thick length, trying to capture him for longer than a second. The rougher he mounts me, the more my arousal amps up and drips down my inner thighs. As much as I want to match his strokes, I can't. His hold allows no movement other than my breasts bouncing and my ass jiggling with each impact from his groin. I give in and sag against his hands.

"There's my good Little Girl. You please me. Now, cum for me."

I preen along with my wolf at his praise. Then fall under his erotic thrall as he continues to fuck me. My body responds to his command. The orgasm he abruptly stopped races forward not with tingles. An inferno rages through me. My eyes roll back, my pussy constricts, and my toes curl. All. At. Once.

"*OH, GODS!*"

Rust chuckles wickedly.

"Not the gods, Little Girl. YOUR. FATED. MATE!"

He explodes within me with a roar and triggers a mind-blowing orgasm.

As I pass out from the intensity of it all, my last thought makes me moan.

This is going to be the most excruciatingly tempting four weeks of my life. If Rust keeps this erotic torture up, I may just beg for his claiming bite. Gods help me…

ust

"GOOD MORNING, sleepyhead. Did you get enough rest?"

I snicker and kiss my fated mate on the crown of her head

She's adorable, all tousled, barefoot, and dressed in one of my new t-shirts. It reaches the middle of her toned thighs. The much larger size does little to hide the swells of her tits topped with pebbled nipples. As she turns to sit at the kitchen table, I swat her ass and grin as it jiggles. She yelps and covers it with her hands as she scowls at me over her shoulder.

"I would if you didn't fuck me every five seconds, every single day and night," she responds with an arched eyebrow.

Yeah. I may not have issued my claiming bite to her. However, I initiated a seclusion where I kept her in bed, fucking her often for the last seven days. My goal? Get her hooked on my fine skills and used to begging me—to let her cum, that is. Soon she'll beg for me to make her mine completely. And I cook for her, bathe her, and treat her like a queen. I'm pulling out all stops to secure my fated mate.

Even so, she can be a naughty girl. Not that I mind her spunk. Keeps things spicy. I just don't let her know how much it turns me on.

I cock my eyebrow and let my eyes rove over her body. She begins to flush, but her nipples poke against the soft cotton. The scent of her arousal wafts through the air.

"You do not have that tone of voice when I pound your greedy little pussy, Little Girl. In fact, you barely speak at all. Only moans, whimpers, and howls of carnal pleasure pour from that sassy mouth of yours."

Crimson floods her cheeks as she lowers her gaze.

"Exactly. Now, let's have some breakfast. I planned a fun excursion for us."

She lifts her head. Onyx eyes sparkle in the sunlight from the kitchen windows. She claps her hands and shimmies on the wooden chair.

"Ooh! Where are we going?"

"It's a surprise. So, eat up, and we'll get going," I respond with a smirk as I slide an omelet onto her plate. Then chuckle when she digs in with gusto. "Slow down, babe. No need to rush."

When I turn back to the stove, she slaps my bare ass. I growl.

"Nice apron."

I glance down at the words written on the front and frown at her.

"It reads, *Kiss the Chef*, not Slap the Chef."

She giggles.

"Oops, my bad, *Chef*. Shall I make it better for you?" Her eyes sparkle with mischief.

Yup, my naughty fated mate. And I'd have her no different.

An hour later, the Uber pulls up to the marina. I take Natalie's hand and help her from the car. She glances around at the boats along the dock as we walk towards the end.

"We're getting on a boat?"

"Surprise! We're spending the week on our pack's boat."

Well, technically, it's Jagger's megayacht *Moonbeam*. He designed it with our pack in mind, wanting to provide the members with a luxurious water respite. The 465-foot silver megayacht has five decks tiered from the back with a long front to accommodate a helipad. Twenty cabins sleep up to thirty-six guests. For entertainment, it features a beach club with a garage for water sports toys, fitness center, spa and sauna, swimming pool and hot tub, media room, bowling alley, and a game room. Multiple living spaces include salons, wet bars, dining rooms, library, and an office with a conference room he can conduct business.

I called him to reserve it for my fated mate and me. It'll give us the perfect way to explore the rest of the Florida Keys. I want her to experience all the pack and her new home has to offer. She wants to get the know me. Well, no better way than aboard the beauty.

Jagger was more than happy to arrange our excursion. So happy with his fated mate, he wants the rest of his best friends to have the same joy. Dylan's already set. Now, I'm up. Although, Tag has been pretty mysterious lately. But that's his story to tell.

Natalie and I reach the end of the dock where a crew member waits in a tender to ferry us to *Moonbeam*. Like the rest of the crew, he's a member of our pack. He greets us as I help my fated mate onto the craft. We set off, and she looks at me expectantly.

"Um, we're not staying on this, are we?"

I shake my head and point ahead. She follows the direction and gasps.

"Rust! Do you mean that big boat there?"

I nod with a grin.

She blinks and turns back to face *Moonbeam*.

"Seriously? No, way!" My fated mate squeals in gleefully as she claps her hands and bounces again. "I've never been on a boat. This is awesome!"

Then she turns to me with a frown.

"Your pack—"

"*Our* pack," I correct her.

She nods absently and continues, "Owns this boat? I don't mean to sound crass. But how can you afford it? I mean, you're an ER surgeon. No offense."

I chuckle and lean over to kiss her lips, then drag my lips to her ear.

"My pack is known as the *Billionaire Wolves of Miami*. And I'm a billionaire, along with Jagger and several others. I work as an ER surgeon because I want to help people—not for the money. I'm also our pack's doctor," I murmur, then sit back to watch her reaction.

She doesn't disappoint.

Her eyes widen as her mouth drops open. She starts to speak, then stops, and starts again.

I throw my head back and laugh. She pushes my chest and growls.

"What??? Why didn't you tell me??? You're serious, aren't you? I would never have guessed—"

"Damn, you wound me, fated mate! Am I that bad I can't pass for a billionaire?" I ask with a mock sad face and my hand covering my heart.

She giggles then trails off as the tender approaches *Moonbeam*'s stern. Her eyes nearly bug out of her head when she spies the crew on the lower deck waiting to greet us.

They line up in their dress whites. The captain steps forward as the others stand at attention. Jagger selected him for the position since he's a former naval officer who can't get enough of the sea.

"Doc, it's been too long. The ER keeping you from having some fun? Or maybe not," Captain says as the tender slips beside the much larger boat. While the bosun helps secure the tender, Captain reaches out to lift Natalie to the deck. "Welcome aboard, ma'am!" He smiles.

"Thank you," she responds with a giggle as she glances around at the rest of the crew.

"I agree, Captain. It's time for some R&R," I say as I step onto the boat and take my fated mate's hand. My wolf growled at his hands on her, even if polite. "Natalie, this is Captain. Captain, this is Dr. Natalie Moore, my fated mate. She works in the hospital as an OB-GYN."

He tips his hat and turns to introduce her to the rest of the crew. The Chief Stew holds a tray of mimosas. We take flutes with thanks, and I slip my arm around my fated mate's waist.

"We'll get going with the itinerary you submitted. Once we're further out, we'll anchor so you and Natalie can enjoy the watersports," Captain says.

"Great. I'll take her on a tour for now," I respond and guide her up the stairs to the next deck.

As expected, the megayacht amazes her. She oohs and aahs over just about every room, nook, and cranny. We end in an upper cabin just as the megayacht stops. She turns from the windows and points to her sundress.

"Rust, you should have told me we were going somewhere for more than a day's outing. I don't even have a toothbrush, let alone a bathing suit for watersports."

I smirk and stride towards her.

"As you already know from experience if we were alone, you'd walk around naked, including skinny-dipping. But have no fear. I asked Sage to select clothes she thought you'd need, and I ordered your favorite toiletries for you. They're in the closet and in the en suite bathroom."

She throws her arms around my neck. I laugh between her kisses.

"But if you keep this up, you won't leave this cabin," I warn as I nudge her belly with my semi.

"Oh, no you won't! I want to explore all this beauty has to offer. Tonight, you can ravish me. Maybe on that sunbed on the top deck…"

She winks and sashays into the closet. I watch her hips sway and groan as I stride to the en suite bathroom. I'll never get enough of my fated mate.

When I reemerge, she's adjusting the skimpy triangular top of a white string bikini. The piece doesn't even cover the fleshy sides of her lush tits and her ass! What the hell was Sage thinking? I growl and stalk forward.

Natalie jumps, and her tits almost pop out.

"What?" She asks, then rolls her eyes as I tug at the top, trying to stretch it across her tits. She swats my hands away and growls. "Cut it out, Rust! It's a bikini, for goodness sake."

Despite wolf shifters being accustomed to seeing one another naked whenever we shift, I can't help the possessiveness that clouds my mind. She huffs and scoots past me for the door. I grumble as her ass bounces. Fuck! My fated mate is going to kill me.

~

NATALIE

. . .

"RACE YA AROUND THE BOAT!"

I laugh as I zoom on my jet ski past Rust, who's wiping his aviator sunglasses on his board shorts. And boy, does he wear them well. Thick, muscular thighs flex beneath the fabric. His ample package rests between them. Even flaccid, he's magnificent. My mouth waters as I smack my lips. Ummm…

I snap out of my reverie and fishtail the jet ski to splash water all over him. Get him as wet as me. He yells. I hear the revving of his engine and shoot ahead. He gives chase as we fly across the sparkling turquoise surface of the Gulf of Mexico.

We spent the last twelve days cruising along the Florida Keys from Big Pine Key and around Key West. What started as a week-long excursion turns into two. With so much to explore, Rust extended our trip. And I'm beyond excited!

I've never had so much fun, and he treats me like his queen—so attentive in every way. The doubts I had on mating based on the horrible experiences I witnessed fade every day. Rust is nothing like the male wolf shifters of my former pack. He brings me joy and gladdens my heart.

At night, I pretend to sleep so he'll drift off and I can watch him while he's at his most vulnerable. His handsome face relaxes, and he appears boyish. Sometimes, a smile plays at the corners of his full lips. But if I move, his eyebrows knit as he reaches for me with a growl. Even in sleep, he wants to keep hold of me.

If it were two months ago, it would piss me off a male wanted to keep me under his thumb. At least that's how my mind would interpret it then. Now, not so much. It's his way of making sure I'm safe and, of course, close to ravage. Again, something I no longer mind. In fact, I can't wait for him to unleash that anaconda in me. The absolute carnal bliss he bestows on me is beyond mind-blowing. I couldn't deny him, even if I wanted to. I'm addicted to Rust.

So much so, I wonder what it would be like for him to claim me in the age-old manner of our kind. The thought makes my heart soar. I'd given up on having a mate. My expectation was to follow my career path and keep to myself. Now, I see the benefits of having more, of having a mate and a pack.

Rust says he'll introduce me to everyone once we return. I'm nervous as all hell. But he assures me they'll accept me and reminded me of Jagger and Sage's welcoming words. I so hope they're true. If the way *Moonbeam*'s crew treats me, it is. The males are friendly but keep their distance since Rust growls whenever they come anywhere near me. The she-wolves go out of their way to make me feel comfortable. I appreciate them all.

As I zoom past the megayacht, the crew cheers with wolf whistles and claps. With Rust gaining on me, I loop around the massive boat. A glance over my shoulder reveals he's right behind me. He whoops and grins as the engine of his jet ski revs. Waves rock mine as he zips past me with a triumphant howl. I growl and pick up speed.

I catch up to him seconds before we reach the megayacht's stern. I throw my head back and howl. He joins in, and the crew's voices rise with ours. My heart lifts with as our glorious melody rises on the wind.

We turn the jet skis over to the deckhands and dive into the crystal-clear water.

It slides over my skin like a warm caress. I luxuriate in the sensations as I channel my inner mermaid. My arms stretch with hands together while my legs press as one to mimic a fish's tail. I flick my feet to propel forward.

Colorful fish swimming amongst the coral below catch

my eye. They dart in and around the yellow-green mounds with star shapes on it. During a snorkeling lesson, the deck-hand explained it's lobed star coral native to southern Florida and the Caribbean. I give them one last look before I shoot for the surface.

"Gotcha!"

I gasp for air as firm hands grip my waist and propel me from the water. I fly backwards—arms and legs flailing—to drop into the water with a giant splash. Not quite the Little Mermaid…

"Why you!" I splutter as I resurface and swim towards Rust.

He laughs and swims in the opposite direction. His powerful arms and long legs slice through the water with ease. He stops a distance away and spins to face me. He smirks as he dips his head backwards into the water and smooths his shoulder-length hair with his hands. The dark ginger color gleams in the sunlight.

"Come here, Little Girl," he says in a gruff baritone as he crooks his finger.

My eyes flick to the megayacht. It floats in the distance with no crew visible. Since we're the only boat around, I needn't worry about strangers witnessing what I know Rust intends to do to me. However, the idea of someone observing him ravage me clenches my pussy.

As though reading my naughty thoughts, he chuckles devilishly and beckons once more.

Forget the mermaid. I practically run on the water to reach him. My arms go around his neck as he pulls me flush to his body. His mouth descends on mine for a scorching kiss. Tongues twine. Teeth nip. He swallows my mewls as I wrap my legs around his hips.

The anaconda doesn't disappoint. Already thick and long, it prods my pussy entrance. I hump him like a feral she-wolf as I growl with carnal need. My mouth leaves his, and I stare at him with hooded eyes. I purr the words I know will send him over the edge and unleash the savage side of his wolf. I want untamed Rust.

"Fuck me, Rust."

His hazel eyes flash golden as his nostrils flare. A low growl rumbles in his chest. The vibrations skitter over my skin. My nipples bead. So sensitive—even through my bikini top—they rub against the dusting of hair on his chest. I hiss.

He dips his head as he lifts me from the water. His teeth move the fabric away, and his mouth engulfs a nipple. He suckles. Hard. I throw my head back and moan as my fingernails dig into his wide shoulders. He grunts at the pain but doesn't stop lavishing my breast with sucks, nips, and tugs. His mouth moves to give attention to the other one.

My eager pussy grinds against his eight-pack abs. Even without the water, I would slide along his body, eased by the juices leaking from my core. I lower my head to his.

"Rust, please… I need you inside me."

My swollen nipple pops from his mouth. He tilts his head back to stare up at me. A feral gleam sparks in his wolfish eyes.

"How badly do you need me, Little Girl?"

"*Oh, gods!*" I groan, closing my eyes as his warm velvet voice rolls over me.

A bite to my nipple makes my groan morph into a yelp. My eyes pop open to find him staring at me with a cocked eyebrow.

"So badly," I pant.

"So be it."

He reaches between us and unleashes the anaconda. The slit of his plum-shaped tip winks at me before he uses it to push the gusset of my bikini bottom aside. One upward thrust, and he impales me.

"RUST!"

My scream bounces around us. Surprised seagulls mimic my cry as they take flight. I continue with each toe-curling thrust. Caught in a state of sheer rhapsody, I cling to him, letting him take full control of our carnal pleasure.

His cock swells impossibly bigger. The snug fit triggers another orgasm, and I wail. His grip on my hips tightens painfully sure to leave marks. He buries his face in my neck as he roars through his release. Hot cum bathes my pussy. The walls contract to milk his cock of every last drop of his seed. My mouth opens on a silent wail.

I startle when fangs graze the juncture of my shoulder and neck. The contact ends abruptly as Rust jerks his head away. He stares at me, dismay on his handsome face.

"Sorry. I got carried away," he says in a tortured voice. His fangs glint in the sunlight with the serum male wolf shifters secrete for their claiming bite. I stare at it, mesmerized. But he pulls me away from him.

Our intimate connection breaks.

The loss of his warmth and the disappointment in his eyes make me rethink my demand we wait. Am I doing the right thing by letting my wounded heart dictate my life?

*ust*

"Are you sure you don't want to join me? We could do a couple's massage or something. I feel bad leaving you while I get pampered."

Natalie scrunches her nose as she scans my face.

It's the last morning of our stay aboard *Moonbeam.* I arranged for an aesthetician and a masseuse to treat her to a spa day while we cruise back to Big Pine Key. They'll give her the works with a body scrub, manicure and pedicure, massage, everything the Chief Stew recommended. Nice, but for a dual purpose. She gets spoiled. Me?

I need a time out.

Three weeks ago, I thought I could withstand the urge to claim my fated mate since we'd be together, and I could seduce her. For a while, the intimacy of sex and shared space satisfied my wolf and me. With her in my arms or on my lap, contentment ran high. I believed she would give in soon. So, I held back.

However, it proves more difficult each time I'm buried in her wet warmth to stop myself from sinking my fangs into her neck to embed my scent in her permanently. The other morning as we fucked in the Gulf and again last night, my fangs descended of their own accord. Serum filled my mouth. I had to wrench my head away and separate us.

The last thing I want to do is claim her without her assent after I promised I wouldn't do it. Not only would it ruin the forward momentum of our relationship. But Sage would have my balls—and cock. I'm pretty damn strong, but I shudder at the thought of losing my junk. Plus, I would lose Natalie and any chance of securing my fated mate.

Then I question whether what I've longed for is worth this torture or not at all. First, her rejection pierced my soul. Now, her ongoing will to deny me claiming her wreaks havoc on my being.

The vision of the male wolf shifter in the Everglades reminds me I don't want to face the madness of not having a mate. It's even worse when the mate is fated and they spend time together. The pain of being apart from Natalie for those three days after she rejected me would seem like a tap compared to the gut-busting punch of absolute denial now. She's embedded under my skin as much as my serum would be under hers—inseparable. It would be like me ripping my own heart out.

I think about Jagger and Dylan. Sure, they had drama with securing their fated mates. But in the end, they made it. Hell, Dylan didn't even believe in fated mates before he met Sasha. He scoffed at the rest of us. Now he's happily mated, and I'm in agony. Fuck!

At this point, I need some advice. I have to talk this shit

out with them. Find out what they did and if it will help me with Natalie.

Thus, I keep a straight face as she scans it. While she's in the spa, I plan to call Jagger and Dylan. Gain their perspectives. Help a brother out…

"I'm sure. Besides, you deserve a bit of pampering. Unless, of course, you don't mind a female rubbing all over my naked body with warm oil as she leans her breasts—"

"GRRR! Do *not* finish that sentence, Rust Ingolf!"

Natalie's eyes blaze as she snarls. Her wolf flicks across her features. Fists form at her sides.

Hmmm. Perhaps she does care. Her possessiveness makes my cock harden. But I ignore it. Time out, Rust.

"Well, then, enjoy," I say as I usher her to the cabin's door. "I'll be by the pool."

I drop a kiss on the crown of her head as we part ways at the elevator. She hesitates and glances up at me with her eyebrows drawn together. I spin her around and spank her ass twice. She yelps and hops into the elevator. I wait until the door closes, then jog up the stairs to the pool deck.

I grab a couple of bottles of water from the Viking built-in beverage center on my way to a sunbed. As I flop down, I pull my mobile from the pocket of my board shorts. I sent a text message earlier, so they expect my call. The FaceTime app rings, and Jagger answers right away. I tell him to hold on while I add Dylan to the video call.

"Okay, so how can we help the Love Doctor?" He asks with a smirk.

Jagger chuckles, then adds, "Oh, don't tease him, D. He called for help, and we'll give it to him without flack."

I nod my thanks to Jagger as I sip from a bottle. Is it too early for aquavit? I sure could use something stronger than water for this conversation. Laughter bubbles from my mouth.

"Private jokes, or what?" Dylan asks with a cocked eyebrow.

"Yeah. On me for having to ask you Mr. Doesn't Believe in Fated Mates for advice on my fated mate. Oh, the irony."

They join in on my laughter. Then Jagger sits up.

"Not all of us can roll around heaven all day. I have a company to run and a meeting in half an hour. So, what's up?"

They listen intently without interruption while I fill them in on my concerns. When I finish, I gulp the rest of the water. Jagger speaks first.

"To answer your question if it's worth the torture, yes. You know the shit Sage and I went through, and it involved more than us. Like Sage, Natalie is an independent female who's used to taking care of herself. Be patient. Imagine coming home to her every night and waking up with her in your arms. I'd walk through Hell for my Sage."

Dylan nods.

"You're right. I denied the truth of fated mates for years. Then I walked into that diner in New York City, and my knees buckled. Me, the toughest of us, MMA cage fighter brought to his knees by a she-wolf a foot shorter than me. When it happens, bro, it happens. And I wouldn't change a damn thing about it. Except for the drama with the fuckers who kidnapped her."

He ends on a growl as his amber eyes flash with his wolf.

I consider their words as I stare at the Florida Keys along the Atlantic Ocean. *Moonbeam* reaches Big Pine Key in a few hours. Back to the cottage for the last week of our alone time. I hope for more. But will accept what Natalie offers so as not to force her. Her reaction to another female with me proves Natalie has grown attached to me. I'll take it as a win.

I thank Jagger and Dylan. We shoot the shit until Jagger's

meeting. Before we hang up, they wish me luck. I shake my head.

"Yeah, well, we'll see. If she doesn't give in, I'll go primal and take what's mine."

Jagger shakes his head as Dylan snorts. They know it's all bravado.

Time to cool off. I toss the mobile on the sunbed and yank my t-shirt over my head. I stride to the pool and dive in.

∾

*N*ATALIE

"*Y*EAH, *well, we'll see. If she doesn't give in, I'll go primal and take what's mine.*"

Instead of surprising Rust, he surprises me. Tears fill my eyes. I back away from the pool deck and rush for the elevator. Thankfully, it's still there. I slip inside and jab the close button. No way do I want him to see me crying. A sob catches in my throat.

I knew he'd break his promises! It's only been a few weeks, and he's gone back on his word. And here I was about to tell him I was ready for his claiming bite. What a sucker I was for believing in him. He's nothing but a liar!

The door slides open, and I hurry down the hallway for the cabin. My hands swipe my face when I see a stewardess carrying fresh linens in her arms. She raises an eyebrow when she spies my tear-stained face. But I shake my head and rush past her.

"If you need anything, Natalie, let me know. The girls and I are here for you."

Afraid my voice will crack, I wave a hand over my

shoulder to thank her. Once inside the cabin, I enter the en suite bathroom to splash cool water on my face. It helps with the redness on my cheeks but not my eyes.

I soak a washcloth in the water and carry it to the bed. With the pillows fluffed behind me, I lean back and place the cool washcloth over my closed eyes. I push Rust's hurtful words to the corners of my mind and focus on my breathing.

Lips pressed to mine startle me awake. I push against Rust's firm chest as I sit up quickly. The washcloth falls to my lap. I stare down at it not wanting to meet his eyes.

"Whoa, babe! Take it easy. It's me. You almost knocked my front teeth out. How would you like your mate to walk around gumming?"

I ignore his joke. Although it's appealing.

"We're twenty minutes away from Big Pine Key. Otherwise, I would've let you sleep—"

"You can't *let* me do anything!" I snarl as I scooch across the opposite side of the bed away from him. I hop off and stalk to the closet.

I don't want anything from him, including the clothes he bought for me. So, I strip out of the silk caftan and pull my sundress on. It slips past my face, and Rust stands in the doorway.

He frowns as his eye flit over my face.

"What's wrong? Did something happen with the aesthetician and masseuse? I'll let the Chief Stew know."

I growl and push past him. He snags my arm.

"Hey, talk to me. What the hell happened? And what do you mean, I can't let you do anything?"

I snap my head around and glare at his hand on my arm, then at his face and back. He takes the hint and releases his grip. I snatch away and storm for the door. As I open it, it slams shut. Rust's palms press on either side of it, boxing me in. I glare at him over my shoulder.

"Move dammit!"

"No! Tell me what's going on, Natalie."

His lean, muscular body presses all around me. He towers a good nine inches taller. His citrusy, musky, and spicy cologne mixes with his pheromones and saltwater from the pool. The intoxicating combination overwhelms my senses. Rust weakens me.

My forehead leans on the door as I sag.

"Baby…"

He breathes the word into my hair as he drags his nose along my head and down to my shoulder. His knees bend as he presses the fronts of his thighs to the backs of mine. The anaconda unwinds against the crack of my ass.

I bite my tongue to hold in a desperate moan. However, my hips don't get the memo. They undulate to rub my ass along his cock.

"Mmmm… Baaaby…"

My palms slap the door to give me leverage. He has other plans and covers them with his as he entwines our fingers. His teeth nibble at my neck. My knees give out. He groans and braces me with his powerful thighs. The sharp tips of his fangs score my flesh. Warmth drips on the spot. With a throaty moan, my eyes close. I tip my head to give him better access.

"MINE!"

"Rust, Natalie, the tender is ready for you."

The bosun's rap on the door knocks me into reality.

Rust growls viciously. His fingers tighten on mine.

I hear the bosun gulp as he backs away from the door.

"Um, ring Captain when you're ready," he says hurriedly.

"Wait!" I cry and wiggle to free myself from Rust. If I let the bosun get away, Rust will continue with the claiming bite. I won't let it happen, no matter how enthralled I was a moment ago. "Rust, let's go!"

He remains unmoved. I worry he'll go through with like he said. Then he blows a ragged breath and steps back. I sigh in relief and bolt out the door.

The bosun waits at the end of the hallway, as far from the door as possible. He peers past me for Rust. I don't turn around. But I hear him behind me. Judging by the shock on the bosun's face, Rust must look a sight. I sneak a peek.

His narrowed hazel eyes darkened, filled with a feral gleam focus on me. The tips of his fangs dip into his lower lip. Color suffuses his cheeks. A glance at his groin reveals the anaconda standing tall directed at me. A growl rumbles from his chest.

I shudder and swing my gaze forward. The closer I get to the bosun, the more threatening the growl. The bosun flattens himself against the wall and exposes his neck in submission to avoid Rust's wrath. I never thought he would frighten me. But now, I tremble in the face of his need to claim me.

Skirting around the bosun, I head for the elevator. No way do I want to be responsible for Rust attacking him. A wild vision of Rust ripping him from limb to limb flashes in my mind's eye. No way.

It's just a few more feet to the elevator. As much as I want to dash for it, I know better than to run from a predator. So, I keep my pace steady but not quick. The door opens when I press the call button. As I step inside, I glance over my shoulder. Rust bustles in and crowds me in the corner. A sharp cry slips past my lips.

Once again, he brackets me with his arms. His hair hangs in his face as he stares down at me with feverish eyes. His wolf flickers beneath his skin, altering his features. They shift from human to wolf and back again, as though Rust fights for control. His hot breath comes out in huffs.

I stare up at him wide eyed, too afraid to move and risk pushing him over to the feral wolf side.

"Rust, please," I say in a breathless whisper.

He squeezes his eyes shut and shakes his head as if trying to dislodge his wolf's hold. When they open, anguish replaces the wildness. His forehead drops to mine.

"Natalie… What you do to me…"

The elevator door pings open.

"Rust, back out and keep your hands up!"

Captain's commanding words surprise me and piss Rust off. He growls low in his chest. The wolf returns as he swings around to face Captain.

"Stay. Out. Of. This." Rust snarls as his hands form fists at his sides.

"RUST STAND DOWN! NOW!"

Another commanding voice fills the air. Captain holds an iPad in front of him. Jagger—the imposing Alpha of their pack—glares with flashing ice blue eyes from the screen at Rust.

Rust snarls but lifts his hands, unable to withstand his Alpha's command. Rust casts a glance at me.

"ENOUGH, RUST! Go with Captain. Do *not* fuck around. You will not like what will happen to you."

He steps off the elevator and follows Captain, who keeps the iPad trained on Rust. Jagger continues to glare at him.

"Natalie, come with me."

The Chief Stew's voice drags my gaze from Rust. I look at her, and she nods brusquely as she beckons for me to follow.

I glance back at Rust, who's surrounded by every male on the megayacht. My heart sinks. Tears fill my eyes. But I slap them away angrily.

Rust brought this on himself! He's the one who lost control. And do not forget he said he would force you!

I harden my heart once again hurt by a male and follow the Chief Stew. She guides me to a tender where a deckhand waits to transport me to Big Pine Key. I thank the Chief Stew and ask her to give my thanks to the rest of the crew. Without a backward glance, I step onto the tender.

CHAPTER 13

"WHAT THE ACTUAL fuck did you do?!"

Jagger demands as I sit in his office on *Moonbeam*. His ice blue eyes glare at me from the iPad.

Fuck!

I lower my face into my hands. What the actual fuck did I do? I lost control. Fell over the edge. Succumbed to the madness. My worse fear.

All I see is Natalie's stricken face. All I smell is the odor of her fear.

Fuck!!

I don't need Jagger to harp on me. I already regret my actions. What I said I wouldn't do, I did, and worse. She'll probably never want to speak to me again. My heart breaks.

To top it all off, the entire crew witnessed my abysmal behavior. The bosun, worse of all. If he spoke to Natalie—or the gods forbid, touched her—I would have torn him apart. Talk about embarrassing.

And where is Natalie? Is she still aboard or did she leave on the tender?

I need to speak to her. Apologize and let her know I didn't mean to lose it.

"—need to take some time for yourself. Natalie doesn't need to see you right now. You're lucky Sage doesn't realize yet. Well, at least I don't think she does. You would notice. Are your balls still in place?"

I grunt and tune back in to Jagger's words.

"Listen, I admit I was wrong. But you just don't understand. I was about to initiate my claiming bite when the bosun knocked on the door. Damn! I couldn't help myself. I lost my shit," I respond, miserable as all fuck.

Silence descends.

I glance up at the iPad. Jagger stares back at me. He nods in understanding.

"Okay, I get it. However, you scared the shit out of the bosun. Captain said he had peed his pants. I mean damn, Rust. You scared him that bad?"

Now, I feel even worse. Never have I lost control. I'm a Dom, dammit! I thrive on control! Obviously not with my fated mate. Or at least she was.

"I didn't mean it. The urge to claim my fated mate took control. You've known me all my life. When have I ever lost control?"

Jagger nods.

"Damn. I recognize what that feels like. Sorry, bro. However, as your Alpha speaking, you need to apologize to the crew. As for Natalie, I'll ask Sage to speak with her. As Luna of our pack, she's responsible for the she-wolves," he says, then chuckles. "I'll use my best skills to persuade Sage from shrinking your junk. At least one of us will get something good out of this mess. Any opportunity to ravage my sexy as fuck mate, I'll take it."

I'm happy for Jagger. But my cock and balls shrivel at the thought of Sage enacting her promise. Now that my mind is clear, the magnitude of my error hits hard. He's right, I need to apologize to them. But first to Natalie.

"Listen, I'll apologize to the crew. But first, I need to apologize to Natalie. Talk to her to let her know I didn't mean to lose it. Hopefully, she'll forgive me. I'll call you back after I talk to her."

Jagger stares at me, then shakes his head.

"Natalie left on the tender. You are not to speak to her until after your Luna meets with Natalie. I'll call Sage now and ask if she can use her teleportation magick. She can reach Natalie in seconds. If she says Natalie is receptive to you, then you may speak with her. Do not test me on this, Rust. Best friend or not, I will punish you if you disobey your Alpha's command. Are we clear?"

I BITE BACK A GROWL, knowing he's correct. As Alpha. As my best friend, not so much. But Jagger earned my respect years ago. I will not go against his word.

"Crystal," I respond.

He eyes me a moment, then nods.

"Good. I will reach out once Sage makes her assessment."

He ends the call.

I drop my head into my hands again. How the hell did I let it get this bad?

As I wait for his call, the urge to call Natalie tempts me to ignore Jagger's command. I jump from the sofa and pace around the office. I'm on edge, and my wolf yearns to break free. Suddenly, the walls close in on me. I need air.

With a growl, I stride towards the door. The knob won't turn. Damned if Captain didn't lock my ass in here. Frustration and anger wash over me. I throw my head back and bellow. The sound would surely reach beyond the walls except Jagger's office is soundproof to prevent sensitive information from being overheard. I punch the door and howl in pain. In my ramped up state, I forgot he reinforced the door, ceiling, floor, and walls. His office serves as a safe room. Or in my case, a prison.

I stalk over to the wet bar and grab the bottle of aquavit. Perhaps if I drink all of it, the amount will override my system and dull my emotions. I slump on the couch and tip the bottle to my mouth. Guzzling it down, I finish half of it. Nothing.

I set the bottle aside and pace. Time goes on forever until at last the iPad rings. I snatch it from the coffee table and accept the FaceTime call. Jagger's grim face appears. My heart sinks.

"Sage spoke with Natalie. She doesn't want to talk to you and asked for you to let her go—"

I hurl the iPad across the office. It hits the wall and shatters to the floor. A gut-wrenching howl rips from my chest. No fucking way! This cannot happen. How could she reject me again?! I know I messed up. But damn not bad enough she wants nothing to do with me. Especially since I told her about the madness.

My mind fractures, and my wolf surges forward. I retreat to allow the feral beast to take over.

～

Natalie

. . .

ONE MINUTE I'm sitting on the back porch of the cottage bawling my eyes out, and the next Sage appears in front of me. Out of thin air! She scares me so badly my wolf literally jumps out of my skin. But she barely stands before Sage commands I shift. And damned if I don't. Too shocked to speak, I sit here mouth agape until she suggests we go inside and I dress. I glance down, only then remembering my tank top and yoga pants shredded. My mind isn't right.

She follows me inside and sits on the sofa while I continue to the bedroom. When I reemerge, Sage smiles at me. Her emerald green eyes glow as though lit from within. Their brilliance emphasized by her warm toffee complexion. Curly ebony hair cascades to her waist, cinched by the belt of her silk wrap dress. Long, toned legs—crossed at the knee—end in stilettos. I thought she's stunning on video. But in person, she radiates beauty and power.

"I know my grand entrance startled you. But Jagger wanted me to reach you as quickly as possible."

When I continue to stare at her in shock, she tilts her head.

"Oh, I see. Rust didn't tell you I'm a witch turned wolf shifter. Okay, let's start from the top. And do sit. I won't bite," she says with a giggle. Then continues as I join her on the love seat. "I'm Sage Waters, the High Witch and leader of the Coven of the South. Now, add Larson to my name as I am the fated mate of the Alpha of the Miami Wolves Pack and the Luna. Jagger bestowed me with the gift of wolf shifter when he claimed me. I used my teleportation magick to reach you in seconds. Good?"

I've heard of witches but never met one. And to meet the High Witch, well, damn.

"Good and thank you for the clarification. Rust only told me you and I are the same age," I respond, then shake my head. "You didn't have to come all the way here. I've already told him to let me go."

My voice catches at the end, and I have to cough to clear it.

"Would you care for a bottle of water? I need one," I say as I rise from the love seat. She nods, and I head to the kitchen. When I return, I give her a bottle and continue. "I don't mean to sound rude. I'm sure you're busy and don't need to waste your time."

Sage studies my face as she sips water.

I fidget under her intense scrutiny. Even my wolf tucks her tail and shies away. Just as I open my mouth, Sage speaks.

"You don't mean that, Natalie. Deep in your heart, you know you and Rust belong together. Fated to be one for all time. I understand you're wounded from past emotional trauma. He does, too. But you're a wolf shifter and know how males are single-minded when it comes to their mates. Add being fated, and it's more narrow minded. Wouldn't you agree?"

I consider her words. I can't deny their veracity. However, they don't change my mind. I heard what Rust said about claiming me against my will despite his promise. Then he lost it and would've attacked the bosun! For a male to lose control frightens me. It reminds me of Sam and his cohorts. I shudder and wrap my arms around myself.

No matter what, I must protect my heart. It's had enough heartache to take anymore. My only option is to restart the serum. Hopefully, it blocks Rust from scenting me as his fated mate, and he can go on without madness overtaking him. This last week of my leave of absence gives the serum enough time to suppress my wolf before I return to Miami and the hospital. I'll just avoid the emergency room. Problem solved. Although my wolf throws her head back and howls mournfully. Sorry.

I turn to Sage determined to live my life as I see fit and not conform for a male I cannot trust. Not even one who's my fated mate.

"Yes, I agree with you. However, Rust broke his promise to me. He intended to claim me without my consent. He said so and acted upon it. I cannot trust him. So, please, let me be."

I rise from the love seat. Sage follows and reaches into her handbag.

"Here's my number. You don't have to be alone, Natalie. Call me anytime," she says, then smiles when I take the card. "I will relay your wishes to Jagger, and he will speak with Rust. Now, don't get nervous. I'm leaving the same way I came."

"Thank you, Sage. Know that my intention is not to hurt Rust. My heart comes first."

She nods and lifts her hand in farewell.

I blink, and she's gone.

The room suddenly feels empty, as does my heart.

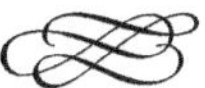

 agger

"Fuck!"

I grab my mobile and pull up the security app. The view of my office on *Moonbeam* appears.

Rust—or rather his wolf—rampages. The massive red beast rakes his razor-like claws on the leather sofa as though gutting prey. Instead of entrails, white stuffing flies around him like puffs of smoke. He snarls and growls with each swipe.

"Dammit, Rust! Stop!"

He pauses and cocks his head at the sound of my voice over the speaker system. For a moment, I think he's going to listen. But no.

He spins, bounds across the office, and leaps onto the large wooden desk. His front leg knocks over the crystal lamp. It shatters on the floor. The pen holder follows the same path. Montblanc and Waterman fountain pens scatter.

His claws seek purchase on the polished surface. Trails of scratches appear. Stable, he throws his head back. An ominous howl erupts from his mouth.

His hazel eyes narrow at the camera. The golden flecks glitter as he snarls viciously. Tongue flicks between bared teeth. Ears flatten to his giant head. His stance displays a challenge to my authority as Alpha.

Completely uncharacteristic behavior for Rust. Like Viggo, he's the fun-loving one with a good sense of humor. Sure, he's an Alpha Dom. We all are. But he's not inclined to challenge me as the Alpha of our pack.

No. This outrage comes from hurt. Hell, I know the loss of a fated mate… I get it. But to let his wolf take over. Not acceptable.

"Shift, Rust! Shift. Now!"

I instill my Alpha command into my words and through the bond I share with members of my pack. If this doesn't get through to him, I fear he may have succumbed to the madness. I keep my eyes trained on him through the security camera. It's the best I can do from this distance.

He glares back. Body rigid. His tail wags in a high up position in a show of dominance and aggression. A low growl rumbles in his chest.

Fuck! He won't concede.

With a growl, I slam my fist on the desk. Then switch to the phone app.

"Tag, Rust succumbed to madness… Listen, I don't have time. Meet me in my office now."

I end the call and dial Karl—the head of my personal security and pack enforcers. He enters my office through the door connected to his. A grim expression appears on his face as I recount Rust's madness and show the live feed from the security camera.

Unable to get out, his wolf prowls around the office.

Intermittent snarls and growls filter through the speaker. No sign of the man remains. Shaking my head, I turn away from it to alert Captain. He and the crew will leave Rust locked inside until I arrive.

Another call to my pilot to prepare the Larson Enterprises, Inc. Sikorsky S-92 Executive Helicopter.

"What the hell's going on with Rust?"

Tag draws my attention from the mobile screen. I beckon for him to see for himself. He stands gobsmacked.

"Ginny, I'm gone for the day. Reach me on my mobile. Reschedule my appointments," I tell my administrative assistant through the intercom as I jump from my desk chair and head to my private elevator. "Tag, Karl, let's go."

We ride the elevator that connects my office to the garage and to the roof where the helicopter awaits. Karl must have alerted the rest of my security team since they stand beside it. They greet me as Alpha with respective nods while I step aboard. Tag and Karl climb in behind me. Tension fills the luxurious cabin as each of us retreats into ourselves. Concern for Rust and his wellbeing remain at the forefront. His challenge was nothing but the madness. Hopefully, he's not so far gone that I can't pull him back from the abyss.

My fated mate must sense my turmoil. A lightness lifts some of the tension as I answer her call.

"Hi, babe. We're on our way to *Moonbeam*... Tag, Karl, the rest of my team... No! I do not want you to... I know you can take care of yourself. That's not the point. Rust is unpredictable right now... Do not go anywhere near him until I arrive, Sage! Do not push me. Do you understand? Good. I'll see you soon."

"Let me guess, she used her teleportation magick and beat us to the megayacht," Tag says wryly.

I roll my eyes to the heavens with a prayer to the gods for strength. My fated mate wants to kill me. I know it…

I press the intercom built into my seat to ring the pilot to go faster. We zip through the air and arrive in less than forty minutes.

Captain greets me solemnly. I pat him on the shoulder as I jog to my office with the others behind me. I stop in my tracks at the sight of my office door wide open. What the absolute fuck?! I swing my head to face Captain. He shakes his head vehemently.

Tag steps in front of me, followed by Karl and the rest of my security team. I wave them off and push past. This is a delicate situation involving my best friend. No one will interfere. Well, except for…

NATALIE

"OWOOOOOO!"

The hairs on the back of my neck rise. I jump from the love seat where I must have fallen asleep. My eyes dart around the cottage's living room in search of the ominous howl. No wolf. I rub the back of my neck as I walk to the back door cautiously. But instead of fear, a sense of loss and pain envelopes me.

I wrap my arms around myself as I peer out the pane of glass. Nothing in the backyard appears out of the ordinary. A glance out the front windows reveals the garden and path clear. I rub my arms as a shiver trails down my spine. Something is very wrong.

As I pad back to the living room, another howl fills my ears. It's not from outside. The menacing cry originates in my head! What the hell?! Again, no fear. Instead, my heart aches. I press my palm to my chest and rub the spot.

I sit on the edge of the love seat and close my eyes. I steady my breath and reach out to the source. In my mind's eye, I see Rust. But not as the man. Rather, a ginormous red wolf.

Its feral eyes focus on me. They narrow, then widen, as if in recognition. *Natalie...* Surprised to hear Rust call my name, I reach my hand out. However, the wildness seeps back into the wolf's glowing golden eyes. It throws its head back and howls before it bolts away out of my reach.

"Rust!"

My eyes snap open and fill with tears. He needs me. Oh, why was I so stuck in my old beliefs? Why couldn't I have given in to what I know I want as much as he does? My gods! What a fool!

I glance around the coffee table, then grab Sage's card. My hands shake as I hold it and pick up my mobile. She answers on the first ring. A second later, she stands before me again.

"Sage, it's Rust! He's lost to his wolf! Please help me get to him. He must still be on the boat. I saw him. He needs me..."

I trail off as another howl fills my head. My eyes close in anguish.

"Natalie, it's imperative you remain calm and in control. I will take you to Rust. But you cannot help him if you are weak. You must be stronger than his wolf to bring Rust back. If not, we may lose him forever to the madness. And Jagger will have no other choice but to—"

"No! Don't say it! I'll do it. I'll be strong. I—I can't lose Rust. I was wrong. This is my fault!"

Sage nods and holds her hand out to me. I grasp it without hesitation.

"Once we reach *Moonbeam*, I will take you to Jagger's office. I can go inside with you—"

"No, I will do it alone. I won't risk your safety for my mistake. Thank you, Sage. Can we go now?"

She nods, and the living room disappears. I blink, and we're in a hallway outside a door on the boat.

"I'll wait here for you. Be strong, Natalie."

I squeeze her hand and turn the knob. They locked the door.

"Hold on," Sage says.

The lock clicks, and the door opens a crack. Sage and I exchange nods, then I step inside, shutting the door behind me. I lean against it. The lock reengages.

The office is in shambles. Stuffing from the furniture is strewn all around the room. Shards of broken glass from liquor bottles, a lamp, and picture frames glitter on the floor. Paintings hang askew on the walls. The acrid stench of urine mingles with musky pheromones and the spilled alcohol. My nose wrinkles as I hold back a gag.

My eyes dart around. But I can't find Rust or the wolf. A low growl catches my attention. I gasp as the red wolf emerges from behind the massive wooden desk opposite the sitting area. As in my vision, its eyes gleam and narrow on me. It moves with the graceful stealth of an apex predator. And I'm its prey. The hairs at my nape lift again, and I shudder.

Be strong, Natalie.

Sage's words sound in my head.

I nod and take a deep breath, ignoring the rancid odor. My wolf paces on the fringes of my being. But I won't let her come forth. The gods only know what Rust's wolf would do if it encountered mine. No. I have to appeal to the man.

"Rust, I know you can hear me. You called to me. And I came—"

A growl cuts off my sentence. Only a few yards separate me from its gaping jaws. Sharp fangs glint from the overhead lights. It continues to stalk towards me.

You can do this, Natalie.

I straighten and lift my chin. My onyx eyes flash with my wolf as I curl my lip. The giant beast hesitates. Its intense stare would make a human lose control of all bodily fluids. But I'm not a human. I am a strong she-wolf, determined to save my fated mate—even from himself.

"Rust! Listen to me. I'm sorry. You're right. I'm wrong. You're my fated mate. We belong together. Forever. Come back to me and make me yours, my love."

The wolf lifts a paw to step forward. I recall Rust's command to me when I launched myself at him in the cottage. My shoulders square, and I stand tall. Glaring at the wolf, I command it.

"SHIFT! NOW!"

Shocked at my boldness, its eyes widen. But its hackles remain raised. Its feathery tail high. Not yet ready to cede domination, it growls.

I issue my own threat as I clench my fists.

"SHIFT! NOW!" I surprise myself with the ferocity of my snarl. Even more so when a sudden crackling and a flash reveal a naked Rust on his hands and knees. His skin ripples as the ginormous wolf retreats beneath it. Rust shakes his head as though dislodging the last vestiges of his beast. Then his eyes lift to mine.

My heart stops.

We stare at one another in amazement.

Slowly, he rises. All magnificent six feet, six inches of sculpted lean muscle in plain view. And an incredibly colossal cock, fully erect and dripping with pre-cum. My pussy clenches, and I mewl as I sag against the door. The need to be strong ebbs from my body, replaced by the need for my fated mate.

His nostrils flare, and he tips his head back to inhale deeply. I know he scents my juices, even above the mess his wolf caused. He rumbles in his chest appreciatively.

My arousal amps at his citrusy, musky, and spicy cologne mixes with his pheromones. My wolf whimpers in need and rolls to her back in submission. I want to join her. I glance at Rust from beneath the thick fringe of my eyelashes.

He approaches with the swagger of an Alpha male about to claim his fated mate. Taut muscles flex in his thighs with each step. The anaconda bobs.

"Natalie…"

The gruffness of his voice sends electric pulses along every nerve in my body. The synapses flash and spark more heat in my already molten core. I whimper in response as my nipples tighten to painful peaks, and my pussy throbs. I rub my thighs together to lessen the ache.

"NO! MINE!"

Rust closes the distance between us in two long strides. One hand grips the back of my neck while the other rips the front of my cotton sundress in one go. It flutters open to reveal my braless breasts. The cool air tightens my sensitive nipples further.

He drops his head and engulfs as much of my breast as his mouth can take, then he draws back to suckle the nipple.

Erotic pleasure zings straight to my core. My fingernails dig into his shoulders as I try to remain upright and not puddle on the floor at his feet. Indecent moans pour from my mouth. My hips undulate, seeking his groin to rub my pussy against for release.

My nipple pops from his mouth. He stands and glares down at me. Displeasure rolls off him in waves.

I gulp.

He spins me around and yanks my hips back. My palms brace against the door. He spanks my exposed ass. A weighty palm lights fire beneath it upon each connection. I dance on my toes, trying to evade his punishment. He bands an arm about my waist and spanks even harder than before.

I cry out. But as the spanking continues, a peace settles over me. I let go, give in to his dominance. His control of my pleasure. The pressure to fight his claiming me recedes giving more space for the peace to flourish. I sigh and hang my head.

He detects the change in me. A few more spanks alternating each ass cheek, and he slows the rhythm. My panting decreases with it as my arousal soars. His palm rests on my ass. My back arches as he leans into me. Warm breath skitters across my ear.

"Do you understand you are mine now and forever, my fated mate?"

My mouth opens to respond. But instead of words, a strangled cry emerges as he slams his engorged cock inside my tight pussy. My arousal eases his passage. However, the stretch burns as my core strains to accommodate his massive girth and length. It hurts oh so good. I cum with legs shaking and knees wobbling.

"Y—Y— Yessss!"

He grunts and pistons his hips. Each thrust drives me onto my toes and ignites the heat in my well-spanked ass. Palms slap the door. Eyes roll to the back of my head as another orgasm rockets through my pussy. My entire body quakes.

"Gods, yes!"

The steady slapping of skin on skin, low and husky

growls, and desperate moans reverberate around the office. Sweat trickles down my spine to collect at the small of my back as I arch to take Rust to the depths of my core. The scent of our raw fucking fills my nostrils, and my wolf howls in carnal pleasure.

My pussy walls flutter as the anaconda grows impossibly larger and thicker. The base expands to form his knot, locking us together at the entrance of my core. I scream and writhe at the burn. His free hand snakes around my hip to tug at my clit. Stars explode behind my closed eyelids. I scream his name as my pussy gushes.

A hand swipes the sweat-dampened damp hair stuck to my neck. Then long, tapered fingers enclose my throat like a collar. The other arm tightens its grip around my waist. Warm breath skims across the bared skin at the juncture where my neck meets my shoulder. Hot liquid drips on the sensitive spot. Then pain radiates through me at the same time as his cock floods my pussy with his seed. Blood trickles down my shoulder. I howl from the piercing pain.

Rust increases his holds on my throat and waist as his extended canines coated with his scent serum sink into my delicate tissue. He opens his mouth, then bites the same spot to ensure his scent lodges beneath my skin. He guarantees to mark me as his permanently, with no room for doubt. His head shakes to intensify his claiming bite.

"MINE!"

He growls the singular possessive word, then licks the spot to initiate the healing with his saliva. The rumbling in his chest soothes my cries. Still intimately connected, he lowers to the floor and cradles me on his lap. He buries his face in my hair and murmurs gentle words of love.

I cuddle against him as my eyes drift close.

A kiss to my lips rouses me. My eyelids flutter open to find Rust's handsome face smiling at me.

"Hello, my fated mate. We need to get up. Jagger will be here soon."

The memories of Rust as his menacing wolf, him shifting and claiming me rush through my mind. I return his smile and reach up to cup his cheek.

"Hello, my fated mate. But how do you know?"

He taps the side of his head and grins.

"Our Luna told me."

I giggle, knowing exactly what he means. Then I gasp.

"Did she hear us?"

He shakes his head and tells me the office is soundproof, and she wouldn't eavesdrop on such an intimate act.

I sag in relief. Then wrap my arms around his neck as he lifts me to my feet. I glance down at my torn sundress and arch an eyebrow at him.

At least he has the decency to lower his eyes remorsefully.

"Sage will fix us up," he says, then glances around the office. "And this too, thankfully. I did a bit of damage."

I scoff and lift my sundress for a bit of modesty before Rust opens the door and stands behind it. Sage enters. She scans my face, then Rust. A beatific smiles spreads across her face. She makes no comment about our appearances. Instead, she glances around the office. Within seconds, it's back to its pristine condition. I gasp when a silk caftan covers my freshly washed body and my hair tumbles down my back in glossy waves. A glance at Rust reveals he's spiffy, too. And just in time.

"Sage?! Rust?!"

Jagger bellows as he runs down the hallway. He appears in the doorway. His eyes flit about the office until they settle on Sage. She wiggles her fingers at him. He growls and stalks into the office. Crimson floods her cheeks at the words he murmurs in her ear. Spoken too low for Rust and me to hear. But enough to make her blush and bite her lower lip. A THWACK, and she hops with a yelp. I offer her an empathetic smile as I place a hand on my heated ass.

"Alpha, I apologize for my loss of control. I will apologize to Captain and to the crew, especially to the bosun. Even though Luna repaired the damage I caused, I will accept whatever penance you wish for it and for my behavior."

Rust ends with a bowed head as a show of respect.

But I can't let him shoulder all the blame.

"Alpha, if I may," I start, then continue when he nods in assent. "I will take the majority of the responsibility since Rust reacted to my rejection of him as my fated mate for the third time."

I pause and turn to him.

"I overheard your conversation by the pool. It upset me you would claim me without my consent. Rather than telling you the reason for me rejecting you again, I ran away. From now on, I promise to communicate better and to work on my trust issues."

Rust pulls me to him and lifts my chin.

"I apologize. I said the words out of frustration. Know I would never break a promise to you. However, I understand it from your viewpoint. As for communication and trust, I know just what you need."

A shudder runs through me as he ends with a seductive, low timbre to his voice. I stare into his hooded eyes—

"All right, hold that thought," Jagger says, breaking the sexual thrall Rust cast upon me. "Sage and I accept your apologies. Since your actions were because of madness from the loss of your fated mate, your apology to Captain and to the crew will suffice. Now, why don't you spend the last week aboard *Moonbeam* for your seclusion, then meet the pack in the Everglades? You can complete your mate bonding ceremony, and we'll celebrate with a pack run."

Rust glances at me, and I grin. He kisses my forehead and turns to Jagger to agree.

"I do have a question," I start, then continue when the others turn to me. "I know Sage as a powerful witch can speak to us through our minds. But how was I able to hear the howls of Rust's wolf and him call my name?"

"Our fated mate bond. Even though you rejected me, each time we were intimate, the bond strengthened. My wolf's anger, along with my distress, coursed through the fledgling tether we share. Now that I claimed you, the bond seals our connection. Reach out through it to gauge my emotions."

I close my eyes and cast about until I detect a steady thrum from my heart to his. My wounded heart swells with the love he sends to me. With a joyful smile, I open my eyes and beam at my fated mate. He kisses me softly. We part, laughing at a cough.

"Well, I take it crisis averted?"

A handsome, brawny male wolf shifter an inch taller than Rust stands in the doorway. The newcomer's emerald green eyes flick to each of our faces as he cocks a sable brown eyebrow. Just as with Rust and Jagger, the evidence of their Viking heritage appears in his imposing size.

"Mr. Grumpy! I didn't realize you were here. Allow me to introduce you to my fated mate, Dr. Natalie Moore, now Ingolf. Natalie meet Tag Dahl, our pack's beta and COO of Larson Enterprises, Inc. One of my best friends."

Tag growls at Rust but smiles at me.

"Problem solved, I'm heading back to the office. Jagger?"

He smirks at Sage.

"I have important business to attend to with my naughty

fated mate. I trust you can hold down the fort in my absence."

A grin plays at the corners of Tag's full mouth. He nods and leaves the office with a backward wave.

Jagger and Sage bid us congratulations before they disappear. Her giggles fill the room, then fade with them.

"Ready to be ravaged, my fated mate?"

I loop my arms around Rust's neck to pull him down for a passionate kiss. When we part for breath, I respond with a purr.

"Yes, as long as you promise to give me what I need for communication and trust."

He smirks.

"Oh, Little Girl, we have a special place for that lesson. I will take you when we return to Miami after you meet my parents and the pack in the Everglades. For now, we will make do with what we have available."

An unexpected spank to my ass makes me yelp and jump even as my pussy warms at the thought. I cannot wait for what my fated mate has planned for me.

CHAPTER 15

atalie

"HOW BEAUTIFUL! I've heard of the Everglades from nature shows I used to watch with my sister Amanda as pups. But to see it in person and from this height reveals its magnitude and natural splendor. And your pack—"

"*Our* pack, my fated mate."

I giggle at Rust's correction.

A week later and I still forget the Miami Wolves Pack is my new pack. I guess it's because the last seven days of our seclusion, Rust kept me in the cabin. We made love or cuddled in the bed for hours. He fed me on his lap from the tray left outside the door. We bathed or showered, washing each other. At night, we swam naked in the pool, then made love on the deck. I only saw Captain and the crew as Rust and I disembarked. So, yeah, I kinda forgot about anyone except for my fated mate.

He chuckles when I remind him.

"So, as I was saying… *Our* pack has a camp in the midst

of the Everglades. How nice it must be to enjoy the vast amounts of land free of worry humans may see us. As excited as I am to meet everyone and to run as a wolf, I must admit I'm a tad bit out of touch with my other half. It's been so many years I haven't shifted regularly, even before the you know what."

Rust glances at the door that separates us from the flight attendant and pilot aboard the pack's helicopter. Like on *Moonbeam*, they're members of the pack. Rust nods in understanding.

We decided to tell Jagger and Sage about my suppression serum since they're our Alpha and Luna. Rust assures me it's best they know. Plus, Sage may be able to refine it with her magick and definitely secure its safety from the wrong hands.

"I must admit I noticed you were a bit clumsy when you shifted and moved at the cottage when I arrived," he says, then cups my cheek when I pout. "However, there's no need for you to be concerned about your wolf. The connection we have with our other halves doesn't disappear without use. She'll help you the more you shift. And I'll help you relearn our ways. Sound good?"

I turn my head to press a kiss to his palm and nuzzle against it as I purr my agreement.

"Good girl," he murmurs before he slants his mouth over mine.

His tongue coaxes mine to tangle. I lean into him as he swallows my moan. He pulls me onto his lap where the anaconda unwinds beneath my core. I circle my hips to encourage it to come out and play. Rust groans and squeezes my ass cheeks in each hand. He nips my lip, then trails open-mouthed kisses along my jaw and throat. His tongue flicks over his claiming bite, and I mewl.

"Rust, Natalie, we're five minutes from landing."

The disembodied voice of the pilot interrupts us.

Rust growls in frustration and buries his face in my neck. I stroke his hair before I slide from his lap and settle on my seat reluctantly. He entwines our fingers as he leans his head against the sumptuous leather of the cushy chairs.

"I love you, my fated mate," he murmurs with a smile.

I bring our joined hands to my mouth and kiss his knuckles as I stare into his intense hazel eyes.

"I. Love. You. My. Fated. Mate."

I punctuate each word with a kiss, and he grins.

As we land, I glance around the area cleared for a helipad.

"We're near our pack's camp. It's the place we come for pack runs and trainings. For generations, the virtually untouched area of the subtropical wilderness allows us the freedom to be in our wolf form without prying eyes. Over the years, the original pack grounds grew from temporary cloth shelters to simple wooden cabins and now to luxurious residences scattered around the Alpha's house and clubhouse. Glamping—or glamorous camping, as Signy, Jagger's younger sister—calls it. Sage cast a cloaking spell over the entire area for miles as added protection from outsiders.

"A few families and enforcers choose to remain here, not wanting the hustle and bustle of Miami for their principal home. On days like this one, when the humidity is low, the sun sits in a cloudless sky, and fresh air abounds, who can blame them?"

"It's even more amazing on the ground," I say as Rust takes my hand and leads me to an SUV where Jagger and Sage wait for us. I return their waves of greeting.

Sage pulls me in for a hug.

"You're glowing! It must be all that sea air," she says with a wink.

I giggle and respond, "Absolutely, it was relentless!"

We burst out laughing as Rust and Jagger chuckle at Sage's euphemism. Then they herd us into the SUV. I climb in the backseat behind Sage while Rust rides shotgun. Jagger starts the engine. We leave the crew to tend to the helicopter. They'll ride to camp in the other SUV.

Rust points out different spots as we go along. He and Jagger tell stories from their youth about the adventures they and their best friends got into. Sage and I laugh with them. The vision of Rust and Dylan running from hornets after the two hit the nest with rocks on a dare from Viggo brings tears to our eyes.

I smile happily at the thought of meeting Dylan, Viggo—Jagger's younger brother—and the other pack members. Already, the joy of having a positive pack lightens my heart.

We round a bend and the camp sprawls out before us. Rather, the glamp since every cabin is a rustic mansion of logs and stones in various styles—some ranch and others multilevel, with and without front porches. They surround an open park-like square in the middle, where a lovely garden displays colorful flowers and bushes with wooden benches. Lanes crisscross the land to provide access to the various homes and structures. Members of all ages mill about. Their laughter and conversations fill the air. Content smiles spread across their faces as they interact. Those in wolf form mingle with the others without a care. It's a picturesque village with the incredible Everglades as the backdrop.

I feel right at home.

Sage reaches for my hand and squeezes as she smiles.

"Welcome to our pack's Everglades home, Natalie."

"Indeed, welcome!" Jagger adds as he glances over his shoulder at me. He turns to Rust. "Sage and I figured you wouldn't want to shack up with the bachelors in their lodges, as usual. So, we prepared one of the guest cabins for you and Natalie. If you decide to choose another, let us know."

"Oh, but Natalie, it's the one next to the Alpha's cabin as a place of honor for important guests, and it's decorated nicely. Not that any of the residences lack luxury! I agree with Signy about the glamping!" Sage adds with a giggle.

"I'm sure it's perfect. Thank you both so much! I feel so welcome already!" I respond as I squeeze her hand and smile at Jagger. "It's been so long since I had family and the love and support of a pack. You make me feel so special."

My voice catches, and Rust spins around on the seat. He leans over and cradles my face between his hands.

"We're your family now, my fated mate. Do not feel sad. And if you do, I will comfort you," he says earnestly. I close my eyes and a tear trickles down my cheek. He smooths it away with his thumb. "I love you, Natalie Ingolf!"

"Speaking of Ingolf… Signy, Sasha, and I put together the overall plan for your mate bonding ceremony. We set it for tomorrow evening. But you have final approval. So, when we get to your cabin, the girls and I intend to whisk you away," Sage says, then glances at Rust with a devilish grin. "Unless, of course, you wish to join us."

His eyes bug, and he flops back onto the seat.

"Uh, hard pass."

I giggle as I dab my face. Sage joins in. Jagger speaks up.

"He couldn't, anyway. The guys and I have plans for our newly mated best friend," he says mysteriously. "A new tradition Dylan came up with."

"No strippers!"

Sage and I shout at the same time.

All four of us bust out laughing. Jagger assures us they would never allow any strippers at their gatherings. Sage and I high five.

Jagger stops in front of an impressive cabin—to say the least. It's a two-story mansion with large river stones around its base and split timber above. Instead of a porch, it has a balcony with a glass wall on the second level that runs the entire length of the front facade. It overlooks the center square. It's more than nice.

We climb out, and Rust scoops me in his arms like a bride. I giggle and wrap my arms around his neck. He strides across the threshold and only puts me on my feet when I protest as Jagger and Sage enter behind us. She takes me on a tour while Rust and Jagger head to the deck off the great room.

Aside from the great room, the home features on the main level a guest bathroom, media room, den, chef's kitchen, and dining room. The second level has four bedroom suites with attached baths. As Sage said, the furnishings are posh but comfortable. I tell Sage it reminds me of a Ralph Lauren home. She laughs and says most of the pieces and accessories come from his home decor collection. I giggle and flop onto a vintage leather chair in the great room. She sits opposite me on the other.

"So, you're happy, then?"

I grin wider than the Cheshire Cat.

"Oh, absolutely! Rust treats me like a queen and loves me beyond measure."

"Good! I won't have to shrivel his family jewels. Now, let's get the girls over to handle business."

We chat while we wait for Signy and Sasha to arrive. I can already tell Sage will be a great friend to me. She's funny, has a mind of her own, and loves deeply. I admire her loyalty to her fated mate, coven, and pack. Their love match was even more complicated than Rust's and mine. Gah!

"Hello!"

"Hey there!"

"Hiya!"

Sage and I glance up to find several members of the pack enter the cabin. An older couple must be Rust's parents since the she-wolf rushes over to me with her arms outstretched. I rise from the chair, and she embraces me.

"My dear! I'm so happy our son found his fated mate. Let me get a good look at you," she says as she holds me at arm's length and inspects me from head to toe. She smiles. "Beautiful and smart! I understand you're a doctor, too."

"Honey, let me welcome her, too," her mate says as he smiles at me. "And yes, Rust did well for himself. I'm his father, Rudolf, and this is his mother, Frigg."

"I certainly did!"

We turn at Rust's voice. He saunters into the great room with Jagger and puts his arms around my shoulders. He leans over and kisses his mother on the cheek and claps his father on the shoulder.

"Well, done, son!"

"So, you're the one who captured Rust's heart?"

A younger, gorgeous she-wolf with waist-length jet black hair and ice blue eyes arches an elegant eyebrow at me. Her cool gaze assesses me. We're the same height at five feet, nine inches. But somehow, she looks down at me. I bristle. Then she throws her head back and laughs.

"And thank the gods! One less *big brother* to hamper my lifestyle!" She says with warmth in her gaze as she strides towards me. "I'm Signy Larson—Jagger and Viggo's younger sister. Hence their besties adopted kid sister. Ugh! Welcome to our pack!"

I shake her hand as Rust nudges her with a chuckle. She swats him away and sticks her tongue out. He laughs even harder. The rest of us join in.

"And this is Sasha—my fated mate—and I'm Dylan."

It seems as though all the males in this pack are downright sexy. Golden eyes peer at me from a foot above. I smile and turn my gaze to Sasha. She's an ethereal beauty with ash blonde waist-length hair. Her dove gray eyes sparkle set in an oval-shaped face of alabaster skin. She hugs me with one arm since her pregnant belly makes it impossible for a full embrace.

"Nice to meet you, Natalie," she says in a Russian accent. "I understand you're an OB-GYN. No offense to Rust. But I'd love for you to deliver my baby girl."

"Oh, that's not even a question. No way will Rust continue as your doctor now that we have a capable she-wolf doctor in our pack," Dylan says with a growl.

Everyone laughs at his possessiveness.

"It would be my honor to care for you and your pup. I can tell you don't have much time before you deliver her," I say as I eye Sasha's heavily pregnant belly, then turn to Rust. "I don't imagine you plan for the delivery at the hospital."

He shakes his head.

"No, that's too risky for human interference. We have a state-of-the-art hospital on the pack's private island, Moon Island, in Biscayne Bay in Miami. And no offense taken, Sasha. In fact, I'm thrilled to pass all the care of the she-wolves to my fated mate. And no, she will not tend to the males!"

Again, everyone laughs.

"What did we miss?"

"Hardy har har."

A male wolf shifter strides into the great room ahead of Tag. I recognize the ice blue eyes from Jagger and Signy and guess he's Viggo. The dark ginger red hair resembles Rust's, but the features match his siblings. Another striking Viking male.

"Viggo! Let me introduce you to Natalie, my fated mate. Natalie, this is Viggo—"

"Jagger and Signy's brother. I recognize the resemblance!" I cut in as I wave at Viggo, then turn to Tag. "Good to see you again, Tag!"

He smiles and nods.

"All righty then. We shall leave you she-wolves to your business. The guys and I are outta here!" Jagger says. He winks at Rust's father and adds, "Care to join us for a bit of mischief?"

The older male chuckles and declines the invitation. He heads out the door with a wave. Rust kisses me breathless and joins his buddies after Jagger and Dylan kiss their fated mates. Signy makes gagging noises while Viggo and Tag roll their eyes. Once they're gone, Sage turns to me.

"Now, let's get started."

"ENOUGH WITH THE fancy mansions for the Everglades! Time for us to get back to the male style and rough it. No built-in espresso machines. Don't even start me on the steam showers. Forget about the manicured lawns. We're leaving it all behind from now until noon tomorrow. Get changed and grab your packs, fellas. We're out!"

Viggo glances at me. I turn to Tag. He cocks an eyebrow at Jagger, who snorts.

"For real? D., what the hell do you have planned exactly?"

"Since we're bonding ourselves to our fated mates one by one, I figure we should renew our best friends' bond each time one of us pairs up. Remind ourselves we got each other's backs. No male left behind type of attitude."

We express our agreement, then a feral gleam lights his golden eyes as he chuckles wickedly and rubs his hands together.

"Now for the good part… We hike to the spot we used to hang out at as pups. Pitch tents. Hunt as wolves. Explore. I arranged a few activities for us, including airboat races and fishing. So, if you're finished asking questions, let's. Get. At. It!"

Pumped up, he claps his hands for emphasis.

"Yeah! Let's do this, like Brutus!" Viggo exclaims as he fist bumps with Dylan. Then they throw their heads back and howl.

Jagger, Tag, and I glance at each other, then join in their call. It reverberates around Dylan's great room. My heart soars with it, excited to spend time with my boys. We end with exploding fist bumps and change into the new gear Dylan laid out for us—tank tops, cargo pants, socks, and heavy boots. The packs slip onto our backs before we head out.

"We each have a satellite phone in our packs. So, you won't be completely disconnected from the world, you wusses," Dylan adds as we tromp along the path headed for the tree line.

As we pass beneath the pine trees, I send a blast of love through the tether Natalie and I share. I grin as my heart swells with her response. Being with my boys is great. But nothing beats my fated mate.

~

"Rust! You're back! I missed you, baby! How was your Guys' Getaway?"

Natalie jumps to her feet from where she sits on a chaise lounge and races across the deck, arms outstretched. She stops abruptly a few feet away and wrinkles her nose.

"Um… You're stinky. What did you guys get into? Or what didn't you get into? Ewww!"

"Oh, no, Jagger! Don't even think about—"

Sage squeals as he dips his shoulder into her belly and lifts her onto his shoulder. Her long hair tumbles from the bun. Curls bounce as he jogs past Natalie and me. Sage's giggles trail behind them.

I turn my hungry gaze on my fated mate. She lifts her hands up, palms out, as she backs away from me, shaking her head. I growl low in my chest. She shudders visibly as her pupils dilate. The outline of her plump nipples appears beneath the thin cotton tank top. The tip of her tongue darts out to moisten her lips.

"Rust..."

Her sultry purr causes blood to rush to my already thickening cock in the confines of the cargo pants.

Twenty-four hours for Dylan's rugged adventure prove too long of a separation from my fated mate. I'm hungry for her. Stinky or otherwise. Her backing away only triggers my hunting instinct. The predator in me howls, eager for the chase.

Natalie must sense my mood through our bond. Her hooded eyes widen before she spins and scampers towards the other end of the deck. I watch in appreciation as her ass in skimpy shorts jounces with each hurried step. I allow her a head start, then howl as I pursue her through the glass accordion doors. She shrieks and runs for the stairs. I lope after her.

"Rust! Our mate bonding ceremony is in a few hours! You can't just ravage me now! Oh!"

I swipe her calf as she races up the stairs. She catches her balance on the banister and rushes on.

"You're incorrigible, Rust Ingolf!"

I chase her all the way to our bedroom suite. She peeks over her shoulder as she flings our suite's double doors open. I growl. She hops like the frightened hare my wolf devoured last night. Now, it's her turn.

Before she reaches the bedroom's doors, I lunge forward and grab her by the waist. She sails through the air and lands on the bed. She scrambles to her hands and knees. The silky curtain of her midnight hair covers her beautiful face.

But it's her perfectly round ass that draws my attention. I allow my claws to extend and drag one from her ankle and up her inner thigh, leaving a trail of goosebumps in its wake. Her legs quiver as she moans and drops to her forearms, forehead on the bed. The position elevates her ass, and I rumble in approval.

The claw drags along the gusset of the minuscule shorts to trace her folds. A line of moisture appears on the white linen. She arches her back with a throaty moan. Her ass rises higher. I lick my lips, greedy for a taste of her honey.

The claw slips beneath the gusset. She gasps as it scoops some from her dripping pussy. I suck on the claw and growl. She shudders from the animalistic sound. Her whimpers increase my desire to devour her.

With one swipe, the claw rends the shorts in two. The pieces flutter to the bed as she gasps. The claw retracts, and my hands grip her hips. I lower my mouth to lap straight from the fount. Her body convulses as I force orgasm after orgasm from her pussy. Her honey gushes into my mouth. I swallow it down with satisfied grunts.

I reach for the zipper of my cargo pants. She cries out at the sound of the teeth parting. I fist the base of my cock, then slam home in one brutal thrust. It sinks within her wet heat to bottom out at her womb. My groin cradles her ass while my heavy balls slap her engorged clit. I grunt when her pussy walls clamp on my cock like a vise.

She moans and tosses her head as her pussy stretches to accommodate my girth. To ease the burn, my thumb and index finger slip beneath the hood of her clit to tease the sensitive nub. She bows her back as her pussy juices gush on my fingers and drips between her knees. Her natural lubricant coats my cock.

I grip her hips and pummel her pussy. The insistent need to fuck her outweighs gentle lovemaking. Our bodies smack together in a carnal rhythm. Her desperate moans mingle with my hungry growls. The air around us explodes with the musky scent of sex and sweat.

It's a quick and dirty fucking. A few thrusts, and I go off like a geyser. Hot seed shoots into her womb. A savage roar punches the air. Sated, I collapse on top of her, flattening her body to the mattress. She bears my weight with a throaty moan.

~

Natalie

"You look gorgeous, Natalie."

"You don't need any makeup. That glow outdoes any blush!"

"So pretty."

"Rust will fall in love with you all over again."

Through the trifold mirror in the bedroom's sitting room, I smile tearily at the girls and his mom. Sage rearranged the room for my mate bonding ceremony preparation space. A rolling rack of exquisite dresses stands to the side with shoes and sandals arranged below it. Lace and silk lingerie rests on a dressing table. Champagne bottles sit in a sterling silver bucket with crystal flutes and strawberries on the coffee table. It's wonderful except it's missing my Mom and Amanda.

Signy hands me a tissue with a smile.

"I know you must miss your family, especially today. We can never erase your pain or replace your sister and mother. But we adopt you into our pack and our circle of girlfriends. You have us, now, Natalie."

The others gather around me for a hug. The sadness in my heart lifts, and I smile with happiness.

"Thank you. It means so much to me."

A knock at the door followed by Rust's father's voice.

"May I come in?"

Frigg unlocks the door, and he smiles at her as he strides in the sitting room. He stops a few feet from me. His smile widens.

"Natalie, how lovely you are," he says, then continues after I thank him. "It would be my honor to walk you to the ceremony bower."

Once again, tears fill my eyes. I nod, unable to verbalize a response.

"Now, we can't have you all weepy as you greet your fated mate. Allow me?"

I turn to Sage and nod. She grins and works her magick. Immediately, the tears stop and my cheeks dry. A rush of elation sweeps through me. I giggle and thank her.

"Shall we?"

I slip my arm through Rudolf's.

The girls and Frigg bustle out ahead of us. We get into the golf carts and make our way to the open, park-like square.

Amidst the garden and benches stand rows of long rectangular tables with white tablecloths and white wooden chairs. Floral arrangements line the center with buckets of Champagne. Chafing dishes with a variety of foods and beverages sit on tables to the side. A separate table holds a four-tiered cake. Columns of intertwined tree branches and flowers strung with thousands of fairy lights surround the area to allow for the celebration to continue after the sun sets. A ceremony bower with the same treatment stands at one end. I smile at the magickal fairy-tale, all thanks to Sage.

The pack gathers in front of the bower while Rust waits beneath it with Jagger. Sage slips from the first golf cart and circles the pack to stand opposite Rust and Jagger. He grins at her. But Rust only has eyes for me.

He looks up the aisle as I alight from the second golf cart. Our eyes connect. His glow with a love so fierce, my heart skips a beat. A pulse reaches through our tether. I smile brightly at my fated mate as Rudolf escorts me down the aisle. Rust strides towards us, nods at his father, and scoops me into his arms. I giggle and wrap my arms around his neck. The pack wolf whistles and claps. He turns for the bower and settles me on my feet.

"Natalie Moore, I claim you as my fated mate to protect, love, and cherish for all time. To bear my pups and to stand by my side. I love you, Natalie Ingolf, my fated mate!"

I swallow back tears of joy, then clear my throat to respond.

"Rust Ingolf, I claim you as my fated mate to protect, love, and cherish for all time. To bear your pups and to stand by your side. I love you, Rust Ingolf, my fated mate!"

More shouts and howls of rejoicing fill the air.

Rust scoops me up and swings me around. My head goes back as I howl with joy. He joins me for a song of love. Then he carries me back up the aisle as the pack congratulates us. We settle at the head table with Jagger, Sage, Rudolf, Frigg, Viggo, Tag, Dylan, and Sasha. Once everyone takes their seats, Jagger and Sage stand with flutes of Champagne.

"It is my great pleasure to welcome Natalie Ingolf as the fated mate of Rust Ingolf to our Miami Wolves Pack—"

Cheers interrupt him. He waits with a grin for them to finish.

"Natalie is an OB-GYN and will assume the role of doctor for all she-wolves—"

The males clap and stomp their feet. Jagger chuckles. He and Sage raise their flutes.

"Tonight, we celebrate Rust and Natalie's mate bonding with good food and fellowship, followed by a pack run. Join Sage and me in welcoming Natalie to our pack!"

I laugh as the space rings with the howls of dozens of wolf shifters. Rust grips the back of my neck and kisses me passionately. More howls and whistles fill the air.

"Now, let us feast!"

Jagger says, then he and Sage sit.

During dinner, every member of the pack introduces themselves and offers well wishes. Their heart-felt welcome gladdens me. Nerves flitter away with the breeze. I lean against Rust, and he tucks me against his side.

"You take my breath away, my fated mate," he says as he places a kiss on my temple. "How are you doing?"

"Thank you, my fated mate. Marvelous, darling! Simply marvelous."

He chuckles and kisses the tip of my nose.

I sigh, content to be held and loved so dearly.

We eat, drink, and dance as the sun sets. Soon, the pack grows restless, ready for our run. Jagger senses the change in mood from festive to eager. He rises and announces the start of the pack run. Everyone strips where they stand and shifts amidst crackles and flashes.

As I slip out of my dress and sandals, I glance at Rust, who stands naked. Only the wolf paws on his sculpted pecs cover his divine body. He smiles encouragingly.

"I've got you, babe. Your wolf has you, too. Now, shift."

My body follows his command. In seconds, I'm on four paws. I lift my gaze to him. He winks and shifts. My wolf purrs at the sight of his massive brown wolf. He approaches and nuzzles my throat. My body vibrates at his touch. He rumbles deep in his chest, then throws his head back and howls.

Soon the sultry Everglades' night resounds with the howls of dozens of wolf shifters. Leaves rustle as creatures of the night hasten to their lairs to avoid the apex predators on the loose. A barred owl hoots as it takes to the air wings flapping to reach the sky. In the distance, a Florida panther yowls to remind us how cats hate dogs before it too slinks away. The hum of winged insects remains as a backdrop to our calls. The pack makes its presence known and silences the rest of the wetland.

Above, the waxing gibbous moon signals redirection, adjustment, and flexibility. I take it as a sign for new beginnings with my fated mate and my new pack. I'll relearn my wolf with his help. And I will let go of the rigidity caused by my wounded heart. It's time for healing.

I throw my head back and howl.

Around me, the pack stamps their paws and rejoins my call. I revel in the camaraderie and am as eager as they to sprint through the saw grass marshes and pine flat woods. Jagger and Sage set off. His giant silvery white wolf and her smaller ebony one rush for the tree line. Rust nudges my flank, and we follow. I match his pace. Shoulder to shoulder, we run together. Our paws land with each step silently.

The invigorating run heightens my senses. My body tingles as the wind ruffles the dense coat of my midnight and white streaked fur. My eyes adjust to the darkness. The landscape appears as though daylight reveals it. Scents of the Everglades inhabitants fill my nose. At once, I feel carefree.

Along the way, Rust romps and teases me affectionately. I respond with yips and barks. Excitement sparks in the air around us.

Miles later, we rest on our haunches. I take the time to familiarize myself with the new surroundings. Several members pair off and separate from the pack. Rust nudges me and rises. He darts away, and I give chase. We reach a cluster of dense pine trees. He moves beneath the low hanging branches. Inside, a patch of ground covered in pine needles makes the perfect hideaway.

He turns to me and rumbles. I quiver with need as he approaches. Without prelude, he mounts me. I howl and paw the ground with my front feet. He takes me with feral growls. My slick eases his savage thrusts. His front legs tighten around me as the base of his cock expands to form his knot.

I whimper as my pussy contracts. More than our mate bond, we lock together physically. His hot seed fills my core as he howls. I join his carnal song.

While we remain as one, he rumbles to soothe me. Once his knot deflates, we separate. I whimper and rub my body against his before I curl up on the bed of pine needles. He lies beside me as my eyes drift closed.

My last thought of how happy I am for what's to come makes me purr.

ust

"You know, a she-wolf could get used to this swanky lifestyle."

I chuckle at my fated mate as she waggles her eyebrows seated beside me in the helicopter.

We just lifted off with Jagger, Sage, Dylan, Sasha, Tag, Viggo, and Signy. The rest of the pack members—including my parents—fly in other helicopters or drive back to their Miami residences. Everyone was excited about the pack's newest addition. Over breakfast, several members told me how happy they were I found my fated mate, who could care for me as I have for everyone else. I couldn't agree more.

Especially as I grin at her now.

"Well, get used to it, babe. I plan to spoil you rotten!"

Everyone laughs.

Jagger pulls his mobile from his pocket and accepts a

call. He puts it on speaker since it's from Magnus—Alpha of the Los Angeles Wolves Pack.

Natalie reaches for my hand as she stares at the mobile like it's a rattlesnake set to strike. I squeeze her hand reassuringly. She nods.

"Hello, Alpha, I have you on speaker with my Luna, beta, Natalie, Rust, and my most close confidantes. What news do you have for us?"

"Hello, Alpha. Good and bad."

Natalie gasps as her eyes widen. I pull her onto my lap and rumble to soothe her distress.

"Give us the bad first."

"That Sam is a wily fucker. He escaped my enforcers by squirreling down some hidden hole he has beneath the floorboards of his house. It took them a few days. But they found him hiding out with a pregnant she-wolf. The female was more than happy to be rid of him."

"Well, thank fuck!" Jagger says. "But if him being captured is the bad news, what's good?"

Magnus chuckles.

"My head enforcer met his fated mate! I gave him my blessing as the pack's new Alpha. He'll have the rest sorted out quickly."

"Excellent—"

"Uh, excuse me, Alpha," Natalie says, then continues when Jagger nods. "What happened to Sam?"

Magnus growls.

"The dumbass thought he could challenge the new Alpha. And got his throat ripped out."

Natalie sags with relief, then asks, "Would you and the new Alpha mind if I visited the pack? I would like to visit my family's graves and check on the she-wolves."

"Absolutely! Let me know when you and Rust want to

come. I'll arrange everything for you. And my congratulations on your mating."

We thank him, and Jagger ends the call. All eyes turn to my fated mate.

"Thank you. You do not know how much this means to me. A peace I haven't had for many years settles over me. I truly appreciate your kindness."

She bows her head humbly.

"You're welcome, Natalie. Your wellbeing—as with the rest of our pack—is Sage's and my top priority. We do whatever we can to help."

My fated mate nods, too overcome for words. I rock her in my arms and nuzzle the top of her head. She buries her face in my neck. After a while, she calms and returns to her seat with a smile.

I point out landmarks as we fly to distract her from any sadness and to remind her of her new home and family. She thrills at the coastline and vastness of the Atlantic Ocean. I tell her we'll go swimming on South Beach. Soon, Miami's skyline comes into view. The pilot takes us along the barrier island to give my fated mate a bird's-eye view of the city.

When we land atop the beachfront building on Ocean Drive where the bachelors live, she stares out the window in awe. Viggo and I hop out. I turn around and help her from the helicopter and grab our bags. We bid the others goodbye before we leave the rooftop for the elevators.

"So, we have a new resident. A she-wolf at that, huh?" Viggo asks.

I shake my head and respond, "Not for long. I'm no bachelor, and my fated mate needs a residence. One she can make our own."

"Where will we go?" She asks as we board the elevator.

"I have a bayfront plot on Moon Island near Jagger and

Sage and Dylan and Sasha. I'll take you there after I put our things away here. We can build a residence to your liking."

Her eyes widen as her mouth opens and closes a few times. I place my index finger beneath her chin to draw her mouth closer, then slant mine over it.

Viggo groans. I chuckle and slip my arm around my fated mate's waist when the elevator doors open on my penthouse floor. Mine is the highest in the forty-story building with Viggo's next in age order. Natalie waves goodbye, and we step into the entry foyer.

"If the entry is fabulous, I can't wait to see the interior!" She quips as she glances around the space where two glass and steel tables with bouquets of white flowers flank steel double doors etched with wolves.

I smirk as I press my palm to the plate, then push the doors open. I drop our bags inside. With a flourish, I scoop her into my arms bridal style and carry her over the threshold. Her giggles morph into oohs and aahs as the Atlantic Ocean comes into view through a wall of windows across the expansive living room.

"My goodness, Rust! This is spectacular!"

She wiggles to get down, then rushes to the glass wall as soon as her feet touch the white marble floor. I follow and wrap my arms around her as she stands gaping at the unobstructed view.

Two cruise ships on the horizon and several megayachts float on the turquoise water. A person on a parasail powered by a speedboat flies by in the clear blue sky. Higher still, a plane displays an advertisement banner for a luxury condo. I chuckle when I see it's one of Larson Enterprises, Inc's new properties. I point it out to my fated mate, and she shakes her head in amazement at all of it.

"Are you sure we want to move? I mean, this place is phenomenal, and I haven't even seen the rest of it!"

I'm a possessive fucker. The idea of my fated mate riding the elevator with the male wolf shifters of our pack makes my wolf snarl and bare his fangs. Nope. Not happening.

"Sorry, babe. I will not allow the horny bachelors of the pack to ogle you on a daily basis. Do you want me to go feral, or what?"

She giggles and nudges me with her elbow.

"Are you a wolf or a caveman, Rust Ingolf?"

I bend down to press my lips to the delicate shell of her ear and murmur, "I'm a possessive male who will protect his fated mate at all costs."

She shudders, and I chuckle wickedly.

"Come, I'll give you a tour since it'll be a few months before our residence on Moon Island will be ready. You have until then to enjoy the penthouse. If that's a consolation for you."

She shakes her head but takes my hand.

We finish the tour in our bedroom suite. Her laughter and comments end as she stares at the king-size bed. I frown.

"What's the matter?"

She nibbles on her lower lip as her eyes flick between the bed and me. I shrug and raise my eyebrows.

"Um… I love the room. But… um… I don't want to sound like a prude or anything. But the bed. I'd rather not sleep where you had sex with other females. Sorry. Not sorry."

I chuckle, and her brows knit as she turns away. I rush behind her and grab her by the waist.

"Are you jealous, my fated mate?" I croon in her ear.

She pushes at my hands. I hold tighter.

"Now, you know what I would feel if we stayed here amongst all these males," I say, then continue when she stills. "However, other than my mother, no female has ever entered my residence. You are the only and the last lover to writhe beneath me in my bed. Do you understand?"

I finish on a growl with a thrust of my hips. Her jealousy makes my cock instantly hard.

She mewls a breathless yes.

"Now, let us make good use of *our* bed."

~

*N*ATALIE

"O*KAY*, now, a James Bond car! What will you shock me with next?" I ask as Rust leads me to something straight off the big screen in the posh action-packed movies.

"Oh, my fated mate, it only gets better. Just you wait."

I slip inside as he holds the door open. It's so low, I almost fall in! He reaches over and pulls the safety belt across me. Then places a kiss on my lips before he strides around the front and slides into the driver's seat. I roll my eyes at how easily he made it.

We're on our way to Moon Island. He'll show me around our pack's private island and take me to the plot for our new home. I'm so excited, I bounce on the luxurious leather seat. I turn my gaze out the window. People in other vehicles stare at the car—rather Bugatti La Voiture Noire, as Rust told me. I can't blame them. It's a masterpiece. They can't see me through the tinted glass, but I smile anyway.

We zip along MacArthur Causeway, leaving South Beach behind. More cruise ships docked at the Port of Miami await passengers. Their sheer size makes me wonder how the ships remain afloat. Soon, we turn off the causeway and pull up to intricate wrought-iron gates. Rust tells me they're the entrance to Moon Island. Two members of the security team sit in the guardhouse. They recognize Rust's car and wave.

He lowers his window and returns the gesture. I lean over and tell them hello. They greet me with warm smiles.

The gates' swing inward as the sensor detects its counterpart installed in the car. We drive through and along what Rust points out as the main road. He points out more sights as we drive along the entire island.

Homes ranging from ranch style to two- and three-story line the road. Some front Biscayne Bay, while others have interior views. On the other end, in the interior of Moon Island, a mini town offers options for those who prefer not to leave our protected land. A school for younger members of the pack, restaurant, deli, pizza shop, beauty salon, and barber shop are available.

The wealth of our pack continues to astound me. Never would I have imagined I would be in a situation like this one. I chalked my life up to being single and working hard at my career. Now, I have a fated mate who dotes on me and a new practice as the doctor for the she-wolves of our pack. Thankfully, Rust promised he won't force me to stop my work at the hospital or to have pups right away. I shake my head unbelievably. Now, I consider having pups even if not now. I guess that's what love and security will do for me.

As we pass a driveway covered in stone pavers leading to a Spanish-style ginormous mansion, Rust tells me it's Sage and Jagger's home. Okay, wow. I press my nose to the window as I try to get a good look at it. Rust chuckles and says we can call and see if they're up for a visit after we go to our plot nearby. I nod enthusiastically.

"That's Tag's residence next door. And this, my fated mate, is our plot set on Biscayne Bay, with direct water access. The acreage will allow for a home as large as Jagger and Sage's residence. We have a few architects and interior designers in the pack. I worked with two of them for the South Beach penthouse. Come on, we can walk the land so you can get a feel for it."

He hops out and helps me from the supercar.

I tilt my head back and let the glorious Miami sun shine on my face. A deep inhale brings the scent of saltwater and fragrant gardenia and jasmine flowers to my nose. Paradise!

Rust leads me to the edge of the property where mature palm trees rise tall and flowering bushes grow on the grass lawn. It extends uninterrupted from the road to the bay. Birds chirp in the palm fronds and bees buzz around the bushes. It's extraordinary.

"What do you think? Can you envision us here with a palatial home and room for our pups to run and play? Once you're ready, that is."

I rise on tiptoe and cup the back of his neck to bring his face closer to mine. I rub the tip of my nose against his, then press our foreheads together.

"I can envision it and so much more. When can we meet with the design team?"

"Hello, there, Rust and Natalie!"

Surprised, I turn to find a male wolf shifter and a she-wolf approaching us. They wave. I wave back, then lift an eyebrow at Rust. He grins.

"How about now?"

I laugh. My fated mate wastes no time!

A short while later, they leave with a follow-up meeting set in a few days. They'll present their ideas and sketches. I gave some input but can't wait to see what they come up with since they know the Miami style better than me.

Once they're gone, Rust takes my hand and leads me to the water's edge. He cups my face and stares at me with so much love, I feel it through our mate bond. I return it twice fold. I love my fated mate!

He pulls a small navy blue suede box from his jeans pocket and opens it.

My heart skips a beat.

Nestled in silk, a giant diamond ring sparkles in the sunlight. Rainbows glint off its flawless surface. I guess the oval-cut diamond is at least fifteen carats and set in platinum, with smaller round diamonds on the band. Unbelievable.

"I would have given you your wedding ring at our mate bonding ceremony. But it wasn't ready, and I didn't want to rush the custom piece. I selected an oval cut to match the shape of your gorgeous face," my fated mate says as he lifts the ring from the box and takes my left hand. He slips it on my ring finger as he continues. "Now, with my claiming bite on your neck and my ring on your finger, no one can wonder whether you are mine, Natalie Ingolf."

He lifts my hand to his lips and kisses it.

Tears blur my vision.

He rumbles deep in his chest and pulls me into his arms. I nuzzle my cheek against his heart, relishing its steady beat. One that only beats for me.

"Now that we handled the details for our new home, I will fulfill my promise to teach you to communicate better and to trust me. I told you I know just what you need. Tonight, I will show you, Little Girl."

CHAPTER 18

R*ust*

"WHAT'S ALL THIS?"

My fated mate stops and stares at the gift boxes on our bed as she adjusts the towel wrapped around her freshly showered body. She approaches the bed. Her fingertips glide over the glossy black wrapping paper and matching bows. Her eyebrow arches as she glances at me over her shoulder.

I cross the floor and plant a kiss on the bare flesh as an arm bands around her waist. The other hand tugs the towel. It drapes down her body. I cup a full tit and brush the pebbled nipple with my thumb. She moans, and I tweak the sensitive bud.

"Gifts for you, Little Girl."

I skim my fingers down the flat plane of her belly and cup her bare mons. My fingers delve between her wet folds to tease her swollen clit. Her head falls back against my shoulder as her hips gyrate. She bleats when my fingers spank her pussy.

"Be still. Now, open them."

I step away to watch her reaction to the erotic presents. My erect cock throbs in anticipation beneath my black leathers. I stroke the bulge languidly. Soon it will fill her wet warmth.

She touches each box, then decides on the smallest one. The bow slips free to the floor, followed by the discarded wrapping paper. The top lifts. She pushes the black tissue paper aside. Her eyes widen as she holds up the strands of pearls and black silk ribbons to her throat.

"Oh, Rust! This is gorgeous! Thank you, my love!" She gushes as she turns to me with a bright smile.

I chuckle and shake my head as I take the pearls from her hand.

"You're welcome. But the piece is not a necklace. Here, I will put it on you properly. Widen your stance."

She frowns but does as I command.

Standing behind her, I loosen the silk bows and slide the portion shaped like a triangle between her thighs and hold it to her mons. The double strand of pearls slips between her ass cheeks. She gasps as they glide along both sides of her clit and stroke her back entrance—which I will claim soon. I re-tie the bows at her hips.

"That's how you wear your pearl thong, Little Girl," I say in a voice roughened with carnal lust. Then slap each ass cheek. I groan as they jiggle enticingly. I add two more for sheer pleasure. She mewls and shimmies her hips.

"Next gift, Little Girl."

She takes a deep breath. A startled gasp slips from her parted lips as the pearls work their magic. Wide eyes peek at me over her shoulder as she hesitates.

I reach over and spank her ass in quick succession.

"When I tell you to do something, you do it naughty girl," I admonish.

"Y—Yes, Rust," she stutters.

"We will discuss more details in a moment. But you will call me Sir when we play—not Rust. Do you understand?"

"Yes, Sir."

Her cheeks flush crimson as she bites her lower lip.

Fuck. Me.

My cock leaks with pre-cum.

She turns to the bed and surveys the gift boxes. The rectangular one catches her eye. She removes the ribbon and top. A pair of six-inch, black marabou mules emerge. She blinks.

"Uh, Sir, they're fabulous. But I've never worn heels so high."

I take the mules and crouch before her. A tap to her calf, and she lifts her foot. I slip one on, then repeat for the other. I press kisses to her thighs, mons, belly, and to each nipple as I rise. Now, she stands three inches shorter than me. My erect cock nudges her lower belly. Perfect. As I expected.

Her pupils dilate.

"Do you trust me?"

She nods.

I clasp her chin between my thumb and index finger.

"Words, Little Girl. I will have your words."

She blinks, but responds, "Yes, Sir."

"There's my good girl. Next."

She bites her lip and spins around, then gasps as the pearls and my cock arouse her further.

I remain behind her as she bends over to reach the largest box. My fingers skim her hips. Tugs to each silk ribbon presses the pearls closer to her clit and puckered hole. She moans and bucks with a mini orgasm. The scent of her arousal wafts into my nostrils. I growl.

Her hands tremble as she opens the box.

Beneath the tissue paper lies an exquisite hand-crafted black corset with pearls. The sculpting design creates an hourglass figure with lace panels across the front in a butterfly shape and nipped in at the waist with a narrow strip of velvet. Elastic trim crisscrosses to form the shoulder straps, center panel, and outer panels of the lace.

She lifts it with an awed expression on her face.

"Astounding," she breathes.

"Here, I will help you."

Deftly, I place the corset on her and adjust it for a perfect fit. A bow around her neck and tiny ones between her amble tits lifted just right and at above the pearl thong make her look like a present. My present.

I step back. My mouth curves into a devilish smile as I twirl my finger for her to spin. She blushes but keeps her glittering onyx eyes on mine, glancing over her shoulders with each rotation. My feral grin spreads. My wolf howls.

"Come, Little Girl, or we will never reach our destination," I command as I rip the wrapping paper from the last box and remove a black Burberry trench coat. She slips her arms through the sleeves. I place my arm around her waist to keep her steady in the fuck-me mules. "Now, we go."

We ride the elevator down to the garage and slide into my one of my supercars. She remains quiet during the short ride along Ocean Drive. But the sexual tension is palpable as she fidgets in her seat and my cock throbs in my leathers. The musky aroma of her arousal fills the supercar's interior.

I guide the supercar into a driveway directly across from the Atlantic Ocean in a South Beach historic, beachfront gated mansion. She glances through the windshield, then out her tinted window.

"Where are we?" She asks as she squints at the discreet gold plaque with to Club Sol & Mani Miami written in a script font.

Cole—the club's valet and a young wolf shifter—opens her door.

"Good evening, Rust, Natalie."

"Good evening," we respond in unison.

She giggles as she takes his hand and rises from the low supercar. I growl at him for touching my fated mate. He raises his hands palms out and rounds the back of the supercar. She offers him an apologetic smile as I place my hand on the small of her back and usher her to the side. Laughter from members as they frolic in the mosaic-tiled pool within the sun-filled courtyard floats in the balmy evening air.

"Welcome to Club Sol & Mani Miami the luxury, members-only club owned by our pack."

She frowns and glances down at herself, then back at me with an arched eyebrow.

"If you think I'm going dancing in this risqué outfit, you have another think coming, mister!"

I hold back a chuckle and put on my stern Dom face.

"Oh, naughty girl. You will learn to trust me. All the more reason tonight's lesson is so important," I say. She lowers her eyes. "The club provides a safe space for those in the BDSM lifestyle. And as you know, I am a Dominant. You, my Little Girl, are a submissive."

Her eyes jump to my face as her mouth opens to protest. I place a finger on her lips and shake my head.

"You will give in to your submissive nature. I will guide you as your Dom—a highly skilled Dom. You display all the signs of a sub. You will recognize and appreciate them under my guidance. Now, come the night promises much pleasure."

We enter the club through the scrolled wrought-iron and glass doors.

"Good evening, Rust, Natalie. Enjoy," the doorman says with a smile.

We pass him and enter the opulent lobby where two she-wolf greeters stand behind a podium.

"Hello, Rust and Natalie!" They chorus cheerfully. "We're so excited for you! We'll take your coat, Natalie. Go right in."

She smiles at them, then glances at me questioningly. I untie the trench coat belt and unbutton it. Her lips part. I cock an eyebrow. She takes a deep breath and relaxes. I slip the trench coat off and hand it to the greeters.

A couple enters behind us.

My fated mate balks and places her hands over her ass. I rub her arms until she settles, then place my hand on the small of her back. I increase pressure to urge her through the double doors behind the greeters.

We enter Exhibition where demonstrations and performance rooms provide entertainment—or inspiration. The Dungeon provides a spacious section devoted to public forms of BDSM play. Those not in the lifestyle may think it's a medieval dungeon for torture with the St. Andrew's Crosses, spanking benches, chains suspended from the ceiling, and more. To those who enjoy the lifestyle, the pieces and assorted whips, floggers, canes, and implements are to be expected.

Which is why I chuckle when she gasps and freezes. Her wide eyes dart about Exhibition, taking in the sights. Four male wolf shifters surround a she-wolf spread out on a leather padded table. Her hands and mouth work three cocks while the fourth plunges in and out of her pussy. She moans and writhes in ecstasy. A she-wolf sits on her calves bound by red silks artfully arranged by a male wolf shifter trained in Shibari. Other demonstrations range about the space. The sounds of carnal pleasure and the scent of sex mixed with heightened pheromones blend for a hedonistic atmosphere.

"This way, Little Girl," I murmur in her ear.

She wobbles unsteadily by the distractions. I tighten my hold and lead her to a secluded area.

"What are Sage, Jagger, and the others doing here? They're Doms and subs too? Is this a party?"

"You'll also learn to stop thinking so much and go with the moment, Little Girl."

We stop where the others gather. Jagger and Sage greet us along with Dylan, Sasha, Viggo, and Tag.

"Your corset is fabulous, Natalie!" Signy exclaims, then winks at me. "Nice choice, Rust. You did well!"

"Thank you. I love your lingerie set. I just wish I knew what was going on," my fated mate responds, and glances at me.

I spank her ass, and she yelps.

"Unless you want to perform our collaring ceremony with a heated, red bottom that matches the soles of your mules, I suggest you remember what I just told you about thinking, naughty girl."

"Yes, Sir."

"Good girl," I praise her, then continue. "Our friends gather to celebrate our union as Dominant and submissive."

Jagger holds a navy blue suede flat box for me. I press the cabochon clasp to open the lid.

A custom-made collar rests on the silk lining. Tiny sparkly diamonds cover the intricate platinum lacework of the three-inch wide collar and the lock. I lift the delicate piece and place it around my fated mate's neck. The soft click of the closure makes my cock pulse. Mine!

"Natalie, I give you my collar as a sign of my love and my

vow to teach you communication and trust. My collar always shows your status as a partnered sub—my sub. You will obey me in all sexual interactions unless you want all play to end with the use of your safeword, *red*. For a Dominant to place a collar on a submissive equals the pair's commitment to their D/s relationship. On some levels just as important as a wedding ring is to a marriage. I have never collared a sub. Only you. Do you understand, Little Girl?"

Tears fill her eyes. She opens her mouth to respond but can only nod.

I lean over and brush my lips over hers as I murmur words to settle her.

"Yes, Sir." She responds with determination as she traces her fingertips lightly over the exquisite craftsmanship of my collar, then rests them on mine.

My heart swells with pride. My cock swells with carnal lust.

The others clap. Sage, Signy, and Sasha hug my fated mate while my best friends clap me on the back. They're Doms and understand the significance of the collaring ceremony.

A pulse of need rushes to my heart over the tether. I turn to find my fated mate surrounded by her friends. Yet her eyes focus on me. I nod and return her message with a strong one of my own. Her lips part on a gasp.

"Well, fellas, my sub has need of her Dom. Thank you for witnessing our ceremony. Good night!"

They chuckle as I prowl towards my Little Girl to take her to my private suite upstairs. Sage, Signy, and Sasha scatter at my presence, chattering like little birds. I bend and dip my shoulder into my sub's belly to lift her onto my shoulder. She squeals, and I spank both ass cheeks, cupping one to hold the fire inside. She gives in and hangs submissively.

Yeah, she's a natural sub. And it will be my absolute carnal pleasure to draw her into my BDSM lifestyle.

atalie

"NATALIE! Sasha is in labor! Can you come to Moon Island's hospital now?"

Dylan's panicked voice sounds through my mobile as I leave the day's last patient in an exam room at the OB-GYN department.

It's been a week since I last saw Sasha and Dylan at Club Sol & Mani Miami. I thought then she seemed close to delivery. But she assured me she was fine and still moving about with ease. Well, things change!

"Absolutely! I'll be right there—"

"Go to the hospital's roof. I sent the helicopter for you. He'll be there in five minutes... It's okay baby, Natalie is on her way... Ten minutes, that's all, baby. Don't worry. Listen, Nat, I have to go to Sasha. See you soon."

While he spoke, I ran to my office and grabbed my bag. On the way past the receptionists' desk, I tell them I'm gone for the day. Miraculously, the elevator arrives in less than a minute. I burst out on the highest floor, then race up the stairs to the rooftop. As I fling the doors open, the helicopter lands. The flight attendant opens the door and waves me forward. I hop in, and we lift off.

I pull my mobile from my pocket and send a text message to Rust since he's in the emergency room until eleven tonight. Before I put it away, the three dots indicate his response. Dylan already told him, and he'll come after his shift ends.

I glance out the window for signs of the Moon Island hospital. As Rust told me, it's a state-of-the-art facility with all the latest equipment and two operating rooms. They spared no expense to make it the best care facility for our pack. Departments include urgent care, general medicine, obstetrics, and pediatrics. It's rare a wolf shifter requires medical assistance since we have enhanced healing. But accidents can happen that require further help. The most used department being obstetrics.

Over the last week, Rust gave me a tour and introduced me to the staff of nurses, aides, and the head of administration. They expressed their excitement about a female doctor on staff. I set up my office and exam rooms. I met with the midwives for lunch. They shared their knowledge and told me which she-wolves were expecting and which hoped to conceive. I scheduled appointments with each of them. Their mates were relieved and thanked me profusely. So, I'm all set to help Sasha.

The pilot announces our arrival. I jump from the seat and hop out the moment the flight attendant opens the door. We landed on the front lawn, making it easy for me to rush inside and to the obstetrics department.

I round the corner and see Signy, Jagger, Tag, and Viggo in front of Sasha's delivery room.

"Nat! Thank goodness! Sage is in the room with Sasha,

Dylan, and the midwife. Sasha doesn't want magickal help—silly girl! So, hurry!" Signy says as she waves her hands.

"When did she start? Do you know the time between her contractions?" I ask rapid-fire questions as I rush past them.

"Three hours ago, we were eating ice cream, and she complained of a stomachache—"

"Obviously, she was mistaken!" Jagger chimes in.

I nod and push through the door.

"Oh, thank the Fates!" Sage exclaims as she rises from the chair beside Sasha's bed. "Tell me what you need. I'll help without my magick."

I nod and speak to Sasha as I wash my hands and switch to a fresh white coat.

"How do you feel?"

"Oooo… Like I'm going to *castrate* my fated mate!"

Dylan shudders and bows his head.

I bite my lower lip to keep from laughing out loud. The midwife catches my eye and smiles. Then she catches me up on Sasha's vitals. I check her cervix.

"You're not far now, Sasha. I want you to focus on your pup being in your arms soon and how much love you and Dylan have for her. Can you do that for me?"

Her dove gray eyes focus on me. For a moment, I think she's going to curse me in Russian. But she nods quickly and closes her eyes. Dylan presses a cool compress to her forehead. She opens her eyes and smiles softly at him. He sighs and leans over to kiss her lips.

My heart pangs. I turn away from their tender moment. Am I ready for pups now? What would it be like to be in Sasha's place with Rust pampering as best he can between me snapping at him? Sasha's sharp cry pulls me from my musings.

"Let's have another look, Sasha."

I check her again. Not much change. I tell her we'll have

to wait a bit longer, and she growls. Dylan widens his eyes. It's comical to see the fierce MMA fighter scared of his she-wolf fated mate. Poor thing.

My mobile vibrates in my pocket. I glance at Sasha. She leans against the pillows propped behind her back with her eyes closed. Good. I shift my gaze to the mobile screen and smile as I open the text message app.

Hi, babe. How's Sasha? Better yet, how's D.?

My grin widens. He knows his best friend so well. My fingers fly across the screen as I type my response.

She's good. Not much longer to go. D.... He's another story. I hope he doesn't faint! I'll keep you posted. xoxo Your Heart

"I'll go tell the others it'll be a while," Sage says and leaves the room.

I check Sasha's and the pup's vitals. All sounds and appears as expected. She's young and won't have an arduous labor. And since it's her first delivery, it will take longer. But less time than human females. She-wolves deliver faster.

While we wait, I make certain the station for checking the baby after birth along with the bassinet, diapers, blankets, and bedding are prepared. As my fingertips brush the soft cotton, my mind drifts back to the thoughts of me giving birth to Rust's pup. Would we have a female or male? Does he prefer one over the other?

Since he told me he won't force me to have pups right away, he hasn't mentioned a family of our own. He focuses on the two of us. The trips he plans to take me on—like the one to tour the major European cities, including Paris, Milan, Rome, Amsterdam and up to the UK for London and Glasgow. We'll go once I get more time at the hospital. On our days off, we'll go to the Bahamas or back to the Florida Keys. That's exciting. But what if—

"NATALIE! Get this pup out of me!"

I hurry to Sasha's side and place a hand on her round

belly. The pup shifted. I check her cervix, and she's ready. I tell her we're good to start with pushing, and she nods, biting her lip. Dylan stares at me in shock. I smile at him encouragingly. He needs more help than Sasha. I nod at the midwife, and we settle in to deliver their pup.

Thirty minutes later, Inessa Vang makes her glorious debut. Sasha says her name is Russian for pure and symbolic for her and Dylan's love. Tears fill my eyes as they do his at her pronouncement. The midwife and I leave the new family to bond. We go to the waiting room to tell the others who wait anxiously for news. Everyone cheers. Jagger congratulates me on a successful delivery. I smile and thank my Alpha and my friend.

After a while, Dylan enters the waiting room to tell us he and Sasha want to introduce the pack's latest member. We rise and follow the proud papa. I send a text message to Rust, then put him on FaceTime so he can take part in the introduction. Dylan holds his tiny pup to his massive chest and announces her name, Inessa Vang. Her eyes blink open to reveal amber eyes like her sire. We cheer. They thank me for delivering their pup and the midwife for her support before we leave the room.

Sage invites me to dinner with her and Jagger. I tell them I'll meet them at their home after I write my notes in my office. Once alone, I let my mind wander to a family with my fated mate.

Maybe the time is closer than I thought.

EPILOGUE

hree Months Later
Rust

"Your mansion is spectacular!"

"Congratulations on a fantastic property!"

"Damn, bro, you went all out, huh?! Well done!"

Natalie and I stand on the rear lawn of our newly finished bayfront residence on Moon Island. We invited our pack to the housewarming. And I have to agree. The architect and designer captured the modern Miami style Natalie and I want for our home. She loves the style of our former penthouse and wanted it on a larger scale.

The two-story glass and concrete mansion has five en suite bedrooms, two bathrooms, an open floor plan living, dining, and kitchen, media room, family room, gym, infinity edge pool and spa, pool house on the terrace with an outdoor kitchen, and so much more. Manicured lawns in the front and the rear with flowering bushes and palm trees make for a lush landscape. South Beach and the Atlantic Ocean beyond create a spectacular backdrop.

We just moved in yesterday, and already it feels like home. The only things missing are little pups running around getting into everything. Since Sasha gave birth to Inessa, I can't stop thinking about my fated mate and I having pups of our own. Dylan strides around with a puffed chest and shows pictures of his little pup every chance he gets. Then there's Jagger with his twin pups, Harald and Tove. He's no better than Dylan. I don't blame them. I'd do the exact same thing.

I shrug to myself and smile down at my fated mate. She's happy, and that's all that matters to me. My world is complete with her in it. Pups would add more joy. But I won't push the topic. Instead, I'll have patience. When the time is right, we'll have a family of our own.

"Rust? Did you hear me?"

I blink and shake my head.

"Sorry babe. I was in another world. What did you say?"

Her onyx eyes scan my face, then she smiles.

"Sage asked about a nursery."

My heart skips a beat. I cock my head to the side and stare at my fated mate.

"I told her we don't have one."

My heart sinks. But I manage to keep a straight face. I turn to Sage and smile.

"Yeah, we won't need one for a while. We have plenty of time. For now, we're enjoying one another. We have trips planned and fun to be had at Club Sol & Mani Miami. We're good for now."

I ignore the look Jagger sends my way. I don't want to go any further down that path. Instead, I excuse myself and head to the outdoor kitchen where Viggo mans the Viking grill. At least the bachelor for life—as he refers to himself—won't mention pups or nurseries.

"Hey, bro. I've got some burgers ready. You want one? Well, actually, you look like you could use some aquavit."

He turns to the wet bar behind him and pours a two-finger tumbler for me. I thank him and sip it as I watch him plate my burger.

"You know, you could earn a decent living as a cook," I tease.

He rolls his eyes and shoves the plate at me. Then dings an imaginary bell.

"Order, pick up!"

We laugh.

I take a seat at the oval table and smile at the pack members seated around it. My mate bond tether makes me glance up. Natalie walks towards me with a smile. I grin back. Her hair flows behind her, caught by the breeze. The colorful silk maxi dress skims her curves. She looks radiant. I shift in my seat to adjust my burgeoning erection at the sight of my gorgeous fated mate. We may not have pups. But we certainly put in enough practice.

She greets the others at the table, then leans over and wraps her arms around my neck.

"Hey, good looking, what you got cooking?" She asks with a giggle.

I lift the burger to her mouth, and she takes a hearty bite. Her moan makes my cock jump.

"Wow, Viggo knows what he's doing with a grill!" She says after she swallows.

I nod in agreement as I pull her onto my lap. I alternate feeding her and myself until the burger disappears from the plate.

We chat with the others, then mingle with those milling about the property. When the sun sets, the fireworks display begins. The brilliant sparklers light up the sky above Biscayne Bay. Everyone oohs and aahs in delight. The pups of other members laugh and point at each burst of color. I smile at their excitement.

Later that night, my fated mate and I sit on the balcony off our bedroom suite on the second floor, overlooking the bay and ocean. We reflect on the day and how happy we are with our new home. She climbs into my lap to straddle my thighs and nuzzles her cheek against mine.

"I love you so much, Rust Ingolf."

"I love you more, Natalie Ingolf."

"But some things are missing from our life, and I'm not happy about it."

I sit up straight, concerned, and stare at her.

"What—"

She places a finger on my lips and smiles. Leaning to my ear, she continues.

"I want lots of pups with you, Rust Ingolf. A little pack of our very own. Now, *Sir!*"

CHARMAINE LOUISE SHELTON

TAG
THE REDEMPTION

ABOUT TAG THE REDEMPTION: A WOLF SHIFTER FATED MATES PARANORMAL ROMANCE

What havoc can my shy, curvaceous human assistant wreak on my structured life? Drive my wolf feral.

As the beta of my wolf pack—the Billionaire Wolves of Miami—and the COO of our multibillion-dollar corporation, I demand control and order in my life. A serious wolf shifter with no time for drama or a relationship. They don't call me Mr. Grumpy and bosshole for nothing. But the gods have other plans when they choose Wren Byrd as my fated mate. The BBW personifies chaos. But my wolf wants her. Despite the ring on her finger.

All my life others teased me for being more robust and for not wearing a size zero. I'm curvy, darn it! So, when Jonathan the hot man of my dreams proposes, I accept. Then catch him with his sassy and slim neighbor. I accept his forgiveness—who else wants me? Until I meet Tag Dahl, my new boss. The beast of a male sets my soul on fire.

Little do I know he's not all he seems. And Jonathan won't accept he lost. He means to ruin my life…

*Their steamy love story is a standalone in the sizzling **Billionaire Wolves Series** of interconnecting stories featuring wolf shifter fated mates romance. Get a glimpse of their dynamism in other books.*

Anthem: "Live Your Life" T.I. featuring Rihanna
https://www.youtube.com/watch?v=koVHN6eO4Xg

Visit CharmaineLouiseBooks.com

CHAPTER 1

ag

WHY DO they whisper I'm a bosshole? Case in point…

"And that concludes the marketing department's promotion plan for the new build in Naples."

A hush descends in the conference room as fifteen pairs of eyes peek nervously at me. I keep mine laser focused on the male wolf shifter who heads the marketing team for the Naples residential project. He lowers his gaze respectfully as he awaits my comments.

As the COO of Larson Enterprises, Inc. it's my responsibility to manage and to handle the day-to-day business operations of the Miami Wolves Pack's multibillion-dollar company. Including working closely with department heads and supervisors to support the daily activity of employees.

A lot of pieces must move in sync to maintain Larson Enterprises as the top company in the hospitality industry for luxury hotels, fine dining, clubs, and lounges. Founded in Miami by our pack Alpha's family—with Jagger Larson as the current CEO. I'm his second in command as COO and as his pack beta. Both roles I take very seriously.

So much so that I will not tolerate less than stellar work by staff. And that means I have to hold back an irritated growl at the half-ass *promotion plan* presented. I'm surprised the male bothered. He should have known better. And I don't hesitate to express my dissatisfaction. At. All.

"Do you truly expect me to believe you did your research, Jackson?!" I bark, then hold up my hand when he opens his mouth to respond. "Rhetorical question. Obviously, you did *not*. Otherwise, you would recall a similar 'promotion plan' presented three months ago. One I rejected. The same I do with this one. You have twenty-four hours. I expect an *original* plan on my desk."

"Yes, Mr. Dahl, sir," he responds, then slinks to his seat.

As he hovers above it with his hands on the armrests, I shake my head with several tsks. His startled eyes jump to mine. I cock my head.

"Don't you think you should gather your team now? You have your work cut out for you, Jackson."

He stutters a response as he hops up and dashes towards the double doors.

I watch him go, then flick my gaze to the head of business development.

"Sally."

The human female swallows audibly, bobbing her head as she rises.

"Yes, Mr. Dahl, sir."

I sit forward, lean my elbows on the sleek conference table, and steeple my fingers. Next...

Two hours later, I stride past the staff on the executive floor on my way to my suite of offices. We employ wolf shifters and humans. Best for our kind to hide in plain sight and all. Although we've been here a hell of a lot longer than the humans.

Several millennia ago, Scandinavian Viking wolf shifters sailed from the Old World and landed along the East Coast of what's now the United States. The six packs headed by best friends who sought new lands moved throughout the continent to form territories, with ours settling here. We maintain close ties with our brethren through friendship, mating, and business. Plus, our Ruling Council gatherings keep us informed of happenings throughout the packs.

Our Miami Wolves Pack is the most powerful pack in the South. Because of the success of Larson Enterprises, other packs refer to us as the *Billionaire Wolves of Miami*. Further reason for me to ensure I fulfill my responsibility to take Jagger's CEO vision for the company and turn it into an executable business plan. Correction, a *flawless* executable business plan. So, call me bosshole all day. And sometimes all night.

I round the corner to my office suite and nod at my administrative assistant, Beth. The she-wolf scampers to her feet from behind her desk outside my office and hands a file folder to me. Her head tilts back since I tower over her at six feet seven inches.

"Here's your speech for the charity gala tonight, Mr. Dahl. Communications made your requested edits, sir."

"Thank you, Beth. My date is aware of the time I'll pick her up?"

"Yes, Mr. Dahl. I spoke with Katrina an hour ago. She confirms she will be ready. Your lunch delivery is on its way up now. Both Mr. Larsons, Dr. Ingolf, and Mr. Vang wait in your office."

I figured as much since the opaque treatment blocks the clear glass wall. Jagger must have activated it knowing we'd want privacy for our weekly Guys' Lunch. Today it's my turn. Naturally, I'm hosting it here in between meetings.

More than likely, I'll hear about it from them since I'm always in the office. So what? Unlike Jagger and Dylan, I don't have—nor do I want—a mate that keeps me tethered to her side. Or like Viggo, who can't stay out of any female's panties. Rust is the only one as tied to his job as I am to mine. He's in the emergency room as a critical care surgeon more than anyplace else. Inwardly, I shrug. Outwardly, I nod at my assistant.

"Thank you, Beth. You may leave for your lunch early."

"Thank you, Mr. Dahl."

I open the double doors of my office. My best friends lounge on the white leather sofa and chairs in the sitting area with their feet up on the coffee table and armrests guffawing. Thank the gods my office is obscured and soundproof with this lot.

We've been friends since we were pups. My father Branson was the enforcer for the former Alpha Marcus— Jagger's father. Jagger and I were born a few weeks apart and inseparable for twenty-eight years. My mother Ylva teases the former Luna Sigrid she stole her only pup. Rust Ingolf and Dylan Vang are a year older, while Viggo came along two years later as Jagger's younger brother. The five of us share a strong bond as best friends, even going so far as to get wolf paw tattoos on our pecs. Well, Jagger wussed out, claiming he has no interest in marring his perfect body. Regardless, we treat each other like blood brothers. And that includes getting on my nerves kicking back on my furniture with no care whatsoever…

"Hello, gentlemen. A pleasure, as always."

They pivot as one pack. Heads cock. Eyes sharp. Nostrils flare. Then the grins spread across their faces, laughing at the scowl on my face as my eyes flick between their feet and the furniture.

"Why hello there, Mr. Grumpy!"

"How's your grumpilicious day going, bro?"

"Why the sour face? Don't you love us anymore?"

"I hope your status meeting went better than the expression on your face…"

I shake my head as I loosen my silk tie and shrug out of my bespoke suit jacket. Oh, yeah, we're all billionaires, and they're dressed in similar high-end apparel. Young, sexy AF, and wealthy beyond our wildest dreams.

"Hello. Again. My day would be better without your boots on my white leather sofa. I can't get rid of you, so I'm forced to love you. Other than a wreck of a promo plan, the meeting went well, surprisingly."

A knock on the door cuts into their uproarious chuckles. I stride over and open it. Beth leads the delivery person to the conference table beside the floor-to-ceiling wall of windows.

As they arrange the gourmet meals from a Larson restaurant at each chair, I glance at the view always captivated by the stunning panorama. One of the tallest buildings in the city, The Larson Tower in Downtown Miami Bayfront stands seventy-five floors high across from Biscayne Bay. Beyond its azure waters—where jet skiers zip by and megayachts cruise along—lies the Atlantic Ocean. Its dazzling turquoise surface extends to the horizon as far as the eye can see. I inhale and relax. The clamoring of the guys as they pull out chairs and check who has what food interrupts my all too brief respite. I roll my eyes and drop into a white leather executive chair.

We shoot the shit about the latest Miami Dolphins football game, Viggo's new blinged out watch, and our upcoming deep-sea fishing trip to the Bahamas. My mobile vibrates in my pocket. I groan at the photos on the screen.

"What's up?" Rust asks as he peers over my shoulder. He barks out a laugh. "For real? You've gotta be kidding me!"

He snatches my mobile and passes it to Dylan, who guffaws and passes it to Viggo and on to Jagger. Until I grab it back with a growl, emerald green eyes flash with my displeased wolf.

"What the hell is Katrina up to?"

I sigh and run my fingers through the short length of my sable brown hair.

"She's accompanying me to the charity gala tonight. I thought she behaved well at the hotel opening last week and figured she'd be a suitable candidate for another social event. Obviously, she thought more of the invitation."

Dylan chuckles and smirks.

"You don't say? If the lingerie pics under the guise of 'Which, do you prefer?' didn't clue you in, I don't know what would!"

I groan and respond with a terse not interested and no need to get dressed at all since you won't join me, then toss my mobile on the table.

I'm no monk. I like to fuck. A lot. But I keep my life segmented by work, social events, and sex and keep the participants separated. The luxury, members-only BDSM lifestyle club on Ocean Drive—Club Sol & Mani Miami— owned by our pack provides me with willing she-wolf submissives to satisfy my Alpha Dominant kinks. And even there, I play with several subs. I never let the thought of one being a favorite form in their heads. So, no, I don't need lingerie photos of Katrina. She lost her spot in the social events segment for good. But now, who to take I ponder as my head shakes.

Viggo studies me with ice blue eyes so like his brother's

but has fiery copper red hair. I cock my head at the younger wolf shifter.

"Why don't you hire another assistant who can manage your social calendar and attend events with you? As an employee, she won't expect to become Mrs. Tag Dahl. Better yet, hire a human female. Then it's zero chance of her thinking she's your mate. We may fuck a human female. But it's been decades since a male wolf shifter turned a human in our pack. No wrong ideas or vavavavoom photos!"

He snaps his fingers and sits back, arms crossed over his muscular chest. A triumphant grin appears on his face.

I stare at him.

A human female assistant to handle my personal affairs with no endgame to mate with me? No coy smiles or hair flips? Actual conversations and not double entendres? A business professional who expects a paycheck and not a diamond rock? Well, damn! Let me contact Human Resources right now.

A grin spreads across my face as the idea settles in.

"Hell yeah, Viggo! That's just what I need. In fact, I'll email the head of HR—"

My mobile skitters across the smooth surface of the table like a hockey puck. Dylan's massive mitts catch it as he grins at Jagger.

"Not now, you're not. You're having lunch with your best friends. Work can wait," Jagger says with a smirk. "And I'm telling you that as Alpha, CEO, and best friend. No room for dispute or negotiation, bro."

I roll my eyes and sit back.

These guys are lucky I do love them. Or else I'd kick their asses.

"Now that you dumped Katrina, who will you take?"

I shrug in answer to Rust's question.

After seeing the she-wolf's unwanted photos, I'd rather

go alone. Although, having a female on my arm keeps others at bay. Well, for the most part. I've had a few approach me the moment my date stepped away to the ladies' room. I may be a bosshole. But I'm still a gentleman and made it clear I was with someone. Tonight, I won't be in the mood to dodge hopeful females.

"Take Signy. The social princess is always up for an event if her calendar allows a last-minute engagement. Give her a reason to wear one of her beloved haute couture gowns."

Viggo's suggestion pulls me from my musings. His and Jagger's younger sister is the pack princess and a little sister to me. So, again, no chance for mistaken expectations. Perfect!

"Damn, bro, you're on fire today, huh?" Dylan teases with a smirk. "Trying to get Brownie points or what?"

Viggo throws a handful of French fries across the table in response. Herbs and Parmesan cheese crumbles drop to the surface. Dylan picks the fries up and pops them in his mouth.

I growl, and they laugh.

"Listen, I'm not due to the ER for another few hours. I have no interest in saving either of your asses from Tag's wrath. So, cut the shit," Rust says as he eyes them.

Dylan grabs him in a headlock and noogies his head.

I refuse to play referee—or preschool teacher—and ignore them. Instead, I snag my mobile to call Signy.

"It never ceases to amaze me how well you scrub up. I remember you as a pup chasing behind your brothers and the guys to prove you're just as tough."

Signy rolls her ice blue eyes as I tease her.

She's a gorgeous she-wolf and dressed spectacularly in a

signature red Valentino haute couture gown with a matching clutch and strappy stilettos. Her waist-long ebony hair piled atop her head in an easy bun and blood red lipstick offer contrast to the elegant gown. Ruby and diamonds sparkle on her ears, neck, finger, and at both wrists. An absolute stunner.

Which is exactly why her brothers and the rest of us run interference with any male who dares to get close to Signy. Only the best and the most worthy male will court the pack princess. At twenty-four, she has plenty of time before she mates. Not that she has a choice. Especially since Jagger nixed the attempt by an Alpha from out west to claim her.

"Tag, that was decades ago! Now, come on or, we'll be late, Mr. I Have an Overseas Call I Can't Skip."

She loops her arm through mine and drags me towards the front doors of the bayfront mansion she lives in with her parents. I help her into the back of my chauffeured Bentley Bentayga and round the back to slide in beside her. An enforcer for the pack serves as my driver and personal security, along with a second enforcer who rides in the passenger seat.

She bleeds my ear about her latest exploits—social events attended, philanthropic work—pack gossip, and her next trip to Europe for fashion week. I indulge her like a good older brother, even though my mind drifts to my business trip.

"—And the cow jumped over the moon."

I frown and lift an eyebrow at her. She shakes her head.

"You weren't listening to a word I said, Tag. Let me guess, you have some important business on your mind?"

I open my mouth to protest, but she lifts her hand to stop me.

"That's why you need to take a hint from your boys and

find your fated mate. Then you won't only have Larson Enterprises to occupy your mind."

Thankfully, the luxury SUV stops in front of the Larson Miami Hotel & Resort, saving me from responding. Without a word, I hop out and stride around to her side. The enforcer holds her door open while I extend my arm. She places a dainty hand on my forearm as a brilliant smile spreads across her face.

Immediately, cameras flash from the paparazzi covering the charity gala for local society papers and websites to national and international media outlets. They call Signy's name since she's a regular on the social scene.

She alights from the luxury SUV with grace. Her gown flows behind her as I escort her down the red carpet. She's a beauty amidst the other patrons lined up for photos or chatting with the camera crews. We pause in front of the step and repeat where the Larson Enterprises, Inc. logo blazes behind her. She smiles and points at it with a red-polished, manicured fingernail. The paparazzi go wild. The flashes blinding. I stand aside and respond to emails on my mobile.

A tug on my arm alerts me to Signy's return to my side. I smile, and we head inside for the rooftop ballroom with an outdoor terrace. The night goes as planned. We mingle with others during the cocktail hour. Females know better than to approach me with Signy on my arm. Her eyes flash if they come anywhere near me. I send my thanks to Viggo.

After my speech and dinner, Signy wants to get some air. Although I think she has her eye on a particular human male. Like I'll let that happen. But again, I indulge her.

We step through the opening created by the wall of glass sliding into side pockets. Others have the same idea of enjoying the evening breeze off the Atlantic Ocean, creating a glitzy crowd of designer gowns and tuxedos. Their laughter and the buzz of conversations float all around.

I glance at my Patek Philippe timepiece. Another thirty minutes, and we're out. I let Signy guide me in the direction the human male took.

I stop, stunned.

Eyes narrow. Nostrils flare. Cock thickens. A rumble grows in my chest. The urge to howl grips my throat. I inhale deeply.

Carried on the breeze across the rooftop, the faint scent of cinnamon sugar caramel apples wafts towards me. The unique scent I inhaled as my first breath when born tantalizes my senses. The scent of the only she-wolf destined for me.

My fated mate.

 ren

"HELLO... Earth to Wren Byrd... Come back to the room, chica."

I blink to clear my unfocused gaze and turn to my personal trainer turned best friend, Maya Alejandra Perez Garcia. Her jet black eyebrows knit together over her expressive topaz eyes. Looking at her gorgeous face makes my thoughts wander again to last night's unpleasant encounter.

Maya is everything I'm not. A former fitness model with proportionate curves whose body makes men fall at her feet. Five inches taller than me at five feet, nine inches. Not to mention her confident, outgoing, and independent personality. The only commonality is our age of twenty-five. Gee...

Her eyes narrow as they scan my face. Undoubtedly, the misery from last night appears on its fullness. She places her hands on her hips and arches an eyebrow.

"Spill it, Wren. What happened?"

My eyes slink away as I shrug. Instead of responding, I head to the treadmill for my warm-up before our training session begins. I ignore the panorama of Biscayne Bay out to the Atlantic Ocean while my fingers fiddle with the digital display panel. The treadmill belt starts slowly.

"Oh, no you won't," Maya says as she slams her palm on the big red stop button. I grip the side rails and glance at her. "Before we begin, we need to clear your head so you can focus on yourself and not on whatever upset you. This way."

I follow her to the corner of the gym on the top floor of my luxury condo building in Brickell. She rolls two large stability balls to the floor-to-ceiling windows. The expanse of the glass allows the brilliant Miami sun to shine on us as we settle on the balls. I wobble before I find my balance.

Maya sits with ease and flicks her long ponytail over her shoulder, bare in a white crop bra. She rests her hands on her lithe thighs covered in the matching leggings. Her expectant gaze focuses on me. Obviously, there's no chance to avoid an answer.

I adjust my black t-shirt over my soft belly. My palms slide along the black joggers. All black everything, I mean, it's the best color to cover flaws, right? Inwardly, I roll my eyes. Outwardly, I sigh. Might as well get this over with.

At least Maya is my best friend and won't judge me. She'll definitely have loads to say after she finishes cursing in Spanish. I wince at the thought. Fortunately, the gym is empty now. No one to overhear me recount the disastrous night. Ugh!

"I caught Jonathan with his neighbor."

My hot fiancé with his sassy and slim neighbor—again my complete opposite—to be exact. Last night when I arrived at his condo to surprise him with dinner from his favorite restaurant, the front door was ajar. Concerned, I pushed it open and crept inside, not wanting to alert an intruder to my presence. When, in fact, *I* was the intruder.

My jaw dropped when I found him not in an uncompromising position with a home invader. But in one with his blonde neighbor who always makes snide comments about me or wrinkles her nose at the sight of me. Of course, Jonathan says I'm being overly sensitive and imagining things. But them in the living room with her naked on her knees between his spread legs and her head bobbing while his leans back against the pillow was no figment of my imagination.

In my haste to get away, I backed into the wall and knocked a painting to the floor. Their heads jerked in my direction. His eyes widened while hers gleamed. She even had the audacity to lick her puffy lips. I covered my mouth and spun on my heels, dropping the bag with dinner. Jonathan calling my name as the sound of him scrambling to his feet spurred me on. I reached the door and ran down the hallway to the elevators. Frantically, I pressed the call button. The blasted doors didn't open before he caught up to me.

Shirtless and adjusting the erection that tented the front of his joggers, Jonathan grabbed my elbow and hauled me to his condo. I tried to pull back, but he was determined. The neighbor slipped out his door with a maxi dress now covering her slim figure. Jonathan ignored her and turned his back. She winked at me before she sashayed towards her door. Tears blurred the vision of her trim hips swaying.

"For fuck's sake, don't get so emotional, Wren. It's not what you think."

I pulled my arm from his grasp and glared through my tears.

"Oh, really? My fiancé's manhood in the mouth of

another woman should not upset me? Is that what you're saying, Jonathan? Seriously?"

He scrubbed a hand down his face and murmured what sounded like *at least it was in someone's mouth.*

I choked back a sob and spun around for the door. His audible words stopped me.

"Wren, she means nothing to me. I lost an important client today. Cassie stopped by for a screwdriver and one thing led to another. I just had to let go of the frustrations. You know your uncle. He was beyond pissed."

Uncle George—the CEO of Byrd Capital, our family's financial company, and my late father's older brother. My guardian since my parents, Ethan and Connie, died in a boating accident sixteen years ago. More like I'm his burden. He happily introduced me to Jonathan to marry me off to a man who can take me off his list of responsibilities and who can run the company when he retires. Naturally, Uncle George doesn't believe a woman can man the helm of our family's business. Despite me being the sole heir since he's unable to have children with my Aunt Gretchen— rather, Wretched Gretchen—he prefers an outsider. And I know from experience how angry he can get when disap- pointed.

I folded my arms across my middle.

Jonathan took it as a sign I was caving in and placed his hands on my shoulders. At six feet, he bent his knees to align our gazes. He fixed me with an intense stare as his turquoise blue eyes met my mink brown ones.

Before he speaks, I cut in.

"She came to borrow a screwdriver or to get screwed? Which is it, Jonathan, since it certainly appeared the latter to me!"

He had the good grace to flinch but shook it off. His blond hair—longer on the top—tumbled over his forehead.

He gave me his signature hot hunk smile—the same one I fell for when Uncle George introduced us two years ago.

Jonathan was more than elated to meet me. At the time, he was doing well with the company. The son of Uncle George's friend from Harvard University and a family close in social ranking to ours. Uncle George sees it as a power match. I see it as a hot guy who's attracted to me—for once. Six months ago, he proposed, and I accepted. Now, my uncle grooms Jonathan for the CEO role. Meanwhile, I'm a socialite and the dutiful fiancée. Boring!

"Come on now, Wren. You have to believe me. Cassie means nothing. What she did meant nothing. You're the only girl for me, babe. And I'm the only guy for you. You know that, don't you?"

He didn't wait for my response. Instead, he planted a chaste kiss on the top of my head as he stood and squeezed my shoulders. A glance behind put a smile on his handsome face.

"Wow! That smells like food from STK Steakhouse. What a pleasant surprise. Thanks, babe. I'm starving!" Jonathan said as he sauntered past me to the bag I had dropped. Confident I'm pacified, he put the horrible situation behind him with ease.

I turned and watched his taut butt flex beneath the cotton joggers. He's right. He is the "only guy for me." What other hottie would want a chubby like me for a wife? None.

I sighed then and sigh now as I finish my sorry story.

Maya's topaz eyes flashed throughout. Now, she jumps to her feet and curses as she storms around the gym. Fluent in Spanish, I nod along glum until she grabs my hands and yanks me to my feet. Did I mention she's strong?

"Wren, you've come so far in your confidence level. Remember, you are so much more than you give yourself credit for. You're worthy of a man who loves you, respects you, and would end the world for you! Do. Not. Settle. For. Less!"

Maya's impassioned response brings tears to my eyes. I can only nod, too emotional to speak.

"You know, I think you should dump his cheating ass. But I will support you no matter what you decide. However, I will not allow you to let his trifling behavior derail your wellbeing progress!"

She squeezes my hands and nods towards the gym's bathroom.

"Go rinse your face with cool water. We have work to do, chica!"

"Wren, did we not decide you should wear the black ballgown with three-quarter sleeves and high neckline? What are you doing in that flashy dress?"

Wretched Gretchen's midnight blue eyes would widen if she didn't have Botox injections regularly. Instead, she blinks rapidly. One auburn eyebrow twitches slightly, unable to arch.

Regardless of her nature, my aunt looks elegant as always. This time in a goldenrod-colored strapless pleated silk-faille gown. The column silhouette with voluminous, draped panels that skim the sides pool at the floor accentuates her tall, willowy figure. The folded neckline and gathered waist add to its sculptural feel. Makeup and hair coiffed to perfection. Diamonds drip from her ears, neck, and wrists. She's regal.

However, I'm no slouch with the gown Maya helped me to select instead of the frumpy one Wretched Gretchen advised. *It will hide those not so pleasant parts of your physique, Wren, dear.*

The gown skims my BBW figure—as Maya calls it—and ends in a fishtail hem that cascades to the floor. Crystals form a pattern to mimic a chandelier on the moss green stretch silk jersey. Thin straps at the shoulders dip to a v-neckline offer a glimpse of my full breasts. Thanks to the Spandex Goddess, I'm nice and sleek.

Strappy sandals add five inches to my five feet, four inches. A colorful crystal minaud in the shape of a butterfly rests in my palm. Minimal makeup and my mahogany hair falling in lush waves to the middle of my back complete my look.

I lift my chin proudly as I respond to Wretched Gretchen.

"*You* decided the black ballgown. However, *I* prefer this one."

My heart hammers in my chest as I wait for her response.

When she and Uncle George brought me into their home at nine, I was a regular-sized child. But the grief of losing my parents caused me to withdraw. I sought solace in food. The resulting weight gain drove my aunt to put me on every diet known to man. They worked for a time. But I hid snacks in my room and ate late at night after they went to bed. At weigh-ins, she couldn't understand the lack of weight loss and the increase of pounds. Until she found cookies in my backpack. Her steely gaze sent shudders through me. Even now.

She scrutinizes me from head to toe as she circles me like a bird of prey. Stopping in front of me, her lips form a ruby slash on her stunning face.

"Well, at least you left your hair out. I've always said it's your best asset, Wren, dear."

"All right. Let's get going. We don't want to be late."

Wretched Gretchen and I turn to Uncle George's

booming voice. He and Jonathan enter the living room. When he and I arrived at my uncle and aunt's oceanfront mansion on Fisher Island, Jonathan went to the study, saying he had to discuss something with Uncle George.

I've never been happier to see them. Relieved to avoid further scrutiny, I pivot and head for the front doors.

"Wren, what the hell do you have on?!"

Well, maybe not…

As the limousine slides in front of the Larson Miami Hotel & Resort, I don't wait for the valet to open the door. Eager to escape the thick fog of tension, I push the door open into his hand, then nod in thanks as he helps me from the limo. Jonathan emerges after me and takes my elbow. He's all smiles for the flashing cameras on the red carpet.

The charity gala is a big event on Miami elite's social calendar. I'm sure he expects to make business connections with the wealthy guests. Whatever.

Drawing on Maya's words, I straighten my spine and force a smile onto my face. Regardless of the naysayers, I will do my best to embrace being a BBW.

The verdict is still out on my relationship with Jonathan. I only came tonight to avoid questions from Uncle George and Wretched Gretchen. I do not wish to disclose what happened to them. At. All.

We make it through the cocktail hour, mingling with others. Jonathan takes every opportunity to inform people he's with Byrd Capital, and I'm his fiancée, Wren Byrd. They smile politely. Some women give me the once-over for having a hunk. But I ignore the flutter of self-doubt gnawing in my belly.

I'm surprised by Jonathan's attentiveness. He's portraying the perfect fiancé despite last night's fiasco. I shudder at the memory of him bowing out, claiming an early morning meeting when I cuddled up next to him on the sofa after we ate. I nodded, not wanting him to notice how much he wounded me. He was all ready for his neighbor. But me… Not so much.

"Wren?"

I blink out of my musings at the sound of his voice.

"It's time to move into the ballroom for dinner. I'm sure you're ready to eat."

Now, I blink to hold back tears. However, Jonathan turns towards the doors and misses my reaction. I will the tears away and let him lead me to the tables. Just a while longer, and I'll make an excuse to leave.

I rely on the social skills imprinted on my brain from the moment my uncle and my aunt became my guardians. He didn't want me to embarrass him in any way. So, the table conversation flows. After dinner, the couple on Jonathan's left announce they're going onto the outdoor terrace for cordials.

"Come on, they're brilliant prospects," he murmurs in my ear, then stands and helps me from my chair.

I nod around the table at the others. They return the parting gesture.

Half listening to Jonathan gush about the couple's potential to save his lost deal, I plan my escape. Once outside, I accept a proffered cordial from a server and take a sip.

"Oh, my," I say as I hold back from Jonathan. He glances over his shoulder at me. I frown and shake my head. "I—I don't feel so well. It's best if I leave. Now."

He scowls then turns to the couple a few feet ahead of us.

"Really, Wren? Didn't I just say the guy's company would make up for the deal I lost? I can't leave now," Jonathan says, fully irked by my sudden illness. There goes the attentive fiancé.

I shake my head and pat his arm.

"No. You stay. I'll have Uncle George's driver take me home. They won't need the limo any time soon. And don't you worry about me. I'll make it out of here without your help."

Jonathan graces me with his hot hunk smile, completely oblivious to my sarcasm. Poor thing.

"Great! I'll call you tomorrow."

I watch as he rushes to the couple. The man has his arm around the woman's waist, leaning close to her ear. Their cheeks press together. She giggles and cups his face. The love they share is clear on their cheerful faces.

Now, why can't I find a man who will stare at me like I'm his moon and stars and not scowl like I'm a pesky burden?

CHAPTER 3

W*ren*

"YOU KNOW, I was thinking about what you said about reducing your dependence on your uncle. A client told me about a job opening at her company, Larson Enterprises, Inc. She's in the Human Resources department and learned the COO wants a social assistant. Someone who can help him with his social calendar, like scheduling events, coordinating functions, and attending them with him. Yada, yada, yada. I thought about you since that's your thing, Ms. Socialite. She said the salary was pretty high for the position. The COO wants someone he can trust and knows her stuff. Not someone who will look for a big fat diamond ring. He's a sexy as sin billionaire, by the way. I looked him up."

Maya giggles.

We finished an outdoor session in the park next to Biscayne Bay and went across the street to Pura Vida for açaí bowls. Sitting on the open field of grass surrounded by palm trees blowing in the balmy breeze, the morning sun shines on us, making her topaz eyes sparkle. I grin back.

The thought of a job that pays me enough I won't need to rely on Uncle George's monthly allotment and makes me responsible for myself fills my heart with happiness. I could prove I'm capable and not flighty like my father. Never do I think of my Dad in that way.

But Uncle George rarely lets a day go by he doesn't remind me how disappointed he is in my father not taking his place at Byrd Capital. He thinks my father wasted his life and married beneath the family. Even my name irks Uncle George. *Wren Byrd. Bird Bird. Such a silly name!*

Silly or not, it's my name. One of the few things I still have from my parents.

Uncle George told me I was to begin my new life with him and Wretched Gretchen fresh. *Leave that nonsense your father instilled in you and whatever he gave you behind.* At nine, saddened by the loss of my parents, and unable to stand up for myself, I had no choice but to obey his command. My name, memories, and photo albums survived. I cherish them. Even now, my heart clenches. I miss my parents constantly.

A chance to get from under Uncle George's control would be a win. I'll use all the etiquette classes and event planning sessions he and Wretched Gretchen insisted I take part in. Social connections the Byrd name generates prove an added bonus. I'm on the list for invitations to the best galas, fundraisers, and intimate gatherings in Miami and beyond. I find it hilarious the very means to escape and to prove I can make my own way in life comes from them!

Laughter bubbles up. I let it tumble from between my upturned lips until tears leak from the corners of my eyes. I laugh even harder when Maya joins in. So thankful for her, I throw my arms around my best friend. After we catch our breath, I sit back.

"How do I apply?"

"Atta girl! I'll send a text message to my client right now," Maya says as she whips her mobile from her duffle bag.

I watch as her fingers fly over the mobile screen. She pauses, then grins and types some more. Eager to know what's being said, I peer over her shoulder. I can't make out much. So, I sit back and pull my knees to my chest. Please, oh, please, oh please! I chant inwardly until Maya drops her mobile back in the bag and grins at me with a thumbs up.

"You're all set for an interview tomorrow morning at nine. I texted the details to you. She's excited to meet you since I kind of name-dropped who you are and all. Gotta use what you got to get what you want, you know," Maya says with a wink. "I have back-to-back client sessions. After, I'll come to your condo. We'll pick the best outfit and hairstyle. Sounds good?"

I hug her again.

"Absolutely! Thanks so much, bestie!"

A hot guy in a tank top and stretch-shell shorts lopes over and drops next to her. She startles as he says, boo. With a wry look, Maya folds her arms across her full breasts and tells him he'll do ten extra burpees double-time. He groans and falls to his back with an arm over his face dramatically. His head tilts towards me, and he winks. We laugh at his antics.

I bid them goodbye as I gather the empty açaí bowls and my crossbody bag. So excited for the job, I all but skip away clicking my heels! I toss the bowls into the trash can and head to my car.

A smile spreads across my face as I near it. My most recent nod to the more confident me is my birthday present —a BMW i4 eDrive40, the electric Gran Coupe. Upon first glance, the mineral white metallic exterior is simple. However, on closer inspection behind the tinted windows, the red leather interior gives a glimpse of my budding sassiness. Plus, it's better for the environment.

Naturally, Uncle George called it a ridiculous waste of more than $70K for a car with a gaudy interior. I held my tongue as he signed off on the purchase with his AMEX Centurion Card. Then I giddily slid behind the wheel, just like I do now.

I close my eyes as my fingers tighten around the steering wheel.

"Wren Byrd, you will get this job, do well at it, and prove to Uncle George you are more than capable of taking care of yourself. Live your life!"

Happy, I sing aloud the lyrics from my personal anthem playlist as the warm sun and breeze fill my car. At a red stoplight, a little girl in a car beside mine giggles as she watches me belting out Rihanna's lyrics from T.I.'s "Live Your Life." I grin at her and hope she never has to deal with controlling people. Ever. When the stoplight changes to green, I wave at her. She puts her palm on her window and smiles. A good sign. My heart soars higher.

I thank my condo building's valet as I step from my car and slip a tip into his hand with a smile. He thanks me with a nod and slides behind the wheel. I hurry to the lobby, eager to get upstairs. The doorman greets me with a tilt of his head. I smile my thanks and wave at the concierge who wishes me a good day. It certainly is one!

As always, the endless expanse of the Atlantic Ocean beyond the floor-to-ceiling windows of my living room takes my breath away. The view from the fifty-fourth floor of my condo can't get any better.

Virginia Key, Fisher Island, and Dodge Island appear between the Atlantic Ocean and Biscayne Bay as I walk through the oversized living room with buttery soft sand-colored leather sofas and chairs. The golden sand-colored floor tiles angle toward the wall of windows to draw me closer. Out on the terrace, my gaze drops to my uncle and aunt's oceanfront mansion on Fisher Island.

My heart races at the sight of where I spent most of my years growing up miserable. I close my eyes on a long inhalation, then open them at the same pace on the exhalation. Maya's deep cleansing breath technique clears the negativity.

"Live your life, Wren Byrd!" I exclaim as my hands clap and my curvy hips shimmy. "Time to shower, put together your résumé, and check out your closet for a killer interview outfit!"

Hours later, Maya arrives. She showers and changes into a t-shirt and yoga pants in the second bedroom suite. It's become her home away from home.

"Okay, show me what you got," she announces as she steps into the sitting room, where I wait for her to finish. I jump to my feet and take her hand.

She giggles as I drag her down the hallway to the third bedroom suite converted into a dressing room. It's one of the few Wretched Gretchen's suggestions I agree with since I have tons of formal attire, evening wear, handbags, shoes, and accessories, not to mention regular daywear. It might as well be a posh mini boutique on Manhattan's Fifth Avenue. However, I donate the worn-once designer gowns to fundraising auctions to benefit various charities. Uncle George can't call that wasteful!

"Nice options, Wren! I really like that yellow suit. It brings out the rich mahogany color of your hair if you wear it loose down your back. Oh! The belted midi dress is so feminine. Hmmm… You can never go wrong with my fellow Venezuelan, Ms. Carolina Herrera, you know…"

I grin wider than the Cheshire Cat as Maya makes her way down the row of clothes. She has such an expert eye. I value her opinion.

"Well, you want to go for chic and confident with your appearance, giving the air of a wealthy socialite. One who knows her stuff. Can handle an Alpha billionaire boss," Maya says as she taps a manicured fingernail against her full lips. Her assessing gaze sweeps over the outfits slowly.

My grin stretches further when she points at the navy blue sheath with matching waist-length jacket.

"This is it, chica!" Maya exclaims. "With those stilettos and your hair loose. Just accent your eyes, leaving your lips with a subtle pink stain."

"Perfect! I'll carry my powder blue top-handle bag since it fits my résumé portfolio. Will you take a look at it? I want to be sure I missed nothing."

We chat while I put the other items away before heading to the den where I left my laptop. Maya gives some recommendations on my résumé, and I make the changes. With a flourish, I place five copies in the portfolio. Maya claps enthusiastically, then grins.

"Okay, I'm hungry. Let's order some sushi. We can catch up on our fave *Bling Empire*. I rescheduled my morning sessions so I can spend the night, then help you get ready."

"Thanks so much, bestie!" I say as I throw my arms around her for a big hug. "You're the best bestie a girl could ever want!"

We laugh as Maya pulls out her mobile and places our delivery order. I grab the flat-screen television remote and switch to Netflix, settling in for a fun night. Excited butterflies flutter in my belly. I can't wait to start my new job. The power of positive thinking—another of Maya's techniques—makes me smile happily. You've got this, Wren Byrd!

～

"WELL, Wren, you impressed my colleagues and me with your education at Harvard, your experience with not only attending significant galas, but organizing them, and with your willingness to work long hours and on the weekends as necessary.

"Mr. Dahl has high expectations for all of Larson Enterprises' employees, especially for those who work with him in a direct capacity. As his social assistant, you would work closely with him.

"However, I must emphasize the need to maintain complete professionalism at all times. Mr. Dahl has the need of a trusted employee, not of a female interested in using the unique working situation as a means to marriage. Am I clear?"

The Head of Human Resources pauses to peer at me. Her fathomless obsidian eyes reach into the very depths of my soul.

I agree, then force myself to sit still under her intense scrutiny. Again, it's something I learned because of Uncle George and can apply it towards me getting this job.

After an almost imperceptible nod, she relaxes back in the leather seat behind her desk.

"Mr. Dahl is on an extended business trip and cannot meet you. However, he wants the position filled before he returns next week. My team and I have a few other candidates to interview before I make the final decision. Either way, we will be in touch. Thank you for meeting with us, Wren. My administrative assistant will see you to the elevators. Good day."

～

*T*AG

"GOOD MORNING, MR. DAHL."

"Hello, Mr. Dahl, sir."

I nod brusquely in response to the greetings from staff as I stride through The Larson Tower lobby towards the executive floor elevator.

Even though it's been weeks since the charity gala, I'm still on edge. No matter how much I searched the terrace, ballroom, hell, even the entire hotel, I couldn't find the she-wolf with the unique scent of my fated mate. Talk about frustration.

But I set the pursuit aside because of a business trip the next day. Not able to cancel it, I had no other choice but to spend the past three weeks in our Charleston, Atlanta, New Orleans, and Houston offices.

At least once every other quarter, I show up unannounced. No better way to gauge productivity and to check on staff behavior than to catch them unaware. Rarely do I find problems requiring reprimand since our leadership team does an excellent job of running their offices.

Most of the team comprises members of the Miami Wolves Pack. Their loyalty and respect keep them on the straight and narrow. Naturally, their share in the profits as pack members serve as serious encouragement. The human team members do not disappoint—most of the time.

It was a successful trip. But I'm glad to be back at headquarters.

I check the time on my watch. Before the weekly staff meeting at nine, the Head of Human Resources—a she-wolf —has my new social assistant scheduled to arrive at my offices. I reviewed her application—along with the other top five candidates—and agree on paper she's the best choice. I added a sixty-day trial period clause in her contract just in case. She doesn't appear Katrina-like. But who knows?

My mobile chimes with an incoming text message. I take it out of the breast pocket of my bespoke three-piece suit. I smirk at the mobile screen. Viggo invites me to a party for a popular human female singer at Club Hati—one of Larson Enterprises' venues in his portfolio. He chose the name as a nod to Norse mythology. The wolf Hati chases the moon, across the night sky. His counterpart the wolf Sköll chases the sun during the day. They do so until the time of Ragnarök when they will swallow the heavenly bodies. The club caters to wolf shifters and humans.

I shrug. Why not? I could use a distraction after these past few weeks. My wolf and I need more sexual release than my hand allows, but nothing more than a one-nighter. At this point in my life, I don't want a relationship and none of the drama that comes along with one.

And that includes pushing aside the dull ache for my fated mate's touch. It's best I can't find the elusive she-wolf. Undoubtedly, I *can* find a nice morsel to feast upon at the party and get my mind off a fated mate. My cock twitches at the thought as I reply to Viggo's text.

Punching in the code for the private elevator, I adjust the burgeoning erection then step inside. The elevator will automatically go to the executive floor since it's the only stop besides the lobby. As the doors close, a female's manicured fingers—one with an engagement ring—slip between the bit of space. I frown. Only the C-suite uses this elevator. The rest of the staff take the general elevators. Who the hell is this?

Then it hits me dead on this time.

The tantalizing aroma of cinnamon sugar caramel

apples. The scent of my fated mate—the only she-wolf destined for me.

Forget burgeoning. My cock punches the front of my trousers instantly. A growl rumbles in my chest. My wolf throws his massive brown head back and issues a feral, lust-filled howl. My nostrils flare as I inhale deeply. Emerald green eyes flash as they narrow on the slit between the elevator doors.

Who *are* you?

The doors slide open.

A petite human female in a body skimming green dress that stops at the midpoint of her shapely calves ending in fuck-me stilettos with a sexy touch of toe cleavage enters. The fit of the dress accentuates her mouthwatering tits and luscious curves. Lustrous mahogany brown hair ripples down her back. Soulful mink brown eyes widen as her pouty lips form a perfect O. A rose flush licks at her exposed collarbone, up her throat, and to her cheeks. The first taste of her arousal teases me, increasing the saliva pooling in my hungry mouth.

The doors slide close.

CHAPTER 4

ren

"Whoa, Wren! Look at you. Your new boss better watch out or he just may fall in love with you at first sight regardless of the no employer-employee relationships stipulation!"

I giggle at Maya's compliment, then glance down at the new outfit for my first day at Larson Enterprises.

The goal isn't to make Mr. Dahl fall for me. Rather, I want to combine the style of a socialite with my budding confidence.

The jewel green midi dress flatters my BBW figure. The interlocking twist drape bodice, darted seams, and fitted skirt highlight my curves just enough without going beyond professional. Flesh-tone slingbacks lengthen my legs and give my generous butt a nice lift. A hunter green top-handle bag finishes the look.

"It's not too much, is it?" I ask as I nibble my lower lip, now concerned. "I don't want to give off the wrong impression. Maybe I should wear the—"

"Oh no, you won't. This is perfect. You're not going to work at a corporate law office. The company is in the hospitality industry—clubs, hotels, restaurants. Plus, you're his *social* assistant, not his accountant."

Maya picks up my handbag and ushers me out of the dressing room towards the front door of my condo. I laugh and take the bag, then loop my arm through hers. We part in the garage. She hugs me and tells me good luck. I grin and thank her.

The drive to The Larson Tower takes no time. I bop to the music from my encouragement playlist to pump me up. Beyoncé's "Run The World (Girls)" blasts from the surround sound. My left foot taps to the beat. Yes!

I don't even care when a guy in a sleek sports car frowns at me. Instead, I wave and zip ahead when the traffic light changes. My confidence rises with the speedometer— although I stay within the posted limit. Let's not go crazy, now!

In the lobby, I present my employee badge to the security guards behind their station, then follow where a guard points to the elevators. As I approach one, the doors begin to shut. Not wanting to risk a late arrival to meet Mr. Dahl, I rush forward and slip my hand in the gap. Relieved, I step inside.

I freeze.

The provocative scent of vetiver seamlessly blended with citrus, rich spices, and fresh woods fills my nose as the cologne sensuously molds around my body. Nipples tighten, that sensitive nubbin at the apex of my thighs pulses as my gaze settles on an impeccably dressed man. He's so tall, my eyes only reach his powerful chest. They scan up his muscular body to broad shoulders and to a face kissed by Aphrodite herself.

A dimpled chin with a dusting of sable brown stubble

leads to a kissable mouth. The nostrils of his nose flare. My breath hitches as his flashing green eyes narrow on me. The intensity of his stare heats my cheeks.

Before me stands Tag Dahl—the most gorgeous man I have ever seen. The photos online fail to capture his masculine beauty. And his charismatic pull.

The doors close behind me.

I gasp at the sound of a low growl. If a man wasn't standing there, I would bet a wild wolf lurked within the elevator shaft. A shiver snakes down my spine, and I don't think it's from fear.

"Who *are* you?"

His gruff, smokey voice skitters over my skin like a lover's teasing caress. The promise of the carnal pleasure to come.

My mouth opens to respond. But words can't form. I blink and breathe through my open mouth. Before my next attempt, I cough to clear my throat. Like steel to a magnet, our eyes find one another again. A yearning grows deep within me. My lips part.

The lights flicker.

With a frown, I lift my gaze to the ceiling.

The elevator jounces.

It drops a few feet.

The lights flick off.

Pitch black.

Instead of words, a scream rips past my lips as I tumble against Mr. Dahl. Strong hands hold me close to his firm chest. The scent of his cologne makes me dizzy with need. I bite back another cry mixed with an unexpected lusty moan.

"I've got you," he growls, a deep rumble in his chest.

There's that wolf again. Now, I know the sound emanates from him and isn't a figment of my imagination.

Just like your father. You have the most vivid imagination!

A nervous giggle bubbles up as my mind replays a memory of Uncle George complaining about my creativity. He found my hidden stash of drawing pads, where I sketched the fantastical creatures I read about in my favorite story books. Witches, wolves, trolls, fairies, elves, and more filled the pages. They were my escape from my depressing reality.

But it's my fear of tight places that strikes panic in me. If Wretched Gretchen felt I misbehaved, she locked me in a dark closet for hours. Her threat to throw away my photo albums kept me from telling Uncle George. I knew he wouldn't care since he wanted me to forget my parents all together.

Now, I cling to Mr. Dahl. Fingers scrunch his soft wool suit jacket. My heart thuds as I bury my face in his chest. Hysteria grips me.

"It's all right. The elevator stopping will alert the building maintenance and the security staff," Mr. Dahl says. His warm breath blows across the crown of my head as he curls his enormous body over me. "I'm going to let go of you with one hand so I can hit the intercom button. Do you understand?"

My fingers grip tighter. A sob escapes.

A large palm strokes my back as a rumble vibrates beneath my cheek. I feel it throughout my body—a calming rhythm.

"Mr. Dahl, sir! Are you all right?"

A disembodied voice breaks the moment.

He stiffens. The strokes and the rumble cease.

I whimper.

His hand and the vibrations resume as he responds.

"Yes. What the hell happened?!"

Although he's soothing me, I sense his anger and frustration. I try my best to calm down. I don't want to make the situation worse. God forbid we're stuck here for more than a few minutes. I shudder. He growls.

"Tell me something. Now!"

"Yes, sir, Mr. Dahl. There's no issue on the security end. The Head of Building Maintenance is checking his system as we speak, sir. Please give us a moment. We will respond as soon as possible."

Another displeased growl follows.

"Fine. Tell my administrative assistant I'm stuck in the elevator. I also have a Ms. Wren Byrd due in my office. If she's checked in, tell her, too. Otherwise, have Beth contact her."

"Yes, sir, Mr. Dahl. Right away, sir!"

I lift my cheek from his chest to glance up at him, then remember he won't be able to see my face. I'm nervous to tell him I'm Wren Byrd since he bit the head off the security guard. Geez.

"Um… Mr. Dahl?"

"Are you all right? It won't be long. I know you're frightened. Just try to relax. I'll keep you safe. As you heard, they're working on the situation."

He tightens his grip on my waist with one arm and strokes my back with the other hand.

It feels so good to be held lovingly. I haven't felt such warm affection since my parents. Tears burn my eyes. But I hold them back. I must remain focused.

"I understand, sir."

I pause when a ripple runs through him. A moan threatens to slip out of my mouth. I swallow it back down with a shake of my head.

So inappropriate, Wren! I chide myself.

But I can't help the sensations flowing through me. I

close my eyes, take a deep cleansing breath, and try again with more conviction.

"Mr. Dahl, sir, I'm Wren Byrd."

He sucks in a breath. His body turns rigid. The moment he steps away from me, the loss of his heat chills my soul. I cry out.

"I—I... This comes as a surprise. Excuse my inappropriate behavior. It didn't occur to me you are my new social assistant."

Each word spoken drives a nail into my heart.

My arms wrap around my torso in a protective manner. The darkness and closeness of the stuck elevator threaten to overwhelm me. His loss makes it a thousand times worse. I regret admitting my identity, dammit!

"Mr. Dahl, sir," I try again, speaking in the direction he withdrew. "I appreciate your... behavior. I must admit, it calmed my nerves. You see, I'm afraid of close quarters and the dark makes it unbearable."

A rumbling comes from his corner.

My knees weaken in relief.

I reach for the wall as they buckle.

But before I hit the floor, strong arms embrace me. His heat and intoxicating cologne engulf me. I sag against him once again. Tears pool in my eyes, squeezed shut.

"Thank you," I sigh as my arms wrap around his waist. Despite the facts he's my new boss and we have a non-fraternization clause, I hold Tag Dahl with all of my might.

～

Tag

. . .

MY ENHANCED VISION allows me to see Wren Byrd clearly in the elevator's darkness. Her eyes set in a face etched with fright, stare pleadingly in my direction. She can't see me but senses my presence. My wolf claws beneath my skin. He wants to break free and comfort what he considers his fated mate. It takes more effort than I expected, but I tamp him down. He returns to the fringes of my being with a disgruntled howl.

I recall the movie "The Gods Must Be Crazy" and how a foreign object causes such chaos in a peaceful, controlled environment. Instead of a Coca-Cola bottle dropping from the sky to disturb the people, Wren Byrd—my human social assistant—lands in my arms. She bears the unique scent of my fated mate. The only one for me. And she's a *human* female. Not a she-wolf. And she's engaged.

No. Fucking. Way.

I'd fall over laughing hysterically if I thought this was some sort of dumb prank Viggo—the jokester of our group—pulled on me. Unfortunately, it's all too real.

Her delicious scent fills my nostrils as I hold her close. The instinctive urge to comfort her causes a soothing rumble to emanate from my chest. My feral wolf howls, disturbed by our fated mate's distress. We want to console her in more ways than rumbles and back strokes.

My aching cock wants to drive into her warm, wet pussy made only for me over and over and over again. Until she writhes beneath me, screaming my name in carnal bliss, not in abject fear. Then expand my knot to seal us together as my seed floods her womb, placing my pup in her belly.

Mine!

Fuck. Me.

But I cannot allow this to happen.

For one, I'm not interested in a relationship beyond

satisfying my sexual needs. I'm too busy for it and don't want the drama. So, it's good she's engaged.

Two, she's a human. No male wolf shifter in our pack has turned a human into a she-wolf in for-fucking-ever. It's dangerous and can cause her death. Not something to do on a whim driven by the attraction to a fated mate.

Three—and above all—Wren Byrd is an employee of Larson Enterprises, Inc., my social assistant, my subordinate. We have a non-fraternization clause in her contract. I cannot get involved with her. No way.

This whole situation is screwed.

"Mr. Dahl, sir?"

"Yes?! What's the status?" I snap as my barely contained frustration and anger threaten to overflow. As it stands, my control hangs on by one wolf whisker. And damn if it's not about to fray as her sweet scent entices me.

"Yes, sir. Maintenance confirmed there's a fault in the machine room. He estimates the repair's completion in… um… twenty minutes. He apologizes for the inconvenience, sir."

I growl, knowing the security guard will sense my displeasure since he's a member of our pack. My keen wolf hearing picks up his thick swallow.

"Do all of you realize this could have been a major disaster?! I want a full report on my desk in thirty minutes, including the status of all elevators, their repair and inspection histories, warranties, etc. Do you understand?"

"Y—Yes, bet—ah, Mr. Dahl. sir."

I narrow my eyes as I glare at the intercom for his almost slip-up in referring to me as our pack beta. Not good. At. All. A human would wonder what he means. And I have one trembling in my arms as we speak.

"Ms. Wren Byrd is here with me. Be mindful of your

choice in words. Also, no need to inform her of my situation."

Another stuttered acknowledgment, and the intercom falls silent.

My mind returns to the dilemma.

I can't have Wren Byrd as my fated mate.

Can I have her as my social assistant and not issue the claiming bite?

My wolf stares with flashing emerald green eyes as the serum to initiate her transformation into a she-wolf drips from his exposed fangs.

Talk about pure havoc wreaking my structured life and driving my wolf feral. This curvaceous human female's been in my life for less than ten minutes and shit's already turned upside down.

As though sensing the inner conflict roiling within me, Wren Byrd whimpers. Her fingers clutch at my back. The softness of her lush body molds to the hard planes of mine calling to my cock like a Siren.

My wolf howls demandingly.

I stiffen.

Fuck. Me. Or. What.

CHAPTER 5

ag

"Mr. Dahl, sir?"

Fortunately, the security guard interrupts my thoughts. I use his call as an excuse to gently extricate myself from Wren Byrd. Her soft gasp nudges the heart I'm trying to harden. My wolf paces on the fringes, eyeing me. I ignore all of it and respond.

"How's the progress?" I bark into the intercom speaker.

An audible gulp answers my question.

"Do not tell me there is no change in the status. Do not disappoint me."

A different voice responds.

"Excuse me, Mr. Dahl. We don't have the part required for the repair. The elevator company rep will arrive with it in thirty minutes based on traffic—"

I shout.

Wren wails.

Silence on the other end.

I ream the Head of Maintenance out for not having the proper supplies on hand. The situation could be a lot more critical as in a pregnant female on board or a medical emergency. I demand a full accounting of the elevator systems by the end of the day. He apologizes profusely and assures me they will fix the problem as soon as the rep arrives. I end the communication and pivot to check on Wren Byrd.

My heart clenches at the sight of her huddled in the corner. Eyes closed. Knees bent with her arms wrapped around them. She rocks back and forth. Her lips move. Even with my keen hearing, the words are too low to decipher.

I rush over and crouch in front of her. Hands on her shoulders, I stop her movement.

"Ms. Byrd, I know this must be an unimaginable horror for you. However, as you heard, the crew expects to get us out of here soon. Until then, rest assured, I will allow nothing to happen to you. We will get through this situation together. Do you understand?"

She mumbles incoherently as tears stream down her pale cheeks.

My protective instinct kicks in. I drop to the floor. One arm wraps around her shoulders to angle her body into mine, while the other arm encircles her and clasps my opposite hand. She melts against me with the top of her head beneath my chin and her knees pressed to my chest, curled into a ball. I can't help but to notice she fits with me perfectly.

My nose burrows in her hair. A deep inhalation suffuses every cell in my body with her unique cinnamon sugar caramel apples scent. One by one, the cells spark, crackling with electricity. The sensation spreads from my heart out through each limb. It ignites my brain like a headstart jolt from a jumper cable.

Engaged or not, Wren Byrd is my fated mate.

Whether or not I want her.

The realization unsettles me.

My wolf? He struts, tail high.

I ignore his triumphant parade.

The rest of the time, I hold Wren close. The rumble emanating from deep within my chest soothes her. By the time the lights flicker on and the elevator ascends, she's quiet with her eyes shut. I cradle her in my arms and rise.

We emerge onto the executive floor to find half a dozen people gathered at the elevator doors, including the staff nurse. Ignoring the others clamoring, I tell her to follow me to my office suite. Wren's care takes priority above all else.

I lay her on the sofa in the sitting area of my office and stand.

Her eyelids flutter but don't open. She mumbles again as she reaches for me.

As I stare down at her, I have to admit I miss the warmth of her body. My arms feel empty without her in them. My fingers flex with the urge to grab her close.

A polite cough reminds me of the staff nurse and Beth's presence. I nod and stride to the built-in beverage center. Removing two bottles of water, I return to the sofa and place one on the coffee table.

Wren's eyes open as the staff nurse speaks to her gently. But instead of looking at her, they scan the room until they find mine. Her sad mink brown orbs tug at my heart. I rub the ache in my chest.

In my periphery, Beth's eyebrows raise to her hairline in surprise. The staff nurse glances at me over her shoulder, hand suspended with a moist cloth.

It's then I notice the rumble started again.

As mated she-wolves, they recognize the sound of a male wolf shifter soothing his mate.

Fuck!

They'll suspect something between Wren and me. I cannot have staff or pack members aware of this unresolved set of circumstances. From a company standpoint, Wren is my subordinate. As for the pack, they'll question a human female being turned. And as the Alpha, Jagger would need to know first.

Beyond all that lies the problem of me being undecided. For once in my well-thought-out life, I have no idea what to do. It's not a simple solution.

The magnetism to a fated mate proves irresistible, especially for the male wolf shifter. The inherent urge to care for, protect, and to breed the female is instant and increases over time. If the mate bond cannot complete, the male suffers from madness as he loses control of his wolf. Roles reverse and the wolf becomes the dominate. No pack allows a rampant wolf. They kill it. And that damn sure is not a part of my life plan.

Plus, I can't harm Wren. She's practically comatose from getting stuck in the elevator. Not that I don't empathize with her. But the transition from human to wolf takes a toll on the body and adjusting to being a wolf shifter impacts the psyche. She's a fragile human and may not survive the claiming bite or handle the mental aspect of it all.

And she's engaged to another male.

What a clusterfuck.

So, I back away from the sofa, where Wren stares beseechingly at me. She doesn't understand the reason for the attraction she feels for me but knows she needs it. She continues to seek my comfort without looking at Beth or the staff nurse.

Again, my heart clenches. But I fight the urge and maintain a stoic expression. I refuse to add to the potential gossip.

Behind me, my office door bursts open.

"Tag, damn. How are you and Ms. Byrd?" Jagger asks as he storms inside. His ice blue eyes survey the scene, then focus on me. A slight frown draws his white blonde eyebrows together. Imperceptibly, he sniffs the air. The frown deepens. He opens his mouth to speak. But I cut him off.

"Beth, get Ms. Byrd whatever she needs. She will remain on the sofa until I return momentarily," I say, then nod at Jagger to follow me before I march from my office and shut the door. "Let's talk in your office."

He nods.

We enter his office suite next to mine. He tells his administrative assistant Ginny to hold his calls as we pass his reception area, where she sits at her desk. I shut his office door while he strides to the desk. He presses the privacy button to darken the glass walls. I slump on a sofa. My hands drag down my face with a growl.

"Okay, what the hell is going on? Why do I sense a bond between you and Ms. Byrd? Hell, I even sense her as I do members of our pack. Talk to me, Tag."

He lowers his massive frame onto the chair opposite me. Keen eyes focus on my face.

As the Alpha, Jagger has a connection to each member of the Miami Wolves Pack. He can sense our emotional states and detect danger to us. Similar to the bond shared between mates. It's his internal radar.

And right now, I wish he didn't have it. I'm no closer to knowing what to do and not ready to discuss it. However, he is my Alpha. I must heed his command, especially as his beta and his right hand. It is the order of the pack.

I scrub my face again as I shake my head and blow a breath.

"Wren Byrd is my new social assistant. *Human* social assistant."

I pause to roll my eyes to the ceiling as though the answer lies above. Yeah, well, I've already established the gods must be crazy. So, I doubt I'll get any sane guidance from them. At least, none that I want since they made the fated mate pairing to begin with. Annoyed, my mouth twists to the side.

"There's more to it than that, Tag. Spill it."

Right. It certainly is a lot more.

"Wren Byrd is my fated mate. A human female. Not a she-wolf. And she's engaged."

I drop the bombshell and sit back as it detonates in the room.

Jagger's mouth drops open.

Mine twists.

"Are you absolutely certain?"

"Cinnamon sugar caramel apples."

He frowns.

I lean forward with my elbows on my knees and steeple my fingers.

"The aroma of my first breath when I was born—cinnamon sugar caramel apples. Wren Byrd bears that unique scent. Funny enough, I first detected it the night of the charity gala a few weeks ago. Out on the rooftop terrace. I searched but couldn't find her anywhere. Today, she steps onto the executive elevator—still not sure why security directed her to it—and her scent overpowered me. My wolf went feral."

I sit back and growl in frustration.

"So, yeah, I'm absolutely certain she's my fated mate. However, I have no clue what to do about it."

Jagger stares at me for what seems like an hour, but really is only a minute. He stands and paces the floor. His hands slip into the trouser pockets of his suit. The same height as me, his long legs cross from one end to the other quickly. He stops and focuses on me.

"An engaged human female. Damn, that's messy bro. If the memory of our pack history serves me correctly, it's been at least thirty years since a transition took place. It was before we were even born. But it stands out sadly."

He returns to the chair and leans forward, eyes intense.

My gut churns. I already know it's not something I want to hear. At. All. I close my eyes a moment, then reopen them, determined to face reality no matter what.

"The male wolf shifter fell in love with a human female. He explained his true nature to her. She accepted him and wanted to be one with him in all ways. He asked my father as the Alpha for permission to grant her the gift. He agreed based on past experiences.

"Prior to them, others were successful, or, for whatever odd reason, the transition didn't take fully. Those partial transitions resulted in the females not being able to shift, but they gained the traits to live longer and better health."

He pauses.

I lean forward, needing to know the outcome of the last pair.

Jagger nods and continues.

"Sadly, the human female died. She never recovered from the claiming bite. Her agony drove the male mad since he blamed himself. When she passed away, he went into the Everglades and never returned. My father and several males searched for him. They only found his remains left by a panther."

I recoil.

Just as I thought. I can't risk Wren's life. She may be my fated mate and the attraction is powerful. But I will not subject her to agony. It was bad enough to watch her tremble in the elevator and to lie comatose on the sofa. Not happening. No. I resign myself to end Wren's contract and to avoid any contact with her. It's for the best.

"Hold on, Tag."

Jagger's voice pulls me back to the room.

"An important difference is key," he starts and waits for me to look at him. I face him. "Remember, I said he fell in love with her. They and the partial transition pairs were not fated mates. The successful ones were."

My eyes bug. No way!

He nods.

"You confirmed Wren is your fated mate by her unique scent. The chances of her transition being positive are high. You'll have more of a hard time getting rid of the fiancé and explaining your true nature to her, so she accepts you. Then she would have to give you permission to bestow the gift. It is her decision to become a she-wolf. I will not allow you or anyone else to force a human female or a she-wolf to complete a mate bond. And if she doesn't agree, we can't have a human know of our existence. The risk is too great. So be sure you've gotten her to fall for you completely before telling her what we are. Are you clear?"

"Yes, Alpha."

Not only are the gods crazy, I must be too.

Wren's contract has the sixty-day trial period clause in it. I have two months to figure out what the hell to do.

CHAPTER 6

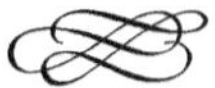

"OH, honey! I'm so sorry! What happens now?"

Maya sits back from hugging me.

I still can't believe that whole elevator fiasco. One minute, I'm all excited about my first day at work. The next I'm face-to-face with my new boss, struck dumb by his sexiness before the elevator falls apart! Then I'm thrown into his strapping arms, where I proceed to lose my damn mind. And not just from claustrophobia but from his alluring masculinity.

Even now, hours later, my nipples pebble. They're so sensitive the silk bra makes them ache. I press my thighs together to soothe the needy warmth pooling in my core just at the thought of Tag Dahl. The beast of a man who yells at others. Yet he's a giant teddy bear holding me close.

I wrap my own arms around myself in a sorry attempt to mimic his sweet embrace. And the way his sizable hands caressed my back. Oh, and I can't forget the rumble in his massive chest. The vibrations did all sorts of things to my lady bits. My goodness!

But I would have appreciated it more had I not panicked. Thanks, Wretched Gretchen…

Genuine fear gripped me. But his presence eased the terror. Unfortunately, the amount of time we spent in the elevator finished me off. I couldn't function despite his attempts to calm me. I retreated to the depths of my being, as I did years ago. My safe space welcomed me like an old friend.

I didn't rouse from it until the staff nurse spoke to me in soothing tones. My only waking thought was to find Tag Dahl. When our eyes connected, I felt instant relief. His mere presence touched me deep inside. The rumble resonated within. But when he left abruptly, my heart sank.

I watched him leave the office. When the door closed behind him, I turned my head and closed my eyes. A sense of loss washed over me. With him gone, I returned to my safe space.

The staff nurse declared I was in shock and needed to rest. She placed pillows beneath my legs and a cashmere throw over me. His administrative assistant handed a bottle of water to me and asked if I needed anything else.

I shook my head and thanked them.

They told me to stay put until Mr. Dahl returned. I murmured my assent while inwardly I prayed he wouldn't be long. I must have dozed off because I awoke to him calling my name. My eyes fluttered open.

"Wren, how do you feel?"

His emerald green eyes appear darker, more like jade as he stares at me. Concern fills them as he studies my face intently.

I have the urge to cup his cheek. My eyes lower to his lips. The urge to nibble on the plump lower one makes me draw my own into my mouth. I drop my gaze. A growl snaps it to his face.

A flash of something crosses it before he turns away and strides to his desk. His muscular legs make quick work of the distance. But it's too far for me.

I sit up and swing my feet to the floor. Our eyes meet again when he folds his body into the leather chair behind his desk. A frisson runs through me. I tremble and wrap my arms around my torso.

With grace unexpected of a man his size, he leaps to his feet and hastens back to me. He crouches and removes my slingbacks. His touch causes sparks to skitter across my skin. His fingers pause, then he places my legs on the pillows. The throw covers me.

"Do not move," he says in a thick, rough voice. "The staff nurse says you are in shock. Be still."

His commanding tone takes me by surprise. I gasp. His eyes snap to mine. If I'm not mistaken, a carnal hunger lurks in their depths. But he blinks, and the moment passes. Perhaps I was mistaken. I shake my head and lean against the pillow.

"I—I just wanted to answer your question, Mr. Dahl, sir," I stammer as I watch him from beneath the thick fringe of my eyelashes. For some reason, I want to show him I'm not challenging him in any way—merely responding.

He grunts a nod.

I take it as permission to continue.

"Well, I'm a bit embarrassed by—"

"No. Do not feel that way, Wren."

I swallow as that tone tingles over my body.

"Go on."

I blink and nod.

"It's claustrophobia. So, thank you for keeping me calm. Usually, elevators don't bother me so much. I recognize the doors will open soon, and I can get off. This time... Well... You know," I end on a shudder and pull the throw tighter around me.

The rumble fills the space between us.

My head jerks in his direction.

"What is that sound you make?"

I bite my lip when his cheeks flush. The sound stops. I miss it immediately and wish I hadn't said a word about it. Big mouth, Wren!

He clears his throat and buttons his suit jacket. I admire the way it drapes over his body, so well tailored to enhance his fit form. He coughs politely, and I blush at being caught staring at his crotch. I can't help it being at eye level or noticing his broad length along a thigh. Holy moly.

My eyes track up his body to his handsome face. Another flash crosses it.

"I have meetings to attend outside of the office for the rest of the morning. You stay here until you feel better. Then go home. Beth will arrange a car for you. If you're up to it, come in tomorrow morning at nine. Otherwise, inform her you're unable to make it. No rush. I want you at your best, Wren."

Why did my mind hear, I want you flipped over on the sofa, knees wide, back arched, pussy bare and dripping???

I press my thighs together, thankful the throw hides the movement. Talk about embarrassing...

Get a damn grip, Wren Byrd! I'm no virgin. But such lustful thoughts never entered my mind before. And Jonathan certainly doesn't evoke them. He's handsome to thrill me. But in the bedroom? It's pretty cut and dry. No steam and definitely no spice.

But my new boss? That's a whole other naughty story.

"Yes, Mr. Dahl, sir. I appreciate your understanding since this is my first day, and it didn't go quite as planned. However, I expect to make it in tomorrow. I hope you have productive meetings."

He watches me for a moment, then nods and strides from the office.

As though he took the air from my lungs, I gasp and flop back on the sofa.

My focus returns to Maya to answer her question.

"Now, I go in tomorrow and not make a fool of myself," I say, then giggle. "I wish I could take the stairs!"

Maya falls back against the sofa and laughs. I join in until a stitch forms in my side. She wipes the tears from her eyes as she sits up.

"Chica! You crack me up. What a way to pivot from an unpleasant situation. Good for you!"

I grin and shake my head.

"Oh, Maya, I have a confession."

Her eyes widen as her eyebrows rise.

I bow my head and mumble.

"Speak up, Wren! You have me on pins and needles here."

"I'm attracted to Tag Dahl."

She gasps and covers her mouth with both hands.

"I know. I know. He's my boss. The non-fraternization clause. Manager and subordinate. Blah, blah blah. I'm a mess and can't help it!"

I admit to my erotic fantasies. Maya sympathizes.

"Okay, I get falling for that sexy as sin hottie. But what about Jonathan? What have you decided?"

Ah, yes, my not-so-faithful fiancé.

After the charity gala, he sort of called me, not the next day as he said he would do. Rather, a few days later, he sent a text message asserting he was busy. Then he had a business trip he extended to a Guys' Getaway. He returned yesterday. I haven't heard from him other than brief conversations or texts.

Not that I mind.

It gave me time to realize we're not right for one another. I choose to value myself more than being happy a hot guy wants me as his wife. Who knows if that was the first time he cheated on me? And maybe with others besides his sassy and slim neighbor, for all I know. I'd rather be alone than with a man who doesn't respect me.

Now, Uncle George, on the other hand, will have a conniption when I tell him my decision. Undoubtedly, he'll attempt to berate me and to make me change my mind. However, I'll stand firm. Well, at least try to ignore whatever hurtful things he may say. I won't marry Jonathan, regardless.

"Hi, honey, I'm home!"

I sit up with a gasp.

God, please let this be my vivid imagination. Please!

As though I conjured him up, Jonathan struts into the living room from the entry foyer. His turquoise blue eyes glitter at the running joke of his announcement when he arrives at my condo. Right now, I don't giggle. Instead, I fight to keep my eyes from rolling heavenward. Thanks for nothing.

Maya folds her arms over her chest. She pins him with a fierce glare. Topaz eyes flash.

"*Bueno, habla del diablo,*" she mutters under her breath with a toss of her waist-long hair. "I'll stay, if you want me to."

I give a slight shake of my head.

"*Hola,* Maya, lovely to see you as always," Jonathan smirks. They have an open dislike for one another. Who could blame Maya?

The more I look at him now, the more I see the jerk she always said he was. I sigh at the time wasted.

"*Adiós, tramposo,*" she responds, then turns and hugs me. "Call me later."

I nod and watch her leave.

Jonathan glares after her. Once she's out the door, he huffs.

"What the hell? A tramp? I'm far from a bum!"

I stifle a giggle. Better he thinks she called him a tramp and not a cheater—the actual translation.

"You need better friends than her, Wren. How many times do I have to tell you no one makes friends with the help, including personal trainers. Your uncle and aunt agree with me."

Anger boils up from my core like a dormant volcano spewing lava to the sky. I rise from the sofa. My fists bunch at my sides. I narrow a scorching glare at him. Through clenched teeth, I snarl.

"How. *Dare*. You."

Jonathan's head jerks back so fast he may suffer whiplash. His mouth gapes, stunned by my ferociousness. Eyes skitter across my face.

"Maya is far from the help! She is my best friend. If your head wasn't so far up your ass, you would pay attention to me and know I told you she comes from a wealthy Venezuelan family, as in petroleum. And even if she didn't, she's still my. Best. Friend!"

His mouth gapes like a fish out of water. Shock registers in his eyes. Along with dollar, no bolívar signs. What an absolute jerk!

"You know what, Jonathan? I'm glad you're here. It saves me from having to make a phone call."

He shakes his head to clear it and cocks it questioningly.

I remove the engagement ring from my finger.

His eyes bulge as I jam it into his chest.

"I will not marry you. It's over."

Stunned, he stares at me. When he recovers, he shakes his head.

"All because I said you need better friends? For real, Wren? Give me a break. Now, cut it out and put your ring back on."

He reaches for my hand.

I tuck both under my crossed arms.

"No. And if you believe the only reason is your rudeness

to Maya, you are beyond clueless, Jonathan," I say with narrowed eyes. My heart races, but I refuse to back down. "You cheated on me with your neighbor, and who knows who else? You tell me I don't satisfy you—"

"Now, hold on, Wren. I never said that—"

I hold up my hand, palm out.

"You don't have to. Your body language speaks volumes. A few pokes, and you roll off and take a shower. Am I that gross to you?" I shake my head. "You know what? Don't answer that. Whatever you say is irrelevant. Just go, Jonathan. We're done. I am done with you."

I storm past him. He grabs my arm. But I snatch it from his grasp and continue to the entry foyer. I ignore his calls to stop. As I fling the door open, I turn and point at him.

"You, out. Now!"

"Come on, Wren. You can't be serious. How about we compromise? I'll give you some time to get yourself together. When you're ready, I'll be waiting. Deal?"

He approaches me with his hand outstretched for a shake.

I stare at it like a poisonous snake set to strike the death blow.

"No. No deal, Jonathan. Despite what you may think, I never agreed to marry you because of what my uncle intends for my betrothed. I fell in love with you. And what good did it do me, huh? A *tramposo*! That's what I got. No, thank you. Now, go, Jonathan."

The veil falls from his countenance. A nasty sneer appears as he narrows his eyes and curls his lip. Nostrils flare.

The vehemence makes me step back. I clutch the door, pulling it closer to me like a shield. What the hell?

"You know what, Wren? I don't have to take your bull-shit. You're lucky to have someone like me even bother with someone like you—a fat, frigid, pathetic girl. But I tell you this much. Your uncle will not allow you to bail on this *marriage*. It's a deal you will commit to whether or not you want it. So, get over yourself. I'll see you around, Wren."

Jonathan drops the engagement ring on the table and stalks past me. He casts another disgusted glare over his shoulder as he presses the elevator call button.

Heart racing and tears in my eyes, I slam the door.

CHAPTER 7

ag

"Yes, Mr. Dahl, Sir. I will get those notes for you right away."

I watch Wren's generous hips sway in a form-fitting skirt as she sashays to the conference table. She bends over it, reaching for the file folder on the opposite side. An arm extends across the surface. The other grips the edge. Her back arches and lifts that mouth-watering round ass in the air. It's like a red flag before a bull. Or, in my case, a delicious morsel dangled in front of a hungry wolf.

A growl emanates from deep within my chest.

She shudders and tosses her long mane of glossy mahogany brown hair over her shoulder. Wide eyes peek at me. Gold glints in their mink brown depths. She wiggles her hips.

My tongue lolls.

My cock thickens.

It weeps a tear of pre-cum.

Slowly, she rises.

"Do. Not. Move."

I growl and leap to my feet. Like the famished apex predator I am, I stalk my prey. "Stretch out across the table. Palms flat. Head down. Ass up."

Her soft mewl sends my wolf baying.

I tower over her. Hands grip her hips. A foot kicks hers further apart. As wide as the tight skirt allows. My enhanced hearing picks up the increase in her heart rate. My nose detects her musky arousal. She moans.

A claw extends.

The sharp tip cuts her silk blouse from the collar and along her spine. The soft fabric slips down her sides to pool on the table. A flick of my wrist, and the bra fasteners pop. The black lace joins the silk. I trail the claw further down her spine. Goosebumps follow in its wake.

She shivers. And not from the cold. A lusty moan pours from her slack mouth. Her hips roll.

I smirk.

My hand brushes the voluptuous curve of her ass. I swing my arm back. My palm lands with a satisfying THWACK on one large globe. The soft flesh jiggles beneath my hand. The sensation zips up my arm and down to my erect cock. It twitches, eager to get in on the action. My wolf scratches to be free. To take what he knows is ours to have.

I agree.

My arm rises and spanks the other ass cheek.

This time, Wren cries out. She dances on her tiptoes. She mewls when I squeeze her hip.

"Do. Not. Move."

I growl in her ear. My warm breath tickles the delicate shell. I trace it with the tip of my tongue. She starts to shiver, then catches herself. She moans. Pressed against her, I angle my pelvis for my cock to rest at the crack of her ass. Her whimper makes it thump in my trousers.

"If you want this, Red, you better obey."

Yeah, she's the innocent little girl to my beast of a wolf. And I will corrupt her in every imaginable way. Just how I know she wants it. Nice and filthy. Isn't that what all good little girls really want?

I smirk and stand.

The skirt proves no match to my capable hands. It rips in two. Only three strings circle her hips and slip between her ass cheeks. I pluck the G-string from her body, sniff it deeply, and place it in my pocket. My eyes lift to find her peeking at me, crimson colors her cheeks. I curl my lip and growl. She closes her eyes and shudders with a soft cry.

I chuckle wickedly.

My palm beats a quick staccato on her ass. Left, right, underside, right, left, underside. Again, and again. She yelps and pants. The sweet ambrosia of her arousal fills the air. I'm dizzy from it. Three fingers trace her puffy lower lips, slick with her juices.

A desperate moan seeps from her mouth. She shifts her pelvis to catch my fingers on her engorged clit. Her moan turns into a strangled cry when I spank her pussy with those same fingers.

"Oh! Oh! Oh! Oh!"

"Did I not command you to remain still, naughty girl?" I growl in her ear. "Now, you will not cum on my cock. But *I* will cum. Down. Your. Throat."

She whimpers as I spin her around. I tear the remnants of her blouse and bra from her body. Ripe tits bounce freely.

Their thick nipples tighten, begging to be suckled. With a growl, I oblige them.

My mouth latches on to one plump tip. It hardens further as my tongue circles around it. I nibble on the succulent morsel, groaning. Fingers tweak the other nipple, keeping it primed for me. My sizable hands easily toy with the hefty weight of her double Ds. I make a savory meal of her tits.

But my cock threatens to explode in my trousers.

My mouth pulls from her tit with a wet pop.

"On your knees, Red."

Her mouth forms a perfect O.

I smirk and brush my thumb around it, smearing the red lipstick. Soon it will stain my cock.

"Now."

Our gazes remain locked as she lowers to her knees. The erotic sight causes my cock to strain painfully along my thigh. Time for my release.

"Take my dick out."

The red on her cheeks deepens. But she obeys my command. Delicate fingers reach for the placket. They tremble as she opens the closure and lowers the zipper. My trousers drop to the floor, leaving the black boxer briefs. My dick pulses beneath them.

She sucks in a breath.

"Continue."

She nods and slips her fingers in the waistband, then tugs. Slowly, she reveals my v cuts, feathery happy trail, and the tops of my thighs. As the thick base of my cock emerges, she licks her lips.

I groan.

Her eyes flick up to mine. A naughty gleam sparkles in her eyes. The tip of her little pink tongue darts out. She draws it back in extra slow.

I fist her hair and yank.

"Think carefully about teasing me, naughty girl," I chide, then continue. "Take my dick out."

"Yes, Sir."

My heavy balls draw up. I growl.

Quickly, she pulls the boxer briefs down to my ankles. As she lifts her head, I tighten my grip on her hair and fist my cock. She watches as I stroke the girth of my shaft. The bulbous tip an angry red and shiny with pre-cum. I tap it against her lips.

"Open," I growl in a feral voice, more wolf than man.

She mewls as her lips part.

I feed my thick length into her mouth inch by inch until she gags. I push more as I growl for her to relax her throat. Tears trickle down her flushed cheeks. Her fingernails dig into the backs of my thighs. But she obeys. My cock pulses as it stretches her throat. I bite my lower lip on a groan.

"Fuck, Red. You take my dick like a good little girl."

She bobs her head as her eyes shine with pride.

When her nose meets my groin, I hold her still with both hands tangled in her hair. After a few seconds, she pushes against me. I hush her and hold on a bit longer, knowing she can take it.

"Breathe through your nose, like a good little girl."

She swallows.

I groan.

After she relaxes again, I pull out at the same slow pace as I entered. She sputters around my tip as saliva drips from the corners of her mouth.

I praise her some more before I slide back in, faster this time. At the back of her throat, she gags a moment, then remembers to relax. I ease down her throat. This time, I only hold her to me for a moment, then snap my hips back to withdraw. Another snap and I surge forward.

My toes curl as my balls fill with seed while I fuck her face. Her moans vibrate along my shaft, testing my control. But when I see Red reach her fingers between her legs to fuck herself, I lose it. My breath turns ragged. I grow diamond hard in seconds. I take her mouth and throat with pistoning strokes.

Her fingernails form half-moons on my thighs. She gags.

A tremor shoots from the base of my spine to my balls. I throw my head back. My roar reaches the ceiling. The violent climax unleashes thick ropes of my seed into her belly. My fingers dig into her scalp as I try to ground myself. My eyes roll to the back of my head as my knees wobble.

My cock falls from her mouth with a trail of saliva. I drop to the floor and pull her onto my lap. My face buries in her sweat-dampened hair. The scent of cinnamon sugar caramel apples mixes with the pungent aroma of pheromones and musk. I'm in heaven. I breathe her name against the crown of her head.

She wraps her arms around me and burrows closer. Her soft sigh brings a smile to my lips.

The sharp trill of my mobile disturbs our carnal bliss. I groan and dig for it in my trouser pocket. I can't find it. It goes on and on and on…

I wake with a jolt.

Warm, creamy jizz coats my eight-pack abs and pecs.

Glancing around my bedroom, I realize my alarm woke me from a dream. The intense dreams shared by fated mates before they meet or complete their bond. They're like premonitions. Signs you're to meet your fated mate soon. The dreams will only increase in intensity and frequency until the pair fulfills the bond.

Just great.

My inner Dom wants kinks satisfied.

My wolf runs feral.

I'm no closer to a solution.

With a frustrated groan, I roll from the king-size bed and stalk to the en suite bathroom.

How the hell will I get through fifty-nine more days?

CHAPTER 8

 *ren*

"Do. Not. Move."

"If you want this, Red, you better obey."

"On your knees, Red."

"Now."

"Take my dick out."

"Continue."

"Open."

"Breathe through your nose, like a good little girl."

Even though it was only a dream—albeit the most realistic erotic fantasy in history—Mr. Dahl's passionate dominance as he issued filthy commands makes me wet. Again.

He used my mouth without restraint for his carnal pleasure. Ruthless. Unstoppable. Wild.

I loved it.

Every single second of it.

Naked at his feet being used so deliciously, my body thrummed. I was no longer the shy, I'm thankful for what you give me lover. No concern for how my more robust figure appeared. Instead, a part of me I never knew existed rose to the forefront. She relished in his savagery. She sought to please him, to gain his praise—like a good little girl.

Oh, God!

So filthy!

So right.

She wanted more and sought her carnal rhapsody. Her fingers cupped heavy breasts and pinched the nipples, tender from his wickedly skillful mouth. The touches offered a taste of satisfaction but not enough. More!

Fingers trailed down her belly in search of her aching, greedy core. They skimmed over her bare mons and traced her slick seam. A soft cry around his girth resulted in a lusty groan from him. Power raced through her. She controlled this man with her willing mouth. Her confidence soared.

Pleased, she slipped a fingertip between the dripping folds. Still not nearly enough. His fervent thrusts provided a hint to her satisfaction. She mimicked his movements and thrust her fingers deep inside her dripping pussy three times. *Yes! Yes! Yes!* She thought triumphantly. The pads stroked her sensitive G-spot. She shattered in orgasmic bliss.

Her heavy-lidded eyes met his flashing ones. He growled and took her mouth with dominant force. His cum shot straight down her stretched throat to fill her belly like a torrent. No need to swallow.

She watched entranced as a long string of saliva swung between her mouth and his cock when he slipped out. She preened with the knowledge she brought this sexy, dominant man to his knees. Content, she wrapped her arms around him and burrowed against his firm chest with a soft sigh.

Can I be that *good little girl* in real life? For Tag Dahl?

Stop it, Wren Byrd! He is your B-O-S-S. Enough!

Yeah, wistful thinking.

I set my naughty fantasy aside and stare out the window of the Larson Enterprises Mercedes-Benz sedan. Since I left my car in the company's garage yesterday, Beth arranged a second car to bring me to work this morning.

Now, I need to focus on making up for a not-so-great first day. That is, if I can step onto the elevator without fainting.

"Good morning, Beth," I say a bit sheepishly as I approach her desk. My eyes dart past her to the empty office. No sign of Mr. Dahl. I shift my gaze back to her.

She smiles and rises from her leather chair.

"Hi, there, Wren! You look much better. How do you feel today?" She asks as she rounds her desk.

My cheeks heat with embarrassment. I duck my head.

"Aaw, don't let it bother you. Things happen. Now, let's get you settled."

She gestures to the desk opposite hers on the other side of the double doors of Mr. Dahl's office. The desk and chair match the modern decor of his private reception area. The neutral palette of sand, tan, and white appears on the wall and floor treatments and on the furniture. I place my black crocodile handbag on the sand-colored wooden desk while Beth pulls out the matching leather chair.

"Have a seat. I'll help to you log into the network. IT generated your credentials and created your email address," she says as she opens the new laptop. "Remember, the employee handbook states staff cannot use the company's laptop for personal activities. Mr. Dahl is a stickler for protocols. You do not want to get on his bad-bad side, as opposed to his bad side, or the gods forbid his bad-cubed side. You'll learn the scale soon enough."

"Thank you, Beth."

I make a mental note of the stickler part. The beast expects the rules to be followed. Check. I certainly don't want to fall on the worse side of his personality. I prefer him as a teddy bear.

Speaking of which…

"His office is empty. But he told me to be here at nine. Is he in a meeting?"

Beth's fingers hover over the keyboard. She turns her head and eyes me for a moment. Her scrutiny makes me shift in the chair. I lower my gaze to the laptop screen.

"We're all expected to be here at nine. I arrive half an hour earlier just in case Mr. Dahl needs anything unexpectedly. You may want to consider doing the same," she says with an unreadable expression. "As for his whereabouts, he's out of the office at meetings this morning. He'll meet with you at two this afternoon."

It's not so much her words as it is the tone and the subtle implication that make me blush. It's as though she's aware of my against-the-rules attraction to him. Just the thought of his brawny body causes heat to gather in my core. I press my thighs together.

Beth's nose twitches, then her eyes narrow slightly.

The ring of her office phone catches her attention. She hurries to her desk. As she adjusts the headset and talks to the caller, her eyes remain on mine.

I avoid her gaze and busy myself with arranging my desk. From my handbag, I remove the sterling silver frame with a photo of my parents and me on St. Jean Beach in St. Barths. It was one of the happiest times we had before their accident. I want to have the pleasant memory near me as I work to make myself independent of Uncle George.

For a moment, I wonder why I haven't heard from him since I ended the engagement with Jonathan. I'm sure it'll be a big to-do. My spirit sinks at the thought. Then I shake my head. No. I will not allow them to taint my day.

I smile at the photo to dispel the negativity. Warmth envelops me. My heart leaps as I imagine my parents' words of encouragement.

With that positive thought, I reach into my handbag for my writing folder and pen. Others may use iPads or other electronic devices for their planning. But I prefer the old-fashioned pad and pen. I guess it's the artist in me.

I place my handbag on the cabinet behind me. Out of the shopping bag, I lift potted white orchids and set it next to the frame. I take out the other orchids and carry them to Beth's desk. Her eyes widen as I place the flowers on the corner. She's still on the phone, so I smile and return to my desk.

A moment later, she squeals and claps her hands. No longer assessing, her eyes shine as she smiles at me.

"Wren, they're gorgeous. Thank you!"

I smile back and respond, "Orchids are associated with wealth, luxury, and good fortune. They enhance career success. The perfect gift for my new work buddy. At least, I hope we can be friends."

She giggles and walks over with her arms open. I stand for her hug.

"Of course! You know, us girls have to stick together. I love Mr. Dahl to death. But he can be brusque and try me. It'll be good to have someone to share the brunt of his demands and moods. Plus, at lunch, I'll introduce you to Ginny and Dana. They're Mr. Jagger and Mr. Viggo's admins."

She nods toward their office suites.

"But before all of that, let's get you up and running. Then I'll give you a tour of the executive floor. I want you situated before Mr. Dahl arrives. He's not grumpy. We're ecstatic!"

I join in on her giggles.

The morning goes by in a whirl of activity. After the tour, Beth places a stack of mail in my inbox with a wide grin.

"My gift for you. Or rather, for myself! I won't have to handle Mr. Dahl's social life *and* professional aspects. Those are invitations, letters for donations, so on and so on. He's a popular guy. Everyone wants a piece of him. If you need any help, let me know."

She winks and spins on her high heels. She practically skips to her desk and sits in her chair, crossing her long, toned legs with a flourish. Just as the phone rings. She laughs and mouths, "Busy, busy, busy!"

I giggle and shake my head.

Time to get to work.

So engrossed in organizing the life of an extremely popular billionaire, I startle at the knock on my desk. I glance up to find Beth flanked by two other young women I assume are Ginny and Dana. The trio grins.

"Lunchtime!" They chorus as Beth rolls my chair away from my desk.

I laugh and grab my handbag while she introduces me to the other two. We chat as we head to the elevator. I ignore the twinge in my belly. They glance at me with concern, and I smile. But I wonder how they could tell I was nervous.

The executive elevator opens behind us with a ding.

Mr. Jagger strides out, followed by Mr. Dahl.

My heart flutters as our eyes connect. His emerald greens scan my face before they travel down my body. Section by section, my skin heats beneath his gaze.

"Good afternoon, Mr. Larson, Mr. Dahl."

Beth's greeting draws his eyes from me to her.

I blink and turn to her as she continues.

"You returned earlier than expected. Would you like us to delay our lunch, sir?"

His eyes flick to me briefly.

"No, I have some phone calls to make," he responds, then returns his gaze to me. "Wren, you look better."

"Yes, Mr. Dahl, sir. I feel better, thank you," I all but stutter. To my relief, his face remains stoic.

"Good. Enjoy your lunch. When you return, we will meet to discuss my expectations."

He nods and turns to Mr. Larson, who speaks with Ginny.

I force myself to look away. As a distraction, I pick up the conversation with Dana. Like my namesake bird, I chatter incessantly. Except house wrens usually do so in response to large animals that may be predators. Only humans here, but nervousness causes me to rattle on.

Finally, Ginny rejoins us, and we step onto an arriving elevator. As the doors close, I glance up to find Mr. Dahl watching me. A tug pulls at my heart. I nibble my lower lip.

The doors slide close.

~

Tag

"If you're finished ogling Wren, we can continue our discussion."

I blow a breath and turn away from the elevator. Jagger chuckles.

"You better work on your poker face, bro. Otherwise, the entire office will know you have the hots for your assistant."

He guffaws and slaps me on the shoulder.

If we weren't in the office, I'd wrestle his ass to the

ground. Instead, I growl and shake his hand off. My reaction only makes him laugh harder. Damn, the start of day 59 goes from a wet dream to a schoolboy drooling. Jagger is right. I must do better.

We talk as we walk, then part at the entry to my office suite.

"Try not to bang her on the sofa after lunch. You know I like to stretch out on it when I need to think outside of my office suite," he says, chuckling and heads to his offices.

I growl and storm towards the doors to mine. The bouquet of fresh flowers mixes with Wren's scent. It permeates the air and every fiber of my being. My wolf sits on his haunches with a feral grin on his face. I shake my head and step forward.

The glint of silver catches my eye.

I move to her desk and lift the picture frame.

A young Wren—around eight or nine—stands between a man and a woman I assume to be her parents. Their carefree smiles shine brighter than the sun above them. Her facial features resemble a soft, feminine version of her father. She inherited her luxurious mahogany hair and full figure from her mother.

According to her background check, her parents died when she was nine years old. It must have been shortly after they took this photo. They were a lovely family.

My heart clenches as I return the frame to her desk.

It makes me wonder what having a family with Wren would be like. Her belly round with my pups. Going on a beach vacation like her parents. Maybe even a group trip with Jagger, Sage, their twins and Dylan and Sasha with their daughter. Which of us would our pups take after? Would they be able to shift? More importantly, would Wren survive the transition? Hell, would she want it?

My mobile vibrates in my trouser pocket.

I scrub a hand down my face before I answer the call. It's a project manager for a new resort with a major problem. The perfect distraction—work. Finished with the call, I throw myself into the rest of my day's plans with zeal. Anything to not ponder potential impossibilities.

Movement outside my office draws my attention. Wren and Beth stand in the reception area talking to Ginny and Dana. With their backs to me, I soak in Wren.

Her hair piled atop her head shines in the overhead lighting. The exposed column of her neck meets her shoulder. The exact spot for my claiming bite.

My fangs punch through my gums and drip with the serum to bestow the gift. At the thought of making her mine, my cock thickens. As a shower and not a grower, my length remains the same while the girth expands. I have to adjust my cock down my thigh thanks to the instant arousal.

Wren glances over her shoulder, and our eyes meet. I yank my hand from beneath the desk. She blinks and flicks her eyes between my hand and the desk. Again, she bites on that lush lower lip. I growl, wanting to taste the sweet flesh.

Ginny and Dana walk away. Beth heads to her desk, then notices me through the glass wall. She nods and says something to Wren, who also nods. She rushes to her desk. A moment later, the intercom buzzes. I will my fangs to retract then answer with my eyes on her.

"Yes, Wren?"

Her name on my lips makes my cock pulse.

"Uh, Mr. Dahl, sir, it's almost two o'clock. Are we still meeting?"

"Yes, Wren. You may come."

My lips twitch as her cheeks pinken and she stutters an affirmative response. Interesting, she caught the double entendre. I get the sense she's interested in me. But enough to welcome me as her fated mate?

I watch her as she rises from her desk chair and grabs a leather portfolio, pen, her mobile, and a folder. Her grip-worthy hips move with naturally sensuous grace. She's petite, around five feet, four inches. But the fuck-me heels add another four inches to her height. The silk blouse and pencil skirt remind me of the dream.

My cock leaks.

Ordinarily, I would conduct the meeting at the conference table. Given my massive erection, I'll stay put. I gesture to the guest chair opposite my desk.

She perches on the edge and places the portfolio and mobile on the other chair. The folder she balances on her lap as she holds the pen.

To further test my theory, I send a burst of desire through our fledging mate bond. Her pupils dilate as her lips part. The outlines of her plump nipples appear through the silk. She shifts in the chair. The portfolio slips to the floor. She leans over to pick it up. No engagement ring. A fresh development.

I can't resist and leap from the chair. My hand reaches the portfolio at the same time as hers. Our fingers touch. Electricity zaps us. Her hand jerks back. She gasps. I growl. She blinks. Angling my body to avoid poking her in the eye with my stiff cock, I rise and hand the portfolio to her.

Seated behind my desk, I clear my throat. Expectant eyes stare at me. Yeah, Wren Byrd is definitely interested. I smirk.

"Shall we begin?"

 *ren*

"WHAT THE HELL is going on in that little head of yours, Wren?! Or have you lost your mind?! You're just like your father, not wanting to do your part for the family. I arranged this marriage for the betterment of the family. You are the sole heir. After I retire, Byrd Capital cannot cease business because you don't want to marry Jonathan. He's the suitable candidate for the role of CEO. I don't give a damn he was with his neighbor. You will marry Jonathan!"

I bristle at Uncle George's offensive words.

How dare he insult my father and me? It always has to be my uncle's way. Anything else is unacceptable. He's more concerned with a business merger than the bonding of two loves or with Jonathan's infidelity. And if my uncle trained me to run Byrd Capital like I asked so many times, Jonathan wouldn't even be in the picture!

"Wren, I agree with George. Women of our standing do what we must for the family. The idea of princes and glass slippers is unrealistic. You're twenty-five. I was married to George by then, as expected of me. It's time for you to grow up and face your responsibilities."

"Here, Wren, give me your hand."

My head swivels from Wretched Gretchen to Jonathan.

His cold eyes send a chill down my spine. I glance at his raised hand. He holds the engagement ring in his fingers. What the hell?!

"How did you get that? You left it in my condo."

"Don't be daft, Wren. I used my access code. Here. Put it on."

He reaches for my hand.

I jump to my feet and glare at Uncle George.

"No! I will not marry Jonathan! And stop speaking disrespectfully about my parents and me! I've had enough of it!"

I spin on my heels and rush through the living room.

"If you walk out of that door, Wren Byrd, it will remain shut to you forever. You refuse to support this family? This family will no longer support you. You will be on your own. Think very carefully on your next move."

Tears blur my vision now turned red.

Un-fucking-believable!

So be it.

I know my worth, even if they don't.

I straighten my spine and hold my head high then march out of the Fisher Island mansion.

"WREN, Human Resources sent your request for an advance on your salary to me. That's an unusual request. Would you mind explaining the need?"

My face flames red. I wish I could disappear from in

front of Mr. Dahl and erase his memory. I had no idea HR would inform him of my appeal.

It's been two weeks since the blowup with George. I refuse to refer to him as an uncle since no blood relative should treat one in the manner he treated me. He made good on his promise to not support me. He closed my bank accounts and my credit cards. I had a few hundred dollars in cash on hand. My condo? Well, I learned Byrd Capital holds the deed. The following morning, I received a forty-eight-hour notice to vacate the premises. Maya came over, and we loaded my necessities into her Mercedes-Benz G-Wagen and my car. Fortunately, the title is in my name. I've been living with her ever since.

Tears fill my eyes. I try to stop them from falling. But it's no use. I bawl. A real ugly cry—sobs, snot, saliva.

Mr. Dahl rushes to my side and hands a handkerchief to me. He asks questions. But I just shake my head. I'm beyond distraught.

The only saving graces have been my best friend and my job. But I'm no freeloader. I have to contribute for staying with Maya. Even though she tells me no and refuses the money. It's the principle of the matter. But a couple of hundred dollars don't go far, and I've only had one paycheck. I have excellent credit and opened credit cards to help. But I must pay them each month. Not to mention I need a place to live.

The waterworks flow faster.

Suddenly, I'm scooped from the guest chair. My eyes fly open. I'm nose-to-nose with Mr. Dahl. His brows knit together over eyes darkened to jade with worry. Then I hear the rumbling. Its vibrations reverberate through my body. My eyes close on a hiccup. I relax against him as he carries me like I weigh a feather. I open them again when I feel his muscular thighs under my butt. He's sitting on the sofa, and I'm on his lap. Eek!

I squirm to get up. But he growls low in his chest as he tightens his grip. My gaze swings from his face to the glass wall. Thank goodness the privacy shading blocks the office's interior. I'd be mortified if Beth or someone else witnessed me on the boss' lap.

"Do. Not. Move."

I gasp. Those are his exact words and commanding tone from the dream. And I've experienced plenty more erotic fantasies of my boss in the past few weeks.

My head whips towards him.

His eyes flash. An air of dominance emanates from him. I lower my gaze and settle on his lap.

"Now, tell me what happened."

∾

*T*AG

BY THE TIME WREN FINISHES, my blood boils thick in my veins. My wolf runs, gnashing his teeth and snarling. Who the fuck abandons their own flesh and blood over utter bullshit? It's not as though her uncle couldn't groom her as his successor or hire a trustworthy CEO. Arranged marriages are common, even amongst wolf shifters. But not against the she-wolf's will. Just like Jagger stopped Signy's arrangement.

And to put Wren out on the street with nothing but a few dollars, items, and her car? Thank the gods for her friend Maya. Now, she's someone who's deserving of Wren. Not that fucker Jonathan. The dumbass. He didn't know how to treat Wren. For him and her family to call her names because of her body type? That's nuts! She's perfect. Soft in all the right places. A female who can handle a big male like me.

I shake my head as my cock agrees. No need to give her a reason to jump off my lap. I'd rather she straddles me. Cut it, Dahl!

"I didn't realize HR would inform you of my request. I'm utterly embarrassed."

Wren hangs her head. A tear drops to her hands folded in her lap.

I capture her chin between my thumb and index finger to turn her head.

"No need for *you* to be embarrassed. It's your uncle who should feel that way. No real man would neglect his family, especially a female. He should cherish and treat you well. Even more so since you lost your parents at such a young age. But don't worry. I'll take care of you."

She blinks in surprise.

I don't. My fated mate needs me. I can't leave her. I won't leave her. She is mine to protect, care for, and to love. Yeah. I'm a goner. Decision made.

She opens her mouth to respond. I put my finger against her lips.

"Go into my private bathroom and wash your face. Then come back here to me."

She nibbles her lower lip.

This time, I lean forward and nip the succulent flesh with my teeth. She gasps. I growl and swat her hip.

"Go."

Her pupils dilate. Her unique scent of cinnamon sugar caramel apples mixes with the musky aroma of her arousal as her desire flares. She jolts when I squeeze her hip. I nod towards the bathroom door. She scrambles from my lap and rushes for the door.

My cock thickens at the sight of her ass jiggling beneath her silk dress.

Mine!

When she disappears behind the door with a furtive glance at me, I smirk and whip out my mobile. Call complete, I rise and put on my suit jacket. My fated mate steps out of the bathroom. Her eyes are red but clear. The color in her cheeks lessened. She smooths her dress and walks over to me.

"Get your bag."

Without hesitation, she scurries for the doors to my office. My inner Dom watches, pleased at her naturally submissive behavior. Oh, the things I will do to her soon. I follow her out and turn to Beth.

"Wren and I have a project. We won't return to the office today. Leave when you're done."

Beth's eyes widen. Then she realizes her faux pas and nods. Surreptitiously, she glances at Wren, who stares at the floor. Crimson colors her cheeks again. The gossip will start for sure now. I no longer give a damn. Wren Byrd is mine.

I place my hand on the small of her back and guide her to the executive elevator. She stops and glances up at me, trepidation in her eyes. Before she can speak, I do.

"Wren, do you trust me?"

Her eyes flick to the elevator and back to me. She nods.

I cock an eyebrow.

"Words, Wren, I will have your words."

A soft breath escapes her parted lips.

"Yes, sir."

My cock pulsates.

"There's My Sweet Girl."

Her mouth-watering tits rise on a deep inhalation. Slowly, the air dispels.

I press the call button. Other than the rumble from my

chest, we ride down in silence. I guide her around the corner to the other bank of elevators. The concierge greets us and hands a slip of paper to me. I thank her and head towards the last elevator.

"If you don't mind me asking, where are we going?"

I glance down at my fated mate and smile.

"It's a surprise."

"Okay."

We step onto the elevator reserved for the top levels of The Larson Tower. I press the button for the seventieth floor. A few people join us. I stand behind my fated mate with my hands on her shoulders to ground her. I keep the rumble low so she can feel it, but others can't hear it. She leans against me. I grin like the Cheshire Cat.

We're the last ones off. The doors open to a foyer with two sets of double doors. I gesture for her to step out and guide her to the pair to our left. I glance at the slip of paper and type in the access code. Then step back for her to enter.

"Oh. My. Goodness! This is spectacular!"

She glides over the white marble floors towards the wall of twenty-foot-high windows. The vast Atlantic Ocean serves as the backdrop. She stands in silhouette against its turquoise waters. However, its beauty pales compared to my fated mate. Her eyes glow as she faces me.

"What a surprise! I've never been so high above Biscayne Bay. This view is breathtaking."

She takes my breath away. I put my hands in my trouser pockets to prevent them from pulling her into my arms. Instead, I turn and nod at the rest of the space.

"The view is only part of the surprise. This, My Sweet Girl, is your new residence."

Her mouth falls open. She spins from the windows. Her eyes dart around the oversized living room, entry, towards the stairs, and back to me.

"No way."

"Yes way. Come, I'll give you a tour."

I extend my elbow to her. She stares at it then up at me. I wait. She has to make the move of acceptance. She takes a deep breath and loops her arm through mine. My grin widens.

Hers grows as she takes in the three bedroom suites, four bathrooms, chef's eat-in kitchen, dining room, media room, and office. We return to the living room and sit on a leather sofa, facing the panoramic view.

My fated mate sits too far away from me. I slide over to her side. She watches me but doesn't move. Good girl.

"Thank you for thinking about me, Mr. Dahl. I truly appreciate it. But I cannot afford this condo. Not even with an advance on my salary."

She laughs softly.

"And speaking of salary, I need to return to work. Earn my keep and all," she adds as she rises.

My hand shoots out and clasps her wrist. She startles.

"Wren, I don't expect you to pay for it. This is one of Larson Enterprises' corporate condos. They're used by visitors. So, there's no fee. You can stay here for as long as you like. Give you time to get acclimated to supporting yourself. And you'll save on gas."

The corners of her mouth quirk up at my lame joke. However, she shakes her head.

"I can't possibly accept your gracious offer, Mr. Dahl. I left one situation dependent on someone. It's not possible for me to put myself in the same situation again. But I thank you."

I growl in frustration. Why can't I get her to see it's for the best without freaking her out about being my fated mate? I can close multibillion-dollar deals. But words escape me with Wren. Think quick, Dahl!

"Sit a moment."

She pauses, then lowers herself to the sofa. Our knees brush. That zing of electricity sparks between us. She gasps. It's my opening.

I take her hands in mine. Go for it, Dahl.

"Wren, I'm going to be honest with you," I start and wait for her eyes to meet mine. "I know you are my social assistant and company policy forbids a personal relationship between a manager and a subordinate. But I can't help my attraction to you. It's natural. Something I can't stop. Something I don't want to stop."

I pause to gauge her reaction. She remains still.

"You feel it too. Don't you?"

She hesitates, then nods. I cock an eyebrow.

"Yes, Mr. Dahl, sir."

I shake my head.

"Tag, Wren, call me Tag."

"Yes, Tag."

"I propose you end your employment contract with Larson—"

She sucks in a breath and frees her hands from mine. Shaking my head, I grab them back before she stands.

"Let me finish," I say, and she stills. "I propose you end your employment contract with Larson Enterprises *and* sign an independent contractor agreement with me. The only changes would be the elimination of the non-fraternization and sixty-day trial clauses and an increase in your pay to allow for health insurance coverage. The agreement would include the condo too."

My fated mate purses her lips.

"That office you gushed about would be *your* office. And when I need to entertain guests for dinners and such as you think makes sense for my social endeavors, you can host the events here. Until you find a place you prefer, you live here too. It's a win-win situation. You maintain your independence with a generous package and a place to live and I keep my social assistant with no barriers to us exploring our mutual attraction."

I squeeze her hands.

"What do you think?"

My fated mate studies my face. I keep an open expression, so she won't find any deceit. She nods, then her eyes rove around the living room.

My wolf senses pick up her increased heart rate and her excitement. I wait patiently, knowing she'll accept my offer.

She purrs.

"Shall we begin?"

CHAPTER 10

 *ren*

I FALL into the dark green depths of Tag's eyes as he stares at me with unabashed, blatant hunger. What a moment ago was a soothing rumble morphs into a carnal growl. Erotic energy swirls around us, replacing the zaps of electricity at our innocent touches. My heart races as he holds me in a sexual thrall.

"Think carefully about teasing me, naughty girl."

"I wouldn't dream of it, Sir."

Tag jumps from the sofa with an animalistic grace. His feral eyes focus on me. Seconds later, I hang upside-down over his shoulder. I squeal and wiggle to get free of his hold. A spank to my ass stills me.

"Behave. Naughty. Girl," he says punctuating each word with a spank.

My pussy clenches. I moan wantonly.

"Where are you taking me?" I pant.

He jogs up the stairs two at a time. I bounce and grab his waist. His grip under my butt tightens.

"To spread you out on the bed and feast on you for hours. If you're a good little girl."

My pussy gushes. A long, low moan slips from my mouth.

Oh, God!

So filthy!

So right.

Perhaps I can be that *good little girl* in real life for Tag Dahl, after all. But will he accept my extra-curvy figure naked, like in my fantasies? My heart lurches at the thought he'll wrinkle his nose in disgust like Jonathan's neighbor or call me names like he did. I hope—

"OWEE!! Wh—What was that for?"

Tag's palm rests on my stinging butt cheek. The heat from the spank radiates from the spot. The sting follows.

"Stop thinking so hard, naughty girl."

I fly through the air. Arms and legs flail. With an oomph, I land amongst fluffy pillows on the king-size bed. I rise on my elbows and toss my hair out of my face. My eyes narrow on Tag, then half-mast at the sight of him stripping.

He doesn't say a word, just keeps his eyes locked on mine. The suit jacket drops from his broad shoulders. He tosses it to the sofa. Maintaining eye contact, he crouches and unties his shoes. He stands and toes them off. One knee after the other bends to remove the socks. He places gold cufflinks on the table and pulls the dress shirt from his trousers.

I sit up, not wanting to miss the reveal of his chest. My teeth draw my lower lip into my mouth.

He shakes his head and stalks towards me. He crawls from the foot of the bed up my body. I hold my breath. His thumb rests on my lower lip, then pulls it from between my teeth. He leans over and licks the plump flesh. I mewl.

Eyes still on mine, he reverses his crawl and stands. His fingers loosen the silk tie. He tosses it over his shoulder towards the sofa. Neither of us bother to check where it landed. Slowly, methodically, he unbuttons his shirt. The sides flap open. I growl in disappointment at the white undershirt blocking my view. He chuckles wickedly.

He grips it behind his neck and yanks the offensive garment over his head. The undershirt drifts to the floor. I'd say good riddance. But the air whooshes from my lungs, leaving me breathless.

What I imagined being a muscular chest proves I'm not so creative. He's magnificent. Carved like Adonis with his v cuts, eight-pack abs furrowed to perfection, and his chiseled pecs with paw-print tattoos on each one. Who would expect this serious man to have not one but two tattoos? A bad boy in disguise? I'll take him. Thank you!

Bulging biceps flex as he reaches for the leather belt at his narrow waist. I lean forward with my tongue hanging out in anticipation of his next reveal. Judging by the thick length along his thigh, he won't disappoint.

Again, he chuckles. The smirk on his face is well deserved. The pants drop to the floor. Outlined beneath black boxer briefs is a log. It twitches, and I jump. Fingers trace the length and circle the head. I blink to be sure I didn't imagine the moisture on the boxer briefs near the tip of his cock. No, it's there.

Oh, God!

My thighs press together as my core aches to be filled to the max by him.

He tilts his head back with nostrils flared. His abs tighten as he inhales deeply. A growl slips from his mouth on the exhalation. Intense eyes flash.

My fingers bunch the duvet, and my toes point when he strips the last article of clothing from his body. His ginormous cock springs free. It points directly at me. The tip glistens. My tongue darts out to lick my lips.

I groan deep in my throat as he fists the base of his dick, strokes up, then tugs the plum-shaped head. More cream leaks from the slit. His sac swings like a pendulum.

My eyes sweep across the muscular planes of this real-life Adonis. I hum my appreciation.

"You like my body?"

I nod vigorously, then add a few verbal yes, Sirs.

"I like yours. Now, show me."

My jaw drops, flabbergasted.

No. No. No. Me? Stand and strip for him? Ah, no.

I switch my gaze to the floor-to-ceiling windows. Sunlight streams inside, bathing the room in brightness. Not even a shadow to hide my flaws. Never have Jonathan and I had sex in a room so lit up. It was at night with the blackout shades drawn and maybe a couple of flickering candles in the corner. This? No.

So caught up in sheer panic, I don't notice the bed shift as Tag sits beside me. I squeak when he cups my face and turns it towards him.

"Wren, you are a beautiful female with a sinful body a man like me worships from your head to your toes. You're my own lush playground. I want to lose myself in you. Bring you pleasures you never knew existed. Make you cum on my tongue, on my fingers, on my cock. Mark you in every way as mine. Do you understand?"

Now, my jaw drops for another reason. To hear a man say such beautiful things amazes me. A man like Tag Dahl? Floors me.

I study his face for any artifice. Only eyes full of honesty stare back at me. Even my heart warms as though he touched deep within me. Relief floods my overwrought system.

On a sigh, I nod.

He raises an eyebrow.

The corners of my mouth lift as I respond verbally.

"There's My Sweet Girl. Now, strip so I can feast."

I scamper off the bed. Then yelp when he spanks my butt. I rub the spot as I glance over my shoulder. He winks and stretches out on the bed with his cock tall like a flagpole. My mouth waters. I forget my body issues and the sting.

With a deep breath, I draw on my inner vixen and put on what I hope is a sexy striptease. My prayers are answered. When my black silk thong lands atop the matching bra and my dress, Tag throws his head back and howls. His eyes land on me full of savage hunger.

Once again, he sounds more wild animal than a man.

I shiver. Goosebumps spread over my exposed skin. At the same time, red-hot sparks skitter across my body, igniting white-hot passion. Nipples pucker and core clenches. Slick coats my inner thighs. My arousal wafts to my nose. The musky scent makes me wetter. Needier. A whine rises in the back of my throat.

"Come to me, mate."

My knees turn to jelly at Tag's guttural command. Quick as lightning, he leaps from the bed and catches me. Powerful arms carry me to the bed. He uses his knees to reach the center and lays me down. He stares at me with a sensual, possessive, fierce expression. An internal furnace heats me up.

I cup his stubbled cheek. My thumb brushes across his full lips. He sucks it into his mouth and nips the tip. I gasp as erotic tingles shoot up my arm. Then moan as he trails open-mouthed kisses in their wake. My eyes flutter close.

A shudder rolls over me when he reaches the sensitive juncture of my shoulder and neck. He pauses and licks the spot. I angle my head to give him better access. He growls his approval. Warm moisture trickles down my back. He jerks his head away and sits up. My eyes snap open.

"Tag? Are you all right?"

With his face averted, he answers a gruff yes.

I ache to see him and take his face between both hands. He lets me turn his head. I sit up and kiss the closed eyelids. His ragged breath tickles my neck. I kiss every inch of his handsome face. But he remains rigid. My hands glide to his tense shoulders and knead them as I brush my lips over his closed mouth.

"Fuck, Wren."

He bands his arms around me and rolls me beneath him. His enormous body covers me. It blankets me in his heat. His mouth devours mine. He swallows my moans while groans of his own fill my ears. He kisses me breathless, then presses his forehead to mine.

"Tell me yes, Wren. Just say yes, baby. Please."

His eyes filled with anguish and yearning plead with me.

I don't know what he wants me to say yes to. But at this point, I'll give this man whatever he wants. He's treated me better than anyone since my parents. No judgement. No disappointment. No disgust. Instead, he's cared for me, considered my needs, and provided solutions. And the attraction? I feel it as intensely as he does. I yearn for him too.

"Yes, Tag, yes, yes, yes."

"Oh, gods," he groans as his eyes squeeze shut.

I press kisses to his face and murmur soothing words as I caress his back.

His eyes open. A wild glow rises from their dark green depths.

"I really need you, baby. Bare, with nothing between us. I need to take you rough now. After, I'll be gentle. I promise. Okay?"

"Yes."

He growls.

His knee wedges between my legs. Eagerly, I spread them. A finger strokes my soaked seam. He growls and fists his cock. The head slips along my lower lips, collecting the juices. His hips snap back and surge forward. His tremendous girth breaches my folds. I keen from the thick invasion. His tip hits my cervix. I buck.

"Hold on to me, baby."

I wrap around him like a monkey, all arms and legs.

He planks above me on his toes with one hand around my waist and the other gripping the headboard. I don't know what to make of the position until he starts to move. And by God does he.

Thrusts like a speeding locomotive pound me into the mattress. He withdraws to his tip and slams back in. Our groins crash. Skin slaps against skin. His sac smacks the underside of my butt cheeks. He's raw and single-minded.

I love it!

I scream his name as a toe-curling orgasm takes me by surprise. The first I ever had with penetration. Already Tag gives me pleasure I never knew existed. Another one rolls on its heels. Turning the aftershocks into never-ending electrical currents. I cry out, thrashing my head from side to side. My inner walls clamp on his magical cock, greedily wanting more.

He bellows. His grueling pace increases. The headboard slams against the wall. Our bodies—slick with sweat—slip and slide with his forceful thrusts. His grunts and growls fill the room. The scent of primal sex surrounds us. It's animalistic fucking.

I hiss from the stretch and burn of his ginormous cock in my tight pussy. It hurts oh so good. Then his cock swells. It grows impossibly larger. I moan as it drives deeper into my ravaged core.

Without stopping, he takes my hands and raises them above my head. Palms press to the headboard. He twines our fingers and buries his face in my neck. Sharp teeth graze my throat. My back bows from the bed. Every cell in my body explodes from carnal desire. I want this man to possess me.

"YES!!!"

I scream without being asked a question. My body knows an answer is due.

Tag roars.

His mouth leaves my neck. He rears back on his haunches, yanking me with him. I straddle his muscular thighs. He grips the back of my neck with one hand and wraps the other arm around my waist. Securing me to his body. He pumps up into me once, twice, then slams me down. He grinds against me, burrowing his dick to the root. Like a geyser, his cock spurts his release in a series of scorching spasms.

Another orgasm blows my mind. I throw my head back and cry out in wild abandon.

～

*T*AG

F*UCK*. Me.

First, I call her mate.

Then, I almost issue the claiming bite. Not once. But twice in only round one of making love.

Wren drives me to lose all control.

My wolf roared in frustration when I held back. Hell, I roared along with him. The urge so strong to make her mine nearly undid me.

But I need her permission. And she needs to understand what it all means, including the risks. Not to mention Jagger will lose his shit if I claim Wren unbeknownst to her.

I scrub a hand down my face and peer at her between the fingers.

She lies sated, blissfully unaware of my inner turmoil. Her cheeks flushed and lips kiss swollen. Her tousled hair spreads out on the pillow. I have the most gorgeous fated mate. And she doubts her beauty. That dumb fuck Jonathan. But if he hadn't been a moron, I may never have met my fated mate.

She's agreed to my proposal, told me yes without knowing what I wanted, and most of all, she trusts me.

I will not allow a lack of self-control to ruin us before we even get started. I have time. No. We have time. And I won't muck it up.

CHAPTER 11

"THAT'LL DO IT. You're officially an independent contractor specializing in social engagements and event planning with me as your first client. Congratulations, Wren!"

Tag grins and hands me the countersigned agreement and my corporation documents.

In less than twenty-four hours, he arranged for Larson Enterprises' legal department to write up and to file the necessary paperwork. He's determined to get me situated quickly.

Which is why we're in his office with the head of the department on a Saturday afternoon. I'm sure she'd rather spend her weekend doing something more fun than explaining legalese to me.

I smile at her gratefully, then turn my gaze to Tag.

"Thank you. Thank you both so much. This is beyond exciting!"

"You're welcome and good luck to you, Wren," she says

and turns to Tag. "If you don't require any further assistance, I'll take my leave."

"No. Thank you."

She smiles and leaves.

As I watch, the glass wall darkens. I turn to Tag.

He's staring at me with hooded eyes filled with carnal desire. I shiver as he rises and takes my hand.

Wordlessly, he leads me to the conference table, places my palms on its surface, pulls my hips back to lengthen my torso over the table, and flips my dress up. He kicks my legs to spread them. I oblige and widen my stance. His hands caress my butt cheeks bare since I don't have any panties on.

Automatically, my back arches and lifts my butt higher into his hands.

He growls in appreciation, then squeezes each mound and pulls them apart. His growl deepens as he stares at my exposed rear.

My head jerks around.

His flashing eyes lift to mine.

"I will claim each of your holes, including your ass. But not today. You must build up the ability to accommodate my size like a good little girl."

My forehead drops to the table with a thud as I moan.

He chuckles wickedly as my juices trickle to the floor. Then his mouth is on me. I buck against him. With a chastising growl, he grips my undulating hips to still them. He devours my pussy like a ravenous man, grunting and groaning with carnal satisfaction.

I lose count of the orgasms. One follows the other for endless pleasure. My entire body shakes. Incoherent cries of passion pour from my mouth in pants. Just as my juices gush down Tag's throat.

He rises, smacks each butt cheek, and thrusts his massive

cock inside of my quivering core. It contracts around him, squeezing like a vise. He growls barbarically.

"You like how my big cock claims every inch of your little pussy?" His voice thrums in my ear.

My palms slap the table as I respond with a garbled cry.

"I'll take that as a yes. So, I'll give you more."

He withdraws slowly. I feel every ridge, every vein, and every inch of his dick. I mewl, then scream when he slams back in with one brutal thrust. It lifts me to the tips of my toes and pushes the edge of the table into my pelvis. Another long, slow stroke followed by another slam, again and again until I'm a spluttering, wet mess.

"Cum for me once more, like a good little girl."

I shake my head, too sensitive for more.

He licks the side of my sweaty neck.

"Yes. You. Will."

The last stroke sends me over the edge. I cum screaming like a banshee, shaking violently beneath him.

He roars and fills my core to overflowing with his hot, creamy seed. His thrusts slow down to a lazy place, gently slapping his groin against my ass. He lowers his torso to my back. I moan softly as he trails kisses along my neck.

"I've had the fantasy of fucking you on this table for the longest time."

Oh, God!

~

*T*AG

"I'M glad I could get my things from the office and leave a note for Beth. I didn't want to disappear without letting her know what happened. It's so sweet you'll keep my orchid on your coffee table."

"It will remind me of you while I'm in my office all alone, without my hot assistant to make the day more enjoyable."

My fated mate giggles and shakes her head.

"I can't wait for you to meet Maya. She's not just my personal trainer, but my best friend. It's thanks to her I embrace my body—"

"*I* want to embrace your body."

She nudges my shoulder and rolls her eyes.

After a quick shower in my private bathroom and I changed out of my suit, we head to Maya's condo to get Wren's things. I'm looking forward to meeting her best friend. Wren speaks so highly of her, and she stood by my fated mate when others abandoned her. I owe Maya my allegiance.

We leave Downtown Miami Bayfront and head to South Beach. As we cross MacArthur Causeway, we pass Moon Island—the Miami Wolves Pack's private island in Biscayne Bay, across from South Beach.

I long to move my fated mate into my bayfront mansion. But we don't allow humans on the island. It's our enclave where we can live in our wolf forms unencumbered. The natural landscape of Moon Island provides protection from unwanted eyes. Then Sage—our Luna and Jagger's fated mate—cast a spell to obscure the island even more. She's the High Witch and Coven of the South leader with remarkable magick, even more so since her mating with Jagger.

For the time being, I'll have to be satisfied with my fated mate living above my office suite in the residential portion of The Larson Tower. Soon, she'll be with me in our home. If she accepts me as a wolf shifter, that is. Not wanting to dwell on it, I tune back in to her ramblings.

I steer my Rolls-Royce Black Badge Wraith onto Ocean

Drive. Maya's condo isn't far from the beachfront building where the pack bachelors live. I'm glad I don't see any of them out and about, especially Viggo. He'll enjoy teasing me nonstop. Once things settle with Wren, I'll introduce her to the pack. Not before.

"There. That's Maya's building."

I park and help my fated mate from the coupe. She giggles when I lift her from the seat and plant a kiss on her lips. I stand her up and close the door, then take her hand. She directs me to the private elevator. On the ride up, she smiles at me and squeezes my hand. Her eyes sparkle. I grin. My wolf struts.

The elevator doors open directly into the condo. A stunning human female squeals and rushes towards us. Her jet black hair flows behind her. She throws her arms around my fated mate. They giggle and dance around.

I slip my hands in the pockets of my low-slung joggers and watch their exuberant greeting. But Maya doesn't forget I'm there. She loops her arm through Wren's and faces me. Topaz eyes pin me with a no-nonsense stare. She extends her hand.

"I'm Maya Alejandra Perez Garcia and Wren's best friend," she says as I shake her hand. "She tells me you treat her well. Good. However, should you fuck with my best friend, I will have your balls, Tag Dahl. Got it?"

"Yes, ma'am," I respond, biting back a chuckle, then I turn serious. "I thank you for being a best friend to Wren. Her family did her wrong. But you stood by her. Wren is extremely important to me. I owe you my allegiance."

Maya assesses me for a moment. She nods.

"Excellent. Welcome to my home, Tag," she says with a smile.

"Thank you," I respond, grinning.

I follow the girls through the palatial duplex penthouse.

Wren tells me she and Maya will gather her things so I can wait in the living room. Maya offers me something to drink and gestures towards the wraparound terrace. I decline a beverage and head outside. I call the movers and answer work emails while I wait.

After a while, Wren pokes her head out the door and tells me they're ready. I kiss the crown of her head and wrap my arm around her shoulders. They piled boxes in front of the service elevator. I send a text message to the movers. They come upstairs. In no time, they have the boxes loaded on their van. I send a text message to the concierge to tell him to allow the movers access to Wren's duplex.

She rides with Maya back to The Larson Tower. I follow.

I call Jagger and tell him about the latest developments. He's fine with them and agrees it's a good idea to separate Wren from the company because of the non-fraternization policy. We end the call as I pull into the garage.

It's amazing the girls still chatter on. I shake my head and follow them to the elevator. Once again, I'm told they'll take care of everything. I don't mind. At. All.

The concierge stocked the kitchen with Wren's favorite foods and the wet bar with my preferred liquors. I pour two fingers of Macallan Scotch into a Baccarat tumbler and head to the media room to watch basketball.

"There you are! I thought you left."

My fated mate appears in the doorway. Maya peers over her shoulder.

"You won't get rid of me that easily, babe," I say as I stand and stride towards them. "Did you finish everything?"

Her cheeks pinken. Maya giggles.

"Oh, you're good, Tag!" She says.

I bow, sweeping my arms wide.

They burst into giggles.

"Well, if you're done, how about we order some dinner?

Binge on Netflix. You know, whatever you two do on a night in."

They glance at each other and double over laughing. They laugh so hard tears slip down their cheeks and snorts mix with their giggles. I can't help but join in.

"Not just good. But *really* good!" Maya chokes out, dabbing her glittering eyes.

"Told ya!" My fated mate says and turns to grin at me.

My heart soars. Then doubt emerges.

Gods, let her accept me and be mine forever.

I snap out of it when she wraps her arms around my neck—standing on tiptoe—and presses her lips to mine. I envelop her in an embrace. Lifting her from the floor, I swing her around.

"You better believe it, Wren Byrd! And never forget it!"

Maya claps.

I put my fated mate down and drape my arm over her shoulders.

"So, what'll it be? Whatever's your favorite spot, I'll get them to deliver."

They start rattling off different restaurants, narrowing down to two. Then turn to me for my preference. Of course, I go along with my fated mate. Maya throws her hands up.

"Now, you're not so good, Tag!" She huffs as her arms fold across her chest.

I grin, and respond, "How about we order from both places? I don't believe in limits."

My eyes drift to Wren. Hopefully, she'll have an open mind when it comes to me being a wolf shifter and her being my fated mate. Not to mention her transition.

"Great idea! Lucky for you, you bounced back to my good side."

I chuckle and whip out my mobile to place our orders. The girls settle on the sofa and switch from my basketball game to Netflix. I don't mind. I sit next to Wren with a grin on my face. It even stays in place as they start some historical romance series called *Bridgerton*.

Viggo would have a field day.

But it's okay. I'll rack up points wherever I can get them. I add her best friend approves of me to the list. When the time is right, I'll have the conversation with my fated mate. For now, I'll make her fall in love with me.

CHAPTER 12

*W*ren

"BY THE GODS, I'm the luckiest male in the world."

I glance over my shoulder to find Tag leaning against the doorframe of the bedroom suite I converted into a dressing room.

He included a stipend for clothing and accessories in our agreement when I told him I wasn't able to bring my gowns and such from the Brickell condo. And I'm glad he did since tonight we attend the most important gala on the Miami social calendar. Plus, it's our first engagement as a couple and I'll meet Jagger and Sage as Tag's girlfriend. With Byrd Capital as a sponsor, George and Gretchen will be in attendance. Jonathan will probably show up, not wanting to miss an opportunity for networking.

Butterflies flutter in my belly.

I place a palm on it atop the silver sequined stretch-tulle gown. I'm glad Tag likes it. It makes me feel sexy. Although strapless, boning in the fitted bodice offers support for my ample bosom. From the fitted and draped waist, the gown falls loosely at the hip to pool on the floor. My leg plays peekaboo through the thigh-high slit. Strappy stilettos lengthen my leg and add height to my petite frame.

"Don't be nervous. You look gorgeous."

Silent like a predator, Tag slipped behind me. His arms encircle my waist, placing his hands over mine. He stares at me through the reflection in the full-length mirror.

I lean into his body, drawing from his strength.

"Thank you. I must say, you wear a mean tux, Mr. Dahl. So debonair!"

He smirks.

"Thank you, Ms. Byrd," he responds, then kisses the crown of my head and steps back. "However, you're missing something."

My eyebrows knit together as I face him.

His eyes sparkle like the jewel they resemble as he bites his lush lower lip. He reaches for a shopping bag next to his black patent leather dress shoe.

I recognize the gold logo for an Italian jewelry atelier.

He withdraws a large flat box and holds it out to me. I glance up at him. He cocks an eyebrow. My fingertip presses the gold closure. The lid lifts to reveal a ruby and diamond suite. I gasp at the magnificent matching brooch, earrings, necklace, and bracelet. The flawless gemstones sparkle like fire and ice.

"Rubies signify love, commitment, passion, protection, and wealth. All that I offer you along with my heart forever, My Sweet Girl."

Tears blur my vision.

Tag sets the box on the center island and sweeps me into his arms. He buries his face in my hair and inhales deeply, then murmurs words of love. I clutch him tightly. He holds me until I calm.

"Come, let's rinse your face."

I nod and let him lead me to the en suite bathroom. He puts a towel over my gown and moistens a washcloth with cool water. Carefully, he dabs my face. Fortunately, I always wear waterproof mascara. The rest of my makeup I fix quickly. He stands by and smiles encouragingly.

When I'm done, he takes my hand again. He puts the necklace on me while I slip the earrings and bracelet on. I turn to the oval mirror and clip the brooch to my hair, swept up at the back of my head. The piece is perfect for an exit statement. I face Tag.

"*Bellissima!*"

"*Grazie, amore mio.*"

He grins and drapes the gown's matching cape over my shoulders. I loop my arm through his, and we leave the duplex.

Jagger and Sage's limousine pulls up just as Tag and I exit The Larson Tower. A second SUV stops behind it. I glance at Tag questioningly, and he tells me it's security. I nod in understanding. Two multibillionaires and me dripping in millions of dollars' worth of jewels need a troop!

A security team member steps from the passenger's side of the limo and opens the door with a nod. Tag nods back. Jagger calls for Tag to get in first, so I don't mess up my gown. The guard helps me inside. I smile at a beautiful woman a few years older than me who must be Sage as I sit beside her. Jagger and Tag sit opposite us.

"Sage Larson Waters, I'd like to introduce you to Wren Byrd, my girlfriend. Wren, this is Sage, Jagger's wife."

I smile and extend my hand to her.

"It's a pleasure to meet you, Mrs.—"

"Oh Wren, no need to be formal. Call us Jagger and Sage," she says with a warm smile. Her emerald green eyes glow against her toffee complexion. "You're radiant. I love your gown and jewels!"

I stare at the robin's egg size diamond pendant dangling from a diamond necklace she wears with other pieces and smile.

"And I love yours too!"

She giggles as her gaze flicks to her husband. He smiles at her lovingly. She faces me.

"Jagger just gifted them to me tonight," she says, as a blush rises on her cheeks. He chuckles, and her cheeks redden further.

As I glance at the smirk on Jagger's handsome face, I get the sense she thanked him very well. My gaze shifts to Tag. He winks at me. Yeah, I'll thank him equally well later.

"Tell me about your new business, Wren. I could use your help for events I have coming up for my luxury custom-made jewelry company, Sage's Gems & Jewels."

I snap my fingers.

"Now, I know why you look familiar! I read about you in the latest issue of *Ocean Drive Magazine*. I'd love to work with you!"

We chat about her upcoming collection and the events until the limo stops at the gala's venue. We step out from both doors. The guys follow us. Tag holds out his arm, and I slip my hand around it. We follow Sage and Jagger up the red carpet.

Cameras flash and the paparazzi call our names. I fall into my socialite persona—slight smile, perfect posture, measured steps. We pose in front of the step and repeat banner where the Larson Enterprises, Inc. logo appears beside Byrd Capital.

As I smile for the cameras, my gaze flicks around the sea of people. I don't spot George or Gretchen. They must be inside.

Tag leans over and murmurs in my ear, "Don't worry about your uncle and aunt. I won't let them upset you."

I squeeze his arm and whisper my thanks. He beams at me.

We move inside, where we greet people we know. Tag introduces me as his girlfriend to anyone I'm unfamiliar with. Some women respond cordially while others appraise me. Whenever I feel uncomfortable, Tag guides us away and tells me how beautiful I am.

He makes me feel adored. How I love this man. And it is love. My heart warms. When we return to the duplex, I'll tell him just how I feel.

Before the cocktail hour ends, Sage and Jagger approach us. They make a striking couple with their opposite appearances. Her long ebony hair to his short white blond cut. Warm emerald green eyes to chilly ice blue. Petite and curvy to imposing and muscular. As they pass, people watch in admiration.

"Wren, I'm going to the powder room. Would you care to join me?"

Jagger shakes his head.

"One day, you'll explain to me why females go to the bathroom in pairs."

"When you find out, tell me, bro!"

Sage and I ignore their chuckles and head to the powder room to freshen up. We enter the anteroom and check our reflections in the mirrors above the vanities. Voices from the interior reach us.

"And to think he's with her. Again."

"Of all the fabulous women in Miami, he has *her* on his arm?"

"Oh, please! There must be a reason."

They giggle.

The hairs on the back of my neck rise. Instinct tells me

the women refer to Tag and me. I know I've gotten looks at other events we've attended. But we weren't arm-in-arm like we are tonight. Now, they bare their vicious claws.

I turn to leave. But Sage catches my arm.

Her narrowed eyes blaze. She shakes her head.

"Do not allow them to run you off, Wren. Nothing they say is true. They're spiteful and jealous. Come on."

She hooks arms with me and marches to the main part of the powder room. The three women notice us. Malice covers their faces.

"Wren, look who we have here. Moe, Larry, and Curly. The three stooges dressed in last season's collections from the dustbin. How sad they don't have your beauty and grace. Pity. Perhaps then they could've snagged Tag. Ah, well, too late. Let's return to our devoted and loving men, shall we?"

We spin on our heels, leaving the three stooges with their mouths hanging to the floor.

In the hallway, we bust out laughing.

"Did you see their faces?"

"Cracked and on the ground!"

We continue laughing as we approach the ballroom. Then the smile falls from my face.

*T*AG

"You know now is a great time for a resort in—"

My chest tightens. Something is wrong. Anxiously, I glance around for my fated mate. I spot her with Sage. Okay. But on closer inspection, I see her uncle and aunt and a guy in front of them. Fuck no!

I charge through the crowd, ignoring Jagger's call. I

sense him following me. Then his curse as he sees the direction I'm heading.

My enhanced hearing picks up my fated mate's cry when that fucker yanks her arm. Oh, hell no! Rage like I've never experienced courses through every cell of my being. Adrenaline pumps through me. My wolf snarls and claws beneath my skin. Enraged, my red vision tunnels on the guy.

"Get your fucking hand off her!"

My bellow causes heads to turn. I ignore them and launch myself at him. We crash to the floor. My fists pummel his face. Snarls rip from my throat. His blood flies with each punch landed. The sickening crunch of bone doesn't satisfy me. My wolf wants to tear his throat out. As do I.

Multiple arms grab me from behind and hoist me up. I fight with all my strength to break free. My tunnel vision still focuses on the fucker. He lies on the floor unmoving. But it's not enough. He. Touched. My. Fated. Mate. MINE!

My wolf breaks the surface.

Then I black out.

∽

WREN

"WHAT DO you think you're doing, Wren?! You keep showing up at events with Tag Dahl. What does a man like him want with you? You better not smear the Byrd name with your shenanigans!"

George's angry tirade on the heels of those nasty women's comments makes my moment of happiness plummet. And to castigate me in front of Sage makes it worse. I'm so embarrassed I could fall through the floor. And then the door to the powder room closes behind me. Snickers let me know the women heard what he said.

I freeze as flashbacks of George and Gretchen berating me hit me over and over.

Sage says something. But I don't hear her.

A tug on my arm snaps me out of the fog.

Jonathan's angry face is inches from mine. His fingers dig into the tender flesh of my inner arm. He yanks me, and I stumble with a cry.

"Hey! Stop it!" Sage exclaims.

"Get your fucking hands off her!"

Tag runs over with an expression of pure rage. He collides with Jonathan and knocks him to the ground. Straddling him, Tag punches his face repeatedly.

Gretchen screams. George pulls her away and watches from a distance. His cold eyes glare at me as though it's my fault.

I shake my head and turn back to Tag. He continues to beat an unconscious Jonathan until the security team member and others pull Tag off him. Tag tries to fight free. But they hold him firm. Then his features shift. I frown, confused. He looks like—

"Wren, come with me."

A mountain of a man blocks my view. I try to get around him, needing to see what happened to Tag's face. But the man moves with me, then turns me around. I hit his chest with my clutch.

"Get off me! Let me get to Tag!"

Jagger appears.

"Wren, this is Blake. He will take you home. Go. Now."

For some reason, I'm compelled to obey Jagger's command. I nod and let Blake guide me down the hallway, away from Tag and the commotion. When I glance over my shoulder, Blake blocks my view again. He increases his pace to where I have to jog beside him. He keeps a firm hold of my arm and waist to prevent me from falling.

We hurry through the lobby and out the revolving doors. He puts me in the back of the SUV and jumps into the driver's seat. As we pull away from the curb, I shift in my seat to glimpse any sign of Tag. Nothing appears out of the ordinary, nor do I hear police sirens. I watch until the SUV turns a corner, and the venue disappears from view.

As I straighten in the seat, tears fall. I can't make any sense of what I saw happen to Tag's face. It appeared his bones were realigning. His eyes changed to that deeper shade of jade. But somehow appeared animalistic. Almost unrecognizable.

And the strength he possessed and the ferocity. He was unhinged!

My God, have I fallen in love with a madman?

CHAPTER 13

"WHAT THE FUCK, Tag?! You almost shifted in front of humans! I get you were upset about Wren. But to lose *all* control?! You beat that guy unconscious and shifted. Thank the gods Sage was there. Or we'd all be screwed. Total chaos."

Jagger has every right to be pissed.

I screwed up big time.

Never ever in my entire life has rage consumed me. It blinded me to all except that fucker with his hands on Wren. My. Fated. Mate. My female touched by another male and in a rough manner? Hell no!

I don't regret breaking his face one bit. He deserved it. To mistreat Wren verbally and mentally was bad enough. She left him, and she's now with me. But he touched her. Physically yanked her arm hard enough to make her cry out.

Unacceptable. I'll rip his arms from their sockets and beat him with them if I get to him again.

The blood in my veins churn from a simmer to a full boil. I jump to my feet, needing to work off the pent-up anger. My hands scrub my face as I stalk around the den of my mansion. Jagger forced me in here since the room doesn't have windows I can go through to escape.

Again, he was right since chaos still reigns in my mind. Thoughts of getting my hands on that fucker, pissed since I lost control, and my wolf howls incessantly.

I rub the ache in my chest.

Wren.

I need my fated mate.

But Jagger refuses to let me go to her until I calm down and regain control. He told me she witnessed the beginnings of my shift. Confusion filled her face. She tried to get to me. But he used his Alpha command to compel her to leave.

When Jagger told me she went home in the care of another male wolf shifter, my blood pressure skyrocketed. I stormed towards the door. He forced me back and told me that's why he couldn't let me see her yet. I had to get a grip.

Instead, he sent Sage to stay with my fated mate. Once again, our Luna prevented a catastrophe of epic portions. If humans learn of wolf shifters in Miami, they will hunt us down, then go in search of others. It would endanger beings besides wolf shifters. The secret existence of the paranormal world would end. And it would be all my fault.

Fortunately, the incident took place in the hallway with fewer people present. Sage cast spells to shroud the area and to stop time. Everyone froze. It didn't impact Jagger, our security team, or Wren. I blanked out when my wolf took over—again, a new happenstance. Jagger tells me he had to use his Alpha command to force the reversal of my shift.

After Sage conjured clothes for me, a few of the security team brought me home.

Jagger stayed with Sage. She used her magick to repair the fucker's face and to erase everyone's memories of my attack before she released the other spells. He made me feel like an ass when he pointed out how she never wants to tamper with people's minds because of her and his experience years ago. I forced her hand. She used her teleportation magick to travel to Wren at The Larson Tower. Jagger came here with the rest of the team.

His ice blue eyes bore holes in my back as I stalk around, prowling like a caged animal. Tension swirls in the air. His disappointment in me proves palpable. As his beta, it's my responsibility to set an example for the rest of the pack members. For me to lose control in general is bad. But to beat a human male to a pulp then shift into my wolf all in public equates to a serious problem.

If only he and Sage witnessed my lapse in judgement, fine. However, our security team consists of pack enforcers. Not a good look for them to watch me go ballistic. Chances are they won't gossip since they don't commonly share what they do for the Alpha and beta. But the impression I made needs to be addressed. They're in the living room in case Jagger needs them. When I pull my mind from the brink, I'll speak with them.

Right now, I want my fated mate.

"Did Sage erase Wren's mind?"

Jagger blows a disgusted breath. He glares at me.

"*That's* your first question, Tag? You better be more concerned with your punishment than with Wren. She's fine. You are not."

For a minute I forget about him being my Alpha and glare back. Jagger doesn't miss my challenge.

He rises from the chair. Even though we're both six feet,

seven inches and built like powerful Vikings, he draws on his Alpha traits to increase his stature. He appears taller and brawnier. His eyes darken to cobalt and flash with his silvery white wolf. The corners of his lips curl to reveal his elongated fangs. A low warning growl emanates from him. Fingernails lengthen to sharp claws. His Alpha command hits me in the chest like a sledgehammer.

I stagger back.

"Tag, you have been my best friend since we were pups. Do not go Dylan's route and challenge me when you know you shouldn't. Do you want years to pass before I allow you back in the pack? Think carefully on your answer."

I growl and whirl around. My fists punch holes in the wall. Plaster crumbles to the floor. Bones crack. Pain races up my arms. I howl more from the agony Wren may not accept me as a wolf shifter than from the ache coursing through me.

And here I worried I'd muck it up between us because I said something wrong. No, I just let her witness me beating her ex and shifting into a wolf.

The gods aren't crazy. I am.

~

WREN

"HI, MAY I COME IN?"

I nod as I open the doors wider for Sage to enter the duplex. The concierge surprised me when he rang the intercom to tell me she was downstairs. I hoped Tag would be with her. Disappointment washes over me when I don't see him.

Half an hour passed since I left the gala. Too upset to

think straight, I left my gown on. My mind still can't make sense of the whole scenario. How badly Tag beat Jonathan. A relentless machine punching again and again. And the sound of Jonathan's bones breaking. I don't even want to think about it.

I shiver and wrap my arms around my torso as I close the double doors. Sage scans my face as she waits for me to get it together. I gesture towards the living room. She follows me and sits on the sofa. She has on her gown. So, I guess she came here directly. I lower myself on the other end, then hop up remembering my manners.

"Would you care for a drink?"

Sage nods.

"That fiasco calls for the bottle," she says with a wry smile.

"Yeah. What do you prefer? Tag has—"

My voice catches as I say his name aloud. I drop onto the sofa with a ragged sob. Arms wrap around me.

"Oh, honey. I know it's upsetting. Jagger is with Tag at his mansion on Moon Island. Don't worry, he's fine."

I blubber harder.

What the hell happened to my teddy bear? He turned into more than the beast the office staff dreads. An uncontrollable wild monster emerged and went on a rampage. His eyes flashed and his facial features morphed into what appeared to be a wolf.

But that just can't be!

I must be mistaken, which is why I tried to get to him. But Blake prevented me. Dammit! Then I realize Sage may know something. I sit back from her embrace and stare into her eyes. I search their emerald green depths as I ask her about Tag.

"You said he's fine. But I thought I saw his face change. I —I mean… somehow his features shifted. I've seen his eyes flash. But this time it was different. It was as though another force was behind them."

I pause and shake my head. My words sound crazy to me. How must they sound to Sage? She must think I've lost it. I peek at her to gauge her reaction.

She stares back without a change in her expression. I'd have thought she would show surprise or tell me I was mistaken. Or bonkers. Weird.

"It must have been the lighting or… or… something. I—I don't know. But I want to talk to him. I *need* to talk to him. He's not answering his mobile. Will you call Jagger so I can speak to Tag?"

I rub the ache in my chest. Something feels so very wrong. Instinct tells me Tag can fix it. Even if my mind tells me he's a madman, and I need to stay away from him.

Sage stares at me a moment, then places her clutch on the coffee table next to my open sketchpad. Her hands pause as she opens the handbag. They reach for the sketchpad. Slowly, she turns the pages.

"Did you draw these pictures?"

I nod and shrug.

"Yes," I answer as I stare at the fantastical creatures on the pages.

She pauses on one where a male and a female wolf romp with three pups amongst pine trees near a marsh. It's the most recent sketch. Where I used to draw a variety, now wolves dominate my thoughts—and my dreams. Wolves!

"Sage, I really need to see Tag. I know where Moon Island is but not his mansion. Can you take me to him?"

"Why don't you go change while I call Jagger?"

My heart leaps as I rush from the living room. Less than ten minutes later, I return to find Sage waiting in the entry foyer. We leave and head to the garage for my car. The ride doesn't take long. We turn off the causeway and pull up to intricate wrought-iron gates—the entrance to Moon Island. Two members of the security team sit in a guardhouse. Sage leans over from the passenger side to wave at them through the window. They recognize her and wave as the gates open.

She directs me towards Tag's home. As we drive along the main road, I admire the posh residences ranging from ranch style to two- and three-story. Some front Biscayne Bay, while others have interior views. We pull into the driveway of a grand Mediterranean Revival style mansion on the bay.

The glass and metalwork double doors open. Tag rushes out, followed by Jagger. The car barely stops before Tag opens my door. I put the car in park as he unfastens my seatbelt. He groans as he swoops me from the seat and buries his face in my hair. His heart slams in his chest. The familiar rumble wraps around me as he strides back inside.

I notice nothing or anyone. My arms tighten around his neck. I meld my body as close to his as possible. I inhale his intoxicating cologne mixed with his natural masculine scent. My body responds with need. The urge to make love to him overrides all else.

"Tag," I moan.

"I've got you, My Sweet Girl," he croons, and I melt.

"Tag, don't fuck up. I'm dead serious."

I lift my head, having forgotten about Jagger and Sage. He narrows his eyes at Tag, who grunts in acknowledgment. Sage whispers in Jagger's ear and takes his arm to usher him out the door. I drop my head back on Tag's shoulder.

He climbs the stairs three at a time and jogs down the hall with ease. We enter the primary bedroom suite. He lowers me to my feet as my body slides along his. An arm bands around my waist while a hand cups my butt. He presses me close. My breasts flatten against his chest as our pelvises grind.

"I love you so much, Wren."

"Oh, Tag. I love you so much too!"

He growls and slams his mouth on mine. Once again, he sounds like a wild wolf. But I don't care. The ravenous kiss obliterates my mind. His demanding tongue pushes past my teeth and sweeps through my mouth. He tastes and conquers me all at once.

Toes curl in my flats as fingers tug his hair. I mewl as he ends the searing kiss with nips, licks, and sucks down the column of my throat to my shoulder. I shiver when he rakes his teeth against the sensitive flesh.

"Tell me you belong to me, Wren. Tell me you'll be mine forever."

My fingernails dig into his shoulders through the thin cotton of his t-shirt. I arch up into him, trying to seal us together. I want nothing between us. I need him more than imaginable.

"Yes, Tag. YES!"

He growls and lifts my maxi dress over my head. He rips my simple cotton bra and matching G-string from my body. The gusset catches my clit, and I gasp. He drops to his knees, parts my slick folds, and kisses the engorged nubbin. The flat of his tongue laves my pussy from clit to slit. I dance on my toes as he eats me out with savage growls.

Before my knees collapse, he scoops me up and carries me to the king-size bed. He sets me on the edge and stands between my thighs. With his eyes on mine, he yanks his t-shirt off. I pull the drawstring of his sweatpants and push them from his narrow hips. His erect cock pops free. I lean forward and press my lips to the swollen tip. My tongue darts out to lap at the bead of pre-cum. I moan at his salty taste.

He groans.

"Need. You. Now."

He crawls over me as I scoot backwards to the center of the bed. His eyes, then mouth fasten on my bobbing breasts. I fall back to my elbows and moan as he suckles the plump nipples. He reaches between us and lines his cock with my core. A snap of his hips plunges him inside to the root. I whine at the instant stretch. He rumbles and places open-mouthed kisses in the hollow between my breasts, then up to my mouth open on a throaty moan.

He wraps his arms around me as he rocks in and out of my core. I wrap my thighs around his hips. My softness molds to the hard planes of his big body—a perfect fit.

We continue to move as one locked in a passionate embrace. I cry out as orgasms ripple through my pussy. Tag groans as my inner walls clench around his massive girth. He shifts the angle of penetration. The adjustment causes the tip of his cock to drag along my clit and against my G-spot.

I writhe beneath him as another orgasm builds. It starts from my toes to crackle up my legs until it explodes in my core. Legs stiffen and toes curl. My fingernails leave crescent moons as I cling to Tag's back. A garbled cry tumbles from between my parted lips. Eyes squeeze shut as the after-shocks roll through me.

My pleasure triggers his release. He rises to his knees and pulls my legs over his shoulders. His hands drop to the bed above my shoulders. Arms bracketing me in place. He stares down at me with eyes full of feral dominance and desire. Then his hips surge forward. Powerful thrusts drill me into the mattress.

I slide up. But his arms prevent me from moving too far. I grab them to ground myself. My breasts bounce with each pistoning thrust. Bent in half, my knees reach my ears. His big body dominates mine.

"MINE! Mine! Forever!

I scream in carnal rapture as a spine-tingling orgasm detonates.

Tag curses as his cock swells deep within me and copious amounts of his seed fill my womb. I pass out from the intensity.

I awake to Tag cleaning me with a warm, damp washcloth. I reach up and cup his cheek. He turns his head and kisses my palm, then looks at me. I frown at the worry in his eyes.

"You trust me, right?"

I nod, then answer, "Absolutely."

"I have something important to tell you."

He closes his eyes and takes a deep breath.

CHAPTER 14

WREN'S MOOD switches from sexual bliss to worry as she stares at me with soulful eyes. I worry too. How the hell do I tell a human I'm a wolf shifter *and* she's my fated mate? The concept of a paranormal being alone will cause her to doubt me. Add to it our connection? Then the claiming bite and her transition?

I blow a breath and close my eyes to gather my words. I open them and take her hands in mine, praying to the gods she won't run from the house screaming.

"Let me tell you about how I got here."

She raises her eyebrows but doesn't ask the question.

I go on to tell her about our Viking origins and arrival here, leaving the part about being wolf shifters out for now. She nods when I finish and smiles.

"That's all? After I saw your face at the gala, I thought you were going to tell me you're a werewolf! I knew I was hallucinating. Too many paranormal romance novels have me imagining things."

She giggles and squeezes my hands.

What the hell are paranormal romance novels?

But she's not far off. I'm paranormal, and we love each other. At least, I hope she still loves me after I tell her the rest.

"Wren, I'm not a werewolf. They're bloodthirsty and murderous creatures who can't control themselves."

As I say the words, I realize they describe my recent behavior. Well, damn. I shake my head, knowing that lapse was an anomaly. Completely uncharacteristic of me.

"I'm a shapeshifter. The kind that can shift from a man into a wolf at my will."

She stares at me.

I fight the urge to pull her onto my lap and snuggle into her to pretend as though I said nothing. But I have to be honest. I wait for her to speak.

"You're not joking, are you?"

"No."

She pulls her hands. I refuse to let her go and hold on tighter. My eyes implore her to stay. I want to issue the command she does not move, appealing to her submissive behavior. But it's more important she asks questions or tells me her thoughts. I get my wish. But not the words I hoped for.

"You're a monster! Let me go! Get off me!"

Her cries wound my heart and soul. My wolf howls in despair. I wrap my arms around her hips and lift her onto my lap. She pummels my chest with her fists. Her body shakes.

"You probably killed Jonathan! Oh my, God! I've had sex with a monster! No!!! Let. Me. Go!"

She slaps my face.

I don't stop her. I deserve her anger. Besides, my enhanced healing repairs any damage to my body within minutes. Her scant hits do nothing. Her words inflict damage. I tell myself she's just saying all those things because she's upset. She can't possibly mean them, especially after she told me she loves me and we made love. I won't let her take that away from me—from us.

"Wren, listen to me. I know you're upset—"

"Upset?!" She shrills. "You think I'm upset?! I'm beyond upset, Tag! You lied to me! Knowing you're a wolf shifter and didn't tell me. You let me fall in love with you. You're as bad as Jonathan! Both liars! I hate you, Tag! I hate you..."

Her words trail off as she sobs. Tears spill from her eyes. They slide down her reddened cheeks and drip on her heaving breasts. She stops hitting me and covers her face with both hands. Her body trembles.

My heart breaks.

However, she's right. I lied to her by omission. But at the same time, how could I tell her—a human—about my true nature? Look at how she reacts now, even after admitting she trusts and loves me. If I told her sooner, who knows what she would've done?

I have to get her to accept me. If not, Jagger says he'll ask Sage to wipe her and Maya's minds of me completely and move her back to Maya's condo while they were in a resting state. It would be as though Wren never knew me. And I cannot have that happen. She's my fated mate. She's mine.

"Wren, baby, please listen to me," I plead as I rock her in my arms and rumble. "Look at it from my perspective. No humans—other than those who are mated to shifters—know of our existence. Since time immemorial, our kind has lived alongside humans and survived because we keep our abilities a secret. Think of what would happen if scientists learned of our existence. They would capture us and conduct experiments. We would die."

I pause to let her absorb the impact.

She stops squirming but remains tense. I take it as a good sign.

"Now, think of how I've been with you. You admit you trust me. You say you fell in love with me—as I have with you. Have I done anything other than respect you, care for you, protect you?"

She shakes her head, then opens her mouth.

I know what she's about to say and speak first.

"Yes, I beat that fucker. And I'd do it again. You know why?"

She shakes her head. I cock an eyebrow.

"No."

"Because he hurt you. He put his hands on you against your will and yanked you so hard you cried out. I will allow no one to hurt you. Didn't I tell you that earlier about your uncle and aunt?"

"Yes."

"Do you know how I knew from all the way across the ballroom?"

"No."

I place my hand over her heart and her hand over mine.

She raises her eyes to my face.

"You feel the connection we share, don't you? That sense of the other's presence and emotions?" When she agrees, I continue. "That's called the mate bond."

Her eyes widen.

"Y—You called me mate before."

"Yes."

"In my PNR novels, that's the same as marriage between humans. You feel it with me?"

"Yes. Even more so since you, Wren Byrd, are my fated mate. Do your books explain the meaning?"

Her jaw drops. I use the tip of my index finger to close it. She nods her head.

"Are you telling me you and I are fated to be together by the gods? Oh, my God! You always say, 'the gods!' I assumed you misspoke. The more I think about it, you act like the Alpha heroes in my novels. But that's fiction! This is real life, Tag! I—I need proof."

I figured she'd ask. I slide her onto the bed and rise.

"Remember, even in wolf form, I'm still me, Tag. I love you and will never harm you. Don't be frightened. Do you understand?"

"Yes," she whispers as she sits up and stares at me intensely.

My body relaxes. This time, I allow my wolf to take over, not giving him full control like earlier. Ordinarily, my other half lives on the fringes of my being. Always ready to spring forth at my command, then retreat at my will. An ability born of our kind so long ago and marks us different from full humans.

The sensations of my bones reshaping and muscles lengthening to shift me from my human form to that of my great sable brown wolf block out my fated mate on the bed. Crackling and a flash find me on all four massive paws within moments.

I swivel my enormous head to pin her with my flashing gaze.

Her mouth gapes as she stares, enthralled. Curious eyes take me in from my snout to the tip of my feathery tail. Every inch of my body thrums from the intensity of her stare. Frissons of electricity roll through me.

The desire to go to her, rub my body on hers, and cover her in my scent proves hard to resist. But I will. My fated mate has to come to me. Accept me and my wolf. I sit on my haunches and wait.

"C—Can you understand me?"

My head nods as my eyes remain fixed on hers.

She gnaws the corner of her bottom lip. I want to suck it into my mouth. A few minutes pass before she scoots across the bed. She picks up my t-shirt and slips it over her head. A toothy grin spreads on my face seeing her in my clothes. She's well over a foot shorter than me. The hem reaches above her knees barely.

She pauses and gasps.

I cock my head, then realize my teeth. Duh! I close my mouth. On further thought, I lower my belly to the floor with my snout between my front paws in a less threatening posture.

My fated mate approaches me with measured steps. I don't move. Hell, I don't even breathe.

"So, you understand me. Can you talk?"

I whine in the back of my throat and glance up at her.

She nods.

"Can I touch you?"

I yip and thump my tail on the floor.

She smiles and kneels in front of me. Tentatively, she extends her hand. Again, I hold my breath and stare at her with pleading eyes. When her small hand lands between my ears, I close my eyes and sigh. Her touch calms me. I rumble in my chest.

"Oh, you like that huh?" She asks as her palm smooths my fur. "I cannot believe I'm actually petting a wolf shifter. Talk about a vivid imagination. Wow."

I want to bristle at the petting reference. Wolf shifters are not dogs. But I let it go. My fated mate is smiling. That's what matters—not my ego. I yip and press my head up into her hand.

She leans on her other hand and crawls further along my body to touch my flanks and back.

The all-fours position makes my cock thicken wedged between my belly and the floor. How I want to mount her on her hands and knees and issue the claiming bite. I close my eyes and will myself to stay in control.

"You're much bigger than regular wolves."

In every way, baby.

She continues to murmur her findings as I lie still. Finally, she makes her way around my entire body. She sits with her legs tucked to the side.

Daring to touch her, I crawl forward and place my head on her lap. She startles at the size compared to her small lap. I nuzzle against her rumbling in my chest. She places her hand on my neck and pats me. I close my eyes and inhale her unique scent mixed with our combined sex. Never a better aroma existed.

Both lost in thought, we sit in silence.

Then my mobile rings. I growl. My fated mate yelps and scoots away. Damn.

In a blink, I shift back. I cup her cheek and smile.

"Sorry, baby. I didn't mean to startle you. I just hate my mobile disturbed us. Give me a minute. It's probably Jagger checking on you."

I jump to my feet and snatch the mobile from my sweatpants pocket. Yup, Jagger.

"Yeah."

"What's going on?"

I glance over my shoulder at my fated mate. My t-shirt is halfway over her head. I frown.

"Wren, what are you doing?"

She bites her lower lip as her cheeks pinken. Then tosses the t-shirt to the bed and picks up her dress.

"I need to go."

My stomach drops. No! I can't let her leave. Not now, before we resolve everything. And I haven't told her about the transition.

"Jagger, listen, I gotta go."

"Tell me what's going on first."

I stalk over to Wren and take her hand. As I answer Jagger, I stare into her eyes, talking more to her than to him.

"I told Wren about being a wolf shifter. She trusts and loves me. I love her. That's what's most important. We need to finish our conversation. I have to go."

"Fine."

I end the call and toss my mobile on top of my sweats, then squeeze my fated mate's hand. I lead her back to the bed. She's hesitant. I turn and stroke her cheek. Her eyes close. I kiss the top of her head and scoop her into my arms, carrying her the rest of the way.

I sit with her straddling my lap and my back against the headboard. My body temperature runs high. But I want her comfortable in the air-conditioned bedroom. So, I tuck the sheets around us.

"Tag, I don't know what you want me to say," she starts as she gazes at a spot over my shoulder. "It's a lot to digest. I don't know."

Taking her chin between my thumb and index finger, I bring her gaze to meet mine. I keep my expression open so she can see I'm being completely honest.

"Wren, I know it must sound absurd to you. But you saw me shift—"

"Wait a minute! Are Jagger and Sage wolf shifters too?" She shrieks, then her eyes widen. "Moon Island! Is everyone living here like you?!"

"Yes, to both."

She covers her eyes with one hand and shakes her head, mumbling to herself. My ears pick up parts of it. It can't be real. Unbelievable. Incredible. Can only happen to me. I let her talk it out while I rumble and stroke her back. Abruptly, she swats my hands away.

"Stop making that noise and touching me! I can't think straight when you do it!" She cries and pushes both palms against my chest. "I. Need. To. Go. Now."

I catch her hands and hold them to my heart.

"Wren, there's more."

She inhales sharply. Her eyes narrow on me.

"Like all male wolf shifters, when I was born, my first breath carried the scent of my fated mate—cinnamon sugar caramel apples. At a charity gala at the Larson Miami Hotel & Resort a few weeks ago, I caught the scent on the breeze. Were you there?"

She blinks in surprise and nods.

"I searched but couldn't find you. Three weeks later, I caught your unique scent in the elevator. I smell it on you now, mixed with my signature. There is no doubt you are my fated mate, Wren. You may not understand. But it's true. And not every male finds his fated mate. It's rare. Something we cherish."

I search her face, willing her to accept me. She doesn't fight me. So, I continue.

"Most wolf shifters mate within our kind. Sometimes a male wolf shifter and a human female fall in love. Our pack has had a few such pairings. The last being at least thirty years ago. Perhaps your books have occurrences?"

She breathes a yes.

"When our kind mate, the male issues a claiming bite, here," I say and skim the juncture of her neck and shoulder with my fingertip. She shivers, then her eyes pop.

"Of course! That's why you always lick and nip me there."

Now, I nod.

"I've wanted to claim you from the first moment your scent filled my nostrils and every time thereafter. But I controlled myself and my wolf, who knows you're ours.

"Not only will it be a claiming bite for you where a serum lodges my scent in your skin permanently. But it will enact the transformation of you into a wolf shifter. I'll be in human form, and the serum will drip from my extended canines. I will gift you with the ability to be one with me in every way.

"It involves the risk your body won't accept the transformation. You may take it completely and shift. Or not, and only benefit from our longer life spans and enhanced abilities. Since we're fated mates and based on past wolf shifter-human fated mate bondings, you will be fine.

"However, the choice is yours. I will not force you. I love you and want us to have a family and spend the rest of our lives together."

Tears fill her eyes.

I lean forward and kiss her lips softly. My forehead presses to hers, and I inhale her breath.

She leans back.

"Well, since we're being honest, I have to admit PNR isn't my first fascination with fantastical creatures. As a child, I read fairy tales and fell in love with that world. They helped me to escape from a sad reality. Now, I enjoy the spicier side of that world with my romance novels."

She pauses as her cheeks flush.

"I've had constant dreams about you and wolves for weeks now. I thought it was just my imagination running wild with my books. Then my drawings changed from wolves, witches, fairies, vampires, and other what I thought were fantastical creatures to only wolves. Sage saw my sketchpad earlier and asked me about it."

Now, my mouth drops. My fated mate closes it with a slight smile.

"But I still need time to think about all you've told me, Tag. It's a lot to accept. You must understand," she says, then arches an eyebrow. "From my perspective."

"Touché," I nod in acknowledgment of her using my words back at me.

She smiles and climbs from my lap. I catch her hand.

"Wait. Where are you going?"

She frowns and responds, "Home. I need space to think, Tag."

I shake my head.

"I can't let you leave Moon Island, Wren."

CHAPTER 15

ren

"I WANT you to stay here with me in our home. Otherwise, you will stay with Jagger and Sage next door."

My mouth gapes, then I sputter in shock.

"You have to be kidding me, Tag. I can't stay here surrounded by wolf shifters. I'd be scared to death!"

He cocks his head as his lips flatten.

"You do realize you've been 'surrounded by wolf shifters' for weeks now?"

I frown, thinking I've only interacted with Jagger a few times in passing and Sage tonight. What is he talking about?

"Well, let's see. Beth, Ginny, Dana. Remember them? How about pretty much seventy percent of Larson Enterprises' staff?"

My mouth drops. The way I'm going tonight, I might as well turn into a fish. But how the hell didn't I realize they were wolf shifters or she-wolves or whatever?!

Then, as I think about it, I recall the way Beth's nostrils

flared slightly or how her gaze could be so piercing, like a predator. The stealth-like movements of the security team. So many nuances I didn't pay attention to. Just like Tag said, they walk amongst us undetected. No one thinks any differently about them. One would have to know what to look for in order to tell them apart from regular humans. Amazing.

"Were you 'scared to death' being in close proximity to us?"

I have to admit I wasn't. At. All.

They treated me no differently than any full human.

"No."

"And do you truly believe I would allow anyone—human or otherwise—to harm you?"

My heart tells me absolutely not. However, my brain still sticks on their numbers.

It shocks me to know there are so many of them. Larson Enterprises is an enormous company. This island has dozens of residences. Another revelation hits me.

"Besides Miami, are there others?"

"Yes."

"A lot?" I ask tremulously, visualizing millions of wolf shifters around the world.

"Yes."

Another thought occurs to me.

"You said you're a shifter who can turn into a wolf. Does that mean there are *other* kinds of shifters?"

"Yes."

My mind goes back to the fairy tales. I've always wondered if the different creatures and their stories held a bit of truth. People speak of and write what they know. It may not make sense to me. But I'm not arrogant enough to dispel the possibilities completely. I just never thought they'd be true to this extent. I mean, Tag is a wolf shifter and I'm his fated mate? What???

It's too much to wrap my head around now. It's late. I've had enough with the drama and the emotional rollercoaster. My brain needs to shut off. I wish I could reboot the whole damn day!

Tag must sense my anxiety. The rumble reaches my ears as loving warmth touches my heart. He squeezes my hand and watches me with soft eyes.

I'm oh so tempted to fall into his arms, bury my face in his chest, and fall asleep. But I do need space. He's too much. My thoughts jumble in his presence. I just can't believe he refuses to let me leave. What the hell?!

"Tag, I need to sleep and not here. I don't want to stay with Sage and Jagger. I want to go home, get into my bed, and close my eyes. Why is that a problem?"

The corners of his mouth droop. Pain flashes in his eyes.

"We can't risk anyone finding out about us, Wren. And before you say it, I trust you. But a slip-up can happen. Look at what happened to me the night of the charity gala, and I need to guard our secret with my life."

I growl in frustration and yank my hand from his grip. I march in a circle, waving my arms in the air.

"What the hell does that mean? How long do I remain captive? What about work? When do I see Maya? What about my life?!"

I spin around and glare at him. I'm tired and frustrated. If I seem like a petulant child, so be it.

He rises from the bed with that predatory grace I should have recognized before and do now. Sorrow mars his handsome face.

My heart clenches. I rub at the ache in my chest where our mate bond floods with his emotions. My sadness blends with his. I hate we feel this way. I miss the warmth. How can we get back to before? Is it even possible? Do I really want to?

"Wren, I can't say that I wish things were completely different. If that were the case, you wouldn't be my fated mate," Tag says as he strides towards me. He shakes his head. "I will say my life plan didn't include a relationship now. Work and pack were all that mattered to me. And as you know, I lead a highly structured life. It brooks no room for unexpected situations."

His fingertips brush against my cheek as a gentle smile lifts the corners of his mouth. Warmth seeps through the mate bond. My heart flutters.

"Then you came into my life like a whirlwind," he says and chuckles. "Hiding from me. The elevator getting stuck out of the blue. A distraction at work. Gossip amongst the pack. A fight where I shift in front of humans. On top of it all, my wolf going feral, eager to claim you. I lost control for the first time in my life."

He shakes his head as his smile widens.

"You made me realize having you as my fated mate supplants all else. I want us to be together. Badly. I don't want to stop your life. I want to be a part of it," he says, then smirks. "Well, the largest part, of course."

I sigh in relief.

"If you truly trust and love me, then give me the chance. No. Give *us* a chance. I'll even take time off from work. We'll go to the Everglades. Our pack has a camp there where fewer members live. We'll stay in my cabin. You can experience life with me and the pack with the knowledge of our kind. Everyone will welcome you and answer all questions you have. If after a month you choose to walk away, I will not stop you. Do you agree?"

I stare up into his emerald green depths. Hope shines within them. How can I dim that light when I want to walk in its warmth forever?

"Yes."

A smile bursts across his face as he whoops and lifts me from the floor. He spins around, then lowers me to my feet. His mouth covers mine for a tender kiss. He brushes his lips against mine, then stares at me fiercely.

"I love you, Wren Byrd and vow to make you accept us before the month ends."

~

"My parents took me to the Everglades when I was around five. We rode on an airboat. I remember how green the area was and the alligators slithering in the water. They scared me. But my parents held me between them. They told me the gators can't get me, but I could eat them. After the ride, we ate fried alligator strips. Not my favorite."

I laugh, and Tag joins in.

We're flying above the marshland in his spacious luxury helicopter.

Before we left Miami, I called Maya to let her know I was going on a trip with Tag for a few weeks. She clapped gleefully. We stopped by my condo for me to change and to pack. I brought my sketchpad and my laptop, even though Tag says we won't work. I have some open activities I can't neglect. Besides, I saw his laptop case. He's too much of a stickler to leave his responsibilities unattended. I don't mind.

A knock on the door separating the cabin from the crew area and cockpit draws my attention from the window. Tag calls for them to enter.

"We land in fifteen minutes, beta. Would you care for anything before?" The flight attendant asks.

Tag introduced me to the crew as his fated mate. Just as he predicted, they greeted me pleasantly. Once we were airborne, he told me they're members of the pack. The flight attendant is a young she-wolf mated to the pilot. The co-pilot is an unmated older male.

Tag smiled when I told him I recognize the term beta from my PNR novels. He gave me more details about his role and that of the beta's mate. My heart swells each time he teaches me more about wolf shifters and his pack. Including their official name—Miami Wolves Pack.

I told him their nickname of *Billionaire Wolves of Miami* was apropos given Larson Enterprises' holdings, Moon Island, and his helicopter. I laughed when he told me about his private jet and *Moonbeam*—Jagger's 465-foot megayacht the members have access to. Yeah, they're an über-wealthy pack.

Tag glances at me with a raised eyebrow. I smile at the flight attendant and decline. We ate a decadent breakfast of eggs royale with caviar and Maltaise sauce during the flight. Yum! So, I'm nice and full.

He declines too, and the flight attendant leaves us. Tag takes my hand and brings it to his lips. He brushes them over my knuckles.

"Ready?" He murmurs as his eyes stare up at me. The bright sunlight makes them sparkle like emeralds.

I pause to think about it. Would I ever imagine I'd be about to spend a month in the Everglades as the only human amongst wolf shifters I never knew existed? Ah… That would be a firm no. However, as George always told me, I have a vivid imagination. If I can swoon over an Alpha carrying his mate to ravish her in my novels, why can't I experience it in real life with my fated mate?

"Yes!"

Tag's eyes spark. He cups the back of my head and kisses me senseless. I swoon against him with a contented sigh. If he keeps this up, he'll have me convinced in no time.

The helicopter lands in a clearing. We thank the crew.

Tag helps me out and grabs our bags. He leads me to a Range Rover where a male wolf shifter stands. He raises his hand as we approach.

"Greetings, beta!"

"Ulf, good to see you!" Tag responds, then turns to me. "Wren, this is Ulf. He's in charge of our Everglades property. Ulf, meet my fated mate, Wren Byrd."

He extends his hand with a broad smile.

"Welcome, Wren! Nice to meet you. If you need anything, my mate and I, along with the others, are here for you."

"Thank you so much, Ulf. How kind of you," I respond with a smile, shaking his hand.

He takes the bags from Tag and loads them in the SUV. Tag helps me in the backseat, then settles in the passenger seat. Ulf hops in, and we drive off.

Tag gives another lesson about the pack's camp.

It's the place they go for pack runs and trainings. For generations, the virtually untouched area of the subtropical wilderness allows them the freedom to be in their wolf form without prying eyes. Over the years, the original pack grounds grew from temporary cloth shelters to simple wooden cabins and now to luxurious residences scattered around the Alpha's house and clubhouse. Glamping—or glamorous camping—as Signy, Jagger's younger sister calls it.

Tag explains how a few families and security members known as enforcers choose to remain here, not wanting the hustle and bustle of Miami for their principal home.

I don't blame them. On days like this one with low humidity, a clear blue sky with the sun shining above, and clean air to fill your lungs, who wouldn't want to be here?

As we drive towards the camp, Tag and Ulf point out spots of interest. They share stories about various escapades over the years. I giggle as Tag recalls how Viggo and Rust—Jagger's younger brother and the pack doctor—snatched eggs from an alligator's nest and she chased them up a tree.

Soon, we round a bend. The pine trees open up to reveal the camp. It sprawls out before us. Rather, the glamp since every cabin is a rustic mansion of logs and stones in various styles—some ranch and others multilevel, with and without front porches. They surround an open park-like square in the middle, where a lovely garden displays colorful flowers and bushes with wooden benches. Lanes crisscross the land to provide access to the various homes and structures.

A few pack members walk along or sit on porches. Their laughter and conversations fill the air. Cheerful smiles spread across their faces as they interact. The only surprising difference being some members in wolf form going about their business like it's an ordinary occurrence. Otherwise, the camp is an idyllic enclave with the spectacular Everglades as the setting.

Ulf pulls up to a two-story mansion-size log cabin with a wraparound porch. Red flowers in window boxes add vibrant color to its wooden facade. Double doors hand carved with the face of a wolf gazing at the center square as though watching over the camp. The wolf reminds me of Tag's role as pack beta to care for them.

"This is us, babe. The one on the left is Jagger and Sage's cabin," Tag says, pointing beyond the windshield.

"If you call ritzy mansions cabins!" I laugh and hop out of the SUV. "I guess like the cottages of Newport, huh?"

The guys laugh as they climb out. Ulf gets the bags while Tag sweeps me from my feet. He carries me to the doors. I turn the knobs, and he strides inside.

"Welcome to our Everglades home, my fated mate."

I glance around at the double-height great room filled with comfortable leather furniture and a massive stone wall with an oversized fireplace. A wall of windows brings the scenery inside. The back porch expands to a deck to accommodate multiple seating areas and a swanky outdoor kitchen. An eat-in chef's kitchen and dining area finish the space. It reminds me of a layout in *Architectural Digest*.

"It's gorgeous, Tag," I breathe, awed by the home.

He grins and sets me on my feet, then takes my hand.

"Time for a tour."

Besides the great room, the home features a guest bathroom, media room, and den on the main level. Spacious four bedroom suites with attached baths take up the second level. The primary bedroom suite has a double-sided iron and glass fireplace between the sitting room and the bedroom.

Tag flips a switch, and the fireplace roars to life. He turns to me with a feral gleam in his darkened eyes. He scoops me up and carries me to the giant, hand-carved, four-poster wooden bed.

"Time to welcome you fully, my fated mate."

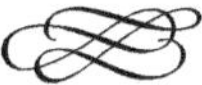

ag

"I BET we'll beat you guys!"

Wren yells as the 600-plus horsepower engines of the airboats rev to life. She adjusts the noise-canceling headset and puts on goggles.

Ulf chuckles as she gives him two thumbs up. He glances at me for approval, and I nod. Even though my wolf is none too pleased my fated mate is in his boat and not mine. But it was her idea to race me through the sawgrass marshes. And whatever makes her happy, I'm willing to do.

Just as I have these last two weeks.

Every question she asks I or a pack member answer. We go on hikes with me in human and wolf form. My wolf loves it when he gets a chance to interact with our fated mate. He doesn't even mind her scratching between our ears while making baby talk. Soon he'll let her put a collar and a leash on us. She enjoys group mealtimes where we gather in the dining hall to eat as a pack for breakfast or dinner. It's one way we keep our communal bond strong. Ulf's mate and several other she-wolves make certain to include Wren in activities where she may learn more about our lives. They garden, collect herbs and plants, and babysit the young pups. I indulge whatever keeps a smile on her face.

So, I smile and give her the thumbs up. She claps her hands, then grips the metal handrail. A pack member on the shore waves a flag. The airboats zip ahead. My fated mate's shouts make my wolf panic. But he calms at her laughter. I shake my head.

We race through open channels, skimming across the shallow waters. Coastal mangroves rise from roots that resemble legs. Beneath them, leatherback turtles and West Indian manatees forage for food. A pair of bald eagles soar above, calling to one another with high-pitch whistles. Near the shoreline, a great egret stands as still as a statue, waiting to snag its next meal.

A brilliant sun shines on my fated mate's excited face as she points at the sights. The wind whips tendrils loose from her long braid. The sun glints off the rich mahogany brown strands.

I recall the many times I wound her hair around my fist as I pounded her pussy from behind. The erotic recollections make my cock twitch. I shift on the bench and shake my head.

We turn a corner and the pack member navigating my airboat taps my shoulder. I follow the direction his finger points. Up ahead, alligators churn the water in a feeding frenzy. Their death rolls as they tear apart their prey disturb the peaceful scene.

Our airboats slow down.

"Listen, give them a wide berth. Ulf, you guys go first. We'll follow. Do not go near those gators," I command into the headset's built-in radio. "Wren, hold on tight. Do not move."

"Yes, beta."

"Yes, beta."

"Yes, Tag."

Her bright smile disappears as she eyes the predators warily. A couple of white-tailed deer made the fatal mistake of getting too close to the water's edge. The alligators lurk beneath the surface. They grab prey before they even know what happened. My poor fated mate doesn't understand the ways of predators. She'll have to learn.

Once we pass the voracious gators, the airboats resume their speed. Relieved, my fated mate turns and gives me the thumbs up. I return the gesture with a broad smile. She's happy again. All is well.

We return to the camp's docks from a different direction. I jump off the airboat and help my fated mate. She grins at me and wraps her arms around my neck. I hold her around the waist and swing her around. She throws her head back and laughs.

The sight of her bare neck and shoulder makes my wolf howl. We want to claim her sooner rather than later. But I'm a patient male. She's almost ready.

"That was so much fun!" She exclaims as I set her on her feet. Then she frowns. "Well, except for those alligators. They frightened me. So many in one spot. That poor animal. They ripped it apart."

I take her hand and lead her to the SUV.

"It's the way of nature, babe. And they caught two white-tailed deer."

Her frown deepens.

"That's even worse."

I open the passenger-side door and lift her onto the seat,

then shut the door. I round the front and sit behind the wheel. Taking her hand in mine, I squeeze it.

"Wren, predators eat prey. It's the circle of life. Wolf shifters are apex predators. We hunt and eat animals."

She chews on the corner of her lower lip as she considers my words. I wait until she speaks. Her eyes avoid mine.

"Does that mean I would have to hunt and eat innocent animals if I transition?"

"Yes. But remember, it's instinct for a predator to do so. Once you transition, your wolf will want to hunt. You will learn to enjoy the thrill of the chase and the satisfaction of your meal. Don't you enjoy a good steak?"

I smirk as her eyes narrow. She huffs and yanks her hand from mine.

"Whatever. Drive, Tag."

I chuckle wickedly and poke her side. She squeals, slapping at my hand. I keep tickling her until the smile returns on her face.

"But I don't eat my steak *raw!*" She quips once she catches her breath.

"Pity. It's oh so delicious, my fated mate," I say as I smack my lips.

She growls and rolls her eyes, plopping back in the seat, arms folded across her chest. But the corners of her mouth curl up in a smile as she stares out the window.

I place a possessive hand on her thigh and drive. When she doesn't swat it away, I smirk. Another win.

She relaxes as we drive along the road to camp.

My mobile rings. I answer it through the SUV's system. Jagger's voice fills the interior.

"How's it going?"

I glance at Wren. She smiles.

"You're on speaker. My fated mate can answer," I respond with a wink at her.

"Hi, Jagger. Thank you for asking. Everything is great! The pack welcomes me and treats me no differently than anyone else. You have a gorgeous camp. Such a lovely retreat from Miami. I love it here."

"That's great to hear, Wren—"

"Indeed, it is! And Tag treats you well, too, I guess?" Sage asks cutting in with a giggle.

My fated mate's cheeks flush as her eyes dart to mine. I smirk.

"Yes, you guess correctly," she responds.

"Excellent! We won't hold you. Call if you need anything," Jagger says as Sage voices her agreement.

"Thanks!" We reply in unison, then laugh as I end the call.

She shifts in the seat to face me.

"I like Sage and Jagger. It's really nice of them to check in on me."

I squeeze her thigh as I nod.

"Yes. And remember, as Alpha and Luna, the pack's happiness ranks high for them. One reason everyone respects them. They genuinely care for each member equally. As you've experienced, our pack is well balanced."

She lowers her eyes and nibbles on her lip.

"What's the matter?"

"But I'm not part of your pack."

～

WREN

. . .

FOR A SECOND, Tag's eyes dim. Then he squeezes my thigh and grins.

"Not officially yet, my fated mate. That happens after I claim you, and we complete our mate bonding ceremony."

In Maya's words, he's *not just good. But really good.*

"We'll see, Tag Dahl."

He nods as his grin widens.

We continue on in companionable silence.

My thoughts move to the claiming bite and the transition. I asked a few of the mated she-wolves about the bite. They say it's done during sex at the point of orgasm. So, although it's painful—you know, sharp fangs puncturing flesh and all—it intensifies the pleasure of the orgasm. A hyped-up climax, they giggled.

My nipples pebbled, and my core clenched. It sounds incredible. However, that's not the part that worries me. It's the transition. They had little knowledge about it since they're born she-wolves. Like Tag already told me, they know decades ago was the last occurrence. But they told me the turned she-wolves would be happy to speak to me. However, they're in Miami on Moon Island.

I'm sure Tag would arrange for me to meet with them. To learn about their experiences would help me a lot. I glance over at him. Even though he keeps his eyes on the road, he smirks. I roll my eyes.

We reach the camp and park in the garage. Tag helps me from the SUV. I hold his hand as we walk to his cabin. Now's as good a time as any to ask about the turned she-wolves.

"I want to learn more about the transition," I start.

He peers down at me and nods.

"Ask away, babe."

I shake my head.

"The she-wolves I spoke to about it and the claiming bite

tell me the turned she-wolves would speak with me about their experiences. Will you arrange for me to meet them? Maybe when we get back?"

He tilts his head thoughtfully.

"How about I set up a video conference call? That way, you won't have to wait another two weeks."

"Perfect, thanks," I respond, happy he doesn't mind me asking more details. It's not that I don't trust him. But I want first-hand accounts.

He pulls out his mobile and makes calls as we continue to the cabin. By the time we get inside, he's scheduled the call in thirty minutes. I rush upstairs to shower. When I meet him in the den, he has the flat-screen television set for the call. He kisses the top of my head and leaves me to speak with the she-wolves in private. I smile at his thoughtfulness.

Moments later, the call connects. Three older she-wolves appear on screen. They greet me with warm smiles. I thank them for taking the time to speak with me. They wave me off, saying it's their pleasure.

"I'm not sure how much Tag told you. But I'll tell you a bit about me and where we are with our relationship."

They nod and voice words of encouragement. I give them a summary from the elevator to now. When I finish, I tell them my concerns about the transition. I also ask they share their experiences not just with the claiming but as humans adapting to being she-wolves.

Each one tells her story. Like me, they're fated mates. Prior to meeting their male wolf shifters, they never knew of the beings' existence. It happened where the males approached them after detecting their unique scents. Like Tag, they wooed the women without mentioning their true natures.

Two of the women fell in love with their fated mates right away. The third rejected hers initially. All admit they felt the attraction and later learned it's the mate bond. What changed the third she-wolf's mind was the persistence of her fated mate. He never gave up. Like Tag.

Once the women committed to the relationships, the males confessed. All three balked. But the solid foundation of love developed proved stronger than their fear, anger, and shock. They accepted their fated mates and decided to be one with them in all ways. The males claimed them.

Like the born she-wolves, the women felt pain and pleasure in the bite. They blush as they describe it to me. Heat rises in my cheeks too. I can't speak for their cores. But mine aches for Tag.

When they describe the transition, I perk up, not wanting to miss any detail. After the bite, they felt woozy and drifted in and out of sleep for a few days. They couldn't remember much more other than their fated mates never let their sides. The males fed them soft foods and liquids. Days later, they awoke invigorated, stronger than before.

Their wolves appeared on the fringes of their beings. The males taught the new she-wolves how to connect with their other half through their minds and to call them forward to shift. The women describe it as their bodies painlessly realigning to the shape of their wolves in moments. They remain in full control of their bodies and their minds. The world appears more vibrant.

They laugh at the increase in their sexual appetites. I giggle, thinking if mine grows anymore, I'll never get out of bed. As for the hunting, they agree with Tag—it's nature.

One woman didn't transition fully. But she lives longer with better health. The pack treats her equally.

They completed the mate bonding ceremony—the wolf shifter's version of a wedding ceremony—after their transition. Their eyes grow dreamy as they recall their special days. Each of them gave birth to healthy pups. They laugh when I ask if the babies came out human or wolf. Relief sweeps through me when they confirm human. I couldn't imagine giving birth to a four-legged miniature wolf!

Overall, they love their lives with their fated mates, family, and the pack. The women assure me pack life does not differ from human families. However, wolves remain loyal and dedicated to the wellbeing of all pack members. The hierarchy of Alpha, Luna, beta, enforcers, and down keep the pack in order. The Alpha and Luna are fair and loved by all.

The women laugh and tell me to ask Sage about her experience. They tell me it's even more extraordinary than theirs. I make a mental note to ask Tag if she would mind sharing.

By the end of the call, my nerves lessen. I'm eager to get to my fated mate. With many thanks and their well wishes, I end the call.

My body thrums with need of my fated mate. I rush from the den, checking the rooms I pass. In the great room, I glance out the wall of windows. My heart swells.

Tag stretches out on a chaise lounge sipping scotch.

I admire him for a moment. The late afternoon breeze ruffles his sable brown hair. He shaved the five o'clock shadow this morning since it grew to more of a beard these last two weeks. The dimple in his chin adds a softness to his strong jawline. A long-sleeve t-shirt covers his broad shoulders and sculpted torso. Low-slung joggers encase his long, muscular legs. They cross at the ankles as they extend to the very end of the chaise lounge.

My fated mate's masculine beauty and strength call to my feminine desires. My core softens as my juices flow, preparing for him to take me. Every cell in my body explodes with desire. I whine in the back of my throat as the pressure builds in my core. On weak knees, I cross the great room and slide the glass door open.

"I sense your need for me. Come, my fated mate."

He turns to me with eyes as smoky as his gruff voice.

A strangled, lust-filled cry slips past my lips as I rush to his side. He sets the crystal tumbler on a side table and opens his arms to me. I fall into them, straddling his thick thighs. My fingers dig into his shoulders as I stare into his eyes.

"Tag Dahl, I love you with every fiber of my being. Wholeheartedly, I accept you as a wolf shifter and as my fated mate. I wish to be with you forever and to bear your pups. I ask you to make me yours in all ways."

He responds with a low and husky growl as he leans forward and licks the juncture of my neck and shoulder.

My core clenches on an orgasm. I cry out in surprise as my fingernails dig into his shoulders. Another lusty growl and my core clenches again.

"Oh, Tag… I need you… inside me," I pant, grinding my pussy against his burgeoning erection. It bobs beneath me, and I moan, increasing my pace. A swift smack to my ass halts my movements. I cry out in half pain and half pleasure.

"I give you your pleasure, naughty girl," he chides in a raspy voice.

"Oh, please, Sir. Please!"

He grunts and lifts the hem of my sundress around my hips, exposing my bare pussy. Since we've been here, he doesn't allow me to wear panties. And in the cabin, I rarely wear any clothing.

I pull on the collar of his long-sleeve t-shirt, needing to feel his heated flesh beneath my palms, aching for skin-to-skin connection. He obliges and yanks it over his head. My eager fingers reach for the drawstring of his joggers. I tug it and pull on the waistband as my mouth waters at the outline of his long, thick cock. He raises his hips. The joggers lower to his thighs.

My fingers wrap around his shaft. It's so wide, the tips don't meet. I stroke up and squeeze the plum-shaped head. He groans as a bead of pre-cum leaks from the slit. I scoot back on his thighs and bend over to lap at the thick, milky seed.

His fingers grip my hair. He pushes my head down. I open my mouth. His cock slides along my tongue to the back of my throat. I gag, then relax with a hum. He groans and grinds his hips. I bob along his cock until it swells.

With a snarl, he pulls me up, fists his base, and glides his shaft along my dripping folds, coating it in my arousal. I moan, greedy for more. He doesn't make me wait. He aligns his cock with my entrance and thrusts up as he grips my hips firmly. Fast pistoning strokes bring us to climax quickly. Our bodies shake from the intensity. My passionate cries and his primal howl resound through the pine trees.

Birds take to the air, squawking their dissatisfaction at being disturbed. Small animals scurry to their burrows. None want to face the Everglades' apex predator.

But I do.

I angle my head to bare my neck to my fated mate. Despite my desire to be claimed, my body tenses as his mouth lowers. Instead of sharp fangs, soft lips press to the spot. Then he sits back. His hooded eyes regard me.

"Aren't you going to bite me?" I ask when my breath evens out.

Tag trails a fingertip along my neck and shoulder. The sensuous touch combined with his warm breath on my sweat-dampened skin makes me shiver. I mewl.

"Not tonight, my fated mate. We must prepare."

CHAPTER 17

"THERE THEY ARE!"

I grin at my fated mate as she bounces beside me, pointing at the approaching helicopters. I chuckle to myself, as much from her excitement as my own.

During her call with the turned she-wolves, I sensed her emotions change from nervousness to happiness, then to strong desire. My own emotions mirrored hers. I decided a relaxing glass of Macallan Scotch would settle my nerves.

Giving her complete privacy, I stayed on the back deck. As she neared me, the level of awareness increased. The mate bond pulsed with her need for me. I sent mine of hers back. When she arrived at the sliding door and paused, I all but leaped to my feet and carried her caveman-style to our bedroom suite. But I maintained my control.

Her poignant words touched my very soul. I'll forever remember them and the expression of pure love on her beautiful face. Even now, my heart soars higher than the approaching helicopters. I squeeze her hand and grin wider than the Cheshire Cat.

"Yup, right on time! My boys always come through, babe."

After we made love on the deck and showered, we Face-Timed Jagger to give him the fantastic news. He and Sage congratulated us—him with a piercing wolf whistle and her with delighted squeals. Wren giggled while I beamed with masculine pride.

I patched Rust, Dylan, and Viggo in on the call.

Rust agrees it's best he oversees her transition. His medical experience will help her through it, if necessary. And like Jagger, he believes she will survive the process since we're fated mates. That's the one thing I didn't mention to her. No need to cause unnecessary panic. Plus, Sage confirms Wren will be a remarkable she-wolf, alleviating any residual concern. Natalie—Rust's fated mate—offered to help too, since she's a doctor.

Dylan and Viggo offer their support. We teased Viggo he's the last male standing. He scoffed and bragged he'll forever be a playboy. Sasha—Dylan's fated mate—congratulated us with a Russian saying for a happy, prosperous life.

For now, they're the only ones besides the pack members here we share the news with. Once Wren recovers from the transition, we'll announce our status to my parents and to the rest of the pack. They'll come to camp to witness our mate bonding ceremony. Afterwards, we'll celebrate with dinner and a pack run through the Everglades. Then I'll take my fated mate into seclusion for the rest of the month.

The helicopters land one after the other on the spacious helipad. The rotors slow as the doors open. My boys, their mates, and in Jagger and Dylan's cases, their pups emerge. I smile when Signy follows Sage, who carries Tove. Jagger's younger sister waves. I return the gesture with a grin. Judging by the shopping bags she carries, the pack princess fashionista wants to help Wren with her dress for the ceremony.

"Who's she? She looks familiar."

My fated mate's question draws me from my musings. I smile and tell her it's Signy, explaining how she used to accompany me to social events. Wren recalls her photos from the society columns. Yup, that's Signy.

I guide Wren forward. She raises her hand in greeting.

"Hey! Good to see you guys!" I say as I one-arm hug the guys and nod at the females, then step back. "Everybody, this is Wren Byrd, my fated mate."

Jagger inclines his head while Sage embraces her. The others approach and introduce themselves. The she-wolves with hugs, and the males with respectful nods. Even though we're best friends, males know better than to touch another's female. Wren's face glows with each greeting, and she coos at the pups.

We pile into the SUVs and drive back to camp. After they drop off their things, everyone comes to our cabin. They join Wren and me on the deck. Viggo heads to the outdoor kitchen to start up the grill for lunch. The others sit around the large oval table.

I pull a bottle of NV Billecart-Salmon Brut Rose Champagne—Wren's favorite—from the ice bath in the center. She claps as I pop the cork and fill her flute. Jagger opens another bottle. Once everyone has a glass, I take Wren's hand. She stands beside me, and we raise our glasses.

"My best friends, I thank you for joining my fated mate and me as I claim her, and she transitions. Your support and love are invaluable. We thank you."

"Hear, hear!"

"Congratulations!"

"*Vot vam!*"

"You sucker!"

Everyone cracks up at Viggo's declaration. I shake my head at the male two years younger than me.

"Give it time, bro. You'll be panting after some female soon."

"Yeah. And I hope she gives your sorry ass a hard time!" Dylan quips.

"Not me, bros!" Viggo responds as he tosses back his Champagne. He sets the flute on the table with a wink at Wren. "I hope you keep a happy smile on Mr. Grumpy's oh so cheery face, little sis!"

I throw a handful of ice at him.

He ducks, chuckling and heads to the grill.

"Meanwhile, I'll rustle up some grub, even for the latest sucker," he tosses over his shoulder.

Jagger glances at Rust. He turns to Dylan. I nod. Then the three of us bum rush Viggo. We knock him to the deck wrestling like we did as pups. He yelps and flails his arms. But we overpower him.

I leave the others holding him down and remove the bottles from the ice bath. I carry the oversized sterling silver bucket over to them. The guys step back, leaving Viggo on the deck. He raises his arms as I dump the water and ice on him. He shouts. We laugh.

"Get used to cold baths, bro. The she-wolf you'll lust after will give you blue balls!" Jagger guffaws.

The girls chastise us for being mean and offer Viggo help. They gather around him and help him to his feet. Over their heads, he winks at us. We growl.

"Thank you, my little sisters. Your mates and brother are savages. I shall return to the male's cabin, change, and return to cook you a delicious feast."

He bows his head. Water drips from the long copper

strands. The girls fuss over him until he disappears around the side of the cabin.

"Not nice, Tag!" My fated mate chides, wagging her finger.

I grin and nip it.

She gasps as her pupils dilate.

"Stop right there," Jagger says. "We have details to discuss."

Reluctantly, I loosen my bite on her finger. I drape my arm over her shoulders and return to the table. The others join us. We leave the sun to melt the ice and to dry the water.

"This afternoon, I'll issue the claiming bite. That way, we have the rest of the day and evening to watch over Wren. Rust, you and Natalie will be on hand while I stay in the bedroom. I think it's best she recovers there than in the infirmary. What do you think?"

Rust and Natalie consider my plan. They glance at one another as though communicating silently. Then Rust answers.

"That's fine. Once you're showered and Wren wears something comfortable, call me. Nat and I will come over to check her vitals. We'll get a reading now, so we have a baseline. We'll stay in a guest suite. That way, we're close, even though only Jagger and Sage's cabin separate ours from yours. Time could be of the utmost importance."

I nod, then turn to Jagger.

"Alpha, what do you think?" I ask deferentially.

"It's a solid plan. Sage and I will stay in another guest suite for the same reason. In addition to Rust and Natalie's medical expertise, Sage will use her magick if necessary."

Wren's head whips towards me. Her eyebrows rise to her hairline. Mouth round.

"Magic?" She croaks. "Like a magician?"

I'd laugh at the comical sight. But I know she's surprised. I clasp her hand and turn to Sage.

"Not m-a-g-i-c, Wren. M-a-g-i-c-k as in witches."

Sage pauses to give Wren a moment to absorb her words. Wren blinks. Her eyes flick from Sage to mine and back. Sage smiles.

"Your drawings are not so far off, Wren. Wolves, others, and witches. You see, we're older than any of the other paranormal beings…"

Sage goes on to give Wren a brief history and ends with her formal titles. She also explains how she handled the fight situation and healed that fucker. My fated mate listens enraptured. Then she nods.

"Yesterday, the turned she-wolves told me you have an even more extraordinary experience of becoming a she-wolf. I wondered what they meant and planned to ask you about it. Would you mind?"

"Of course!"

While we listen to her story, Viggo returns. I feel a tad bit bad and help him to gather the platters of food from the kitchen. We have a major spread of salads, spicy sausages, lobster, shrimp kebabs, and steaks. I chuckle, recalling my fated mate's reaction to the alligators. Lunch is a carnivore's delight.

I leave our pack's master chef to do his thing and rejoin the others.

"Talk about a paranormal Romeo and Juliet!"

Wren exclaims as Sage nods. Jagger kisses her temple as he wraps his arm around her. She nestles against him with a contented smile on her stunning face.

I take my fated mate's hand and kiss her cheek. That's the love I want for us—unbreakable. She smiles up at me, and my heart fills with the love she sends through our mate bond. I return mine to her. She cups my cheek.

"Enough with the lovebirds snugglefest. We have just as important plans to make. And time is of the essence!"

All eyes turn to Signy.

"Wren, the girls and I need to know what theme you want for your mate bonding ceremony and the dinner. We won't discuss your gown with you-know-who around. But the other stuff is fair game."

Sadness comes through the mate bond. I lift Wren's face. Tears fill her eyes.

"What's wrong, babe?"

She sucks in a sob and shakes her head.

"I just wish my parents were alive. My Dad would walk me down the aisle, and my Mom would help me pick out my dress. Even Maya can't be here," she finishes with a hiccup.

I dab her eyes with a linen napkin. The soothing rumble rises in my chest as my other hand rubs her back.

"Wren, I am so sorry about your parents. Unfortunately, we cannot allow humans to know of our existence except in cases such as yours. So, I can't do anything about your best friend. However, it would be my honor as your Alpha and friend to walk you down the aisle," Jagger says.

She covers her mouth with her hand and nods vigorously. Her emotions roll through our tether. I smile at Jagger in thanks. He nods.

"The rest of us share our condolences too, Wren. As for your friend, she may not be here. But there's no reason you can't retain your relationship with her after you transition. You can never reveal yourself or us to her," Sage says, then continues. "And as your Luna and friend, the girls and I will ooh and aah with you as you choose your gown. We'll help you prep too. Just as others did for me, Sasha, and Natalie."

The girls chime in their agreement.

"And…"

We turn to Dylan. He gestures at Jagger, Rust, and Viggo.

"The guys and I are your new big brothers. We vow to protect you with our lives. Should you ever need a thing, call and we will be there for you."

Wren's shoulders shake as tears spill down her flushed cheeks. She clears her throat and glances around the table.

"Thank you. Thank you all so much," she whispers.

Signy lightens the mood by steering the conversation to the ceremony and dinner. I zone out but continue to stoke my fated mate's back while I rumble low. She relaxes and talks excitedly about the plans.

I sense a stare and look up to find Jagger watching me. He nods his head, a satisfied expression on his face. I nod back.

After a while, Viggo calls for the girls to collect their lunch. The tantalizing aroma of the grilled meats makes my wolf sit up, tongue lolling. I agree. We're about to feast. Once they fill their plates, the guys get their portions. We thank Viggo for another delicious meal. He grins and raises his flute.

"May your bellies always be as full of good food as your hearts are with love."

The girls swoon.

Jagger glances at Rust. He turns to Dylan. I nod.

"LOSER!" We shout.

He winks as the girls smile adoringly at him.

Always a player.

~

WREN

. . .

"THEY'RE ALL SO GORGEOUS! I don't know which one to pick!"

I widen my arms at the array of gowns Signy hung on racks in the sitting room of my bedroom suite.

She has superb taste. Not one would I cross off. They vary with hemlines from floor length with trains to ankle, midi, and above the knee. The fabrics range from silk to lace to chiffon. And she didn't stop there with options. The colors include the expected white and off-white. But the blush pink and floral gowns prove good competition for the traditional ones. All flatter my figure.

Signy bustles over. Her fingers flip through the gowns. She pauses at one, shakes her head, then continues her perusal. Then she snaps her fingers.

"This one! The floral chiffon gown is light and airy. Perfect for an outdoor ceremony in the humid Everglades evening. The plunging v neckline shows off your boobs while the waist cinches to accentuate your hour-glass figure. The draping detail lets the gown flow around you. You'll resemble an enchanted forest goddess!"

Signy's elaborate description hypes me up.

"Yes! I love it, thank you!"

The girls agree with claps and snaps of their fingers. We giggle and toast with Champagne.

"Now that you've chosen your gown, how do you envision the ceremony bower and table settings? It'll take place in the square before sunset," Sage asks.

"I'd love to incorporate the beauty of the Everglades."

She nods and an image shimmers before us. It solidifies to reveal the square decorated with columns of intertwined tree branches and wildflowers strung with thousands of fairy lights. They surround the area to allow for the celebration to continue after the sun sets. Amidst the garden and benches stand rows of long rectangular tables with pale green tablecloths and matching wooden chairs. Floral arrangements line the center with buckets of my favorite Champagne. Chafing dishes with a variety of foods and beverages sit on tables to the side. A separate table holds a four-tiered cake. A ceremony bower with the same treatment of wildflowers, tree branches, and fairy lights stands at one end.

"Oh, Sage, how beautiful," I breathe.

She smiles and says, "I kept it in the theme Natalie and I used for our ceremonies, but changed the colors. Let nature stand out. Plus, it goes along with your enchanted forest goddess gown. I'll have it all set up for you. Magick!"

She wiggles her fingers. We laugh.

"Okay, a male has but so much patience, you know!"

Our laughter bubbles over as Tag bellows outside the closed double doors. My teddy bear is morphing into Mr. Grumpy.

"Hold on a minute, Tag!" Sage calls out, then she does her thing, and the dresses disappear. She winks at me. "Well, Wren, enjoy your claiming!"

Sasha and Natalie titter. Signy rolls her eyes. They file out, making comments to Tag that make his cheeks redden. He glances at me over their heads. A thrill rushes through me.

This is it.

Tag closes the double doors and stalks towards me. His ravenous eyes lock on mine. Single-minded determination settles on his handsome face. The apex predator targets its prey. He moves with grace, persistent in his pursuit.

My heart pounds. My entire body quivers in need for this powerful male. I mewl as a blast of desire zips through our mate bond. It travels from my heart to my core. My lower belly heats from the intensity.

"Are you ready for me to make you mine in all ways, Wren Byrd?"

His deepened voice filled with passionate dominance skitters across my heated skin.

I moan a yes, holding my arms out to accept him—all of him.

He scoops me up with a growl and carries me into the bedroom. I slide down his body as he places me on my feet beside the bed. He grips the hem of my tunic and pulls it over my head. It drops to the floor as he unfastens my shorts. They slip down my thighs. I step out of them and kick them to the side. Naked, I stand before him.

His eyes darken with unchecked lust before they disappear behind his t-shirt, and he yanks it off. I rip the placket of his jeans. The buttons pop free. The head of his erect cock peeks out. I shove the jeans down his hips. He kicks them off.

He walks me backwards until I fall onto the bed. He flips me over and pulls my hips up until I rest on all fours. His palm slides up my spine, pushing between my shoulder blades. I lower to my forearms and toss my hair over a shoulder. He growls at my bared neck. I wiggle my ass. He spanks it with another growl. I groan as the erotic pain radiates through me. The moan deepens in my throat when he slams his cock inside my wet pussy.

Immediately, he sets a brutal pace. His groin slaps against my ass while his heavy balls kiss my engorged clit. The pounding continues as our cries and musky scents fill the air. His cock expands. He increases to a frenzied pace. His arm bands around my waist. A hand grips my shoulder. He lowers his torso to my back, still thrusting. I cry out in surprise when the base of his cock expands and locks behind my pelvis. His knot! Just like my novels. I scream.

His warm breath huffs against my neck and shoulder.

Warm liquid drips on the spot. I stiffen, knowing what comes next. A searing pain blanks my mind as his sharp fangs puncture my tender flesh.

"MINE!"

He growls like the wild beast he is. His mouth opens again, then clamps back down on the same spot. He shakes his head to deepen the claiming bite.

My skin sizzles. The serum rushes through my system just as his cock spurts his seed deep into my womb. My pussy contracts, milking his cock of every drop. I keen. Then all goes black.

"—BEEN four days. She doesn't eat. What's happening to her? I can't lose Wren!"

As Tag's anguished cries draw me from a dreamless slumber, I awake to pain in my chest and blinding light.

"T—Too bright..."

My words come out in a harsh voice. My dry throat makes it difficult to speak.

"Wren???"

"Tag."

The now darkened room explodes in cheers.

I'm pulled from soft pillows and crushed against his muscular chest. Hot tears spill in my hair. He cries my name over and over. The pain in my chest morphs to solace and happiness. I wrap my arms around my fated mate.

My fated mate!

"Did you say four days passed? Since you claimed me?"

"Yes," he replies gruffly.

"Tag, let me check Wren's vitals."

At a male's voice, I glance over Tag's shoulder to find Rust, Natalie, Jagger, and Sage standing around the bedroom. Tag growls. Rust holds up his hands, palms out. Natalie steps forward.

"Tag, I'll check her. Will you allow me?"

He nods and moves to sit beside me, one protective arm around my shoulders. His gaze flicks between the others and Natalie. Slowly, she approaches. I pat his thigh.

"My love, it's all right. I'm fine. In fact, I feel fantastic! It's okay for Natalie to check me. All right?"

He grunts his assent. The caveman.

I smile at Natalie and sit up. I notice a silk nightgown covers me. My beaded nipples press against the soft fabric. No wonder Tag freaked out at Rust! I pull the sheet up. Tag squeezes my shoulder.

Natalie checks my vitals, reflexes, eyes, and my hearing. When she's done, she declares I'm in perfect condition. And I feel it. All senses heightened. The world is in sharp focus with amplified sound.

"Excellent news! Wren, you pulled through like a champ!" Jagger says as he smiles broadly.

"That's our girl!" Sage chimes in. "Now, for your mate bonding ceremony tomorrow. Whoohoo!"

I glance up at Tag and grin. He relaxes and grins back. He drops a kiss on the crown of my head, and I snuggle against his side.

"Well, that's our cue!" Rust says with a chuckle. He takes Natalie's hand and heads for the door.

"We'll have food sent over for you. They'll knock and leave it at the door," Sage says as Jagger places his hand on the small of her back.

He nods and ushers her from the bedroom.

Before the sitting room doors close, Tag pounces. I giggle and wrap my arms around him.

"You're truly okay, baby?"

"Absolutely! I've never felt better. And I see my she-wolf on the periphery. Will you show me how to shift?"

He nuzzles my neck, kissing the claiming bite that's already healed.

"Yes, and so much more."

I shiver at the inference in his words, especially since he nudges my thighs apart with his knees. I widen my legs to cradle him against me. We spend the next few hours doing *so much more.*

"WE'RE SO happy for you and our son, Wren!"

"Yes, darling, welcome to our family and to our pack!"

I promised I wouldn't cry on my mate bonding ceremony day. But the kind words from Branson and Ylva—Tag's parents—choke me up. Tears shine in my eyes as I return their embraces. Tag rubs my back when I return to his side and hold his hand.

First a fated mate and new friends, then a new family and a whole pack. I'm the luckiest girl in the world.

"Thank you so much! I feel so lucky to have all of you in my life, especially my fated mate," I respond as I look up at him.

I raise to my tippy toes to kiss his lips when I notice tears shimmering in my teddy bear's eyes. He wraps his arms around me and lifts me as he deepens the kiss. When he finally puts me down, I peek at his parents.

They beam at us. I smile back, so elated.

"We hate to interrupt your first introduction. But we have to get Wren ready for their ceremony."

Sage enters the great room with Signy, Sasha, and Natalie. They grin and beckon me with crooked fingers.

I laugh and kiss Tag on the cheek, then extend my hand to Ylva.

"I would love for you to join us."

She smiles and clasps my hand.

Jagger, Dylan, Rust, and Viggo enter and take Tag away for some kind of bro bonding. Branson declines their invitation and heads to the clubhouse to meet up with the older males.

After a couple of hours being pampered by pack aestheticians, the girls help me to dress. Sage uses a glamour spell for my hair and makeup. I twirl in the trifold mirror, grinning at my reflection. Jagger comes, and it's time to meet Tag at the ceremony bower. Jagger helps me into a golf cart while the others follow in separate carts.

"So, you're truly happy with everything, Wren?"

"Yes, Alpha, so thrilled. Thank you for welcoming me to your pack."

"*Our* pack. And you're more than welcome. You make an excellent addition."

I smile all the way down the aisle where my handsome fated mate waits for me to exchange our vows.

"Wren Byrd, I claim you as my fated mate to protect, love, and cherish for all time. To bear my pups and to stand by my side. I love you, Wren Dahl, my fated mate!"

He slips a ginormous emerald-cut diamond ring set in platinum on my finger. It glints in the sun. He assures me when we shift back, jewelry reappears intact.

I swallow back tears of joy, then clear my throat to respond.

"Tag Dahl, I claim you as my fated mate to protect, love, and cherish for all time. To bear your pups and to stand by my side. I love you, Tag Dahl, my fated mate!"

I slip a platinum band on his ring finger.

The clearing explodes with shouts and howls of jubilation.

Tag scoops me in his arms. I throw my head back and let my she-wolf howl with her joy. Tag joins us for a song of love. Then he carries me back up the aisle to the pack's shouts and howls of celebration reaching the sky. He sets me down next to our table and kisses me senseless. The voices of others as they take their seats don't stop my male from claiming my mouth.

"When the happy couple comes up for air, we can toast their new bond."

I laugh against Tag's lips. He nips my lower one and stands to his full height.

"We're ready, Alpha."

Jagger chuckles. He and Sage raise their Champagne flutes. We follow their lead.

"Miami Wolves Pack, tonight we welcome our newest member, Wren Dahl, to our family—"

Everyone cheers. Once they settle down, he continues.

"She is Tag's fated mate. Once human, she fully transitioned to a she-wolf."

The pack murmurs their congratulations.

"Tonight, we celebrate Tag and Wren's mate bonding with good food and fellowship, followed by a pack run. Join Sage and me in welcoming Wren to our pack!"

I push back the tears and laugh as the square fills with the pack's howls. Tag cups my cheek and kisses me until my toes curl. More howls and whistles fill the air.

"Now, we eat, drink, and be merry!"

Jagger exclaims and downs his Champagne, then he and Sage sit.

While we eat, each pack member introduces themselves and congratulates us on our bonding and me on my successful transition. The three turned she-wolves introduce me to their fated mates. I hug the females and tell them their kind words helped tip the scales in favor of me accepting Tag and being a wolf-shifter. He thanks them and claps their mates on the back.

As we dance, Tag tells me how gorgeous I am. My heart swells with gladness. After we eat the cake, the sun sets. Jagger announces the time for the pack run. I glance at Tag nervously. He brushes his lips against mine and murmurs how he believes in me.

While the pack strips and shifts amidst crackles and flashes, I slip out of my gown and sandals. No one pays attention to my nakedness or comments on my size, especially amongst the sleek and lithe she-wolves. Tag clasps my chin between his thumb and index finger.

"You are my beautiful fated mate. No one compares to you, Wren Dahl. Now shift for me, baby."

At his command, my body morphs into my mahogany brown she-wolf. I embrace the now familiar shift and the wolf. I tilt my head up to stare at my fated mate, then tip it further to howl with the others. Pride from Tag fills my heart through our mate bond. I lower my head and find his giant sable haired wolf before me.

He throws his head back and howls, then nudges my flank with his snout. He races past me to join our Alpha and Luna at the head of the pack. I follow to take my place by his side as the mate of the beta. My new family parts to let me through.

As I approach with head bowed, our Alpha and Luna bark in acceptance while the beta stands tall. Then our Alpha turns, followed by our Luna. My mate yips at me and follows.

I race after them, overjoyed to have a genuine family again.

CHAPTER 18

"I THINK I'll leave my social clothes at the duplex. Wherever we go will be based on the mainland, anyway. I can get dressed there. Oh, and I'll leave makeup and stuff. I'm so glad we're keeping that residence so I can hang out with Maya there. It won't be like I'm lying. It's still our home and my office."

I try hard to pay attention to my fated mate. But she's bent over in her walk-in closet in our Moon Island bedroom suite. The bottom curves of her generous ass play hide-and-seek in the skimpy shorts. My mouth waters.

"Tag? Are you even listening to me?"

She spins around and straightens with her hands on her hips. Her face set in a scowl until she sees mine full of lust.

"Oh, no, mister! You've kept me tied to the bed for twelve whole days and nights. You're insatiable. Not that I mind. But now, I want to get settled in my new home. Promise me you'll behave."

I'm tempted to say after one more round. But she arches an eyebrow and folds her arms under her succulent tits. Now, my mouth salivates for their plump juiciness. But I shake my head to clear the carnal thoughts.

"Fine. However, if I help you, you'll finish faster. Then we—"

"Ah, ah. Nope. You'll just distract me with all that sexiness you have going on. Give me ninety minutes, then you can ravish me," she says with a wink. "Now, go. Hang out with Dylan. He and Sasha just returned from their time in New York City. She says he's caught up in an MMA video game. Since he fights for real, he acts like he's the players. You can work off some tension playing the game."

Not a bad suggestion. I pull out my mobile, tap on the screen, and turn it to face her.

She frowns and steps closer. Her tinkling laughter fills the closet.

"Tag Dahl! You are such a stickler. A ninety-minute countdown? Give me a break."

I smirk and wave the mobile in the air as I back out of the closet ticking down the seconds. She waves her hands to shoo me out as she giggles. I shout the latest number when I reach the double doors of the sitting room. She shouts for me to get a life.

I chuckle. She is my life. And I've already got her.

At the bottom of the steps, my mobile rings. It's Rust.

"Hey—"

"Listen, come to the ER. Wren's uncle just came in. Heart attack. I'm the attending. Gotta go."

The call ends. I race up the stairs four at a time, calling her name. She runs into the hallway.

"What—"

"Your uncle had a heart attack. We gotta go, now!"

Her eyes widen.

I grab her hand and pull her back to her closet. I help her switch out of the booty shorts into jeans and flats. She takes off the t-shirt and puts on a bra, then replaces it. I glance around for her mobile and notice three missed calls. She has it on silent. Damn! I grab her wallet and a bag, shoving everything inside. I take her hand and hurry for the garage.

While we zip towards the hospital, she checks her voice messages. They're all from her aunt. Tears stream down my fated mate's cheeks as she talks to her. He's in surgery. They were at the club playing golf. He collapsed. She tells her aunt we'll be there soon and ends the call.

I rub her thigh as I rumble in my chest. She remains silent, staring out the window. We pull into the parking lot near the emergency room entrance. I slide the Bentayga into a spot. Wren jumps out before I can get to her. She runs towards the sliding doors. I catch up to her easily and race through the doors beside her. A nurse directs us to the waiting room. We hurry down the crowded hallway, dodging gurneys and staff. We burst through the door. Wren spots her aunt and rushes over.

"Any word?" She asks, sitting next to the older woman.

She glances up with red-rimmed eyes. Her face puffy and tearstained. She shakes her head and covers her mouth as she sobs into a wet handkerchief.

Wren wraps her arms around her as tears stream down her face. Despite the woman's mean behavior towards her, my fated mate still shows compassion. I send soothing vibes through our mate bond. She glances up at me with a watery smile.

"I'll go see what I can find out. Rust is the attending physician. Maybe Natalie can get us some answers."

Wren nods and continues to console her aunt.

I jog to the nurses' station. They can't give me information since I'm not listed as kin. I stifle a growl and whip out my mobile. Natalie answers on the first ring.

"Hi—"

"We're in the ER. Wren's uncle had a heart attack. Rust is the attending. I can't get the nurses to tell me anything. Can you find out?"

"I'm on my way."

"Thanks."

As I return to the waiting room, the mate bond pulses with anger. What the hell?! I race to the room.

That fucker is arguing with my fated mate. Here we go again. But this time, I control myself and my wolf—even though he snarls viscously.

"—off, Jonathan. Now is not the time for your nonsense! Leave me alone."

Wren whisper yells at the fool. But I can hear her clearly across the room.

"If your uncle dies—"

She slaps him so hard, his head snaps sideways. I may be in control of my wolf. But hers flashes in her eyes. I rush to her side and block her with my body from him. Then I reach back to put a hand on her arm. I glare down at the fucker, who's seven inches shorter.

"Get the hell out of here, or I will have security escort you off the premises."

He glares up at me.

"Who the hell are you?"

My lip curls as I snarl, "Wren's pissed husband. Now. Get. The. Fuck. Out."

He balks. Then moves to the side to glance at her around me. I move with him, keeping her safely behind my body.

"Is there a problem here?"

I maintain eye contact with him and use my periphery to see the newcomer. It's a security guard with Natalie. I nod.

"Yes. This jerk is not a member of the family and needs to be escorted from the premises."

The guard takes him by the arm and leads him away as he shouts obscenities.

I turn to my fated mate.

"Are you okay?"

She nods. I'm thankful her eyes returned to their mink brown.

"I'll go check the chart and come back," Natalie says and hurries away.

I guide Wren back to her aunt, who shakes her head.

"So uncouth."

Yeah.

Natalie returns and tells us all the information she can find out, which isn't much since he's still in the operating room. But she stays with us since it's the end of her day. We wait in silence.

Hours later, Rust comes out. He strides towards us. I gauge his body language and note the tension around his eyes and in the set of his shoulders. I take Wren's hand in mine.

"Mrs. Byrd, Wren, he's stable. But it'll be a while before you can see him. He's being transported to the ICU. I wanted to come to you as soon as I could. His heart suffered extensive damage and with his age, we can't give a definitive prognosis at this time. However, we did our best. Now, we wait for his body to heal. Do you have any questions?"

Her aunt asks if she can see him through the window. Rust says he'll check with the ICU. Then his pager goes off. Her aunt gasps. But he shakes his head and tells her it's another patient. He leaves, promising to have word from the ICU sent to them and a nod at Natalie.

"I'll check for you," she offers and leaves the waiting room.

"You know, Wren, your uncle loves you dearly. You may not think so. But he does. So do I. We just want what's best for you," she glances at me and nods. "I know who you are. You make a good match for Wren. I was never fond of Jonathan."

My fated mate's eyes widen in shock.

Her aunt pats her arm and falls silent again.

WREN

"You can go in to see him now, Wren."

I nod at Aunt Gretchen.

She's aged these past eight days. The stress of waiting for Uncle George to awake from the induced coma added wrinkles around the corners of her eyes and between her eyebrows normally Botoxed smooth. Still fashionable, she wears Chanel from head to toe—a sheath dress with a cardigan around her shoulders and ballet flats. She reaches into her 2.55 handbag and pulls out a handkerchief to dab her eyes.

My heart clenches. I glance up at Tag. He offers an encouraging smile. I rise from the sofa in the hospital anteroom of Uncle George's private suite and head towards the bedroom. At the door, I glance over my shoulder at my fated mate. He smiles and nods his head. I enter the room.

The beeping machines and antiseptic products assail my new enhanced senses. I shake my head as my nose wrinkles. The raspy sound of my name brings my attention to the bed.

Uncle George lies on his back with the bed adjusted so it's elevated. Tubes stick in his nose and hands. He appears frail and swallowed up by the bedding. But his eyes still hold their light, even if dim.

I walk over and sit on the chair beside the bed.

"Hello, Uncle George. Don't speak. I won't stay long. I just want to let you know I'm here and hope you get better."

He lifts his finger resting beside him. My eyes drop to a legal-size manila envelope next to it. My name—written in bold lettering—stands out. Surprised, I lift my gaze back to his face.

He opens his mouth. But words don't come out.

"No. No. I'll get it," I say as I reach for the envelope.

I open it and scan the contents. It's a copy of his will. And I'm still the sole heir. I inherit all, including Byrd Capital. A separate fund provides Aunt Gretchen with a monthly allotment until her death, then the fund reverts to me. I stare in shock.

"Uncle George, thank you. But we'll table this for a much later time. You focus on improving your health. I'll visit you every day. Now, get some rest."

He stares at me for a long moment. Then his eyes flutter closed. His breathing remains steady.

As horrible as he treated me, I do not wish him any harm. I return to my fated mate, take his hand, and bid Aunt Gretchen a good night. I tell her I'll see her in the morning. Then leave with the male whose love I never have to question.

CHAPTER 19

 *ren*

"NO! Absolutely not, Wren Dahl! Skip yourself right back up those stairs and put on some real clothes. I kid you not, female."

My fated mate thunders as I stand on the bottom step in our duplex. I spent the day with Maya. So, Tag met me here.

We're about to leave for Club Hati—one of Larson Enterprises' exclusive dance clubs—for our first Date Night with Sage, Jagger, Sasha, Dylan, Natalie, and Rust. We invited Viggo. But he declined, not wanting to be *the ninth wheel.*

I feel bad for him since he's the only one not mated out of his brother and best friends. When I asked him about it, he winked at me and said he doesn't mind multiples, just not with males. I chucked him on the shoulder. He grinned with sparkling ice blue eyes. The handsome billionaire playboy would rather continue to play than to mate. He's the youngest of the guys. So, who could blame him?

I'm young too and want to look sexy despite my fated mate's protest. I glance down at my merlot colored mini dress.

It's short and flirty. The pleated bodice with a halter neckline and revealing open back gives way to a softly pleated skirt that skims my thighs. A wide, laser-cut belt nips in my waist. The black leather contrasts nicely with the mini dress' rich color and softness. Paired with sky-high strappy stilettos, the mini dress and shoes lengthen my newly toned legs. All that running around as a she-wolf and wrapping my legs around my bucking bronco trimmed them better than squats!

I glance back up at Tag and pout my glossy pink lips. Sashaying forward, I bat my eyelashes at him, purring in my chest.

"Oh, my love, I wore this for you," I say, then spin in a slow circle making the skirt lift to reveal my bare booty. Facing him, I continue. "So, while we're grinding on the dance floor, your hands can roam freely. No encumbrances."

I step into him. My breasts press against his eight-pack abs. I tilt my head back to pin him with a sultry gaze. His cock twitches against my lower belly. With my fingertips, I trace his sculpted chest beneath the black v-neck silk sweater. They swirl around his nipples and tweak them. His chest vibrates with a growl. My sensuous exploration continues as I trail my fingertips up to press against his mouth.

"Do I not please you, Sir?"

The growl increases as he nips my fingers. I yelp and draw them back. But he grasps my wrists and sucks on the digits. Smoldering eyes bore into me. He pulls my fingers from his mouth with a pop. While his eyes remain on mine, his tongue darts out to lick the length of each finger. Then he closes his hand around them and strides to the double doors.

"We leave now, you Siren. Or, I will have my way with you on *this* floor, not the one in the club."

My body thrums. But I want to go out with our friends more than to party in the sheets at home. We'll have plenty of time to get our groove on. So, I all but skip behind him with a satisfied grin on my face.

Tag helps me into the Wraith. As he shuts the door, my mobile rings. I slip it out of my sequined clutch and check the screen. It's Sage.

"Hey, we're in the car now. Where are you guys?"

"Oh, good. We just turned onto the causeway. Instead of taking separate cars, we're in the Sprinter. See you in a few!"

She ends the call as Tag slips behind the steering wheel.

"That was Sage. They're on their way now, too. I can't wait to dance. Whoop, whoop!"

My fated mate chuckles as he drives towards the garage's exit. We arrive in no time.

The sedan stops in front of an Art Deco building in a prime spot located on Ocean Drive that offers unobstructed views of the Atlantic Ocean. The building stands three stories with a rooftop lounge and has a sleek linear appearance with stylized ornamentation. A sectioned-off outdoor area offers seating for dining and drinking at the bar.

Two men in custom-tailored black suits flank the entry. A queue extends around the corner of people in expensive attire patiently awaiting admittance to the club. Not surprising given Club Hati is for the über-wealthy and influential, too refined to behave boorishly. The hopeful patrons are not rambunctious as one would ordinarily see waiting outside a South Beach nightclub.

One doorman opens my door while a valet waits for Tag to emerge from his side.

"Welcome to Club Hati, Wren," the doorman says extending his arm.

They're members of our pack. The doormen are enforcers, perfect to handle any issues at the club should they arise.

I place my hand on his arm, and he lifts me from the seat. Did I say they're huge? Taller and bulkier than Tag. I thank the doorman as my fated mate removes my hand from his arm with a low growl. The doorman bows his head respectfully to the beta and wishes us a good evening.

I don't comment on Tag's possessive behavior. He's already none too pleased with my mini dress And I want to have fun tonight. He leads me through the outdoor area to the front doors. I notice women watch him appreciatively. My she-wolf and I snarl. Mine!

"Now, you know how I feel, Siren," he murmurs in my ear. "So, behave."

I huff as we enter the club. My she-wolf howls.

The air vibrates with the pulse of the music. The scent of expensive perfume and cologne mixes with an enticing aroma the club pumps through the ventilation system. Colorful lights change periodically.

My gaze roams around the lavish club full of the glitterati. Celebrities, socialites, fashionistas, and billionaire tycoons wear their sexiest, most revealing outfits. With my enhanced senses, I distinguish wolf shifters from humans easily. Bottles of top-shelf liquor and magnums of champagne sit atop the tables in the VIP booths. Assigned female servers in figure-fitting white tube mini dresses carry bottles with sparklers. The patrons applaud.

Those not fortunate to have a booth stand two deep at the three bars or perch on stools at high-top tables surrounding the dance floor. Bartenders stay busy serving drinks to those gathered.

The dance floor teems with gyrating bodies. Females dressed in more revealing outfits than mine dance with hot males. Partiers shake their things.

My clutch taps to the beat against my thigh as I follow Tag. He weaves through the crowd, a head above most others. I can't see beyond his back, but I know we reach our friends when I hear Jagger's greeting.

I step from behind Tag and wave. They cheer and raise their cocktail glasses in the air. A server offers Tag and me a tray of drinks. We select a scotch and a mojito, then raise our glasses in a toast with our friends.

"Here's to the first of many Date Nights with awesome friends!"

Everyone seconds Jagger's declaration before we sip our drinks.

Tag sits on a leather banquet and guides me to his lap. He tugs at the hem of my mini dress when it rides up my thighs. I lean over and whisper in his ear all the filthy things I want him to do to me. When I add on the dance floor, his cock thumps beneath my butt. I wiggle my hips and purr.

"Come on, girls, let's dance for our boys!"

Natalie rouses me from an almost-sex-induced thrall.

I wink at my fated mate and give my clutch to him. Sasha takes my hand and tugs. I rise and follow her with the others to the dance floor.

The DJ's music and callouts have everyone bouncing to the beat. I throw my hands up and shake my hips. In the crowd, no one will notice how high my mini dress rises. But I know Tag will. I twirl and bump my hip against Sage's. She giggles and shimmies.

"The DJ plays the best music!" She says as she bumps her hip against Natalie's side.

Sasha flips her waist-length ash blonde hair over her shoulder as she twirls on the dance floor. Her dove gray eyes—like her silver chain-mail micro mini dress—sparkle in the lights.

We move to the sensuous pulse of the music. A few males make their way over to us. We shake our heads and form a tight circle. Who's interested in any others when you have sexy as sin fated mates? The males take the hint and move on to more willing partners.

I lift my gaze towards the DJ, then shout.

Maya dances on a platform next to his booth. Lost in her own world, she has her eyes closed and moves seductively to the beat. She must have changed her mind from when I asked her to come with us earlier.

"That's Maya, my best friend. I'm going to get her," I tell Sage as I point. She nods, and I make my way through the throng of dancers.

Maya doesn't see me. But the DJ does. I gesture at her. He nods. A moment later, he strides over and taps her, then points at me. Her eyes widen, and she waves me up. I turn and point at the others. Maya nods and waves for them to come up, too.

A bouncer helps us navigate the steps in our high heels. I throw my arms around Maya's neck. We hug. Then I introduce her to the others. She grins and hugs them too. She goes to the DJ and whispers in his ear. He nods. She returns and winks at me.

Soon the music blends to T.I.'s "Live Your Life."

Giggling, I hug my bestie.

We turn to the others and start dancing as I belt out Rihanna's lyrics.

I have the best of both worlds. My fated mate and our pack and my best friend and work. What could be better?

EPILOGUE

wo Months Later
Tag

HERE WE GO AGAIN. When will they learn to not test my patience? I pin the presenter for the new hotel project with a disdainful look. He gulps.

"You do realize the hotel is a historic property in a historic district. Zoning does not allow any changes to the building's facade. Did you not get the memo?"

I cock an eyebrow and wait for whatever excuse he comes up with. And he doesn't disappoint.

He blathers on about wording in the zoning document he suggests we use to *get around the rule.* I let him keep talking to dig himself deeper into a pit from which he will never rise.

Those gathered around the table stare at him incredulously. Some appear to will him to shut up. Others lower their gazes. None want to incur the beast's wrath.

Sure, I'm not as harsh post-Wren. She pointed out how I

could be a little less grumpy. I try my best to satisfy my fated mate. So, the whispers of me being a bosshole have lessened.

But my patience is already thin since Wren hasn't been well these past few days. It's unusual since she's a wolf shifter now. But since she's a transitioned and not a born she-wolf, we can't compare her healing abilities with theirs. Anomalies can happen.

If she doesn't feel better, she promises to ask Natalie to examine her when she finishes her day at the hospital. But, that's hours from now.

I glance at my watch for the hundredth time since this meeting started. Another thirty minutes to go. Then I have more meetings to attend. I can't believe of all the days, this one has back-to-back appointments. The last site visit is across town. So, it'll take a while to get back to Moon Island. Damn!

A polite cough brings my attention back to the conference room.

"I missed that last part. Repeat it."

The presenter blinks like a scared rabbit at my gruff command. He gathers himself and drones on.

With a sigh, I pay attention.

As soon as the meeting ends, I jump from my chair and stride out of the room, mobile to my ear. Wren answers on the first ring.

"Hi, my love."

The annoyance fades as her voice soothes me. I never expected to fall in love, and now I can't live without the love of my fated mate. A smile spreads across my face.

"Hi, to you, babe. How do you feel?"

She goes quiet.

I stop in the middle of the hallway. My heart thuds in my chest. Is the transition reversing? Is she experiencing side effects months later? Does she need another claiming bite?

"Talk to me, Wren. You've got me losing my mind here, babe."

"No, no! Nothing to worry about. I'm fine. I feel better, in fact," she responds, then continues. "But don't you have a ton of meetings to attend? Don't let me keep you. Get your work done, Mr. Dahl, Sir."

Relief weakens my knees. I brace a hand against the wall and hang my head. This female is going to kill me. My blood pressure lowers, and I continue to my office suite.

"You take priority over all, my fated mate. Never forget that. But I do need to go," I say as Beth looks at me expectantly with a file folder in her hands.

"I love you," Wren whispers. "See you when you get home."

A tug at our mate bond causes me to rub my chest. Beth averts her eyes. I take the folder and stride into my office, shutting the door.

"I love you, too," I reply gruffly and end the call.

I turn at the knock on my door. It opens, and Jagger pokes his head in.

"Ready to go?"

"Yeah, let me grab my laptop."

Hours later, I climb out of the Bentayga and tell my driver I won't need him or my security team tomorrow. It's Friday. I'll work from home and keep an eye on Wren.

Inside our mansion, I pause and listen for my fated mate. I don't want to call her name in case she's taking a nap. Besides not feeling well, she sleeps more.

No sound of her on the first floor. I bound up the stairs and stride towards our bedroom suite. The double doors stand closed. I open them softly and stick my head in. I glance around the sitting room. She's not on the sofa. Her scent is faint. But not strong enough to suggest she's in the bedroom.

I close the doors and spin on my heel. Then I notice the door to the closest guest bedroom suite stands open. I frown, wondering why she's in there. My ears detect a scratching sound. I hurry my steps.

The furniture in the room is gone except for a table with her sketchpad and a bottle of water. She wears one of my long-sleeve t-shirts and sits cross-legged on the floor in front of the largest wall. The pencil in her hand makes the scratching sound as she draws on the surface. She's so focused, she doesn't notice my approach.

Not wanting to startle her, I whisper her name. Her head snaps around anyway. Then she smiles and rises.

"Oh, you scared me! I didn't hear you," she says as she stretches her back and walks towards me.

"Sorry, babe," I murmur against her lips as she tilts her face up. After a soft kiss, I cup her cheek. "How do you feel? Did you go see Natalie at the island's hospital? What are you doing in here, anyway?"

She giggles and presses a finger to my lips.

"One question at a time. Although I must say, they're related," she replies, smiling broadly. "First, I want to show you something."

She leads me to the table and points at a drawing on the page. A male and a female wolf romp with three pups amongst pine trees near a marsh remarkably similar to the Everglades. It's so realistic, I could reach out and touch their fur or hear the playful growls of the exuberant pups. She points at the date. It's months ago. Before that unfortunate night of the gala.

"Remember, I mentioned how Sage flipped through my sketchpad after the gala?" She asks, then continues when I nod. "This is one of them she saw and found it curious I drew such a picture. I didn't know about you being a wolf shifter. But wolves dominated my dreams. I drew this and didn't think any more about it. Until today."

She glances up at me with tears in her eyes.

My heart lurches to my throat. I bite my lower lip to keep from speaking, wanting to hear her say it. But afraid I'm wrong.

She gestures towards the wall and the beginnings of a mural replicating the drawing. Then she widens her arms to encompass the entire room.

"I thought this room with the wall taken down to open it to the one next door would make the perfect"—she takes my hand and places it under the t-shirt against her warm skin—"nursery for our three pups."

Her voice waivers as tears slip down her cheeks.

My mouth gapes as my eyes fill with tears. I can't speak. I drop to my knees and lift the t-shirt. As I stare at her rounded belly, the tears flow.

She twines her fingers in my hair. Her soothing purr reaches my ears. Our mate bond floods with love and joy.

I lift my gaze to her face.

"Y—You're pregnant… with my pups? T—Three of them?"

She nods, then gnaws the corner of her bottom lip. Her beautiful face glows. Eyes radiant with love.

I wrap my arms around her hips and press three kisses to her belly filled with my three pups. My eyes close as my forehead leans against her warm, soft skin.

She strokes my hair and asks, "Are you happy, my love?"

As I rise to my feet, I lift her in my arms and swing her around. I let out a jubilant howl. My fated mate giggles and throws her head back to join me. Our wolves take up the call. The cries echo around the empty nursery. Soon it will ring with the sweet coos of our precious pups. My heart soars higher than the moon above.

"Am I happy? Unbelievably ecstatic! You make me the luckiest male in the universe and beyond, Wren Dahl! I love you more than the air I breathe. You complete me, my fated mate. You and our pups mean more to me than you can ever imagine. Thank you, my love."

"I love you and our pups so much. Thank you, Tag Dahl, for not giving up on us. I've never been happier in my whole life."

She cups my face and covers my mouth with hers. I hold her aloft and return her kiss with unbridled passion.

And this is what I live for. My fated mate's happiness and now our pups.

They're my greatest wins.

CHARMAINE LOUISE SHELTON

VIGGO
THE OBSESSION

ABOUT VIGGO THE OBSESSION:
A WOLF SHIFTER FATED MATES
PARANORMAL ROMANCE

I'm the playboy prince who vowed it would never happen. Then it did. And she became my obsession.

Every female, she-wolf and human, wants a piece of me. So why should I choose only one? Unlike my brother—the leader of our pack, the Billionaire Wolves of Miami—and our best friends, I have zero interest in settling down with my fated mate. If she even exists.

But then Maya Alejandra Perez Garcia walks into my club.

I love the life I made for myself in Miami, away from my controlling family in Venezuela. They allow me to leave until I turn twenty-five. Now, they demand I return to marry a man of their choosing, not mine. Before I go, I have one night to do as my heart wants. And it's Viggo Larson, the sexy as sin man who watches me with smoldering eyes.

How could I know my steamy act of rebellion would result in a surprise and Viggo having one of his own?

*Their steamy love story is a standalone in the sizzling **Billionaire Wolves Series** of interconnecting stories featuring wolf shifter fated mates romance. Get a glimpse of their dynamism in other books.*

Anthem: "She Bangs" Ricky Martin
https://www.youtube.com/watch?v=5ihtX86JzmA

Visit CharmaineLouiseBooks.com

CHAPTER 1

 *iggo*

I vow to not end up like the others.

No.

You won't catch this billionaire playboy prince of the pack chasing after his fated mate. Facing death to save her. Being rejected. Losing all control. In front of humans, no less.

Not this wolf shifter.

Although I would risk all to save my fated mate. If I had one. Which I don't. And have no interest in one at the moment.

As the youngest at twenty-eight of my best friends—including my older brother by two years, Jagger Larson, our pack's Alpha—the single life suits me just fine. A plethora of females—she-wolf and human—want a piece of me. So why choose only one? I can have the pick of the pack, no pun.

Plus, my work as the President of Clubs and Lounges for

Larson Enterprises, Inc. keeps me busy and out with late nights several times a week. It's our family's multibillion-dollar company founded in Miami with Jagger as the current CEO. We're the top company in the hospitality industry for luxury hotels, fine dining, clubs, and lounges.

Initially, Jagger was hesitant to select me to run the clubs and lounges. I persuaded him I could handle the role because of my years of not only hanging out at them but also managing a few. The hot and happening Miami nightlife is right in my wheelhouse.

He relented to a trial, and I give it my all. My division generates a sizable amount of revenue each year. Now, Jagger admits his fun-loving and smart brother increases overall profits for Larson Enterprises regularly.

But it's not enough.

I want to shed the perception as the younger brother who makes his way on the back of the pack Alpha and as the carefree jokester with the loftiest achievement of banging multiple females in a night. No. My goal is to prove I'm my own male to be taken seriously. I won't become a boring bump on a log. But others will view me as responsible and respected.

Which is the reason I'm slogging through quarterly numbers with the CFO—a member of our pack—instead of joining Jagger and our best friends for a night at Club Hati. Tag Dahl—the pack beta and COO of Larson Enterprises—called earlier to tell me about the plan to hang out. Normally, I would be all on it. However, two things stopped me. My division numbers' projections are lower than expected and me being the ninth wheel.

Tag is the most recent of the five of us to meet his fated mate Wren Byrd. Jagger was the first to leave bachelorhood when he found Sasha Waters—the High Witch and the leader of her coven—again. Dylan Vang, the rogue wolf who didn't even believe in fated mates, fell hard for Sasha Volkov. Rust Ingolf—our pack doctor—overcame the rejection of Natalie Moore to claim her as his fated mate.

Which leaves me... The last male standing.

So, as much as a night of partying with my buddies appeals to me, joining them with their females dulls my enthusiasm. Not that I don't like them. They're my new sisters added to my actual younger one, Signy. However, I'd rather study spreadsheets until my eyeballs fall out than to witness powerful wolf shifters going gaga over their females and I don't have one. Again, not that I want one. So, no thanks.

I told Tag as much. Of course, he ribbed me and said he couldn't wait for me to meet my match. I ended the call with him guffawing.

"All right, Viggo. This explains the difference in the numbers. Here, look at this column..."

The CFO shares his laptop's screen to the television mounted on the wall across from the conference table in my office on the executive floor of The Larson Tower.

I scrub a hand over my exhausted ice blue eyes and swipe it through the longer top strands of my fiery copper red hair. Determined to find the cause, I focus on the detailed spreadsheet. An hour later, I unfold my muscular frame and stretch all six feet, six inches with a groan. Then thank the CFO for staying late. We part ways in the garage.

The engine of my Ferrari 488 Pista purrs to life. As I maneuver the streets of Downtown Miami Bayfront, headed for my beachfront penthouse on Ocean Drive, I decide to swing by Club Hati. After hours of numbers, I can use a drink and the distraction of a female—or two.

The supercar stops in front of an Art Deco building in a prime spot on Ocean Drive that offers unobstructed views of the Atlantic Ocean. The building stands three stories with a rooftop lounge and has a sleek linear appearance with stylized ornamentation. A sectioned-off outdoor area offers seating for dining and drinking at the bar.

Two males in custom-tailored black suits flank the entry. A queue extends around the corner of people in expensive attire patiently awaiting admittance to the club. Not surprising given Club Hati is for the über-wealthy and influential, too refined to behave boorishly. The hopeful patrons are not rambunctious as one would ordinarily see waiting outside a South Beach nightclub.

I chose Club Hati for the name as a nod to Norse mythology. The wolf Hati chases the moon across the night sky. His counterpart—the wolf Sköll—chases the sun during the day. They do so until the time of Ragnarök when they will swallow the heavenly bodies.

A valet waits for me to emerge.

"Good evening, Mr. Larson," he says as he bows his head respectfully.

He and the doorman are members of our pack. Enforcers who are perfect to handle any issues at the club should they arise.

I enter the club where the air vibrates with the pulse of the music. The scent of expensive perfume and cologne mixes with an enticing aroma the club pumps through the ventilation system. Colorful lights change periodically.

My gaze roams around the lavish club full of the glitterati. Celebrities, socialites, fashionistas, and billionaire tycoons wear their sexiest, most revealing outfits. With my enhanced senses, I distinguish wolf shifters from humans easily. Bottles of top-shelf liquor and magnums of champagne sit atop the tables in the VIP booths. Assigned female servers in figure-fitting white tube mini dresses carry bottles with sparklers. The patrons applaud.

Those not fortunate to have a booth stand two deep at

the three bars or perch on stools at high-top tables surrounding the dance floor. Bartenders stay busy serving drinks to those gathered.

The dance floor teems with gyrating bodies. Females dressed in revealing outfits dance with metrosexual males and macho types. Partiers shake their asses in hopes of hookups.

Pride fills my chest as I weave through the crowd—a head above most others—bound for my office. With floor-to-ceiling windows perched above the dance floor, my office offers the perfect spot to survey the activities.

In addition to employing wolf shifters and humans, Larson Enterprises' establishments cater to both. Best for our kind to hide in plain sight and all. Although we've been here a hell of a lot longer than the humans.

Several millennia ago, Scandinavian Viking wolf shifters sailed from the Old World and landed along the East Coast of what's now the United States. The six packs headed by best friends who sought new lands moved throughout the continent to form territories, with ours settling here. We maintain close ties with our brethren through friendship, mating, and business. Plus, our Ruling Council gatherings keep us informed of happenings throughout the packs.

Our Miami Wolves Pack is the most powerful pack in the South. Because of the success of Larson Enterprises, other packs refer to us as the *Billionaire Wolves of Miami*. Further reason for me to ensure I succeed in my responsibility to generate revenue through my division.

With a nod at the security guard standing at the foot of the staircase leading to my office, I jog up the steps. Once inside, I make a beeline for the wet bar in the corner. Crystal decanters filled with clear and amber liquids glow in the low lights. Striding towards the wall of one-way windows, I sip on Scotch as I watch the happenings below.

Then notice my brother and best friends with their fated mates in the VIP section.

They're clustered together on white leather banquettes with their drinks on low tables in front of them. Their faces radiate with the happiness of true love.

For a moment, a twinge zaps my heart. What would it be like to have a partner the gods choose for me as The One? A she-wolf who senses my needs and my emotions through our bond? Who will spend the rest of her life with me and bear my pups?

Nah!

I shake my head to dislodge the slipup and toss back the rest of my drink.

Wren leads the females to the dance floor. She's the first human turned into a she-wolf by a male wolf shifter in our pack in decades. Thankfully for Tag, she had a successful full transition. Some humans die. Others cannot shift but live longer with better health. The pack treats all turned she-wolves equal to those born as wolf shifters. Then there's the mental aspect of it all. It's a lot for the mind to process the concept of being a wolf shifter.

I don't know if I could handle waiting to see if a human mate will survive my claiming bite. Normally, a male wolf shifter issues it to lodge his scent via a serum in a she-wolf's skin permanently marking her as his mate. The scent wards off other males. Once issued, the pair can never part or the male wolf shifter will go crazy and lose control of his wolf.

However, the claiming bite is also the only way to turn a human female into a she-wolf. The serum enacts the transformation. The process can last for days while she remains in a coma to allow her body to change on a cellular level. A deep sleep they may or may not awake from. And if they do, will they maintain their sanity?

A shudder runs through me.

I pivot and stride to the bar to refill my drink.

Back at the glass wall, I scan the crowded dance floor. The DJ has the partiers gyrating to the slamming music. Even though it's muffled by the wall, the sound reaches my ears easily.

The DJ is an upcoming local favorite. I like to give people in the community opportunities to excel as Jagger did for me. I make a mental note to tell the club's manager to schedule the DJ for a few more nights this month. If he keeps packing the dance floor, we'll put him on the regular rotation.

My head bops to the beat as I gaze at the DJ. Then it snaps to a stunningly beautiful female on a platform next to his booth. Lost in her own world, she has her eyes closed and moves seductively to the beat.

Glossy jet black hair sways to brush her round ass. And that's only the beginning of her curvy, tight body. Bountiful tits—almost too full for my sizable hands to cover—play peekaboo from behind the deep v-neckline of her silver mini dress. Tiny crystals dangle from it and shimmer with each shake of her grip-worthy hips that flow out from a narrow waist. Long, toned golden legs end in sky-high, fuck-me strappy sandals. More crystals dazzle as her feet glide across the floor in time with the beat.

My cock punches a hole in my bespoke suit trousers.

Mesmerized, I watch the female.

Then Wren appears and throws her arms around the beauty's neck for a hug before she introduces her to the others. The beauty grins and hugs them too. Even from this distance, her expressive topaz eyes glitter more than the sparkling crystals that adorn her sinful body. She saunters to the DJ and whispers in his ear.

Jealousy unfurls hot in my chest. The visceral reaction surprises me. I watch as he nods, and she returns to Wren.

When the music blends to T.I.'s "Live Your Life," they embrace again. The beauty's hips sway as they dance and sing. She spins as she throws her hands up and shakes her mouth-watering ass. The hem of her mini dress rises to expose more of her golden skin. She twirls and bumps a hip against Wren's. The beauty giggles and shimmies some more, hypnotizing me with her seductive spell.

Fuck. Me.

Inexplicably drawn to her like a moth to a flame, my feet lead me from the office, down the stairs, and into the shadows near the DJ booth. This close, her beauty surpasses that of any female I've ever seen. Her eyes hooded, golden cheeks flushed, and lush mouth curled up make me wonder what she'd look like as I brought her to a screaming climax on my impressive cock.

It thumps along my thigh, eager to make the fantasy a reality. The heel of my palm strokes down against its length to soothe the burning ache of instant desire. A throaty growl slips from my mouth.

Then my nostrils flare.

A whiff of my first breath as a newborn pup slams into my system. The unique scent of fragrant frangipani mixed with fresh coconuts and salt carried on a tropical breeze from the Caribbean Sea fills my lungs anew. It triggers an ancient and unstoppable chain reaction.

An electric current weaves its way to zap my brain, alerting my entire body to a specific presence. Eyes flash silver with my wolf as enhanced vision zooms around the club and my head tilts back on a deep inhalation to pinpoint the location. Heartbeat speeds up faster than the Ferrari going from 0 to 100 in 2.9 seconds. My cock pulses with the pounding rhythm as it grows diamond hard and pre-cum oozes from the tip.

My wolf claws at my skin to break free for the carnal hunt.

I all but throw my head back and howl like a feral beast maddened by lust and the urge to claim. To possess. To breed.

My fated mate.

She's here.

And I will have her.

Now.

Or tear this club apart.

Nothing and no one will keep her from me.

MINE.

 *aya*

THE TROPICAL SUN warms my skin as I hike along the steep trail in Waraira Repano National Park on the edge of Caracas. My golden skin glistens from a sheen of sweat. Thighs and calves burn from the two-hour climb to the hidden waterfall. Beneath the tank top, sweat trickles down my spine to the waistband of my cargo shorts. I adjust the straps on the backpack as it slips from my damp shoulders, then swipe a loose strand of hair from my brow.

Ahead, the trail widens as the trees separate. The sound of rushing water overtakes the cries of querrequerre birds and the scurrying of small animals in the undergrowth. All indicate my arrival at the base of the waterfall. The water cascades over the cliff to form a crystal-clear pool. Its surface dappled by the sunlight promises a refreshing reprieve from the heat.

I grin at the sight of it as my pace quickens to reach my

goal. A glance around confirms no other in the vicinity. Only a few colorful butterflies flitter amongst the abundant flowers around the edge. The surrounding grass empty. All alone. Perfect for me to skinny-dip.

With a whoop, I shrug my backpack off and drop it to the ground. Crouching, I untie my boots then remove them, flexing my toes as they emerge from thick wool socks. I stand and shimmy out of the shorts and hipster briefs before I yank my tank and sports bra off. The clothes land in a pile on the backpack as I remove the hair tie and shake my head. The tips of my jet black hair tickle the curve of my butt.

My head tilts back as I raise my arms, fingers spread to the cerulean blue, cloudless sky to bask in the sun. A deep inhalation expands my chest. Brown beaded nipples point towards the sky as I bend backwards and rise to my toes for a much-needed stretch. On an exhalation, I straighten and dash into the natural pool.

A squeal pops from my mouth as the unexpected chill of the water sluices over my heated skin. I take a deep breath and plunge beneath its surface. Tapping into my inner Ariel, I press my legs together and flick them like a tail as my arms propel me forward. I swim a few laps as I luxuriate in the tranquility of the tucked-away jewel of the park. As I float on my back, I close my eyes and let go.

The hairs on the back of my neck rise. The tingling sensation of being watched bursts through my bubble of solitude. I peek from behind the thick fringe of my eyelashes to scan around the pool. Slowly, my head turns to take in the entire area. Nothing. And it's silent, as though a predator lurks in the tree line.

The last things I want to confront are a jaguar or a bear. Hell, I'd even face a wolf before those two. I shudder and wade towards the grass as my eyes continue to search for any sign of a large animal. It's doubtful any of them are in this part of the park. But I'd rather be on land with a chance to run than floating in the water.

Once my feet touch the grass, I hurry towards my backpack for the satellite phone. As I reach for the bag, a low growl reaches my ears. My head jerks in the sound's direction. I gasp at the sight of a giant red wolf with ice blue eyes. They flash silver as the wolf's gaze scans my body from head to toe. The rumbling in its chest washes over me.

My heartbeat quickens. Pupils dilate. Nipples pucker. Pussy quivers. My wobbly knees give out, and I land on my ass. But my eyes never leave the red wolf. Which, I swear, narrow then zoom to the apex of my thighs. I snap my legs together. He growls. I shiver, mouth slack on a moan.

I watch, captivated by his lethal power as he stalks towards me. Frozen in place, I whimper when his front paws land above my shoulders and his back legs part mine. His massive head lowers. I cry out, expecting him to rip my throat out. Instead, he nuzzles my neck as he rumbles deep in his chest. The vibrations roll through me, easing my soul. On a sigh, my eyes close as my head lolls to the side, exposing my vulnerable throat. His rumble morphs into a word.

"Mine."

Startled, my eyes pop open.

Bottomless ice blue eyes stare down at me. Fiery copper red hair trails down the face of the most gorgeous man I've ever seen. Chiseled cheekbones and strong jaw blend with long eyelashes and lush, full lips. Lips I can't stop myself from staring at with the hope they'll cover mine for a toe-curling passionate kiss.

"Mine."

I gasp at his possessive tone. He takes advantage of my open mouth and slants his over it. His tongue slips inside and tempts mine to join his in a tango. My gasp becomes a lusty moan. My back arches as my fingers grip his bulging biceps. Of their own accord, my legs wrap around his narrow hips and lock at the ankles. My heels dig into his firm ass to draw him to me. He lowers from a plank. The weight of his muscular body so much longer than mine presses me into the soft grass. My softness and curves mold to the hard planes of his body. I welcome him like an old lover even as my mind wonders what happened to the red wolf.

Balanced on his forearms, he reaches between us and fists his long, thick cock. With one brutal thrust, he plunges inside of my soaking wet pussy. I scream into his mouth as he stretches my inner walls with his girth. The bulbous tip bumps my womb. He grips the back of my neck and grinds his pelvis into mine. Locked in position beneath his hulking frame, I can only take what he gives me. With. Pleasure.

He rocks in and out of my spasming pussy with measured thrusts. My furled nipples brush against his firm pecs. The slight hair teases my sensitive flesh with each pass. He swallows my soft cries as they mix with his groans. Wave after wave of pleasure roll through my entire being as we move in sync like we've known one another for all time.

His controlled thrusts quicken to pistoning strokes as he makes demands of my body. He drops his head to suckle on my nipples, moving from one to the other until I writhe beneath him.

An orgasm starts in my toes and shoots up my thighs to detonate in my pussy. My back bows as my mouth jerks away from his. A scream rips from my throat. It reverberates around us. My body convulses from the intensity and continues to peak as he pummels into my pussy.

His feral growls join my screams to surround us with

our mating cries. And it is a mating as he claims me for his own. His possession as clear as the sky above.

"Mine!"

His roar punches the air.

I shudder as another orgasm rips through me. It robs me of all ability to think and to speak. I can only feel. And he feels divine as he plunders my pussy. Then I cry out as he withdraws. He flips me onto my hands and knees before he plunges back inside my dripping core. I drop to my forearms with my face in the grass. I moan at his increasing thrusts.

The base of his cock swells. I yelp at the burn as he widens the entrance to my pussy. Instinctively, I wiggle away from the invasion. But he grabs my hips to still me. My fingers claw into the ground as he forces me to take his expanded cock. His groin slaps against my ass again and again. Breath escapes my lungs on the last thrust before a torrent of his seed jettisons into my womb.

Hot liquid drips on the back of my neck. A searing pain robs the last bit of air from my lungs. As I pass out, he growls.

"Mate!"

"Maya!"

"Maya, are you listening to your father and me?"

My mother Esmerelda Ariadna Garcia Diaz asks.

Her question rouses me from reliving the erotic dream from last night. It was the most vivid I've had over the last few weeks. They started as snippets during the night, with little more than the ghosting of another in my mind. The progression to a shadowed figure as though seen through a veil or a haze lasted longer. But last night… Oh. My. God.

My pussy clenches and moistens at the carnal memory. I shift on the seat of my Mercedes-Benz G-Wagen to ease the instant ache in my core for the mystery man. Yeah, to top it all off, I don't even know who he is. Aargh!

"You know, Maya, your father and I have been very lenient with you your entire life. Maybe too much. Do not allow our indulgence to influence you. You must come home now. It is your duty to our family…"

I bite back a moan—I mean a sigh, *focus, Maya*—as she drones on.

She and my father, Ricardo Armando Perez Gonzalez, call in their chit. They expect me to return to Caracas from Miami now that I'm twenty-five. The deal was to allow me to remain in the city after graduation from the University of Miami. Allow me the chance to live my life as I wished from eighteen until now.

I was thankful for the reprieve from my family. I love them to death. But I don't want to live under their rule. And a powerful rule it is since we're one of the wealthiest families in Venezuela and the world with the combination of my parents' families' petroleum companies through their arranged marriage.

And now it's my turn.

They want me to come home to marry a man I don't even know except by name—Emerico Tonio Santana Rodriguez. A man ten years older than me and a widower. Great, just great… Sure, he's only thirty-five and handsome. But still. He's not my choice. Don't I deserve to have my happily ever after like the women in my romance novels? I think so.

So, I delayed my return as much as possible.

My life in Miami is just as I want it. I've always been health conscious and met a woman at the gym who introduced me to fitness modeling. I successfully competed for three years, then became a personal trainer and wellness coach to help others on their fitness journey. And I'm damn good at it.

Even now, I wait in my truck for my client turned friend Wren Byrd. Our training session starts in five minutes. Unfortunately, my parents caught me before it started otherwise, my mobile would have been off, and I'd have missed their call. The call I've been dreading for months since my birthday.

Funny enough, the dream started right after I turned twenty-five.

Who the hell is this stranger who invades my dreams to tempt me with mind-blowing sex and the yearning for my soul mate? Why can't he appear and save me from my fate with Emerico? Dream lover, where are you???

A knock on my window jolts me.

Wren beams at me from outside the truck. My best friend just married the man of her dreams. Lucky girl.

Me?

"*Papá, Mamá*, I'm sorry. But my client just arrived. Can we continue our conversation later? I can call you tonight after my day ends."

They grouse but relent.

I'm not spoiled. But I am their baby girl—the youngest of their children with my brothers Odalis and Patricio three and two years older than me. All of them let me get away with more. However, I'm afraid the arranged marriage won't be one of the times.

With a sigh, I hop out of my truck and hug Wren.

"Hi, chica, don't you look all bubbly. You must be ready for your session, or Tag put it on you real good!"

She giggles as her face reddens and her mink brown eyes dance.

"Yes, and yes! Girl, I didn't know a male could be so voracious."

I grin and nod, thinking about the loser fiancé she had before she married Tag. What a difference a good man can make in a woman's life. Gee, I hope to know one day…

"Well, I'm more than happy for you, my friend. Now, let's get to it," I say as I grab my duffle bag from the back seat and loop arms with my bestie. "But don't think I'll go easy on you since you already had a workout for the day. No, ma'am!"

"I wouldn't expect anything less from you, drill sergeant!"

We giggle as we walk into the park next to Biscayne Bay. Other people exercise or play with their dogs on the open field of grass surrounded by palm trees blowing in the balmy breeze. The morning sun shines on us to start a new day in Miami. Just where I want to live my life as I wish.

Another sigh escapes. Wren pauses to glance up at me since I stand five inches taller than her at five feet, nine inches. Her eyes search my face for an explanation. However, I don't want to burden my newlywed bestie with my future husband drama.

"Let's start your warm-up with a jog to that spot over there. Ready, set, go!"

Wren yelps as I break free and charge ahead. Surprisingly, she catches up to me with ease. Not for the first time, I wonder how my BBW bestie is more fit since she married Tag. She was gaining strength and stamina with our thrice weekly training sessions. But her change in a few weeks is remarkable. I watch as she passes me then raises her arms in victory with a whoop.

The rest of the session goes just as smoothly, and I make a mental note to adjust her regimen.

"Tag and I are going to Club Hati with some other couples tonight. Come! I want you to meet everyone and hang out. It's been too long since we shook our booties, Maya."

I think about the impending phone call with my parents later and sigh.

"As much as I'd love to let loose, I have other plans," I respond, then continue when she pouts. "I know. I know. But I promise next time. Okay?"

"Fine. But I won't let you finagle your way out of it," Wren says, then hugs me before she heads for her car. She glances over her shoulder and waves.

I wave back with a forced smile. How I wish I could be so happily in love.

"Hey, there, Maya! I'm ready."

I pivot to find my next client. Drawing in a breath, I place a smile on my face and move on with my day.

Hours later, after the phone call with my parents and my promise to return home within the week, I decide to join Wren at Club Hati after all. I could use an escape from reality. I shower and change into a vintage crystal-embellished chain-mail mini dress and strappy sandals. My hair flows down my back with pink lip gloss and a bare face since I know I'm going to dance it up and don't want makeup dripping on my skin.

Which is why I take an Uber the short distance from my beachfront duplex penthouse to the club and not drive. I want to drink without concern for overindulging. And since Wren will be there with Tag, I have no worry about anyone getting out of hand with me.

I arrive at Club Hati and grin when I spot my friend in the DJ booth. I make my way to him since I can survey the club from the height of the raised booth to spy Wren. He greets me with a wink and points to the platform next to him. Happily, I walk to the steps where a bouncer helps me. I don't see my bestie, so I let the music take me away.

Eyes closed, I sway to the beat until the DJ taps me. I open my eyes, and he points to the stairs. My eyes widen. Wren stands next to the bouncer. My face splits in two as I wave her up. She turns and point at women with her. I nod and wave for them to come up, too.

The bouncer helps them navigate the steps in their high heels. Wren throws her arms around my neck for a hug before she introduces me to the others. My grin widens as I hug them, too. I motion for a moment and go to the DJ. I whisper in his ear to play Wren's anthem—T.I.'s "Live Your Life." He nods, and I return and wink at my bestie.

When the music blends to the song, she giggles and hugs me. We face the others and start dancing as Wren belts out Rihanna's lyrics. We dance from one song to the next.

A tingle at the back of my neck makes me pause and glance around.

Smoldering molten platinum eyes stare at me from the shadows.

Recognition dawns and a shiver courses through my body.

CHAPTER 3

 *aya*

I can't believe my eyes. It's the man from my dreams.

What type of psychedelic-ness is happening? How did he appear in my dreams and now stand in the shadows, watching me with an intense, heated stare? What the hell?

As the questions race through my mind, a nudge to my side interrupts their flow and any logical answers I can think of. I glance over to find Wren bumping her hip against my leg. She laughs and shimmies to the music.

I open my mouth to speak but need answers. My head swings back to the man. A niggling in the back of my mind tells me I know him from somewhere besides my dreams. And there's no doubt he's the man in each and every one of them, including the ones with his face obscured. My heart knows the truth. It races in my chest as I stare back at him, too entranced to dance.

"Hey! What's wrong?"

I blink as Wren talks over the music. She frowns and scans the dance floor. Her eyes widen when she notices the man. His eyes flash silver, and she gasps.

"What is it? Who is he?" I ask, frantic at her reaction to him as I glance between them. "Do you know who he is?"

Wren nods and places herself between the man and me.

"He's Viggo Larson, my Al—um… the younger brother of Jagger Larson and Tag's best friend. Do you know him?"

I shake my head and recall the names Wren mentioned over the last few months—Viggo amongst them. Relief washes over me. If she knows him, he can't be some weirdo. My gaze shifts to him.

His head tilts back as though he's sniffing the air.

Okay, maybe he is a bit odd.

"I could use a drink. Come back to the VIP section with me."

I flick my gaze to Wren, then back at Viggo. He's as handsome in person as he was in my dreams. Well over six feet, with an athletic build beneath his tailored suit. The contrast of his straightlaced appearance to the longer hair pulled in a knot with tattoos on the shaved sides of his scalp makes me wonder what kind of man he is. By the way women stare and nudge each other, they find him as attractive as I do. I bristle with jealousy when one approaches him.

He bends down and seems to sniff her, then shakes his head. His piercing eyes return to me. A jolt of electricity shoots through my body. I shake my head.

"Um, I'm going to dance a little longer. I'll come by after," I respond to Wren.

She eyes me, then glances over her shoulder.

"Are you sure?"

"Yes," I respond without hesitation.

She pauses before she nods and walks off, taking the other women with her.

I barely notice since my eyes remain riveted to Viggo Larson. The attraction between us is palpable. He continues to watch me despite another woman who stands before him, shaking her ass. I arch an eyebrow and turn my back. I'll give him a show he won't forget, and no woman can top.

My hands skim my hips and along my sides until my arms rise above my head. My hips move rhythmically as my ass wiggles to the beat. Only a moment passes before sizable hands grip my hips and a massive erection wedges between my butt cheeks. Warm breath blows across the delicate shell of my ear as a raspy voice growls.

"Mine!"

~

VIGGO

HER!

The unique scent of fragrant frangipani mixed with fresh coconuts and salt carried on a tropical breeze from the Caribbean Sea fills my nostrils as I stalk closer to the beauty. All other females fall to the wayside. Their attempts to seduce me fail. My wolf recognizes his fated mate and wants no other. Neither do I.

When she turns her back to me and moves sensually, a howl threatens to leap from my mouth. I charge forward and grip her hips, pressing my front against her back to let her feel just how much I want to claim her.

Her scent engulfs me, triggering my senses. Serum leaks from my elongated fangs. My pheromones peak. My cock thickens and lengthens to the point of pain. I growl with need.

"Mine!"

She mewls as she leans against me. Her fingers pull at the hair tie, releasing my fiery mane. I groan as she tugs the long strands and trails her fingernails along my scalp. The bite of erotic pain heightens my obsession with her. She likes it rough. Perfect.

I growl low in my chest and undulate my hips, rocking her onto her toes. My cock pulses, eager to plunge into her pussy. The musky aroma of her arousal wafts up to my nose to blend with her unique scent. The thudding of her heart rings in my ears. My vision tunnels blocking all else around us.

We move as one to our own erotic beat.

My balls grow heavy as they fill with seed. Saliva and serum fill my mouth. The urge to claim her increases with each sway of our bodies.

Suddenly, she spins in my arms. Her gorgeous face tilts up. Topaz eyes gleam in the low light. The tip of her little pink tongue darts out to moisten her full lips. I watch, wondering how it will feel wrapped around my cock as I fuck her throat.

"I want you. Now."

My eyes jump to hers at the unexpected demand delivered in a husky, accented voice.

Without hesitation, I scoop her in my arms and stride down the stairs, across the dance floor, and up a flight from my office to my private suite. I added four suites exclusive to select members who want to continue their dancing between silk sheets. And I plan to do so and more with this beauty in my arms.

Inside my suite, I carry her to the bed and slide her down my body until she stands before me. Both hands cradle her face between them as I angle her head back to stare into the depths of her glittering eyes. They're still topaz. No hint of her inner wolf.

Fuck. Me.

She's a human female, not a she-wolf.

In my lust-filled haze and nostrils filled with her unique scent, I failed to notice she lacks the distinction of a wolf shifter. I lower my face to her neck and inhale deeply, hoping I'm mistaken. No. She's human.

My eyes squeeze shut on a frustrated groan.

The one thing I had no interest in enters my life.

The fear she'd be a human comes to pass.

I can't have her.

But my wolf refuses to back down. He pins me with a ferocious glare before he throws his head back. The piercing howl vibrates throughout my entire being. It shatters my resolve. He stares triumphantly.

Fine. I'll give in for one night. But I won't issue the claiming bite. I will not risk her life. Then we'll part ways. Better for me to face the possibility of madness from losing my fated mate than for her to die at my hands.

"Viggo?"

My eyes open as I startle, not expecting her to know my name. She smiles and places her hands on my chest to slide her fingers along the lapels.

"Rest easy, *amante*. I only ask for one night. Nothing more."

I lose myself in the depths of her topaz eyes. My hands clutch her face as my mouth crashes to hers. Only. One. Night. She gasps at the ferocity of my kiss. I take advantage of her open mouth to slide my tongue inside her wet warmth. It sweeps around to savor every bit as growls rumble in my throat. I will make the most of the night and the morning.

My tongue coaxes hers to meld with mine. Her sweet taste and soft cries drive me wild. I need more. So much more.

My hands slide down her body to grip the hem of her mini dress. With a flick of my wrists, it lifts and drops to the floor. I step back to admire her beauty. But she brings her hands up in an attempt to cover her bountiful tits. Oh, no. That will never do.

I lean forward and lift her hands away. Then my head lowers to lick her nipples. They're hard as pebbles and as delicious as ripe strawberries. The flat of my tongue laves one while my thumb and forefinger pinch and pull the other.

She mewls as her fingernails dig into my shoulders. Her back bows to present her tits to me for more attention. I oblige and suckle her plump nipples. Hard. She hisses but pulls me closer, eager for more.

My hands cup her round ass and squeeze each cheek. I lift her from her feet, and she wraps her arms around my neck. In one swift move, I toss her to the bed and watch as her tits bounce when she lands sprawled on her back. Wide eyes stare up at me in surprise. I growl and rip at my tie.

My clothes join hers in a pile on the floor. Naked, I stand by the bed staring down at her as my fist grips the base of my turgid cock. I squeeze then glide up, maintaining constant pressure over the thick, long, shaft. The plum-shaped tip drips with pre-cum. I smear it with the pad of my thumb over the head, biting back a groan. My wolf pants, tongue lolling, eyes bright, focused on the beauty.

No need for names.

Only. One. Night.

Braced on her elbows, hooded eyes follow my hand as it strokes my cock. Her lips part as the tip of her tongue slips out.

With a groan, I prowl from the foot of the bed and over her body until my knees bracket her shoulders, forcing her onto her back. My cock bobs in front of her face. Wide eyes stare at its enormity. Her jaw opens and closes. I smirk and fist the base of my cock then tap the tip against her lips. They part on a mewl.

"You will suck me. Every. Single. Inch."

Now, her mouth widens to accept my girth. I watch as my cock disappears inside. It brushes the soft palate, sliding deeper. Her eyes close as she struggles to take all my cock.

"Breathe through your nose. Relax your throat and let me in."

Her eyes pop open to lock with mine. So fucking gorgeous. I cup the back of her head as my cock moves beyond her gag reflex. She blinks and sputters. But I don't stop.

"Take me. All of me."

She nods.

"You're doing so well, beauty. You feel so good sucking my big cock in."

She blinks rapidly as my cock stretches her throat. The impression as it widens her neck makes my balls draw up, ready for release. She hums. The vibration travels along my cock straight to my heavy balls.

With a savage roar, I withdraw then snap my hips forward to plunge back in. She sputters as my movements increase in pace with thrusts and drags along her tongue and down her throat. When her lips kiss my groin, I let loose a torrent of jizz.

She struggles as her fingernails dig into my bulging thighs.

But I hold her firm commanding she breathe and consume every drop. When my hips slow to languid thrusts, releasing the last of my seed into her belly, I cup her face.

"Now, I will fuck your pussy, making you cum until you beg me to stop. Before we part, you will know I fucked you long and hard, ruining you for any other male. Do you understand?"

Her head bobs.

My still hard cock slips free. I swipe the tears from her eyes and lower my mouth to hers for a toe-curling kiss. She clings to me as I swallow her soft cries.

***

Maya

"ONE MORE, baby. Cum for me one more time..."

My well-used pussy spasms at Viggo's barked command. Juices leak past his giant dick buried deep inside my core. Even after hours of having sex, I still cannot believe my pussy stretches to accommodate his size. But the oh so delicious ache confirms it did each and every time. Just as it does now as the morning sun filters through the windows.

We barely slept.

He's like a feral beast who can't get enough. He's had me every which way possible—standing, against the wall, on all fours, planked above, kneeling. Incredible stamina.

I can barely keep up. He has me panting as though I ran the New York Marathon back-to-back three times. My arms ache and thighs burn. Talk about a never-ending workout session!

But this is just what I wanted. Only one night to do as I please before I return to Caracas and to the fate I never wanted. And I plan to leave Miami with a bang!

"Come on, baby..."

I draw on my reserves and tighten my pussy walls

around his dick pounding inside of me. He growls as it throbs and grows larger. The orgasm starts in my toes, zings up my legs, and zaps my pussy. A hoarse scream tears from my sore throat—another hole he's plundered repeatedly. *Ay Dios mío.*

My entire body quakes from the earth-shattering impact. Boneless, I sag on his lap, thighs quivering around his hips.

He bands his arms around me, pressing me closer to his sweat-drenched chest where paw print tattoos mark his pecs. His hips jut up in the last throes of our fucking. He snarls as he cums. His body twitches as he buries his face in the crook of my wet neck.

I'm in a daze until hot cream coats my womb.

"Viggo! The condom! Did… Did it break?"

A feral growl sends shivers down my spine, even as my pussy clenches.

CHAPTER 4

 *iggo*

MY WOLF GROWLS.

He wants to breed her. Issue the claiming bite to initiate her transformation to a she-wolf. Make her his forever.

For a moment, I hold her close as images flip through my mind's eye. Her belly round with my pup. She places my hand on a spot he kicked. Her gorgeous face glows as she smiles up at me. While we frolic in the Everglades with them in our wolf forms. My pup's excited yips as he chases a rabbit across the grass—

"Viggo!"

Fuck.

The images fade replaced by her face only this time it glows from post-coital bliss even if her eyes stare in shock. I have the urge to cover her kiss-swollen lips with mine and drag her beneath me to pound her pussy—

"Viggo! You are not getting hard inside of me right now! *Ay Dios mío…* Let me go!"

Her palms press against my chest as she slides off my lap. She sucks in a breath and winces.

I feel bad for fucking her so hard. But I needed to get her out of my system since we'll never be together again. Unfortunately. I growl and shake my head. Enough! Now, focus.

"—don't believe in it. And then this happens."

I missed the first part of her sentence but don't miss her pointing to our combined juices dripping from her other swollen pussy lips. I bite back a growl as my cock thumps against my eight-pack abs. The head still slick leaks pre-cum through the remnants of the condom.

"Look what your monster dick did"—she gestures at the sheets as she crawls from the bed—"I have to take a shower. Hopefully, I can wash most of it away. I don't think I'm ovulating since I just had my period. Ugh!"

She stands staring at her inner thighs as my seed drips from her pussy. A frown mars her face when she glances up at me. It deepens when I sit entranced by the sight.

"Hey! Up here. You know what? Never mind," she says, then spins on her heel and marches to the en suite bathroom. Her ass jounces with each step. Damn.

I snap out of it when the door shuts behind her. My hand scrubs over my face as I consider the situation.

I've always worn a condom, and it never broke. I have zero experience with this scenario. A she-wolf doesn't get pregnant outside of her heat. Since she's human, I guess the ovulation thing she mentioned prevents her from getting pregnant. We don't have a ton of information on the mating of male wolf shifters and human females for reference. Fuck if I know. I'll take her word for it.

My wolf whines, wanting to join her in the shower. I'm not so sure she'd welcome me. Or the boner I'm sporting.

Besides, now's as good a time as any for the clean break. No pun intended.

I stride to the walk-in closet and throw on a pair of joggers. My cock tents the front, and I will it flaccid. Picking up my mobile, I wonder if she'd like breakfast. We ate before the kitchen closed for the night. But the number of calories burned makes me hungry as fuck. My metabolism is faster than a human. But I'm sure she's famished too.

Even though I want this to end now, I can't let her go without a decent meal. I'm a playboy, not a cad. Plus, she's Wren's friend. And I don't want Wren pissed at me for poor treatment of her.

Decision made, I place an order for delivery then plop on the bed. Nope. Don't want her to come out of the bathroom to find me lounging as though ready for another round. Instead, I sit at the café table by the window and check my messages.

A few minutes later, she emerges wrapped in my robe. She's tall but slight. The damn thing engulfs her with the belt around her waist twice. I hate to admit it, but she looks good in my clothes. I wouldn't mind her in the shirt she tosses on a chair as she searches for her mini dress. Her dress?

"Hey, I um… ordered breakfast. It'll be here in ten minutes. Afterwards, I can give you a ride home."

She shakes her head and tendrils of jet black hair slip from the topknot. They frame her face flushed rosy from the steam of the shower.

Again, I have the urge to cover both pairs of her swollen lips with my mouth and take her back to bed. My wolf and cock agree as both spring to stand tall.

"No. But thank you. I need to get home. It's not far. I'll get another Uber," she says as she unwinds the belt. I watch as she shrugs out of the robe and slips the dress over her head. It covers her glorious body from my hungry gaze.

My wolf whines. I groan.

She glances at me and cocks her head.

"You sure do make a lot of animalistic noises," she says, then adds. "Not that I mind."

The rosy glow on her cheeks deepen to crimson, and she ducks her head. She picks up her sandals and sits on the edge of the bed to slip them on her feet. She bends her knee, and I catch a glimpse and whiff of her pussy.

Fresh arousal greets my nostrils. I inhale deeply, hoping to imprint the tantalizing aroma along with the frangipani and coconuts on my mind. An indelible reminder of my fated mate, who will never be mine. My eyes close with a deep inhalation.

"Viggo?"

My eyes open as I exhale.

"I'm ready and the Uber will be here in three minutes. Will I be able to unlock the door to the club?"

I shake my head to clear it as I rise.

"No. I'll walk you out."

We walk through the empty club in silence. I demand my wolf back down as he paces and snarls. I don't need him to act up now. We're almost in the clear. A peek at her reveals a stoic expression on her face. Thankfully, she's not still upset about the condom.

I unlock the door and gesture her ahead of me. She pauses and glances at my face.

"Well, thank you for a lovely time, Viggo. Goodbye."

My heart constricts at the finality of her words. As the air rushes from my lungs, I cover the spot on my chest with a hand. I blink and nod, unable to speak.

She peers into my eyes for a second before she walks to the Uber.

I watch as the SUV pulls onto Ocean Drive. As it makes a U-turn, she raises her hand in farewell. Pain laces through me, and I lean against the doorframe. My head hangs as my wolf throws his back for a mournful howl.

~

MAYA

"WHAT ARE the chances of me getting pregnant after a condom broke and I'm not ovulating?"

I hold my breath as I await an answer from Dr. Carmela Fuentes, my gynecologist. She knows I don't believe in birth control since they use synthetic hormones, and I put nothing in my body that's unnatural. Call me an extreme health nut all you want.

It's not like I've had many lovers. Viggo is only the second, and it's been over a year. So, no need for anything beyond a condom. Who knew his massive cock would break it? Aargh!

"Maya, it can still happen. You know my recommendation—"

"No. Okay, so I'll just have to wait and see. I truly doubt it, not that I'm an expert. Kindly email my medical records to my gynecologist in Caracas. Thank you, Dr. Fuentes."

I end the call and lean back against the chaise lounge on my terrace. The Atlantic Ocean spreads out before me. Its turquoise water sparkles like diamonds in the morning light. Jet skiers zip by and megayachts cruise along while a parasail carries a couple above its surface. I inhale and relax on the exhale.

Only a few days remain before I leave Miami. I refuse to spend my precious time worrying about anything, including the potential of a pregnancy. I have other things to focus on. Over the next few hours, I call my clients, cancel other appointments, and organize my move with Idania—my mother's personal assistant.

By the time I finish, I need to go for a run to clear my head. After I change into a crop top with matching shorts and sneakers, I pull my hair into a ponytail and attach my mobile to the armband. Popping earbuds in, I head for the beach.

The balmy breeze from the Atlantic Ocean does little to ease the warm rays of the sun. But I don't mind. I love the Miami weather. Hell, I love everything about my adopted city. I let my mind wander as I run along Ocean Drive. Then Club Hati comes into view.

My eyes lift to the windows where I guess Viggo's suite is based on the times he fucked me against the wall of glass. I bite my lower lip as a moan erupts from my throat. Despite the heat, my nipples pucker beneath my sports bra. I dash by the club. Better to put it all behind me.

However, my mind disagrees. It replays the hours we shared. Sure, we had lots of sex. But a few intimate moments took place between us. When food arrived from the kitchen, he sat me on his lap at the café table and hand fed me bits of steak. I balked. But he had none of it. I moan as I recall how he swatted my butt when I wrapped my tongue around the asparagus spear like it was his dick. Later, he recreated the scene, much to my delight. His cock is as beautiful and tasty as it is large.

He's a work of art—all sculpted lean muscle, long legs, sizable hands, handsome face, captivating ice blue eyes. Man, oh man, is Viggo Larson H-O-T.

Too bad we don't have a chance.

The thought is like ice water dumped over my heated body. I gasp and stop, placing my hands on my knees to catch my breath. I didn't think he'd have such an impact on me and would be the perfect one-night stand for a last hurrah. But I can't stop thinking about him even while focused on my calls or while running. He's gotten under my skin.

Call from Wren Byrd.

In my ear, the disembodied voice of my mobile announces the call from my bestie. How apropos.

"Hey, chica!"

"Hey, nothing, missy. What happened last night?"

Good grief. My bestie's radar is on full alert. Since I hadn't heard from her after she gave me the side-eye last night, I figured she'd forgotten about the heated exchange between Viggo and me. Guessed wrong. Plus, I have to tell her the day has come for me to return to Caracas.

"We need more than a phone call for this convo. It requires a face-to-face. How about I come to your new place with Tag?"

Wren pauses.

I've noticed she's always hesitant for me to come to Moon Island, where Tag has a beachfront mansion. It's a super exclusive private island in Biscayne Bay, across from South Beach. I've only gotten glimpses of it as I drive by the wrought-iron gates with a security booth off the MacArthur Causeway. I'd love a chance to see it before I leave. But her response nixes it as usual. I'll have to ask her why the secrecy.

"How about I come by your place in an hour? I'll bring some of your favorite snacks. We'll drink mojitos while you tell me everything. And I mean every single detail. Good?"

"Fine, Secret Squirrel. But in exchange, you'll have to tell me why you block me from Moon Island."

She's silent a moment, then responds, "See you soon, chica!"

I shake my head as I end the call and check the time. An hour gives me time to finish my run and shower before Wren arrives. I cast a last glance at the third-floor windows of Club Hati. With a sigh, I jog away.

An hour later, Wren and I sit on my terrace. A frosty mojito pitcher and a tasty variety of finger foods—including my favorite Cuban beef patties and grilled shrimp kabobs—sit on the table between us. The second I finish my first bite of an empanada, she pounces.

"So, what happened?"

I stall for time with a sip of my drink. She's my bestie, so I have no problem sharing. Well, aside from the exact details of Viggo using the flat of his tongue to make me cum so hard I saw stars before I blacked out...

"First, I have some bad news."

She gasps as wide eyes scan my neck.

"Viggo didn't bi—I mean hurt you, did he? I wasn't going to say anything. But his scent is all over you!"

I blink, confused.

"What do you mean? I showered twice since I left him. How do you smell him on me?" I ask as I lift my t-shirt for a sniff. "I only smell my citrus bodywash. Are you sure?"

Her cheeks flush scarlet as she shakes her head. Her mahogany hair forms a curtain, blocking her face from my questioning stare. She mumbles a response then speaks louder when I huff.

"I don't know. Maybe his cologne lingers in your hair or something? Never mind that. Tell me the bad news. You're scaring me."

"My parents called yesterday to demand I return to Caracas for the arranged marriage. I leave in a few days. It's terrible!"

"No! You can't go! I thought they changed their minds since your birthday passed months ago. Can't we do something to dissuade them? Look what happened with Jonathan and me until Tag came along. Don't let them force you to marry someone you don't love, let alone even know. It's unfair and cruel!"

Tears well in my eyes as my best friend offers suggestions to change their minds. But I've always known I'd have an arranged marriage. It's just the way it works in our circle, no different from Wren's. She was lucky to meet Tag before she made the mistake of marrying that *tramposo* Jonathan and went against her uncle's arrangement. I see nothing that can help me. I'm pretty resigned.

"It's okay, Wren. But you have to promise to visit me. And I'll fly up a few times a year. We can still be besties, even long distance," I say with a forced smile. No point in ruining our last few days together. "Now, let me tell you about that hottie, Viggo Larson. He reminds me of those sexy Vikings from the TV shows. Boy, oh, boy!"

Her frown changes into a smile as she giggles at me, fanning my face. She listens intently as I give her the deets. Her eyes widen when I tell her about the animalistic noises he made and how his eyes flashed silver. From time to time, her gaze flicks to my neck. When I ask why, she waves her hands and tells me to continue. I shrug and finish with the broken condom.

"What?!?!?! You're not on birth control, and I doubt you'll take emergency contraceptives."

"Don't worry. I just finished my period. No ovulation, no pregnancy. I'm glad my last Miami hurrah was with Viggo. Too bad we hadn't hooked up when you first met Tag. If I'd known Viggo is his best friend, we would have gone on double dates! But I'm grateful and a firm believer in things happen when they should. Now, let's get drunk!"

CHAPTER 5

 *iggo*

Thank you, Miami, for being such an amazing part of my life for the past eight years! I'll miss you! Adiós!

My heart skips a beat.

Maya's gorgeous face stares at me from my tablet.

As has become my habit over the last few days, I stalk her social media posts. My mind wouldn't stop thinking about her. So, I checked Wren's feed, found the link to her best friend, and learned her name.

Maya Alejandra Perez Garcia.

I devoured each post, wanting to learn all I could about the beauty. A former fitness model turned personal trainer. No wonder she has such a banging body. My wolf growls at images of her with male clients, especially when she touches them.

However, seeing her soothes my wolf and gives me a reprieve from his constant whining and snarling. Sure, I want to howl too. But I believe it's best we stay apart. The risk to Maya is too great even if I ache to be with her. So far, losing myself in her social media staves off any sign of madness.

But this latest video nearly undoes me.

I only caught the end of her live stream, so it stops in moments. The only clues I have to her whereabouts is the area around her as she spins, holding the camera up for a selfie. She's on the beach, close to Club Hati.

I don't need my wolf's urging to race from my beach-front penthouse further up Ocean Drive. Once I hit the street, my pace slows to avoid stares at my superhuman speed. As the breeze enters my nose, I scent the air to pinpoint her location.

Unfortunately, it's a busy Saturday with throngs of tourists and locals. They stroll along on the sidewalks and blanket the beach. I zip around them until I get to the spot I guess she stood. Only a trace of coconuts and frangipani lingers amongst the other scents.

My eyes dart about, frantic to find Maya. I don't spot a female in a white tank top and leggings amongst the myriad of other beachgoers or on the sidewalk. It didn't take me but ten minutes. But it's enough time for her to disappear.

With a frustrated growl, I storm back to my condo. All is a blur until I reach the garage and bump into a male wolf shifter.

The Miami Pack owns the forty-story building for unmated males to live if they don't live on Moon Island with the rest of the pack. It's our principal residence where Jagger, Tag, Dylan, and my parents with Signy have mansions. Not too long ago, Rust lived on the top floor since he's older than me. My penthouse takes up the one below his former pad.

The male takes one look at me and throws his hands up

as he bares his neck in submission. I grumble an apology and stalk to my Ducati. The motorcycle engine revs and the back wheel screeches as I drive out of the garage.

I head to Moon Island, where I expect to get answers from Wren. She'll know what the hell Maya's talking about. I zig and zag my way along Collins Avenue to the causeway. Minutes later, I turn off the causeway and pull up to the intricate wrought-iron gates—the entrance to Moon Island. Two members of the security team sit in a guardhouse. They recognize me and wave as the gates open. I nod and rev the engine, eager to pass through.

I make a beeline for Tag's home, ignoring the posh residences ranging from ranch style to two- and three-story along the main road. I pull into the driveway of his grand Mediterranean Revival style mansion on Biscayne Bay. Turning off the engine, I hop off the bike and jog to the glass and metalwork double doors. The doorbell chimes, and I pace, waiting for Tag to open them.

"Where's Wren?"

"The fuck you mean, 'where's Wren?' What do you want with my mate?"

He snarls as his emerald green eyes flash with his wolf just below the surface. An inch taller than me and bulkier, he puffs up his chest possessively.

I'm already on edge and curl my lip, baring my fangs.

"Hold on there, boys! Play nice."

Wren steps between us with her arms outstretched. She flicks her gaze from one to the other. My expression gives her pause.

"Did something happen with Maya?"

Tag frowns and sniffs the air. Then a sly grin spreads across his face as his eyes gleam with mirth.

"Let me guess… You finally met your match, playboy!"

He guffaws while I growl.

"To answer you, Wren, nothing happened aside from the other night. But I need to know what she's talking about in her live video."

Wren nods and gestures for me to follow her into the house. Tag brings up the rear, still chuckling. Fucker.

"Let me see what Maya posted first," she says as she sits on the sofa and picks up her mobile. She nods as she listens to the entire post.

My heart clenches anew.

Maya left for the airport.

"Where is she going? I—I want to say goodbye."

Wren shakes her head as she stares at me. Pity fills her eyes.

"Why not?" I demand, wolf bristling.

"Easy, bro. Watch your tone with Wren."

"It's okay, Tag," she says, then turns to face me. "What is Maya to you, a one-night stand or something more?"

I shrug, trying to make light of it before I respond.

"I'm not sure. We had a good time. It's just weird she didn't mention leaving. Where is she going?"

Wren studies my face. I put on what I hope translates to a nonchalant expression even while my wolf rages inside. Wren sighs.

"Well then, it shouldn't matter to you, and you came all this way for nothing, Viggo," she says with an arched eyebrow. Her challenging expression lets me know she sees right through my facade.

"Fine. She may be my fated mate. At least her unique scent and my wolf's reaction make me wonder."

Wren gasps and covers her mouth with her hand.

"Oh, no! I mean, that's good. But..."

She trails off, and I jump to my feet.

"But what, Wren? Tell me!"

Tag growls and leaps to his feet. He pushes me back onto

the chair and hovers over me with fangs extended and eyes feral. I glare back with a snarl.

"I want answers! No more hemming and hawing."

"Okay, okay. You're right, Viggo. If Maya may be your fated mate, you deserve to know the truth. Tag, baby, please sit. You'd act the same way if you needed information about me."

Tag narrows his eyes at me, but his wolf returns to the depths of his being. He pivots and sits beside Wren, taking her hand in his.

She kisses his cheek, and he smiles down at her. Their obvious love makes me ache for Maya even more. I close my eyes as my hand rubs my chest.

"Viggo, don't go berserk."

My eyes pop open as alarms ring in my head. This will not be good. I can sense it but nod, wanting answers.

"Maya is from an extremely wealthy family that arranged for her to marry a—"

A bestial roar splits the air. It reverberates around the living room.

My vision reddens as my wolf surges to the forefront. The sensations of my bones reshaping and muscles lengthening to shift me from my human form to that of my great red wolf block out all else. Crackling and a flash find me on all four massive paws within moments. Ignoring Tag and Wren's cries to stop, my beast runs for the open sliding glass doors. He bounds onto the deck, over the side, and lands on the grass before racing to the center of the island.

Another perk of our private island provides is a safe place for members of the pack to run in wolf form unencumbered. We run as a full pack in the Everglades a few times a month. The vast expanse and relative safety the subtropical wilderness offers makes an ideal setting for our numbers.

However, now, the island's oasis calls to me. I need to outrun the pain in my chest and the frustration in my mind. My fated mate is bound for another. Flying to another male's arms. A forlorn howl pours from my throat.

I run past fragrant gardenia and jasmine bushes. Their floral scents fill my nose. But don't mask the unique scent of Maya. I can never forget it. With a snort, I dash between some palm trees.

Glimpses of other pack members in wolf form appear amongst the foliage. Not wanting to interact, I increase my speed and head towards the other end of Moon Island. I run for what seems hours. A normal wolf would have tired by then, muscles strained to capacity. As a wolf shifter, my body heals quickly unless silver is involved. Then it can be fatal.

I drag my weary body back to Tag and Wren's deck. My best friend rises from a chair and holds a t-shirt and a pair of joggers in his hand. Gone is the possessive anger in his face, replaced by concern. Unfortunately, the pain in my heart doesn't abate as I shift and put on the clothes. Not that I mind being in the buff. Another distinction between shifters of any kind and humans, nudity is natural. But Tag doesn't want my ass out with Wren nearby.

I run my fingers through my wild hair and drop onto the chair next to his. He hands a tumbler filled with amber liquid to me. I toss it back in one gulp then refill it from the decanter on the table. Downing that one, I pour another and lean forward with my elbows on my thighs and my head hanging. I twirl the tumbler and watch the sunset as prisms in the crystal.

Tag sips his Scotch in silence, giving me the time I need.

"Here's to not wanting a fated mate to having one for a night then losing her to another," I say as I raise my glass in a mock toast. "But you know what? It's for the best. She's a human, and I will not risk her life with the transformation into a she-wolf."

Tag cocks his head and pins me with an intense stare.

"You do realize Wren was a human female before I claimed her, right? So, why can't you do the same with Maya?"

"It would kill me if something happened to her. You know that woman the male wolf shifter turned all those years ago died?"

"And the wolf madness that overtook him? What about that?"

"Well, I'll just have to wait and see."

~

MAYA

"WE'LL LAND in just over three hours, *Señorita* Maya. Would you care for a beverage before we take off?"

"No, thank you. Once we're airborne, I'll have some water and a light meal."

The flight attendant bows his head and returns to the crew compartment.

My parents sent one of their private jets to deliver me back to Caracas. I left Idania to finish up the loose ends in Miami. She'll return on a commercial flight in a few days even though I offered to wait. But my parents insisted I return immediately. They probably think I'll run away. I wish I could.

With a sigh, I stare out the window as the jet taxis to an airstrip of Miami International Airport. I can't believe I'll be in Venezuela in a short while. I'd hoped this day would never come. However, I knew it would. What I didn't expect was to miss not only the city I've called my second home but the man who I can't stop thinking about. The one-nighter I thought would end in hours still dominates my thoughts days later.

I haven't heard from him. I'd figured he may try to reach me through Wren. But he didn't. No word. Not a peep. He didn't even show up to my going away party Wren threw for me at Sol Beach Club last night. So, I guess I was just another night's fuck for him. Well, it's what I wanted. But why does my heart ache and my head swivel to watch Miami drop away through gray clouds?

Once it's obscured by the stormy fluff, I lean back in the plush leather chair. My eyes close as tears flow down my cheeks like raindrops from the clouds in the surrounding sky.

CHAPTER 6

aya

"I KNOW this is your engagement party. But I still don't understand why you don't want to wear the white gown I picked for you. This dress is lovely on you. Why wouldn't you want to wear white, Maya?"

My mother frets about me as I stand in the living room of my parents' penthouse in the Los Palos Grandes neighborhood. It has a view of Waraira Repano National Park. Seeing it reminds me of the dream I had with Viggo shifting from a wolf into a man.

Weirdly, my dreams of him have only increased over these past two weeks since I left Miami. Many nights I awake from the intensity of an orgasm as I cry out his name. The sheets tangle around my sweat-drenched body as they cling to me while my heart beats against my ribs. My eyes open to the empty bedroom of my apartment and not to

Viggo's handsome face above me. My heart and body ache for my Viking lover.

Even now, a flush creeps from my breast to my cheeks.

I shake my head to clear it before I face my mother. The gold lamé gown swirls around my ankles. The draped origami folds turn back to reveal the length of my legs while the strapless top and open back show off my toned arms and back. Black stilettos and clutch complete my look.

Why should I wear white when the gold complements my skin better? Who cares about it being for my engagement party? I'll wear what I please to have some control over the night.

"*Mamá*, I prefer this dress. But thank you for your thoughtfulness."

"You do, *cariño*. Emerico will be proud," my father says as he and my brothers stride into the living room. "He's on his way up now."

I avert my gaze as he kisses my cheek. For a moment, my heart constricts and my breathing falters. I fear a panic attack will drop me to the floor. A gasp escapes my parted lips, and I cling to my father's forearms to steady myself on legs that threaten to give out.

"Are you all right?"

In response to Patricio's question, I nod my head, not trusting my voice. I sense his gaze as he studies my face. We're closer than I am to Odalis. So, I know better than to return Patricio's stare. He'll see right through me.

"*Señor* Emerico Tonio Santana Rodriguez."

My stomach flips as the butler announces my intended fiancé's arrival. A business trip kept him away until now. I press a hand over my belly to will away the distress. I suck in a breath then give myself a silent pep talk and send a prayer for strength to get through this farce of a marriage.

"Emerico! Here's your blushing bride!"

My father grins wider than the Cheshire Cat as he holds my elbow and turns to face Emerico. His brown eyes assess me from head to toe. Under his scrutiny, my back straightens, and I lift my chin. *You can do this, Maya!*

"A pleasure to meet you at last, Maya. How stunning you are."

He extends his hands as he approaches me. I guess he's six feet tall since I have an inch on him in my stilettos. When his lips press to my cheeks, I fight the urge to recoil. His warm breath laced with cinnamon makes my stomach churn. I bite back a gag and paste a smile on my face.

"The pleasure is mine, Emerico," I manage, without a hitch in my voice.

He turns to my parents and brothers to shake their hands and to kiss my mother's cheeks. I watch as she fawns over him, and the men grin. My stomach roils again.

"Maya, may I have a word with you on the terrace?"

I swallow back bile knowing he's going to propose so I'll have the engagement ring on before we leave for the party. Hundreds of guests gather in the hotel's ballroom, eager to congratulate us. The official press release goes out in the morning. Soon photos of the happy couple will splash across websites, newspapers, and magazines. *Vogue* plans a cover feature to follow me from the engagement party through the wedding day. Designers vie to dress me. I couldn't care less.

Drawing on my strength, I nod and place my hand on his offered forearm. I catch my mother smiling up at my father with tears in her eyes. Great…

Emerico closes the glass sliding door behind us and leads me to the table, where he helps me into a chair. I smile my thanks and adjust my gown. His gaze drops to my legs and travels up to the top of the slit. I cringe and cross my legs, placing my hands on the dress to keep it closed. He frowns and settles in the chair next to me.

"Maya, we may not know one another. But I want to assure you I will treat you with the utmost respect, care for you, and support you in the means you're accustomed to as a woman of your standing. In return, I require your respect, faithfulness, and for you to bear my heirs. You will want for nothing. Do you understand?"

I swallow back a retort and agree. No use in prolonging the inevitable. And on cue, he removes a navy blue velvet box from his tuxedo jacket pocket. Tears well in my eyes, not from joy. Rather from a profound sadness that sucks the air from my lungs. Once again, I press a hand to my belly and breathe deeply to invoke calm in my body.

"Don't cry, *bella*," he says, mistaking the tears leaking from my eyes for happiness. He hands a handkerchief to me and waits while I dab my eyes.

I want to throw myself on the floor and bawl. But I suck it up. *Get it over with, Maya.*

He reaches for my left hand and slides the pear cut diamond ring on my finger. It's loose, but he smiles.

"We'll get it sized tomorrow. Tonight, I want all to see you belong to me, Maya Alejandra Perez Garcia."

He leans over and presses his mouth to mine.

I can't open it for fear I'll vomit. So, I make a smacking noise and lean back in the chair, using the excuse of wiping tears from my eyes. He grins and stands.

"Come, *bella*, let us celebrate our union," he says as he extends his arm.

I can only nod as I loop my arm through his.

My family cheers when we re-enter the living room. My mother oohs and aahs over the ring. It's gorgeous, but from the wrong man. I can only think of Viggo and what it would be like to marry him. An arm around my waist draws me from my musings. I glance up to find my second oldest brother.

Patricio pulls me aside.

"Is this what you truly want, Maya?"

Topaz eyes so like mine stare down at me as he searches my face for the answer. It's no use in going back now. So, I force a smile on my face and nod.

"All will be well, brother of mine. Thank you."

He studies me for a moment longer. Then Emerico calls to me. I smile once more at my brother and move to my fiancé's side.

"This is the start of a beautiful partnership between our families. Let us enjoy this night and many more to come!"

My head bows as I swallow a sob while the others cheer.

It is done.

~

Viggo

"Oh, Viggo! Yes. Yes. Yes!"

I pound into Maya as she writhes beneath me, screaming my name. Her forehead rests on the silk sheets with her delectable ass up high gripped between my hands. I stare as my cock thrusts in and out of her hot, slick pussy, stretching it to a gaping hole I want to explore.

Her pussy walls clamp onto my cock like a vise, eliciting a feral growl from the depths of my soul.

"Who's pussy is this?! Who do you belong to?!"

I snarl as each thrust drives her deeper into the mattress.

She keens with another toe-curling orgasm. Her pussy milks my cock, demanding me to fill her womb with my seed.

Not yet.

"I will not cum until you give me three more orgasms. Starting. Right. Now!"

I emphasize each word with a forceful thrust. My balls slap her ass as my tip strikes her G-spot.

She screams for no more, even as she rocks her ass back against my groin.

"You're a contradiction, little girl. Do you want this or not?!"

"*Ay Dios mío! Sí! Sí! Sí!*"

Her wail as she cums hard stiffens my cock. But I refuse to give her my knot to prepare for my seed to fill her womb and make her belly round with my pup.

"Two. More!"

She pants and claws at the sheets. The silk rips as she tosses her head side to side. Desperate moans pour from her slack mouth.

"Viggo! Please!"

One hand slides around her hip to cup her bare mons. Two fingers delve inside while my thumb circles her clit. When I pinch the sensitive bud, she clenches her pussy walls as her back bows.

"There's my good girl. One. More! Do you want my seed to coat your womb or not?!"

Her head bobs as she pants. Then she yelps when my palm connects with her ass for a resounding spank.

"Words, little girl! I will have your words!"

"*Sí!*"

I growl barbarically as she strangles my engorged cock. My balls fill with seed as the tingle lurking at the base of my spine becomes an electric bolt of lightning. It wends its way to my balls, along my cock initiating my knot, and zaps the tip to release a copious amount of my seed deep within her womb.

"Only. Mine. Forever!"

I bark in her ear as my knot locks her to me. Hot, creamy seed bursts forth to create my pup inside my fated mate. My hips continue to piston as her pussy milks my cock for every single drop. When I have no more to give, I collapse on top of her, pushing her to spread out on the bed.

The weight of my body covers her as my face buries in her neck. My fangs extend with serum dripping from them. I push her sweat-dampened hair aside and clamp down on the juncture of her neck and shoulder, issuing my claiming bite. She will bear my scent and transform into a she-wolf. Mine for all time.

Still locked together by my knot, I roll us to our sides and envelop her with my body. One hand cups a tit and the other her mons. With my face buried in her hair, I let sleep take me.

The ringing of my mobile awakes me from yet another dream about Maya. I groan when I realize it's a wet dream as jizz pools on the body pillow I'm wrapped around and on the tangled sheets. Great. Now, I've reverted to a randy teenage male. I scrub a hand over my face as I turn off the alarm on my mobile.

I cast a longing glance at the silver-framed photos of her on the nightstand. In one shot, she's on the beach in a white bikini. She's radiant as the sun shines on her glistening golden skin and her topaz eyes sparkle. She's laughing at the person holding the camera. My wolf growls as I wonder for the hundredth time if a male captured her beauty.

I turn to the pillow beside mine, where I placed a copy of the selfie she took one morning when she awoke in her bed. I never understood why people posted such images on their social media for all the world to see a private moment. But I'm damned glad Maya posted one. Her tousled jet black hair fans around her head as sleepy eyes stare up at the camera. Her full lips curve into a secret smile. Again, my wolf growls. Who the hell put that sated look on her face?

Two weeks of nightly dreams starring Maya and surrounding myself with her images do nothing to ease the constant ache in my chest. I drop back onto the pillows and unlock my mobile. A photo of Maya in a flexy-bendy yoga pose greets me as my wallpaper. I study the lines of her body in the white unitard. Long, toned, curves in all the right places. I groan as my cock thickens and lengthens. I give it a few strokes to ease the ache before I check the Google alerts I set to track her name over the Internet. If any news bears her name, I'll know all about it in moments.

Stalker much? Hell, yeah. She's my obsession. And I don't give a damn.

If I can't have her, I will know what she's up to.

Wren gave me the rest of the story about the arranged marriage and return to Caracas. I had my guy run an extensive background check on the fucker she's engaged to. No red flags. But I monitor him too. If he hurts her, I'll rip his throat out with my fangs and eat his heart straight from his chest. I can't have Maya. But I'll be damned if I let anyone hurt her.

No recent news on the alerts.

I close my eyes a moment and let my mind replay the latest dream. If only she were here beside me, sated and cuddled in my arms. My wolf whines. He's inconsolable. But I ignore him for the greater good. No harm to Maya.

After a while, I roll out of bed and stride to the en suite for a shower. Time to face a new day. Without my fated mate.

"Brother, you look like shit."

"Yeah, Viggo. Not getting much sleep?"

I roll my eyes at Jagger and Tag as I lower into a seat at the table on the executive floor of Larson Enterprises. It's time for the weekly division update meeting. We're the first ones in the conference room. Now, I wish I wasn't trying so hard to be taken seriously and arrived last. Anything to avoid my older brother and best friend's stares.

"Tag told me about Maya. My question is why didn't you come to me first?"

I shrug and spin my pen on the table's sleek surface. Tag wouldn't have known if I didn't have to ask Wren for answers. With my brother and our best friends mated, I prefer not to go into the details of my current abysmal love life. Best to stick with the stalking than to have in-depth discussions and Jagger putting the kibosh on it.

"Not an answer, Viggo. I'm asking as your older brother, not as your Alpha. Talk to me. I'll help."

I glance over at him as I consider his offer. He knows what it's like to lose his fated mate, even if he didn't remember until years later. I check my watch. We have ten minutes before the others arrive. I spill the whole sorry tale.

"Damn. That's a tough one. But you realize she may survive the claiming bite and transition. Isn't it better to try than to lose her forever?"

"I told him the same thing," Tag adds. "Look at Wren. She's adjusted just fine. But I understand your concern. Hell, I nearly lost my mind waiting for her to awaken from the transition."

I pause to consider since it's getting harder to be apart from Maya knowing she's with another male who plans to marry her. Then I shake my head.

"She doesn't know what she is to me, and it's better to keep it that way. Let her live her life. Better only I suffer than something happens to her—"

"Or she rejects you."

My eyes widen at Jagger's comment. Could that be it too? There's a chance she won't accept me as a wolf shifter.

Freak out at the enormity of the situation. Then I'd have to ask Sage to wipe Maya's mind so she can't tell other humans about us. That would be a major catastrophe for not only wolf shifters but other paranormals. Humans would hunt us down for science and drive us into extinction.

I shudder at the thought.

"Maybe. But I won't have to worry about that now, will I?"

Jagger doesn't have time to answer since the doors open and the heads of divisions walk in. He and Tag eye me for a moment before he starts the meeting.

I sigh in relief.

I dodged a bullet… A silver bullet.

iggo

"You know you should have spoken to me about Maya. I'm a female and can give you my perspective better than your boys. What do they know about how a female feels? They can only comment on secondhand info and what they think is the case. Now, tell me everything from the beginning. Correction, not the sex part. Leave all of that out, thank you very much. Eeew!"

As bad as I feel, I can't help but to chuckle at my younger sister's expression as she puts a hand over her mouth and gags. The sun glints off her oversized shades as she shakes her head and wrinkles her nose.

We're at Sol Beach Club on South Beach—another of Larson Enterprises' properties under my purview. It's across the street from Club Sol & Mani South Beach, the flagship of six exclusive, luxury, members only BDSM clubs for wolf shifters. The beach club is an extension of it but also caters to humans and other paranormals.

It's Saturday, so Signy insisted I *quit moping at home and hang out* with her for the day. She showed up at my penthouse and waited while I got ready. Now, we sit cross-legged on the raised sunbed in our cabana. The white canvas curtains remain tied to the four posts for an unobstructed view of the azure waters of the Atlantic Ocean as it stretches to the horizon. A teak table with eight white canvas and teak chairs stands at the foot of the sunbed, where we'll eat lunch later.

It's a busy morning with the other cabanas, low sunbeds, and chaise lounges occupied. Most people opt to keep the umbrellas closed to take advantage of the warm sun. Their colorful bikinis and board shorts add to the tropical atmosphere. Sun glistens on oiled skin or dries the droplets from a dip in the water. Still others sit at the restaurant and bar for brunch.

Sol Beach Cub South Beach proves another of my successes for our family's company.

I take a deep breath and inhale the saltwater breeze. It bears no resemblance to Maya's unique scent. But it still reminds me of her. With a sigh, I face Signy and tell her what happened, leaving out the sex and, of course, the stalking.

"Oh, Viggo. You should give Maya the chance to decide what she wants to do. You can't make such a decision one-sided. It impacts both of your lives."

I run a hand through the length of my hair, loose from the bun. A tug to the ends pricks my scalp and clears my head.

Everyone keeps telling me the same thing. Was I wrong in letting Maya go without revealing what I am, who we are to one another, and letting her decide the course she wants her life to take? Is it too late? What the hell should I do now?

As though sensing my thoughts, Signy places a hand on my arm. She takes her sunglasses off to stare into my eyes. Like Jagger and me, she has the Larson trait of ice blue eyes. Hers show concern as she speaks.

"Viggo, it's never too late to go after the one you love. And Maya is your fated mate. You know it's true, so stop trying to deny it. She's not married yet and deserves the right to know what fate plans for her."

She squeezes my arm and smiles.

"You can thank me later. Now, let's go for a swim. Last one in is a rotten egg!"

She leaps from the sunbed with the grace of a she-wolf and races for the water. Sand flies with each step. Males turn to stare as she zips by in a white bikini, all long legs with waist-length black hair flying behind her, and giggles in her wake.

I glare at them as I chase after her. They flinch at the ferocity. The wolf shifters don't dare to challenge me. Humans lower their eyes. No fucker is good enough for my baby sister! The males who come to court her will face Jagger and me first, not to mention Tag, Dylan, and Rust. Good luck, suckers.

I catch Signy up by the waist and wade into the water. She squeals and flails her arms when I throw her into a wave. She reemerges spluttering as she wipes her eyes. I chuckle and dive in. She jumps on me and pushes me further beneath the surface. We tussle like we did as kids when she was more tomboy than glamour girl. It's fun to let loose with my little sister.

We go for a swim then float on our backs, staring up at the cloudless blue sky. My ears pick up the chatter of human females around us.

"He's so tall."

"Damn, he's sexy AF!"

"I wonder if they're a couple."

"Get a look at what he's packing in those board shorts. Oh!"

I close my eyes and roll over to swim away from them. Not too long ago, I'd have flirted with the females and fucked them all if they were game. Now, no interest whatsoever. Only one woman will do for me. And I'm still not convinced I can have her.

"Hey, let's get some Jet Skis. I'll race you," I say to Signy as I swim up to her.

She grins, and we swim to the water sports section. A male who's a pack bachelor recognizes us and rushes to help. His eyes zoom in on Signy. I growl low in my chest. He bows his head in deference to the pack prince and princess. Signy rolls her eyes at me and sashays to the life vests as she giggles. We gear up and hop onto the Jet Skis.

We zip along the shore, going north to Mid-Beach, then south past South Beach to Fisher Island and back. Signy makes figure eights, and I skim over their wakes. We spot a few sea turtles and a pod of dolphins. Boaters wave as we go by. Once we return to the beach, we decide it's time for lunch.

After quick showers to rinse off the saltwater, we sit at the table in front of our cabana. A server comes by and takes our orders of grilled seafood and French fries. We laugh and talk while we sip mojitos.

"Now, the party can get started!"

"Make way!"

We glance up to find our brother, Sage, Tag, Wren, Rust, Natalie, Dylan, and Sasha approaching. They wave, and I turn to Signy. She grins and winks.

"You didn't think I'd leave them out of your Stop Moping Day, did you?"

I chuckle as Dylan drags me from my seat and lifts me in a bear hug. The MMA fighter laughs.

"Feeling better after your baby sister had to cheer you up?"

I grab him in a headlock, and we tussle. Jagger, Tag, and Rust pile on until we're rolling around in the sand. The girls shout for them to stop teasing me and being bullies. Didn't I mention they love me the most?

When I break free, I give them hugs and swing them in the air despite growls from their mates. We settle at the table with Rust and Natalie on the edge of the sunbed. The server appears with platters of food instead of the plates I expected. Obviously, they planned this. We dig in and enjoy each other's company for the rest of the day, then change and party at Club Hati later that night.

The next morning, I awake to my usual routine—roll over and smile at Pillow Maya, sit up and study her photos on the nightstand, then open my email for Google alerts.

The joyful reprieve from the day before dissipates.

Maya Alejandra Perez Garcia Engaged to Emerico Tonio Santana Rodriguez

The Ultimate Merger of a Petroleum Conglomerate

Emerico Tonio Santana Rodriguez Claims the Prized Caraquenian Socialite Maya Alejandra Perez Garcia

Maya Alejandra Perez Garcia Is All Smiles For Her New Fiancé

I click dozens of headlines. As each article blathers on about the happy couple, my wolf's rage increases. My skin feels too tight and can't contain him. I will him to stand down. I won't have another break like I did at Tag's mansion. Taking a deep breath, I return to the websites and study Maya's face for any sign she truly wants the fucker.

Even though she smiles, her eyes remain distant. The closer I look, I notice her body language speaks louder than the headlines. He may have his arm around her waist—*grrrr* —but she angles away from him. In another photo, her hand rests stiffly on his arm. Yet in another where they dance, the camera catches a frown on her face hidden from his view. She's not the glowing bride-to-be the articles profess.

Signy's words come back to mind: *She's not married yet and deserves the right to know what fate plans for her.*

And she will.

~

MAYA

"OH, Maya! Look at all the coverage of your engagement party! It's international news, darling! Your father is so pleased. Our stock increased overnight in anticipation of the merger with Emerico's company…"

Roaring in my ears drown out my mother's voice as she goes on and on. The tablet she placed in front of me on the breakfast table blurs, then all goes dark.

"—passed out. I don't know what happened. Perhaps it's nerves?"

I crack one eye open despite my head beating like a bass drum. The pale yellow walls with paintings hung on them let me know I'm on the sofa in my mother's sitting room. A servant must have carried me here. I groan as a wave of nausea hits me.

"She's awake. Let me go."

My mother's heels click on the tile floor. The sweet scent of her perfume worsens the unease roiling in my belly.

I roll to my side with one hand cradling my head and the

other my stomach. A wave of dizziness forces me onto my back again. A pitiful moan slips past my parted lips as my eyes close.

"Maya, don't move. You fainted at the table. Rest. I'll ring for some tea."

I listen as she speaks to the butler, who leaves the room for the kitchen. My mother returns and sits on a chair.

"You look pale. How do you feel?" She asks as she places the back of her hand on my forehead. "No fever. Do you hurt anywhere?"

"My head and stomach," I manage to respond as I hold back a gag from her perfume. "*Mamá*, no offense. But your perfume is too much for me."

She huffs and rises.

"Well, then. I'll wait over there, or shall I leave my sitting room?"

I groan at the bite of irritation in her voice.

"Never mind," I mumble.

The butler returns with a tray and pours tea. Roused by the aroma of peppermint, I sit up. The first sip soothes my belly. I sigh, thankful for the relief.

"As I said before you fainted, the reaction to your engagement pleases your father. In fact, Emerico called to join us for dinner. He wants to go over the timing for the wedding. I suggest a year for enough time to prepare and for your gown to be made. He's more inclined to six months. It seems he's eager for an heir..."

And then the tea tastes like bile.

However, I will myself to make it through the day.

Idania arrives, and my mother explains she will assist with the wedding preparations. Despite not having a firm date, she presses on. They schedule interviews for wedding planners the next day. Those selected will return with vision boards three days later. All are eager to snag what promises to be the wedding of the decade.

I do my best to match my mother's excitement. When she asks if I have any preference for colors or season, I respond in what I hope is an upbeat tone. She nods, pleased with my answers. She's even happier when I tell her I trust her vision and would rather she take the lead on the whole affair. Her hazel eyes shine as she beams.

"Wonderful, Maya! I think that's for the best. You focus on acquainting yourself with Emerico. I had Idania put together a dossier for you," she says and hands a binder to me. "She's gleaned the most important information about him. You study that and impress him with your knowledge. He'll appreciate a wife who knows him well and his preferences."

I take the binder and flip through it.

Photos, a family tree, relevant dates, favorite foods, clothing sizes... a complete dossier on Emerico Tonio Santana Rodriquez.

"Thank you, *Mamá*, Idania."

While they continue to chatter about the wedding, I read about the man I'm set to marry. He's not so bad. As far as an arranged marriage goes, it could be a hell of a lot worse. A man twice my age, boring, cruel, evil stepchildren. But he's still not Viggo. I sigh and flip the page. Best not to think about him.

My mother calls for a lunch break. But it's a continuation of the wedding preparation as she and Idania discuss ideas for the menu. I struggle to swallow past the lump in my throat.

We return to the sitting room, where they jump right back in. I study the dossier and respond to simple questions, including my preference for the gown shape. I say mermaid. My mother wants a ballgown. Uncaring, I give in.

At last, she calls an end to the day's preparation since she wants me well rested before dinner with Emerico. I glance down at my empty finger. He took the ring to resize it after he dropped me off at my apartment. More than likely, he'll have it tonight. And will happily slide it back on my finger.

Me not so much. Oh, well.

As expected, Emerico places the ring on my finger while we drink cocktails in my parents' living room. He leans in to kiss my lips. A slight tilt of my head as I pretend to admire the ring causes his lips land to on my cheek. I step back and hold my hand out to my mother. Her coos distract him from my slight. The beginnings of his scowl change into a grin as she exclaims how incredible the ring is. I smile more at the successful evasion than at the sparkler on my finger.

The butler announces dinner, and Emerico offers his arm. I slip my hand around it with a smile. No need to push too far so soon. My brothers take seats across the table from us while our parents sit at each head.

The conversation flows with my mother going straight to the wedding planning. I sit back sipping wine while she gushes on and on. Emerico glances at me from time to time. I nod and smile as though truly into it. I congratulate myself on an excellent performance.

"Well, Esmeralda, you and Maya have accomplished a lot in one day. I'm glad since I still prefer the wedding date in six months. We have the means to get all of Maya's wishes achieved by that time. Don't you agree, *bella*?"

I lift my wine and smile, "As you wish, Emerico."

He grins, and I tip the glass to my lips, draining it.

The countdown begins.

iggo

"So, the playboy prince of the pack found his match, and now he wants to fly down to Venezuela to claim her?"

Jagger chuckles as he shakes his head and runs a hand through his white blond hair. Ice blue eyes sparkle with glee as we sit on the deck of his beachfront mansion on Moon Island. He lifts his snifter of Scotch and grins.

"I have to give it to you. You go from no interest to obsessed in a flash of a wolf shifter's eye. What are you going to do when you get there?"

I tell him Signy's suggestion and add, "Make her mine forever."

He cocks an eyebrow.

"Signy did not say to go that far. She said to let Maya decide," he states, then raises a hand when I protest. "I get wanting to claim your fated mate desperately. Trust me, I've been there, bro. However, as your Alpha, I forbid you forcing her to mate. You will not issue the claiming bite without her permission. She must understand all it entails to transition into a she-wolf. But before you tell her anything, you must be sure she will not reveal us to other humans. Are we clear?"

And that's the thing. I have to tell Maya about what I am without exactly giving the full details. It will take time to feel her out. Anyone unaware of the paranormal world will either scoff at it, run scared, or rat us out. My hope is she will be open to it since her best friend is a she-wolf now.

"We're clear. I'll profess my love for her and ask her to return to Miami with me. Dump that fucker fiancé. I want to fly there now. But I know you need to speak with the local Alpha to get permission for me to enter his territory. Will you reach out now?"

Jagger studies me for a minute before he picks up his mobile.

I listen as he makes a few calls to get the Alpha's contact information. It takes a while since the South American wolf shifters are not members of our Ruling Council. But with their connections, Jagger gets the Alpha's mobile and email address. I wait as he calls.

I bite back a growl as I listen to Jagger's side of the conversation. They're on a pack run for the next week, and the Alpha doesn't want any wolf shifters in Caracas without him present. He'll call Jagger when they return.

"The good news is he gave you permission. In the meantime, come up with your strategy to win Maya's heart, lover boy."

He chuckles and sips his drink.

"Might I suggest you write a letter baring your soul to her?"

I turn on my chaise lounge to find Sage walking towards us with a charcuterie board of meats and cheeses. Jagger jumps to his feet to take it from her. Her emerald green eyes shine as she kisses his cheek and thanks him. His lopsided grin makes me laugh.

"Oh, so who's the lover boy, Jagger?"

He growls as he places the tray on the table, then purrs at Sage, pulling her onto his lap. She giggles and leans against him, then faces me.

"Signy and Wren told us girls all about your predicament, Viggo."

I groan and swipe a hand over my face. Leave it to Signy…

"Don't be embarrassed. You know you're our favorite"—she yelps when Jagger nips the mark from his claiming bite—"Don't be jealous, my love. We want Viggo to be happy too."

He grouses, and she pats his cheek before turning back to me.

"I met Maya at Club Hati the night you met, and we hung out at her going away party—"

"What going away party? Why didn't Wren tell me?"

Sage raises her hands palms up and shrugs.

"It was a Girls' Night Out. Sorry. But if it makes you feel any better, she didn't dance with any of the many guys who approached her."

I growl as my wolf snarls. Jealousy sparks through me as I envision some fucker grabbing her ass or gripping her hips. My vision tunnels—

"Now, now, Viggo, relax and listen to me."

I nod, knowing my voice will come out raspy with my wolf so close to the surface.

"I don't need my magick to sense Maya's attraction to you. When Signy mentioned your name just regarding the club, Maya's face lit up. She asked Signy about you. So, write a letter. Women adore love letters."

She tilts her head and smiles at Jagger. He grins and kisses her lips, murmuring words too low for me to pick up even with my enhanced hearing. She cuddles against him and nods at me.

"Thank you, Sage. That's a great idea, and I'll leave you two lovebirds to go write it now."

They wave as I stride around the house for my Harley on the driveway. There's only one place to inspire Maya's love letter. I turn right and ride a few doors from theirs. I roll onto the concrete-pavers driveway of the three-story glass and concrete modern mansion and hop off my bike.

A year ago, I built the residence for a future I imagined would include my family. I haven't spent the night yet. But this is where I will bring Maya. No way will I have her stay in my Ocean Drive penthouse with a bunch of horny bachelors. We'll make this our own home.

I enter through the oversized glass door and pause to admire the view of Biscayne Bay spread out past the open-concept great room. Its turquoise water glitters like the quartz flecks in the floor. Nothing covers it since I left it unfurnished, expecting my mate to want her touch on the place.

As I walk through the house, I make a mental note of items we'll need right away. I'll order a bed and linens for the primary suite, a sunbed and table for the deck, and floats for the pool. The one room I completed is the eat-in chef's kitchen, since I love to cook. Our first night home, I'll fix her a meal fit for a queen—my queen. With a grin, I add stocking the refrigerator and pantry to the list. Tour complete, I slide the accordion glass walls separating the great room from the outdoor living areas.

The infinity pool blends in with the bay for an expanse of azure waters. I strip out of my t-shirt, jeans, boxer briefs, socks, and boots, then dive in. The cool water sluices over my body as I swim a few laps. My mind wanders to thoughts of Maya and me skinny-dipping under the stars before I carry her to the side and ravish her sexy as fuck body.

My cock hardens, and I lift myself out and stretch out on the lawn. One arm bends behind my head while the other hand fists my dick. I close my eyes to a vision of Maya stepping from the pool with water dripping in rivulets down her golden skin. Hooded eyes caress my body, landing on my cock. Her full tits jiggle with each step. Narrow waist flares to grip-worthy hips, then tapers to long, toned legs. Her steps continue until she stands above me, feet planted on either side of my head.

I stare up into the pink paradise of her slick pussy. It's not only water dripping down her inner thighs. She's soaking wet. For. Me. My lips part and my tongue slips out as she lowers gracefully to her knees. I reach my hands up to grasp her hips, drawing her pussy down to my hungry mouth. A deep growl rumbles from my chest.

She shivers as my tongue traces her pussy lips. I tease her with several passes before I spear my tongue past her folds. The tip strokes her G-spot, and she cries out on a shudder. Her hands drop to the ground above my head as her hips gyrate.

I nip her inner thigh and growl.

"Be still! Only I give you pleasure."

She mewls and tenses her thigh muscles.

My mouth returns to her pussy for a feast. Tongue, teeth, fingers bring her to the edge again and again until she's a panting, dribbling mess. I lap at her juices, inhaling the fragrance of her musk mixed with her unique scent.

"Cum for me, my beauty. Cum for me now!"

My tongue wraps around her clit and sucks hard.

Her legs tremble as she cries out in Spanish. I smirk at her calling for her God.

"Not God, baby. Viggo—your fated mate."

Her pussy gushes.

I roar as my cock shoots ropes of jizz in the air. It dribbles down my hand and onto my eight-pack abs. My hips pump as my fist keeps a tight hold to coax every bit from my heavy balls. Spent, I sag into the grass as Maya's name slips from my lips.

Soon I will spill my seed inside of you. No condom at all.

Once my body recovers, I wash off in the outdoor shower, then add towels to the list... I sit on the grass to let the sun dry my body while I write the letter to Maya. A grin spreads across my face as I type it out on my mobile's note app. It doesn't take long since I don't hold back. I let my thoughts flow. Satisfied, I close the notes and pull up my contacts.

If I can't get to Maya for a week, I need eyes on her at all times. After a few calls, I connect with a human surveillance team who can have boots on the ground in Caracas tomorrow morning. They'll use their system to track her and have men watching her around the clock. They'll report on her every move, and if she's in trouble, they'll step in.

They're not me. But it's better to have some idea of what's going on aside from Google alerts.

I sit and watch the activity on the bay while my mind wanders. After a while, I dress and ride back to Ocean Drive. A couple of males get on the elevator discussing their latest conquests in lewd detail. I roll my eyes. Yeah, this is not the place for Maya.

My fully furnished penthouse feels emptier than the mansion with nothing in it. I sigh as I head to my bedroom suite. Then grin as I think about how I'll have Maya home soon. My wolf grins with his tongue lolling from the side of his mouth. For the first time in weeks, we agree.

~

Maya

"Hey! I was just thinking about you! How's everything going?"

Wren's smiling face appears on my mobile when she accepts my FaceTime video call. But her smile fades as she peers closer at me.

"Maya, what's wrong? You don't look so good, honey. Are you ill?"

The tears I've been holding all day spill down my cheeks as a sob bursts from my chest. It heaves as I let it all out. Wren waits patiently, offering words of comfort until I get a hold of myself. I wipe my face with a tissue and pick up the mobile.

"My period is late."

Wren's gasp makes me cry anew.

"Oh, Maya! I'm so sorry. I didn't mean to make you cry. Let's think this through. Okay?"

I snuffle and nod.

"How late are you? And are you always regular?"

"A week and yes," I wail.

"Okay. Oaky. Um… Let me look up the symptoms."

She types away on her mobile while I try to get it together.

"Okay, let me know if you experience any of these… metallic taste in your mouth, nausea, sore breasts?"

"Yes, to all. Oh, Wren! What am I going to do if I'm pregnant? My parents will have a fit, and Emerico… I don't know! *Ay Dios mío…*"

Wren's silence makes me look at the mobile screen. She bites her lower lip with her eyebrows furrowed. I know that look, and I won't like what she's about to say.

"Um… You should tell Vi—"

"No! I'm not ready to tell anyone but you, Wren. I mean it! Do not tell Viggo or Tag. Promise me!"

Her eyes widen as she stares at me for a moment. Then she nods slowly.

"I promise. It'll be hard since Tag reads me like a book"—she raises her hand when I cry out—"But I won't give in. You're my best friend, and it's your body, your decision. I support you completely. You need to go to the doctor for confirmation. For all we know, it's just nerves about your wedding messing with your hormones. You won't be the first bride-to-be who misses a period because of stress."

That hadn't occurred to me. My stomach unclenches as I sigh in relief.

"Yes! Yes! That's it, Wren. You're so smart, chica! I'll make an appointment with my doctor. Hopefully she can see me tomorrow. Let me go so I can call. I'll call you back."

We end the FaceTime, and I call my doctor's office. I say a prayer of thanks when her secretary offers an afternoon time. It's perfect since it won't coincide with the caterer's meeting. I'll make an excuse to leave my mother and go see the doctor.

I cling to Wren's thought of stress's impact on hormones. It's a likely cause. Not the broken condom and Viggo's super sperm. At least that's what I tell myself…

I call Wren back. She tries to take my mind off the situation by asking me about the wedding until I grimace. She changes tactics and asks when she can come to visit. That perks me up, and we make plans for her to come in a couple of weeks.

Later that night, I dream of wolves running amongst pine trees and high grasses of a marsh. A pup yips as it chases a butterfly in a patch of wildflowers. For the first time in weeks, I wake rested with a smile on my face.

Then I remember my appointment and tears well in my eyes.

Maya, you are so screwed and not in the right way, chica!

Somehow, I make it through the day's wedding preparation itinerary and escape with the excuse of going to the gym. My mother thinks it's a great idea to keep fit for Emerico. I exchange an eye roll with a forced smile before I kiss her cheeks and hurry from the caterer's kitchen.

During the cab ride, I stare out the window, lost in thought. If I'm not pregnant, great. If I am, well, I'll have to tell Viggo at some point. But I won't depend upon him to raise my baby. However, since he's in Miami, my parents will probably not want to see me for a while, and to avoid the press, I'll move back to my second home. At least I'll have the love and support of my best friend.

My mobile chirps with a text message. A smile appears on my face at Wren's name on the screen.

No matter what, we're in this together! I love you! Call me with news.

Tears fill my eyes as I respond with a smiley face emoticon. My hands shake too much for more typing. I return the mobile to my handbag just as the cab stops in front of my doctor's office. I take a deep breath and pay the fare before I step out to face my fate.

CHAPTER 9

 *aya*

*Y*OU'RE *P*REGNANT, *Maya.*

My doctor's words reverberate in my head as I sit in the waiting room of the OB-GYN she recommended. Since the doctor is popular with socialites, I was afraid to come for fear word would leak before I can speak with my family and Emerico. But she's the best in the city, and I will provide the best for my baby. But I keep my sunglasses on for a bit of anonymity.

"*Señorita?*"

I jolt when a nurse appears next to me. She smiles.

"The doctor will see you now. Kindly follow me."

I gather my handbag and mobile, then follow her down a hallway lined with photos of newborn babies and ecstatic parents. My heart clenches as I wonder if Viggo will be elated or pissed. We were only in it for the one night, nothing more. Now, I'm pregnant. How could I know my steamy act of rebellion would result in a surprise?

The nurse stops by the open door of an examination room and gestures for me to enter. Frozen, my gaze flicks between the table with stirrups and the ultrasound machine. I startle when the nurse calls my name. She smiles again.

"Kindly change into the gown behind the door. The doctor will be with you shortly."

I nod mutely and enter the room.

I shiver as the cold air wraps around my bare skin. The thin cotton gown does little to warm me as I perch on the edge of the examination table. My unfocused eyes stare at the wall where more photos hang. The colorful images blur into a kaleidoscope, making me dizzy. A polite cough draws my attention from the wall to the door. I blink.

"Hello, Maya, I'm Dr. Morillo. It's a pleasure to meet you. I understand your doctor confirmed you're pregnant and you would like me to provide a full examination?"

"Yes."

"Well, let's get started."

She proceeds to exam me, then checks the file and frowns. Alarmed, I sit up.

"W—What's the matter? Is something wrong?"

"Ah… this is the file your doctor sent with the numbers from your hCG test. Your hormone levels are much higher than expected at this stage. Are you certain you conceived only five weeks ago?"

I blink in confusion and count back, then nod.

"Absolutely. I remember the morning the condom broke. Five weeks ago."

She nods and smiles.

"I'm sure it's nothing to be concerned about. Errors can occur. I suggest you retake the test now."

I slide from the exam table and walk to the en suite bathroom. My heart pounds as I complete the sample. I leave it on the sink for the nurse.

She takes it and disappears while the doctor makes notes. The nurse returns, and the doctor scans the new numbers. The frown returns. My heart skips a beat as I place a protective hand on my slightly rounded belly.

"Well, these numbers coincide with the original ones. Normally, this level would indicate a pregnancy at the eleven-weeks mark. Interesting. But we will proceed based on your five weeks…"

I attempt to concentrate on her words about supplements, nutrition, and appointments. But my mind sticks on the different hormone levels. Why?

"Should I be concerned?" I ask, interrupting her sentence.

She pauses and considers me before she responds.

"Based on the rest of your exam and numbers, you're an extremely healthy young woman. It's obvious you take great care of yourself," she says and smiles reassuringly. "Each woman's body varies. I see no other issues. So, do not worry. You don't want to stress yourself or your baby."

I study her face for any sign of an untruth. Finding none, I nod and refocus on her recommendations. I don't mention my return to Miami. Instead, I tell her I'll have to check my calendar before I schedule the follow-up visits. By the time I leave, I feel a bit better but exhausted.

As I walk through the front doors, the sidewalk tilts and my vision darkens on the edges until only pinpoints of light remain. As everything goes black, a woman's scream is the last thing I hear.

"*Señorita?*"

My eyes open to a stranger's face. The top half covered by aviator sunglasses prevent me from seeing his eyes. But concern fills his voice. Held in his arms as he kneels on the ground, I glance around.

Others gathered around us, stare and point. A camera clicks. The flash blinds me. I close my eyes to block the glare as white bursts dance before them. The man curses at the photographer but doesn't let me go. I clutch his arm and sit up.

"I—I'm fine. Thank you. I'll get a cab now."

His attention returns to me. He studies my face, then nods and rises, lifting me with him. I tighten my grip on his arm as I wobble on my heels.

"Careful, *señorita*. I've got you. Let me get you in a cab. You need to get home and rest."

I mumble in agreement as he guides me to the sidewalk. A cab waits at the curb. He opens the door and helps me inside. He and the driver exchange a glance and a nod. I tilt my head, thinking the driver seems familiar. He pushes his sunglasses up and faces forward.

"*¿Adónde, señorita?*"

I give him the address to my apartment and settle back in the seat. The stranger smiles and pats my arm. Before he closes the door, he tells me to take care of myself and my baby. Surprised, I stare at him. He points to the doctor's office and smiles as he shuts the door. Of course, the gold plaque by the entry displays the doctor's name and practice. I place a hand on my belly and offer him a weary smile, then close my eyes.

"*Nosotras estamos aqui senorita.*"

My eyes open, and I glance out the window to find we arrived at my building. The doorman steps forward as I pay the fare. Again, I study the driver. He thanks me and averts his face as he checks the side-view mirror. I shake my head and step out of the cab.

Once inside my apartment, I shower and slip into a cashmere v-neck lounge dress. A bit of nausea leads me to the kitchen for a cup of peppermint tea and some crackers I started keeping in stock. Curled on the sofa, I FaceTime Wren. She answers on the first ring. Her worried face fills the screen.

"Well?"

"I'm pregnant."

Her lips press together as she nods.

"Okay. Is everything all right? Nothing odd?"

My breath hitches.

"Tell me!"

"The doctor says my hormone levels are higher than normal for five weeks, more like eleven. She told me not to worry. But it scares me. What if something's wrong with my baby? I couldn't bear it!"

Wren shakes her head vigorously.

"It's okay, trust me. Don't you worry at all. And do not stress yourself out, promise?"

I nod, and she continues.

"Take tonight to rest and adjust to the news. Don't make any decisions or say anything to anyone until we talk tomorrow. You look tired, no offense. Go take a nap. Okay?"

I nod and end the call. Pressing my hand to my lower belly, I lower to my side and let my eyes drift shut. Tomorrow. Tomorrow, I'll decide what to do. Once again, wolves fill my dreams. But this time, Viggo leads them.

VIGGO

"WHAT?!?!?!"

I growl and jump to my feet as my guy in Caracas tells

me Maya fainted outside of an OB-GYN's office. My wolf snarls and bares his fangs, pacing at the edges of my being. I listen as the human tells me all the details he gleaned. They checked the doctor's digital files but didn't see one for Maya yet. They'll get back to me once they have it.

But I don't need him to tell me anything.

Maya is pregnant with my pup.

She hasn't been in Caracas long enough to be pregnant by that fucker. My stomach churns at the thought of him even touching her and to have sex? Hell to the no!

Mine!

I end the call and dial Jagger.

"Maya's pregnant with my pup. I must get to her now. Right now, fly from Miami to Caracas. I will not wait for that Alpha. It's been a week, and he should've called by now. Well, too fucking late. I'm out!"

"Hold on. Let me call him right now. You call the pilot to get a jet ready."

I end the call and get on the line with our pack's pilot. He promises to ready the flight plan for no later than an hour. I'll take a helicopter to Miami International and get there in ten minutes. While I rush upstairs to pack a bag, Jagger calls to confirm the Alpha returned and is aware I'm on my way. As if I cared. Maya needs me and nothing and no one will keep me from her and my pup.

My Harley zips to Moon Island's helipad. I leave the bike in the hangar and race to climb aboard the helicopter.

"Okay, let's go. Let's go!"

The pilot nods but doesn't take off.

"What's up? We gotta go!"

The door slides open. Jagger hops in, followed by Wren, Tag, Rust, and Dylan.

My mouth drops.

"You know I can't have my younger brother go to another pack's territory to get his fated mate without me."

"Damn right!"

"Hell, yeah, bro!"

"You can't go anywhere without backup, Viggo."

"And Maya is my best friend. She needs me too!"

I grin as they settle in the leather captain chairs and tighten their seatbelts.

Wren pats my arm and smiles.

"I'm glad you're going to get Maya, Viggo. She's so scared—"

"You spoke to her? You already knew and didn't tell me?"

Tag growls and leans around Wren.

"Back the fuck up, Viggo. Wren didn't tell me either, and I'm her mate."

She shakes her head.

"I promised Maya I wouldn't say a word to anyone, including Tag. She wanted to confirm her guess and time to think about her next steps—"

"Next steps! She's coming home, and that's final."

Wren flares her nostrils as Jagger growls. His Alpha command hits me in the chest like a sledgehammer. I fall back in my seat.

"Nothing is final, Viggo. I told you Maya must give you permission. Do not disobey me. I will not warn you again."

Tension flares, but I back down to his will.

Rust clears his throat.

"As the pack doctor and mate to the pack OB-GYN, I cannot allow you to issue a claiming bite while Maya is pregnant. She is human. We do not know how her body will react to the transition under normal circumstances. Being pregnant ups the risks to her and to the pup. You will wait until after she gives birth."

My stomach flips.

I forgot about the whole human aspect. Dammit! I was wary before. Now, I'm scared as fuck. I drop my head to my hands and lean my elbows on my thighs. This is more than I expected.

"It's going to be all right, Viggo," Wren says as she pats my back. "Maya is a strong woman. But don't push her. Let her decide her next steps. I truly doubt she'll leave you out of them."

I nod and sit back, staring out the window. MIA appears in the distance. Soon we'll touch down in Caracas, and I can hold Maya in my arms. I'll give her all the love she needs. But I won't let her tell me no. No matter what Jagger and the others say, I will bring Maya home to Miami, and we will be together.

And if that fucker tries anything, I'll rip his head off.

We board the private jet, and the pilot confirms we'll land in a little over three hours. Shortly after takeoff, my mobile vibrates with an email. My pulse quickens at the sight of Maya's OB-GYN file. I scan the notes and her concern about the hormone levels. Fuck!

"Rust, I need you to take a look at this," I say as I sit on a chair across from him stretched out on a sofa. "It's Maya's medical file. Tell me what the hormone levels mean. The doctor is curious about them. We don't need her to get nosy and stir up shit. That won't be good for any of us."

"Damn," he says as he swings his long legs around and takes my mobile. He reads through the file and nods. "Well, I wouldn't worry about it. Maya's body is adjusting to a wolf shifter pup. She won't have human ranges for anything. We don't have a point of reference since the few humans turned she-wolves transitioned before they became pregnant. My guess is Maya will deliver sooner than nine months. By this rate, I'd say in six or so. Natalie will exam her and run tests if Maya comes back with us. If not, I'll see what I can do down there."

He glances at Jagger and calls him over.

"Listen, Viggo has Maya's medical record, and the doctor has questions about the numbers. You need to be aware since we may need to delete Maya's records. We don't need any info lingering that humans can study. They did blood-work too. We'll erase everything."

"Fuck! All the more reason for you to persuade Maya to return to Miami. I investigated her fiancé. He will not be happy since their marriage included the merger of his and her family's companies. The stocks have already increased. No one will be happy, least of all them. I'd say offer a bride-price if they put up a stink. We'll go back to Viking times for that one, bro. As long as she agrees."

My nostrils flare at the last bit, and Jagger cocks an eyebrow. I sigh and take my mobile from Rust, then return to my chair.

They leave me alone while I stare out the window, mind racing. I'm certain Maya will return with me, especially once I tell her how I feel. But I'll wait to tell her about being a wolf shifter until after she gets to Miami. I don't want to scare her off. Then I'll have to really go back to Viking times and kidnap her. Jagger will lose his shit. I say a prayer to the gods since this was their bright idea and hope Maya will come of her own free will.

Regardless, she. Is. Mine.

We land, and I send a message to my guy as we ride in Suburbans to a hotel near Maya's apartment building. I want to be as close to her as possible and booked rooms while on board the jet. My guy will meet us there with the latest news.

Jagger confirms the local Alpha will stop by to meet him and help where he can.

At the hotel, we stride in like we own the place. The staff at the reception desk perks up and checks us in without delay. Jagger, Tag, Wren, and I take the three-bedroom President's Suite while Rust and Dylan stay in two surrounding suites.

I pace the floor while we wait for the Alpha and my guy to arrive. The Alpha arrives first, and Jagger makes the introductions.

"Alpha, we appreciate you giving permission for us to enter your territory. As I mentioned, Viggo's fated mate is a human—Maya Alejandra Perez Garcia. You may know her family."

"Of course. Very influential in Venezuela. I read she's engaged to Emerico Tonio Santana Rodriguez, another prominent businessman. You say she's your fated mate, Viggo?"

"Absolutely. She bears the scent I first inhaled as a newborn pup. Maya is mine. I do not give a damn about Rodriguez or his prominence. She's also pregnant with my pup, not that it's your concern. I'm doubly invested in bringing her back to Miami."

He nods.

"Fine. You have my full support. Contact me if you need any help. Good luck, my friend."

The Alpha extends his hand, and we shake. He continues the gesture with the others before Jagger walks him to the door. He returns with my guy, and we sit around the dining room table.

"What's the latest? Is she still at home?"

He goes on to tell us Maya hasn't left her apartment since one of his men drove her home. He and another alternate as cab drivers as they follow her. If she's not with her mother and needs a cab, they pull up before anyone else. It's a suitable cover. Others follow in cars and trail her on foot when she goes somewhere. They have a handle on her routine.

When I ask when she's likely to be alone, he tells us she hikes in the park every other morning. Tomorrow is the next expected day. He provides details, and we plan to follow her until she's deep enough inside I can approach her without being seen. Wren will remain at the hotel, despite her protest.

That night, I toss and turn in bed, unable to sleep as my mind and wolf run wild. When I doze off, Maya fills my dreams. Her smiling face stares at me until the sunlight filters through the sheer curtains. I jump up and stare at the silver-framed photo I brought with me.

Soon, you will be in my arms. Forever.

 aya

EACH TIME I hike in Waraira Repano National Park, it brings me solace. Before it was for the arranged marriage and losing the life I wanted to live in Miami. Today, it has an additional benefit. Being in nature, surrounded by the abundance of life, reminds me of the baby growing in my womb. A new life dependent upon me for nourishment, protection, and most of all, for love.

My heart swells with joy for my little one. The unexpected consequence of my decision to live as I want before resigning myself to Emerico may upend my world. But my baby is my *Pequeño Tesoro* and I will cherish my little treasure always.

The first smile since the doctors confirmed my pregnancy spreads across my face. I place both hands on my lower belly. It's more pronounced than yesterday, as though overnight my baby decided it would show the world it exists. Worry makes my smile falter. Perhaps there's more to the abnormal hormones than the doctors believe. *Stop it, Maya.* I push the negative thoughts away and continue along the trail.

The sound of rushing water quickens my pace. I can't wait to take a dip in the refreshing waters, a cleansing for my spirit. I step past the trees and onto the grass surrounding the waterfall's crystal-clear pool. Sunlight sparkles like diamonds on its surface.

Eager to cool off from the long hike, I lower my backpack to the ground and lift the hem of my tank top. As it covers my face, a menacing growl sounds behind me. I spin as my hands drop the tank top back in place. But the image before me makes me wish I couldn't see its beady eyes and mouth gaping with teeth as long as my fingers. It shakes its giant head. Saliva drips from its fangs.

Fear freezes me to the spot. My heart races as I watch the bear rise to its hind legs. Paws the size of skillets tipped with black claws swing in the air. A vision of them ripping into my belly jolts me from the trance. I glance around for anything I can use as a weapon to protect my baby. A thick branch lies a few feet to my left. I decide to dart right to trick it to run in that direction so I can double back and pick up the branch.

Howls fill the air.

I stop with one foot raised. The hairs on the back of my neck rise as a tingle spreads through my body. My eyes shift from the bear to the trees behind it. Five massive wolves break from the brush and charge the bear. Their mouths are wide with fangs just as lethal snap. The bear lumbers to turn towards his foes. The wolves circle it. A red and white one rush between the bear and me. Their heads reach my shoulders, leaving only the top of the bear in my view.

I back away towards the branch, keeping my eyes on the

scene. Better for me to have a means to defend myself than to stand here and get slaughtered. But by which of the beasts?

Once my fingers wrap around the thick tree limb, I hold it in front of me like a bat. My head swivels as I seek an escape route. But the only clear path is the trail, and the beasts block it. The pool offers no shelter, and the surrounding dense vegetation prevents a clear pass.

A roar of pain captures my attention.

The black wolf clings to the bear's back. Its jaws clamp around the thick neck. The bear reaches around. But the brown wolf and the second red one sink their fangs into the bear's front legs as they flail. The white wolf leaps onto the bear's chest. Its claws dig into the bear's shoulders and rear legs before it roars and rips the bear's throat out. A gurgling growl marks the end of the bear. It collapses to the ground. Blood seeps from multiple wounds and gushes from its ravaged neck. The wolves throw their heads back and howl.

Bile rises in my throat. I brace myself on the tree branch and retch.

"Maya."

Hands clasp my waist and pull me flush against a muscular body—a naked, muscular body. I scream and bash the branch on the back. The body doesn't flinch. The hands tighten their grip.

"Maya, it's me, Viggo."

My eyes focus on the chest in front of me. The familiar wolf paws on the pecs surprise me. My gaze lifts up and up until it settles on his face, streaked with dirt and blood. His fiery copper red hair is wild around his head. The tattoos on his scalp stand out even more. I gasp and struggle to free myself from his vise-like grip.

"How are you here? Why do you have blood on your face?" I ask then I remember the bear and the wolves. I try to peek around his wide chest. "Wh—Where are the bear and the wolves?"

He swallows audibly then takes a deep breath.

"The bear can't hurt you. It's dead. I'm one wolf, as are Tag, you know, and my brother Jagger, Rust, and Dylan."

My eyes dart over his face. Not wanting to believe him. Impossible! How the hell can they be wolves?! I may not know his brother and the other two. But I've been around Tag dozens of times. He's no wolf!

"He is, as are the rest of us. Trust me, Maya."

I blink. Did I speak aloud?

Viggo nods at my spoken thoughts again.

"Maya, I will explain all to you. But first we need to get rid of the bear before anyone comes along. I'm going to rinse off in the water. You stay right here."

When he moves to the side, I peer around him. The four wolves sit beside the bear. They watch me. I gape at them.

"Tag?"

The brown wolf stands. I jump back and stumble on a rock. Quick as a flash, Viggo grabs me.

"Careful, Maya! They won't hurt you. Neither will I. Let me rinse off."

My mouth opens and closes like a fish. I give up on a verbal response and shake my head. This isn't real. I must be dreaming like I did weeks ago when the red wolf appeared here. Red wolf??? My head swings to Viggo who stands waist deep in the water, watching me as he washes the grime off.

"Are you the red wolf?"

"Yes."

My knees give way. But before I crumple to the ground, Viggo catches me.

He bends down and presses his forehead to mine.

"I didn't expect to tell you this way. But it'll be okay, Maya. I promise. Trust me, my love. Please."

I don't know what to say, so I remain silent. Then another thought occurs to me.

"Wren! Does she know?"

The brown wolf chuffs. My gaze whips to him. He nods his head and chuffs again. I gasp and cling to Viggo to stop from dropping to the ground. He holds me tighter.

"Come. I need my backpack to put on some clothes. We'll head down the trail while the others handle the bear. They'll catch up to us," he says as he picks up my backpack and wraps an arm around my waist, tucking me into his side.

I don't want to think about how they'll *handle the bear*, or about them being wolves, or about Wren knowing and not telling me. I don't want to think at all. Instead, I nod and let him guide me from the clearing, giving the dead bear and humongous wolves a wide berth.

I close my eyes as we pass them. The stench of blood and gore roils my stomach. I whimper and pull against Viggo's grip. He loosens his hold when he realizes I'm sick.

"Oh, Maya, I'm sorry. But we couldn't let the bear harm you," he says as he holds my ponytail away from my face.

My body relaxes as a deep rumbling wraps around me like a soothing weighted blanket. When I straighten, I notice the sound comes from Viggo. It vibrates from his chest, straight to my soul. Tears fill my eyes as I wrap my arms around his waist and press my face into his chest. His heart beats strong beneath my forehead. My eyes close as I sob.

So much happened in the last few weeks. My mind needs a rest.

Viggo scoops me up and carries me past the trees. He sets me down while he puts on his clothes, then lifts me into his arms again. I protest when he turns down the path.

"Viggo, it's too far for you to carry me. I can walk."

He shakes his head as fierce determination shines in his ice blue eyes.

"Maya, you and my pup are mine to care for, protect, and to love. Forever. You rest. I'm here now. We will never be apart again."

Tears threaten until my mind replays his words.

"Your p—pup?"

He nods and glances at my belly. The tank top fails to hide the noticeable bump.

"I know you're pregnant—"

"Did Wren tell you?!"

"No. Your scent changed. There's a fainter one blended with yours."

I blink.

Of course, he can detect smells. He's a damn wolf!

"Wait! You said 'pup.' Is my baby a wolf too? Will I give birth to a wolf?!"

"I don't believe so—"

"You 'don't believe so?' What the hell does that mean? Don't you know? You're a wolf! You should know!"

"Maya, please calm down. You're upsetting yourself and my pup. I'll explain everything when we get to the hotel."

The possibility I'm hurting my baby makes me close my mouth and my eyes. I visualize an infinity pool extending to azure waters. A gentle breeze casts ripples across both. *Peace and tranquility. Peace and tranquility.* I repeat the mantra timed to my breaths, releasing my mind in meditation. I relax against Viggo with hands on my belly.

"Maya, we're near the parking lot."

Viggo's soft murmur in my ear brings me to my surroundings.

"I need you to promise me you won't say anything to anyone about what happened with the bear and, most importantly, about us being wolf shifters. Humans will experiment on us and hunt us into extinction, as has happened in the past. Promise me."

I pause to consider. But the impassioned expression in his eyes and the fact I'm carrying a wolf shifter baby-pup set my decision.

"I promise, Viggo. I can't have anything happen to my baby."

A flash of hurt crosses his face. Oops. I didn't mention him.

I cup his cheek.

"Or to you."

He closes his eyes and inhales deeply as he nuzzles against my palm. My heart clenches. Truly, I couldn't stand it if something happened to him.

"Thank you," he says, then cocks his head. "The others are right behind us. Let's get you in the SUV."

He strides across the parking lot.

A man hops out of the driver's seat. I gasp.

"You! You're the man who helped me yesterday."

He bows his head, and I swing my gaze to Viggo.

"Did you have me followed?"

The fierce determination reappears as he lifts his chin.

"Absolutely. I couldn't get down here for a week, and I needed to be sure you were safe."

I should be angry he invaded my privacy. But the part of me that yearns for support—not to mention the renewed need for him—warms to his possessiveness. I cup his cheek again and smile.

"Okay, okay."

His eyes light up as he grins. The man opens the SUV's door, and Viggo places me on the middle of the first row. He puts my backpack on my lap before he shuts the door. I watch as he talks to Tag and the others, I guess to be the wolves. They're all huge, well over six feet, and muscular. I thought Viggo resembled a Viking warrior. The others do too.

They pile into the SUV, smiling at me. Tag gets in last and sits beside me.

"Hiya, Maya," he says and chuckles.

I'm surprised the serious man can crack a joke. I grin and shake my head.

"Hi, Tag. Fancy seeing you here."

The one with the white blond hair turns around from the passenger seat and smiles at me.

"I'm Jagger, Viggo's brother. It's a pleasure to meet you at last."

I return his smile and thank him.

The others introduce themselves as Dylan and Rust. I recall which wolf did what damage to the bear. It's still hard to believe. But here they are, and the bear? Well, *handled*.

We ride to the hotel in silence while Viggo holds my hand on his thigh. He squeezes it when we pull up to the entrance. I nod and take a deep breath. Soon I'll have answers.

However, the question is, am I ready?

~

Viggo

MY HEART nearly burst from my chest when the bear appeared ahead of us on the path. His growl confirmed he spied Maya. Without hesitation, we dropped our backpacks and shifted, rending our clothes as our wolves leaped forth. As a pack, we charged. Instinctively, I put myself between the bear and my fated mate. Jagger bounded beside me. The others circled him, preventing his escape.

My only thought was to protect Maya. Each of us took turns attacking the bear until Jagger issued the death bite. Immediately, I shifted and rushed to her side. My heart clenched as she threw up. Arms held her close, needing to wrap her up in safety.

I'm thankful she didn't fight me too much. But now that we're in the hotel, I hope she'll remain open to what I have to tell her.

The door to the President's Suite opens as we walk down the hallway. Wren races out, arms outstretched.

"Maya! Thank the gods you're fine!"

Her head jerks up in surprise to find her best friend here. Then she hurries towards her. They embrace with joyous cries. Tag and I usher them into the suite while the others follow.

"Wren! Why didn't you tell me?!"

A sheepish expression appears on her face as her eyes dart to Jagger and Tag. Our Alpha speaks.

"Maya, do not be upset with Wren. No one may speak of our kind to humans. Allow Viggo to explain all to you. We'll wait in the living room."

He nods at me.

I step forward and place a hand on Maya's lower back. I guide her to the library and shut the door. She sits when I gesture at the sofa. I perch on the coffee table and place my hands on her thighs between mine. My eyes go to her rounded belly. Pride swells in my chest. My pup. I lift my gaze to her face. My mate. Mine!

"Maya, I want to start by saying I missed you the moment you stepped out of Club Hati. The need to be with you was strong. I lost my shit when I saw your farewell video post. I ran to find you. But you were gone. When

Wren told me you left for an arranged marriage, the pain was so great I shifted and rampaged for hours. The only reason I didn't come for you then was my concern for you as a human and what it means to be a wolf shifter."

Tears slip down her cheeks as I speak. My fingertips brush them away.

I can't resist the urge to kiss her. She doesn't pull away when I lean in slowly, giving her enough time to deny me. Our lips touch, and lights flash behind my closed eyelids. Electricity zings from our locked mouths along my jaw and down to my heart. It pumps faster as the kiss deepens.

She mewls, and I groan.

My hands glide along the outside of her thighs to grip her hips. They dig into her flesh. She scoots forward. I growl and move over her, turning and pressing her into the sofa. My erect cock tents the joggers. The tip nudges her pussy, hidden by shorts. Her hips lift and knees fall apart to welcome me. I don't hesitate.

In seconds, we're naked. My cock bobs against my abs. I fist it and guide it to her pussy. Again, I move slowly, giving her the chance to say no. Instead, she moans and lifts her hips as her fingernails dig into my biceps and her ankles lock behind my ass.

My cock sinks inside her wet warmth, and we groan in unison as we meld as one. Fully bare with no condom or remnants of one. I take a moment to breathe before I spill my load as her pussy throbs around my dick.

"Viggo, please. I need you. So badly…"

Her hips undulate as her pussy sucks me deeper. I bottom out with my balls kissing the bottom curve of her ass. I place her hands above her head to brace them on the armrest. On either side of hers, I place mine. Planked above, I stare into her topaz eyes darkened to obsidian by her lust blown pupils. Her mouth hangs slack as she stares up at me.

"I need you more than you can imagine, my love. I'll take you hard now. Later, we'll make love."

Before her chin meets her chest in a nod of affirmation, my hips draw back and snap forward. Her elbows bend and fuller tits bounce as I drive her up the sofa. Her mouth opens in a silent scream. She sucks in air as I withdraw, then keens.

My mouth crashes to hers and swallows her carnal cries. Our tongues tangle as our pelvises collide in a frenzied, desperate need to connect. Her juices coat my cock, easing its way into her tight pussy. I growl as she clenches around me.

"Cum for me as many times as you need, baby. Cum hard for your mate!"

She keens as her pussy walls constrict. They quiver along my length as I slam into her with enough force to move her further up to the sofa. One hand lowers to cradle the top of her head to prevent it from hitting the armrest.

I rise to my toes, using my ass and thighs to power on. Skin slaps against skin as the scent of our fucking rises to fill my nostrils and to urge me faster. The sofa creaks in protest. But I don't slow. Not when my heavy balls draw up and electricity zings along the backs of my thighs to the base of my spine, and down my cock.

I pound Maya's pussy harder. My knot forms and locks behind her pussy wall. She screams and writhes beneath me as her fingernails claw the silk. It rips as she screams my name. My fangs elongate, dripping with serum. But Rust's warning not to issue the claiming bite while she's pregnant jumps to the forefront of my mind.

I yank my head back. With my wolf so close to the surface, a primal roar rips from my throat. Our bodies spasm as we climax together. My arms and legs give out. Before I crush her with my weight, I turn us to the side.

Nestled against me, she pants. Her sweat-dampened forehead presses to my neck.

"Viggo… what is that?"

I stroke her back and rumble to soothe her.

"My knot. It expands at the base of my cock to lock you to me while my seed travels to your womb. I didn't release it the first time we were together, even though I wanted to."

She mewls and whimpers as it stretches her pussy.

"It'll get better the more you get used to it. In about fifteen minutes, it'll deflate. Rest now, my love."

She snuggles closer, and our legs intertwine.

I continue to rumble until her breathing evens out. Once she's asleep, my eyes drift closed. Later. We'll talk later.

CHAPTER 11

aya

"Hello, my sleeping beauty."

My eyes open completely as I stretch languorously in the sumptuous sheets. Then I frown and sit up, glancing around. Viggo grins.

"I laid it on you so good, I knocked you out. A sofa is no place for a long nap. This is my room in the suite. If you're rested, I'll bathe you in the shower, and you'll eat before we talk."

"Mmmmm… sounds good," I purr as he scoops me from the bed. My arms wrap around his neck. A girl could get used to this treatment.

Not only does Viggo bathe me, but he also makes me cum on his tongue until my legs shake. He dries me and massages lotion into my skin. Then he carries me to the walk-in closet where he drops a silk caftan over my head. He dresses in a t-shirt and low-hanging joggers sans underwear. My mouth drools as he tucks away his delectable cock. He smirks when he catches my heated stare.

"Later. I heard your stomach growl as I dried you. Wren ordered your favorite foods. They're in the warming drawer. Come, time to feed you and my pup."

He scoops me up, and I grin.

"You spoil me, Viggo."

He shrugs his wide shoulders.

"What else am I supposed to do?"

We enter the living room to applause. My cheeks flush crimson. Without a doubt, they heard my screams. I duck my head against Viggo's neck. His shoulders shake as he chuckles.

"Aaaw! No need for embarrassment, Maya. Not much gets past our enhanced hearing. You'll see," Wren says.

"Hold on. You said, 'our enhanced hearing.' How is that?"

Wren opens, then closes her mouth as her eyes flick between Viggo and me. He shakes his head.

"We were a bit too busy to talk. Let me get her and my pup fed. Why don't you join us in the dining room?"

He strides through the living room without waiting for an answer. In the dining room, he settles me in a chair and goes to the kitchenette.

Wren and the others trail in. She sits next to me and smiles.

"Tell—"

"Nope. Not a word about anything until you've eaten some food," Viggo interrupts as he returns with a tray loaded with platters. He sits on my other side and places the tray in front of me. As he puts a selection of meats on a plate, he continues. "You'll need loads of protein. Right, Rust?"

"Yes. And don't let it alarm you if you crave less cooked

meat," he winks as my eyes widen. "Not to freak you out or anything."

Wren pats my arm and smiles.

The thought of consuming raw meat makes me think of the bear. But instead of nausea, my mouth waters. What the heck? *Ay Dios mío!*

While I eat, the conversation flows easily. As Viggo commanded, no one mentions wolves, pups, or anything related. When I finish two plates, he grins and strokes my belly.

"Nice and full, my little one?"

Everyone laughs.

Rust and Dylan clear the table while the rest of us return to the living room. Viggo puts me on his lap, and I snuggle happily in his arms. Tag does the same with Wren, and we smile at one another. Jagger sits beside Viggo and looks at him expectantly. Viggo nods.

I listen in awe about the history of wolf shifters and their pack's arrival in what's now Miami so long ago. The notion of other paranormal beings intrigues me, especially learning Sage is the High Witch, the most powerful of all. I realize folklore holds some truths. I just never thought I would be in the middle of one. And definitely not pregnant with a half human wolf shifter pup!

However, concern rises when Viggo tells me about the claiming bite and transition. Rust not recommending Viggo do it since I'm pregnant alarms me. If it has the potential to harm our pup, what can it do to me?

As though sensing my worry, Viggo squeezes my thigh.

"Maya, that's why I hesitated to claim you the first night we met. I won't sugarcoat the enormity of the transition—"

"But Tag bit me, and I'm fine."

My head jerks in Wren's direction. Until now, she

remained silent. Her eyes shine with a strength I never saw before. She rises.

"I'm going to shift and show you. Come with me," she says as she extends her hand.

I eye it warily, then remember, this is my best friend. She will never lie to me. Perhaps an omission, but that's okay, given the circumstances. I place my hand in hers.

We go into another bedroom where she strips naked and tells me not to be frightened. She closes her eyes and holds her arms out to the side, palms facing forward. Her body transforms amidst crackling and a flash. A mahogany brown wolf stands on all fours in front of me. Shocked, I gasp and cover my mouth.

Not even in my dream of the red wolf or today have I seen a shift. The impossible is very much real.

Wren shakes her wolf body and sits on her haunches. The same mink brown eyes of her human form stare at me. They flash gold with the presence of her wolf. She's majestic.

I step forward with my hand outstretched. She lowers to her belly, and I kneel beside her large body. Her wolf is not as massive as the guys. But still bigger than a regular one. Her fur is dense beneath my palm. It slides from her head along her back. Her feathery tail thumps on the floor.

"Wow, Wren, you're incredible, chica," I breathe as I sit on my heels. "Did it hurt?"

She shakes her head, and a moment later she's back to human Wren. She puts her clothes on and grins as she hugs me.

"See! A piece of cake. And I'll tell you this… After a shift, you'll be super horny, and Viggo will jump your bones! Oh! And the claiming bite is the most erotic thing ever!"

We giggle as we head to the living room.

The guys turn to watch us walk in. Viggo opens his arms,

and I trot over. He pulls me onto his lap and kisses my cheek as his hands cup my belly.

"All good? Not scared?"

"Amazing!"

Everyone laughs.

Then Jagger speaks.

"So, Maya, do you wish to become one with us, allow Viggo to claim and mate with you, accept the transition into a she-wolf?"

Viggo tenses beneath me. I turn from Jagger to him. My eyes scan his face.

"Is that what you want, Viggo?"

"With all my heart. You are my fated mate, Maya. I will never want another female. We belong together as the gods intended. You are already mine."

I take a deep breath before I answer.

His mobile vibrates, dings, and rings beneath my butt. He frowns and slips his hand in his pocket. His scowl deepens as he listens to the person on the line. He ends the call and shifts me to sit on one leg. His fingers fly across the screen.

"What is it?" I ask as nerves creep up my spine.

He growls.

"The fucker who took a photo of you outside of the OB-GYN's office sold it to the media. It's splashed across the Internet."

He turns the mobile around.

Maya Alejandra Perez Garcia Fiancée to Emerico Tonio Santana Rodriguez Pregnant!

Proud Papá Emerico Tonio Santana Rodriguez

Baby Makes 3 for Maya Alejandra Perez Garcia & Emerico Tonio Santana Rodriguez

Is It A Shotgun Wedding for Maya Alejandra Perez Garcia?

"No!!!"

I jump from Viggo's lap and race to the library for my backpack. He runs behind me, calling my name. I snatch the mobile from the inner pocket and turn it on. Immediately, it chimes with alerts.

I sink to the sofa as my father's voice thunders over the speaker. It's the first of many voicemails and text messages, not only from him, but from my mother, brothers, and Emerico.

Viggo growls and pulls me onto his lap as he takes the mobile from me.

"Enough! Do not listen to their bullshit, Maya."

"Oh, honey! They're cruel and selfish!"

I glance up to find Wren and the others crowded around us. Scowls darken their faces. Their eyes flash with their wolves.

"This wasn't how I wanted them to find out. I was going to tell them today," I wail as tears pour down my cheeks.

Viggo holds me tighter and rocks as his rumble begins. Wren sits beside us and pats my back as she murmurs words of support. Their comfort helps the pain slicing through my heart. But does nothing to prevent me from facing my family and Emerico.

~

VIGGO

"WHO THE HELL ARE YOU?"

"Are you pregnant, Maya?

"Is this the bastard who knocked you up, *fiancée*?"

It takes every ounce of control for me to wrangle my wolf. Yelling at me is one thing. But shouting at Maya makes him feral. And me. My arm tightens around her waist as we stand in the doorway of her parents' living room.

Maya insisted she speak with her family right away. She changed into a dress and heels Wren selected along with the other items I asked her to buy for Maya while we went to the park. Tag agreed it was better to let Wren stay busy shopping than to sit in the hotel. I expected Maya to wear them for our return trip to Miami, not to speak to her incensed family.

But here we are.

Jagger and Tag rode with us. They wait in the SUV for any word from me to come up to the apartment. Sage used her teleportation magick to reach the hotel. While we're gone, Rust will go with her so she can erase the doctors' minds of the hormone levels and their and my surveillance guys' files. Dylan remains with Wren while she supervises maids to pack our things. They have our back.

Just as I have Maya's back now. I give her a squeeze before I address her family.

"If you want to speak to Maya, you better do it with respect. I will tolerate no one hurting her, including you. Do you understand?"

Five pairs of stunned eyes stare at me.

"How dare you come into my home and—"

"I'll cut this short. Maya is pregnant with my baby. She will return to Miami with me where we will marry. I will care for, protect, and love my family with a fierceness you cannot imagine. If you wish to be a part of her and our baby's lives, choose your next words very carefully."

Her father splutters while her mother gasps and clutches her pearls.

Her brothers stare—one with vehemence and the other assesses me.

The fucker's face flames red. He stalks forward, pointing his finger.

My lip curls as my wolf snarls at the threat.

He hesitates.

"Last. Chance."

I growl, skin itching as my wolf claws beneath its surface.

"The engagement is off," the fucker says as he glares between Maya and me, then he turns to her father. "As is the merger."

He storms past us. Fortunately, he has the sense to not bump into me, only to cast a last glare. I narrow my eyes in return. The front door slams shut. Maya jumps with a soft cry.

I cup her face, tilting it up to mine.

"It's okay, my love. We'll leave once you have your say."

She nods as her eyes close briefly. When she reopens them, resolve glistens in their depths.

"*Papá, Mamá.*"

They face her with displeased expressions.

I hear her swallow and squeeze her waist to encourage her. She nods.

"I only learned I was pregnant yesterday afternoon when that photo was taken. It was not my intention for you to find out through the media. I planned to tell you today—"

"You disappoint me gravely."

"How could you have done this knowing you were to marry Emerico after your twenty-fifth birthday?"

"You made a fool of our family and ruined a profitable merger for our company!"

Before I can respond to her father, mother, and brother, the one who watched me intently whirls on them and shouts.

"Stop! Do you hear yourselves? You. You. You. All your

concern is not for Maya and how she must feel with a surprise pregnancy. No! You focus on yourselves. Not to mention it's archaic to arrange a marriage, anyway."

He strides towards us and opens his arms.

"*Hermana*, are you okay?" He asks his sister as she nods and falls into his embrace with a sob. He holds her as they exchange words too low for even my hearing. When they part, she smiles softly. He extends his hand to me. "I'm Patricio, Maya's second oldest brother."

"Viggo Larson," I respond as I shake his hand. "Thank you for caring about your sister. I understand it wasn't expected. But no one may question her. No. One."

I say the last words as I glare at her parents and older brother. Then I turn to Maya.

"Did you wish to say anymore, my love?"

"Yes," she replies and faces her parents. "I never meant to disappoint you. I resigned myself to a life not of my choosing and returned to Caracas willingly. However, I take back my life and will return to Miami, as Viggo said. Should you wish to reconcile, I am open to it. I will always love you. Farewell."

She nods at them and hugs Patricio before she takes my hand. I eye each of them and nod at Patricio. He nods in return.

"I will always love and support you, Maya. Let me know when I can visit. I want to be present for the baby's birth and your wedding. And Viggo, you better do right by my sister. Or you will have to answer to me."

"I would expect no less from a brother who loves his sister."

Maya nods as tears shine in her eyes.

I squeeze her hand and lead her from the living room. Once inside the elevator, she falls into my arms. I scoop her up and rock her as my rumble fills the elevator. I stride through the lobby, ignoring the questioning glances of other residents.

Jagger hops from the passenger seat of the SUV and opens the rear door. I slide in, cradling Maya to my chest. He closes the door and returns to his seat. He glances over his shoulder at me. I nod.

"To the hotel and then the airport. Rest easy, Maya. We'll be home in no time."

 iggo

"I'VE ALWAYS BEEN curious about Moon Island since I moved to Miami. When Wren told me she and Tag have a place here, I couldn't wait to visit. But she always had an excuse. Now, I realize why…"

Wren giggles as her best friend turns from the helicopter's window to arch an elegant eyebrow.

"Oh, Maya! You know I tell you everything. I just couldn't say a word about the island."

Maya smiles, the first since we left Caracas. She remained quiet when we returned to the hotel, then slept in the bedroom aboard the jet. I held her close, hoping the rumbling would offer comfort. Now, I lift her hand to my lips and kiss the knuckles.

"I will fulfill your curiosity. Tomorrow, I'll give you a tour after Jagger and Sage introduce you to the members of our pack who live on the island. The rest live near or at our camp in the Everglades."

"Once you're on the island, you'll see its true splendor. To protect us from prying eyes—or the curious—I cloak the island with a spell. Upon looking at Moon Island, it resembles the surrounding Venetian Islands, Hibiscus or Palm Islands with mansions and docks along the water and interior with more homes and a park. People move about. However, it's an illusion. No one sees us. We're free to roam about in wolf form…"

As Sage talks, I watch Maya's face. Still adjusting to our Luna being a powerful witch and turned she-wolf, Maya listens intently. Her topaz eyes widen in surprise.

"Wow, who knew! All this time, I thought I saw real people as I zipped by on a Jet Ski. It's so real. I'd never think otherwise."

Sage wiggles her fingers and winks as she says, "Doing my best to keep our pack safe."

Jagger strokes her back as he murmurs in her ear, "Thank you, baby."

Her grin widens as they stare at one another.

Before I fell hard for Maya, I would have joked about their lovey-dovey behavior. Now, I squeeze Maya's hand. My heart swells when she smiles at me and leans her head on my shoulder.

Moments later, the helicopter lands on the island. Golf carts await us. We exchange goodnights and drive to our homes. I'm excited to see Maya's reaction to ours. Along the way, I point out the others' residences. She's impressed. But when we pull into our driveway, she claps her hands and bounces on her seat.

"Ooh! Is this your house?"

I shake my head, and she sits back, peering over her shoulder to the main road.

"It's not my house. This is our home."

I grin as I jump from the golf cart and jog around the front to her side. I scoop her from the seat. She throws her head back and squeals with glee. I carry her over the threshold of the oversized glass door. Her head turns to the accordion glass walls. The lights of South Beach fill the night sky on the other side of Biscayne Bay. The moon reflects on its inky black surface. How apropos where we met and the symbol long associated with wolves stretch out before us. I take it as a positive sign from the gods and grin.

"Welcome home, my love."

She cups my cheek, pulling our faces together for a kiss.

"It feels good to be here. To be with you," she whispers against my lips. "You don't know how much I missed you. I was so scared. And now it's the three of us."

My heart clenches at the sadness in her voice. I can't imagine how she must feel after her family's reaction. Thankfully, Patricio has more sense than the rest of them combined. But I'll make it up to her.

"I missed you so much, Maya. We're together now. And it's not just us. You'll join the Miami Wolves Pack fully once I issue the claiming bite and you transition—"

I trail off as she shakes her head and averts her eyes. Her arms loosen from around my neck. Hands press against my chest as she tries to stand. My heart stutters beneath her palms.

"What? What's the matter?" I ask, not really wanting to hear her response. Instinct tells me I won't like it. At. All.

"Viggo, let me down. We need to finish the conversation we had at the hotel before your mobile blew up about the photo."

Instead of responding, I stride across the floor and up the stairs. Inside the primary bedroom suite, I sit on the bed. Maya squirms.

"Viggo! I can't believe you take me to your bedroom when I want to talk seriously."

"I've never lived here. There's only basic furniture I ordered for your arrival until you make this into our home. Tell me what's wrong."

She wriggles on my lap, but I tighten my grip.

"I can't sit on the bed?"

"No. Tell me."

She sighs and runs her fingers through her long hair. It cascades down her back, brushing my fingers as they grip her hip. Her gaze focuses on the headboard. Then she speaks.

"Jagger asked if I wish to become one with your pack, allow you to claim and mate with me, accept the transition into a she-wolf. I asked what you want because I'm unsure. We"—she gestures between us—"don't know one another. One night and equal longing doesn't equate to us knowing one another enough for such a major commitment, especially me becoming a wolf shifter and losing my humanity…"

My grip tightens as my heart races. I thought we were of like mind, even more so after I explained fated mates. Apparently, not. I remain silent. Let her divulge all obstacles. Then I'll plan my strategy. Maya will be mine regardless.

"I wasn't lying when I told my parents I would return to Miami, as you said. However, I didn't affirm the rest. There's no doubt I'm attracted to you. The pull is strong, and I truly missed you. But I need to know you better before I commit to marriage or a mate bonding ceremony. And the claiming bite to transition… At this point, I don't see it happening. Yes, it's incredible how well Wren adjusted to it. But I need more time. My pregnancy delaying the possibility of transition is a sign."

She pauses and gestures around us.

"You want me to stay here and make it our home. Well, my interest in Moon Island and this being a clean slate are more signs. Between now and the birth of our baby-pup, we have over seven months to build our relationship."

She cups my face and stares into my soul.

"Believe me. I want us to be a couple, a family. To have the love and support of your pack. However, I'm still undecided about the transition. That's a hell of a big ask. Give me time. Let's not rush. I hope you understand."

With a sigh, she presses her forehead to mine.

"Okay?"

Thoughts run through my head as my heart pounds in my chest.

Even apart, I've grown attached to Maya. Awaking to her face on her pillow beside me and on the nightstand. Following her activities through past social media posts and her time in Caracas via bloggers, media outlets, and detailed updates from the surveillance team. Plus, the extensive background check provides more about her life. I have a hell of a lot more knowledge of her than she knows of me.

Her wish to learn about me better makes sense.

I'll give her that. But not claiming her as my fated mate? To not bear my mark? Not prove she's mine for all males to see? Out of the question now that she carries my pup.

Over a month without her, followed by news of her pregnancy, and coupled with Wren's positive recovery, lessens my fear of losing Maya during the transition. In my heart, I do not believe the gods would be so cruel as to give me my fated mate, then take her from me.

If I must defy Jagger—my brother and Alpha—to issue the claiming bite against her will, so be it.

~

MAYA

AT VIGGO'S SILENCE, I lean back to scan his face for a reaction to my decision.

His eyes flash silver.

Now knowing he's a wolf shifter, I see the eyes of the red beast within him. My heartbeat ticks up. But I remind myself to relax. I doubt Viggo will ever harm me.

The appearance of his wolf means his emotions run high. Whether it's with anger, as with the bear, with passion while we have sex, or with hurt from my words. I don't want him upset with me. But I won't leave one controlling situation for another. He must understand I get to make decisions in my life.

I wait for him to answer.

Viggo blinks, and the wolf retreats. A fierce determination replaces it. He nods.

"I guarantee after you give birth to my pup, you will bear my mark and join me beneath the mate bonding ceremony bower."

My mouth drops. No. He. Didn't.

He cocks an eyebrow. His finger lifts to my chin and presses up closing my mouth.

I growl.

My eyes widen as my hands clap over my mouth.

What the hell???

Viggo throws his head back and barks with laughter. When he lowers his gaze, it shines with the beast.

"You see, my fated mate, your body knows what it is despite your protests. You carry my pup—a wolf shifter—in your belly. Your genetic makeup blends."

He rises and carries me to a walk-in closet and sets me on the island. He kisses the tip of my nose. His smug chuckle makes me want to growl again. But I hold it back. With a wink, he waves his hand at a wall where all kinds of clothing hang. Then strides to the wall of drawers.

"Signy—you know, my younger sister—shopped for you. I asked her to get some items to carry you over until you went for yourself. As you can see, she filled your entire closet," he says, as he riffles through a drawer. "I said no underwear. She called me a caveman and did as she pleased. Ah… this I like."

He lifts a pale pink silk negligee with cream lace bra cups and a matching robe.

"How about you shower and change into this while I cook dinner?"

He lays the pieces on the island and stands me on my feet. His hands squeeze my hips as he bends his knees to bring our eyes on level. I quirk my lips to the side. He grins devilishly.

"Oh, my little Maya, don't bother to fight it. You know you're mine, and I will make it so. Be a good girl and meet me in the kitchen. I promise your mouth will water for more than my cock."

He turns me towards the door that must connect to the bathroom and spanks my butt. I yelp in surprise as I cover it with both hands. He smirks at my glare, then strides from the closet. I shake my head and let the growl I held back tumble past my lips.

"I heard that, my little wolf!"

"Fuck you, Viggo!"

"Oh, you will…"

I can't help the smile that lifts the corners of my mouth as I continue into the bathroom. I know it should irritate me he sort of disregarded my decision. But the delicious thrum in my pussy from the spank and his parting words overrule.

The smile widens when I spot my favorite toiletries on one vanity. Signy must have spoken to Wren. How thoughtful! I must call her with my thanks.

Not long after, the tantalizing aroma of steak wafts through the air as I enter the kitchen. Indeed, my mouth waters. However, it's not just the food that flares hunger inside my core.

Viggo stands at an impressive stove. Bare chested, his lats and triceps flex as he stirs a saucepan. Fiery copper red hair pulled up in a bun reveals what he calls pack tattoos on the buzzed sides of his head. Black low-slung joggers dip beneath the v cuts at his narrow waist. My eyes track down the long, muscular legs to his toes. My core clenches for the sexy as sin Viking wolf shifter.

"See something you want, Maya?"

I swallow, then quip, "I thought a caveman would prefer his woman pregnant and barefoot in the kitchen, not the other way around."

His hand stills. Slowly, he pivots. His eyes sweep over me from head to toe. The heat in his eyes hardens my nipples. I shift on my feet to ease the ache in my pussy. A smirk tilts his full lips.

"So, you admit you're my woman?"

Before I can respond, he continues, "Good girl."

He leans a hip against the cabinet as he folds his arms over a firm chest. The paw prints move over his pecs. Biceps flex. He cocks his head as his tongue moistens his lips.

"You'll be delighted to learn I enjoy cooking and, as everyone tells me, the food is damn good. So, you will never have to be in the kitchen other than to watch me create dishes to delight you."

He pushes off the cabinet and prowls towards me. His eyes linger on my belly. He crouches before me and places his hands on each side. His lips press to the center before he peers up at me through the thick red fringe of eyelashes a woman would cry for. His eyes flash.

"But I want you pregnant as often as the gods grant us. My son will be the first."

Viggo kisses my belly again and rises with the effortless grace of a predator. His fingertips stroke the sides as his lust-filled eyes train on mine.

I blink to break his carnal spell.

"And how do you know the baby-pup is a boy?"

A smirk full of secrets lifts his lips.

"Instinct. Now, come sit so I can feed you and my pup," he says as he swings me in his arms and carries me to a corner banquette. "Get ready for me to rock your world. Tonight is only the beginning of my Woo Maya Plan."

He growls the last part in my ear as he places me on the leather bench. He sniffs, and I feel his lips spread in a grin.

"I scent your arousal, my little wolf. No worries, I won't only feed you. But I'll feast from your bountiful body every. Single. Day. And. Night."

My eyes flutter closed on a purr as his lips trail from my ear along my jaw to the pulse in my throat. His teeth nip the area as he issues a possessive growl. I shudder. Head lolls to the side to bear my neck. He rumbles and licks the spot before he rises.

My hooded eyes open to watch him stride to the oven. The thick muscles in his legs bunch beneath the joggers. When he returns with one plate loaded with steak and vegetables, his massive cock tents the soft fabric.

Again, I can't decipher whether the aroma of the food or the vision of the wolf shifter causes me to drool. But I do know the next few months will be long and full of temptation. The question is, will I remain strong or fall prey to the red beast?

iggo

"I CAN'T BELIEVE how much is on the island. I figured it only had mansions. This is a self-contained world for wolf shifters!"

Maya giggles as we ride along in a golf cart for the tour of Moon Island.

We left our home, and I pointed out Tag and Wren's grand Mediterranean Revival style residence, followed by Jagger and Sage's Spanish-style one. Rust and Natalie's modern home sits on the other side, next to Dylan and Sasha's Spanish-style one. Each mansion ranges from eight- to ten-thousand square feet. Homes perfectly sized for loads of pups to run, ours included.

As we passed pack members, they wave. Maya returned their gestures and smiled at me. I told her they know who she is even though they'll gather at the clubhouse in a few hours for her formal introduction. Not much is missed on the island since word travels fast. So far, no negative comments arouse despite Maya being human.

I didn't expect any. As the pack prince and beloved by all, they'll support me. And if they don't, they'll tell me why. Again, no one will disrespect or hurt Maya—pack included.

We're on the other end of the island after passing through the more dense interior where we run as wolves amongst the pine trees and foliage. Here, a mini town offers options for those who prefer not to leave our protected land. A school for younger members of the pack, restaurant, deli, pizza shop, beauty salon, and barber shop are available. And the hospital where we're headed for Maya's OB-GYN appointment with Natalie.

So, yeah, it's an entire world separate from the human one right at their doorstep, or rather the wrought-iron entry gates.

"It is. Which is another reason I brought you here instead of my Ocean Drive penthouse."

She raises her eyebrows in surprise.

"I used to live there, close to Club Hati. The vibrancy of the neighborhood and the vicinity to the beach makes it a perfect spot. I'd love to see your place."

"I can take you. But the building is for the pack bachelors, and there's no way I'd have you stay around a bunch of horny males. I teased Rust when he only stayed there with Natalie until the completion of their mansion. I thought he was being dramatic. Now, I understand why."

Maya rolls her eyes as she shakes her head.

"Seriously? And you don't think you're a caveman? Good grief, Viggo."

"Never said I wasn't," I respond with a smirk, then chuckle when she shakes her head again. "Here we are."

I hop out of the golf cart and help Maya. She glances around the hospital's all-white modern lobby where a receptionist sits behind a desk.

"Hi, Viggo!" She says as she rises and smiles. "You must be Maya. I'm Janice. Welcome to the Miami Wolves Pack. Natalie waits in her office. Rust is on duty at the emergency room on the mainland."

Maya beams and returns Janice's hug.

"Thank you! It's so kind of you to welcome me since I'm human. I must admit your greeting lessens my nerves about the pack introduction later."

"Mostly, we're an open pack. Some were upset about our Luna being a witch. But they got over it. Jagger does not tolerate the mistreatment of any pack member, no matter their origins. Plus, you're with pup. We treasure the little ones as the continuation of our kind. We can talk another time. I don't want to delay you from your appointment. It's just few come to the hospital since wolf shifters heal on their own generally. So, no one for me to talk to. Which is a good thing! I'll see you at the clubhouse!"

Maya grins as Janice shoos us toward the corridor where Rust and Natalie have offices.

True, it's rare a wolf shifter requires medical help. But accidents can happen that require further help. Rust insists on maintaining a state-of-the-art facility with all the latest equipment, two operating rooms, exam rooms, labs, and several patient rooms. They spared no expense to make it the best care facility for our pack. Departments include urgent care, general medicine, obstetrics, and pediatrics. The most used department being obstetrics. Staff besides receptionists include nurses, aides, and the head of administration.

"Hey, Nat!" I say as we enter her office.

She lifts her head where midnight hair streaked with a snow-white widow's peak falls over her shoulder to her waist. Onyx eyes brighten as she smiles.

"Viggo, Maya! Come in. I'm so excited for you!" She says, walking around her desk. Her belly—rounded with Rust's pup—presses against Maya's as she embraces her and grins at me. "Let's sit and chat before the exam. Do you want water or some juice?"

"A water would be great, thanks," Maya responds while I decline.

Natalie gets the water as we settle on the sofa. She hands Maya a bottle and sits on the chair.

"I'm glad you agreed to me as your OB-GYN. I'm experienced with human and wolf shifter births. My speciality is critical care obstetrics. Plus, with all the tests, particularly blood, performed during pregnancy, we can't allow curious minds to question the results."

Maya places the bottle on the coffee table and nibbles her lower lip. The scent of fear fills the air around her.

Automatically, I rumble as one arm wraps around her shoulders and the other hand rests on her belly. The need to soothe her and my pup kicks in.

She leans into me and places her hand over mine.

"What's the matter?"

"I'm scared since I'm human and you're a wolf shifter," she says, then shifts her worried gaze to Natalie. "Do you think our baby-pup will be okay? Already I'm larger than the photos online, and the doctors were concerned with the levels of my hormones. I want nothing to happen to our baby-pup. I want it healthy like any other."

She whispers the last as her eyes drop to Natalie's belly.

She nods with a reassuring smile and responds, "I understand, Maya. Any pregnancy has risks to the mother and baby or pup. I've spoken with the turned she-wolves about their pregnancies and births. None had complications—"

"But they transitioned before they became pregnant. They were she-wolves at the births. I—I'm human, and Rust says it's not advised I transition at this stage. No one else gave birth as a human. I'm scared."

My heartbeat trips at the anguish in Maya's voice. She has mentioned none of her concerns to me.

Natalie sits beside her and pulls her in for a hug.

"Oh, Maya, I understand and don't blame you. Your situation is unique to our pack. However, I reached out to other pack doctors and midwives. Those with a human female giving birth to a pup connected me with them. Only two, but enough to share their experiences. They confirm similar differences in the test results and a shorter pregnancy of six months instead of nine. Hence the higher hormone levels during earlier weeks. They offered to speak with you in case you need reassurance."

I sigh with as much relief as Maya.

Natalie smiles at us and returns to her chair. We talk more about the information she learned before she examines Maya. Then my pulse quickens when Natalie starts the ultrasound.

On the monitor, a tiny face with distinct features appears, followed by the body where hands and feet show fingers and toes. Natalie grins.

"Would you like to know the gender?"

"Yes!" Maya and I shout in unison, then laugh with Natalie.

She changes the position and hovers.

"A male! Yeah, baby! I knew it!" I whoop as I fist pump the air. I lean over to Maya's ear and murmur, "My instinct is never wrong. Trust your fated mate. We were meant to be together as wolf shifters, my love."

She nods as emotions flit across her face.

"You and your pup are in excellent health, Maya. Enjoy your pregnancy and your mate."

I grin at Natalie's last words. She winks and hands a soft cloth to me to clean the gel from Maya's belly.

"When you're ready, come to my office. We'll schedule your follow-up visits and answer questions you may have," she says before she leaves the exam room.

I turn to Maya and kiss her lips.

"Feel better, now?"

"Yes, so much. A little boy. No wonder I'm so horny with so much testosterone flowing in my system!"

"Ha! Even better!"

She giggles even as her eyes heat. I kiss the tip of her nose and remind her we meet with the pack after this appointment with no time for hanky-panky. She growls, and I chuckle at my little wolf.

~

MAYA

"GREETINGS MIAMI WOLVES PACK! I sense your excitement about our newest arrival. Your Luna and I are pleased to introduce you to Maya Alejandra Perez Garcia!"

My heart races as I stand on the raised platform and face the pack at the clubhouse.

The two-story structure accommodates their meeting space, recreation rooms, and a grill that serves burgers, fries, shakes, and other backyard-style food. The meeting space fits the large pack, set up with tiered seating and two aisles that lead to the raised platform.

Murmurs arise. Members shift in their seats to get a

better view of the human who sits beside Viggo. Jagger raises his hand to call for silence.

"Maya is Wren's best friend and the fated mate of Viggo. She is pregnant with their male pup. At this time, as a human, Viggo cannot issue the claiming bite to initiate their bonding and her transition. However, Maya is off-limits to any male."

Viggo growls and leans forward, fists clenched.

The males lower their gazes in deference to the pack prince.

I sigh in relief since Wren told me males could challenge Viggo for me as we're not bonded despite me carrying his baby-pup. Her revelation further explains his reluctancy for me to stay at his Ocean Drive penthouse. Surrounded by single males could cause complications within the pack. I have no intention of causing any division. I want everyone to accept me.

"Does anyone have questions?"

Jagger gazes around the space. He nods at an older male who rises.

"Yes, Alpha, if I may?" He says, then continues after Jagger nods. "How do we know Maya won't tell other humans about us?"

"Good question, Frode. She swore allegiance to our pack. As a mother to a future pup, Maya's loyalty is to wolf shifters," he responds, then surveys the crowd. "Any other questions?"

A female stands.

"Yes, Alpha, if I may?" She continues at Jagger's nod. "Where will she stay? On Moon Island or elsewhere?"

"Here, in the home she shares with Viggo. Next?"

Soon the questions end. Sage joins Jagger as he motions for me to stand. Viggo rises beside me. He takes my hand and squeezes it as we face the pack.

"Maya, Luna and I vouch for you and welcome you to the Miami Wolves Pack. Your safety and happiness rank as high as any member," he states, then turns to the pack. "The meeting is over. Kindly welcome Maya!"

They clap and approach the platform to introduce themselves. Three older humans transitioned into she-wolves make their way to the front. They offer me reassurances and their phone numbers with plans for dinner in a few days. I thank them, and they move on.

I notice a cluster of she-wolves flick their gazes between Viggo—who never leaves my side—and me. When I catch their eyes, one stares defiantly while others either avert their gaze or smirk. Not one to back down, I match the stare.

Unexpected possessiveness flares in my chest. I excuse myself and stalk towards the group. Viggo calls my name. But I wave him off. Wren appears at my side. The she-wolves watch as I make my way through those waiting to introduce themselves. I ask for a moment and continue on until I stand before the ringleader.

"Is there a problem?"

Her lips twitch into a sneer as she flicks her gaze over me.

"Ask Viggo."

My nostrils flare.

"Really, Bridget?"

I keep my eyes on the she-wolf as Viggo appears in my periphery. He steps between us, blocking her from my view with his larger frame.

"We fucked, as I did with the others. Do not attempt to make Maya believe it was more. Wolf shifters have voracious appetites. Now, my fated mate feeds me well. I have zero interest in anyone else."

He eyes each of the females until they lower their gazes,

then takes my hand and pivots. He puts a hand on Wren's back and guides us to the platform.

"Maya, they mean—"

"No need to explain, Viggo. What you did in the past remains there, along with my—"

He growls as his wolf flashes in his narrowed eyes.

After my reaction to those females, I understand. I cup his cheek and reach up on tiptoe to brush my lips across his mouth. He leans down and nips the lower one between his teeth, then growls.

"Mine and only mine. I will hear nothing of any other male."

"Yes, Viggo," I breathe, aroused by his dominance.

His nostrils flare.

"Come, you'll meet the rest of the pack over the next few days. Right now, you have need of me."

He scoops me and nods at those standing in front of us. They laugh and whoop as he carries me from the clubhouse. Jagger and his best friends' guffaws sound loudest. Viggo ignores their teasing, including those who stand outside as he sets me on the golf cart seat and hops in.

His hand massages my thigh as he drives to our home. Once there, he carries me inside and up to the bedroom where he sits me on the bed. Heat rushes through my body as he strips naked. His gorgeous body with a ginormous cock bare before my eyes makes my pussy flutter. In moments, he removes my dress and lingerie. He puts an arm around me and moves on his knees to the middle of the bed. He pivots and lifts me to straddle his face.

I nearly cum from the sound of his growl as his hands grip my hips. The fingers dig into my flesh as he aligns my pussy with his mouth. A moan slips from my parted lips when the tip of his tongue brushes against my heated pussy lips.

My knees widen to spread my thighs, giving him better access. They quiver as he eats me through two orgasms. My cries of pleasure echo around the empty bedroom.

He kisses both inner thighs then slides up to a seated position with his back against the headboard. His flashing eyes stare into my hooded ones as his dick breaches my folds slowly, inch by delicious inch. Fully seated, my ass rests on his thighs and my fingernails dig into his shoulders. He withdraws just as agonizingly slow. One thrust of his hips, and I'm impaled on his incredible girth. The bulbous tip grazes my G-spot, then press against my womb.

"Aaaahhhh, baby…"

"Fuck yes… So tight, Maya… All mine!"

Once my core adjusts to his size, Viggo's grip on my hips tightens. He lifts me to his tip, then flexes his muscular thighs to snap up and bring me down at the same time.

Shooting stars dance before my closed eyelids as I grip his shoulders to brace myself. So fucking good…

He sets a controlled tempo of slow and deep stokes. His flashing eyes never leave mine after he commands me to open them and to not look away. His hooded gaze burns with passion.

I'm mesmerized.

He continues his thrusts but refuses my cries for release. His commands of *not yet* set my thighs aquiver and my breath to come in pants.

Viggo bands his arms around my waist and hoists me into the air with ease to settle me onto my back. His knees brace on the mattress. His mussed hair falls into his eyes as he places his hands on either side of my head to loom over me.

Did I say sexy AF, or what?

His hips go berserk as he pistons in and out of my greedy little pussy, my thighs tight around his hips.

Squelching joins his grunts and my moans. He rides me like a thoroughbred stallion, taking his mate in heat.

My fingernails dig into his biceps as I hold on for dear life.

"Cum… for… me… NOW!" He demands.

The pent-up orgasm rips through me from the top of my head and up from the tips of my toes. My body arcs off the bed as I throw my head back, my mouth open wide in a silent scream. The muscles of my pussy spasm. My juices gush as Viggo tweaks my engorged clit.

Another orgasm followed by another has my mind floating in erotic bliss. The sensation of his dick expanding, then jerking as his hot seed spurts in copious amounts to paint my pussy walls and to fill my womb sends another orgasm through me. It's enough to put another baby-pup inside of me.

A carnal roar rips from his mouth as he yells through his climax to the ceiling.

The air is rich with the scent of our arousal and the mingling of our perfume and cologne with our natural musk. I inhale deeply and close my eyes to savor this moment.

Still hard within me, Viggo lowers his head to my heaving chest. We remain locked in our embrace until our breathing returns to normal.

I brush my fingers through his damp hair, wanting skin-on-skin contact beyond the intimacy of our groins.

He lifts his sated gaze to mine.

"Only you, Maya. No one since, and no one after. I am yours and you are mine," he declares as he holds my chin in his fingers. "I will allow no one to hurt you. Only I will give you pain and know that pleasure will always follow."

I nod as he caresses my lips with the pad of his thumb.

"I love you, Maya."

With a contented sigh, I nuzzle against his neck. Viggo Larson is mine. All. Mine.

CHAPTER 14

$\mathcal{M}$aya

"WREN, I still cannot believe you're pregnant with triplets, and we'll give birth around the same time! Talk about besties! Our baby-pups will grow up together. Your little girl will have three brothers instead of two to watch over her!"

I clap my hands as we walk into the Bal Harbour Shops. Viggo and Tag follow behind us. Sage suggested we get clothing for the baby-pups from some stores she and Sasha bought items for their pups. We called ahead and made appointments with personal shoppers to help us with our selections.

Over the past three weeks, I've adjusted well to being pregnant and knowing about the paranormal world. The nausea subsided while my hunger and energy increased, not to mention my sex drive being over the top. Viggo loves it all since he can cook tantalizing dishes for me and do his best to keep up with my stamina. I'm well fed and bred!

Each evening, he shifts into his wolf for our stroll before dinner. He says it's his favorite way to unwind after the office. I love our strolls since we bond while he's a wolf getting me acclimated to the whole wolf shifter side of him.

Pack members wave or stop and chat with me if they're in human form. Wolves keep their distance since Viggo's wolf doesn't want any others near me. The first time one approached, he jumped in front of me, hackles raised, and snarled. They dropped to their backs and bared their necks and bellies in submission. Word spread, and they know better than to come near me.

And no other she-wolves treat me poorly since Sage held a session for the female members of the pack. The Luna reminded everyone to respect each other. She further stressed once a pair mates, former lovers should not refer to their trysts. Some females mentioned instances Sage addressed to ease their minds. The she-wolves who stared at me apologized, and we moved on. I admire Sage's leadership and respect her as the Luna and a friend.

I consider her, Natalie, and Sasha as close friends. We bonded quickly after a Girls' Night In at Sasha's home. She sent Dylan to Jagger and Sage's home to hang out with the guys. We cooked dinner and binge-watched *Vikings: Valhalla* on Netflix. We agree our guys are sexier than those in the series, and they're some hotties! Later that night, I told Viggo the Norwegian prince turned me on. He growled and showed me why no one compares to the Miami prince.

As promised, the turned she-wolves invited us to dinner with their mates. Wren and Tag joined us. As we ate, each one told her story. They're fated mates—like Viggo insists we are. Prior to meeting their male wolf shifters, they were unaware of the paranormal world and the various beings.

The males approached them after detecting their unique scents. They pursued the women without mentioning they could shift into wolves.

Two of the women fell in love with their fated mates right away. The third rejected hers initially. All admitted they felt the attraction and later learned it's the mate bond. What changed the third she-wolf's mind was the persistence of the male. As Viggo does with me, he refused to give up or let her deny him.

Not until the women committed to the relationships did the males reveal their true natures. Their initial reactions were disbelief, fear, and anger. Fortunately for the males, their love proved strong. In time, the women accepted them and decided to be one with them in all ways. The males claimed them.

As with born she-wolves, the humans felt pain and pleasure in the bite. Their cheeks reddened as they described their experiences. The males sat back with smug expressions. Viggo caressed my thigh beneath the table. Aroused by their words, I barely contained a moan.

But their descriptions of the transition brought my attention back from carnal thoughts. After the bite, they felt dazed and slipped in and out of sleep over a course of three to four days. They could only recall the males' constant presence as they fed them soft foods and liquids. In time, they awoke revitalized, more robust than before.

Their wolves appeared on the fringes of their beings. The males taught the new she-wolves how to connect with their other half through their minds and to call them forward to shift. The women described it as their bodies painlessly realigning to the shape of their wolves in moments. They remain in full control of their bodies and their minds. The world appears more vibrant.

They laughed at the increase in their sexual appetites. I

giggled, thinking if mine grows anymore, I'll never get out of bed and Viggo would never get to the office. He squeezed my leg knowingly. My cheeks flushed crimson.

Unlike the others, one woman transitioned partially. However, she lives longer with better health. The pack treats her just as they do with the other turned she-wolves.

They completed the mate bonding ceremony—the wolf shifter's version of a wedding ceremony—after their transition. Their eyes grew dreamy as they recalled their special days. Each of them gave birth to a healthy pup. I nodded, remembering Natalie confirmed the human females from the other packs birthed pups in human form too.

Overall, they love their lives with their fated mates, family, and the pack. The women assured me pack life differs little from human families. However, wolves remain loyal and dedicated to the wellbeing of all pack members. The thought of my family's silence other than Patricio and his weekly FaceTime calls made me sad. Viggo rumbled in his chest and put his arm around my shoulders to tuck me against his side.

The women ended with their admiration of the Alpha and Luna since they're fair and loved by all.

Grateful they lessened my nerves, I thanked them. Their positive experiences encouraged me to consider Viggo claiming me fully. But first, I must give birth to our baby-pup.

Along with decorating our new home, we selected the suite closest to ours as the nursery. It comprises a bedroom, playroom, and bathroom. The color palette of greens, blues, and tans makes it a calming space. Bleached wood furniture, hand-painted tiles, and boat accessories keep with the nautical theme. Now, we need clothes for our little one.

Wren smiles brilliantly as she places a hand on her babies bump. Dressed in a silk wrap dress that clings to her

BBW figure, she radiates happiness. I'm so proud to see her not only transform into a she-wolf but into a confident female no longer doubtful because of her horrible ex-fiancé. Tag loves and appreciates her, as any smart male should.

"I know, right? I wasn't so surprised when Natalie confirmed I was pregnant. But when she told me one pup was three, I fainted on the exam table! Naturally, Tag is overjoyed," she says as she glances back at him with a loving smile. "Natalie, me, and now you are pregnant. Sage says the pack shares our excitement."

"Five births within weeks of each other. Incredible. I can't wait to hold our little one."

Wren links arms with me and nods.

"Who would have expected we would be pregnant now, anyway? Funny how fate works," she says, then glances up at me. "As you always tell me, everything happens for a reason, Maya. Trust in it. Viggo truly loves you. He'll suffer wolf madness if you deny your bond. Don't worry. You'll be fine."

I nod since the desire to be one with him increases every day. But I still have time to choose whether I accept his claiming bite and transition or live amongst the pack as his human lover. No need to rush my decision.

We reach the first of three boutiques for children's clothes. Wren and I ooh and aah over the window display with tiny hand-knit onesies, caps, and blankets. Viggo stands beside me and wraps an arm around my waist, drawing me into his side. I place a hand on my baby bump as I lean into him with a contented sigh.

"It still amazes me you're carrying my pup inside of you. Soon I'll hold both of you in my arms," he murmurs as he stares at my reflection in the display window. "I love you both so much, Maya."

My heart clenches. It's times like these my body longs for his bite. To be his forever. I turn into him, wrapping my arms around his waist as I bury my face in his powerful chest. I inhale his cologne mixed with his natural scent, wanting to imprint it on my mind.

He rubs my back and rumbles, making the world fall away. We're in our own bubble of bliss. One I never wish to leave.

~

VIGGO

As I HOLD Maya in my arms, I sense the warring in her mind, as I have recently. I can sense her struggle with the transition. Prior to dinner with the turned she-wolves, Maya was more resolved to not transition instead wanting her humanity. Their experiences combined with that of her best friend cause confliction for Maya.

I also add in to the mix my wooing of her. The more time she spends with me in wolf form, the more comfortable she becomes. Especially when Wren and Tag as wolves join us for walks. It was his idea to help sway her.

Then there's her time on Moon Island interacting with the pack. Movie night in the clubhouse, getting her nails done at the salon, going for pizza all immerse her in our everyday lives. They show we're no different from humans if she sets aside the wolf part.

However, if she denies me after she gives birth to my son, I will take it back to the Viking days and claim her. Jagger's wrath be damned. I'll take my fated mate and pup to another pack or go rogue like Dylan. Maya is mine, and no one or nothing will stop me from completing our bond.

I loosen my hold around her and lift her chin with my index finger. Her eyes shine with love in a gorgeous face aglow with impending motherhood. I brush the pad of my thumb over her lips.

"Let's get my pup ready."

The smile that spreads across her face could make the gods sing.

"Yes, Viggo. And I love you too."

I suck in a breath, and she kisses my thumb. I cover her mouth with mine for a passionate kiss.

"Oh, get a room or get inside the store."

We break apart, laughing at Tag's wry remark. Mr. Grumpy shakes his head and ushers Wren inside. We follow laughing.

"Welcome to Bonpoint!"

A salesperson greets us as the door closes. She glances between Maya and Wren's rounded bellies. I can't believe Tag put three pups inside of her. I'll have to up my game.

"Thank you," Maya and Wren say in unison, then giggle.

"We have appointments," Maya adds.

The salesperson nods and confirms their names. She introduces herself as the shopper for Wren and calls to a female folding a sweater. She walks over and introduces herself as Maya's shopper. We pair off and sit on sofas to discuss our needs. When the shopper asks about our budget, Maya hands her the AMEX Centurion Card and grins at me.

One of the first things I did following Maya's arrival on Moon Island was to arrange the Black Card along with bank accounts for her. I scheduled monthly fund transfers and automatic payments to cover her expenses. Maya will never worry about the cost of a damn thing. She can buy whatever the hell she wants. Her parents can go kick rocks since they cut her off. Fuckers.

Her eyes widened in surprise when her card and her bank details arrived. She didn't realize I was a multibillionaire on my own, aside from my family's wealth. I invest wisely.

I grin back at her as the shopper pockets Maya's card.

We spend the next few hours in two stores before we break for lunch. The girls decide only Italian food will do. They lead the way to Carpaccio. The hostesses do a double take when they glance up from the podium. Their eyes flick between Tag and me with interest. We place our arms around Wren and Maya. Growls vibrate in their chests. The hostesses blink.

"A table on the patio for four."

They nod, and one hurries to gather the menus before she leads us to the sun-drenched patio. Tag and I help the girls into their chairs, then sit. The hostess hands the menus to us, careful to keep her gaze down as Maya and Wren glare at her flushed face. She mutters an *enjoy your lunch* before she scampers away. If she had a tail, she would tuck it between her legs.

Tag and I glance at each other and laugh.

"Not funny," Wren snarls as her wolf flashes in her eyes. The petite beauty did not appreciate the other females ogling her mate. Nor did Maya, who growls in agreement.

I press a kiss to her check as my hand kneads her thigh beneath the table.

"Only you, my love. Only you," I murmur against the delicate shell of her ear, then trail kisses along the column of her neck. A nip to the juncture of her shoulder makes her yelp. I lap the spot and kiss it. A reminder of the claiming bite I will issue.

When I sit back and smirk, her hooded eyes stare at me glistening like the precious stone their color resembles. If she continues to react this way, she'll give in to me without me forcing the bond. Either way, it will happen.

A server appears. He rattles off the day's specials and

takes our drink orders. When he steps away, Maya and Wren chatter about the dishes they crave. In the end, they decide on a smorgasbord with citrusy Riviera salads, Margherita pizza, and paper-thin, succulent beef, tuna, and salmon carpaccio. Their mouths watered for the special of linguine with lobster, shrimp, mussels, and clams in a red tomato sauce. I order it so they can have some. Tag goes for the sirloin steak with green peppercorn, brandy, and cream.

While we eat, talk centers on the items we found so far, what is missing from their lists, getting toys for the nurseries, and all pup things. A goofy grin remains on my face. I glance up to find Tag smirking at me. I shrug, completely busted. What can I say? I'm an excited papa-to-be. He nods in agreement as his gaze slides to Wren. We chime in as needed. But they keep the conversation going until we finish and they're ready for the last store.

When we drive up to Moon Island's entry gates, the security guards wave and gesture to the building where they place deliveries. Tag and I hop out of Maya's new Mercedes-Benz G-Wagen I purchased to replace the one she sold when she left Miami. We load the packages from the stores into the back. With an abundance of bags, Maya and Wren hold some on the back seat. They giggle as we pile the bags on the floor and their laps. Before I shut the door, I zerbert her golden cheek tinged rosy as she laughs. Her topaz eyes sparkle. So beautiful. And all mine.

We drop Tag and Wren off first. I help him carry the bags inside as Wren hugs Maya. The couple wave as we drive off. At our home, I park in the four-car garage and help Maya from the truck. She wraps her arms around my neck and grins.

"What a great day! I'm so happy."

I nuzzle my face in her neck where I will place my mark and breathe in her unique scent. The intoxicating aroma of fragrant frangipani mixed with fresh coconuts and salt carried on a tropical breeze from the Caribbean Sea fills my lungs anew. I say a silent prayer to the gods, thanking them for my fated mate, who I will claim soon. My wolf can barely wait a second longer, and neither can I.

 iggo

"So, how are things going with Maya? What did she decide about the transition? Not much time left since she'll give birth in a just over a month."

Jagger asks as we stroll along the interior of Moon Island. Glancing at me, he cocks a white blond eyebrow.

I take a moment to consider.

During the past ten weeks, she's expressed her love for me and happiness we're together with my pup on the way. She hasn't mentioned the transition—neither as a no or a yes. More often, I nip the spot on her neck. She no longer swats at me or wiggles away. This morning, she moaned and tilted her head to the side to give me better access. I increased the pressure of my fangs. She mewled as the scent of her arousal wafted to my nostrils.

Her reaction tempted my wolf. With great effort, I lifted

my mouth away from her neck as the serum dripped from my fangs. The warm liquid pooled at her collarbone, and she moaned. My wolf remains on edge despite Maya and me being a couple. His patience wears thin. He wants to claim her fully. Now. As do I.

"She's amenable."

He pauses and faces me. He folds his arms across his chest. Muscles ripple as he cocks his head. Ice blue eyes regard me intently.

"Care to elaborate?"

Not really. But judging by his dominant stance, Jagger speaks as pack Alpha, not as older brother. His concern focuses on Maya, a potential member under his protection. Even from her fated mate, should she not wish to proceed with the bonding.

I run a hand through my hair, tugging on the loose strands. The bite of pain clears my head.

"We're in a good place. She's happy, excited about being a mother, tells me she loves me every day. She made my mansion into our home, blending our styles into a harmonious sanctuary. You know she's into crystals, feng shui, and all."

I glance over his shoulder at movement behind him. An elder couple approaches. They stop to talk. Once they move on, I start to walk.

"You missed a question."

Jagger's statement stops me mid-stride.

Naturally, he didn't forget about the transition.

I turn to face him. He raises an eyebrow.

"She hasn't said no," I say, hedging. Then he growls as his wolf flashes in his eyes. "Fine. She's more responsive when I nip her neck, no longer pushes me away. I expect she'll consent after she gives birth."

He studies my face. Satisfied, he nods.

"Excellent. I expect you to obey my command, Viggo. Do not try me."

"Yes, Alpha," I respond with fingers crossed behind my back. I keep a straight face to prevent him from detecting any deceit.

His eyes narrow and nostrils flare as he scents the air. My eyes remain lowered out of respect. He steps forward, and I brace for impact. His arms raise.

"Good to hear, bro!" He exclaims as he claps me on both shoulders and presses his forehead to mine. "I want you to experience the unfailing love of a fated mate and the joys of fatherhood. Sage has changed my life from a playboy like you to a happy husband."

"Months ago, I would have laughed. But after meeting Maya, that's all I want too."

He squeezes my shoulders and pivots.

"You've matured so much since you joined Larson Enterprises. Every year, you offer new recommendations that prosper and your division reaches—if not surpasses—its revenue goals. You've impressed not only me but our business partners. During many meetings, one will mention you and one of your projects. You've made a name for yourself in the industry. Excellent."

He glances at me and nods.

"Now, with Maya and a pup on the way, you will have more responsibilities. I believe you will be as great a father as you are a businessman. I'm proud of you, Viggo."

My chest swells with pride. At last, the recognition I wanted and more.

"Thank you, Jagger. You don't know how much that means to me, brother."

While we continue our walk, I launch my own list of

questions for his advice. After a half an hour of baby prep talk, babymoon, and push present—push present???—suggestions, diaper changing hits or misses, and post-natal intimacy, we shoot the shit. We part at his driveway.

"See you in a few hours."

"Yup, see you at the clubhouse."

I wave and head down the street and onto my driveway. Inside the mansion, I call for Maya. But no answer. I check my mobile, then call hers when I don't see a text message. She went to the salon with the girls to gussy up for the pup shower this afternoon.

"*Ciao, Mi Amor!*"

"*Ciao hermosa.* How's it going? Almost done?"

In the background, Signy giggles about Sasha's joke. Her distinctive Russian accent stands out from the others. Maya giggles before she responds.

"Wonderful! We're almost done. Natalie and Wren sit at the dryers. We'll leave in a few minutes. How was your walk with Jagger? Sage wants to know if he's home yet."

"Good and yes. I left him at their house a few minutes ago. I won't hold you up. See you in a bit. I love you."

"I love you too. *Besos para usted, Mi Amor.*"

We end the call with the girls teasing her about blowing me kisses. I grin and jog up the stairs to shower. I'd wait for Maya. But I doubt she'd want me to mess up her hair. When I step out of the bathroom with a towel wrapped around my hips, I hear a sound in her walk-in closet. I stride over.

"Hey, babe, you're back already—"

But the words get stuck in my throat. Before me is a dick hardening sight.

My eyes travel over her lush body covered in a black silk bra and thong. Since we skinny-dip, no tan lines mar her flawless golden skin. Long, silky waves cascade to brush her round ass. It gobbles up the thin strip, emphasizing the fullness of each cheek. I lick my lips as my mouth waters.

"*Hola, Amante,*" she purrs.

My hungry gaze lifts to her reflection in the trifold mirror.

Maya glances over her shoulder at me with a lust-filled expression in her eyes. She narrows them seductively when she sees my mouth hanging open and my eyes fixed on her enticing bottom. She shimmies her hips and her voluminous breasts bounce in the silk demi cups.

With a low growl, I loosen the towel to free my dick. I advance with a predatory gleam in my eyes. With a snap of my wrist, the thong rips. She gasps as it pinches her clit. My cock thumps at her cry. I release the bra hooks and growl as her ample tits slip from the cups. She whines as I knead the heavy mounds and tweak the plump nipples to distended peaks. I bend my body over hers to lower her into a ninety-degree angle, ass high. A hand lowers to cradle her pup bump.

My growl deepens when I line my rapidly hardening shaft with her seam and impale her instantly. Both of us groan in mutual satisfaction as we join as one in absolute carnal rapture.

Since I entered Maya with no preparation—yes, she definitely drives me mad—I spank her ass to give her pussy time to grow accustomed to my girth and length. I move at a slow, rhythmic pace. Her juices coat my cock as her arousal catches up to mine. The feeling of being bare inside of her is indescribable. My cock feels every surface of her pussy walls, including the texture of her G-spot that I brush my tip against each time I re-enter her core. The increased movement of her ass hitting back against my groin pushes my dick deeper within her drenched folds. My tip touches her womb.

Again, my inner caveman surfaces and grunts as I mount Maya and increase my pace, plundering faster and harder, wanting to plant my seed deep into her fertile womb. I adjust my grip, placing one hand on the top of her shoulder to hold Maya in place. The other hand I place under her opposite thigh to lift it, changing the angle to go even deeper. The sounds of our mating reverberate around the room.

I feel her walls tremble, milking up and down my cock as I squeeze her clit with the fingers under her thigh. She tosses her head back and wails my name as she convulses with her orgasm. I lift her off the floor to drive up into her pulsating pussy. Mad in my desire to fuck her raw, I chase the orgasm brewing at the base of my spine.

"Fuck yes, baby… Take it… Take all of it… YES!" I shout, my voice gruff with desire.

My movements become disjointed as I feel Maya cum for the fourth time and my dick swells deep within her sopping wet pussy. I shift to face the wall and brace her against it as I ram into her again and again until I can't hold back any longer. I grip her hips tightly and possessively bite the sensitive area where her shoulder meets her neck as my orgasm rips through my body. My cock jerks deep inside of her, erupting with seed that coats her womb. I can't stop thrusting like the feral beast I am claiming its mate until every drop of my jizz spews from my tip.

My knees weaken and I lower us to the floor, pulling a boneless Maya into my lap. My spent dick falls from her pussy that's dripping with our combined essence. I stare at the puddle forming beneath our entwined legs, transfixed by our coupling. She sighs and lays her head against my chest where my heart beats helter-skelter.

"Sorry I messed up your hair."

~

MAYA

"SURPRISE!"

I place a hand over my heart as Viggo removes the silk blindfold from over my eyes. I glance around to find Wren and Natalie equally surprised. Their mouths form perfect Os as they clutch Tag and Rust. The pack continues to chant. I glance up at Viggo.

He grins and kisses my cheek.

"Surprise, Hot Mama. The pack wants to celebrate the upcoming births with a pup shower."

A smile replaces the questioning expression on my face. I wrap my arms around his neck and whisper thanks. Keeping a hand on his arm, I face those gathered on the lawn behind the clubhouse. They wave and whoop.

"Thank you! Thank you so much!"

Wren and Natalie echo my sentiments. We move forward to join the pack. They decorated in shades of pink, cream, blues, and grays. Sofas and chairs arranged around six throne-like chairs with tables and chairs covered in white linen fill the space. To the side, rows of tables laden with delicious smelling food make my stomach growl. Still more tables overflow with gifts. Digital photo booths with frames of our names and drawings of wolf pups stand to one side. Stations labeled with various games sit throughout the space. Instead of a baby shower limited to women, they included the guys for a full pack affair. It's a giant party!

Jagger and Sage step forward. The crowd quiets.

"We're excited to have new additions to the Miami Wolves Pack! Today we celebrate the mothers who will give us such precious gifts. Thank you, Natalie, Wren, and Maya."

We thank the Alpha and Luna. Sage embraces us and guides us to mingle with the others. Viggo remains by my side with his hand on my lower back. Just his touch causes tingles to radiate through me. His unexpected, aggressive fucking drove me wild. *Ay Dios mío.*

He must sense my renewed arousal. His hand strokes up my spine to grip the back of my neck. He gives it a squeeze, and my knees wobble. He chuckles and braces my back against his front.

"Easy, greedy girl. I'll ravish you again later."

"Promise?" I ask breathily, then moan as he leans down and nips my neck before sliding his teeth up to my ear.

"Promise," he rasps in a voice thickened with desire.

A shudder runs through me. This male right here…

Wren's squeal pulls me from the lust fog.

I glance over at her where she stands beside a game station. She waves a piece of paper in her hand as she giggles. Tag takes it from her and reads it. He smirks and whispers in her ear. Her cheeks blossom bright red. He chuckles and kisses her cheek.

"Whatever that is, I want some of it."

We laugh at a single she-wolf who fans herself. Another female bobs her head in agreement. A handsome pack bachelor sidles between them and drapes his arms over their shoulders. He flicks his gaze between the two.

"I volunteer myself for whatever pleasures you desire."

One nibbles her lower lip while the other winks. They walk off, heads bent together.

"All righty, then!" Another male says as he guffaws. "We'll have another pup shower in a few months."

"Yes, there's something about mate bonding ceremonies and births. Everyone gets the itch," a she-wolf adds.

Viggo tucks me against his side and moves us along. We chat with others as pack members acting as servers pass through with trays of finger foods and glasses of iced tea. We enjoy the games and take photos before we settle down at the tables for a late lunch.

Afterwards, Sage and Sasha lead us to the throne-like chairs. They hand us gifts to unwrap as the pack watches from the sofas and chairs. Dozens of onesies, hand-crocheted blankets, plush wolves, books, toys, and more pile up on the tables behind us. We'll need a truck to bring the gifts home and a second nursery to put them in.

Everyone is so loving and don't differentiate my baby-pup from Wren and Natalie's pups. My heart swells. Viggo and I exchange several glances. He's as thrilled as I am. His handsome face flushed with joy as he laughs and holds up a wooden train set. The whole affair turns into a fun fete we enjoy for hours.

A sharp cry from Natalie quiets the space. Rust jumps to his feet as she places her hands on her both sides of her belly. She glances up at him and nods. He barks orders to clear the way and to bring a golf cart from the front of the clubhouse. Dylan races to get one. Jagger rushes to Natalie's side and asks Rust how he can help.

In moments, Rust has Natalie in the golf cart and drives to the hospital with Jagger and Sage. Dylan and Sasha hurry for another cart. Viggo and Tag insist Wren and I go home despite our protests, citing the excitement may be too much for us at this stage of our pregnancy. The pack agrees with the overly protective males and offers to deliver the gifts. Viggo scoops me up as Tag does the same with Wren. They carry us to golf carts and take us home.

I wave as they turn into their driveway. Wren crosses her fingers, and I return the gesture with a prayer for Natalie. I place a hand on my baby bump as I wonder what she experiences. Viggo covers my hand with his. I glance at him.

"Don't worry. Natalie will be fine. Rust will deliver his pup as he did for other she-wolves and their little ones before Natalie joined the pack. It'll be your turn soon, baby. And then I will make you mine."

CHAPTER 16

aya

"THESE ONESIES ARE TOO CUTE! Look at the little wolves doing cartwheels!"

Sage giggles as she holds the tiny outfit up.

"I love it!" Wren exclaims. "And get a load of this one with teddy bears!"

We're in my baby-pup's nursery six weeks after the surprise baby shower. It was so much fun to play the games and to open the many presents while we interacted with the pack members.

But the biggest surprise was Natalie giving birth to a healthy male pup. Rust delivered him with no problem, as Viggo said he would. With her advanced healing, Natalie recovered in a few days. However, she took a leave of absence from her OB-GYN duties at the mainland hospital. Thankfully, she confirmed she will handle the deliveries for

Wren and me, much to Tag and Viggo's relief. They got all growly at the possibility of Rust covering for Natalie. Cavemen…

Since the shower, I've had the urge to nest. Hence reorganizing the gifts we received along with others delivered in the last few days from the other five major wolf shifter packs. I've even reordered my baby-pup's supplies in his bathroom!

Sasha says it's a natural instinct to use the burst of energy I've gotten to prepare for his arrival. It's no different from mama birds, cats, and other humans—male included.

I drive Viggo nuts with moving his things into an order I think works best. The other morning, while I was in the library reorganizing the books to make room for the first editions of *The Bobbsey Twins* and *Winnie The Pooh*, he came in asking where I put his ties.

He didn't quite understand why I moved them from their drawers to racks behind his suits. I figured he picked a suit, then would move down the row to pick a tie.

Well, no. So, I spent an hour putting them all back.

I roll my eyes at the memory. Then straighten up to glance at the onesies Signy and Wren hold.

"Oh, those came from Garrett Moen, the Alpha of the New York Wolves Pack. A baby boutique in New York—"

A sharp pain in my lower belly and lower back makes me double over with a cry. The pain radiates down my legs, making my knees buckle. I whimper and clutch my belly when I realize I'm falling.

But instead of hitting the floor, two sets of hands hold me up.

"We have you, Maya!" Sasha exclaims.

"Deep breaths, Maya," Sage tells me calmly. "Focus on your breath."

They maneuver me to the glider, and I sit gingerly. The bracelet on my wrist beeps. A second later, my mobile rings.

Viggo.

Concerned he would be at the office when I went into labor, he purchased a monitor to track vitals, particularly for erratic or elevated heart rates that deviate from the norm. Plus, it has a fall detection and a GPS tracker for the location of the wearer. He gave one to Wren and one to me. The app connects to the monitor, then alerts Viggo, Tag, Natalie, Rust, Jagger, and Sage.

Sasha answers my mobile while Sage checks my vitals.

"Maya! What's happening?!" Viggo asks over the speakerphone.

I start to speak, but another cramp hits me and knocks the breath from my lungs. Instead, a pitiful moan spills from my lips as I grimace.

All morning my back bothered me, but I just assumed it was gas from the French onion soup I ate last night. I craved the crouton and broth. It was yummy then, but it repeated on me... So, I ignored the pangs.

Wrong.

"I'm on my way there!" Viggo shouts and disconnects the call.

Sage asks me questions while Sasha answers Natalie's call. They relay my answers to her, and she advises we come to the hospital even though my water hasn't broken. Since we can only guess at my due date, Natalie doesn't want to risk me going into labor at home. She will meet us at the hospital.

Just as they stand me on my feet, Dylan rushes through the nursery room's door. He takes one glimpse at me and scoops me from the glider. He rushes for the door. Sasha grabs my hospital bag. Sage helps Wren. Signy follows.

"Hold on, Maya, I got you!" Viggo says as we hurry down

the stairs. "Just breathe like Natalie taught you."

"Yes. Don't worry, just focus!" Sasha adds with a nod. "You and your pup are all good!"

I smile at their words. But the grin gets wiped off my face a moment later when I feel a popping sensation, along with a slow trickle of fluid between my thighs.

OMG!!! Did I just pee on myself???

Embarrassed, I peek at Sasha, then Dylan. She doesn't notice. However, he picks up on my discomfort.

His nostrils flare as he cocks his head to the side. He nods and tells me not to worry.

I glance down at my lap, then at him with wide eyes as we walk through the front door Sasha holds open. I'm wearing a white off the shoulder loose tunic and black leggings. At least the dark color will hide the evidence of my oopsie. Although I'm certain it ruined my silk thong and his sweater.

He nods in understanding and turns to Sasha.

"Babe, before you put Maya on the golf cart's seat, can you place a towel down?" he asks.

She nods, and Dylan's gaze shifts from me to Sage to Wren.

"Did your water break?" She asks softly.

I flush bright red and nod.

"It's okay, Maya. That's good! Your pup is on his way!" She exclaims with a smile so full of happiness my heart flutters with joy.

Then Wren cries out.

We turn to her in unison as Dylan sits me on the seat. She grasps her belly and frowns. Sage says it's Wren's time too. Dylan lifts her into his arms and places her next to me. We huddle together as he gets behind the wheel and Sage, Sasha, and Signy hop in. Soon we arrive at the hospital.

Natalie and two midwives wait for us. As the midwives

push us in gurneys down the corridor, she tells us Rust is on his way from the hospital and Viggo and Tag will land at the helipad soon.

They place Wren and me in separate patient rooms. As we part, we stare at each other scared, until Natalie assures us we'll be fine. Sage and Signy go with Wren and Natalie while Sasha stays with me. Dylan excuses himself as his mobile rings. The midwife helps me to change into a clean gown and robe, then makes me as comfortable as possible on the bed.

I settle back and focus on my breathing. *Stay calm, Maya. You can do this!*

"Fuck!!! What the hell did you do to me, Viggo Larson?!?!?!"

I scream at the top of my lungs as I glare at him. Daggers don't even come close to the dangerous weapons of mass destruction I'm throwing in his direction.

He stares back at me wide-eyed with his mouth agape. My Viking warrior is no longer in control. He's in shock.

I've been in active labor for almost seven hours. Seven. Fucking. Contraction-Filled. Hours…

"How much longer, dammit?!?!?!" I screech.

The contractions come faster and last longer now. I want to bear down. A lot of pressure stabs my lower back, worse than before and now in my rectum. I want to push, but the midwife tells me not yet.

After Natalie settled Wren in her room, she prepped me for the first stage of pregnancy, pre-labor. She explained in first-time pregnancies, it can take six to eight hours for my body to be ready for the actual delivery. Once my cervix dilates to ten centimeters, she expected the second stage to be as short as twenty minutes or as long as a few hours.

Hell to the no, no, no! Not another minute, let alone a few fucking hours!

"Let's have the midwife check your cervix. Since the contractions are coming closer together and occur for ninety seconds, you may be ready," Sage suggests as she massages my calves.

Sasha agrees, and Sage steps out. Jagger and Dylan sit in the waiting room.

Since Wren and I are in labor, they split between my room and hers. I haven't had a chance to speak with my bestie, so I don't know how far along she is in labor. I only know hers will be quicker since she's a turned she-wolf.

Right now, I can't think past this pain honestly.

Ay Dios mío.

"Let's have a peek, Maya."

I raise my gaze to see the midwife and Sage walk through the door. She helps me to lean back against the pillows while the midwife peeks under the sheet.

"Well, well, well, your cervix dilated to ten centimeters. I'll get Natalie now," she says with a warm smile and a gentle pat to my knee.

"Oh, thank you, Lord!!!" I cry.

Viggo takes my hand in his and smiles as he says, "Babe, you're doing so well. Soon it'll be over, and we'll have—"

He yowls as I grip his hand with all my strength when an excruciating contraction rocks me to my core.

"Fuuuck!!!" I bellow, followed by a string of curses. I call Viggo every name I can think of and then find some more.

The midwife chuckles as she heads to the door.

"Viggo, would you like me to have a look at your hand?" She asks over her shoulder.

"No, thank you. That's all right," he grunts as he rubs his hand.

Sage rises from the chair and reaches for Viggo's hand.

"It's not the best idea to hold a female's hand when she's in labor," she laughs as she massages his hand with her fingertips. "Ask your brother and Dylan. I'm sure I broke one or two of Jagger's fingers!"

Viggo groans, "Lesson learned, Sage, thanks."

Natalie enters, and I say a silent prayer.

"Sounds as though you're ready for me, Maya," she says. "Let's have a look."

Viggo growls softly when she takes a seat on the stool at my feet and lifts the sheet. She smiles at him reassuringly before she lowers her head and peers between my legs.

"All right, Maya, we're in the second stage of labor. The time to push is now," she says.

"Thank the good Lord!!!" I cry as another contraction hits me.

"He's crowning. Get ready to push, Maya," Natalie raises her eyes to mine and nods. "All right, now! Push!"

At once, I curse myself for not accepting the epidural when I had the chance. My and my not wanting to put anything unnatural in my body… I feel as though I have a hundred of Viggo's massive hard dicks battering my pussy for hours with no end.

"AAARRGGGHHH!!!" I growl as I bear down.

"Breathe with it, Maya. Breathe," Sage says as she stands to my right, just in my line of sight. "Focus on your breath."

I take a deep inhale in preparation to increase the pressure within my belly and contract my abs. Holding my breath before I let it go as I push our baby-pup out.

"That's it, my love. You're doing well," Viggo murmurs as he strokes my hair that Sage put into one long braid down my back.

My mind knows it's not his fault. Well, not entirely. But I just can't think straight at a time such as now.

"Shut up, Viggo!!!" I growl as I slap his hand away from me with a kyber crystal-powered super laser stare from the

Death Star. It's strong enough to destroy an entire planet. Or a Viking.

Viggo opens his mouth, then thinks better and closes it. He glances at Sage, and she shakes her head, suppressing a giggle.

It's rare one sees the powerful wolf shifter at a loss and not in charge of a situation.

More contractions, more choice words, more killer looks, more pushing, and our baby-pup makes his debut.

~

VIGGO

MY PUP IS BORN!

Holy shit! I'm a father, a Dad, a *Papá*.

"Viggo, you may cut the umbilical cord now."

Natalie's words pull me from my pleasant musings, and I glance at her. She hands a pair of sterile scissors to me with a broad smile and a nod of encouragement.

I shift my gaze to Maya, my fated mate, my love, the mother of my pup. Her topaz eyes—softened by the miracle she achieved—stare back at me from a face flushed red and damp from the exertion of nine hours of labor.

My heart swells and my eyes well with tears. I lean over to kiss her on her lips, then press my forehead to hers as I close my eyes on a silent prayer of thanks to the gods.

"I love you, Hot Mama. Thank you," I murmur huskily as tears slip down my cheeks.

Maya reaches a small hand up to wipe the moisture away. She brings her wet fingertips to her lips, then places them on mine.

"I love you, *Papá*. Thank you, my love," she whispers in a

hoarse voice. "Cut the umbilical cord so we can hold our son."

She pats my cheek and sighs, exhausted from the delivery.

With a nod, I turn to Natalie and do the honor. The pediatrician takes my pup off to the side in order to care for him. I split my gaze between her actions and Maya, who's being comforted by Sage. I confirm she's fine, then turn my full attention to our pup.

"How is he?" I ask as I watch possessively over the doctor's shoulder while she tends to him.

She smiles at me and responds, "He's in excellent health! All ten fingers and toes! He weighs 7.8 pounds. An acceptable size for a male newborn. Congratulations, Viggo!"

Relief washes over me. Then anxiety sweeps in when she places our freshly cleaned son in my arms. When I look at her in a panic, she smiles encouragingly.

I glance down at his mottled face. He may be tiny, but the weight of responsibility hits me in that moment. My son, the fruit of my loins. I am his father. His safekeeping ranks as my utmost priority, along with his mother.

"Viggo? What's taking so long? Is he okay?"

Maya's soft voice filled with concern calls me back to the room.

"He's perfect, my love. See for yourself," I respond as I stride over to her and place our pup on her chest.

Her face lights up with such love and joy when she stares at him. Tears stream down her cheeks. Her fingers tentatively touch his soft jet black hair, and his eyes open slowly.

Ice blue eyes and jet black hair. The perfect combination of his parents.

Maya peers up at me and smiles angelically.

"Your baby-pup, my love," she whispers. "He looks like you, like a true Viking. Are you pleased, Viggo?"

I nod, overwhelmed, and I bury my face in her damp hair.

An hour later, a freshly washed Maya holds our pup to her breast as she feeds him for the first time. They're skin-to-skin to help him stay warm as he gets used to being outside of her womb. Natalie explained it's a great way for parents and pup to get to know each other right away. Our pup welcomes our gentle touches, and this closeness can help us bond with him.

I rub his back beneath the blanket, wanting him to recognize his sire, too. My hand is so much larger than his narrow back. I smile and pull my mobile from my pocket to take a video and some photos.

Maya giggles and pats the bed beside her.

"Come, sit, *Papá*," she says, with a twinkle in her hazel eyes.

I smirk when, for a moment, my mind drifts to the fetish. But that's not our thing. Although we'll try anything once…

"Stop it! Viggo…" Maya laughs. "Sit with us before others come in. I'm just sad my family isn't here. We didn't have time to tell Patricio. Hopefully, he can visit soon."

As tears fill her eyes, I cup her cheek. I won't let those fuckers ruin our first family bonding moment. When Maya sleeps, I'll reach out to Patricio to invite him to visit—not on Moon Island, of course. I'll arrange for Maya, our pup, and me to stay at a visitor's apartment in The Larson Tower while he's here.

I turn my mind away from negative thoughts and focus on what truly matters. I have my family of Maya, our pup, and me. Our family unit that fits inside of the Miami Wolves Pack. Now, I know how Jagger and Dylan feel. To have my own is the most incredible sense of responsibility. Mine to care for, mine to protect, mine to love forever.

Mine!!!

"Tell me, did Wren give birth to her triplets?" Maya asks. Her eyes pop in concern for her best friend, even on the heels of her delivery.

I smile before I put my mobile in front of her to hold it as our pup suckles at her breast. With a few swipes, I load the video Tag sent earlier.

"Here, see for yourself, babe," I say as the screen fills with a grinning Tag angling his mobile to capture Wren, their pups, and himself.

"Hi, bestie! Guess who made their debut?" Wren trills.

Tag moves his mobile closer to their tiny faces. Their little rosebud mouths purse, and they open their eyes to reveal emerald eyes like their sire.

"My sweet pups. Can you believe it?" Tag says in awe.

Wren gazes at him with such love. Then faces the mobile again, and her mink brown eyes shine.

"Now it's your turn to send a video message!" She laughs.

"Yes!" Tag adds as he waves before the video ends.

Their intimacy tugs at my heart. This is what Maya and I have now. I'm beyond ecstatic.

As I put my mobile down, it vibrates with a call. A glance at the screen shows Jagger's name. Maya and I have been so focused on enjoying these first few moments with our pup we hadn't communicated with him, Sage, or the others.

"Hey, bro! We're all good. Give us a minute before you come in to meet your newest pack member!" I exclaim.

Maya laughs as she puts him on her shoulder.

I rub his back to help him burp. The greedy bugger. While Maya fixes her nightgown and robe, I cradle our pup to my chest through the opening of my button-down shirt. He's warm from Maya and smells like a newborn, just as I remember Signy.

"I'm all set, Viggo," Maya says on a yawn.

"You need to rest, babe," I respond and continue when she starts to object. "We'll announce his name, make the video, and take some more photos. Afterwards, everyone leaves. It's important you take care of yourself, *Mamá.*"

She grins and nods in agreement.

I place our pup back in her arms, and she nuzzles his hair, inhaling his unique scent. Before I let the others in, I take a moment to stare at my little family.

All mine!

As soon as they walk in, Sage makes a beeline for Maya and our pup. She coos softly as she strokes his chubby leg.

"How are you, Maya?" She asks. "You look so happy. But you need to rest. We won't stay for long."

Jagger agrees, "No, we won't keep you. Only a quick peek. You need your rest."

I chuckle to myself, thinking how alike my brother and I behave. He and Sage are couple goals.

"Congratulations, Little Sis, bro! You did it," Jagger says as he fist bumps with me. "Now, what do we call the little one officially?"

My face splits in two nearly as I wrap my arm around Maya's shoulders while I pat our pup's back. Maya turns him around to rest against her big boobs so he can face everyone. I hand my mobile to Jagger for him to take the video.

"Meet Ulf Larson!" I announce, beaming.

"Ulf! I love his name!" Exclaims Signy as she claps her hands. "It means wolf in old Norse."

"It sounds badass!" Dylan grins, his golden eyes twinkle with mischief.

My brother grips my shoulder and smiles. "Well done! A strong name for the newest addition to the Miami Wolves Pack. Tag and Wren had healthy pups. Today is a great day for our pack!"

I grin at my brother even as my wolf howls.
Time to claim my fated mate.

CHAPTER 17

$\mathcal{M}$*aya*

"MAYA, you look incredible! I'm so happy for you and Viggo. Congratulations!"

Patricio pulls me into his arms as tears slip down my cheeks. It's so good to see my brother.

Viggo told me he had a surprise for me. We drove to The Larson Tower, with Ulf sleeping in my arms. I had no idea the surprise was Patricio.

It's been a couple of weeks since Ulf's birth. The next day, Viggo gave me a push present of an incredible blue diamond heart-shaped pendant on a delicate platinum chain. The heart aligns with mine to represent our little Ulf's heart beating in sync. I haven't taken it off since Viggo placed it around my neck. I treasure it but not nearly as much as I love Viggo and Ulf. They are my heart.

However, it beats quickly as my brother hugs me close. No more words pass between us. Yet we speak volumes.

731

Viggo stands to the side with Ulf held against his chest. I sense his watchful eyes on us. Even though he invited Patricio to Miami and we speak every week, Viggo remains leery. Not that I blame him.

It's been hard not having the support of my family all these months. Complete silence from my parents and Odalis. At first, I thought they would give in. I even called and sent text messages. But they went unanswered. I didn't tell Viggo, convinced he'd fly down to Caracas and have it out with them. After a while, I realized it's not worth it.

I chose to live my life as I pleased, and I will.

I dry my eyes and smile up at my brother. His handsome face lights up with a genuine smile full of love. My heart sings.

"Thank you, Patricio. I'm so happy you're here! Come sit. Do you want something to drink? Are you hungry?"

My mothering instincts expand beyond little Ulf. I find myself having the urge to care for others, too. Wren laughs and tells me I can come mother her triplets any day while she takes a much-needed nap. I join in her laughter knowing she'd have it no other way. Her trio of adorable wolf pups is her top priority, with Tag coming in a close fourth!

Natalie's pup is so sweet. He's bigger than the other four and not just because he's a few weeks older. She and Rust say it's because they're born wolf shifters. It will be interesting to see if Ulf and Wren's pups differ. However, I don't worry about it. Ulf is bigger than a human baby. As with my pregnancy, he's at a more advanced stage at a younger age. So, I'm sure he'll keep up with everyone else.

Viggo says his pup is absolutely perfect. I agree!

Wren and I introduced them to the pack a week after we gave birth. We gathered in the clubhouse meeting space. It was so different from my first time standing before the pack. I wasn't nervous they wouldn't accept me. Or, if I'm honest, terrified they'd eat me. The she-wolves who made innuendos about their dalliances with Viggo oohed and ached over Ulf as much as they did the other newborns. The space vibrated with love. I couldn't be happier.

But not as happy as I am now as I sit beside my brother in a guest apartment. I realize Viggo had us come here to avoid Patricio visiting Moon Island. It's best to let him believe Viggo and I live here than to make him aware of the protected island.

Patricio turns to Viggo and opens his arms with a smile.

"May I hold my nephew, Viggo?"

He hesitates, then crosses the distance between them. I can sense his need to protect our pup. I smile as he approaches. Our eyes meet, and I nod. He returns the gesture and places our pup in Patricio's arms. Viggo ensures my brother holds Ulf's head and cradles him to his chest. Viggo eyes Patricio as he holds him. Satisfied, he steps back and perches on the edge of the sofa beside me. I place a hand on his thigh and squeeze. He smiles while his gaze remains on our baby-pup.

"He's a handsome boy. The darkens of his hair combined with his pale blue eyes is striking. He'll be a charmer like his *Tío* Patricio!"

He chuckles and winks at Viggo. He doesn't crack a smile. My brother shakes his head and clears his throat. He glances between Viggo and me with serious eyes.

"Listen, I understand you're wary of our family, and I do not blame you in the least. They were wrong. I tell them every day," he says, then focuses on me. "Maya, you must live your life and not wait for our family to accept what happened. You know how stubborn *Papá* is, and *Mamá* follows right behind him. Odalis will do anything to please our father."

He flicks his gaze to Viggo and glances down at Ulf before he continues, "You have your family now. And of course, you will always have me. Do not allow ours to drain you of the joy you share with Viggo and Ulf. Focus on the gifts given to you. Do not miss out on a moment with them. Promise me, Maya."

I nod, too emotional to verbalize a response. Viggo strokes my back as he presses a kiss to my head. He murmurs comforting words for a moment before he faces my brother.

"Patricio, I appreciate your words. I'm sure it's difficult for you to go against your family to support Maya. They don't deserve either of you."

My brother inclines his head.

I take his words to heart. It's painful to know he's told them repeatedly how wrong they are. Yet I hear nothing from not one of them. It's foolish of me to hold back my life. I bring my gaze to Viggo and smile. I make my decision.

~

VIGGO

I SENSE a change in Maya after her brother tells her to move on. My wolf grins with tongue lolling, convinced she decided to accept my claiming bite and to transition. To be one with me forever. I send a silent prayer to the gods my instinct is true. Then another one to get Patricio out of here and into his guest apartment. Not polite. But I don't give a damn. I want to be alone with Maya. Now.

Unfortunately, they spend hours talking. To make the time go faster, I go into the kitchen to prepare dinner. Maya's appetite increased since, as she told me, she burns loads of calories breastfeeding Ulf—and me. I can't get enough of her sweet milk.

I prepare one of her favorite dishes, shredded beef in a tomato sauce with roasted vegetables. The first time I made it and she smacked her lips, I teased she wanted it because it instinctively reminds Ulf of an animal his wolf hunted. She refused to eat the dish the second time, then asked me to cook it a week later. I chuckle to myself as I stir the red sauce.

My mind drifts to the other morning.

My enhanced hearing detected Ulf snuffling in the nursery while Maya slept peacefully. Wanting her to let rest, I decided to feed him from a bottle. Quietly, I slipped from the bed and left our suite. I strode with a purpose to his nursery. He waved his arms in the air, making sucking noises. A grin spread over my face as I crossed the room to his crib. With each step, my heart soared.

Who'd have thought the playboy prince of the pack focused on proving I'm my own male to be taken seriously would meet my fated mate at the club, fall madly in love, and have a pup?

Hell nah!

But here we are, and there I was picking up Ulf with a stinky diaper. I couldn't help but to chuckle at the irony. I'm ready for family life. Wow!

"Viggo? Did you hear me?"

I glance down at the sound of Maya's voice. She places a hand on my back and stares at me with questioning eyes.

Caught in my thoughts, I didn't detect her enter the kitchen. I smile and kiss the crown of her head.

"Sorry, my love. I didn't hear you. What did you say?"

She studies my face, then smiles.

"How's dinner going? Do you need any help?"

I glance over her head, looking for Ulf. Patricio stands by the island holding him. He smiles.

"I'm not handy in the kitchen. But I can pour the wine."

I realize I should give him a break. At least he attempts to be a part of Maya's life, and now Ulf's. I nod.

"Sounds good, thanks."

He walks over to Maya. She takes Ulf from his arms and sits at the island.

"The food smells delicious. What is it?" Patricio asks.

I offer him a taste as I tell him about Maya's favorite dish, leaving out the wolf shifter part. I smirk over my shoulder at her, and she grins.

"So, my tastes changed. I'll admit it."

We eat alfresco on the terrace with the panoramic view across Biscayne Bay, abuzz with water lovers, to the azure Atlantic Ocean. We fall into a companionable conversation through the meal to after-dinner drinks. The entire time, Ulf sleeps peacefully in his bassinet between Maya and me.

Patricio leaves with plans to spend the next day with Maya while I care for Ulf. We'll meet up again for dinner. It pleases me to see her eyes bright with happiness. No matter what happens with the rest of her family, she has her brother's love.

We bathe Ulf and settle him in his nursery for the night, then head to our suite. Maya slips her hand in mine and leans into me as we walk along the hallway. I bring our entwined fingers to my lips and kiss her knuckles as I inhale frangipani and coconuts. She sighs and smiles up at me.

"Viggo, make me yours in all ways, *Mi Amor*."

 *aya*

"Mmmmmm... Mmm mmm... Aaahhh!"

My eyes roll. My head flies back on my neck. I snap my legs together against the sides of Viggo's head. I jackknife off the bed. It's the third orgasm he's pulled from me since I awoke to his tongue laving my pussy. I'm incoherent at this point. My swollen pussy lips and engorged clit can't take any more of his licks, nips, and probes.

"Ooohh, Viggooo!" I wail as my body continues to convulse.

He growls his disapproval and nips my inner thigh. Then he adds two of his thick fingers to the mix. The strumming of my G-spot causes another orgasm to rise from the base of my spine.

I cry out from the unexpected sharp pain and toss my head from side to side. My bound wrists struggle against the silk belts attached to the ornate wooden headboard. Not only is Viggo my Viking warrior, he's resourceful. He made good use of the sumptuous robes in the en suite bathroom by repurposing the belts as restraints. I can only move my lower body fully and tug my arms fruitlessly.

"Bad girl," he admonishes as he parts my lower lips to spank my sensitive clit.

The moist sounds of flesh meeting flesh are a trigger for my body to respond with another mind-blowing climax. I mewl as it ignites my body in pure ecstasy.

"Be still, or I'll force you to cum five more times," Viggo threatens.

Ordinarily, that may sound like a phenomenal idea. But not after multiple rounds last night and this morning. I hate to admit it, but my body needs a break. He's determined to make my experience with his claiming bite a memorable one. And damn if it won't be. I'm so boneless, I'll never walk again!

"Viggooo… Please!" I beg.

Relief floods my system when he prowls up my body, leaving a trail of open mouth kisses on my heated skin. His ice blue eyes—now silver with lust—never leave mine. Hypnotized, I watch his approach. Only when I catch sight of his massive cock in my periphery do my eyes veer from his.

Viggo's dick is a sculpturesque piece of art. Hard as steel, covered in velvety soft skin. Veins and ridges stand in relief. The bulbous head reddened with need glistens with a drop of pre-cum on its slit. Its ten-inch length and girth too wide for my fingers to meet. His heavy balls swing at the base like a pendulum. The tantalizing sight makes my mouth water. I lick my lips. He chuckles.

"Hungry for what you see, my little wolf?" He asks as his voice thrums in my ear.

I nod and whimper my response.

He grips the base of his big dick and feeds the tip an inch inside of me.

I groan.

"Open up for me. I need to feel your tight pussy wrapped around me, milking my cock," he growls in a voice rough with desire.

Conditioned to respond to her mate, my body drains of the tension to allow him unrestrained entry. We groan together as he breaches my pussy lips. Once fully seated, Viggo stills. Entranced by the sensation of my pussy clenching around his pulsating cock, we don't utter a sound. Only the rapid beat of our hearts fills the air.

Not until my hips rise of their own accord demanding movement, does Viggo pull out to his tip then piston back inside of me. He wanted to give me the time I needed for my mind to catch up with my body in its appetite for more.

"Oh, baby... You feel so fucking good... So hot and wet..." Viggo grunts as his passion builds.

I writhe beneath him. My wrists pull against my restraints, aching to wrap my arms around his neck or grip his biceps for stability. Instead, all I can do is open and close my fists on air. He feels so good. So very good. But I need more.

Viggo takes one hand from my hip and places his thumb in my slack mouth. Without hesitation, I suckle it with fervor, pretending it's his dick. Once it's sopping wet, he pops it from my mouth and lifts me up onto his thighs as he sits back on his haunches.

Upright, he has more access to my body. His lips trail down the column of my neck to wrap around my fully aroused nipple. At the same time, he pulls my ass cheek to the side and presses the pad of his wet thumb against my puckered hole. My muscles in my pussy and ass tighten. He grunts from the strength of them on his dick.

"Aaahhh!" I scream as he plunders my bottom hole with his thumb and uses his muscular thighs to pump his cock up into my pussy.

My back arches and I keen with each bottoming out thrust. It seems as though I'll break in two from Viggo's power. An orgasm comes upon me with the speed of a freight train going downhill with no breaks. A bolt of lightning strikes me. Blinded with my body on fire, I ride Viggo like my life depends upon it.

"Fuuuck… Mayaaa!" He roars as my climax triggers his knot.

Inside of me, the base of his dick swells impossibly larger, locking us together. The tip presses against my womb. I cry out from the burn as it stretches my pussy.

Viggo bands one arm around my waist while the other hand sweeps my long hair to the side. It hangs over my shoulder. His flashing eyes stare into mine as his hand wraps around the back of my throat. I can't move.

He snarls and lowers his mouth to the juncture where my neck meets my shoulder. His hot breath blows across the sweaty skin. Warm liquid drips on the spot. Then pain sears me at the same time as hot ropes of his seed bathe my womb. Blood trickles down my shoulder. Liquid heat explodes in my pussy. I howl and struggle to break free of his hold.

Viggo's hand and arm tighten like bands of steel as his extended canines sink into my flesh. His mouth opens, then clamps back on the same spot. The serum from his canines lodges his scent under my skin to mark me as his permanently and to initiate my transition. He shakes his head to deepen the claiming bite.

Another wave crests over us as we continue to pound fiery flesh against fiery flesh in our frenzy to sate our carnal needs. When the last drop of Viggo's essence flows from his body to mine, we collapse breathless on the bed in a state of sheer euphoria.

"MINE!" He growls against my skin as he licks the bite.

It's the last thing I hear before darkness overtakes me.

~

VIGGO

"YOU TOLD me Maya's body needed to recover from the birth and to wait for six weeks before I issued my claiming bite. I did what you said. Now, five days have passed! How much longer do you think before she wakes up?!"

My gaze flicks between Rust and Natalie as we stand outside of Maya's room at Moon Island Hospital. I pray to the gods my worse fear doesn't happen. I cannot lose Maya. Especially since we have Ulf. Our pup needs his mother. I need my fated mate. Pain laces my heart at the thought she'll never wake up. *Do not take her from me!* I rail at the gods. My wolf howls mournfully.

"Viggo, we spoke with the other packs. The transition time ranges from four days to a week. It depends on the female," Rust says.

"Yes. I know it's difficult, Viggo. But have patience. Maya is a young, healthy, and fit female. I have no doubt she will recover. Give her body time to adjust. It's not a straightforward process to change the body's genetic makeup," Natalie adds as she rubs my arm.

"Why don't you come and sit, Viggo?"

I glance over at Wren, where she sits beside Maya's bed. She smiles reassuringly and holds out her hand. I flick my gaze to Jagger, Sage, and Signy where they stand with Tag, Dylan, and Sasha across the hall.

"I agree. She's connected to every machine possible to monitor her vitals. All is well. Go sit by your mate's side. Give her the comfort of your loving presence," Jagger says.

"Place Ulf on her chest like you did before. She responded well to him," Signy adds.

I listen to my siblings' advice and lift Ulf from his crib. I kiss the top of his head, covered with even more silky, jet black hair. He waves his arms as drool slips from his bow-shaped lips. I wipe it clean with a cloth and lay him on his mother's chest with my hand on his back.

I watch the two most important people in the world—my family. I send love down the mate bond formed when I issued my claiming bite. My heart, body, and soul beg Maya to open her eyes. A few minutes pass with no response. Only the steady pings of the machines sound in the room.

With a sigh, I lift Ulf from his mother's chest and cradle him against mine as I lower my cheek to his hair. I breathe in his pup scent of milk and soap while I murmur my love for him. With a heavy heart, I turn to place him in his crib.

"V—V—"

My heart stutters at the soft sound of Maya calling for me. I spin around to find her eyes fluttering open. She blinks against the light from the window and closes her eyes. Wren rushes to lower the shade, then leaves the room.

"Maya!" I exclaim.

My hand strokes her cheek as I call to her again. Slowly, she opens her eyes. I could drown in their topaz depths as she stares up at me. The corners of her lips curve.

"Viggo, Ulf," she says in a raspy voice. "Am I okay?"

A grin splits my face in two. I lean over and press my lips

to hers. Fingers tangle in my hair as she pulls me closer and parts her lips. Our tongues twine on mutual groans. Ulf babbles in my arms as though telling us enough. I lean my forehead on hers and chuckle.

"You're awake. Thank the gods."

"Viggo, let me check her."

I stand as Natalie closes the door and approaches the bed. She asks Maya questions as she examines her. I finally relax when Natalie confirms Maya is indeed okay, even better than the baseline tests she did before the transition. Pleased, Natalie leaves the room to tell the others.

"I can't believe I was out of it for so long. The whole time, I dreamed of a black wolf. Even now, I can see her in my mind's eye. Is that my wolf?" Maya says in between sips of water.

"Yes, and I will show you how to shift. After our mate bonding ceremony, we'll go to the Everglades camp for a pack run. My wolf can't wait to meet yours."

I turn at a knock on the door and call for them to enter. The gang troops in with whoops and words of congratulations. They gather around Maya, and she grins. She pats the bed beside her, and I sit, placing Ulf in her lap. She kisses his plump cheeks and cradles him in against her chest. With the other hand, she takes mine and kisses it.

"We're so glad to see you awake and strong, Maya," Jagger says, then glances at me before his gaze returns to her. "I know how eager Viggo is to complete your bonding. If you're up to it, the pack would like to celebrate your transition and witness your love with a mate bonding ceremony tonight. Would you like to do it?"

Tears stream down Maya's cheeks as she nods vigorously.

"That's so kind, thank you, Alpha."

Jagger beams at her use of his formal title as leader of our pack.

"Excellent! The Miami Wolves Pack will howl tonight!"

I grin as I brush Maya's tears with my thumb and press my forehead to hers.

"I love you, Maya Alejandra Larson."

"I love you, Viggo Larson."

A few hours later, as the sun sets, we stand before a ceremony bower of fragrant frangipani and jasmine flowers in the middle of Moon Island beneath the swaying fronds of palm trees. Their soft rustling seems to whisper words of joy at our union. The balmy air mixes with the floral aroma for a sultry scent. Whip-poor-wills chirp to welcome the night.

I wear a classic black tuxedo. But it's my smile with such jubilation in my heart that looks best. My fated mate returns my smile with one filled with love as she stands before me.

Signy helped her to select a crystal embellished evening gown with the sparkly stilettos that complement it so well. It hugs her round ass just the way I like it. Sage invoked a glamour spell to apply makeup and to put soft waves in Maya's hair. The tresses flow down her back, away from her radiant face.

We exchange our mate bonding vows with Ulf in my arms as we stand in front of our pack. My heart swells at how the members welcome Maya into our fold. They embrace her fully. Well, not the males or I'll tear their arms from their sockets...

After I slip a family heirloom princess-cut diamond and platinum ring on Maya's finger—the new pack princess— and she places a platinum band on mine, we face the others. The clearing at the center of Moon Island explodes with shouts and howls of elation.

I dip down and lift Maya onto my other arm. She giggles and wraps one arm around my neck while the other hand holds Ulf's hand. I throw my head back and howl. Maya joins in. I kiss her lips. Then, as a family, I carry them back up the aisle to wolf whistles and claps.

Maya is all mine. Forever.

ix Months Later
Maya

"COME, my little wolf. Let's run in the moonlight as wolves."

My pussy quivers at Viggo's rich baritone as he takes my hand. We came to the pack's Everglades camp to celebrate the one-year anniversary of the first night we met. Wren and Tag pup-sit Ulf in their cabin nearby.

It's the place we go for pack runs and trainings. For generations, the virtually untouched area of the subtropical wilderness allows the pack the freedom to be in wolf form without prying eyes. Over the years, the original pack grounds grew from temporary cloth shelters to simple wooden cabins and now to luxurious residences scattered around the Alpha's house and clubhouse. Glamping—or glamorous camping—as Signy calls it. A few families and security members known as enforcers choose to remain here, not wanting the hustle and bustle of Miami for their principal home.

The camp sprawls out around us. Rather, the glamp since every cabin is a rustic mansion of logs and stones in various styles—some ranch and others multilevel, with and without front porches. They surround an open park-like square in the middle, where a lovely garden displays colorful flowers and bushes with wooden benches. Lanes crisscross the land to provide access to the various homes and structures.

A few pack members walk along or sit on porches. Their laughter and conversations fill the air. Cheerful smiles spread across their faces as they interact. The only surprising difference being some members in wolf form going about their business like it's an ordinary occurrence. Otherwise, the camp is an idyllic enclave with the spectacular Everglades as the setting.

Viggo leads me from our cabin and strides to the path lined by ornate wrought-iron lampposts. We walk in silence. He scans our surroundings while I absorb its beauty. The full moon illuminates the grassy areas where an abundance of trees rises to the night sky.

Raccoons scurry to the right. The little bandits lift their gazes from foraging to watch two lethal predators. They detect our wolves. Once we pass, the raccoons return to their dinner.

Rustling within the leaves of a nearby elm tree draws my attention. I narrow my gaze to pinpoint the source. Red furry bodies extend wings. A colony of red bats awake from their slumber to hunt. Not a fan of the creatures, I turn my attention to the left.

Another grassy, tree-filled area stretches to a large pond. Its surface ripples with the breeze. Ducks huddle in nests gathered in bushes along its edge. Beaks appear from beneath their back feathers as they sense our wolves, too.

Viggo squeezes my hand, and I glance up at him. He tilts

his chin towards a cluster of trees beyond the pond. I follow as he changes direction. When we reach the center hidden by low branches, he drops his black backpack to the grass.

"We'll shift here. You first. Our clothes will go in the backpack. Before I shift, I'll put it on. Remember to always stay by my side, Maya. Now, hand me your clothes and sneakers. Then shift."

My black wolf drops her front legs and raises her rear as her tail wags. She's ready to play, and so am I!

I peel off the t-shirt. My full breasts bounce free. The already puckered nipples tighten to peaks as the cool air licks at them. I toe off the sneakers. My hips shimmy as I slip out of the shorts. When I rise with the clothes bundled in my arms, Viggo stares at me. My cheeks flush crimson from his unleashed desire.

A needy whine rises in the back of my throat. He growls in response and stalks towards me. My clothes fall to the ground. Once again, he kisses me senseless. He pulls away, and my body leans towards him, drawn like a magnet to steel. Or rather to his velvet-covered steel rod that tents his shorts.

"I'm not waiting until we get back, little wolf."

I squeeze my thighs together as my fingernails dig into his forearms. *Ay Dios mío!* Does he mean to mount me in wolf form? My wolf leaps to her feet and howls.

"Shift, *mate.*"

His command catches me off guard, but not my wolf. She surges forward. Bones reshape and muscles lengthen as I shift to my black wolf. Amidst crackling and a flash, we stand on four legs moments later. My fur-covered head tilts back to gaze at him.

"So beautiful you are, Maya. Gorgeous," he murmurs as he circles me, trailing his fingertips along my neck and flank. The feathery edges of my tail slip through his fingers. They move to caress my spine and the top of my head.

He crouches in front of me and cups my jaw. "Now, I'll shift, and we'll run. Then mate."

My fur ripples as I shudder. *Yes!*

Viggo strips and adds his clothes with mine to the backpack. He loosens the straps, then loops his arms through. It hangs to the side. Moments later, it fits snug to his massive red wolf. The same wolf from my dreams. My fantasy lover come to life.

Slowly, I approach him with my head and tail low. My wolf wants to guarantee he sees we pose no threat. We are omega to his Alpha. I pause at a low growl. A tentative step forward elicits another low growl. Immediately, I drop to the ground and bare my throat and belly.

He pads forward and nuzzles my vulnerable areas. Hot breath blows my fur as he sniffs and chuffs.

I remain completely still.

He probes between my rear legs and rumbles. The flat of his textured tongue laves my sensitive bits.

I whimper.

He growls low in his throat.

A nip to my flank breaks my stillness. I yelp and gaze up at him. Tempered lust fills his eyes. He jerks his head, and I roll to all fours. A quick shake loosens the leaves and twigs stuck to my fur. He pads from beneath the branches. I follow.

We run and play through the sawgrass marshes and pine flatwoods. The scent of fresh grass, musky-sweetness of fallen leaves, squirrels asleep in their burrows, and unbathed humans flow through the crisp air past my nose. The pads of my feet snap twigs and grip boulders with every bounding step. My heart races as fast as my legs. Free!

Viggo slows and lopes towards a rock formation. He

pauses outside the opening and blocks me from following. He steps inside. Seconds later, his head peeks out. He rumbles and steps back. I enter. My eyes dart around the cave.

Dirt covers the ground with windswept leaves scattered about. The rough surface of the rocks creates three walls and a ceiling. Away from the evening chill, the temperature is comfortable—not that wolf shifters get cold. It's cozy.

Viggo prods me with his snout and shrugs his shoulders. I nod and use my teeth to tug the backpack straps from his body. I watch it drop to the ground. When my gaze lifts, he stares at me like a hungry predator ready to devour its prey.

∽

VIGGO

MAYA'S SCENT taunted my nostrils from the moment we stood outside our cabin. Many times, I had to fight the urge to push her against a tree and plunge my hungry cock deep into her cunt.

But I wanted to find a suitable place for us to mate as wolves for the first time. Now, I wish to take pleasure in her. My wolf howls in agreement.

I prowl towards her—a constant rumble in my chest. She remains still. I breathe in her unique scent as once again I nuzzle her neck, flank, and base of tail. With a possessive growl, I rise onto my hind legs and wrap my front ones around her waist and legs. My thighs bracket hers.

She lifts her tail.

I plunge my aching cock inside of her. She whines and stamps her front feet. I growl as my hips pump vigorously. Nips to her neck and shoulders still her wriggling. My knot expands. Her pussy contracts. She paws the ground, whining as we lock together. I rumble in my chest to soothe her while we remain carnally connected. I want another pup in her belly.

Fifteen minutes later, my knot deflates, and we separate. I nuzzle her flank and lick her snout. She returns my affection.

I step away and send my contented wolf back to the fringes of my being. He retreats at my will. On all fours, I stretch and watch as my beautiful mate shifts. I look forward to more times fucking her while we're wolves.

"Oh, Viggo," she purrs as she stretches. "That was amazing, *Mi Amor*."

She presses her forehead against mine. A yawn interrupts our moment of bliss. She giggles and reaches for the backpack. Handing my clothes to me, she smiles.

"You wore me out, big bad wolf."

Kneeling, I chuckle and tug my t-shirt over my head. When we're dressed, I crawl out our den and scan the area. Maya crawls forward and slips her hand in mine. She stifles another yawn.

"Come. Let's get you home. I'll bathe you and tuck you in for a good night's sleep. I have surprises for you tomorrow."

She bounces on the balls of her feet and kisses my cheek.

Who expected I'd fall so hard for a fated mate I never knew existed a year ago?

And now I love her, our pup, and want another.

The pack prince met his match and more.

igny

"KEEP your head down and hold on, Signy! Hold on! Oh, gods—"

Across from me, the flight attendant shouts from her seat while the pilot and co-pilot attempt to regain control of my private jet.

It jounces in violent turbulence caused by an unexpected blizzard swept in from the Atlantic Ocean as we fly from Miami to New York. When I last glanced out the window, only thick swirls of snow appeared. The white fluffy clouds replaced by ominous gray ones until nothing was visible. I could see not even the wing or its flashing light.

I threw myself back against the plush leather seat and tightened my seatbelt. I reached for my mobile in the seat next to me. But the jet dropped. The mobile flew from the seat and skittered across the floor. I cried out in horror as it crashed against the wall. The cracking of the screen let me know I had no means of calling for help. I couldn't reach my parents or my brothers in Miami. Nor anyone else in our pack. My wolf whined in despair.

The pilot announced they were going to circumvent the storm and reroute from the flight plan to JFK. The monitors showed a chance to avoid the worse of the storm if they flew further north of New York City.

Now, I wonder if anything would have made a difference as the jet banks left and drops several feet. The change in course is so severe, bile rises in my throat. I choke it down as I hold my head between my knees. Tears stream down my cheeks as I sob.

As a young she-wolf, I can survive most damage with my enhanced healing. Only silver can inflict fatal harm. But this? Flying miles up in the sky during a freak snowstorm that blocks visibility for the pilot and co-pilot? Not an easily recoverable situation should we crash.

My heart clenches at the thought. Please gods, no!

How can I go from poring over the latest edition of *Vogue* while listening to my favorite playlist to begging for my life? All I wanted was to go to New York Fashion Week as I do every season. Now, I wish I'd stayed at home.

All thoughts blow from my mind as the front of the jet dips. The seatbelt digs into my pelvis as I hang from the seat. My waist-length black hair covers my face like a curtain. A scream rips from my throat. It blends with the flight attendant's wail.

"We're going down! Brace yourselves!"

The pilot's terrified shouts make my blood run cold.

My ears pop as I scream. My hands reach out but flail with nothing to hold.

The jet jerks up enough for me to sit back with a gasp as my body pulls away from the seatbelt. I swipe my hair out of my eyes and swivel my head. The interior of the jet is a mess.

"Oh, fuck!"

The pilot curses as something drags along the bottom of the jet. Metal screeches, lights flicker, alarms sound. Cold air fills the cabin. Tendrils of smoke follow.

We have no time to react as the jet plummets.

The flight attendant and I stare in stark fear at one another.

My wolf throws herself to the ground. She reminds me to brace myself for impact. Arms lift to the sides of my head as I lower my chest to my knees. Fingers intertwine. I say a silent pray.

Then boom…

Cold. So very cold.

My trembling body wakes me. Every inch screams in pain. I black out.

"—way. Over here!"

"Holy shit! This is the worse crash I've ever seen."

"Where's the rest of it? Fuck…"

"Check her pulse. Is she breathing?"

Calloused fingers wrap around my wrist. Gently, they skim across the skin. A jolt of electricity zips from the touch and up my arm. I cry out.

"She's alive!"

"Thank the gods."

"What about the others?"

No!!! Please let them be alive, too.

Another jolt—but not a pleasurable one—courses through me as I try to sit up.

"Do not move."

Something warm infused with the enticing scents of sandalwood and vanilla covers me. Stubble scratches my neck. A deep inhalation against my skin makes me shudder.

I cry out in a combination of ecstasy and agony. The man hisses. He jerks away.

"No, fucking way," he mutters.

"Do you smell that?"

"She can't be."

Who are these men?

My eyelids hurt as they flutter open. Blurry images in the shapes of three enormous men appear in the darkness. I blink to clear my vision, then reopen my eyes.

Glacial blue ones stare down at me. I watch mesmerized as they darken to cobalt, then flash electric.

The other two men snarl and growl. Surprised, my gaze shifts to them.

But a rumble draws my attention to the first man's face.

The air leaves my lungs as my mouth falls slack.

Jet black hair frames chiseled cheekbones and firm jaw. The silky strands hang to his bulging pecs. Muscular arms fold across his broad chest, covered in only a white tank top. On top of it, dog tags hang from a chain-link and leather necklace. My gaze follows the chain up to his magnificent face.

He studies me with an intensity that makes me tremble, and not from the cold.

THANK you for reading *Billionaire Wolves Miami*! If you enjoyed the book, I would so appreciate your review as they make a huge difference for indie authors.

Want more of Signy's story? Read *Signy's Mates: A Wolf Shifter Fated Mates Reverse Harem Romance* for the start of *Billionaire Wolves New York*. Turn the page for a preview.

Sign up for my newsletter for the latest updates, releases, and a free book at **bit.ly/CLBooksJoinNewsletter**.

Join my Facebook Group **facebook.com/groups/char mainelouisebookscoterie** for a community who love my spicy worlds!.

For early access to my current works, visit my Ream Stories **bit.ly/CharmaineLouiseBooksCoterie**.

Their steamy love story is a standalone trilogy in the sizzling Billionaire Wolves Series of interconnecting stories featuring wolf shifter fated mates romance. Get a glimpse of their dynamism in other books.

Click the Image Below or Visit books2read.com/u/ 4ARKLp For Your Copy

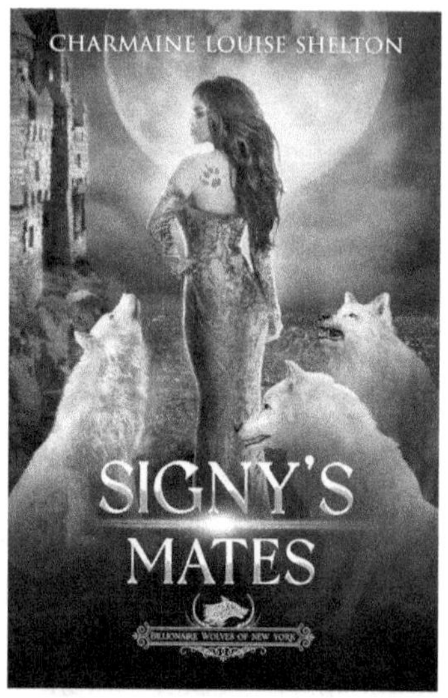

Signy's Mates: A Wolf Shifter Fated Mates Reverse Harem Romance

A Trilogy of Desires Malcolm & Starr Parts I-III

Series Extras

Series Playlist

STEELE INTERNATIONAL, INC. - JACKSON CORPORATION
A BILLIONAIRES ROMANCE SERIES CROSSOVER

Tempt My Desires Lachlan & Haley Part I

Tease My Desires Lachlan & Haley Part I

Grant My Desires Lachlan & Haley Part III

Intrigue My Desires Harris & Kat Part I

Decode My Desires Harris & Kat Part II

Honor My Desires Harris & Kat Patt III

A Trilogy of Desires Lachlan & Haley Parts I-III

A Trilogy of Desires Harris & Kat Parts I-III

Series Extras

Series Playlist

BILLIONAIRE WOLVES SERIES
WOLF SHIFTER FATED MATES PARANORMAL ROMANCE

MIAMI

Jagger The Awakening

(Available in Billionaire Wolves of Miami —The Complete
Collection)

Dylan The Rogue

(Available Exclusively to Subscribers)

Jagger The Temptation

Rust The Rejected

Tag The Redemption

Viggo The Obsession

Billionaire Wolves of Miami — The Complete Collection

NEW YORK

Signy's Mates

Signy Claimed

Signy Forever

Series Playlist

Complete List bit.ly/CharmaineLouiseSheltonBooksList

CharmaineLouiseBooks.com

**To read her current works in progress, visit her Ream Stories
bit.ly/CharmaineLouiseBooksCoterie.**

ABOUT CHARMAINE LOUISE SHELTON

Charmaine Louise Shelton loves a dominant Alpha hero—human, shifter, or vampire—as long as he's a billionaire and sexy as sin! Her romance novels take readers into the heroes' glitzy, glamorous, steamy worlds as they chase after independent women who unexpectedly capture their hearts.

Want to experience some more? Follow her on social media on your favorite channels below. Read her current works in progress at her Ream Stories bit.ly/CharmaineLouiseBooks Coterie. Join her newsletter for the latest updates, releases, and more bit.ly/CLBooksJoinNewsletter.

Find her at:
CharmaineLouiseBooks.com

Fulfill Your Desires.

bookbub.com/authors/charmaine-louise-shelton
tiktok.com/@charmainelouisebooks
youtube.com/@charmainelouisebooks
facebook.com/CharmaineLouiseBooks
instagram.com/charmainelouisebooks
goodreads.com/charmainelouisebooks

DEDICATION

To my awesome and dedicated beta readers and ARC Team, my amazing author friends, and this incredible community for their support.

And most of all to you, my loyal readers who love these couples as much as I do.

Thank you!

Fulfill Your Desires.

xoxo
Charmaine Louise Shelton

www.ingramcontent.com/pod-product-compliance
Lightning Source LLC
Chambersburg PA
CBHW060605100726
47907CB00006B/1510